Hear the Wind Blow

George Collord

ISBN: 978-1-0792-8019-7

DEDICATION

This book is dedicated to my brothers
and sisters of the Thin Blue Line.
We bend but will never break.

ACKNOWLEDGMENTS

At one time or another, every cop thinks he or she should write a book. Why? Because we've all experienced that creepy side of life that no man or woman should see, day and night, for a whole career. It never leaves you. That being said, every shift and every case has the potential for hilarity, tragedy, and mind-blowing violence. Stories play out before our very eyes. We write a lot of them in terse reports but think to ourselves, "If I just threw in a little Hemingway-esque sentence or two, that would have been a page turner!" Then we forget it and go on to the next call.

Knowing this about her dad, Hailey, my younger daughter and editor, challenged me on a mountain hike to write a story about some strange bones along our trail. In a moment of weakness I said, sure, if you'll help me. In a moment of weakness, she also said sure, so I started an outline. She promptly let the real world get in her way, so there I was, stuck, on my own. I refused to give up, but along the journey she kindly checked in with her expertise in the English language and forensic anthropology. Without her guidance, this book would never have reached midway. Hailey is also responsible for the cover art and back cover synopsis, and she urges readers not to look too closely at her poor photoshop skills.

I'd also like to thank three wonderful ladies who are avid readers of crime fiction — Linda Keno, Terra Cohen, and Shalonda Gerdes promised honest feedback. They fulfilled their promises with positive words of encouragement. I continued honing this tale of Delroy Church and his search for truth based on their assurances that they, at least, would gladly accept my book as a present…to re-gift no doubt.

A special thanks to my father-in-law Val, a man who reads trashy novels day and night. He may have taken pity on his daughter and therefore weighed in with a thumbs-up on my pile of prose.

Lastly, I thank the most important person in my life, Valerie, my wife and boss at the school where I volunteer. She took time out of her hectic schedule to read every word…and then ask if I'd paid any attention at all in her fourth grade language arts lessons. She was a saint to put up with my mad typing on her school computer, instead of grading math or spelling papers as I'd been tasked with. She is the Rachel Stern to my Jake.

CHAPTER 1

0300 hours, June 22, 1995

High above the Puma Creek canyon, a silent night hunter launched from its perch. It swept downhill, deftly slicing through the taciturn mixture of sugar pine and Douglas fir. Tufts of ear feathers, adapted over the ages, let it detect and sift the slightest noises, such as the imperceptible skitter of a cautious mouse now stopping atop an outcropping of timeless granite. Sealed fate. The rodent's fatal pause preceded its last moments alive, struggling helplessly, fearfully, in the clutches of sharp talons. Back on the safety of a thick pine limb, a hundred feet above the forest floor, the suffering ended as a sharp beak, curved perfectly for tearing and chunking, stilled the night's offering. Momentarily, the hunter's head swiveled. It sat motionless but attentive. Something foreign had intruded its woods.

Far below, a pair of bouncing headlights meandered up the packed-gravel, logging road that scarred the east side of Puma Ridge via a series of switchbacks. The headlights paused. Doors slammed, and bright stilettos stabbed the darkness. Indistinct voices, almost whispering, mixed with sounds of scraping and grunting. A soft thud gave way to the rattling of rock on rock scattering downhill.

One voice rose.

"Jesus Christ, do you smell that? Enough to make you blow chunks. Well, we ain't goin' down for his illegal shit. What a fuckin' waste."

Doors slammed again. The sound of crunching gravel under angry tires mixed with a cassette player blasting Tim McGraw's "I like it. I love it. I want some more of it…."

Someone laughed, "Throw me a beer, sweet cheeks. Gonna be a long night. We got promises to keep and a head to dump before we sleep."

The headlights jounced back downhill just as a playful, summer solstice breeze teased the still night.

The sated predator did not move. It gazed down intently, its vision easily penetrating the blackness. Watching. Waiting. Presently, a slow tentative movement rose from under a Manzanita clump just below where a dumped form had come to rest. A gray fox, one of nature's scavengers, turned a suspicious head as it checked for danger. Then, after sniffing the form, she ripped at it with her razor-like canines. The wise, impassive face far above cocked right, as if in slight amusement.

♦

October 2018

Jerry Rafferty had climbed Mount Shasta twice, once in high school and again when he graduated from the University of California at Davis five years later. A third ascent of the dormant volcano had been planned this past September, but an early snow had messed that up.

His addiction to the wild country surrounding the crown jewel of the Cascades had begun just before 5th grade. That summer, his parents drove up from Sacramento to spend a week camping at a lake called Karuk that shimmered placidly under the snow blanketed peak. He'd been back every summer since. The 500 acre Karuk Lake was man made. Its dam, finished in 1969, supplied power downhill in the Central Valley where air conditioners sucked up juice six months out of the year.

This October, in place of a Shasta climb, Jerry planned the next best thing. He'd hike the opposite side of the Strawberry Valley, get up high on the southwest slope above Karuk Lake into the conifer-covered Pumas, a lower range west of Mount Shasta. The Pumas butted up against their kissin' cousins, the Trinity Alps and the Klamath Mountains. They were all components of the Coast Range, interior California's protector from dreary, ocean fog.

He aimed to hike above the tree line and camp in the open

briskness, just below the snowpack. On his map, he'd selected a route along an old logging road turned trail that cut up the east side of Puma Ridge. This would get him high enough to connect with the Pacific Crest Trail that ran along the top of the Pumas. The PCT had plenty of good camp clearings along it. He'd find a flat spot above a cliff where he was hoping to have an unobstructed view directly across a wide expanse of ridges and valleys at the lower 48's 14,000-foot answer to Kilimanjaro.

Jerry would not be camping alone. Two late-twenty something colleagues from his CPA firm in downtown Sacramento had jumped at the chance to stretch their legs away from the office. Carrie Buckley and Chris Landau shared Jerry's passion not only for numbers, but also his fear of ending up resembling their pale, rotund, pink-fingered bosses down the hall. A few more years behind a desk covered with balance sheets, lattes, and cinnamon croissants meant flab. Flab on the gut, flab on the arms, and flab on the thighs. No way. 24 Hour Fitness and a healthy longing for the outdoors should keep the fat cells at bay for at least a few more years.

Tax season would not begin in earnest until after the first of the year. All three were granted a long weekend. They agreed to call it a "teambuilding weekend," so technically they'd still be on the job, meaning somewhere in there lurked elusive tax deductions.

Early Friday morning, Jerry stowed all their backpacking gear in the rear of his Jeep Grand Cherokee. One Starbucks drive-through later they were on northbound Interstate 5, flashing past the Sacramento International Airport where they entered the wide open farmland of the Sacramento Valley. The upper half of California's famed Central Valley fanned out before them, a vast collection of orchards, rice paddies, and dense flocks of wild birds landing and taking off from several nature preserves.

Far ahead, growing larger by the mile, beckoned the frosty tip of Mount Shasta. It rose high above surrounding mountains, growing more prominent through the windshield as Jerry sped past the farming communities of Williams, Willows, and then Corning.

Farther north, Jerry stopped for gas in Redding where it was hot and crowded even on a mid-October morning. Redding, known as Satan's Oven by some of the locals, lay at the upper reaches of the Sacramento Valley.

A tattooed panhandler approached Jerry at the pumps. He carried a grease-stained cardboard sign that read *God Bless, Anything helps.* To keep the peace and avoid the lingering smell, Jerry dug out a few bucks. A hand, looking as if it had recently dug in compost, quickly snatched them away. A grunt followed. It could have been "Thanks" or maybe "Thanks for nuthin." He couldn't be sure. He sighed. The still of a wilderness couldn't come fast enough.

Back on I-5, they passed over the state's largest reservoir, Shasta Lake. Below the Pit River Bridge, a few diehard house-boaters had the lake mostly to themselves. The wide ribbon of red dirt shores was a testament to the autumn drain of the lake. The lake supplied fresh water to the Sacramento Delta, keeping the saltwater at bay.

Beyond Shasta Lake, Jerry snaked up the Sacramento River Canyon, home to stream, railroad, and wide curved freeway. Mountains carpeted with thick fir sloped upward on both sides, giving this part of their journey a shaded, claustrophobic feeling. The slate gray Castle Crags rivaled Yosemite's Half Dome, prompting *oohs* and *aahs*. These behemoths glared down at the travelers from the west side of the freeway just south of the small burg of Dunsmuir which touted itself as "home of the world's best tasting water."

Mount Shasta had now grown enormous in front of them. It played peek-a-boo as they negotiated the twisting and turning canyon. Chris and Carrie took iPhone photos through the windshield and Snapchatted them to those co-workers not clever enough to ask first for days off.

They soon passed a metallic road sign that read *Entering Karuk County. Where We Honor Veterans.* The closed in feeling gave way a short time later when they entered a higher, wider, forested Strawberry Valley laid out between the down slopes at the foot of Mount Shasta on the east and the sharks tooth Pumas on the west.

Jerry zipped off the freeway and eased through the two-stoplight village of Sisson. He laughingly informed his fellow travelers that those two stoplights were two out of maybe seven in the entire county.

There was no need to stop as the morning quickly disappeared. Jerry drove west out of Sisson along a severely winding, oiled road toward the Pumas. He fixed an eye on these mountains as they rose ahead of him displaying their intricate green and rusty schemes of fir, cedar, and pine, thinning out upward into the purples and pinks of sun-painted rock. The upper reaches of the Pumas finally gave way to the dazzling white of un-melted, month old snow that draped over ridges above 9,000 feet.

Ten miles after leaving town, after passing the whitecaps on Karuk Lake, after stopping to consult a map twice, and luckily catching the gravel road that ran along Puma Creek, they arrived at the trailhead.

The three backpackers, feeling relieved to be standing and stretching, checked gear and then ate a simple snack of energy bars. Jerry and Chris wolfed their PowerBars for max endurance. Carrie teased them both with her organic bar, boasting that she needed no "inserted protein or artificial sweeteners." For proper hydration, they guzzled "captured at the source" water from collapsible plastic bottles. Go time.

Jerry strapped his 50 lb. Kelty pack firmly on his back. He strolled off first, up the old gravel road, now more of a rutted pathway. Initially, he found himself slipping on loose stones, made so by erosion and the freezing and thawing along the rocky upper banks. He brushed in and out among orphan firs that had sprung up thickly through the gravel bed. Chris and Carrie followed closely behind. Heavy breathing came quickly to all three hikers. Irritated office legs, bent four hours in a car, initially rebelled at the demands, but eventually, oxygen levels in the muscles evened out. The frantic, first pace slowed to an efficient, manageable up, up, and up some more.

As the trio made their ascent, they paused periodically to look out over the Strawberry Valley. Eastward they watched miniature big rigs passing each other north and south on I-5. Distant homes and businesses in and among the trees of Sisson lay helter-skelter at the foot of the gargantuan, silent mountain that loomed behind them.

To Jerry's dismay, the Vente sized coffee and copious amount of water caught up with him sooner than he'd planned. He stopped, stepped to the side, and apologized. He told the others to move on by so he could "check his balance sheet." Chris shook his head. Carrie giggled.

As soon as the others had disappeared around a bend in the trail, Jerry danced to the edge of the bank.

He stood enjoying his yellow stream of relief as it raced downhill like a Lilliputian flashflood, taking out villages, overturning cars, and finally disappearing into the rocky soil about three feet down. That's when he spotted the first bone.

He would have missed it had he not been lost in the fantasy world of death and destruction from the Great Jerry Piss Storm of '18. But there it was, a six-inch breakwater barrier set up by tiny engineers to protect the people of the town from cloudburst rage. The rush of liquid had turned the beige gravel and soil to a taupe, causing the lightness of the bleached bone to stand out.

Curious, he searched around then picked up a branch about the perfect length for a marshmallow roast. Had this been near his campsite, he'd have kept this stick as a poker for sitting and staring into the flames while contemplating the mysteries of the ages.

He bent out over the bank, mindful of the extra weight on his back that had thrown off his normal balance. He grasped the trunk of a fir sapling for safety then reached out and down to insert the tip of his marshmallow stick under the bone. He flipped it over.

Yeah, it's bone. Sweet, but I better catch up with Chris and Miss Organic.

He dropped the stick in the middle of the trail and turned back uphill. His legs worked overtime to catch up with the others. Rounding a corner a few hundred feet later he found Chris and Carrie sitting on matching boulders staring out over the Strawberry Valley at Mount Shasta, iPhones in hand. Chris was commenting on signal strength while Carrie clicked away at nature. Carrie turned her camera on Jerry as he strolled toward her.

Chris snorted that it was about time and asked Jerry if he had "everything well in hand." Carrie flashed an "OMG" eye roll.

The trio continued their hike for another hour before they reached the top of Puma Ridge. From here they could see north beyond the Strawberry Valley into the dry, high desert terrain of the Shasta Valley. Their view extended beyond California, all the way into Oregon. Across the state border stood Mcloughlin, a younger sister to Mount Shasta, posted up at her link in the chain of active and dormant volcanoes that highlighted the Cascades on their run to Canada.

They made camp in a relatively flat clearing protected from the wind by elephant-sized boulders on two sides, a row of scraggly, high country silver tips on a third, and open on the fourth. They each rolled out different colored tents. Their camp, with its bright orange, yellow, and green tents secured with guy lines, reminded Jerry of a downed rainbow.

On the open side, about fifty feet beyond the tents, was a ledge to a hundred-foot cliff. Jerry teetered above it, a bit anxious and dizzy. Looking down at the base, he saw a field of hundreds of scattered boulders that continued downward, disappearing into the mixture of conifers. Farther below was the teardrop-shaped puddle formerly known as Lake Karuk. Stepping back, he tilted his head up and gazed in wonderment directly behind the lake at the rise of the ever-present Mount Shasta. The climb had actually enhanced its dominion. As he watched, waning sunlight turned its snow from a pale rose color to a ghostly white. He breathed deeply of the early evening air laced with the scent of cedar and pine. This was the spot he'd counted on.

That night, the trio sat around their small, flickering fire. They shared scary stories and life experiences. It was just like camping with their parents only different. Now they were on their own, big kids responsible for themselves. They had no mom and dad to tell them to go to bed, but no 's'mores for later either. Naturally, the subject of their work came up. Coincidentally, they'd all gotten into the accounting business because they liked money.

Yeah, I love my job. Well, not really. The money is good. I love my Audi and all, but I don't know if this is what I see myself doing for the next forty years. What about you?

Chris let on that at one time he thought about being a cop, but it was too dangerous. Miss Organic said that was strange because she once thought about joining the FBI, but it was too dangerous.

Jerry offered that he, too, had considered a career in law enforcement. Then he'd looked at the salary schedules. Still, he enjoyed the CSI shows on TV. It seemed the perfect segue into discussing the bone and how he had a feeling there were more of them that he hadn't seen. He sure wanted to take a better look on the way back down. He knew right where the spot was because he'd left a unique stick in the trail. He secretly hoped the soil had dried by the time they got back. Could be awkward.

CHAPTER 2

Roy Church hit print on his laptop. He shoved back from the worn post-WWII desk at the Sisson Substation and stretched his back, sore from sitting in a chair that FDR himself may have sat in. He set his reading glasses down then moved across the low-ceiling, converted living room. Next to a brown, 70's style paneled wall the HP printer hummed. It spit out two sheets of white paper. He read over his report.

On the above date and time, I was dispatched to 112 Shasta View Road to meet with Reporting Party/ Victim Jasmine Hill.

Hill reported that she and her husband left their home at about 0800 hours to go to Wal-Mart in Silverton. When they returned at about 1100 hours they discovered that a decorative porcelain frog was missing from their front step. They searched the area and found the frog lying about 200 feet away in the grassy meadow to the rear (NE) of their home. They saw no one around.

Hill told me there has been an increase in homeless transient type persons in the area. They often smell the odor of burning marijuana coming from the hillside behind their home.

I walked to the meadow where the frog was found and saw a slight path leading into a thicket of willows and small trees. I found a homeless encampment. It was empty.

I checked with neighbors on both sides of the Hills. They saw or heard nothing. The neighbors also mentioned the increased transient traffic.

At this time there are no known suspects or witnesses to the theft.

Recommendation: Forward this report to County Code Enforcement. I will conduct extra patrol checks in the area to identify any transients illegally camping on county land.

Satisfied, Roy dropped the report in the office out-basket marked *Informational.* Another out-basket tray was marked *In-Custody.* Any deputies driving the thirty-five miles north on the I-5 to Silverton for Superior Court the next day would take the informational reports with them to the county seat. There, they'd be filed at "the Main" – the Sheriff's Headquarters. An in-custody report would go directly to the Sheriff's court deputy's desk where it would be copied. Then two copies were walked across the street to the Karuk County District Attorney's Office located in the county jail-court complex. Except for weekend arrests, all in-custody reports had to be processed ASAP so the deputy DA assigned to the case could read it before arraignment hearings that occurred within 24 hours of an arrest. At an arraignment, the deputy DA would hand one copy of the report to whomever an arrestee's defense attorney might be.

Roy smiled to himself thinking of the report he'd slipped into the in-custody tray three days earlier. A rude and frisky out-of-towner from San Francisco had stopped off the I-5 freeway to gas up at the Spirit Station. The Frisco Kid proceeded to berate the "fucking redneck clerk" when the pump proved too slow to his liking. Clerk had definitely smelled the odor of an alcoholic beverage on Frisco's breath prompting him to do his civic duty and call 9-1-1 for drunk drivers, like the sign says.

Roy had monitored the scanner in his Sheriff's SUV. He heard a California Highway Patrol officer being dispatched with an ETA of 15 minutes. Roy was just one minute away, having recently abandoned a fruitless search for a hippie girl who'd sneaked into the nearby KOA campground pool. Roy told Sheriff's Dispatch he'd roll by the station and detain the driver until CHP arrived.

The blue Nissan Sentra, parked just beyond the gas pumps, with the white male adult under a slouch hat, leaning back lazily on the trunk, spelled clue. Slouch Hat, later identified as Arnold Mankins of SF's Parkside District, had actually sneered when Roy stepped out of his SUV.

"Christ. Seriously? A good old boy, country Nazi. Fucking perfect."

It had gone downhill from there, especially when Sheriff's dispatch hit the tone alert seconds after Roy read off the plate on the Sentra into his shoulder mic.

"Victor 12. 10-36, 10-30 Frank. 10851 out of San Francisco County."

Great, the Sentra's a reported stolen car.

"You redneck clowns don't impress...." Arnie had chuckled, just as Roy went Condition Red.

But Arnie had been impressed with the dark, gaping hole at his end of a Springfield Arms .45 ACP.

Roy had always found the Automatic Colt Pistol impressed, unless you were in LA's sprawling Nickerson Gardens HUD Housing complex. Nothing impressed there unless you were Bounty Hunter Blood who'd been to the joint for 187, murder, at least twice. But that was a long time ago.

Turned out Arnie had "borrowed" his grandmother's only mode of transportation, without letting Grandma know. Apparently, he'd been called to Portland for a Voodoo Donut get-together or an Antifa rally or both and had no car of his own.

Arnie had sat sullenly in cuffs in the back of Roy's SUV all the way to Silverton where he was booked on the felony section for swiping a car, 10851 of the California Vehicle Code. It wasn't until Roy had finished his report that SFPD got hold of Grandma. The pissed off old lady said Arnie could drive her car back to San Francisco since towing it there would've cost more than it was worth. It took until the next morning for the stolen car to be removed from the Stolen Vehicle System, so Arnie got to spend the night in lock-up with all manner of country redneck clowns from Karuk County.

Still smiling wryly at the memory, Roy closed his laptop and slipped it into its black leather case. He looked around the room to make sure all his gear was still in his patrol SUV.

He paused at a full-length mirror next to the front door. A sign over the top read, "Look sharp, stay sharp, and stay alive." Good advice. Not so different from what he'd been told by his training deputy his first day in a black and white, the one with LA County Sheriff on the door. Florence-Firestone. A lifetime ago.

"Firestone Station will never die," he whispered to himself, feeling a slight pang while recalling the iconic, ancient LASD station where so much SoCal history had passed.

He took stock of his reflection. Older, thinner, with grey hair and a few wrinkles around his green eyes — okay, more than a few — and sun-splotched arms and hands. Definitely not as ripped as the young patrol deputy who'd hit the streets in 1980. Of course, this was only after doing his obligatory year babysitting in LA County lock-up. All barbell weights and T-bone steaks in those days. Even still, he had a lean, well-muscled look for an old guy. He'd never stopped working out, even if the plates weren't as heavy as in times past. His tan and greens were clean and pressed. Seven bright yellow stripes were affixed to his forearm sleeve, one for every five years of service. His coal-black, basket weave gun belt leather, with keepers evenly spaced, whispered after years of Kiwi conditioner. The break-front holster era with a six-round Colt Python long gone, now replaced with the high-rise Bianchi and a double stacked semi-auto.

Roy checked his watch. Three hours until the end of shift. He stepped out into the mid-afternoon sun. Swirling maroon and gold leaves rustled and drifted across the asphalt parking lot in front of the sub. Might have been a crispness in the air. A hint of frost to come. He still wasn't used to it. He breathed deeply. No smog and no ocean air influence. Pine sap mixed with Manzanita? Maybe.

He keyed his shoulder mic to let Dispatch in Silverton know he was back in service.

"Victor 12, 10-8."

"Victor 12, detail," Silverton came back.

"Go to Victor 12."

"Victor 12, Suspicious circ. Meet the RP, Jerry Rafferty, intersection Puma Creek Road and entrance to southwest side Karuk Lake public parking. RP was hiking in Puma Creek Trail area, found possible bones. RP standing by with maroon Jeep Cherokee."

"Victor 12, 10-4, be en route."

Shading his eyes, he gazed southwest across the breadth of the Strawberry Valley. He could make out the sliver of blue right about where Karuk Lake lapped up against its dam. He reckoned it was about two miles away as the crow flies. The southwest parking lot lay just beyond the dam, hidden by tall firs. He figured he'd be there in less than ten.

To get to Karuk Lake from the sub, Roy had to pass southbound through Sisson on a four block portion of its Main Street. Sandwiched on the east side were a Goodyear tire shop; Ace Hardware; Ghost Mountain Art Gallery; Ron Faraday's Real Estate, which was hawking mountain view properties in its front window; and the United State Post Office, where the American flag flapped under a north wind. The west side of the street was occupied by Magic Crystals and Chai; Clip and Snip: A Professional Hair Salon; Shastafarian Burgers and Brew; Sweet Air, a ski and board shop; and a marijuana dispensary called Shasta Mountain High.

SMH had the most cars in front though none of the stores looked busy. Roy liked it that way. He'd already done busy. This was okay.

Halfway through town, at the pewter colored water fountain outside the town hall, he turned west onto Lake Street. This would take him toward and across Interstate 5 and ultimately to Karuk Lake. The busiest place in town, right off the freeway, was the Black Tail, a classy pancake house that served breakfast 24-7 but also advertised authentic venison tacos. Roy shook his head. Venison tacos. Only in Karuk County.

A few minutes later, Roy spotted the maroon Jeep Cherokee parked in the gravel just inside the entrance to the west side parking lot for Karuk Lake. He flipped on his dash cam and body cam. Three adults, two male, one female, dressed in hiking gear. Force of habit, no matter who, what, or when, made him quickly assess all three for threat level. They seemed Code 4, but it had been drilled into him from the time he'd walked into the LA Sheriff's Academy. Be polite but have a plan to kill everyone you meet. It wasn't something you talked about with civilians, they'd think you were insane, but every good street cop knew the score. Shit hits the fan when you least expect it, so always expect it. And never carry anything in your gun hand, unless you're taking a piss...and then *only* behind a locked door. There are no second chances. Roy had stood graveside a score of times over the years, sadly contemplating his dead comrades who'd forgotten these rules. They'd been taken by surprise and murdered with their guns still in their holsters. In any event, the three hikers looked to be just that, hikers.

Roy parked at a 90-degree angle to the Jeep so that his eyes would never face away from the three civilians.

"Afternoon. I'm Roy Church. Looking for Jerry Rafferty," he called out as he stepped toward the group.

One male, about 30 years, maybe younger, walked toward him.

"I'm Jerry. With a J. I'm the one who called."

"Great. What's going on?" Roy asked. His sharp green eyes focused on Jerry, but still kept track of what the other two civilians were doing.

"Hey man, really sorry to bother you on a Sunday afternoon, and it's probably nothing, but we, my friends Chris and Carrie, and I, we thought we're not going to be those people," Jerry said gesturing to his companions and looking slightly apologetic.

"Those people?" Roy raised his eyebrows with both curiosity and light amusement.

Jerry chewed his cheek a bit with hesitation, but he adjusted his stance to appear a little more self-assured. Roy suspected this increase in puffiness was more for the benefit of the young lady he was with than for him. Jerry answered, "Yeah, the ones who don't get involved. We found some bones up on the trail on Puma Creek. Probably a dead deer, but we can't be sure."

"Okay," said Roy, interested.

"We're accountants," added Jerry, as if that explained the whole situation, or just maybe why they didn't know deer bones from human bones.

Roy listened as Jerry Rafferty explained how he had initially found one bone a few days earlier but had found others when he'd taken another look at the site on his way back down the mountain.

Jerry said, "I had this stick, and I poked the one bone to show Carrie and Chris, and then I found another bone under it in the gravel. So I thought, cool, and I started digging around those bones a little bit more and there's like several more of them. Then we realized we were probably fucking up a crime scene. Oops, sorry for my language." He gave Roy a sheepish smile, running a hand over his short, dark hair.

Roy smiled politely but said nothing, just listened. Let anything nervous and spontaneous spew forth. You never knew.

Jerry continued, "I mean, you see a lot of that on TV and in the movies how you're not supposed to mess with a crime scene, and we thought, well we better call."

"Okay," Roy said. "How far up the trail are they? Can you show me?"

"Oh shit," Jerry said. "We'd like to but we gotta get back to Sacramento. We gotta work in the morning."

"Hmm. Okay," said Roy, calculating. This might be going

nowhere fast.

"But we took photos for you, and we marked the place really well, with Carrie's green hair ribbon, a couple of red and blue Clif Bar wrappers, and a stack of rocks," Jerry added. "And I can show you on my map exactly where the spot is."

Mouth twitching, Roy said, "But did you string up yellow crime scene tape?"

Chris and Carrie, who'd been standing nearby listening, exchanged snickers. They joined Jerry in fooling with their iPhones.

Roy was suddenly overwhelmed with a myriad of photos taken of rocks, trees, Mt Shasta, bones, Jerry pointing at bones, Carrie pointing at bones, and Chris and Carrie pointing down a bank, presumably at bones. In one, the distinct robin's egg blue and vermillion of a Clif Bar wrapper touched the edge of a possible femur. In another photo, he noted a stack of rocks and some bright green ribbons tied to tree branches.

Chris said, "We thought a cairn was called for, so we have a nice little stack for you." Roy thought he detected a note of pride in his voice — clearly the cairn had been his idea.

"Oh, and here's a photo of Jerry walking uphill toward us after he relieved himself all over the crime scene," Carrie laughed.

Roy was impressed with the quality of the iPhone photos. Sure enough, there were bones all right. He'd seen his share of human bones. These looked like an animal, probably a deer. But then there was something about the photos that bothered him, especially when one zeroed in on the scene.

"Was there anything there besides the bones? That almost looks like a piece of plastic," he said.

Chris interjected, "Yes, definitely some bits and pieces of something besides the bones. Not sure what it was, maybe a part of a plastic bag."

"Can I get you to send me those photos?" Roy asked.

"No problem," said Jerry.

"I can give you my phone number and you can text them to me," said Roy feeling IT-like.

"Do you have an iPhone, officer?" asked Carrie.

"Deputy. But yes," said Roy, "Let me give you the number to text."

Carrie laughed. "No need. That's old school. Turn on AirDrop and we'll transfer all the photos right to your phone."

Roy stared at his phone. *Jesus. I just now barely mastered texting.*

A minute later, Roy's iPhone contained several dozen photos of the bone scene, many of them duplicates. In addition, Jerry had suggested Roy photograph his topographical map to have the exact coordinates of the site. The spot Jerry had marked was definitely inside the boundaries of the national forest, so if it turned out to be anything the feds would have to be notified, at least for sake of protocol. Of course, no FBI agent from Sacramento was going to travel 4 hours to look at dead deer remains, but the US Forest Service had one sworn peace officer in the area that Roy could tip off.

Roy wondered how different his career would have been had this young persons' communication technology been available twenty-five years earlier. The army field phone between the front seats of his unmarked, along with his pager, had been the status symbols of the day. Christ.

"Okay," said Roy, taking out a pocket notebook. "I guess we can find the spot. We'll check out the bones, make sure it's all good. Let me get some contact info, and I can let you guys hit the road. All right, Jerry with a J, spell your last name for me, and I'll need date of birth, address, and phone numbers."

Jerry replied, "R-A-F-F-E-R-T-Y, 2310 Angel Way, Sacramento, California."

Roy said, "For a moment there, I thought you might live on Baker Street."

Jerry and the others laughed.

Jerry said, "Yeah, my folks were fans. But I spell my name with a J, not a G."

Roy laughed, "Loved his music. Been a fan myself, right down the line."

Carrie smiled broadly and said, "I didn't know cops had a sense a humor. I like you."

Roy said, "Well, I wasn't always a cop. Never forget where I was the first time I heard those tunes. '78. I was surfing The Wedge on a Takayama Rocket."

Jerry said, "The Wedge? That's like LA. You were a dude!" His eyebrows were raised, clearly impressed with Roy's past life.

Roy replied, "Well, Balboa, but yeah, like LA, Orange County actually. A dude, a long time ago."

Jerry asked, "How did you end up here?"

Roy said, "Ran out of gas on the I-5. No one here believed my cardboard sign, so I had to get a job."

All three witnesses laughed out loud. They were comfortable. Nervousness at talking to a cop had disappeared. Roy had always been good at setting folks at ease, sometimes to their peril, in a penitentiary sort of way.

Roy asked, "About how long did it take you guys to hike from the trailhead to the site? I've not been on that trail."

"Hmm. I'd say fifteen…twenty minutes. We were carrying packs so we weren't going that quickly," Jerry replied.

"See anyone else up there?" Roy asked.

"Nope. Just us accountants."

"Last thing," Roy said, as he looked at his notebook. "Did you file an environmental impact report before you disturbed the rocks for the pile? We're very protective of our ant and scorpion populations up here."

Ten minutes later, Roy watched the Jeep ease out onto Karuk Lake Road, taking the CPA Posse back to the city. He checked the time. Late afternoon. Shadows had grown long. Too late to hike to the bone site? He was torn. Normally he'd have been fine with waiting until the next day, but the plastic bothered him. Plus, there were some angles that didn't really allow him to see all the bones that were on the site. Now that the area had been marked up like Mardi Gras, should anyone pass, the entire site could be compromised more than it already had.

He radioed Dispatch for a Suspicious Circumstance report number. Then he phoned Sheriff's Lieutenant Cyril Savage, the watch commander in Silverton. It was always best to run a potential problem past the guys who'd make the decisions on how to proceed with overtime.

The word came back. No overtime. Check it out tomorrow. Lieutenant Savage had his eye on the bottom line.

Roy went back in-service. There were no calls waiting, so he pulled over on a wide spot on Karuk Lake Road and quickly banged out his report on his laptop. He filled out a face sheet with the horsepower of his Reporting Party and the other two witnesses. Then he got to the meat of the story, short as it was.

On the above date and time, I was dispatched to meet with Reporting Party Rafferty at the Karuk Lake parking lot. Rafferty reported that he and his two hiking companions, Witnesses Landau and Buckley, had discovered some bones alongside the Puma Creek Trail, about one mile uphill from the trailhead. Rafferty actually spotted one bone on the way uphill, then discovered several more at the site on the way back down the trail two days later.

All three wits provided me with cell phone photographs they'd taken of the bones and the surrounding area. They told me they marked the area with green hair ribbon, some blue and red Clif Bar wrappers, and a stack of rocks (also known as a cairn). Wit Rafferty showed me on his topographical map where he thought the scene was. I took a photo of the map showing a marked spot.

I consulted Lieutenant Savage at Sheriff's Main. He advised that due to the time of day I would have to wait until the following day to inspect the scene.

Evidence: Memory card w/24 photos of a portion of Puma Creek Trail. One photo of a topographical map belonging to RP/Wit Rafferty.

Recommendations: At present, this report is for information purposes only. I will follow-up with a US Forestry Law Enforcement officer then coordinate a scene inspection ASAP.

Before the end of the shift, Roy handled two more calls. One was a "488 P.C. dine and dash" from the Black Tail. The other was a "415 P.C. music" which turned out to be a loud stereo coming from a high schooler's rebooted Bronco parked at the dead end of a residential cul de sac. The petty theft of restaurant food required a report, even though the suspects had hit the freeway in a nondescript silver compact. The disturbance of the peace car stereo required only a drive-by, and the music stopped. Then the day was done.

That evening before leaving the sub, Roy sat at a desk and stared thoughtfully at the bone photos. He'd transferred them to his laptop for a better view. Animal bones, no doubt. Not human, he was sure. He'd seen human bones, enough to fill half the cemetery at Forest Lawn. But his guts gnawed over the human factor. The plastic whatever it was. He was relieved that the accountants had been mature and intelligent enough not to disturb the scene any more than they had.

As he studied the soil and rocks, the firs and pines, the wide trail that had once been a road, his mind wandered to another time. A time laced with the scent of damp sand, chaparral, and Joshua trees in an inhospitable landscape. The sounds of Mojave green rattlers warning intruders, and distant jets screaming out of Edwards. It was the desert, the preferred place to dig a shallow grave in the SoCal. But here and now was an old, remote logging road turned trail. Was it the preferred place to dump a body in this part of the state, a part he was still not comfortable in?

Keep it simple. You're just a road dog now. Leave it at that. You can't go home again, Detective Church.

But he couldn't ignore the distant howl of the Santa Anas fixing to blow their firestorm off the arid Mojave toward the Pacific. The death wind.

CHAPTER 3

Monday morning, 0600 hours. Roy was up and dressed. He sat at his kitchen table in a rented two bedroom, two bath converted shop building on a forgotten edge of an estate that overlooked Karuk Lake. The owner of the estate, a San Francisco attorney, came and went from the property's main home at irregular times, mostly in the winter when there was skiing, and in the summer when water sports could be enjoyed. Occasionally the estate's main home, a lodge really, was rented out for big bucks, usually to fellow San Franciscans. Right now it sat empty down the hill behind giant cedar trees, yet visible from Roy's kitchen window. Filtered sunlight glanced off its rough cedar board exterior. Three stone chimneys stood cold and smokeless over a dark green roof. There were no vehicles in its driveway, save a white, five year old Ram pick-up that belonged to Roy. Roy parked it there to make it look as if someone were home. Any dope sick hype from the city would immediately recognize the lame set-up, but still it didn't hurt to try out here in the woods.

For company, Roy had bitter coffee, oatmeal, and the NFL channel. A chatty, animated panel of former players and a female moderator furiously over-analyzed the previous day's carnage. The Rams had won, again. Roy had to stop himself from rolling his eyes.

Figures. I leave LA, the Rams return. They win.

He flipped through the morning news channels. Same old crap. The national Crips party was bagging on the national Bloods party. The Bloods were on their own channel throwing rounds downrange at the Crips. The spinning wheels of political violence continued. Roy shook his head. The advance in technology that allowed him instant access to possible crime scene photos via the iPhones somehow figured into the 24 hour news cycle that never took a break. It was a sure-fire way to keep the partisans whipped into a foamy-mouthed frenzy.

Thinking of the chaotic national political scene, he couldn't help remembering years back when various homicide investigations had required a half a dozen trips or so from the Southland to a deep forest in California's far, foggy, dripping north, just outside Crescent City. Hidden in that impenetrable landscape of redwoods and coastal firs lay the supermax of all supermaxes, Pelican Bay State Prison.

"The Bay," as it was known by cop and criminal, housed nearly 3,500 of the worst offenders the prisons of California had to offer. The shot callers of the four major California prison gangs called a sectioned off area home. The Mexican Mafia, the Nuestra Familia, the Black Guerilla Family, and the Aryan Brotherhood dominated the thousand beds in the 22.5 hour a day lockdown within a lockdown known as "the SHU." The Security Housing Unit was an isolated dungeon inside this toughest prison. The SHU was an attempt to dampen the influence the gang shot callers had over their thousands of members in other institutions and on the streets of the Golden State. The SHU was separated into two cement block fortresses known as C and D Facilities. Incredibly, the top dogs in the prison gangs were still able to send out their lethal directives all over the state. A hit in the southern desert community of Palmdale could be called by a Mafia *Big Homie* from a cell in D-Facility, or a go ahead for a robbery crew to operate in the cool, Central Coast town of Salinas could be ordered by an NF general from C-9.

True, prison could have a positive effect on behavior. Crips and Bloods, who would normally gun each other down on the streets of Compton, were more agreeable toward one another in the joint, under the thumb of the BGF.

On the flipside, the soldados of Los Angeles based *La Eme*, aka Mexican Mafia, were under strict orders to attack and kill when confronted with their Northern California nemeses, the soldiers of *La Nuestra Familia.* The streets and the prison yards ran red with the blood these two sides spilled on their way to dominance and glory. For 40 years there had been no peace between these two warring Latino gangs, nor could there ever be, if their leaders had any say.

Funny thing happened though. Several years earlier, while looking for a witness to a gangland murder, Roy had visited a building at The Bay called the THU, the Transfer Housing Unit. The program in place there was designed to monitor former gang members who had renounced their membership and fully debriefed (truthfully detailed a personal criminal history) with the gang intelligence officers of the California Department of Corrections. It was an incredible moment to watch two previously sworn enemies interact. A few months earlier, they would have shivved one another in the neck the moment a cell door popped. Now, they played basketball and lounged on benches shooting the shit. Roy mused to himself that a THU for disgusted members of the American two party system was long overdue.

He killed his television, checked his watch, and dialed the Sisson office of the US Forestry. The clerk on duty told him Parker Covington, the only federal law enforcement officer in this part of the Trinity-Shasta National Forest, was out of pocket. He'd gone out east on the Reno Highway, past McCloud, some twenty miles away. A damaged road gate needed checking. Roy figured it had probably been vandalized by someone pissed that access to the National Forest had been limited by a bureaucrat 3,000 miles away. He wondered if the Puma Creek Trail had been gated off, or if trees and erosion had made a man-made barrier unnecessary. In any event, he was on his own.

Roy went 10-8, in-service, from his own driveway. Being a resident deputy rendered the commute obsolete. He checked with Silverton Dispatch. No calls of import holding. He was free to head toward Puma Ridge. He'd be afoot for a while, away from his patrol vehicle if the shit hit the fan anywhere in the south county. Dispatch advised him that fellow resident Deputy Tom Hanlon would be 10-8 in about two hours. In the meantime, emergency coverage could roll from Silverton. Dispatch told him that the Silverton's early dayshift deputies, all three of them, would take turns hovering at the south end of the beat in case they had to make a dash down to Sisson.

Twenty-five minutes later, Roy parked at the Puma Creek trailhead. He studied the padlocked, iron pole gate, with a pedestrian pass to one side. Beyond the gate lay huge boulders across the old roadway, presumably placed by a bucket loader to bar vehicular traffic, to deter a breach of the gate. Roy grinned at the typical government overkill that now prevented a terrorist and his truckload of TNT from blowing up the mountain.

He spied fresh tire marks in the soil, probably from where the accountants had parked and turned the Jeep. Seeing only one set of tracks, Roy breathed a slight sigh of relief. That meant no hunters, hikers, illicit lovers, or school class on a fieldtrip had altered the scene in the past 16 hours.

He said silent thanks for his uniform Tuffy jacket that protected him against the bluster of a hostile breeze. Across the valley, half of Mt Shasta was shrouded in gray. He'd checked the weather earlier. It looked to be cloudy with a chance of showers, maybe even some snow above 7,000 ft. It was late October, still warm in the Southland, but here? Well, he'd not been here long enough to say with any certainty what the weather should or shouldn't do this time of year. He crossed his fingers. A murderer's best friend was a rainstorm, although it was true many a flash flood had undone the best laid plans for a covert grave. He shivered. Definitely not flash flood country.

The walk up the incline warmed him in minutes as he negotiated the loose rocks and young trees in the wide rutted trail. He unzipped his jacket and felt cool relief. His heart rate had increased considerably, his breathing now audible. Still, he knew many men his age were waddlers, carrying their portable beer can ledge just above the belt as they followed their portly wives pushing grocery carts filled with sugar and precooked meals.

It suddenly occurred to him that he'd been looking down the entire time, careful not to make a misstep and twist an ankle on a hostile stone. He stopped and turned fully around, his right palm reflexively brushing a cold back strap. He inspected the pale, RV sized granite boulders and dark, mossy outcroppings on the uphill side of the old roadbed. Many were partially obscured by giant tree trunks and thickets of tan oak. He'd seen amateur videos and trail cam photos, passed via iPhones and computer, of the silent apex predator whose haunts he'd now entered.

A hundred pound mountain lion could easily take down a man whose willing neck had been left unguarded. Female joggers in the late evening or early morning hours, or a bicyclist bent down to fix a flat, the cougar was known to stray from its natural prey of deer and family pets. It was rare, but it did occur in this state. The murder of police officers by lowlife assholes was actually rare, but it happened in this state as well. The killings in both cases often had a common theme. The victim had been unaware of the danger and unprepared for it when it rushed at him or her. He chastised himself and resolved to stop, look, and listen every hundred feet or so from here on. At that moment he felt a certain warm comfort in the weight of the Kevlar around his chest and the .45 on his hip.

About twenty minutes into his hike, Roy rounded a curve in the trail and immediately spotted bits of green ribbon tied around several branches, both on the trail and down the embankment. The ribbons didn't say "Police Line. Do Not Cross" but got his attention nonetheless. A pile of rocks, about 18" tall, lay at the edge of the trail.

More force of habit. Roy did not approach the first ribbons, staying about thirty feet back. He took out his iPhone and snapped preliminary photos of the whole celebratory scene which he estimated, based on the wrappers and ribbons, to be about 10' X 20'. He took photos in a circle so he could get a perspective on the old roadbed leading to the dump site. He stepped to the downhill side of the trail and carefully viewed every tree, rock, and piece of brush leading along the trail and bank to where he figured the bones must be. Two chirping tree squirrels paused their game of mating tag on a cedar tree trunk and curiously eyed him. He then slid down the embankment below the trail. Slowly, he made his way over fallen trees, low shrubs, and football sized rocks, carefully inspecting all in front of him before taking quiet, deliberate steps, like an ancient warrior stalking his foe.

He realized that his breathing had slowed considerably, and his vision had sharpened. Calmness, laced with occasional blips of adrenalin, settled over him. It felt natural to be here again, as if he'd never left, had never turned his back.

Within minutes Roy stood over the first bone, highlighted by a colorful Clif Bar wrapper. Based on his experience, this bone was a vertebra, something he would have expected in a deer or dog carcass. No surprise. Just because the accountants had messed with the scene did not mean he would. He would touch nothing. He took a simple gray, plastic, 6" evidence scale out of his jacket pocket. He carefully placed it next to the gray, bleached bone and wrapper. Then he snapped several photos. The scale would give nearly exact measurements in inches or the preferred millimeters to anyone viewing the photos.

Roy sat on his haunches and surveyed the scene in front of him.

The bones were not in a single pile. They were actually strewn downhill for at least ten feet, still partially covered by old leaves and needles. He could see fresh disruptions of the humus around the bones where, presumably, Jerry and the accountants had dug with sticks then placed wrappers next to bones.

Without disturbing anything, Roy clicked more photos. Some of the bones he took for ribs, another for a femur. He reasoned that wild animals must have come upon the dump site and had them a good old time de-fleshing and gnawing. It was highly likely many bones that had been present in the beginning were now hundreds of yards away in some lair, never to be seen again. There was no obvious tell-tale skull or pelvic bone, so he'd have to work with what he had.

He turned his attention to several small, ragged pieces of black, mud caked plastic which were within inches of the visible bones. No doubt about it. This scene had been touched by human hand. Did unknown person or persons dump a dead dog, albeit a big one? Had someone brought their dead canine companion, wrapped in a garbage bag, to this spot? Had a hunter kicked a deer carcass out? Why not butcher it? Was the meat bad? He'd never hunted a deer and knew virtually nothing about the process. The only real deer hunters he'd ever laid eyes on had filled the glossy pages of a *Field and Stream* magazine in a drug store. He and his teenaged pals had feigned interest while scheming how to get to the *Penthouse* or *Playboy* on the top shelf.

He sighed. He had no right to ask questions. He was a patrol deputy. Just take some photos and send them off to a human ID lab. Let the plain clothes guys make the decisions down the road if and when anything comes of it. Unruly rednecks drinking beer on dirt back roads needed his attention these days. Then he saw something else that piqued his curiosity even further.

At first, the rust color blended perfectly with the bark and stone around it, just like a rattler, heard but not seen until it moves to strike or slither away. It was partially buried by curled leaves and dry needles, about 20" inches away from a blue and red Clif Bar wrapper. He could count teeth on the saw blade, the sort of blade one attached to a pruning saw, gently curved, growing in width until it disappeared into the soil.

Roy wondered if the saw was attached to an unseen pole. Unlikely, but you never knew. He'd once found an antennae sticking up out of the sand in Antelope Acres just north of Lancaster. Under the antennae was a restored '74 Mercury Marquis, the model driven by Steve McGarrett in the original Hawaii 5-0 series. Its owner had been a fan, a huge fan, and he was still behind the wheel when Roy pried the door open.

Roy recalled his partner, Sergeant Charlie Criss, peering down at the body from above and behind and saying, "I'll be damned, you were right. Book 'em, Royo. Aloha."

♦

"Victor 12, status?" Dispatch radioed in, keeping an eye on his back.

"Code 4," Roy radioed back, letting his lifeline know it was all good so far.

Roy backed slowly out of the scene and crawled back up on the trail. He dialed the number for the watch commander on his cell phone.

Lieutenant Savage answered.

"Well? Got a serial killer on the loose down there?" he laughed.

"Maybe a serial poacher," said Roy. "Bones don't look human. Dog or deer probably. I can't be sure. Definitely human related debris at the site though, so it is probably a dump, not a natural death."

"Yeah, gotta lotta boys down there'll spotlight a doe then panic when they think a fish cop is onto 'em."

"Just to be safe, I think I ought to send some photos to an expert."

Lieutenant Savage said, "Probably a waste of time. Yours and theirs but let me get the number for you."

"Thanks." Seems Lieutenant Savage could save jurisdictions a lot of overtime with his ability to solve a crime from behind his desk.

Disposition? Case cleared, Waste of Time per Lieutenant Cyril Savage.

Roy copied the number for the Human Identification Laboratory on the Chico State University Campus. In LA he would not have been first on scene. A forensic tech would have already determined animal or human long before his desk phone rang.

Roy dialed the number. A professional sounding voice answered.

"Maya Sanchez, Chico State Human Identification Lab. How may I help you?"

Roy explained to Sanchez, who turned out to be the lab manager, who he was and what he had. She told him to text only the best photos, and she would see what she could determine. She told him he was lucky. There were several grad students and the lab director available, so if he could stay put, she'd share the photos and get back to him within fifteen minutes with some preliminary opinions.

He sent four photos of the scene and six of the various bones. He included one where bits of plastic were visible and the one that had the saw blade in it. He did not say anything about the plastic or saw blade to Sanchez. Sometimes it was best not to plant ideas, so you could get unprejudiced feedback.

As he waited, Roy took a seat on a large boulder in a direct line with the spot at the bank just above the bone field. First, he looked west and pondered what was there. He studied a steep bank of exposed roots, tree trunks, and massive boulders before the view disappeared into a black array of timber. Nothing jumped out.

He turned north. The trail extended upward. Beyond it, in the gray light, lay an expansive view of the Shasta Valley and beyond. Still nothing.

He adjusted his perch to face east and sat mesmerized by the monstrous, dormant volcano across the valley. If only that peak could talk. Whose secrets would it divulge?

He rotated south and stared down the trail, scanning for anything he might have missed on his way up. Someone had driven up it, he was positive. They had stopped here. They had dumped their package of flesh and bones here. They had left. Who were they? Why drive all the way here to dump a poached deer? No wildlife officer, ever, had gotten prints off a deer and then come looking for an unlicensed hunter. Deer weren't protected like a cougar or a wolf. Killing of one those predators neared presidential assassination in eyes of state Fish and Game. They would hunt you across three continents.

Hmm. Maybe I'm onto something.

Why didn't whoever dumped the damn deer, if it was a deer, dump it down in the valley? There he was letting his mind get away from him again. Still, years of body dumps had given him a sixth sense. True, there was nothing overtly murderous about this scene. But what of the trash, the location, the memories sneaking about in his head, the ones for which he occasionally took sleeping aids to escape, and now this seated ritual? He had done his rotations subconsciously today, something he had performed deliberately at every homicide scene since 1987. Red flags fluttered.

His cell phone buzzed.

"Couple of things going on. You have deer bones," Lab Manager Sanchez said.

"Figured as much but, hey, thanks," he said, trying not to sound disappointed.

"Right. Looks like you have some pieces of a plastic bag, maybe, and what looks like the tip of a pruning saw blade."

These folks were observant.

"Somebody dumped the deer bones, maybe, we're guessing, which is something we don't do. However, we would like to ask a favor."

"Sure, what's that?"

"You're still on scene, right? Without disturbing anything, can you get us a better photo of one bone? It's just to the right of a candy bar wrapper, I'm thinking about a foot. It may be nothing, but our Lab Director, Dr. Godwin, would like a better view. He's an anthropologist who is about as good as it gets with these things. We're lucky he was in today."

Roy hung up then carefully slid back down the bank at the same spot he'd done so previously. He took what he thought were almost identical steps along the same path he'd used to get in and out of the scene. He saw the bone, or portion of bone, that Sanchez had mentioned. It looked like a piece of white, bleached bone one inch by three inches or so. Nothing special. He bent down, placed his scale next to it. He took four or five photos from varying angles.

He quickly texted the photos to Sanchez then waited.

A few minutes later his cell phone rang. It was Sanchez.

"We're not sure what to make of this, but there could be a plot twist here. Dr. Godwin says that bone is not definitive for non-human and it is not definitive for human. We wouldn't be able to tell unless we got a better photo. Actually, we'd be more comfortable if we could get it here in our lab and put it through some paces."

"Hmm," said Roy, thoughtfully. The trees above him rustled and creaked with an increasing breeze.

"Hmm is right," said Sanchez. "Now you have to call your boss and give him the bad news."

"Yeah," said Roy. "OT is tight up here."

Sanchez laughed, "Alrighty then. Call us back to tell us if we deploy a team or not. This number is good 24-7. And deputy, if this is a crime scene, you probably know to protect it, right? Not trying to be condescending, but some of the more rural counties have had some issues."

"Yep," said Roy, slowing his speech ever so slightly. "I learned about protectin' crime scenes. No issues here."

He knew how the next call would go.

"Shit. Jesus Christ. Are you sure?" said Lieutenant Savage. "Sometimes these professor types get all caught up. And he was looking at a picture on a freaking phone?" Roy could practically see the doubt on Lieutenant Savage's wide face as he blustered on the other end of the phone.

"These iPhone photos are very clear, sir." Roy said, slowly enough for the lieutenant to understand.

"Well, fuck. Guess I gotta ring the sheriff."

CHAPTER 4

Sheriff Ed Silva examined encroaching, somber clouds as he stretched his arms after stepping out of a luncheon. He paused on the sidewalk under a plastic sign for Pepe's Nugget, *featuring Mexican and American faire.* He mindlessly reached into his shirt pocket for a Gas-X chewable. This time it was the Silverton Rotary club. Last week it had been City of Weed, Chamber of Commerce. Next week was the bi-monthly Karuk Cattlemen's Association. Face time with movers and shakers was mandatory if votes, and funds, were to flow his way two years from now. He didn't anticipate a challenge, but you never knew when a Sheriff's Lieutenant or a local police chief might get frisky.

Silverton Police Chief Calvin "Buddy" Hackett moved into the light next to him, patting the stomach of his yellow knit shirt, the one stenciled above the pocket with "FBI Academy, Quantico." Buddy always wore that shirt on luncheon days.

Silva knew that every police chief and sheriff in America, at one time or another had been given the chance to go for a multi-week "training" course put on by the FBI. It was an opportunity for the FBI to ingratiate itself to locals around the country. Without local and state help, FBI agents were often at loose ends when it came to getting the lay of the land on any number of critical cases. Donating a few shirts for small town chiefs went a long way toward greasing the wheels in rural America. It was the big city police chiefs, the florid faced boys, who extended one hand to shake and another for coin, who kept the accountants for the Bureau up at night.

Today the rotary denizens had been all over him with questions and opinions on a newly proposed Indian gaming casino by the Karuk native tribe. Word was that the casino would be built on Indian land just outside the Silverton city limits.

"Casino means crime, Ed. Organized crime. Look at Vegas," Buddy sighed. "We'll get the spillover. Gonna need a few more officers. Think the tribe might kick in some funding?"

"Oh, I don't know if we're going Vegas," Silva chuckled. "From what I've researched most of the casinos have pretty tight security, and we've got 18 percent unemployment. Give people jobs, and they've got less time for spillover."

"Well, you're the sheriff," Buddy said. "But I don't know. I guess between the two of us we've seen it all."

Silva usually dreaded the vibration of his phone. This time he quickly pulled it from his pocket.

"Sorry, Buddy. Gotta take this." He turned and moved away down the sidewalk.

"Cyril Killer. What's up?" Silva prided himself on coming up with that nickname for the stony-faced lieutenant.

Predictably, Lieutenant Savage was not happy.

"Ed we got a slight situation."

"Go ahead."

"Your boy Roy Church is out with a pile of damn deer bones in the south county on some ridge. He sent photos to Chico ID Lab. At first, they confirmed deer skeleton. Then some knucklehead professor down there got all froggy, and says he can't be sure about one, one, bone. Now they want to do a full-blown crime scene. You know what that means. We're already shorthanded down there."

"Is Roy still on scene?" Silva asked.

The "your boy" comment was not lost on him. True, Silva had lobbied his background guys and had ultimately signed off on Roy Church's lateral transfer request from LASD. He knew it seemed unusual to okay someone that old who wouldn't be hopping fences after burglars. Chances get taken, especially when you're the sheriff. *Sheriff Cyril Savage? Tuck that away.*

"Yep. He's still there."

"One bone?" Silva scratched his chin thoughtfully.

"One effing bone. Deer bones all around it. Duh." Lieutenant Savage's annoyance with Roy Church went unchecked in his tone.

"Okay, well it is Roy Church, Cyril."

Savage replied with mild sarcasm, "Yeah. Old Roy."

"You know his history. Maybe we oughta pay attention."

"Hey, you're the sheriff." Lieutenant Savage chuckled.

Silva took note of the hand washing.

Silva sighed, "Yeah, you're the tenth person today to remind me of that. So, Cyril, why don't we compromise, send a tech down there, snatch up the one bone, send it to the lab and then make a decision?"

"Great idea. That's why you're the sheriff."

"Okay, can you sell it to Church, or do you want me to call him."

"No. I can handle it. That's why I'm the LT."

Lieutenant Savage hung up.

Silva looked back up the sidewalk to where Buddy Hackett was strolling away. He was in a lively conversation with the mayor who had one hand on his elbow. The mayor said something. Buddy laughed hard and slapped the mayor on the back.

Silva exhaled then strolled toward his unmarked parked on the opposite side of Silverton's downtown main street. He glanced both ways. Zero traffic on the cobbled, twisting Old Town street that been restored at significant cost to reflect its Gold Rush past. 18 percent unemployment. He shook his head and popped another chewable.

♦

Roy's cell phone rang. It was Lieutenant Savage.

"Okay, Roy, we put our heads together, and here's what we came up with. We'll send a tech to collect the bone. We'll send the bone to the lab, they positively ID it as a deer, and everybody goes home happy."

Roy interjected, "Okay, but if we collect the one bone and wait for turnaround, we'll have released a possible crime scene to be further disturbed. I doubt we're going to leave it protected for a week."

Lieutenant Savage sounded exasperated.

"It's what the Sheriff wants to do. It's on him. I'll have Dead Fred en route in thirty minutes. He'll be at your 10-20 in 90 minutes. Just stand by until he collects the damn bone. We'll take our chances on anyone messing with your dead buck."

Roy laughed to himself. This was about what he'd anticipated.

"Okay, I'll wait for the tech," he agreed.

He'd met the rotund evidence technician "Dead Fred"

Cavanaugh only once. He'd come down to Sisson from Silverton to process the scene for an unattended death Roy had come across six months earlier. An elderly gentleman, Jimmy something or other, who lived alone, had expired. Neighbors became suspicious when they saw blowflies in the window and no sign of Old Jimmy.

Roy had forced the front door and knew the score before advancing more than a foot. The house was closed up, heat on, and smelled like a pile of dead birds. Old bloated Jimmy was in the bathroom, on his knees, head sandwiched between the toilet and the wall. Elderly people who felt poorly and died could usually be found in bed dead, just out of bed dead on the floor, somewhere dead between the bed and the bathroom, or usually on the floor of the john with their heads between the toilet and the wall. They'd died while on their knees in front of the bowl then slid sideways. No dignity in death.

There had been no signs of foul play, but since Old Jimmy had not been seen by a medical doctor in the last two weeks there was no one to legally sign a death certificate. Therefore, the term "unattended death" applied. Had he been seen and had been expected to expire soon, his doctor could say "no surprise" and release the body over the phone with a promise to sign a death certificate listing natural causes. That would have been an "attended death." Unfortunately, in the absence of the willing doc, California law dictated that a postmortem be conducted. That meant the deputy coroner, instead of a mortuary service, had to come out, remove the body, and take it for an autopsy at which time the exploded heart or raging cancer would be revealed and cause of death suitably determined. The body could then be released to the next of kin. In the meantime, the death scene had to be treated as a possible crime scene. It had to be processed for any and all evidence. This included medications, prints, photos, indicia, and any sign of foul play missed in the initial search by first responders. That meant Dead Fred, his camera, and his evidence kit.

Roy had been around long enough to know better than to ask anybody on the job how he or she got a nickname. He figured Dead Fred was a constant at scenes involving the deceased, and the sobriquet just sorta stuck.

The bespectacled, fifty something, overweight Dead Fred parked his unmarked white van next to Roy's SUV at the trailhead. It was a day for unhappy people.

He shoved his thick legs out of the van. "Well, this is just dandy. I've better things to do than sweat my fat ass up a hillside for a pile of Bambi bones," he grunted. *No hello, how are you?* from Dead Fred.

Roy wasn't keen on making the twenty-minute hike again either, but it had to be done. He helped carry Dead Fred's gear which consisted of a camera case, a double drawer fishing gear sized box containing, among other items, plastic and paper bags, evidence tags, gloves, scales, Luminol, brushes, tweezers, hand sanitizers, safety goggles, and disposable overalls and shoe covers.

Dead Fred left ten times as much gear in the van. He'd been told he was only here to view, measure, photograph, and retrieve a small bone, then package it, and send it off to the Chico State University Human ID lab.

When they got back to the scene, Roy was pleased to see that Dead Fred, in spite of his surliness, was a pro. He didn't just march right in and grab the offending bone. On a note pad, he recorded time and date along with a general location for his work. He took a series of scene-establishing, overall photographs with a high-resolution Nikon digital camera, using a Circular Polarizing Filter to adjust for any glare.

Roy noted Dead Fred had ceased any criticism of the task. Like a pointer on a pheasant, he was all business. He did curse considerably when he slipped and fell on his ass trying to make his way down the bank to the spot where he could move toward the bone field. Roy saw with satisfaction that Dead Fred was using about the same path he had used earlier to approach the scene.

"Yeah, they look like deer bones to me," he called up to Roy who stood about twenty feet above him on the trail. "You know, there are bits of old plastic here. Probably a plastic bag."

"Yeah. I saw them," said Roy. "Looks like a dump site."

"Now which one of these little fuckers am I out here for?" Dead Fred asked.

Roy pointed out the small bleached bone next to the Clif Bar wrapper.

"That little fucker right there, by the wrapper," Roy said drily.

"Okay," said Dead Fred. He pushed his glasses up the bridge of his nose and began photographing his quarry.

"You know, I can see why the lab guys wanted a better look." He called up to Roy. "There is definitely something about this bone."

"What makes you say that?"

"I'm a hunter," he waved his hand in a preemptively defensive gesture. "I know, I'm a fat bastard, but I've been hunting deer for forty years. Killed my first buck when I was ten. Right across the valley over there in McCloud. Anyway, I know deer bones. I don't think this is a deer bone."

"Why is that?" Roy asked. He felt his heart rate increase.

"Well, for one thing it's got what looks like a healed fracture now that I can see it real well. Don't see healed fractures in deer that often. They usually just wander off and die or get eaten. And shit, there are cut marks. Actually a couple of cut marks. Hmm. Very interesting."

"Very interesting," repeated Roy.

"I'm not in charge, but I think we gotta take a better look out here. Hope that rain holds off. Went to a training course once in LA. Some instructor kept sayin' rain was a killer's best friend."

"Yeah. Think I heard that before myself," said Roy. "Can you clean well around that suspect bone for us to get better photos than what I sent to the lab?"

Dead Fred raised his Nikon.

"Uh, yeah, that's why I'm here. But gonna need a brush outta my kit. Think you could bring it down here without fuckin' up my crime scene? I think we got us a bingo."

While Dead Fred grunted and swore on all fours, brushing around the little bone in question, Roy dialed the Chico Lab again and spoke to Lab Manager Sanchez. He explained what had transpired and asked if someone would be available to view an incoming higher quality photo in a few. Sanchez told him Dr. Godwin had left for a class, but she could email him the photo right to his laptop in his lecture hall once she got it.

Dead Fred had carefully removed the soil around the bone with a brush and tweezers. Using a scale he called out, "14mm wide by about 82mm in length. If my bifocals are worth a shit, there are definitely cutting marks on one end."

Over the next few minutes Dead Fred took overall, mid-range, and close ups of the bone. He breathed heavily upon crawling back to the trail. He removed a memory card from the camera and inserted it into a laptop he'd labored to haul up to the site.

"And we got lift off," he said as he scrolled through the shots. "These are bad ass, even if I do say so myself. Let's send these bitches."

"Remember to say it exactly like that on the stand when this thing gets solved," laughed Roy. "Refreshing my memory with my report, I see that at 1630 hours I sent the bitches…."

CHAPTER 5

Forensic anthropology, a subfield of biological anthropology, is defined by the recovery and analysis of human remains, particularly skeletal remains, in a legal context. Forensic anthropologists work with various law enforcement agencies to aid in forensic cases by providing expertise in recovery methods and skeletal biology and analysis. Among other duties, they are often used to help compile a biological profile — age, sex, ancestry, and stature — for unidentified skeletal remains as well as study the skeleton for indications of antemortem and perimortem trauma.

Two professors of Anthropology at California State University, Chico, showed up in a faded green, 15-year-old Subaru Forester hatchback. Dr. Jeffrey Godwin sat behind the wheel while Dr. Sarah Milstein looked at Roy out of the passenger window.

The Puma Creek trailhead got a little more crowded when four grad students and one intern rolled in behind the Subaru in a dusty, maroon Chevrolet Suburban with a Thule cargo carrier on top, ready for the upcoming board season. These vehicles joined Roy's SUV, Dead Fred's van, and Sheriff's Detective Alison Baker's unmarked Crown Vic. Sheriff's Sergeant Bo Jensen had given up his spot and parked in a turn-out several hundred feet back down Puma Creek Road.

It wasn't the cluster of LASD marked and unmarked cars along with those of the LA County Department of the Coroner that Roy was used to seeing. He had no way of knowing if these rural Sheriff's personnel and college civilians had their act together or not when it came to skeletal remains recovery. But it was no longer his problem. He figured he'd be relegated to scene security, and he was okay with that. He was a *road dawg* now.

Dead Fred's photos had caused a chain reaction that began when Professor of Anthropology Dr. Jeffrey Godwin received an email from Lab Manager Sanchez while conducting a class in Human Identification in Butte Hall. He'd heard the ding of incoming mail on his laptop. He'd paused to take a gander and immediately put his class on a YouTube video ironically called "Study of Clandestine Graves and the Human Skeleton." He'd stepped to the side and texted Sanchez.

Human clavicle with healed fracture and cut marks. Is LE still on scene? If so, preservation of integrity crucial.

Sanchez had relayed the text to Roy, who'd then showed Dead Fred.

Sweat still beading on his forehead, Dead Fred smirked and said, "Told ya."

The two took a look around at the late afternoon's serene setting before Roy made a cell phone call.

Dead Fred said, "'Bout to get busy. Wonder who this poor bastard was?"

Roy, phone to his ear, replied, "When we find out, send a Christmas card to the next of kin thanking them for the OT."

Lieutenant Savage had left for the day. Roy got transferred to Sergeant Bo Jensen. Jensen was Karuk County born and raised, but he'd done time in the Sacramento County Sheriff's Department before taking a pay cut and returning home. He didn't hesitate.

"Okay, stand-by out there until I get you some relief. Have Dead Fred stay there until I can get down, probably an hour. Once we find out when the Chico ID squad can get here, we'll decide how to handle the scene. Can you call Chico and get that info?"

Roy noted that Sergeant Jensen had not mentioned OT once.

Lab Manager Sanchez told Roy that Chico could assemble a team and be there in the morning after 1000 hours. Roy relayed this to Jensen.

"Tell them to come ahead," Jensen said. "I'll call the on-call detective, get someone on board. Probably nothing to do tonight but keep the scene secure, we won't have a detective out there until morning."

♦

The weather had held. However, heavy rain was in the forecast for late the following day. The crime scene gods were having a grand time toying with the mortals.

Roy sized up the civilians as the deployed Human Identification Lab (HIL) Team went through their gear.

Two pros, four grad students, and one intern.

He watched as Dr. Godwin and Dr. Milstein addressed the assembled students to make sure they had all they might need. Tyvex suits, booties — probably won't need them —, goggles, gloves, breathable cotton long sleeve shirts, long pants, knee pads, hats, hiking boots, sunglasses, bug spray, sun screen, shovels, buckets, screening trays, dig kit with trowels and extra gloves, stakes, twine, neon tape, pin flags, measuring tapes, cameras, clipboards, multiple forms, compasses, scales, levels, 3 foot metal probes, backpacks with snacks and water, and a winning attitude.

By 1030 hours it was time for a scene briefing. As scene commander, Detective Alison Baker would normally have given the briefing, but she'd just arrived 10 minutes ahead of the college kids and deferred to the uniformed first responder for initial explanations. Bo Jensen pointed at Roy.

He said, "That's you."

Roy was up.

He stepped to the front of the group as they clustered around the back bumper of his SUV. He'd half expected the college kids to be chewing gum, but they looked serious, liked they were opening a letter from the IRS. The two professors looked as though they were about to slice a prime rib. He noted Sergeant Jensen, in dark glasses, stood to the rear with his hands behind his back at parade rest. Dead Fred lounged to one side, bored that he'd have to listen to a rerun. Detective Baker seemed lost in thought as she scribbled in her notepad.

He began.

"Two days ago," *Yes, two days ago. Thank you, Lieutenant Cyril "CSI" Savage*, "I was dispatched to meet with three civilian hikers who'd come across some bones about ¾ of a mile, or twenty minutes, up that trail," he said, pointing to the trail that now finally had garish yellow crime scene tape across its entrance.

He drew their attention to his open laptop screen on his SUV tailgate.

"I understand most of you have seen the photos of the immediate scene. I've got a top map, but Google Earth here shows us the area, too."

He used his pen to point to the center of the screen.

"Right about there is where you'll find it. California Highway Patrol will have a helicopter overhead in a few to take aerials."

He saw Detective Baker scribbling furiously, brushing back chestnut hair that fell over her face. At some point he thought he better tell her that he'd memorialized all he was about to say in a detailed report, a copy of which was on the front seat of his patrol SUV, just for her.

Roy brought everyone up to speed, glossing over the more mundane details of how he'd been spelled for awhile the previous evening, so he could run home and eat, but that he'd been here freezing his ass off the rest of the night. Dead Fred, on the other hand, had been directed to either check into a local motel or return to Silverton, but needed to be on scene bright and early the next morning. Sergeant Jensen had returned to Silverton but had been ordered to return to the scene in the morning to stand by until Detective Baker could get there.

Roy imagined Lieutenant Savage advising Sergeant Jensen to "keep control down there." Middle managers were not so different anywhere you went.

Roy continued, "I-we've declared this trail, from here to the scene and beyond if necessary, a crime scene. As such, each of you will be signing in and out on a log. Name, signature, time in or out, and purpose for entering the scene. As you may or may not know, the log is what helps keep the looky loos, lieutenants and above, on the outside so we, you, can do your work."

Roy realized Alison Baker was staring hard at him. He needed to wrap this up before he came off sounding as if he knew what he was doing.

"Oh, another thing. We've not been through the immediate scene except to get the photos that we sent you. There might be no more than what we see on screen here. On the other hand, this could be a Leonard Lake-like dumping ground. We won't know until you all do your thing. It's always best to assume the worst. Myopia always prevents building the best theory of the case."

Shit, why did I have to say that? Makes me sound pretentious.

Alison Baker was now looking at her iPhone.

Looking up myopia?

"That being said, we've got a county tractor standing by to open this trail back up a little to its previous state, at least so we can get a 4X4 to the immediate scene, in case we end up bringing in lights. To beat the weather."

Bo Jensen was nodding. He'd been busy on the phone all morning following a few of Roy's suggestions. Attack by air, land, and sea. Keeping things under control.

Roy finished, "But we can't alter the trail until we make sure it's been cleared."

Dr. Godwin raised his hand.

"Deputy, might I suggest that with all the bodies we have here, a line search up the trail, especially paying close attention to the downside of the bank," he said. "That way we eliminate the trail first off."

"Excellent idea," said Alison Baker, stepping forward.

I was wondering when you'd show up

Roy saw nodding approval from Dr. Milstein who was already whispering which grad students would be placed where in the line. Enthusiasm danced in eyes of all the college kids. All but one.

Roy glanced at the female intern. All the students had student ID cards clipped to the front of their shirts. The intern's clip read Katherine Hoover. She looked to be early twenties, 5, 6", light brown hair, dark eyes, with a thin build and a very pale complexion.

Hmm, she doesn't feel well. Poor girl. I hope it's not because we're looking for human remains.

Alison Baker had taken over now. She huddled with the professors and students.

Roy picked up his Posse Box from the tailgate of his SUV. The roughly 1" x 8" x 12" silver metallic box had a clip board on top, report forms and writing tools inside. Every cop in America carried one. Every cop in America had left his first Posse Box on the roof of his patrol car. He now carried his second one, the one that would see him through his career on the street.

A scene log was under the clip. Roy strode to the trail entrance and turned to record names and signatures from the worker ants.

A few minutes later, he watched the students, their professors, and Detective Baker, who was in conversation with Dead Fred and his video camera, disappear up the trail. Bo Jensen had gone back downhill to meet the CHP helicopter flying up out of Redding. It was scheduled to land any moment by the Karuk Lake dam.

Roy stood on the outside of the yellow tape. Other than scene security, he was done with this case. His only company were the melancholy sights and sounds of nature. Wind from a coming storm played in the trees, far-off hawks sailed down the canyon past dark cliffs, and plump squirrels twitched and paused on dead logs.

CHAPTER 6

Roy watched the black and white CHP helicopter thunder up the canyon from Karuk Lake. It circled for ten minutes uphill beyond him. He pictured Sergeant Bo Jensen on board snapping aerials of the crime scene. Momentarily the helicopter veered off and disappeared over a ridge to the north.

Roy's radio crackled. It was Detective Baker. She asked him to switch to Channel Two, the radio channel reserved for administrative traffic.

"David 6, Victor 12."

"Victor 12, go ahead" Roy replied.

"Victor 12, Sam 5 is done with the bird and will be heading back to your 20. When he gets there, need you to transport a sick X to Karuk Campground facilities. We're sending her downhill now. Copy?"

"Victor 12, Copy, 10-4."

Old Roy to the rescue for a sick female student. Dollars to donuts it's the Hoover girl.

The "X," a radio term used to designate a female, and Sam 5, aka Sergeant Bo Jensen, arrived at the trail head from opposite ends at about the same time.

There was no doubt the X, Katherine Hoover as Roy had suspected, was way under the weather. Her blanched face and unsteady gait told Roy time was not going to be on his side. He dispensed with having her sign out on the log. He did it for her.

"I am so sorry," she breathed as she got near him. "I'm really ill."

Bo Jensen, alarmed at the sight of the sick girl, said, "I got your post. Get her to the bathroom at Karuk Lake. Make sure that's all she needs.

Roy hurriedly ushered an apologizing Katherine to the passenger seat of his SUV. He ran around to the driver's side. In seconds, he was turned around and bouncing downhill, Code Two and a half. Code Three, the next level, would have required lights and sirens. That seemed overkill out in the woods.

He grabbed his radio

"Silverton, Victor 12."

"Victor 12 go ahead."

"Victor 12, 11-48 an X from Puma Creek Trailhead to Karuk Campground. Mileage 47,113.8."

"Victor 12, 10-4. Your time is 1233 hours."

Roy did not know the history, but it made all the sense in the world to give your mileage and time if you were transporting a female anywhere so no one could later say you stopped along the way for something sketchy. He figured some dumbshit cop way back when had cost a jurisdiction a butt load of cash in a civil suit by getting overly romantic with a passenger on the way to somewhere. It had backfired. Payday for the passenger. Self-insured cities and counties from that time forward required an ounce of prevention. *Give your time and mileage. No mercy if you fuck it up.*

"Oh, God. I'm not going to make it. Pull over!" Katherine Hoover moaned, her hands over her abdomen.

"You gonna throw up?" Roy asked as he slammed on the brakes.

"No, the other!" Katherine cried, clearly mortified.

"Oh shit," said Roy. "Hang on. I got just what you need. Squeeze those cheeks, young lady. I need five seconds!"

Katherine was staggering out of the passenger door as Roy frantically fished inside his bug-out bag for a roll of toilet paper. In more normal unhurried times, he would have grabbed man's best friend out of the rear of the SUV then knelt next to his 2"inch trailer receiver hitch. The Kotula's Off-Road Commode would have slipped in perfectly. It sported 1 and 5/16 diameter steel tubing, covered with a soft padded camo cover, a throne that could accommodate up to 500 lbs. and would have been ready for its queen.

But this was not a normal time, with certain catastrophe about to occur.

"Quick!" Roy yelled as he spiraled the godsend roll over the roof to a frantic wide receiver. He sprinted to the front of the SUV while Katherine hurried to the rear, unzipping and shimmying as she went.

"Oh, God, I am so sorry. I am so embarrassed," Katherine called from the rear as the floodgates opened.

In spite of himself, Roy laughed. That had been too close.

He was a man who'd gotten used to bodily functions. Fluids leaking from the dead and dying had been his stock in trade for decades.

He couldn't help but chuckle to himself remembering Charlie Criss, those many years ago, screaming for him to "pull the fuck over" near the "shore" of Lake Los Angeles — not really a lake but a dry waste of planet Earth south of Edwards Air Force Base. Charlie had dashed off into the blazing sand and cactus for relief. From his hunker down spot behind a big red rock he yelled, "I just shit through a screen door and didn't leave a mark!" They'd resolved to forever avoid Mojave Manuel's, Home of the Big Boy Bandito Burrito.

Roy immediately got on his radio and asked for a 10-36 (confidential) channel, one that could not be scanned. He advised Silverton of the exigent circumstances. He included his mileage at the time of the emergency stop.

The female dispatcher dryly noted, "You made it 2 tenths of a mile. Didn't your kids go before they left home?"

♦

Much later, Roy mused that having sex with someone involved a high degree of intimacy, but taking a screaming shit in front of another human sure ran a close second. He and Kat, as he discovered she preferred, had experienced a moment. Their relationship would forever be tied to this day and time on the side of Puma Creek Road. He would find it humorous, but not surprising, that basic human needs had come to play such a prominent role in the case. Jerry Rafferty had stopped to relieve himself, setting the whole mess in motion, and Kat, having to heed the clarion call of nature, had helped, in the words of the late NFL coach Hank Stram, to "matriculate the ball down the field."

Finding the culprit in a case of food poisoning is not unlike finding a triggerman in a whodunit. On the way to the Karuk Lake campground Roy conducted a forensic interview. The most likely suspect turned out to be a premade tuna sandwich Kat had wolfed at the Travel Stop off the I-5 in Redding on her way up from Chico the night before.

"I thought you all drove up early this morning," Roy said.

"The others did. I came up last night to stay with my parents. I'm from Sisson."

"Really?" Roy said.

"Yeah, I'm just a lowly intern in the lab. The others are all grad students. That's what I want to be, hopefully next year."

Roy, ever the observer and interpreter of subtle human interaction and behavior, had noticed the other four students had cliqued up slightly during the briefing. He'd had it wrong. He had attributed it to Kat not feeling well. Now it made sense. Kat was still on the outside looking in. She seemed like a really nice girl. She reminded him of a little girl from long ago.

"So you want to eventually be the next Professor slash Dr. Milstein?" Roy asked, trying to keep Kat's mind off her lower tract.

"That's my goal," she said. Lamaze breathing. "I am so sorry," she repeated.

Hang on!

"Well, I wish you all the luck. And here we are. Run. Oops, wrong word."

Roy slid to a stop outside the pit toilet at the Karuk Lake campground. Kat launched herself out of the SUV for round two. She didn't take time to close the passenger door.

Roy waited behind the wheel, thankful that he'd not have to remove the portable toilet seat from his bumper. It would not have been a good look racing into the campground where a few campers had curiously glanced up at the marked vehicle far exceeding the posted 5 MPH signs. Still, that device had sure come in handy in country with a dearth of friendly fire stations and hospitals.

Years earlier, Roy had been urged to write a book. Every cop thought about it at one time or another. The life was rich with stories. At the time he'd demurred. But if he ever got the itch, he decided this episode had to be included. Of course, he'd change the names to protect the innocent.

When Kat emerged from the toilet, she did not look good. In fact, she looked much worse. Clammy skin and trembling hands told Roy that Kat was not returning to the crime scene. He got bottled water out of his SUV and gave it to her. She drank tentatively then turned and vomited.

Roy seriously thought of getting her to the Sisson Urgent Care, but she shook her head at the suggestion.

"Do you think you could just give me a ride home?"

Roy kept Silverton apprised of his whereabouts, and, following Kat's directions, soon found himself on Hill Drive, a residential side street two blocks over from the Sisson High School and about a quarter mile from his substation.

Kat's neighborhood was flanked on both sides by wood sided, ranch style tract homes built in the 60's. Brick half walls, lava rock chimneys, and large front yards with rock gardens dominated the street. Lining the street were mature alders, birches, and conifers that normally blocked the direct sun. Now the blazing golds and reds of the falling, piling leaves were opening things up for the coming winter. Roy could imagine the throngs of chattering ghouls and witches who'd be carrying plastic pumpkin buckets in a week's time.

As Roy stopped in front of Kat's house, he noted an older, silver Honda Accord with a black bra in the driveway. A bumper sticker read "I Dig Anthropology," a clue as to its owner. Next to the Honda was an off white, aging Toyota Rav 4. Its myriad of faded bumper stickers read "War is Not the Answer," "Climate Voter," and "Feel the Bern." Standing on the lawn, holding a rake, was a short, white pony-tailed man of about 60, wearing a beige ball cap, a dark green vest, and khaki pants. Roy guessed the Rav 4 was his.

"That's Paul, my stepdad," said Kat. "He's probably freaking out right now."

Paul wasn't freaking out but having the police in his front yard did cause him to drop the rake in a pile of crimson leaves and hurry forward.

"It's okay, Paul. He just gave me a ride home," called Kat who walked shakily across the lawn. "I got really sick on the dig."

Roy sensed that Kat's hurried explanation was to cool Paul's jets. He looked the type who'd lived a probable lifetime of suspicion toward uniformed authority, expressing it more than once around a dinner table or at an annual art and jazz festival.

In spite of Paul's possible antipathy toward law enforcement officers, he told Roy he was appreciative for the ride. He and Kat's mother had worried a bit about her when the other students arrived that morning to pick her up. Kat had expressed a degree of trepidation at going out on the dig but had gone anyway.

Kat, looking forlorn, dejected, and wrung out, turned to Roy and said, "You have no idea how much it means that you took care of me. Thanks so much for the water. I better get inside. Thank you!" With that she turned and trotted toward the front door, closing it behind her.

To Roy's surprise, Paul walked with him to his SUV, his hands jingling some change in his khaki pants-pockets.

"Is it really a dead body up on that mountain? I've hiked it a couple of times," he said. "The kids were all talking vaguely about it this morning. I'm sure it's all hush, hush and official, so I guess you can't say."

"Yeah," Roy replied, "I don't know myself exactly what they have up there. I'm sure the investigators will figure it out."

"Well, if it's a murder victim, I'm not surprised. I moved to Sisson ten years ago from the Bay Area to get away from the crime, but there are some really mean people who live here. Big meth and opiate problem in the county. But you know that already. You have a hard job. Anyhow, good luck, and thanks again for bringing Kat home."

He extended his hand. Roy shook it, reminding himself for the hundredth time not to judge books by covers. You just never knew.

Roy radioed Silverton that he was 10-8, back en route to Puma Creek Road.

A dispatcher acknowledged.

"Victor 12, 10-4. Be advised Victor 9 is en route from the Main to relieve, ETA less than 30."

A blizzard of leaves pelted Roy's SUV as he cruised away down Kat Hoover's street. A south wind had kicked up, flowing north out of the Sacramento Canyon, picking up speed, a harbinger of the coming storm.

CHAPTER 7

The Black Tail Restaurant had opened in 1987. It was the brainchild of Bob Turk, a former car dealer in Redding, and his best friend Howard Jensen, a twenty-year man in the hotel industry. A family environment with solid American food, it served 24-7 on the I-5. The restaurant was immediately at the top of the off ramp with an easy return to either northbound or southbound travelers. A massive thirty-foot-tall sculpture of the titular and elusive woodland creature, a subspecies of the mule deer, stood guard in the parking lot. Bob and Howie, not wanting to go overboard, but not wanting to understate either, had settled on a 4 pointer, four antlers on each side.

Real antlers are made of true bone that is fed by blood arriving via a velvet covering, but this was a fake deer with fake antlers made of aluminum. In September 1997, just as hunting season had gotten underway, this fact seemed lost on one Wyatt "Smokey" Judson, a frustrated and inebriated hunter with a score to settle with a buck, any buck. The top third of one antler was still missing, the victim of a Winchester .308 cartridge fired from the passenger side of a 1986 Ford one-ton 4X4 that disappeared into the night. The round had missed the restaurant, most likely landing harmlessly a few miles south near the I-5 truck scales. At the time, the drive-by sparked more than one rumor that LA gangs had finally arrived. Smokey Judson never owned up.

Bob and Howie had laid out the interior of the eatery in an L shape. A long counter, for the single guy, ran the length of the center, separating the customers from the waiters' prep area and the kitchen. On the outside wall a dozen or more booths joined large windows. Except for a few power lines, the wall of glass afforded an unobstructed view of the mountain most traveling customers had pulled off the freeway to marvel at. Off to the south side of the building lay an airy room for overflow. It featured round and oblong tables of various sizes to accommodate almost any group. This area could be closed off for special events or used by anyone wanting a little more privacy. Today it was occupied by a coffee klatch crew that had come in ahead of the normal lunch crowd to get a jump on identifying and solving the world's problems.

Dewey "CPO" Mendenhall, carrying the Karuk Daily News in one hand, had arrived first, sporting his deep blue *Retired Navy* cap. This particular Chief Petty Officer had seen the world, partied at Subic Bay, and preferred Sisson. George Miller, retired Cal Trans, strolled in next, accompanied by Ollie Johnson, retired metal shop teacher at Sisson High. Last to get there was Johnny Pardeau. He limped in as per usual. A logging accident in '73 had robbed him of his speed.

Late Wednesday mornings were their mornings at the Black Tail. None could believe how the years had passed. Decorating the walls of the restaurant, especially in this back room, were memorabilia and sports photos of every football, basketball, and baseball team that had passed through Sisson High since the 60's. A group photo of the grinning league champs, the Sisson Bears of '68, hung on the wall above their favorite table. Next to that photo was a smaller one. In it, a lone, helmeted Johnny Pardeau, the one who'd gone on, posed with his war face in a Davis Aggies uniform.

An attractive, middle-aged waitress with a name tag that read *Jeanie* came in to take orders.

"You boys got your coffee and waters. Have you decided what you'll have?"

Johnny Pardeau lowered his menu and his bifocals first.

"I gotta take Mary to the doc in Redding this afternoon, probably have dinner later, so I'm goin' light. Just a Forkie Burger and side of Fawn fries," he said.

CPO, snorted, "Hell, I'm starving. Full Muley for me, and extra onions, darlin'."

"CPO must have a date," laughed George Miller. Jeanie joined him.

When Jeanie had left with the orders, the boys got down to business.

"Halloween tomorrow. Weatherman says cold and rainy," said Ollie Johnson. "That'll keep the little monsters to a minimum. More candy for you, Georgie."

"Halloween. Now that was a scary, damn movie. Didn't have all that computer stuff they have today. Miss the old films," sighed CPO.

"Well that killer in the movie must be alive and well. Dumped a body up on Puma Ridge I see," said Georgie Miller as he scanned an article on the front page of the paper.

"Naw," said Ollie. "Dead homeless bum. I read that this morning.

"What's it say, Georgie?" asked Johnny Pardeau. "I haven't heard about this."

Miller read from the article written by a reporter named Amy Douglas.

The Karuk County Sheriff's Department is investigating a discovery by hikers of alleged human skeletal remains found last week on the Puma Creek trail. In a press release, Sheriff Ed Silva revealed that a team of anthropologists from the Chico State University Human Identification Lab is assisting Sheriff's detectives in the investigation. The remains have not been identified. In a phone interview, Silva wouldn't say if foul play is suspected, only that the presence of the remains was suspicious, and that the matter is under investigation. The Sheriff Department is asking anyone with any information to please call the Sheriff's Department's Major Crimes Investigations Section at 530-843-1700.

"I bet it's a body dump by a serial killer," CPO declared. "No homeless bum is going to walk all the way up there and die."

"What if they say it's an Indian burial ground?" asked Pardeau. "Just one more way for the environmentalists to keep us out of the woods. Another place we can't cut trees."

"You used to fall timber up there didn't you, Johnny?" asked Ollie. "Did all of you come back, or did you leave a choker setter under a log somewhere?"

"You know what?" exclaimed Georgie Miller. "I'll bet it's that girl who went missing from Weed back in the early 90's. Gotta be. Everybody figures her neighbor killed her."

"Well, what about the asshole boyfriend who told the cops he got in a beef with his girlfriend and she jumped out of his car over by the lake and disappeared?" said CPO Mendenhall. "I'll bet it's her.

Everybody knew he whacked her and buried her out there somewhere."

"More likely a dead city dude out for a hike. Didn't tell anybody where he was going, he has a heart attack, and nobody gives a shit that he's missing," said Ollie Johnson. "Or he stopped to take a piss and a cougar got his ass. They don't call it Puma Ridge for nothing."

Someone said, "Maybe a dead hippie. One of those Rainbow assholes. Too many of them around here now. Damn, this place has changed since we were kids. Used to be old Italian families and mill workers. Now it's all these crystal loving weirdos who worship the mountain."

Someone else weighed in with, "Place used to be safe. Never locked my doors. Drugs and hippies. Ruining a good town."

"Hey Jeanie, did you hear about that dead body they found up on Puma Ridge?" CPO asked as the waitress came in with a water refill.

"Hope it's my ex-husband," Jeanie said as she poured.

"Shit, I hope it's *my* ex," exclaimed Ollie Johnson. "But she's too mean to die. That gal could hunt a grizzly with a switch."

"Yeah, your ex old lady was a piece of work, Ollie," agreed Georgie Miller. "I heard she has a bearskin rug. The bear ain't dead, just afraid to move."

"Whoa, 5-0 just walked in. Over here, officer, here's the one you want!" laughed CPO while pointing at Johnny Pardeau.

Roy Church grinned and took a table on the other side of the room.

"He looks too nasty for me. Let me get SWAT on this," Roy said, pretending to talk into his shoulder mic.

All the old guys laughed.

Someone yelled, "Jeanie, his money's no good in here. Put his lunch on our tab."

"Thanks, men, but the Sheriff has strict rules. I really appreciate it though." Roy smiled good-naturedly.

"So what's this dead body up on Puma Ridge all about, officer?" Ollie Johnson asked.

"Uh, deputy. Hey, you know as much as I do. Detectives are investigating. If you know anything, or know anyone who might know something, call the Sheriff's Department main number," replied Roy.

"We got it solved," said CPO, "It's an eyewitness to Clinton corruption."

"Shit. Probably true," said Johnnie Pardeau, shaking his head.

♦

An hour after attending the amateur detectives' roundtable at the Black Tail, Roy stepped into the Sheriff's Substation. The air of quiet and calm had been interrupted over the past week by two detectives sent down from Silverton who'd made the sub their base of operations. Alison Baker and her partner on the bone case, Wallace Westwood, were busy debating their next move.

Roy sensed frustration. A week after the dig and no one in custody. Occasionally these matters took time, but some detectives were wired for immediate results. They preferred a rapidly cooling body, a fresh kill with lots of witnesses and physical evidence to point them in the right direction.

The two investigators glanced up as Roy passed by. Alison nodded. Westwood looked bored.

Westwood, mid-thirties with a shaved head over a frame that had admired itself in a gym mirror more than once, tossed down a pen and pushed away from a desk. He stood up, stretched and cracked his neck side to side. Roy noted the cross-draw shoulder rig with the nickel plated .45 on one side, handcuffs on the other.

It might have been the cowboy boots and expensive leather jacket, but a week earlier Roy had immediately pegged Westwood for a detective more in love with the title than the job. He knew the type well. They loved the part, loved driving the unmarked, the lengthy lunches, and not being a slave to the radio. Most of all they enjoyed handing out the business cards to their friends and relatives, the cards that clearly spelled out their title of *Detective*. It was the pinnacle for any cop who wanted to stay a cop and not advance up the managerial chain. Police management was a dark subject for another day. He'd bet that Wally Westwood probably wanted to be known as Clint.

"So, Clint," Alison Baker yawned. Roy barely kept his coffee in his mouth. "Wanna go get some lunch?"

"Might as well. Not doing dick here," Westwood replied. He grabbed his leather jacket off the back of his chair. "Maybe Old Roy can solve his own pile of shit while we're gone. Ha. Jesus what a pain in the ass."

Roy chuckled right along with "Clint." "Not me, young man. Won't catch me taking cases home at night. When the shift is done, the shift is done."

Westwood and Baker beat it out the door, hopped in their unmarked, and were off to a 90 minute lunch.

Roy could just hear them at 1530 hours, "Too late to start anything now, might as well knock off for the day."

Roy looked around the empty sub and at the workspace just vacated for chowtime. The two desks occupied by the detectives were piled with missing-persons fliers, coffee cups, and old police reports. Baker even had copies of Roy's original report from that first day with the accountants, as well as supplemental reports detailing his actions with Dead Fred and the Chico crew. He saw that Baker had highlighted portions of his report in which he'd described his phoning Chico from the scene and requesting the lab respond, instead of excavating the clavicle bone and sending it to the lab per instruction from Lieutenant Savage. Scribbled in the margin were the words "*authorized by?*"

Roy had made sure he'd clearly documented that Dead Fred, the evidence expert on scene, had agreed with his decision to maintain scene integrity and wait to do it right instead of yanking one bone from the scene.

Somebody's got his panties in a knot.

Baker and Westwood had a whiteboard leaning against the side of one desk. In erasable, red scrawl the various theories of the case had emerged.

Transient? Missing hiker? Runaway? MG-Weed? Body dump-domestic? Drug deal GB? Mexican cartel (most likely)? Native Burial? Serial (Green River)?

Roy observed that they'd discounted DB Cooper, Elvis, and Jimmy Hoffa. He wondered if he should add Amelia Earhart or "*funk between fur trappers and 49ers.*"

A yellow sticky note on Westwood's desk read "*SNAFU by Chico?*"

Desperation.

Roy sat and finished a 594 P.C. report, vandalism to construction equipment at the new Black Tail Brewery site adjacent to the restaurant. Someone with a black sharpie had drawn a huge penis on the side of a backhoe. A sign that had read *Coming Soon, Mule Deer Dark on Draught!* had been altered to read *Cuming Soon Dear.* Roy suspected two unidentified 14 year olds who'd been seen racing from the area on bikes. Or, maybe the original Black Angus Restaurant sign vandal had finally paroled and needed new frontiers.

As he drove away from the sub to finish out the shift, he spied a pirate and a demon, getting the jump on All Hallows Eve, wrestling madly through a pile of leaves in a front yard.

To be young and innocent, when evil is fun.

♦

Cedar Stock idled and watched from the 76 gas station he'd just finished filling up at. His eyes followed the Sheriff's SUV as it pulled out of the Black Tail lot next door and turned east, away. Then Cedar eased out onto Lake Street and immediately turned right, into the Black Tail lot.

Automatic on the job. Don't be seen if you don't need to be seen.

A few minutes later he sat at the Black Tail's counter nursing a cup of coffee. He began taking in each line of a front page story on the butter stained newspaper that had been left behind by the four old boys who'd just backslapped each other out the front double doors after hollering goodbye to the waitress who now poised over his cup, question in her eyes.

"No thanks," he said politely.

Jeanie smiled and moved away.

Before returning to the story on the human remains investigation, he glanced out the windows into the Black Tail parking lot where two of the elderly foursome had temporarily remained in sight. Mr. Johnson doubled over with laughter, then straightened and heartily shook a weathered, outstretched hand.

Two years in his metal shop and he didn't recognize me. Hell, I guess it was a long time ago.

Cedar reread the story twice more before dropping a five dollar bill on the counter and strolling outside.

The old boys were nowhere to be seen.

He momentarily regretted not calling out to Mr. Johnson, but then he figured it might have been uncomfortable. There'd been a lot of muddy water passed under life's bridge.

His musing on high school memories halted when he felt his iPhone vibrate.

Truck stop I-5 Lodi Hwy 12 exit mules will be there cowboy ready to ride?

Cedar took a deep breath, glanced down at imaginary Tony Llamas boots, and texted back.

Spurs on. Cut 'er loose, and let's talk punctuation when I get there.

CHAPTER 8

In the 1980's the Mexican drug cartels, picking up the slack left by the vanquished Columbians, monopolized the cocaine market in the U.S. They made a bundle. Greedy as they were, they then invaded California and booted the Hells Angels from the methamphetamine market. They made a killing. Not satisfied, the *paisas,* as they were known in the dope trade, looked to go full Scrooge McDuck and own everything. Time to go green, go natural, go organic, man. Up to this time the Tye Dye Mafia had run the show, mostly in the North Coast region of *Califas.* Counties of Humboldt, Trinity, Mendocino, Del Norte, and Karuk had the best climate, soil, and attitudes for the laid-back agrarians to work their THC magic. The aging hippie, marijuana farmers eschewed violence and generally looked upon the 2nd Amendment as a horrific, unforgivable error by the Founding Fathers. The cartels didn't give a shit what the mellow fellows thought about jack. There were no guns to face, and they moved right in, leaving the stunned and saddened sons of the 60's holding their broken dreams and mouthing the words, "Wow man, not cool."

The Mexicans set up shop in a huge way. Hundreds of acres of illicit marijuana farms sprang up in the sparsely populated woods of the north state. Poor Mexicans from Michoacán, Sinaloa, and Sonora were smuggled in to work their asses off in the hills. The average laborer would haul and install PVC water pipe, then plant, weed, trim, and guard against marauding wildlife on four or two legs. A good crew planted three gardens within a few miles of each other.

The bosses figured one would go down via CAMP agents, the Campaign Against Marijuana Planting, another might fall victim to poor soil, pests, or bad luck. The third would still yield a million dollars, making the whole effort worthwhile. Once every two weeks, a "supervisor" would pick up his farmers along a back logging road and run them into town. There, they'd get more supplies, recharge cell phone batteries, spend a night in a motel so they could shower properly, and place a call to family members back across the border. The workers knew if they effed up, *jodido*, on the job, the family back home would pay, often times with their heads. It was a tough business, but times were hard below the border, and men got desperate.

The cartels made bank as the serfs toiled in the woods. Illegal drug profits in the US reached into the billion plus range. Times were good. Then the voters of California came along and fucked it all up. They legalized weed, both medicinal and recreational. Cartel profits plummeted. Karma had come home to roost. In the words of the last hippie chased off his pot farm ten years earlier, "Bummer, dude."

With legalized marijuana there was joy in the street. Everybody gets high, cheap. *We can all grow our own!*

Unfortunately, life doesn't work that way. If you were a slug who missed work while smoking copious bowls before legalization, you were still the same slug who couldn't get out of bed in the morning without a breakfast blunt to get you motivated to play Xbox. Cultivation of marijuana was cultivation of a crop. Corn and rice farmers get their butts and green thumbs up early and go to bed late. Rinse and repeat. There is a reason most Americans fled the rural life in the last century in favor of a comfortable life in the cities and 'burbs where your food grows on shelves. Being a farmer is a difficult proposition at best.

Admitting to himself he was lazy, had no green thumb, and loved life on the reckless side, Ricky Dunn meticulously planned his crew's home invasions. His second in command, Bobby Dudley, assisted. They were bros. Had been since Silverton High. They'd done time together in the principal's office, served in-house suspensions together, followed one another at expulsion hearings, and roomed together at Juvenile Hall. They got separated for a minute at California Youth Authority but held a joyous, pruno-fueled reunion on a Susanville Prison fire crew. Now they had a can't-miss, get rich quick scheme. All they had to do was mask up, waltz in, put everyone on the floor and load already packaged marijuana into the back of a rented U-Haul. Bobby came up with the U-Haul idea. No sense using one of their parents' vehicles.

Ricky rounded out the Ricky Bobby Crew (a nod to Will Ferrell's comedy Talladega Nights) with Bobby's cousin Cody Barham who had the lay of the land since he'd not been away for several years like them, bouncing around California's gray bar hotels. Cody had connections. He knew guys who knew guys in the vast Silverton underworld, such as it was. One of Cody's guys was his homeboy Tim who had hella connections and an eye for anything sketchy.

Their target was a sweet little set-up brought to their attention through a clap carrying, drug addled Native chick named Virginia whom Homeboy Tim had recruited as a scout of sorts. The idea was to locate a righteous dope pad, send Virginia in to buy some product, get the layout, and then hit it like a SWAT team. Then, while looking for employment, Virginia found the perfect grass processing house about seven miles east of Silverton on a five acre parcel in the long time farming community of Montague. It was run by some "harmless little Chinks from down south." The Asians had gotten a jump on the legalization and had a full season of beautiful buds and flowers packaged and ready to ship to a dispensary in Fresno. Virginia had seen it all. Just sitting there, waiting for the taking.

The "harmless little chinks from down south," named Lor Kia Tong, Touby Lyfong, and Mee Moua, had left the sizable Hmong community in the Central Valley burg of Fresno for Karuk County. Their aim was to establish a profitable cannabis grow for their families who ran the Fresno dope store.

Mee Moua had hired then fired Virginia. He'd depended on her to help package, as in like a real job. Virginia had neglected to show up for work on time three days in a row and got shown the door. Virginia, nursing a mad-on, told Homeboy Tim everything she knew. She'd show them.

Homeboy Tim passed all this valuable intel to his boy Cody who hotfooted it over to Bobby who then told the brains of the outfit, Ricky Dunn, and the plan was set.

They'd considered bringing Homeboy Tim for added security, but the four-way split seemed less of a return on investment than they wanted. Tim was more than cool with being on the outside looking in as long as he got "broke off" on the job. Besides, he pointed out it was his girl who went in as the mole. If the slants backtracked they might land on him, and then it was just an extra step to the crew. He'd seen it in the movies. It was called "plausible deniability." Real spy shit. The others agreed he'd get broke off with a fat commission. Smart business. Then they had Cody rent the U-Haul since he had the license.

Go time.

Unfortunately, the shit hit the fan the moment the white boys stormed the Hmong stronghold, stronghold because the Hmongs were not stupid. They came from violent stock in the hills of Laos where their grandfathers had fought the commies under guidance of the American CIA. Grandfathers had to flee Laos when the Americans turned tail in the early 70's. These people were not going to be taken advantage of again. Virginia the Scout had apparently neglected to mention the bad attitude and firepower the "harmless little chinks from down south" possessed.

The second Ricky and Bobby entered the front door wearing masks and carrying pistols, one of them a six-shot revolver, they were in a world of hurt. Forty seconds earlier Touby Lyfong had been kicked back in a chair talking on his iPhone when he glanced up at a screen wired to a hidden surveillance cam. He spotted the U-Haul as it slid to a stop. The white boys had brought the proverbial knife to a gunfight. The Hmongs were loaded for bear, commie bear, with an AR-15 sporting a 30 round magazine (legal in Texas, illegal in California), a Glock 17, with an15 round magazine (legal in Texas, illegal in California) and a Sig Sauer P226 Legion boasting a 15 round 9mm mag, (also legal in Texas but illegal in California).

Ricky Dunn and Bobby Dudley, who immediately discovered they'd mistakenly gone to Texas as bros in life, suddenly became bros in the hereafter.

The Hmongs could have cleaned up the mess except Cody was in the U-Haul in the driveway waiting for the signal to come inside for his reward. He saw the carnage and hauled ass, dialing Homeboy Tim for grief counseling as he sped west toward Silverton. Cody abandoned the bullet ridden U-Haul on a Silverton back street. He then got a ride from Homeboy Tim. A resident on the street, taking out his garbage, saw the shot up U-Haul. He also saw the car Homeboy Tim picked Cody up in and grabbed a plate. Just in case. Then he dialed the cops.

The rude sound of his cell phone awakened Karuk County Sheriff Ed Silva, at 0400 hours. It was Lieutenant Cyril Savage, filling in for the normal watch commander.

"Ed," he said, "We got a situation. Double homicide, multiple suspects on the run. Gonna need all hands on deck. I think we're gonna need those investigators milking that bone business down in Sisson."

♦

Roy's cell phone rang. He hit the hands free on his dash and answered. It was Sergeant Bo Jensen.

"Hey Roy, Bo Jensen here. Got a sec?"

Shit, a supervisor never says "got a sec" for anything good.

"You bet. What's up?"

"Sheriff is gonna be down there this afternoon. You around? He wanted me to check."

Oh double shit.

"Hey, if this is about the graffiti vandalism to your uncle's brewery site, we've got solid leads. Pot dispensary trying to run him off that land," Roy laughed.

"Nah. Uncle Howie probably doesn't even know he got hit. He's on a trip to Australia. But I saw the report and photos of that wang. A good likeness of me, I'd say."

That's good. He's making dick jokes. Can't be too serious.

"Sure. I'll be around. Any idea what's going on?" asked Roy.

As if you're going to say.

"Something about the bone case, I think. Might have to do with Baker and Westwood getting pulled for the double 187 up here yesterday. Real clusterfuck from what I hear," Bo replied.

"Thanks, Sarge." The call ended.

Roy continued driving, his mind spinning.

♦

At 1600 hours Sheriff Ed Silva walked into the Sisson substation where Roy was just wrapping up a report on a 459 P.C., burglary, of a storage unit on Mott Road just south of Sisson, off the I-5. No witnesses, but a lot of furniture and other household items had disappeared. The victim suspected his ex-wife and her new boyfriend. The divorce hadn't reached final status yet, so a civil issue might be in the offing.

"I haven't got a lot of time, Roy. Damn meetings," said Silva. He looked tired. "Wanted you to know I appreciate how you handled the initial scene on the bone case. You're obviously a pro."

Where's this going?

"Thank you, sir. Didn't do a lot," said Roy.

"Anyhow," Silva continued, "We've got our hands full up in Silverton with the Hmong Pot 187 case. We pulled Baker and Westwood out of here to help out on that. I got the feeling they were spinning their wheels anyhow."

"Tough case. Not a lot to go on," said Roy.

"Well, I was thinking, I doubt if they'll be back on it for a while. Shit is hoppin' everywhere, so if you get some spare time down here and want to look it over, give some input, maybe follow up on any leads in your spare time, feel free. Savage knows I'm asking, so does Gary Lynch, the LT in Investigations. If you need anything on it, they can get it for you. Don't kill yourself on it, and if you come up with anything earth shattering maybe I can shake Baker or Westwood or somebody loose. Your call. Give you a chance to show us how you got all those awards back in the Civil War era," Silva chuckled.

"Thanks, Sheriff, I'm not looking to get back into the detective game, but I'll keep my eyes and ears open."

"Okay, Roy. Like I said, your call. No pressure. But it would be nice to clear that damn thing. Newspaper keeps buggin' me on it. At least I can say we're — meaning you — still following leads."

"Right," said Roy slowly.

No pressure my ass. Voters don't like unsolved mysteries.

Sheriff Silva took a look around the sub.

"I'll have the case file brought down here for storage. No pressure. Gotta run." Silva nodded to Roy on his way out.

Yep, we've got storage room all right. It'll be safe awaiting the return of your boy Wally.

♦

Roy enjoyed the days and nights of changing seasons in his new home. From the front of the substation he could plainly see lights glowing over the tops of trees, coming from the Sisson football field. The distant roar of the local crowd told him the Sisson Bears of '18 were closing in on a championship. The diminutive, late evening monsters swinging their orange and black pumpkin buckets up and down the sidewalks morphed into mid-afternoon children wearing colorful knit hats while carrying orange and brown paper turkeys. The leaves had all fallen, leaving barren, gnarled sticks with damp gray trunks. Low clouds now hid the upper half of Mt Shasta more times than not. He excitedly awoke one morning to a pure white dusting in his front yard. Down the slope, the green asphalt roof of the main house had blanched. This was not the Laguna Beach of his childhood.

He passed the time patrolling the hood. A day's labor for a day's pay. He gave nary a thought to the bone case, even though a black binder containing case reports had arrived at the substation weeks ago. Not his problem. "No pressure" the Sheriff had said. Roy was not interested in getting back into the life where he would lie awake at night planning his next moves, unable to sleep like the gentle, loving woman next to him.

In mid-November he lucked out on the Penis Bandit case. Surveillance video at Sisson High caught two youngsters duplicating their fantasy art on the side of the gym. The school principal had both boys in his office when Roy arrived. One was sullen, the other frightened out of his wits.

After Roy viewed the video tape, he took custody of both boys. He released them to their parents after they signed Notices to Appear in front of a juvenile commissioner thirty days hence. One set of parents was apologetic and chagrined. The other set expressed utter annoyance that a cop had come to their home to embarrass them in front of the neighborhood. That fact was not lost on junior. Along with his parental units, he smirked at Roy as he turned to leave.

That's cool. Without your ilk, we cops wouldn't have jobs. Thanks, Mom and Dad, for providing me with a living.

The day before Thanksgiving, he received a directive via email from Silverton to have his winter tires mounted ASAP. What a kick. No studs necessary in Santa Clarita.

Thanksgiving Day was slow. He'd volunteered to cover a shift for Deputy Tom Hanlon, a family man. Hanlon had promised to drop off a plate for him at the sub. He swore his wife made the best pecan pie in town, and his mother-in-law was a master at keeping the bird moist. Roy thought the gesture nice.

Early Thanksgiving night Roy sat at his desk in the sub marveling at the delicious food dropped off minutes before by Hanlon and his wife Pam. Hanlon was right. Scrumptious turkey and pecan pie to die for. He looked around at the empty room. The radio was quiet. Even the dirtbags suffered from turkey overload and were too stuffed to fight or steal.

Flipping through the beat info board, he examined the *Be on the Lookout* (BOLO) fliers displaying the DMV photos for Lor Kia

Tong, Touby Lyfong, and Mee Moua. All three suspects had been positively identified and were wanted for P.C. 187, murder, as well as several other penal code sections pertaining to possession of illegal firearms. Their whereabouts was unknown. Roy wondered if the investigators up in Silverton had checked with Rochester, Minnesota, PD. The last South East Asian killers he'd dealt with claimed membership in the Tiny Rascals Gang. After a botched home invasion of a Cambodian family in La Puente, in which a mother and her two-year-old were left gurgling out, the responsibles had fled LA County for the frozen Midwest. They'd switched all their names around and were working in an uncle's donut shop when Roy came calling, SWAT team in hand.

His cell phone rang. He examined the number and saw the 949 area code and prefix 315. Laguna Beach, California. He let the call go to voice mail. He could picture the good times on the other end. The palm trees swaying in a warm, salty breeze, music floating and exotic drinks splashing on the deck that extended out over the cliffs soaked by a thunderous spray. He could hear the sound of the PCH above the party, hissing as thousands in Orange County made their way north and south on National Turkey Day. He recalled those years so long ago when the Pacific Coast Highway had taken him past the famous Laguna Beach Greeter to the happy chaos of the Laguna Art Festival or to the half a dozen beaches where he'd pass the day charging the surf, chasing the barrel, and reveling in an epic Eskimo roll. So long ago. A lifetime. He could never return, and he knew the other end of the line understood that. He felt badly. They just wanted to hear his voice and know he was okay. Well, he was okay. He didn't feel like talking. That just brought it all back to the surface.

He stared at the black binder on the shelf for a moment, but just for a moment. No good could come of it.

He bucked out of his chair, grabbed his jacket, and hurried out into the churlish cold.

♦

November faded. Sisson hunkered down for winter. Roy felt a hair anxious when he had to drive in 8 inches of slushy snow to get down his driveway to Karuk Lake Road. The locals were used to the snow. He was not. Still, the exhilarating novelty fell just short of what he thought a long ago native must have experienced seeing his image in a photo for the first time. He wondered if at his age snowboarding was even an option. Perling, or nose diving, in the tepid Pacific was one thing. Launching into an unforgiving cedar trunk in a snowstorm was something else altogether.

Eye catching changes told Roy the season of peace and joy had arrived in downtown Sisson. Multi-colored lights danced merrily in the shop windows, merchants hoping to catch an eye. Dark green wreaths decorated with red bows hung across the main drag. Bright, white lights sparkled among the verdant limbs of the giant Douglas fir growing in front of the town hall. A partially lit menorah graced the front display window of a jewelry store, reminding him of those long passed, dueling holidays in his home.

Late afternoon sun, lying low in the southern sky, greeted Roy as he emerged from taking a petty theft report at the Chevron Mini Mart on Lake Street. An odorous, bulky clothed, address challenged citizen had helped himself to a free bottle of whiskey. The suspect had disappeared, leaving behind his battered cardboard *Need $ for Cannabis* sign. Roy figured the suspect wouldn't get far before he had to sample the loot, all of it. But the thief had proven hard to find, even after Roy cruised the area in his SUV and then searched on foot in a wooded thicket to the rear of the station. Maybe the bum had a camp somewhere else in the brush that Roy hadn't yet discovered. In any event, he was flat gone. Roy returned to the station to let the unconcerned clerk, hey, it wasn't his money, know of the escape.

As he parked, he immediately noticed the black bra on the front of the Honda being fueled. He checked, and sure enough, the "I Dig Anthropology" bumper sticker was there.

Kat Hoover walked out of the station, head down, stepping over oil and spilled diesel. She'd dressed in a pale knit beanie over a shiny, black Columbia down jacket with dark pants and comfortably warm looking boots. No stranger to the turn in the weather. Miniscule snowflakes swirled in and danced around her as she crossed the oil stained concrete. She seemed, if that were possible, a bit thinner than he remembered.

"Hey, young lady," he called to her.

She turned, looking startled when she saw the uniform. Then a smile of recognition crossed her face.

"Oh, God, I was hoping never to see you, ever again," she said, flushing a little.

Roy laughed. "Gee, I wonder why. So how you been? How's school?"

Her smile disappeared.

"Not so good," she said, sounding a bit down.

"Really," he said. "What about grad school and all that?"

"Well. That's not looking good. I got really sick after I saw you last. I missed almost three weeks of school. I actually ended up in the hospital. The food poisoning weakened my immune system, I got the flu that turned into pneumonia. It was really nasty."

"Whoa. Too bad."

"I graduate in the spring, so I could start grad school this next year. But first you have to take a test called Graduate Record Exam or GRE before you can get into grad school. I was so ill I couldn't take it. Now I have to wait to make it up. That means another cycle of waiting to apply to school, probably a whole year. I can't change it, so I have to go with it," she said.

Trying to keep a stiff upper lip, I suppose.

Roy said, soothingly, "You're young. They say roll with the punches life gives you. Builds character. Easy for me to say, of course. I've found that nothing in life is worth having if you've not struggled for it. It's the struggle that builds muscle."

"I know. I just had counted on getting away from here, maybe make something of myself somewhere. I worked so darn hard in school," she replied, wistfully.

"Trust me, a lot of people would love to get away from where they are right now and come *here*," Roy said, with a sweep of his hand. "Take it from someone who knows."

"Don't get me wrong. I love the trees and mountains. It's just the people and memories sometimes. Mostly, I need to make a living, be independent. I can't survive on my own working in a gas station store," she said with a wave of her hand at the door behind her.

She trailed off, looking west out toward the Pumas, now fading from view behind the increasing intensity of snowflakes.

"Hey, people have a way of ruining just about any spot on earth," Roy chuckled. "But I shouldn't complain. I've made a good living off that fact."

Standing there in front of him, the brisk breeze biting at her jacket collar, she looked lost. An ill-advised thought hit him. Maybe it was the gloomy strain in her face, or her brave chin set against the fate that had befallen her through no fault of her own. She'd gotten sick from a damn sandwich. Lightning had struck. It was not as if she'd made a conscious effort on a poor choice, like some homeboy or bank robber. If he were honest with himself he knew the reason for a change of heart, but he couldn't bring that reason to the surface without it tearing at his chest, and he wasn't going to do that. He'd worked hard to build the armored plate that kept the monsters in his memory outside the gates, at least in the light of day.

"So are you home on break?" he asked.

"Yes, six weeks. Hoping for snow at the ski park. In the meantime, I just asked inside if they needed any help over the holidays with extra clerk time. I've worked here before, during the summers."

"Would you rather work on a murder case?" He watched her carefully.

"What?"

She acted as if she hadn't heard him correctly.

"I'm serious. The Sheriff asked me to take a look at the bone case. It sorta got put on the back burner when we had some other stuff jump off. The detectives who were assigned to it got pulled, left some leads that need to be followed up. It's just sitting there," he said.

"Are you serious?" she repeated.

"Sure. Why not? I could use an intern to help with some stuff, and you have a connection to the case," he said. "I'd have to get the okay from my boss, but if you're interested, I'll do it."

"That would be so cool!" she exclaimed, the dejected, wannabe grad student now nowhere in sight.

"Great," Roy said. "Here's my card with phone numbers on it. You got a cell?"

"This is so exciting!" she said.

That night, Roy sat alone in his cabin listening to dripping eaves and the occasional pop from his fireplace. Doubts crept from crevices deep in his mind. He pushed them away. He got up, went to his bedroom and stared at the photos on a nightstand. A lump formed in his throat. He fought it. He then stepped to a window and lit a candle — a candle for the dead.

CHAPTER 9

Sheriff Ed Silva hung up the phone. For a moment he stared thoughtfully out the window of his second-floor office. He had a feeling. He turned and dialed the first floor.

"Cyril, it's Ed."

"What's up, boss?"

"Roy Church is going to take over the Sisson bone case."

"All by himself?"

"Yeah, by himself except I'm authorizing an intern for him."

"Great. We could use getting rid of at least one gleamer we got down here right now."

"Nah. He's got one in mind already. And 10-22 on a background. She's a college kid who worked on the case with Chico Human ID lab, so she's already been vetted by them. Roy really wants her, just her. Sort of a condition for him."

"Okay, so now we got deputies dictating who they work with. Hey, you're the Sheriff," said Cyril Savage.

Fuckin A right. I'm the Sheriff.

"Thanks, Cyril. If he needs anything, he gets its. Okay?"

"No problem. Baker and Westwood gonna be cool with this? They did a lotta work."

"Actually, I think their approach could stand a little scrutiny from an eye like Roy Church's."

Lieutenant Savage changed his tune smoothly. "Sounds good. I was wondering how long we were going to let that thing go unworked."

Were you now?

"So, Ed, is Church going plainclothes? Do we gotta back-fill his position down there?"

"It'll be his call. He said he needs a day or two to get up to speed on the case, and that'll dictate how much free time he needs."

"I'll try to make it work."

Silva almost rolled his eyes. *Yeah, no shit. As if that's not your job.*

"Thanks, Cyril. Appreciate the effort."

♦

At 0930 hours, Roy pulled a thick black binder off the shelf and set it on his desk at the sub. The binding label read *Puma Creek 187*. He went into a back storage room and rooted around until he found what he was looking for. He emerged carrying a yellow legal pad. He set it on the desk. Presently he did what he'd always done.

He rested his hands on the binder, palms down. He could feel it. It was still there. It had not abandoned him. His fingers quivered slightly, the adrenalin rising so ever slowly, the focus sharpening. He pictured some unknown quarry at that very moment. He, or she, could be sitting smugly over a cup of joe. Or maybe he'd just glanced nervously through the blinds following another sleepless night fighting nausea and the dread of waiting. Or maybe he was a soulless wraith still on the prowl.

His partner, Sergeant Charlie Criss, had understood this ritual. He'd kick back at his desk waiting patiently, playing wild card poker off the side of a paper cup of coffee from the ancient Saeco vending machine that had guarded the hallway next to the men's room.

Roy opened the binder and began reading and studying photos. As he read he jotted notes on the legal pad. At 1230 hours he broke for lunch. At 1300 hours he began sifting through a stack of missing persons fliers and reports compiled by the Baker/Westwood duo. At 1445 hours he set the stack aside and stepped to scan a map on the wall.

At 1600 hours he took a ten minute break when Deputy Tom Hanlon stopped by to print out and drop off a report. Then he went back in the binder, staring again at the opening page. His mind turned and twisted, pausing on every detail, looking for anything familiar or the smallest throw away sentences that could open a portal to the past, to dirty deeds done and flights taken to stay free. The introduction to the story was there in front of him, hinting at the road to come, but right now, as he'd expected, it was like reading in a foreign language where only a few words are known. *My name is…Where is the bus station?* But if you kept at it, you could finally pick up enough to find your way home. At 1700 hours, he stopped.

He picked up his cell phone and dialed.

"Hello, Katherine? This is Detective," Roy cursed himself internally, "I mean *Deputy*, Church. Can you talk? Great. Sheriff Silva has given me permission to bring you on as an intern for a few hours a day or however much time you can spare on your vacation. Yeah, I figured you would be. Could I ask you a couple of questions? And when could you start?"

♦

Kat showed up at the sub at 0900 sharp. Roy had been there an hour, prepping for the day. He was pleased to see that she was on time, with notebook in hand, eyes sparkling like a kid with unopened Christmas presents. He figured she probably hadn't slept the night before.

After Kat had hung up her coat, next to his Tuffy jacket, he showed her a desk she could use. He'd removed the pile of papers and binders from it earlier that morning. She immediately sat at the desk, back straight, hands folded in front of her, staring at him expectantly. He wondered if he should throw a stick.

He planned to ease her into the tasks he had in mind for her. But first things first.

"Coffee? It'll help you stay awake. You've got some thinking and reading to do," he laughed.

"No thanks. I was up early with my stepdad. Had just a cup of decaf tea. Don't want to make a mistake while I'm wired."

"Hmm. Don't drink coffee? How we going to make a homicide detective out of you?"

She smiled slightly, a quizzical look on her face.

It dawned on him that he was still in uniform, so the detective comment was maybe a little lost on her. His mind was in the Bureau, but his body was still on patrol. He hadn't wanted to seem too eager to leave the road behind, especially if any other deputies stopped by who might not have gotten the word of his reassignment yet. Be ever careful of appearance and perception, sage advice from Charlie Criss that first day in the LASD Homicide Bureau.

"Okay, Katherine…," he started.

"Call me Kat, sorry," she interrupted. "Everybody does."

"Kat. Got it," he continued, "I've been asked to review the whole case, including all the work done by Detectives Baker and Westwood who were first assigned to it but got reassigned because of a mess up in Silverton."

She nodded, not blinking.

"I took the liberty of calling your lab manager, Maya Sanchez, in Chico. She said you've been a model student intern there and are allowed to view a lot of sensitive material that the Human ID Lab manages. As such, I expect you to use the same level of care when viewing materials on this case. Any complex police investigation, *any* police investigation for that matter, should be treated as confidential."

"I understand. Do I need to sign anything?" Kat asked, her dark eyes serious.

"No. Think of this as an extension of the work you do in the Chico lab. Your word is good enough for me. And since I'm now the case agent, that's all that's needed," Roy replied.

"You have my word. I'll keep anything I learn here completely confidential," Kat stated firmly.

"Good. Let's get started. Let's start with you. What do we do first?"

Kat looked at him blankly.

"I don't have a clue," she said truthfully.

"Great, then you could have made just as much progress as the two detectives who worked on it before us," Roy laughed.

Kat smiled nervously, tucking a loose strand of coffee-colored hair back behind her ear. She opened her notebook and clicked her pen.

"Seriously, though," he said, "Whenever you take on a cold case it's best to start as if you know nothing. If you let a previous investigator brief you verbally or sift through his reports right out of the gate, you hear or see only what he knows. You risk going down the same bad road he did."

He left out the part of the previous day's 9 hour scour job of every scrap of info available to him. *Sometimes experience is granted short cuts.*

Kat, who had regained her composure, chuckled, "I don't even know where to begin investigating a murder. Actually, I thought I'd be making copies or filing reports. I'm just an intern."

Roy replied, "You're not *just* an intern, you're an intern who didn't get sick in my SUV."

"Oh God, can we put that behind us?"

"Ha. Okay, we don't yet know that this is a murder. Everyone assumes so, but for me, right now, it is a suspicious death."

"I don't understand," Kat said, puzzled.

"Well, as unlikely as it is, it could have been an accidental death covered up. Might have been a local mortuary saving money-again not likely. Obviously, the circumstances point strongly toward an unlawful homicide, but a good investigator should not jump to conclusions. Let the evidence lead you, don't lead the evidence," he said, channeling Charlie Criss.

Has it really been thirty years?

Roy continued, "The first error made by the other investigators was to label this case as a 187 on the outside of the case file. Their minds were already made up that it was a murder."

"I've heard the term 187 on TV and in the movies," Kat said.

"I don't want to bog you down with legalese, but 187 is the *California* Penal Code section for murder, or more specifically, for the unlawful killing of a human being or fetus with malice aforethought," Roy replied. "It amuses me when I see a TV show or movie set in another state and the term 187 is used. It has entered our national lexicon as a cool substitute for the word murder, I guess."

"Malice aforethought?" asked Kat. She twiddled her pen between her long, pale fingers as she mulled over the term.

"Yes. Eventually a District Attorney will decide which section to charge in a killing, but to charge with 187, or murder, you have to prove that the killer intentionally injured the victim or was committing another act with what we call wanton disregard for human life, in other words committing an act that any reasonable person could predict would end in the death of another human, such as setting a fire in your nightclub to collect the insurance and not caring that people might die in a stampede. Then murder may be first degree or second degree. And one can't forget manslaughter."

"Sounds complicated," Kat said, eyebrows raised.

"You have no idea," Roy laughed. "We are currently light years away from getting into the mind of the person responsible for the death and dump on the Puma Creek trail."

"Okay, maybe start with what we know about the evidence we have?" Kat offered.

"Excellent starting place. What do we know?"

Socrates would have approved. Don't tell the student, let the student tell you.

Kat began.

"I know that some deer skeletal remains were found just off the Puma Creek trail. They had been scattered. There were bits of old plastic at the same site and a section or fragment of a human clavicle was found among the bones. We also know that the clavicle had cut marks, maybe from a saw, and that there was a healed fracture. We also know that a saw blade, maybe from a pruning saw, was found at the scene. I didn't spend enough time there before, well, you know, to see much else. And all of that I only saw in the photographs."

"Okay, anything else?" Roy asked.

"Well," she said, "I haven't seen the reports from the lab to know whether there is any nuclear DNA for genetic identification or mitochondrial DNA with which to run a maternal line or whether both were too damaged. Maybe if we thought we had a possible match on a missing person we could contact the family and get a DNA sample to compare."

"Not bad." She had zeroed right in on a possible way to ID the victim.

"Anything else?"

"I'm running out of material here," Kat giggled. "No. That's it. What did I miss?"

"Not much. Maybe a few other observations and steps we might make before we jump into reports and evidence," Roy replied. "I will tell you though, since you brought it up, that the other investigators spent most of their time going through missing person fliers and reports both here and around the Western United States. They also sent out requests nationwide for any information on missing people who may have a connection to Northern California."

"I guess that seemed like the obvious, logical step to take," she said.

"It is definitely one initial step for sure, and that is what our other two investigators thought to do. But what if the deceased has never been reported missing?"

"I never thought of that. Why would no one have reported the person missing?"

"No one cares?" Roy replied. "Serial killers pick on prostitutes and homeless transients for a reason. No one gives a rip. No one reports them missing or is taken seriously when they do get reported missing."

"You think this is a serial killer?" Kat was suddenly amped.

"No. No," Roy laughed. "Just a quick lesson in whom to target if you ever take up the dark art of a psycho killer."

Kat laughed. Not as nervous this time. Good.

"So, what exactly is it I'm going to be helping with?" Kat asked, getting down to business.

"One of the ways you're going to help is simple. Your schooling in anthropology, obviously, but also your local knowledge. You grew up here. I didn't. I'm new to the area. I have to learn the territory. You've been around this community for over twenty years. I've been here a year. I'm getting to know the town, local bad guys, but it all takes time."

"Well, I have hiked that trail several times. I can't believe I walked past those bones. Really creepy. You said you're new? You're not from Karuk County? I just thought maybe you were from Silverton."

"No, I grew up in Southern California. That's where I became a cop. I didn't transfer here until last year."

"Oh, okay."

Good, she seemed satisfied with that. He didn't expect her to understand or care about the ins and outs of lateral transfers, or even why one would wish to do such a thing. She just accepted it.

Roy continued, "We're still waiting for a formal report from your lab to give us an idea of age, race, and sex, how long the bones sat there, that sort of thing. By the way, you saw the photos. What did you think of the human bone? Can we tell anything about it? For example, the sex?"

Kat, leaned forward and began rolling her hands in front of her as she spoke.

"Arguably, every bone in the human body can show some degree of sexual dimorphism, but it's difficult to make approximations of sexual dimorphism without having most of the biological profile like age, ancestry, and stature. However, if a bone is extremely robust or extremely gracile and you know the individual is not a sub-adult, then you could make an estimate of male or female, respectively. And it's important to remember, it's always considered an estimation, never a determination."

Roy looked at her thoughtfully.

"Hmm, so in English, as for example in front of a jury of mouth breathers and night school lawyers, you're saying we may have to flip a coin on the sex. Very impressive by the way."

Kat, looking sheepish, said, "Sorry. Just sort of went into school mode there."

Roy chuckled, "No, no. That's why you're here. So what about length of time in the field? What can we tell?"

Kat continued.

"How an element decomposes and degrades has almost everything to do with the environment in which it is left. Any level of protection such as clothing, plastic, et cetera, that can inhibit natural bug and animal access as well as protect it from weathering will slow decomposition and help preserve the element. The acidity of the soil and root etching will also determine how quickly or slowly it decomposes. Seasonality plays a big part as well. If you don't have an environment to study, you can maybe tell a bone that is less than a year at a site, but everything else could be anytime, though you can often tell prehistoric remains apart."

Roy grinned, "Good to know. That narrows it considerably. If it weren't for the plastic and the saw blade, you're saying we could be looking at an Indian burial or a fight between fur trappers and gold miners."

"Pretty much," Kat said. "It is not an exact science. For example, you come across someone who died in a sleeping bag out in the woods. While the upper exposed part of the body might be all bones, the flesh on the lower protected half inside the bag could be intact."

Roy raised his eyebrows. "Sounds tasty. And again, very good job. Someday you'll come across great on the stand. You actually sound as if you know what you're talking about. Trust me, that's half the game in court. Hey, so what about age of the victim?"

Kat's eyes flashed, enjoying the grilling.

"If we're talking a clavicular fragment, it will depend on which end of it we have. A fully fused sternal end of the clavicle would indicate an adult of at least 25. If there is significant degenerative evidence, it could be an adult over 60."

Sharp.

Roy pointed to a Forest Service topographical map on the wall showing Sisson, Karuk Lake, and the Pumas. A yellow flag pin stood out on the Puma Creek trail.

"So, until we get the actual reports that give us some basic info on the bone's owner, how about if we divide the morning in half. In a minute we'll discuss the various reasons to commit a killing and cover it up. But first, let's examine the scene as if we were floating over the countryside in a hot air balloon, slowly and high enough to take it all in."

"Okay," Kat said. She got up and joined Roy in front of the map.

Pointing at the map, Roy said, "It is 10.7 miles from the I-5 off ramp in Sisson, past five intersections of county and private roads, along a lakeshore, across the top of a dam, past a campground to a one-time dirt and gravel road, but now a trail. Does that say anything to you?"

"Seems to me it might be someone familiar with the area," Kat answered. She stared at the map, tracing her finger along a possible route from the Sisson off-ramp to the trailhead.

Roy, watching the route she traced, said, "The odds are you're right, but there is always the chance that a wandering out-of-state hunter found this spot, killed a deer and his hunting partner, accidental or otherwise, and then returned to Oregon or wherever he came from."

"Wouldn't a dead hunter's relatives report him missing?" Kat asked, turning to look at Roy inquisitively.

"You'd think. So that leaves us with the highest probability, which is…?"

"That whoever dumped the deer and body or parts of a body had knowledge of the roads and area?"

"Yes. That is most likely. However, keep in mind the possibility that a whole theory can explode if the right piece of info pops up. Never get zeroed in on just one solution too early. You'll end up missing all the other significant clues in front of you."

Roy rubbed his chin as he stared at the top map.

Kat tentatively put another two cents in.

"I grew up around here. Lots of people hunt, but not as many as used to. Mountain lions have killed most of the deer. Whoever dumped the body with a deer has to be a hunter, right? I don't want to speculate, but the saw marks on the clavicle could be consistent with a meat saw used to cut up steaks on steer or deer carcasses. And you're right, that trail or used-to-be-road is a long way off the beaten path. So do you think our killer or killers still live here?"

"I guess you could say right now we have a town filled with suspects. Of course, principal players may or may not still live here. I'm betting someone who knows them does, only right now they may not know that they know what we want to know. Get it?" The deep lines around Roy's eyes grew more obvious as he tried to contain a smile, but it served only to make his face kinder.

Kat laughed as she followed his complex thought process, and she sat back down at the desk.

Roy could see her early nervousness was gone. She'd been at ease discussing the anthropological aspects of the case thus far. The warmup phase was over. Her mind was unlocked. It was time to refocus.

Roy pointed at a whiteboard on the south wall. He handed Kat a red erasable marker.

"Hope your printing is neater than mine. Time to earn your keep."

Kat grinned, took the marker, and then waited expectantly.

Roy continued, "Let's kick around all the reasons we can think of on why that bone fragment ended up in a bag of deer bones on the side of that trail. Let's start with Mexican cartels. Go ahead and write that up there."

Roy leaned back in his chair. *The fat mouse slumbers peacefully, while the cat takes its first, unhurried steps.*

10 CHAPTER NAME

Kat printed *Mexican Cartel* on the whiteboard.

Roy began, "If this is a cartel dump, we will have a problem. I have to admit that I am not an expert on their activities in this part of the state, but I'm told they have been extremely active. If there is the slightest possibility that they had a marijuana grow up off the old logging road, back when it was a road, then that possibility must be considered. Let's hope that does not become a focus down the road." He blew his cheeks out.

"Why is that?" Kat asked, watching him.

"Because over the last three decades the cartels have been slaughtering each other by the thousands below the border in their drug wars. We would require help from below to positively ID a victim. Unfortunately, the cops down there are often in league with the cartels and there is no incentive for them to seek justice for some paisa up here that ran afoul of his *jefe*."

Kat looked a little blankly back at Roy. "What's a *paisa*?"

Roy smiled. He had forgotten that civilians had often never heard these terms. "It means fellow countryman, roughly. The Mexican nationals involved in the dope trade north of the border generally refer to themselves as *paisas*. When a dope addict or dealer or gangster uses the word, he or she is also referring to Mexican Nationals who fuel the dope supply in this country."

"So for the sake of my new intern job, I'll keep my fingers crossed that one of my neighbors is a killer!" Kat exclaimed, a good-humored smile on her face.

Roy chuckled and said, "We might get lucky and have DNA available to us. Then we can sift through a number of local missing persons first, if we can get samples from relatives. If we're really lucky we'll get a hit. That will make zeroing in on our bad guys so much easier."

"I could make a call to the lab and see if there are any updates on the process," Kat volunteered.

"Great. Be my guest," Roy said, motioning to the beaten-down, black desk phone.

"I've got Maya on speed dial," laughed Kat, tapping her much less dingy iPhone.

Roy listened and watched as the enthusiastic young lady across from him spoke animatedly on the phone. His instincts, so far, had been correct. He experienced a momentary pang of some painful emotion, fought it, and moved on.

When Kat got off the phone she didn't look optimistic.

"The lab report is ready to send. But basically, the most helpful DNA — nuclear — has been too damaged to run through any state system. Mitochondrial DNA might be an option to show a maternal line, but there are no reference samples at this time."

"Again, in English?"

"The nuclear DNA is found in the nucleus of all cells and can be damaged more easily. It's what we would need to show any genetics. MtDNA is heartier and found throughout all the cells, so it is less likely to have been degraded. It will really only show the maternal line of someone's ancestry, not the paternal. So if we happen to come across a possible female sibling, mother, aunt or grandmother of our clavicle owner, we can more easily extract an mtDNA sample from the fragment and compare them for shared ancestry."

"Hence the need to go through local missing reports," Roy said.

Kat added, "Once we take a cross section of the mtDNA, we'll have that fingerprint or formula forever and can compare at any time if we come across a possible family member with a genetic connection to the missing person's mother's side of the family."

"So we wait on that," Roy said. "When we get confirmation via the official report we'll go through *missings* and see if we've got info on area connections as well as medical histories that might show collarbone fractures."

"That would be a fascinating but sorta sad search," Kat said. "I guess we could give a family some finality but also destroy hope."

"It's an ugly biz," Roy said quietly, lips pursed as he considered how true that was.

"In the meantime we complete our first task, that of listing motives. Next up, gang killing, as silly as it sounds," he said.

Kat printed *Gang Killing* on the board. Roy winced slightly as the pen made a horrible squeaking sound, and Kat looked around apologetically having pressed too hard.

"Why do you think or not think this could be a gang killing?" Roy asked.

"Uh, I feel really stupid, but, uh, no, because there aren't any gangs around here? Aren't they all in like LA or the Bay Area?"

"Don't feel stupid. Most people only know gangs from the movies. There are different levels of gangs, from the tagger crews to organized street gangs to the prison gangs who call the shots. One thing they all have in common? Publicity. They thrive on publicity for power and intimidation. To keep membership up they have to be seen as the biggest dog on the block. So, when they kill, they mostly do it publicly. One of the reasons gangsters will shout their gang name as they commit crimes is to get the credit for what just went down. They recruit that way, and they intimidate other gangs and the public at the same time," Roy explained wisely.

"Oh." Kat looked surprised and tucked another stray lock of hair back into her ponytail as she concentrated.

"So, I think we can safely assume this was not a gang-on-gang killing. However, gangs will kill their own on the under, meaning they will clean house quietly. They know word will seep through their own ranks, so the message is clear. Keep in line, don't screw up."

"Oh, I see. Then these gangsters could have killed their own cohort and dumped him in our woods? But how many gangsters hunt deer, too? And how did they find this spot to leave a body?"

"Right you are. The probabilities are very low, with some exceptions."

"Which are…?" She probed.

"When people hear the term gangsters they think ethnic minority, African American, Asian, and Latino. Truthfully, most of the organized street gangs are non-white. However, there are organized white street gangs in parts of the state."

"Here?" Kat asked, startled.

"Some, but mostly in Orange County or Riverside County down south in Southern California."

"So it is again unlikely that a white street gang is responsible?"

"True. But don't forget the predominate ethnicity here in Karuk County is white, so if somewhere down the road we find gang involvement, the involved race is most likely white," Roy said.

"Domestic Violence slash Family Violence, put it up," Roy said.

Pressing, ironically less aggressively on the pen, Kat printed *Domestic Violence/Family Violence.*

"Domestic violence would include husband and wife, anyone cohabitating, or anyone in a dating relationship, past or present. This has a high likelihood," Roy said. "Family violence would be like a parent or mom's boyfriend beating a child to death. The clavicle is most likely from an adult so this is not highly likely.

"Okay. But in a domestic violence case wouldn't a victim be reported missing?" Kat observed.

Roy picked up a stack of Missing Persons fliers.

"Absolutely. So when we get some usable mtDNA, these fliers will become critical for contacting family members for comparisons. Until then, we'll do what we can, which is quite a bit. This exercise we're doing is a way to get all possibilities in front of us."

Two hours later, Roy and Kat stepped back to admire their board work.

Mexican Cartels, Gang Killing, Domestic Violence-Family Violence, Drug Dealers, Revenge Killing, Thrill Kill, Serial Killer, Russian or Any Other Org-Crime, Intra-tribal Feud, Vendetta, Personal Feud, Protection of Another, Witness Elimination, Self-defense Cover-up, Accident Cover-up, Mortuary Short Cut!

Roy stood with his hands on his hips and stared at the list and some of the bullet points added under each category. Then, more to himself than to Kat, he began to speak. His speech quickened as his thoughts poured out.

"If you're a gangbanger you kill it, leave it where it falls. In the city, if you're a panicked husband, you roll your dead wife in a rug and drop her in a dumpster behind a K-Mart two blocks from your house. Or you might drop her in the deep freeze while you dope out your next move. If you plan it, you might take the time to drive a corpse out into the desert. Most killers are in a hurry to get rid of evidence. That's when they make mistakes. Their minds cloud up with paranoia. The blood rushes in their ears. They shake. They hyperventilate. They can't think straight. They see nothing but red lights in their rear view mirrors. Our dumper knew this area, was familiar with it, comfortable going there. This is too far off a main freeway for a transient serial killer. We need the DNA so we can eliminate local missings because this feels like something else."

Kat listened intently, mesmerized by the murmurings.

"Sorry," Roy said. "Just thinking out loud."

"Hey, it sounded good," shrugged Kat.

"At this point we have to work from the theory that the bones, the saw blade, and any other evidence found at the scene arrived in or with some sort of plastic bag," Roy said.

"Could there have been more than one bag? A deer, along with a body seem to be pretty big to go inside one bag," Kat observed.

"Right," Roy replied. "Although we can guess from the cut marks, saw marks, on the clavicle that the body had been cut down. Maybe the deer had too."

"The lab report may reflect that," Kat interjected.

Roy said, "Of course, none of this makes any difference if we can't pinpoint how old this body dump is. Right now we run the gamut of the invention of the plastic bag to whenever that road became unusable. It is imperative that we narrow our time of occurrence. Any ideas, Detective Hoover?"

Kat laughed, looking at her iPhone.

"Says here the first disposable plastic garbage bag was invented in 1950 by somebody in Canada. So that narrows it to almost 70 years."

"Well, that means, theoretically, our killer and his kids have fled back across the northern border and could all be dead of old age by now. That's no fun. Let's keep that under our hats. Otherwise, I'm back in patrol and you're back applying at the gas station," Roy laughed.

"Maybe that's where I belong. I think my brain is fried, or maybe I'm just starved."

"Yep. It's lunch time. But before we break, I need you to add one more possibility to our list of suspected motives, please," Roy said.

Kat uncapped the red pen and waited.

"Aliens," Roy said.

"Aliens," repeated Kat as she began to print. "You mean like illegal aliens?"

"Aliens from Planet Zarkon," Roy finished solemnly.

"What?!" Kat turned, laughing.

"It was a tradition with my old partner and me. We always wanted to leave ourselves an out if we went unsolved," Roy said, a very slight smile on his lips.

God, those were the days.

"That's hilarious," Kat laughed.

"If you lose your sense of humor around death, you get too serious, and you don't last."

"So you've worked on murder cases before, I take it?" Kat asked.

"A few. Enough to pick up some pointers and enough to get us in trouble," Roy replied. He hoped she didn't ask any more questions.

Roy opened the black case binder.

"Look, this is your first day. I don't want to overwhelm you or rob you completely of your vacation time," Roy said with a serious expression. He knew that this kind of work could take a toll, especially if you weren't used to it.

"There's no place I have to be, until tomorrow evening. There is a high school winter reunion," Kat said. "It's sort of a tradition. It always covers the past decade, so there will be a crowd."

"I saw that in last week's paper," Roy said, nodding. "It'll be good for you to leave the murder and mayhem behind for a few hours." He gave her a sardonic smile.

"I'd rather be here working on a murder investigation, believe me. I don't have to answer uncomfortable questions, like 'When are you starting grad school?'" Kat said, with a hint of chagrin.

"Suspicious death investigation," Roy corrected, smiling. "Still, I'd like you to head home for the day, enjoy the afternoon. It'll clear your mind. You can pick it up again tomorrow morning or whenever you can get here. Hopefully we'll have the lab report by then. In any event, I'd like you to read through this case file tomorrow, as flimsy as it is. Feel free to make any notes."

♦

Roy watched Kat back her Honda around and drive away from the sub. He desperately wanted to smile at her youthful vigor and eagerness to jump in. She was smart, articulate, and laughed easily. She had protested mightily when he'd finally insisted that she take a break. She'd accepted his excuse that he had patrol work to take care of before spending more time on the case. He wondered if he was doing right by her. Detective work, for those born to it, could be an addiction. A true detective, unable to give up the scent, could find himself standing at the precipice, no different than a drunk lifting his sack or a hype firing his spoon. Roy felt the light scratching of an itch he had long since buried but that had begun to emerge once again — the itch of a habit he thought he had kicked.

CHAPTER 11

Roy left the sub and drove into downtown Sisson. He turned right at the north end stop light, crossed the Southern Pacific tracks, and pulled to the curb in front of a single story, dark brown building with a green roof. A sign out front read *United States Department of Agriculture, Forestry Service.* Next to it was a second sign that read *Shasta-Trinity National Forest.*

An employee, clad in a tan and green uniform with struggling seams, smiled at him from her chair behind a waist high counter. As she rose and approached him he read a name plate above her left shirt pocket that identified her as *C. Morris.* She ran a hand over her dark, silver-laced hair which was neatly pulled back in a ponytail.

"Can I help you, officer?" Her tone was friendly and professional.

"Uh, *Deputy* Roy Church, and yes, please," Roy smiled back. "Who would I talk to about the history of national forest road construction in a particular part of the county, say the area on which the Puma Creek Trail now runs?"

"You've come to the right spot, Roy," she smiled toothily. "Does this have to do with the body found up there?" She leaned in close from the other side of the counter. Roy detected the scent of Green Jasmine tea mixed with bear claw.

"Possibly. I was just asked to get some info on the old road that is now a trail," Roy replied. "Can you explain to me how that worked?"

A nearly imperceptible faux British accent bubbled up as she rubbed her hands together in delight. Roy guessed she could fire off the tempting titles of her favorite BBC mysteries. Netflix was a godsend to the lonely.

"Well, I read the article in the paper, and I knew right away that our road system would come into play. I actually expected a…detective…a week ago, but better late than never," she laughed.

Had the Hmongs been more accommodating, this moment might never have happened.

"So let me explain how this works. In 2000 the logging road was taken out of our road system. The Puma Creek Road transitioned into Puma Creek Trail, by order of our District Ranger, Roger Parsons. He's gone now. Died of throat cancer. It was a bad time around here, he was a wonderful man."

"I'm sorry," said Roy, truthfully, but also noting the longevity of service. Could come in handy.

She smiled in gratitude. "I apologize, didn't mean to get off topic. The trail is part of our public use program whereby we encourage the public to get to know their national forest on foot rather than by vehicle. Much healthier for forests and humans, don't you think?

"Absolutely. So it hasn't been used for vehicular traffic since 2000?" asked Roy, as he wrote notes in his pocket notebook. "And before that? Do we know when the road was built?"

C. Morris looked side to side to make sure no one else was in the office.

"Well, since you ask, I happen to have that information as well. Do we think it's the body of that poor girl who went missing by the lake?"

"The detectives haven't let me in on that. But right now I think they are working all possibilities. Now, you say you know when the road was constructed?"

"Behind me is a little building, the light green one back there," C. Morris said, pointing through a window behind her at a low slung, wood sided cabin set in the middle of an expansive lawn. There were no lights on. "It's no longer in use. All its records were brought in here."

"And why is that?"

"Well, there used to be lumber mills all over this part of California. Sisson once had three mills running. But the focus as of late has been in preserving the natural resources, not exploiting them."

"Okay," said Roy. He was in no hurry. Sometimes useful info came from out of nowhere or took time.

"Once the number of timber sales was reduced, it was no longer necessary to keep the timber shop–that's what we called it–fully staffed."

"What's a timber sale, if you don't mind me asking?"

C. Morris, paused and looked very carefully at him. She ran her tongue along her back teeth before speaking.

"You're not from around here are you?" The question wasn't hostile, simply curious.

"No, I transferred here from Southern California a year ago." Roy answered. "Not a lot of timber in LA."

"Ah. That explains it. Well, a timber sale is when the US Forest Service opens up a section of the national forest to be harvested in part. That means logging companies can look at the sale acreage and bid on it based on how many board feet of timber they think they can harvest."

"Oh, okay. I think I understand."

"Well, it is a very complicated process, let me tell you. No longer can a logging company just clear cut in the forest. They have to file a plan to selectively cut the trees, leaving enough root systems to hold the soil in the case of heavy rains. Also, there has to be a plan to replant where the trees have been harvested. Then, there has to be a plan to clean up the mess left by the loggers."

Roy wondered if C. Morris would grant a bathroom break soon.

"Right," Roy smiled, "So let me see if I understand. A timber sale was held in that section of the Shasta-Trinity Forest where the Puma Creek Trail runs. A logging company bid on the sale. They won the bid. They built a road. Do we know when?"

"Oh, 1980. I'm sure I told you that already. And we built the road for them. Part of our service as stewards of the forest," C. Morris said.

She leaned in toward Roy and lowered her voice in a conspiratorial tone. "That means our murder was committed after 1980."

She stood back, nodding her head up and down smugly. *Yeah, that's right.*

"And whoever did it is probably still here in this town."

"Wow," said Roy. "Good detective work Mrs. Morris."

"Miss Morris. And call me Cassie, Roy. They used to call me Sassy Cassie," she tittered, brushing a crumb off her shirt sleeve. "But I've settled down over the years. You wouldn't know it to look at me, but I was a Sisson Bear cheerleader in the late 70's," she said, nodding her head.

"Well, you have been a great help, Cassie," Roy smiled as he finished making notes.

"Oh, it's been my pleasure. And it you need anything else, anything at all. I watch all the CSI shows and the Discovery Channel on murder investigations," Cassie said.

As Roy left the building he turned to his right. He caught a pair of eyes following him, like a dog watching its master leave for work. Then she turned and went back to her desk.

♦

Roy had already scrawled, *1980-2000*, on the white board when Kat waltzed in through the front door of the sub the following morning. She chirped, "Good morning," and placed a water bottle on her desk. She then stepped to the oil heater next to a wall and vigorously rubbed her hands together. She seemed, in a word, happy. Working for free, but happy. Maybe she didn't have bills.

It brought to mind Charlie Criss as he stood over a limp form in a yard of broken Old English Eights, the whole scene cast in the yellowish glow of sodium streetlights.

"Ah, nothing like a little human tragedy to turn a profit." Roy could still hear the way his deep voice made the joke, trying to lighten the devastation of the job.

The overtime never stopped, but it couldn't make up for what had been missed.

"Wow, how did you find out that?" she marveled, pointing to the time frame.

"Well, I couldn't count on you, so I had to go out and conduct a little detective work," Roy laughed. "Made a visit yesterday afternoon to the Forest Service. A real nice lady there, name of Cassie Morris, looked through the records and found out when the road was first built, 1980, and then when the District Ranger declared it non-useable for vehicular traffic but usable for recreational purposes in 2000."

"Sassy Cassie! My mom went to school with her," Kat laughed.

"Small town," Roy observed wryly. "Anyway, we now have a theoretical path forward."

"Right. Whoever dumped the body and the deer did it sometime in a twenty-year period," Kat said.

"That is most probable, but do not forget that there is always the possibility that someone packed the plastic bags that far."

"For that much weight and to go that far, I mean I walked it. It's a long way," said Kat.

"Yes," said Roy. "You're most likely right. Just never discount an alternative scenario. That way you don't get caught slippin'."

"Caught slippin'?"

Roy laughed. "Yeah, gangster term. Means you dropped your guard and took a shiv in the neck or the gut."

Kat shivered.

"I don't want to get caught slipping."

"Slippin'. Lose the g. Slang it up," Roy chuckled. "How much time do you have today? I know you've got your school shindig tonight."

"Oh, I can work all day. It's not until 8 p.m."

"Great. Two things I'd like to accomplish, then, one of them is us driving to Silverton to pick up all the evidence and bring it back here. We'll store it in the evidence locker in the back room."

"Sounds good. And the other?"

"Before we go to Silverton I want to go over Dead Fred's report and evidence sheets."

"Dead Fred?" Kat was amused.

"Ha. Forgot you don't know nicknames yet. Fred Cavanaugh, the Sheriff's Department Evidence Specialist. He has to go out on all homicides or suspicious deaths to process scenes. Lots of cops get nicknames. Like gangsters' monikers"

"Dead Fred, okay, I get that. Do you have a nickname?" Kat asked with interest.

"No, not here." Roy said. He quickly changed the subject by opening the case binder to the evidence report filed by Dead Fred.

Of interest were the photos taken by Dead Fred as well as the list of evidence he'd collected at the scene.

"Those trees in the middle of the trail. How old do they look to you, Kat?" Roy asked, handing her a glossy printout of a Dead Fred original digital.

"Hmm. They are either Doug fir or white fir. Maybe fifteen or twenty years old. Only way to tell for sure is to cut them down and count the rings."

"Excellent idea. Probably have to file an environmental impact report for that though. Maybe we better ask Sassy Cassie what the procedure is for getting permission to destroy a tree in the national forest for evidentiary purposes," Roy smile ruefully.

"Seriously. Lots of people around here would show up in the parking lot with protest signs while chanting, 'Tree killer'. They might chain themselves to your police car," Kat joined in.

Roy enjoyed their shared amusement over the hypothetical reactions of some of the Sissonians. "Well anyway the estimated ages of those trees simply corroborates the suggested time frame for road closure until today."

He pointed out the items of evidence that Dead Fred had collected on Puma Creek Trail. They included:

23 ragged pieces of black plastic

1 bottle (40 oz., clear glass, without label)

1 bottle (12 oz., dark glass, without label)

1 broken piece of weathered, light colored (faded) molded plastic, approx. 2mm X 13cm X 13cm (approx. 1/16" X 7" X 7")

1 hard plastic container w/o top 5.5cm X 9.5cm X 15cm (2 1/4"X 3 3/4" X 6"

1 broken saw blade (pruning type) 20cm or 8" long (approx.) Transferred to Chico ID Lab for comparison.

1 bone fragment (suspected portion of human clavicle with healed fracture and cut marks-transferred to custody of Chico State University Human ID Lab)

17 bone fragments (Suspected non-human, transferred to custody of Chico Human ID Lab)

1 Memory card with multiple digital photographs of Puma Creek Trail from trail head to scene on Puma Creek Trail

1 digital video tape of Puma Creek Trail and bone discovery site.

♦

"Anything jump out at you?" Roy asked Kat.

"Only the one human fragment? Maybe?" Kat said, thoughtfully. "Of course, there is the saw blade and the cut marks on the clavicle. Maybe they match?"

"Maybe. Anything else?"

"The torn pieces of plastic from a bag, maybe a garbage bag, and the plastic container had something in it? I'm terrible at this." Kat looked at him sheepishly, and Roy got the impression she felt as though she was rambling aimlessly.

"What about the bottles?" Roy suggested encouragingly.

"One sounds like a beer bottle. The other is too big?"

"Ha. Right, too big for a normal, taxpaying, upright citizen who has never been involved in stolen property, dealing drugs, assault with a deadly weapon, or murder," Roy said, grinning widely. "That bottle is a classic forty-ouncer, consistent with a malt liquor guzzled by the hooptie load by every SoCal gang member or parolee since the 70's"

"Really?"

"Yeah. To see what I mean, just check out a film from the early 90's called Boyz n the Hood. Set in South Central LA. Gangland. The actor Ice Cube constantly sits on his front porch sipping on a forty-ounce Old English 800 malt liquor. Stereotypical."

"You mean LA gangs might have been here?" Kat asked, brown eyes wide.

Roy waved one of his weathered hands dismissively. "No, no. That would seem a bit farfetched. But you never know. However, the LA gang scene spawned a whole generation of bad boys across the country, black, white, brown, and yellow, who saw chugging and sipping forty-ounce malt liquors as a part of their whole criminal persona. Blue collar criminals don't drink wine."

Well, actually they do, but only years later, after they've lost everything. Then they spend their days swapping lies and slapping hands with T-Bone and Cadillac behind a liquor store on Florencia.

"Oh, so you suspect a low life criminal killed someone and dumped a body," Kat dryly observed. "I get it now."

"Case solved," Roy said in mock seriousness.

"And what's a hooptie?"

"Oh, sorry, I fall into the jargon and forget you're a middle class white kid from Sisson who's never been in trouble. It just means a piece of junk automobile, peppered with bullet holes from the homies, backfires cruising down the block. No hubcaps, doors don't work, crawl in through the window, clothes hanger for an antennae. Up here it's something that runs, just short of a yard car, or General Motors lawn sculpture."

"I've been in trouble before," Kat drew herself up haughtily. "In fourth grade I threw a snowball on the playground. I had to stand against the wall of the music room for the rest of recess. I've never been so humiliated in my life."

"Hmm. Chico Lab shoulda done a better background," Roy groused.

Kat, who had taken a moment to drink some water from her blue Nalgene bottle, ended up snorting into her bottle and entering into a brief coughing jag. As her coughs subsided, she continued to chuckle at Roy's comment. Watching her, Roy felt the familiar dread in the pit of his stomach. He moved on.

"What about the clavicular fragment with the healed fracture? How do you break your collar bone?" Roy asked thoughtfully.

Kat answered, "Skiing accident, crash a bicycle, flip a motorcycle or car, play football? There are old men hobbling around here who got hurt back when logging was big. I grew up listening to stories about men who'd been crushed by logs out in the woods. Plus," she pointed out, "the clavicle is the most commonly broken bone in the human body."

"Really? What about a bar parking lot fight with baseball bats," Roy said. "I wonder if the ID Lab can tell the difference between a snapped bone due to a fall versus a broken bone from a blow of some kind."

"Sometimes. It depends on how long the bone has been healed and what kind of treatment the person received to correct any misalignments. And can't we at least check with any missing person we narrow in on to see if they ever suffered the injury?"

"Unless it went unreported," Roy said. "Unlikely, but never discount the possibility."

"If I remember nothing else from this, it will be to never overlook an obscure possibility." She sighed heavily, beginning to see both the roadblocks and endless possibilities that investigators are faced with during the course of their inquiries.

"Then my work is done here, Grasshopper," Roy said.

Kat looked at him.

"Grasshopper?"

Damn I'm old!

"Guess you had to be there. Most popular TV series for a year or so starting in 1972 was *Kung Fu*. 150 years ago young mixed-raced kid learns martial arts from a blind grand master of sorts called Master Po. The old boy imparted wisdom to the kid in every episode, always called him Grasshopper."

"Oh. Like *Karate Kid*?"

"Exactly. But if I have to keep explaining my references, our killer will die first of Alzheimer's in a Del Webb senior community."

"Del Webb? From that show *Dragnet*. That, I remember my mom and dad watching. So we're good!"

♦

Roy drove while Kat gazed out the windows. Northbound from Sisson on the I-5, they whizzed through the windiest town in America — Weed, California. The billboard sign hawking the local brewery now seemed a bit dated touting ale called Legal Weed.

Roy's SUV bucked and snorted, buffeted by the Venturi effect of a harsh wind rushing up the Sacramento Canyon gaining more force from the constriction between Mount Shasta and the Pumas. The tailwind, from its violent expulsion out across the high desert of the Shasta Valley, had Roy joking that he'd wear out his brakes just trying to stop in Silverton.

His memory flashed to that night in the SoCal desert coming back from Vegas. He and Charlie Criss had spent six hours stranded on the shoulder with a sandblasted windshield and a killer in the back seat. The killer whined for hours that his handcuffs and belly chain were too tight and that he had to piss. Eventually, he claimed he'd trade the location of a dead female clerk from an all-night gas station if he could just empty his bladder. Of course, he reneged once he got his way.

Charlie and Roy got a kick out of that one. Nothing lost. A confession under duress was useless anyhow. Besides, they already had the body, a positive ID by several witnesses, a video tape from the 24 hour stop n' rob, not to mention the killer's wallet that he'd dropped at the scene of a hastily dug trough off Highway 138 in the Juniper Hills.

"Why do you think we sought an arrest warrant in the first place?" he'd asked the killer the next morning when he had him in the box.

As they continued toward Silverton, Roy cursed himself for forgetting the victim's name. Julie something, he was pretty sure. But he'd never forget knocking on the door and staring at the faces of her huddled parents who'd gone sleepless for days hoping and praying for good news. Roy had lied to them, to protect them. He'd told them their angel's death had been quick. He crossed his fingers that they would not, could not, bear to attend a trial and listen to his actual truth, and see his evidence that revealed the sickening blow by blow of the ugly end to a beautiful life.

Roy had kept a binder on his desk listing his case load, past and present. For the binder, the dead gas station clerk was just another case number entry, but to Roy it had been one more reason these many years later he'd often find himself at night sitting at the table or on the fireplace hearth with his head in his hands, not moving, not making a sound, unaware of the time passing, his mind sifting through the killings that had destroyed the lives of those left living.

Roy snapped to. He glanced sideways at Kat who was staring at him. She looked away quickly and pointed to a field on the east side of the freeway.

"Those are the Chinese rocks," she said. "Chinese immigrants built those as fences a hundred and fifty years ago. At least that's what my grandparents always told me. Master Po and Grasshopper were here."

Roy marveled at the black and brown stacks of jagged volcanic stones, about 18 inches wide by 3 feet high, running fence-like for several hundred yards through the dead grass up a hillock before disappearing at the crest. It looked like a lot of dripping sweat by someone, some time ago intent on combining thousands of rocks into rattler condos. Little time for mischief in the old days it seemed.

Black beef cattle dotted the adjoining fields and pastures, now dormant and brown in the winter. They grazed lazily on stark green alfalfa bales. Broken bales lay strewn in haphazard lines left by hearty, modern day cowboys who tossed them from the backs of meandering, flat-bed pick-ups. Roy felt guilty from inside his warm SUV watching the bundled-up cattlemen brave the biting chill.

The county, both yesterday and today, exhibited a hard-working, back-breaking spirit. But it did not matter. The Devil's workshop had still attracted idle hands. Someone had died at those hands, hands that Roy knew he'd touch before this was all over.

CHAPTER 12

Roy parked in an *Official Vehicles Only* lot on the west side of the Sheriff's Main. Built on a slight hill, the Main consisted of two floors and a walkout basement setup. The outside of the building had been painted a lackluster tan sometime in the late '90s, and the patches of peeling paint suggested it hadn't been touched since then. After mounting a series of concrete steps from the lot, he opened one side of the double front door and allowed Kat to enter before him. A civilian receptionist sat behind a smudged window of bullet proof glass. She glanced up, saw the uniform, and buzzed a side door. Roy opened it and again let Kat step through first. They were on the main floor where patrol and investigations shared the same level. The floor above was reserved for the Sheriff, his Undersheriff Tommy Sessions, and their administrative staff. A number of conference rooms of varying sizes occupied the balance of the second floor.

Roy had been upstairs a few times, once for an oral board designed for divining his reasons for a lateral transfer that coincided with retirement, and once to Sheriff Silva's office for a welcome aboard meet and greet. He'd been in Undersheriff Sessions's office a couple of times through the lateral process, going over medicals and fitness-for-duty reports. Otherwise his visits had been confined to the first floor where he'd gone for some initial patrol orientation and briefings, along with one state-mandated training day on sensitivity toward minorities and those with sexual preferences other than his own. All pretty innocuous for him. You don't survive in LA by getting excited over some stubble-faced woman with outdoor plumbing, or those who speak dialects more commonly found in countries where there is no plumbing at all.

In a corner office with a glass door, Watch Commander Savage sat behind a cherry colored, L shaped desk studying a massive flat screen computer. He glanced up when Roy knocked on his open door. He minimized an Excel spreadsheet and swiveled his chair to face Roy and Kat. Roy noticed that Lieutenant Savage's chair was much nicer than his own. Perks of being higher-up the food chain.

"Deputy Church, how goes it?" His words inquired after Roy's status on the job, and maybe in life generally. His tone said he was about as interested in an actual answer as he was in prepping for another colonoscopy.

"Fine, sir, just here to gather up the Puma Trail physical evidence and run it back south," Roy answered.

"Well, you know where the evidence room is. Sheriff says you get whatever you ask for. Not sure why you can't just look at it here."

"Well, sir, in a homicide case, any big case really, a reexamination of evidence occurs whenever new facts or theories come to light. That's why I believe it would be much more efficient to have the evidence in Sisson rather than wasting the Department's time and money running back up here," Roy remarked with a polite and professional tone.

"Well, thanks for clearing that up for me," Lieutenant Savage said, slowing biting off the last two words. His light-brown eyes, already beady naturally, became more so as he attempted to mask whatever emotion was threatening to reveal itself. Roy suspected it was a Molotov mixture of distaste, superiority, and slight insecurity.

Roy replied in a friendly tone, "No problem."

Maybe the Sheriff could send you to homicide school if you asked real nice — heck, any school on criminal investigations.

Lieutenant Savage had shifted his beady gaze from Roy to the young lady hovering slightly behind him. Roy piped up, "Oh, this is my intern from the Chico Human ID Lab, Kat Hoover. Kat,

Lieutenant Savage." He gestured between the two as he made introductions.

"Nice to meet you, sir," Kat said, enthusiastically. Roy knew she meant it. She'd never been anywhere near a police station before and was overwhelmed with the experience, completely missing how much disdain dripped from the middle manager's voice and demeanor.

"Likewise," Lieutenant Savage said, smiling, rising slightly from his chair, and sounding halfway civil.

Maybe he smells a future vote?

Apparently he didn't blame Kat for whatever bug had crawled up his ass over Roy. As if Roy didn't know. Anytime an underling has a channel to the throne which involves bypassing gatekeepers, the butt hurt sets in. Enemies get made.

"He was really nice," Kat said as she and Roy strolled down a hallway beyond Lieutenant Savage's office. Roy nodded vaguely back.

Jesus, I might need to warn her about helping search for a lost puppy belonging to a guy with a Russian accent driving a windowless van.

Evidence was stored in the walk-out basement of the building that included a parking lot level sally port used for processing impounded vehicles. Roy and Kat had to bounce down a set of stairs from the first floor to meet the civilian clerk in charge of the evidence room.

Roy signed and dated an evidence withdrawal sheet, but not before having the clerk open the box to verify that all evidence listed on the outside was inside. It wasn't much. All the bones had been sent to the Chico ID lab, along with the broken saw blade. He stared at two bottles, a cracked molded piece of faded gray hard plastic, a small, weathered plastic container, and a baggie of multiple torn pieces of black, soiled plastic. It was all there. No blood, no prints, no DNA, and no suspect or victim ID cards to hang a hat on. But it would do for now. Roy had been working on some ideas from the photos. Here, seeing and feeling the physical evidence, some of it for the first time, he was excited to get it back to Sisson and test out a theory.

He turned to Kat who had been peering over his shoulder into the box.

"Well, that's it. We can catch a drive-through on the way out of town."

"Sounds good," she replied.

As they turned to go, his cell phone buzzed. It was the Sheriff's secretary.

"Deputy Church?"

"This is he."

"The Sheriff would like you to stop by his office before you leave."

Shit.

"Will do."

Roy hung up and said, "Tighten your belt. We gotta run upstairs and check in with the big boss before we split."

"Sounds good," Kat said again, still smiling and taking in everything in as if on a school field trip.

They trudged back upstairs to the first floor. Their path toward the stairs to the second floor took them through the investigators' section. Seated at two adjoining desks were Detectives Baker and Westwood.

Baker had her back to Roy, but he instantly recognized the flaming red hair in a bun, and it wasn't hard to identify the guy with the cross draw .45.

Westwood looked up from a laptop on which he was furiously typing.

"Hey, it's the Sisson Bone Squad!" he called out.

Baker swiveled and nodded, looking first at Roy who'd halted, then at Kat who'd come up beside him.

Kat's probably staring at the .45. Great.

"Sorry to dump that on you," Baker said in a genuine tone.

"What ya got in the box?" Westwood asked, leaning back casually in his chair. Roy noticed with a touch of amused annoyance that this one was also better than his own.

"The evidence that wasn't sent to the Chico ID lab," Roy answered.

Baker had returned to her work, but Westwood cocked his head a little. "What ya doin' with it?"

"We're taking it back to Sisson to examine and then store it there," Roy answered.

"Why couldn't you just examine it here?" Westwood asked, his eyes flicking to Kat and then back to Roy.

Why is it any of your fucking business?

"Well, in a homicide case or any big case really, it helps to have the physical evidence close by to examine if new facts come to light."

Did Lieutenant Savage sit on your oral board when you tested for detective?

Westwood snorted. "Homicide. We got yer homicide. These Asians don't mess around."

He purposely held up, so Kat could see, an 8 X 10 glossy of a dead body, a river of dark red leaking from under it as it lay just inside a front door on the hard floor. Roy assumed it must have been the Hmong's house.

"And you must be Old Roy's young intern we heard about?" Westwood asked. "Detective Westwood." Roy noted there was no "Clint" or "Wally," just Detective. He stood up and offered a hand to Kat who shook it vigorously.

"I'm Kat," she said. "This is so exciting. I've never been around detectives before."

"Well, we like to say in the homicide unit, 'When your day ends, ours begins'," Westwood chuckled. Kat smiled broadly at his unoriginal joke.

"Don't forget, 'We'll solve no crime 'til overtime,'" Roy said, dryly.

"Ha. Good one," Westwood guffawed. He turned ever so slightly so that Kat got a good shot of his shoulder rig.

What a tool. Probably flexing his pecs and cheek muscles.

"Look, would love to stand here and chat, but I gotta get upstairs and see the Sheriff before we leave," Roy said.

"Kat, why don't you stay here while Old Roy goes upstairs and kisses some butt?" Westwood suggested laughingly.

Roy saw Baker's head jerk slightly toward Westwood, but she chimed in, "Yeah, Kat, sit right here, if that's okay with you Roy?"

Roy shrugged and looked at Kat who was soaking in the attention paid her by a *real homicide detective*!

Roy couldn't blame her. He'd been in absolute awe his first time on scene security when the plainclothes boys showed up, the ones who got to go under the yellow tape, the ones the reporters shouted to, the ones the uniformed brass deferred to without question. More than that, they were the ones who knew the answers to the mysteries or would find them soon enough. He'd known at that moment that he was destined to join their ranks, someday, somehow. It had been his ultimate goal, to become a real homicide detective. He never imagined the price he'd pay.

"I'll be quick. Can you hold onto our box while I'm gone?" he said as he handed the box of evidence to Kat.

Westwood reached out and gently took the box from Kat's hands. He set it on the edge of his desk.

"Why don't we just keep it on my desk? That way we can say the chain of custody was never broken with regard to the evidence being in police custody," he said, pleased with himself for having asserted judicial prowess.

Wow. Point scored on the old guy.

♦

Sheriff Ed Silva stood when Roy stepped through his door.

"Have a seat, Roy. Thanks for stopping by," he said. "Coffee?" He pointed toward a full pot on a side counter.

Roy shook his head, no thanks.

Sheriff Silva said, "I'm gonna have Tommy join us." He tapped in a text. Roy laughed inwardly thinking of what old Sheriffs Peter Pitchess or Sherman Block would have thought about texting their undersheriffs.

Momentarily, the door to Silva's office opened and in walked a man of about 45 years. He had the crew cut and build of a former marine, which he was, and the bearing of an LAPD SWAT commander, which he had been. Another SoCal transplant from down the I-5. You could always pick out an ex Southern California cop. They put "the" in front of every freeway or highway number, "The 405, The PCH, The 10, The Pasadena Freeway, and The 101." It didn't matter.

"Hey, Roy. Windy as hell coming up the 5 through Weed, I'll bet," Tommy Sessions said as he shook Roy's hand, his tan face pulled into a genuine smile.

"Okay, down to business because I know you gotta get back," Sheriff Silva said. "Have you had a chance to go over the case? Made any headway, and do you have everything you need?" He steepled his thick fingers together on his desk.

"Well, I've got some ideas, and we just came up today to pick up all the evidence. My intern is downstairs being babysat by Baker and Westwood," Roy said.

"Do you want to go plainclothes? Just say the word," Tommy Sessions put in.

"If you don't mind, I'll play that by ear. Might be advantageous to have the option, depending on where this thing leads me," Roy said.

"Your call," Sheriff Silva replied. "We can't tell you how much we appreciate this."

"Hold that thought, no breakthroughs yet," Roy cautioned good-naturedly. "But I've got a few ideas. We'll see how it goes. Thanks for the intern. I have a feeling she's going to work out just fine."

"We've got state grants for cold cases, so if we have to pull out some stops don't worry. Just keep Lieutenant Savage up to speed. We've got him doing budget numbers for patrol and investigations, but your case may end up off our books."

"Thanks," Roy said, "Right now I'm in the preliminary stages, but if I should need additional resources, need to pay informants, or have to travel out of state, I'll check in with Lieutenant Savage."

"Do that. Let me know your status next week, will you?" Sheriff Silva said. "Okay, then, good luck."

"One thing I'd like you to do if you would," Roy said.

"Name it," Sheriff Silva said.

"Give the media a little nudge. Tell them we're following up on promising leads, but we still need the public's help. I want to shake the tree out there again," Roy said.

Sheriff Silva waved his hands. "Done. Calling KDN right now."

Roy got up to leave. Tommy Sessions followed him.

In the hallway outside, he stopped Roy.

"How are you doing? I mean really, how are you doing?" Tommy asked with sincerity.

"I'm okay, honest," Roy said.

"Got people asking after you, man. You got people thinking about you," Tommy Sessions said.

"I appreciate it, but I'm good," Roy replied. He was touched by Tommy's concern.

"Okay, my friend. You got my number. We SoCal boys gotta stick together. They don't trust us up here. Rams *y* Dodger Blue *por vida*!" Tommy Sessions clapped a hand on Roy's shoulder, smiling.

They shook hands, and then Tommy Sessions turned and strolled off down the hallway. Roy watched him walk away. Even though the LAPD and LASD were fierce rivals at times and would bust each other's chops at the drop of a hat, they were still LA family. Family sticks together. Roy pivoted the opposite way, toward the stairwell, with extra energy in his step and a smile on his face. He wondered if Westwood had pulled out any high school football trophies for Kat yet.

CHAPTER 13

Kat was animated on the way back south, while Roy was in survival mode fighting the headwind.

"So Detective Westwood showed me the case they've been working on. Horrible."

Did he now? Head and gut shots from three separate shooters can leave an ill effect.

"He said they've got several leads and may have to travel to Fresno to find the people who did it. Sounds so complicated."

Roy nodded. *Did he tell you he is not the case agent? Probably not.*

"He and Detective Baker make a good team."

Are you talking on the case or in the Holiday Inn Express?

"Yes, it sounds like quite the undertaking, going after some dangerous boys," Roy said.

"Being a detective must be so complex." Kat sounded impressed.

"It can be challenging, for sure. Not all high adventure like it is on television or in the movies. They never show the detectives, or any cops for that matter, doing paperwork. The reports are endless. The time away from home is…," Roy trailed off.

"You were a detective." A statement, not a question. Out of his peripherals, he saw her shift her body to face him with interest.

Looks as if I still am.

"Yeah, for a while," Roy answered with vague finality. Kat picked up on the cue and fell silent, but Roy could see that she was still watching him.

Roy turned to thinking about Tommy Sessions. Tommy had lost

a team member in a barricade clusterfuck in the San Fernando Valley back in 2005. Bad intel had cost a good man. Tommy had blamed himself for giving a go order that seemed the right call at the time. He'd been blistered a bit in the press, those fans in the stands that were suddenly expert on tactics and weaponry. To them, anything other than a six shooter was suddenly an assault weapon, whatever in the hell that meant. The shooting review board had been less than kind. The whole mess had soured him on life for a minute. But he'd picked himself up off a barroom floor and had two more productive years before the commute on the 14 from Santa Clarita finally got to him. One lateral transfer later and he'd stepped on the fast track in Karuk County given his training and experience. Sheriff Ed Silva had recognized a stud cop and had promoted him quickly to Undersheriff after the previous holder of that title suffered a coronary while sitting at his desk eating takeout from KFC.

Sifting through prospects almost two years ago, Tommy Sessions had come across Roy's lateral transfer application. He'd sprinted into Sheriff Silva's office without bothering to knock. Roy owed Tommy Sessions a debt for sure.

♦

Grainy snow, like frozen sand from a Bahaman beach, peppered Roy and Kat as they dashed inside from the sub parking lot. Roy carried the box. He sure didn't want to break police chain of custody.

The substation was actually a converted and retrofitted home. As such, a back former bedroom had been reinforced as a temporary evidence storage area, with sign in-sign out sheets in a transparent sleeve next to several lockers on one side. A work table for processing stood on the other side, under a window crisscrossed with wire mesh. A shelf next to the table was filled with evidence logging forms, tapes, tags, markers, scissors, plastic bags, envelopes of varying sizes, bottles of chemicals for presumptive tests on suspected drugs, a box of protective goggles and several boxes of nitrile gloves in black, purple, or baby blue, your choice. Kat chose baby blue.

As Kat watched, Roy quickly spread out a section of white butcher paper, a little longer and wider than the work table. She helped him crease the sides to make it form fitting.

Roy set the evidence box on a chair next to the table then opened it. Wearing his own black nitrile gloves he removed the items, each bagged and tagged with a number followed by *FC*, for Fred Cavanaugh. Roy would have bet Dead Fred at one time or another had marked a tag with *1-DF*.

A forty-ounce malt liquor bottle, a twelve-ounce beer bottle, a broken piece of hard faded gray plastic, a small plastic container, light colored, with no top, and a baggie with the torn pieces of a black plastic bag. That was it.

"Well, this is what we go to war with, Kat," Roy declared, standing with his hands on his hips staring at the table.

"This is like one of those cooking contest shows where the mystery box of ingredients is opened and you have twenty minutes to cook up a sumptuous meal for the judges!" Kat noted, also staring at the contents intently.

"Then let's cook, Chef Kat," Roy commented. "What looks good here?"

"I better stick to cold cereal," Kat sighed. "I don't have any more ideas."

"We already know we've eliminated college grads with the forty-ouncer, so let's set that aside," Roy said.

"Whew, that lets my mom and Paul off the hook," said Kat.

"Unfortunately, that still leaves several deputies in the suspect pool, along with all Raiders' fans," Roy laughed.

"Careful, my mom is a Raiders' fan," Kat grinned.

"The dark beer bottle is a wash. Tells us nothing other than that no Mormons were involved," Roy said.

"Or ministers?" Kat said.

"Hmm. Not so sure. There is an old saying. 'If you find four Baptists together, there's a fifth hidden somewhere.'"

"What about the plastic bag remnants?" Kat asked.

"I think we can safely set those aside for the time being," Roy said. "That leaves us with the hard plastic pieces, which is why I wanted to get this box down here. What do they tell us?"

"Well, the plastic box looks like one of those boxes we used to keep our crayons and spare pencils in at school," Kat said.

"Have you ever helped take care of a baby? Or babysat an infant who is still in diapers?" Roy asked.

"No. I babysat my nephew for a whole summer one night. Worst experience of my life. A terror," Kat laughed.

"For my money, this is the lower part to a plastic box of baby wipes," Roy said. "Buy them at any drugstore. Use them for diaper blow-out clean-up."

"That totally makes sense! Sounds as if you have a history in that regard," Kat raised her dark eyebrows, sensing some good stories behind Roy's comment.

"Yes, I have a history. I preferred Huggies to Pampers," Roy said.

So long ago.

"Okay then, baby wipes in a plastic box it is. What does that mean other than there was a baby around when the trash bags were filled?" Kat asked.

"Listen, Grasshopper, baby wipes probably means a baby in the picture, but not necessarily. Always think of an alternative. Baby wipes are not just good for babies. Adults use them as well."

"Ah, another lesson from Master Roy," Kat smiled, bowing her head slightly, her hands together prayer-style in front of her. Her eyes twinkled with delight.

Roy said, "That leaves us with Item 3-FC, the broken molded piece of hard plastic."

"What do you think it is?" Kat asked, picking up the plastic bag and examining the piece close to her face.

"It's part of a bigger object, a cover. I'm betting I know what it is," Roy said. "Can you Google portable CD player?"

In a moment, Kat had a photo on her iPhone of numerous products from the 1980s forward. She narrowed the search to Discman and came back with a dozen shapes and colors for multiple years, starting in 1984 with the Sony Discman D-50.

"Let's throw all those up on the big flat screen." Roy said. He carried item 3-FC into the other room and set it on his desk. He opened Google and told Kat to take a seat. "You're on. Let's go through year by year until we find the best match."

Roy held the plastic cover to the screen as Kat scrolled through the different images of the portable compact disc players that Sony had put out over the years. The overall size remained the same, but subtle differences in the curved lid were apparent.

Kat stopped on one image.

"That's it!" they exclaimed at the same time.

The Mega Bass Sony D-231 Discman ESP matched perfectly with the curvature of the molded plastic.

"What year was it for sale?" asked Roy.

Kat typed furiously on the keyboard.

"Looks like 1995," she said with excitement. "Does that mean we've narrowed the timeframe from 1995 to 2000?"

"Possibly," said Roy reading an article on the screen. "Looks as if these portable CD players sorta faded from view by the end of the 1990's, early 2000's with the introduction of music downloads and iTunes. Disappeared about the same time as the fanny pack. Only people who ever wore those were cops."

"Well, I wouldn't know too much about that time frame here in Sisson — I was just a baby."

"Yeah, I was in Monterey Park in those years. So I can't say what happened around here either."

"Ooh, I love Monterey," Kat said, off on a tangent. My parents took me to the aquarium there when I was five. Got some really good seafood on Cannery Row. Loved the waves and jagged rocks."

Roy laughed, "Wrong Monterey. This is East LA. The Sheriff's Homicide Bureau works there. Spent more than a few years I guess. Could smell the ocean, couldn't see it."

"You said you'd been around detectives and worked on 'a few' murder cases. That's what you said," Kat said, accusingly.

"Guess I neglected to make that clear. In the interest of full disclosure, I did work the LASD Homicide Bureau for over 25 years."

"Seriously?"

She says that a lot.

"I'll tell you about it sometime, but right now you have a school reunion to go to and a weekend to spend sleeping in. We'll see you Monday, young lady."

Kat glanced at her iPhone, saw the time, and jumped up.

"Right," she said as she gathered her coat, laptop, and water bottle. She strode quickly to the door. "I have to scoot. I'll bet you have lots of good stories. I want to hear some later."

None good. Interesting, fascinating, incredible, but none good.

Roy followed Kat through the front door to see her off. He chuckled as she ducked and dodged toward her Honda. The driving snow sand from earlier had been replaced by relentless flakes, resembling a pillow fight gone bad, that now decorated her hair and coat.

He yelled, "Enjoy yourself tonight. Forget all this garbage, and have a great time with your friends. Don't stay out too late, and don't drink and drive,"

"Yes, Dad!" she called back at him, waving goodbye then slamming her car door.

The familiar lump returned to his throat. He thought he might choke. He stepped quickly back inside and closed the door. He pressed his fingers to his temples and took deep breaths.

On a regular patrol day, Roy's shift would have ended. But tonight he dreaded going home and sitting with his ghosts. He pulled the chair back at his desk and tapped a dozing screen. He studied the images of the Sony Discman for a moment. He held the broken CD player cover up for comparison for a second time to reinforce the fact. There was no question. He had a match. Even a future defendant's lawyer would have to concede, but not before getting Roy to admit that Sony had sold millions of these Discman players. *So big deal if my client ever owned one. Does that mean every owner of a white Bronco has murdered his ex?*

Had this been the desert community of Lancaster or the Grapevine village of Castaic or even West Hollyweird and Malibu, he'd have felt on familiar turf, regardless of millions of potential suspects. Here, with scarcely 2000 souls, one or more of them dark in this matter, his vision was fogged, his orientation to history desolate.

Kat would play the part he'd intended, he was sure, but she was young. Sassy Cassie knew the landscape and the people, but she was a puddle of tears waiting to dissolve. The old boys in the Black Tail had the look of deep roots, but they were a sewing circle of gossip, impossible to trust.

The deputies in the South County were all transplants too, one of them no older than Kat. They'd gone through various police academies around California then landed jobs in Karuk County. No help there.

He looked up the numbers for the Karuk Daily News in Silverton and the Redding Record Searchlight in Shasta County. By telephone he found each had a morgue file, a copy, either digitally or on antiquated microfilm, of every issue going back to the early 1900's or beyond. They might be of use.

Then he gazed at a shelf above the printer. It was lined with golden covered, hardback books, twenty of them. There were more in a back room gathering dust. Each had a white label on the binding with a different year. In sequence they documented the students and faculty, including sports, clubs, and candid shots for every school year in the Karuk Union School District. These *White and Golds*, as the yearbooks were known, could very well contain photos of a dead man, a killer, or both.

He pulled *1995* from the shelf, sat down, and flipped to the section on Sisson High. Dozens of faces. Dozens of poses. Grins, smirks, and tentative smiles on the edge of adulthood greeted him. Other sullen or anxious eyes stared at him. Early manhood and womanhood with little clue as to how to proceed. Who, if any, on these pages held long kept secrets?

He closed the book then slow drummed the cover with his two forefingers. Another piece of a jigsaw puzzle that would have made Old John proud.

CHAPTER 14

Cedar Stock stood still, approving of his stacks of wood. A work of pure beauty. Cut and split 16" lengths of lodgepole pine. You could drop a plum bob off the first row. He'd picked up the firewood last September, high up on Military Pass Road on the far backside of Mount Shasta. Seemed a shame to bite into it, but Ma had to keep warm. He tossed fifteen pieces in a dented, blue wheelbarrow and pushed it out of the open-faced shed to a slippery, white sidewalk. He bent his head to keep the blowing flakes from sneaking down the front of his vest.

He dropped the wheelbarrow when he reached the front door, under cover of a slightly sagging overhang, straining under the foot of new snow. He reminded himself to get up there and clean it off before he left. He loaded six pieces in his arm, opened the door, and stepped through into a dark living room. Unpleasant odors wafted by. He grimaced. Been a while since air freshener or a cracked window. Condensation clouded the corners of aluminum framed windows, one of which had a twinkling string of blue and white lights held in place by push pins and scotch tape. A porcelain tea pot rattled on top of an onyx, cast iron, free standing stove set midway of an interior wall. The hissing sound of bacon popping its grease out onto the linoleum floor floated from an electric range in the galley-sized kitchen beyond the living room.

"Cedar, hon, could you please turn the bacon down," Ma asked from the easy chair on the opposite side of the living room. Cheering, dinging of bells, and forced laughter of a smooth host rose from the speakers on a wide screen TV. The shadowy glare dimly lit up Ma's frail form as she turned slowly to gaze at him. Her thinning grey hair needed combing, and the skin under her eyes pulled heavily on her lower lids, exposing the red inner-linings. Jersey Stock had seen better days.

Cedar set the armload of pine next to the stove then swiftly stepped into the kitchen to slide the bacon pan off the burner.

"You've seen the paper?" Ma called to him. "They've got another article. Sheriff says they're following up on promising leads. What do you think? It must be Dina." She wiped at her nose under the oxygen line with a wrinkled tissue. Cedar wondered how long she had been using it.

He wandered back into the living room and sank into a couch covered with a coarse, Mexican horse blanket. The faded yellow, orange, and gray stripes reminded him of the job in San Diego. He'd picked up the couch cover for Ma right before he split for Northern California. She loved it, mentioned it every time he showed up. He always made sure he brought home souvenirs whenever he could. Sometimes there wasn't an opportunity to pick up a nice trinket when he was moving fast. He felt bad about that.

"Don't know, Ma. Maybe." Cedar adjusted his position on the leather couch he had purchased for her a few years back. It was a small price to pay as he sometimes spent the night there, and her last couch had busted springs that would push uncomfortably through the sagging cushions.

"Well, you know I truly believe Pud did it," she continued.

Ma began coughing. Cedar quickly moved to her and wrapped his hand around a bony shoulder. She leaned into him but turned her head away. When the hacking stopped she discreetly spit into her tissue that she then dropped into a plastic bag on the other side of the chair. She adjusted the clear tubing to her nose that ran from a rolling, green oxygen bottle on the floor next her. Then she shakily pushed herself up out of the chair.

There'll come a time when she can't get up.

"I'd like to eat before Oprah comes on. Did you see how she gave all her guests cars? Wish I could have been in the audience."

Cedar helped Ma to the shiny wooden table at the end of the kitchen. Five chairs sat empty. He sidestepped to the stove and filled a paper plate for her. One piece of crisp bacon, a half piece of wheat toast, and one scrambled egg didn't seem enough. He set a glass of juice in front of her. She picked at her plate then lost interest. The juice went untouched.

Cedar sniffed the air.

"I saw that, Cedar. I'm sorry. Would you mind checking the cat box? If Maddy stops by I'd like the place to smell nice. I sure hope she stops by."

"I'm going by Sarah's place later today, Ma. I'll ask her and Maddy to come see you."

"No need to bother Sarah. She and I always seem to get into a disagreement. We've never really got along," Ma said for the thousandth time.

"Sarah's okay," Cedar said, a phrase he had also uttered many times over the years.

"Sometimes she acts like she's the only person in this family who reads. Has an opinion on everything. I read the paper and watch the news all day. I can have an opinion, too." Ma was getting defensive. Cedar didn't want to get her riled up before he had to leave, but he felt the need to defend Sarah.

"She's an in-law, Ma. Sometimes they got it hard fitting into a family, especially one like ours," Cedar said. He knew this conversation by heart.

"What's that supposed to mean? Nothing wrong with our family. Be proud of your Stock name. I gave up mine, a good name too, when I married your daddy." Her chin tilted a little with pride.

"Stock is a fine name, Ma," Cedar consoled her.

"And Sarah did that whole 'her last name hyphen Stock thing' when she and Zack got together. That was insulting." Ma nodded her head sadly. "Could you bring me the newspaper?"

Cedar quickly grabbed the Karuk Daily News from Ma's easy chair. He returned to the table and set the paper next to her.

She pointed to the front page.

"Says right here, Sheriff Silva still wants the public's help on that skeleton on Puma Ridge. That's over by the lake. You know it's Dina. Damn that Pud. Sorry for my language, but you should have talked to him."

Cedar slipped a pair of cheaters from his inside vest pocket. He leaned over and studied the article.

"Ma, it's not my business. You know how Dina was, out of control half the time. Besides, when she went missin' I wasn't around."

"Still, that girl didn't deserve to be dumped on a trail in the woods, like a crumpled up old Burger King bag. That wasn't right."

Cedar sighed. "Look, Ma, I gotta get. I'll clean the cat box on my way out. You gonna be okay? I'll tell Maddy to come see you."

"Well, if you have to tell her, what's the use of having her come? Kids should *want* to see their great aunt, especially if they haven't got a Nana anymore," Ma sighed and pulled the paper back from Cedar.

"You know, maybe we ought to have another conversation about getting you a fulltime housekeeper in here, one who has some nurse knowledge."

"And have her steal from me? Heck, no. And this is just the flu. I'll beat it." This topic fired her up every time.

"Well, what about the elder care facility? They'll take good care of you there," Cedar suggested.

Here it comes.

"Never! Went there to visit your Aunt Becky all those times. Place smelled like Lysol. Folks drooling on themselves in the hallway, starin' at nothing. Becky's roommate moaning and wiggling all night. Drove her crazy No thank you. I'm dying right here, with Oprah."

Cedar got up, his chair screeching across the somewhat dingy linoleum.

"I really gotta go, Ma." He ran his hand through his now greying auburn hair.

"What? You just got here. Thought you were going to play for me. Well, kiss me goodbye." She tilted her age-spotted face up expectantly.

She smelled a little ripe, like biting into Swiss cheese. A Depends check might be in order. Cedar bent and kissed her on the forehead.

"Hey, Ma, can I have the paper? Only if you're through with it," Cedar asked nonchalantly.

"Go ahead. And please check that cat box. You're right, something smells in here."

Cedar knelt next to the blue, hard plastic box sitting on the floor of the hallway that ran from the living room to two bedrooms and a laundry room. He scooped a dozen black turds into a plastic bag as a fat, charcoal colored, long-haired feline rubbed against his leg. He scratched the cat's back for a moment, thinking. Then he got up, opened a back door and dropped the turds in a green plastic garbage can.

"Bye," he shouted. "I'll bring my guitar next time."

He grabbed a fifteen-foot ladder, set it against the front door overhang and climbed up. A few minutes later he stood on the ground brushing snow off his gloves, satisfied that no one would be crushed if the storm kept up.

He hunched in the driving snow as he quickly moved to the driver's door of a jet black, GMC pick-up parked in Ma's driveway. A magnetic sign on the side of the driver's door read *Cedar Stock, Handyman.*

Snow swirled and drove sideways as he crept through downtown Sisson. He shook his head at the front wheel drive compacts that had been forced off the freeway because of poor visibility. Bewildered, frightened looks on drivers' pale faces betrayed them as clueless flatlanders. They faded from mind as the rhythmic scrape of his wipers turned his thoughts to what Ma had said about Pud. Might be something to it. He'd think on it a bit more, analyze the situation.

He turned onto a residential side street and drove the familiar three blocks. He parked in Sarah's driveway next to her green Subaru Outback, noting the half foot of snow on top. No tracks behind the car so she'd not been out in the night or this morning. Good. He stepped out into the frozen landscape and detected a low roar mixed with singing chains one block over. Snowplows would be by soon. He checked his truck bed to make sure he had a shovel for the berm they'd leave behind.

He dashed to the front door of the single-story tract home. He stamped his boots to make sure they were snowless then opened the door without knocking. It was warm and silent in the dark foyer. He breathed deeply, taking in baked bread and something else — a sweet mixture of coffee, vanilla, and cedar that he recognized as the Black Opium perfume by that French dude he'd learned about. He smiled recalling how much he'd paid for Sarah's scent, a special gift for her birthday last fall. A month before her birthday, he'd been thumbing through a magazine he'd snatched off the coffee table at the dentist office. An article featuring a photo of an airbrushed babe in a short bathrobe, with her eyes closed, like she was thinking impure thoughts, caught his eye. So he'd settled in to check it out. He'd gotten an education on expensive smells, about how a good perfume can make a woman not only feel sexy, but confident, and mysterious too. The Black Opium was said to give off a hint of cedarwood. That had closed the sale for him. Clever.

He ventured farther into the house and paused quietly in the living room, listening for any signs of life. Suddenly there was the metallic banging of pans coming from the kitchen, punctuated by the whine of a mixer. She was cooking no doubt. Every Saturday morning in the fall and winter she baked breads and cookies and took them to her church on Sunday. He thought about how those ignorant do-gooders handed out free food to bums who wandered inside long enough to listen to how some god loved them. At the same time, they'd score a cup of coffee and a roll. The church goers didn't understand that feeding these vermin kept them coming around, like campground deer. Instead, you gotta force the herd south to the cities. Nowadays it was getting so even the hostilities of winter couldn't chase them off. He felt a pulse of disgust in his chest. Worthless people.

He stealthily moved forward until he could peer around a corner from the hallway into the kitchen. Sarah was baking all right. She was standing at the double oven on her tiptoes peeking in at a set of rolls. Behind her on an island stood the white mixer surrounded by powdered sugar, an egg carton, flour, rolling pins and little bottles of spices. Damn. For 40 something she looked pretty freakin' good from behind. He wondered if he stood there long enough, she might bend over and pull something out of the bottom oven. He bit his lip.

Her salt and pepper hair looked hella, up in a bun. Still thin, after all these years, even with all the baking she did.

"Hey," he said.

Sarah Stock let out a yelp and whipped around.

"Jesus, you scared the shit out of me, Cedar!" she exclaimed, one hand fluttering to her chest.

Cedar smiled apologetically. "Not supposed to take the Lord's name in vain. Better say one of those Hail Marys."

"I'm not Catholic, Cedar," she laughed, patting her hair in a mildly self-conscious gesture. "I didn't hear the bell ring."

"That's because I didn't ring it," he said, nonchalantly. He felt some melting snow dripping from his shaggy, dark auburn hair. He needed a haircut.

"Cedar, cousin or no, you can't just waltz right into my house. What if I'd had someone here? Besides, Maddy's home. She could have been lounging around here in her pajamas. You'd have freaked her out," Sarah laughed, but it seemed a little strained.

"Who would you have had here?" he asked, betraying his annoyance more than he intended to. "Sure wouldn't be that light-in-the-loafers boss you work for," he muttered.

"Maybe Santa Claus came early!" Sarah tried to joke away her discomfort. "Here, have a roll," she said, quickly changing the subject.

"Looks like a white Christmas," Cedar said, moving on too.

Wish she wouldn't talk that way…as if she's seeing someone.

"Be good for Maddy to have a white Christmas," Sarah said, making small talk. "How long is this storm supposed to last?"

"Rest of the day, as least. Freeway's closed off and on. Tourists all trapped downtown. Parking lot to the Black Tail is a mess."

Sarah poured Cedar a cup of coffee and pointed at a bar chair on one side of the kitchen island.

"Sit there and drink. Maddy should be in any minute. She was out late last night. School winter reunion."

"Saw Jersey this morning," Cedar said carefully.

Sarah plastered a polite smile to her face. "How's she doing?"

"About the same, wants Maddy to come visit."

Sarah cleared her throat and nodded. "I'll tell her. I'm sure she'll go, if the snow's not too bad." She reached up and patted her hair again.

Cedar sat and sipped, watching Sarah as she turned back to check her baking. She opened the oven and removed a cookie sheet with golden brown rolls.

"Let your coffee cool. Wash your hands and you can help me set these on a rack. Be useful for a change," Sarah gibed him, rolling her eyes. She was in a good mood.

Cedar liked it when she talked *that* way. It made him feel wanted, almost as if they could have been together.

Maybe if I'd been around more....

"Uncle Cedar!"

Cedar turned to see an early-twenties version of Sarah come gliding into the room.

"Maddy, baby!" Cedar called back boisterously.

Maddy Stock threw her arms around him and kissed his cheek.

"White Christmas?" she asked, pouring herself a cup of coffee before turning to look through the kitchen window at the chalky world.

"Looks that way," Cedar agreed.

"Started snowing hard last night on my way home."

"Have a good time?" asked Sarah.

"The party at the school was lame, so some of us went over to Kat Hoover's house. That was pretty fun," Maddy said.

"How is Kat?" Sarah asked. "Isn't she going to Chico State? She should be about done I'd think."

"Oh, she's great," Maddy said, her eyes all lit up. "Guess what she's doing."

"I give up," Sarah replied, distracted with placing rolls on the cooling racks.

"Well, you maybe don't know, but she's majored in anthropology. It's like the study of ancient cultures, I think. But I guess they also study bones. She's been working as an intern in a lab at Chico where they bring in dead bodies that get discovered out in the woods or wash up on shore. Then they try to figure out who the person is and how they died by looking at their bones."

"Like the TV show?" Sarah suggested, glancing up at Maddy.

"Yeah, sort of. We talked about that. She said the people she works with say the show is pretty much a joke though."

"Sounds fascinating," Sarah said, dropping an egg and a measured cup of flour into her mixer. Cedar continued to sip his coffee, but he was listening intently.

Maddy continued, "Oh, but that's not the best part. Get this. The people she works for in Chico are helping the police with that dead person that was found on Puma Ridge, so she gets to work here as an intern while she's on break."

"Seriously? Working with the cops?" questioned Cedar. He set his coffee cup down and looked squarely at Maddy who had reached over and grabbed one of the hot rolls from the cooling rack.

Maddy pointed at her mouth as she finished chewing and swallowed a bit of roll. "Sorry. Yeah, she is. She said she can't talk about the case because it's all confidential, but she got to meet some detectives the other day in Silverton who were working on it, I think."

"In Silverton?" asked Cedar.

"Well, they're not working on it anymore. They're working on a murder case where two guys got killed trying to steal some marijuana," Maddy clarified. She broke off a smaller piece of the warm bread and dropped it into her mouth.

"Oh, how terrible, I think I remember reading about that," said Sarah. "Well who is working on the Puma Ridge case with her?" She brushed her hands off and turned to fully face Maddy with interest.

"She said he's a policeman from Southern California. Kind of an old guy. But apparently he has a lot of experience." Maddy shrugged and leaned over to refill Cedar's coffee cup which was still half full. He smiled with gratitude but didn't take a sip.

"From Southern California, huh? What's he doing up here?" Cedar asked casually.

"I'm not sure. But he was a detective down there or something."

"What's his name?" asked Cedar, leaning back in his chair. "I know most of the cops around here. Didn't know one from SoCal."

"Kat kept calling him, Deputy, what was it, something religious sounding? I can't remember. Church, that's it, Deputy or Detective Church."

"That's crazy," said Sarah. "So do they know who the dead person is, or was? I see they keep asking in the paper for anyone who knows something to come forward."

"She didn't say, but she said the detective is really smart, and she thinks he'll solve the case," Maddy said. "It would be so exciting to work on something like that."

"Aren't you studying some sorta law stuff? I could see you being one of those CSI types, Maddy," Cedar said, giving her a toothy grin.

"I took an introduction to criminal justice class at the J.C. It was really interesting. I might ask Kat if they need another student helper with the case."

Sarah turned to regard Cedar and said, "What about that girl who went missing when she was with her boyfriend, what was it, about ten years ago over by the lake? That's really close to where they found the body. You knew them, right, Cedar? I think I've heard you say something about that disappearance over the years."

"Yep, Dina and her boyfriend Pud." said Cedar. "He was a scandalous dude, but I'm sure this new detective is all over that." He gave Sarah a reassuring smile.

"What kind of a name is Pud?" Maddy asked with amusement.

"Been called that as far back as I can remember," Cedar said, shrugging a little.

"How well did you know them, Uncle Cedar? Maybe you should talk to the detective." Maddy suggested.

"Not me. You know the cops and me. We haven't always gotten along," Cedar said, chuckling darkly. "But maybe you could tell this Kat girl that you know somebody who knew the missing girl and her boyfriend real well, and you could get some information if they let you work on the case with them. You don't wanna put it like that, but you know what I mean."

"I don't know…," said Maddy uncertainly.

"Yeah, Cedar, I'm not sure that's a good idea," Sarah added.

"Look," said Cedar, "It's gotta be Dina who they found. But there must be some reason they can't prove it. Otherwise they'da busted Pud already and wouldn't be asking for help. I can't prove it, because I wasn't around back then, but I know he did it. I used to drink with him back in my wild days. He was the kinda dude who never takes lip. Probably snapped. Dina wasn't the easiest." He picked up his coffee again and took a sip.

"Still, her poor family," Sarah said defensively. "I might be wrong, but I think I recall Dina and a boyfriend from years ago. Maybe the same guy, Pud. I don't know. School? I don't think so. Oh well."

"Yeah, too bad he got away with it," Cedar said. "Sure be nice if the cops would zero in on him. I just can't be the one to talk to them. I've got a bad history with them," he stated again.

He stopped there. Didn't want to push.

All three fell silent for a moment, and Maddy turned to look back out the window again. Sarah spoke first.

"How about you play us something, Cedar? There's a guitar in the den." She gave him a brilliant smile, and he felt something stir in his chest. He couldn't refuse her.

"It's been awhile, but I could give it a go," Cedar said good-naturedly.

"Sweet," said Maddy as she turned and hurried from the room. She called over her shoulder, "I've missed you playing."

Maddy returned momentarily with a cheap nylon stringed acoustic guitar with a light tan panel.

Cedar swooped it out of her hands and settled back, his left thumb expertly on the back of the fret board. He hit an E minor and C major plus one or two chord progressions to warm up. He stopped and raised his eyebrows as the chords twanged unharmoniously. He proceeded to tune the guitar and tried again. Sarah and Maddy grabbed chairs and waited expectantly.

"Whadya wanna hear, Maddy?" Cedar asked, playing some simple chord progressions.

"You used to play really beautiful songs for me when I was little. What about one of those?"

"Hmm," said Cedar. Then he began, slowly, with his eyes closed.

Down in the valley the valley so low
Hang your head over, hear the wind blow

Hear the wind blow love, hear the wind blow
Hang your head over, hear the wind blow

Roses love sunshine, violets love dew
Angels in heaven, know I love you

If you don't love me, love whom you please
Put your arms round me, give my heart ease
Give my heart ease love, give my heart ease
Put your arms round me, give my heart ease

"Aww, that is so beautiful, Uncle Cedar." Maddy sighed, nostalgia washing over her. "That one and 'All the Pretty Little Horses' meant a lot to me growing up. I wish I inherited your musical ability"

"Very nice, Cedar," Sarah agreed sweetly.

Maddy came over and hugged Cedar. He thought he'd died and gone to heaven. Sarah and Maddy. In the end they should have been his. Choices made.

"Okay, girls. Gotta bounce," Cedar said, handing the guitar back to Maddy.

"Take some rolls!" Sarah said, rising to drop a half dozen in a plastic bag. She handed them to Cedar. As she did, she reached up and kissed him on the cheek. Always the cheek. And she never asked him why he'd come. Maybe she just expected him.

Nice, real nice.

CHAPTER 15

At about 2100 hours, in early October, 2017, horror invaded the north end of California's iconic Napa Valley. Residents of the hamlet of Calistoga, famed for its mud baths and wine grapes, readied for a fall slumber, unaware of the hell about to slip its leash. At 2143 hours a call came in that a small fire, of unknown origin, had kicked off on Tubbs Lane, a half mile north of the city. The first fire crews on the scene were immediately overwhelmed by a growing monster from Hades. Hurricane force winds descended on them, feeding the infuriated monster, giving it energy to barrel into the hills and valleys to the west. Beyond Calistoga, over a ridge that had been raped by another inferno 50 years earlier, the Venturi-treated wind fanned pitiless flames that raced toward another clueless burg, this one of over 200,000 called Santa Rosa. Santa Rosans living in its northwest quadrant had less than fifteen minutes warning as their homes now lay in a certain path of incineration. Thousands fled in their pajamas, taking nothing more than a wallet, one car, a cell phone, and a diaper bag. The monster obliterated everything left behind.

Over two weeks later, when the final smoke cleared in Napa, Sonoma, Lake, and Mendocino Counties, dozens were dead, and thousands were homeless. Three thousand homes had been destroyed. Lives had been altered forever. The landscape resembled Hiroshima. Entire neighborhoods were now nothing more than smoldering, twisted garage doors, and minuscule piles of broken, charred debris.

But like a good neighbor, State Farm was there, along with a covey of other insurance companies who'd sent their shell-shocked adjusters to inspect the sites along with carefully compiled lists of losses. This phase preceded a virtual Niagara of payouts. Then an army of bucket loaders and dump trucks showed up. After load upon load of bedsprings and concrete chunks had been hauled away, the boys with clipboards and transits arrived. Property lines were reestablished. Behind the scenes, phone calls were placed to sawmills throughout the Pacific Northwest. This is going to be Katrina-like. Stand by to stand by. And oh, by the way, if you know any carpenters, tell them to pack their suitcases. Good times are comin'.

Jesse Wilson could swing a hammer. He'd been framing houses off and on for some thirty odd years. Not every day, because occasionally he'd show up late for work or not at all and get fired. But in a boom economy he and his carpenter's tool belt, or "bags," would stay on the sideline only so long. The next-up, fly-by-night contractor would give him a shot, counsel him on getting his shit together, and provide him with enough paycheck to keep pronto pups and a case of Natty Ice in the fridge.

When the cry went up for troops to march on the vacant lots of Santa Rosa in the fall of 2018, almost a year to the day from the conflagration, Wilson answered the call. Then he began spending his days, starting at 0600 hours, pounding nails, lumping studs, headers, or oriented strand board— known as OSB in the biz — or running a chop saw producing 2 x 6 blocks for fire walls.

He spent his evenings at any one of several low-class watering holes that Santa Rosa had to offer up and down its main thoroughfare called Mendocino Avenue. His favorite was fast becoming Red's Rusty Nail at the corner of Mendo and College Avenue. Red's offered cheap draft beer with a Carpenter's Special Happy Hour (just show your phone with a photo of you balancing atop a wall plate wearing your bags.) A couple of former meth freaks worked the saloon offering cheap blowjobs in the shitter or a hook-up for the real deal in a backseat in the parking lot if you had the cash.

It was in Red's on a foggy Tuesday night when Wilson's cell buzzed. He didn't recognize the number, but as far as he knew there were no warrants out for him, so he answered.

"Yeah? Who's this?" he growled.

"Pud, wassup!" came a smooth singer's voice on the other end.

"Turn around, fool!"

Jesse "Pud" Wilson turned in his seat to stare at Cedar Stock across the room flipping him off and grinning like he'd just shot his wad.

"The fuck you doin' here you sumbitch? I didn't recognize the phone!" Pud excitedly called out, rising, extending a hand, and hugging Cedar bro-style.

"Told you I'd be looking for work, motherfucker!" Cedar exclaimed. "You know me, I can rough in plumbing or hang rock or whatever."

"Oh, fuck yeah," Pud laughed. "You gotta come work on my crew. We been buildin' custom homes on a golf course, and not the bitch-ass stick homes on the flats."

"Think you can hook me up? At least intro me to your boss?" Cedar asked earnestly.

Pud was amped up, excited to see his old friend. "Fuck yeah! And Merry fuckin' Christmas!"

Pud turned to the bartender and ordered up another pitcher. He was just gettin' started.

An hour later, Pud declared he was going to show Cedar where they'd be "bustin' ass" for the next couple of months. He was too wobbly to drive so Cedar, who seemed like he could drink like a fuckin' Russian, offered to take the wheel. Pud dropped his keys on the fog-soaked asphalt of the inky parking lot behind Red's. Cedar bent and scooped them up, tossed them in the air, and deftly caught them.

"See, I can fuckin' drive like Dale Earnhardt. Shit, we need more beer, motherfucker! Hell, fuck beer, let's go JD."

"Fuckin' A right!" Pud slurred back.

Pud had slumped over in the passenger side of his own pickup when Cedar returned from inside a liquor store with a bottle of Jack Daniels in a paper sack.

Ten minutes later, after winding uphill east from the runway-flat Mendocino Avenue, Cedar pulled to the curb on a dumpster crowded street of ghostly shapes. He could make out the partial frames of the massive homes going back up and the darkness beyond that was the Fountaingrove Country Club golf course.

"We're here buddy. Let's check out the house, looks like we can just walk in. That is one big ass great room you got going on!" Cedar marveled.

"How the fuck you know where the job was?" mumbled Pud, his right hand searching for a door handle, slipping off it several times

"Shit, you only told me a dozen times. 3130 Greenskeeper Court, you said."

Pud smiled sloppily, finally grasping hold of the door handle, "Oh yeah, guess I did."

"Hell, I just put it in my GPS and Kazam! We're here. Now show me that king stud you were braggin' about." Cedar's face was partially hidden in the darkness of the cab, but a newly erected streetlight about three yards down the street illuminated the lower half of his face where stubbly reddish-grey hair was in need of trimming. He smiled encouragingly at Pud.

"Fuck yeah," Pud slurred. He opened the passenger door and slid partially to the ground, catching himself just in time. Cedar moved smoothly around the front of the pickup and lended a hand. Pud staggered, with one arm over Cedar's shoulder, to the temporary door of the structure, its interior barely lit by the sodium streetlight.

Once inside the immense great room, Pud sank to the OSB sub floor, his back up against a wall. Cedar slid down next to him and took a long swig off the sack. Cedar handed the sack to Pud who grabbed it with a heavy hand.

"To Dale Earnhardt, motherfucker," Cedar said.

"To Number 3," Pud mumbled. "Feel like I gotta go Number 2." Pud sniggered at that then took a lengthy pull off the bottle. No sack this time. Damn that was fire. But a good fire. He guzzled again.

"Gimme a hit you Karuk County bastard," Cedar laughed. He snatched the bottle away from Pud with a gloved hand, sloshing a little onto the sub floor.

"Man, we had some good times, Cedar," Pud's speech was thick and nearly indistinct.

"You, me, and Dina," Cedar slurred.

"Dina, Dina, Dina," Pud started sniffling. "I miss you, baby. I'm sorry, Dina"

"We all miss Dina, Pud" Cedar said soothingly "Wish I coulda been there for you, Pud. I coulda helped you go another way. But what's done is done."

"What's done is done," Pud said, trailing off, now all weepy.

"Don't worry none, Pud. Life's too short. Anyhow, women been givin' men shit ever since Biblical times. There's even a Christmas story about it," Cedar said.

"Whadya mean?" slurred a teary eyed Pud.

"Well, shit. I mean Mary. Hell, she was ridin' Joseph's ass all the way to Bethlehem."

Pud giggled a slow giggle, like a four-cylinder crawling up a steep grade.

"We ain't got Dina, but we still got Jack," declared Cedar, handing the bottle back to Pud.

Pud raised the bottle.

"To Jack," he whispered. He drank listlessly, the whiskey dribbling out of his mouth and down across his dirty shirt.

Cedar reached over and gently removed the bottle from his hand.

Momentarily, Pud was snoring while leaning against Cedar's shoulder.

Cedar carefully pulled away and lay Pud over on the subfloor. He got up deftly and, using the light on his phone, made his way to the exterior door. There was enough light coming from the street that he could put the phone away. He stepped carefully over strewn cut boards to the curbside where he reached into Pud's truck bed. He pulled out two lengths of yellow nylon rope, one about 50 feet in length, the other ten. He also picked up a hand operated ratchet winch, commonly known as a come-along. He dropped the three items in an empty, white plastic five-gallon bucket.

Cedar returned to the great room where he could hear the halting snore of the dead drunk Pud. About six feet from Pud was the framed doorway to a hallway that he'd scoped out the night before. A header beam lay just under a wall top double plate, between two by six king studs which were nailed to two trimmer studs. Sturdy as fuck. Able to hold a house up sturdy.

Cedar set down the plastic bucket. Then he tossed the longer rope over the upper wall plate and temporarily tied the end off to a two by six horizontal interior wall-nailer block. He fixed a slip knot on the other end of the rope. Then he turned his attention to the snoring, dark lump at his feet.

He reached down and shook Pud's shoulder in an attempt to wake him. Nothing. Then he pulled Pud over onto his back and grabbed his jacket. He dragged Pud into the doorway.

Next, he undid the temporary tie, fashioned another slip knot and slipped around a hook end of the come-along. He released the ratchet and unspooled a length of cable on the opposite hook-end. That hook and cable he looped around a wall nailer block, then reset the ratchet to operating position.

He pulled the other slip knot end of the nylon rope down to Pud. He dropped a crude noose over Pud's head and snugged it on his neck. Pud snored away, oblivious.

Cedar took up the slack. Pud slept. Then he removed his own jacket and pulled Pud up into a sitting position. He knelt behind Pud and threw his right arm around Pud's neck, making a V with his elbow in front of Pud's Adam's apple. With this left hand he reached across behind Pud's neck and grasped his own shoulder. He squeezed his right inside wrist bone against the left side of Pud's neck. Five seconds of squeezing and he felt Pud go limp. Not dead, just out, his carotid artery had been cut off long enough to stop the blood flow to his brain. He'd come to in about thirty seconds, so Cedar had to move fast.

Cedar hit the ratchet and pumped the handle. The rope tightened and began to move, hoisting Pud up. The noose had tightened around Pud's neck. There was no coming back now. He pumped furiously. The come-along, designed to move a ton, did its magic.

Pud swung in the air under the header beam, his feet kicking wildly, his hands grasping uselessly at his throat. Cedar doubted Pud had any idea what was happening to him. The throat grabbing had simply been an unconscious attempt at survival. In a moment, Pud was limp. Cedar heard the drip of liquid from the bottom of Pud's jeans. The smell of deep-down shit clouded his nostrils. *Jesus, worse than Ma.*

When Cedar was sure Pud was dead, he grabbed the plastic bucket and placed it upside down under Pud's wet boots. It was just high enough to take slack off the hanging rope. He grabbed the shorter length of rope and looped it under Pud's arms, tying it around his chest. Then he threw the free end up over the header and tied it off tight. Now he could release the ratchet on the come-along, which he did. Pud didn't move, held in place by the second rope.

Cedar hurriedly undid the come-along then retied the longer rope next to the shorter temp rope. Next, he undid the shorter length of rope. Pud stayed perfectly hanged.

From inside his jacket pocket he removed a plastic baggie. Inside the baggie were two sheets of paper. He took the paper out of the baggie and pressed them into Pud's limp hand. They fluttered to the floor below.

Cedar stepped back and admired his work in the darkness. To see better he turned on his phone light. Pud's neck was getting longer by the minute. His eyes were bugged out, and his shit smell was really getting to Cedar. He kicked the bucket over. Pud swayed.

Cedar lit up the area under Pud to make sure he'd left no footprints in the piss that had dripped. He slipped through the exposed studs in the wall and inspected where he'd had the come-along chain tied on the wall nailer board. A deep, fresh groove, possibly a tell-tale wound, caught his attention.

How hard would anyone look this far away from the body? To be on the safe side he reached down under the subfloor to the crawlspace and retrieved a handful of soil. He rubbed a little in the groove then rubbed some more on the nailer board next to it. Perfect. Nothing fresh to see here.

Before he left the great room, Cedar made sure the two pieces of paper and the bottle of JD were right where they needed to be, on the floor under Ol' Pud on a Stud Wilson.

Damn. That was fuckin' funny, Ol' Pud on a Stud.

Two streets down, Cedar tossed the come-along into the side yard of another custom home under construction. He knew some sketchy sub-contractor would gaffle it before morning break. He'd already tossed the short length of nylon rope into a huge dumpster and had covered it with a broken slab of sheet rock. He tossed the paper sack from the whiskey in another bin. He shredded the receipt and dropped bits of it along the way, feeling a bit guilty about littering.

Five minutes later, Cedar Stock strolled out onto Fountaingrove Parkway, the main in and out to the rebuilding, country club neighborhood. He disappeared into the Sonoma County fog, whistling *Let it Snow.*

CHAPTER 16

The pre-Christmas snowstorm that hit Sisson was a nightmare for front wheel drive compacts but a godsend for Sisson's motels, the local ski-park, and a thousand skiers and boarders within a hundred mile radius of Mount Shasta. Incredibly, many of them felt an illness coming on the night before yet another day of Monday drudgery in the cubicle. Scores of employers fielded early morning phone calls from gravel-voiced workers who insisted on describing in detail how many times they'd thrown up. The most common response heard was, "Man, I hope you feel better." The second was a joyful, "He bought it, let's go." The third was a muttered, "That fucker isn't sick."

There was no need for Kat Hoover to play games. When Roy Church saw how much snow had built up on the sub parking lot, he insisted Kat take a few days and do what needed to be done. He could relate. When the surf was up back in the day, there was only one choice. Call in sick, same as half the other baggers at the Vons Supermarket on the PCH in Laguna Beach. He didn't want Kat ever getting hemmed up in a pre-employment polygraph situation wherein she had to admit she'd once lied to her boss so she could go play in the snow.

The winter holidays being the season of total slowdown, Roy was still waiting for a formal report from Chico before making his next move. So when Kat protested, he reminded her of her age and station in life. Youth is fleeting he told her. Soon enough she'd be saddled with husband, kids, job, car and house payments, and a schedule that required a personal secretary. Besides, it was winter, and winter was the best time to recreate. He fondly recalled the January swells off the Rincon, just south of Santa Barbara, and the pleasant lack of *inlander* crowds on the beach. Catching the right-handed, point break of the "queen" made the next day's baleful looks from the boss or the chemistry teacher worth it.

Today, he ventured tentatively out into Sisson's strange, white world of slow motion. He was convinced that the studs on his SUV were all that came between him and certain death.

How the hell do people drive in this mess?

His training days on the LASD skid pan course sure came in handy. Sliding and counter steering at 15 miles an hour on a mixture of oil and water was not unlike sliding and counter steering at 60 during a surface street pursuit past palm trees and pit bulls. He recalled the hapless wheelman for a carload of armed and dangerous Frogtown homies, who'd just hit a murderous lick in East Los. They hadn't gone through Emergency Vehicle Operations Course updates like he had. The four spinning skins pointing toward the sky, through smoke and flame, had been a testament to inadequate driving skills. It had been a crying shame that Fire and Ambulance got held up on the 10, costing the lives of four youthful armed robbers and killers who'd had so much to live for.

Just south of Sisson, on the Reno Highway, Roy backed up a CHP officer who was trying to take the paper on a fender bender between two flatlander snowboarders from Redding. The boarders had been headed uphill toward the ski park when their day ended poorly due to speed and lack of EVOC training. That didn't stop them from motherfucking each other, which led to blows and blood. The traffic officer took the rip and tear, one page crash report, and Roy took the 415 PC report. He released both combatants at the scene with citations and court dates for fighting in public. He was pretty sure a judge would most likely dismiss the charges as a case of mutual combat by idiots who should have had studded tires like Roy.

He meandered back to the sub to type his fight report and eat a sandwich. He had just wrapped it up when the front door to the sub opened. A head under a hat peeked in. She was a young lady about the same age as Kat but shorter, slighter, with raven hair, and nervous eyes.

"Can I help you?" Roy asked, rising from his desk.

She stepped all the way in, glancing about and stamping her boots on the front mat.

"Uh, I was sorta looking for my friend Kat. Guess she's not here?"

Every kid in America texts their friends so they know exactly where each other are. So what is it you're really here for?

"She's not here today. Took the day to go snowboarding. Did you text her?"

"Oh, my phone's messed up," she said vaguely.

Of course.

"Well, I can text her right now and tell her you're looking for her Miss…" Roy trailed off expectantly.

"My name is Maddy, Maddy Stock. And that's okay — I can catch her later." She flashed a nervous smile and lingered on the mat.

"Okay. Anything else?" Roy asked.

She picked some nonexistent fuzz from her coat front. "No, that's it. Well, actually there is sorta something. Are you Officer Church?"

"Deputy, yes. Roy Church. Have a seat in that chair," Roy said. It was always easier for people to talk once they took a seat. Too much energy spent in anxiously stamping back and forth. Roy had brought in this particular chair, made sure it was slightly lower than his. All about edge, no matter how subtle.

Maddy took a seat and sat up straight while slightly bouncing a calf and rubbing the web of her left hand with her right thumb.

"Can I get you some coffee? You look old enough," Roy said, chuckling.

She shook her head and said, "No, thanks." She seemed to be waiting for him to start off the conversation.

Roy obliged. "Okay, Maddy, now how can I help you?" *Personalize.*

"Are you the person to talk to about the skeleton found on Puma Ridge a few months ago? Kat gave me your name."

"Good for Kat, and yes, I'm the person to talk to," Roy said. "Is there something you think I ought to know?"

She rushed on, "Well, it's probably a waste of your time, but we were wondering if you've looked into the lady that disappeared about ten or fifteen years ago. Her name was Dina."

"Yes, I believe she is one of our missing persons that we're interested in," Roy said. He rolled away from facing her and flipped through a binder until he came to an old missing persons flier. He opened the three rings, removed the flier, and then turned to roll back.

"Is this who you're talking about?" he asked, handing it to her.

She barely glanced at it. "Yes, I think so, Dina Morgan." Maddy handed it back.

Roy summarized the information off the flier. "She went missing on the evening of July 10, 2004, last seen in the area of Karuk Lake. Did you know her?"

"No, not really, maybe I saw her once. I can't remember. I was pretty young. But some of my family knew her and they think a guy did it."

"A guy?"

"Some guy they call Pud," Maddy said. "I don't know him either."

"But some of your family members think this person called Pud is responsible for Dina's disappearance?" Roy asked. "Do you know Pud's real name?

"No. I guess it's not a lot of help is it," Maddy said. She tapped her right foot, like Morse code to a fellow POW.

"On the contrary. It means that good citizens are concerned about bad things in their community and are willing to help," Roy countered. "Without community members stepping up to support, cops can't do their jobs."

"I guess so," Maddy said, smiling tentatively.

Roy's interest was piqued. "So, your family members, do they know something more about Dina's disappearance and just haven't said anything?"

"I don't know. I don't think so." She gave a slight shrug and the outer nylon layer of her snow jacket rustled softly with the movement.

"Do you mind me asking who in your family might be able to help me more on Dina?"

Maddy hesitated. "I'd rather not say. They said they just thought you ought to know about Pud in case you didn't have his name, which you probably already do. They just wanted to make sure, I guess."

Roy reached for a card on his desk.

"Look, if you or anyone in your family would like to talk to me more, off the record or whatever, here's my card. Call me anytime. My cell is on there."

"Thanks," said Maddy, taking the card and squirreling it into her coat pocket. She looked as if she was about to stand up, but Roy wanted to gather some more information from her.

"So how long have you and Kat been friends?"

Maddy settled back into her seat. "We went to school together. I saw her the other night at the high school winter reunion and then later at her house," Maddy replied.

"Did Kat tell you the help she's been to me?" Roy asked.

"Oh, yes," Maddy's eyes grew wider. "She said she couldn't talk about what she was doing, but that she is super excited to help out. It's something I'd love to try if given the chance."

"Are you going to school?" Roy asked.

"I went to the JC for two years, then I had to take a break to help my mom out at her office. But I'm going back. I want to go to Chico like Kat, maybe even become a CSI someday."

"Well, Maddy, you go back to school, and I think you'd enjoy crime scene investigation. Hey, it's been a pleasure meeting and talking with you. I want you to feel free to get hold of me anytime if you think there's something I should know. We'll just keep it between us." He stood up, and Maddy mirrored him.

"Thank you."

"Oh, I'll tell Kat you were by for her, but you'll probably see her before I do. She's taking a few days to catch some air up on the hill."

Before Maddy left, Roy got her full name and cell phone number. Then, glancing out the window, he surreptitiously copped the plate on her green Subaru Outback as she was backing out of the sub parking lot.

Roy smiled to himself as he sat at his desk. He drummed his fingers, thinking. Then he opened the case file on Dina Morgan, which had been the first Missing Person's case grabbed by Baker and Westwood when they'd arrived in Sisson last October. He'd already summarized the case on his yellow legal pad, but he reread the entire file anyway.

Dina Marie Morgan, White female adult, aged 34, 5-4, 110 lbs., brown hair, brown eyes, had disappeared on the evening of July 10, 2004. She was last seen in the company of her boyfriend Jesse Wilson, aka Pud, at a local *beach on the north side of Karuk Lake.*

The previous summer Roy had learned that tourists went to the south side of the lake where there was a pristine campground, a resort store and manmade beach with all the rafts, canoes, and hot dogs an urban dweller in the wilderness could desire. Locals went to the north side and shared the one overflowing trash can, a pit toilet, and red dirt lot on a slant.

It was in the red dirt lot that a fight between Wilson and Morgan jumped off at dusk. According to Wilson, who was interviewed multiple times by detectives back then, the argument had been verbal only. *Right.* The argument had continued as Wilson and Morgan drove back along the north side dirt road toward Sisson. At one point, Morgan had leaped from the slow-moving car driven by Wilson. That was the last time she was seen. Wilson had taken investigators to the spot where he thought Dina had jumped out, but he couldn't be sure because it had been dark, and honestly, he'd been drinking a little.

A lone witness, a kid who'd been out on the lake bass fishing, heard yelling by angry sounding adults from several hundred yards away but saw nothing. This witness corroborated at least part of the Wilson story, giving investigators a specific time and place from which to start.

Sheriff's Search and Rescue had combed the shoreline and the heavily wooded mountainside rising north from Karuk Lake, as well as the Sacramento River Canyon heading downhill toward Shasta Lake. Sheriff's divers from Shasta County had come up and had given the bottom of Karuk Lake a thorough swim-through. Nothing.

It hadn't helped matters for Wilson that the reporting party in the disappearance had been Dina's father, Lonnie Morgan, who'd reported her missing a full week later after he couldn't land a satisfactory answer from her boyfriend as to his daughter's whereabouts.

Jesse Wilson explained his lapse in concern several times to investigators. He guessed Dina just needed some time, and he was willing to let her be out there to chill, to get it together, and work through whatever had pissed her off. They'd had their problems. This was nothing new.

Reading between the lines, Roy sensed Dina had been no stranger to substance abuse. Maybe it was the interview with her rehab counselor who had blamed Jesse Wilson for being an enabler, or the arrest for 11377 of the Health and Safety Code, citing possession of a controlled substance. Another arrest for 647(f) PC, being intoxicated to the point of being unable to care for one's safety or the safety of others, pretty much summed it up. Dina Morgan had not led a life on the straight and narrow. Not surprising, her record mirrored that of Jesse "Pud" Wilson. A match made in Heaven.

Roy scoured the list of persons contacted in the search for Dina Morgan over the years. No one named Stock appeared.

He again noted the entry by Detective Baker that Dina Morgan's mother had passed away years ago, and there were no known siblings. It didn't look as though an attempt had been made to further the maternal side of the family tree. MtDNA might still be a possibility down the line,

Right down the line.

Roy smiled at Gerry Rafferty's late 70's lyric. Nostalgia.

Of course, the biggest obstacle to matching the Puma Creek Trail bone to Dina Morgan was an inconvenient timeline. No one had driven the trail since 2000. Dina Morgan disappeared in 2004. The obvious suspect, Jesse Wilson, didn't seem like the sort of schemer who would backpack a human body part, along with a full deer carcass, a mile and half just to cover his tracks.

A supplemental report written by Detective Westwood stated that Lonnie Morgan had been re-contacted but could add nothing further to his original statements from thirteen years earlier. Maybe no one had asked him the right questions.

Roy wrote Lonnie Morgan's name on his list of *Things to Do.*

In 2004, Sheriff's detectives had set up surveillance on Jesse Wilson. They'd followed him from bar to bar, from drug house to drug house, and watched him get kicked off a building job in Weed. They had to alert Weed PD that a physical fight was in the offing when:

"Suspect Wilson returned to his truck and retrieved a crowbar. He then walked toward a male, later identified as his former boss Randy White, and shook the crowbar at him. The situation deescalated when other workers exited the house under construction and stood next to White. Wilson then left at a high rate of speed westbound on College Avenue. He turned into the Mt. Shasta Brewery then spent the next several hours there. Nothing further of note."

Subsequent contact with Randy White, the contractor, revealed that Jesse Wilson had shown up late for the umpteenth time and was suspected of theft of materials. He had to go.

Over the years, various Karuk County detectives had added to the Dina Morgan file. Whenever a national teletype on an unidentified body came in, comparisons got made. A female's skeleton found in the Utah desert had looked promising for a bit. Unfortunately, Dina's dental records shot it down.

Roy scanned Dina's file and found one supplemental report from 2004 summarizing her known medical records. A court order had opened up her local Sisson doc's files to show her shots as a child and her treatment for an STD later on. Nothing indicated an injury such as a broken collarbone. That did not mean she'd not been treated in an emergency room in another state for a fall off the back of a Harley.

Roy set the Dina Morgan file aside. He grew thoughtful again, turning to stare out the front window of the sub at the fluttering last gasps of a storm that had passed. The bright mid-afternoon sunshine streaming in, made brilliant by the snow's reflection, cheered him a bit, or was it the fact that someone had taken the time seek him out. The Sheriff's Department had received dozens of calls after the first article on the skeleton discovery, a dozen or more after the second article. But Maddy Stock had been the first to actually visit. What did it mean? Maybe nothing.

He reopened Dina Morgan's file, found the phone number for Lonnie Morgan. He dialed it on his cell,

A male voice answered. It was weak and far away sounding.

"Hello," the man said

"Hello," Roy said, loudly.

"Hello, I can't hear you. Hello. There's nobody there," the man said.

"You've got the damn thing upside down, Lonnie!" said an exasperated female voice.

"Oh," Lonnie said. There was a rustling sound and Lonnie's voice came on, strong.

"Hello."

After Roy introduced himself as the deputy working on the Puma Creek Trail mystery which included by default his missing daughter's case, Lonnie became animated, not in a good way.

"Damn cops don't give a shit. Thirteen damn years and all I get is nothing. You talked to the sonofabitch who killed her a dozen times, and he's still walking around free. Goddammit. Don't call me again until that sonofabitch is in jail."

"Mr. Morgan, sir, before you hang up please answer one question about Pud if you know."

"What?" came the bitter question.

"Was he a hunter?"

"A hunter? Ha. All that fucker ever did was hunt for drugs. Worthless no good sonofabitch!"

The female voice in the background yelled, "Hang up on 'em, Lonnie. You'll give yourself another heart attack. Government sucks!"

Click.

"So, for clarification, to the best of your knowledge, Pud Wilson was *not* a deer hunter," Roy said into the phone, to himself.

Roy wondered where Pud Wilson was at this very moment. Probably hanging out in a bar, he thought.

A day later, he'd find that he'd been half right.

CHAPTER 17

Initially, the call came into Karuk County Sheriff's Dispatch early afternoon of Christmas Eve. Death notification needed, a common enough call from out of county in any jurisdiction in Anywhere, USA. People moved away, people died in auto accidents, falls, got run over by trains, got murdered, or committed suicide by hanging themselves with new rope at their job site. Next of kin had to be notified. Best not to see it on the news or in the history books first.

A Sonoma County deputy coroner, at the request of the Santa Rosa Police Department, had taken possession of a body. The deputy coroner had transported it to an address on Chanate Road in Santa Rosa for a to-be-scheduled postmortem to confirm death by strangulation, suspected self-induced. Sonoma County requested that a deputy from Karuk County simply research the next of kin for one Jesse Dale Wilson, aged 49, and notify same that Jesse was deceased. The cause of death was under investigation but appeared, preliminarily, to be death by hanging. If next of kin would please contact the Sonoma County Coroner's Office, they could get information on when the body might be released for transport to a place of final rest, or conflagration, whichever was preferred. The next of kin would also be told that the death was currently being investigated in conjunction with the Santa Rosa Police Department, and that a Detective Jake Stern could be contacted with any further questions regarding the circumstances surrounding the death.

The Karuk County Dispatcher thanked the Sonoma County deputy coroner for the call at the same time she was running Jesse Dale Wilson through the local system to ascertain location for a parent, brother, sister, or uncle who would weep at the sad news. Instantly, though, Jesse Dale Wilson popped up as a POI, Person of Interest, in an unsolved missing persons case for one Dina Marie Morgan of Sisson, California. The detail was rerouted to the investigation section of the Karuk County Sheriff's Department, quickly landing on the desk of Detective Wallace "Clint" Westwood, notable this day for his cross draw .45 under a season-appropriate elf hat.

"Shit, that name sounds familiar," said Westwood to his office mate, Detective Alison Baker, when he got off the phone.

"What name's that?" Baker asked, setting down a cup of virgin eggnog while *Santa Got Run Over by a Reindeer* played raucously from an overhead speaker.

"Some dude named Jesse Wilson hanged himself way down in the big city of Santa Rosa, and we've got him named as a POI in a missing persons case up here in Sisson. He's got a mom in Sisson."

"Uh, Clint, didn't you do the follow-up on that missing girl Dina Morgan, for Old Roy's bone case? Wasn't the suspect named Jesse Wilson? Duh?" She rolled her eyes.

"Oh, right, now I remember," said Westwood. "I've got so many weird-ass Asian words running through my head lately I can spell the sound my keys make when they hit the table."

"Seriously," said Baker. "I'm thinking this whole Vietnam War thing was a huge mistake."

"No shit. Lettin' all those boat people come here, telling them, 'You are a Hmong friends' is costing me my sanity."

Baker got a kick out of that. "Clint, you crack me up." She continued to chuckle as she took another sip of her eggnog.

Westwood's ego had been stroked. "You think I ought to send it down to Old Roy or call Santa Rosa myself? I'm kinda busy, but I was thinking we might steal out of here a bit early so I can 'crack' you up some more, maybe lay a present under your tree. Then I gotta go to the in-laws for dinner. Tradition," Westwood said, blowing his cheeks out exaggeratedly.

Baker snorted and replied, "If you're gonna slide down my chimney, you gotta wear that elf hat! But I'd say you could send the detail south to Sisson after maybe a quick call to the detective in Santa Rosa, get some particulars, and then Old Roy can go make the notification."

"Got it," said Westwood, who began dialing the 707 area code.

Twenty minutes later he got off the phone.

"Not gonna believe this shit. Jesse Wilson hanged himself at his job site. He works as a carpenter in Santa Rosa. Looks like he got real drunk then stepped up on a plastic bucket, ran a rope around his neck, and jumped off."

"What's not to believe?" asked Baker as she glanced back at the paperwork she was filling out on her desk.

"Well, the best part is he had two cut out articles, most likely from the Karuk Daily News, on the Puma Creek bones find. He was reading them before he killed himself. Left the clippings on the floor under his feet."

"Whoa." said Baker, fully engaged now.

"Whoa is right. Sounds like case solved," said Westwood, grinning. "He must have gotten all shook up over the discovery, figured we were closing in. Been working up to offin' himself. I better go talk to Savage."

"Think you better call Old Roy, first? It is his case," Baker pointed out.

"Was his case," laughed Westwood. He got up and strolled in the direction of Lieutenant Savage to take advantage of the open-door policy. The overhead speaker had upped the ante to *Little Drummer Boy*.

Fate, being what it is, Detective Westwood would normally have gone to his supervisor, Lieutenant Gary Lynch, who was in charge of the investigative section. Lynch would have told him to 'quick fuckin' around' and drop the whole mess on Roy Church. However, Lynch had split for an out-of-county, family Christmas gathering, and that had left the next up, Lieutenant Cyril Savage. Lieutenant Savage immediately connected the dots as laid out by Detective Westwood.

He jotted some quick notes and hustled upstairs to see if the Sheriff was still in. This had to be done in person.

Sheriff Ed Silva was himself prepping to sneak down the backstairs so as to avoid anyone drawing the conclusion that he'd abused his authority by getting out early. He was not thrilled to see Lieutenant Savage poking a bald head through his office door like an unwelcome conscience.

"Ed, we got ourselves a situation," Lieutenant Savage began.

Sheriff Silva sighed and sank back in his chair.

"Lay it on me."

Five minutes later, Sheriff Silva was feeling the Christmas spirit move him.

"How sure is Westwood that this Jesse Wilson is good for our Puma Creek bones?"

"Well, from what he says, the Santa Rosa detective is apparently drawing the same conclusion. Wilson was a loner, a drinker, had been on the job for a few weeks. But it all fits. Why else would he cut out the articles from the KDN? He's leaving them as a confession, seems to me."

"Yeah, it sounds really promising. What's Roy Church think?" Sheriff Silva asked.

"We haven't been able to get hold of him yet. That's why Westwood stepped in. I guess Dispatch should have routed the call to Sisson, but it's Christmas Eve," Lieutenant Savage replied, deftly laying fault squarely on the Christ child.

"Okay, get hold of somebody down there in Sisson so we can get the notifications out of the way. About to ruin someone's Christmas," Sheriff Silva said.

"Will do," said Lieutenant Savage. He got up and took the conscience with him.

A few minutes later, as Sheriff Silva was treading carefully down the icy back stairs toward his private parking space, he couldn't shake a minute feeling of unease. He wished Tommy Sessions had been in. Tommy Sessions was a good sounding board on just about everything. He'd make a great sheriff if he were so inclined. Maybe someday he could give Tommy Sessions his endorsement. Right now, though, he wished he could have asked him how Roy Church was going to take the news that others had jumped in his case uninvited. But Tommy Sessions was out of town due to Christmas just like Lieutenant Lynch, aboard a plane, probably over Bakersfield by now, about to land in LA for a holiday family reunion.

Karuk County Sheriff-2, Christ Child-0.

♦

Roy Church hung up his cell and looked at his notes. Something didn't feel right. Lieutenant Savage had been too pleasant. Maybe it was the season, and Savage was just a true Christmas reveler getting into the whole Peace on Earth for a Day thing. He'd wished Roy a Merry Christmas right before hanging up. Not in character. But there it was. Jesse "Pud" Wilson was dead. Roy had the unenviable task of notifying his mother, a resident of Sisson, and handing her two numbers, one for a police detective in Santa Rosa and the other for the Sonoma County Coroner's office.

Savage had told him that Detective Stern had relayed some particulars when he called regarding the circumstances of Wilson's demise. Death by hanging, empty whiskey bottle, and two cut out KDN articles on the Puma Creek Trail bone case.

Roy dialed the SRPD number first.

"Violent Crimes. This is Jake Stern. Can I help you?" came a clipped but polite voice.

"Yeah, Jake, Roy Church here, Karuk County Sheriff's Department. I'm the investigator on a clandestine grave case up here in which Jesse Dale Wilson was a person of interest, mostly because of his connection to a missing person case from about 13 years ago. I understand you've got Jesse in custody down there cooling to room temperature?"

"Yeah, right. Okay. I just talked to one of your people an hour or so ago."

"Yeah, sorry to make you repeat. I just got the call from my LT. I guess he spoke to you briefly, but if you've got a sec, I'd love to get a few more details."

"No problem. Your boy Wilson was working on a house building project down here. We had a hell of a fire fall of '17, lost thousands of homes, so we've got construction crews from all over the country pouring in for rebuilding," he explained.

"Yeah, I saw all that on the news."

"It was something. We had patrol cars burn up, lost a lot of civilians. Still sifting through burned out houses for crispy critters."

"Damn. Sounds awful," said Roy with sincerity.

"It was. Anyhow, like I said, your boy Wilson was working on a really expensive home up in our Fountaingrove Country Club neighborhood. Million dollar plus digs. He'd been there for a few weeks. I interviewed his boss and a few co-workers. They said he was a good carpenter. Seemed like a loner a little bit and showed up occasionally hungover. But that's not unusual in that profession I'm told.

"Might explain a crack or two in my plaster," Roy chuckled darkly.

"Shit, we had to sue over a house I bought in west Santa Rosa," Stern added. "Mold everywhere, crooked walls. But we got a payout and moved."

"What a nightmare. So who found Wilson deceased?" Roy asked.

"Two of his co-workers arrived at about the same time. Get this, there are so many construction crews in town, everybody fighting for spaces to live and what not, and not everyone has kitchen facilities where they live. So the contractor pays one of his guys to pick up breakfast burritos and donuts and basic breakfast food on the run. Makes sure he's got a happy, fed crew in the morning. Second guy shows up early to warm up equipment they use for lifting units of lumber and roof shingles. Anyhow, they found Wilson hanging from a doorframe. Let me check my notes. They call it a header. Heavy board, like a short timber really. Goes above doors in fancy houses, I guess. Anyhow, Wilson was hanging from that."

Roy jotted some quick notes and probed further. "My LT told me there were newspaper clippings and a whiskey bottle."

"Right, two clippings from your Karuk Daily News. I Googled them and found the exact articles, one from last October and one from last Saturday's edition. They are both reporting on your skeletal remains case on a Puma Creek trail."

"Okay, and a bottle of booze?"

Stern sighed. "Yep. The old standby, JD, Jack Daniels. Looks like he drank most of it or spilled it. Tox report won't be back to us for a few weeks, but it's generally what we see around the holidays. We seem to get a lot of suicides, most involving booze. Postmortem will be day after tomorrow what with tomorrow being Christmas."

"Okay. Any idea where he got the JD? A sack with a receipt maybe?" Roy asked.

"Didn't see one. He could have had the bottle in his truck or stopped and grabbed it at a liquor store en route. I can think of a couple along or near the route from the Rusty Nail to the scene," Stern added helpfully.

"No note?"

"No note. We checked where he was living. He was renting out a garage from a guy just a couple of blocks from where I'm sitting. Right now we got carpenters and construction guys holed up in any place with a roof and four walls. We got like thirty cops here in Sonoma County who lost their homes. No one can find a decent place to live. Rent has gone through the roof. It's a mess," Stern said in a weary tone.

"I can't even imagine. Sounds as if the whole place took a nasty body blow. Did Wilson get mail at the garage?" Roy asked.

"Unknown for sure. But don't think so. No indicia in his garage to say otherwise. His only known address was with a mother or some lady with the same last name, up in your neck of the woods. Let me check." There was a brief pause and the sound of shuffling paper. "Yeah, here it is. Lydia Wilson, 4203 Old Stage Road, Sisson, California. That near you?"

"Very near me. When I hang up, I'm headed there to make a notification. By the way, did his landlord notice any strange behavior?"

"No," Stern replied. "Of course, landlord didn't know him very well, and he wasn't real thrilled with us nosing around. He was pretty much taking advantage of the fire disaster situation and gouging for a space in his garage. A cot, heater, a small fridge, and access to a bathroom. Better than a tent under a bridge I guess."

"What about the newspapers the clippings came from?" Roy asked.

"Not found. And we searched, too. Checked his vehicle, trashcans. Nothing. We figured the first clipping he could have had for a few months. The second one? Not sure," Stern said.

Something wasn't quite adding up for Roy. "How'd he get paid?"

Stern answered, "Contractor pays, then they can go straight to any number of check cashing places here. Those outfits take a percentage, but better than having your checks mailed back home."

"Okay. I know I'm asking a lot of questions, but was there anything about the hanging scene that didn't look right? Anything suspicious about it?"

"No, not that I saw. We got some top notch evidence specialists here. I let them comb through, photograph, sketch, and collect everything. Nothing jumped out at us. I can email the digital photos of the scene and his crib to you. Be a minute for the report."

"Thanks, I'd really appreciate that." said Roy. He gave Detective Stern his e-mail address.

"One other thing," Roy said. "Were you able to trace his movements leading up to the death?"

"As a matter of fact, we were," said Stern. "Some of the other workers said he liked to hang out at a local beer joint here called Red's Rusty Nail. I spoke to a bartender who remembered him from last night. I was looking to see if he'd made any statements about being pissed at the world. He'd become sort of a regular. Never caused problems, usually sat and drank by himself."

"Usually?" Roy caught the qualifier.

"Yeah. Actually the reason the bartender remembered last night was because he had a guy join him. They were really yuckin' it up, like they were old pals. Left together before 2200."

"Hmm," said Roy.

"Hmm?" asked Stern. "You think we missed something? And by the way, you ask a lot more questions than the other detective." He sounded amused.

"Well, he's a lieutenant. What can you say?" Roy chuckled.

"Lieutenant? Heard you mention that earlier. Thought he said detective when he called," Stern said.

"When *he* called? I thought you called us," Roy said.

"No, Detective Westwood called me," Stern replied.

What. The. Fuck.

"The Coroner's office probably called you guys for notification. I was actually going to call later to see if there was any background on Wilson that we should include, like prior suicide attempts or known history of depression."

"I see. Well, it's all good now. Listen, do you have the identity of the fellow Wilson left with? Another construction guy maybe?"

"No. Bartender never seen him before. Noticed him right away though. Bartender described him as a 'hard dude.' Bartenders scope out everybody who comes through the door. Never know when they gotta hit 9-1-1. Don't wanna be taken by surprise," Stern explained unnecessarily.

"Can the bartender recognize the 'hard dude' if he sees him again?"

"He's not sure. But if we ever get a name, sounds like a guy who's had his photo taken more than once or twice in county."

"Look," Roy said. "Something is fishy as fuck."

Roy proceeded to give Detective Stern a rundown on the Puma Creek bone case and the Dina Morgan case.

"Trust me," Roy said. "Everyone up here not on the inside of this case thinks the clavicular fragment came from Dina Morgan. The entire town believes that Jesse Dale Wilson killed her, and that we've got her burial site up on a mountain side. We got dozens of calls over the months. I even had a little girl stop by the substation the other day to tell me to look at Pud Wilson."

The Santa Rosa detective whistled when Roy was done.

"You're right. This has the makings of a clusterfuck. Unfortunately, we've already released the scene back to the construction crew. But I don't know what else we could have done there. We treated it as a homicide scene with evidence processing, so I think we're good."

"No sweat. It is what it is," said Roy. "Look, I'm headed to make the notification. Here's my cell number. I think we'll be talking again."

"Great," said Stern "And Merry Christmas, Happy Holidays, all that."

"Same to you, Jake. And *Hanukkah Sameach.*"

"Ha. Very good, but you're not Jewish. Are you?" Stern laughed with surprise.

Roy smiled, "No, my in-laws."

"Well wish them *Hanukkah Samaech* and *Chag Urim Sameach* from me!"

"Will do."

Before Roy could hang up, Stern asked, "They got a temple way up there in the sticks?"

"Nah, Orange County."

"Oh, you a lateral?" Stern asked.

"Yep," Roy answered.

"Me too. Oakland PD, ten years. Now I'm up here in the Wine Country. Bit of a change."

"Los Angeles Sheriff, 34 years. Bit of a change here, too," replied Roy, an incredible understatement.

"Damn. Long time. Patrol the whole time?"

Roy leaned back in his chair; it immediately pushed painfully into his spine. He cleared his throat. "No. A year in custody then eight years in patrol. 25 in the Homicide Bureau."

"Whoa, Nelly. Wait a sec. Did you teach a course in Officer Involved a few years ago? Up here in Los Gatos at Homicide School?" Stern didn't wait for a reply. "I was there. I was in your class. I'll be damned."

"Yes, that was me. That's been awhile," said Roy. He periodically ran into former students from his Officer Involved Critical Incident classes in the Southland, this was a first in NorCal.

"You taught with a partner. Funny as hell, as I recall."

"Yep, Charlie Criss," Roy replied.

"How's he doing?" Stern asked.

"Uh, he passed away a few years back. He was good partner," Roy said, sadness creeping into his voice though he tried to suppress it.

Better than good. The best.

Stern was silent for a second. "If you don't mind me asking, why'd you transfer?"

"Needed a change," Roy said simply.

"Gotcha," Stern replied. He quickly dropped the line of questioning. He must have detected the melancholy in Roy's voice.

"Okay then," Stern said. "Let's keep in touch on this mess."

"Will do."

Roy hung up. He sat pondering. He shouldn't have gotten distracted by Stern's name. Too late. He sucked it up and moved on. Anniversaries would be coming soon. He wasn't looking forward to them. There was something about Stern, though. Maybe it had been the connection to his past. Maybe it was the straightforward, no nonsense approach to the Wilson "suicide," and his willingness not to CYA or hedge his movements thus far. Roy didn't know him, but he liked him.

He switched gears in his mind. He crossed his fingers that too much damage hadn't been done by amateurs sticking their noses in a pro's business. It was something he'd have to deal with. It wasn't as if he'd not had to play political games before. There was nothing like the palace intrigue of a big city police department or the country's largest sheriff's department. Went with the territory. Of course, there'd be a meeting on all this in Silverton, after Christmas. He'd cross bridges then. In the meantime, this bullshit suicide was conveniently providing him with more than enough smoke and fog in which to advance his positions. When the air cleared, he'd be massing at the gate.

CHAPTER 18

Roy turned north on Old Stage Road. It ran north-south somewhat parallel to the I-5 west of Sisson and north of Karuk Lake. Heavy forest loomed on both sides with giant, white apparitions bent over, nearly joining high above the center line. The gaiety of Christmas shined cheerfully from the front porches, windows, and rooflines of homes tucked back under the giants.

He cranked his heater to limber up fingers made stiff from brushing the frozen snow off his windows back at the sub. He knew other cops wore gloves in the cold. Old habits die hard. He just couldn't bring himself to hamstring his gun hand that way in the SoCal. No matter what the temperature. He supposed he'd have to find a happy medium up here. It was freakin' cold!

Traffic was non-existent. Christmas Eve had most folks inside, gathered around a piano, tearing open gifts, or readying the young for sugar plum dreams, so he was able to slink along, searching. With his spotlight he lit up various mailboxes, most of them stuck in five-gallon buckets and pulled back away from the road to avoid the snowplow blades. Sporadically, he spied various brass-colored or white numbers pounded into tree trunks, telling him he was close. Then he spotted *4203* on a black stick with a red reflector a few feet off the right shoulder. Beyond, he noticed a driveway trenching eastward through the drifts.

He turned up the driveway, wondering if he should have walked, but the maintenance yard guy in Silverton had sworn the studs would get him through the Yukon. He hoped like hell there had been a snowplow or snow blower that had cleared a turnaround somewhere in the past few days. The driveway had been plowed at one time, but still there was over a foot of snow on narrow ruts for him to creep through.

This is insane. They'll find me Donner style with my arm halfway digested in my stomach.

Then, had this not been a death notification, he might have chuckled. He couldn't have gotten more stereotypical in his search. Lydia Wilson lived in an actual doublewide with oxidized pink siding and white framed windows which had bed sheets covering them from the inside. The trailer house had been there for some time, since it now had a faded wood frame built over it, with a slanted aluminum roof that kept a few feet of snow off a flat top. A chimney had been installed through the top of the trailer and the aluminum roof. Thick smoke curled and twisted away into the blackness as Roy played his spotlight over the scene. An open carport stood framed to one side, and a black Ford Explorer, late 80's model, exposed its rear bumper to him. Tracks behind the Ford said it had been out sometime in the past few hours. Probably for wine, cigarettes and a scratcher was Roy's guess. He wondered where the hungry pit bull hid. Too cold? Was it inside waiting to pounce on a uniformed leg? Would pay to keep that in mind.

Roy knocked on the door. He'd done this number a hundred times. It never got easier, but he'd learned a thing or two over the decades. Get it over with quickly. Don't string out the waiting with small talk about 'may I come in, and would you please take a seat'. Tell them at the door. The pain between a front door and the couch could be cruel agony for the person about to become a victim.

A porch light flicked on, and the door opened a crack. Low glow from a TV backlit a pink, round face and glasses over a substantial all-day nightgown. Roy guessed late 60's but looked late 70's.

"Roy Church, Sheriff's Department. Are you Lydia Wilson?"

Lydia Wilson looked him over for a moment before responding heavily, "Yes, deputy. Come in." She opened the door wide and Roy stepped in, quickly scanning the interior for others.

"Anyone else in the house?" *More force of habit. How many targets do I have?*

"No, just me. What happened? What's wrong?" Fear in the voice.

"I've got bad news about Jesse. I'm afraid he's passed away."

Sometimes Roy said, "Passed away," sometimes, "Died," and

sometimes, "Dead." He'd used, "Gone" once, only once. It had confused the hell out of a mama whose boy lay in the street a block away, face down in a red rag. He'd fumbled that one. Later, Charlie Criss said he might as well ask at the next one, "Are you the Widow Jones?" When the answer came back, "No," he should say, "Well, I beg to differ."

To Roy it didn't matter that Jesse Wilson was a dirtbag who'd likely killed his girlfriend and disposed of her body. This was not his time to suffer. This was his mom's, and she didn't deserve the pain. No mother did.

He said to her, "Would you like to sit down? Is there someone I can call? I'm so sorry for your loss."

She stared at him for a moment, shoulders limp, eyes moistened. Then she turned and slowly walked to her easy chair where she slumped backward. She picked up a remote control that lay across a Bible on a side table. She turned off the TV.

This gave Roy a chance to glance around the room further. A short string of seasonal lights encircled a fake, tabletop tree, two lights on the blink. A cardboard sign, gold on black, with the words *Merry Christmas*, sat atop a faux mantel over the potbellied stove in the center of the living room. No other decorations.

She didn't look at him, but she said, "You can sit down on the couch if you like. I'm okay. And there is no one to call."

"Thanks," said Roy, "But if it's all right I'd like to sit on one of these." He pulled an open straight-back table chair over to face her, its back to the wall of the trailer. Too difficult to get up out of couch quickly if she'd been fibbing about being alone.

"You must know his history. Not a lot of people want to be around me, think I'll rub off on them. I go to church, but it's not enough. I know he was bad."

He let her ramble. He suspected she'd cried any and all tears for Pud years ago. Roy had sat with many a parent, mothers mostly, who'd remained dry eyed through his entire time with them. How they acted later behind a closed bedroom door or in the shower he did not know.

"You might as well tell me what happened. I've been expecting this visit for the past thirty years."

"Mrs. Wilson–," Roy began.

"Call me Lydia," she interrupted.

"Lydia, it seems Jesse may have taken his own life."

She glanced up sharply.

"Killed himself? What?"

"That's what I'm being told. It wasn't around here. Do you know where he was working?"

"I think he was down in Santa Rosa. He told me he had a construction job there. Seemed happy to be going there. He's had a hard time keeping steady work. Drugs and alcohol didn't do him any favors. But killed himself? How?"

"From what I'm hearing, it seems he might have hanged himself at the place where he worked."

She reached a trembling hand up and adjusted her glasses. "Oh my."

He noticed she hadn't mentioned God, in spite of the Bible on her table. Pud had been cut loose by Lydia a *long* time ago. When your own mother doesn't recommend you to the number one deity, you've reached bottom, down with the whale shit.

"Can you think of any reason why he might have wanted to hurt himself?" Roy asked quietly.

She stopped and looked at him again.

"I think it's obvious. It's all about Dina."

"So you believe he is responsible for Dina's disappearance?"

She paused, clearly trying to choose the right words before speaking. "As his mom, I didn't want to think so at first, but he was not a nice man. I didn't do a good enough job with him. He got mean over the years."

"Hmm," said Roy.

"I didn't really like it when he came by. You wouldn't believe how much he stole from me over the years. I made him move out a long time ago, long before Dina went missing. They lived together somewhere, probably a lot of somewheres. They floated out of here, down to Redding, and then over to the coast, Humboldt County, Eureka, and Crescent City, even down in the Central Valley toward Fresno. Lots of drugs in those places, I guess. But he called me off and on. We didn't talk long. Just asked how I was, told me where he was headed. Like he thought I might care."

"He was still using this address for mailing," said Roy, watching her closely.

She nodded. "Yes, the one thing I allowed was for his mail to come here, he's moved around so much. I'd put anything for him in a bag in the carport. At times there's been mail for months that he'd didn't come by and get. Piled up, mostly letters from the county probably telling him he missed court dates." She tried to give Roy a weak smile, but it came across more as a sad twisting of her lips as she struggled with the memories of her son.

Roy gave her a moment to collect herself before asking, "When did you hear from him last?"

She took a deep breath. "He left a message on my machine that he was going to Santa Rosa to work. That's what I mean about him sounding happy. That was over a month ago. Nothing since."

"Did he have any friends that you knew of?"

"I don't know, druggies I suppose. He and Dina were on that awful stuff they called crank," she shook her head sadly.

"Can you think of any reason someone might send him some recent newspaper clippings from the Karuk Daily News?" Roy pried gently.

"No. Why would they do that? He couldn't read. That was part of his problem. No good in school when he was younger. Couldn't form letters. But they kept skipping him along from grade to grade until he stopped going to regular school," she said, looking away.

You don't say.

"He did work though, in construction?"

"Oh yeah. He was supposed to be a good carpenter. He built the frame over this house in a few days. That was ages ago when he was excited about making money by working hard."

"Really?"

She nodded. "Yeah, I suppose if he could have stayed away from the drugs he could have made a good life for himself."

"Where did he meet Dina?"

Lydia waved her hand vaguely, "Oh, she grew up around here. I think they started hanging out back when they first started that school you go to when you can't get into high school. He was several years older."

"You mean continuation school?" ask Roy.

"Yeah, that's it. Nothing but little druggies and criminals. Bad influence on him," she sighed.

"Did Jesse have any guns that you knew of?" Roy asked.

"I wouldn't know. But I never knew him to have a gun. I thought you said he hung himself."

"Yes, you're right, he did not shoot himself. I was just curious," said Roy.

He paused briefly, letting the moment sink in. Then he continued.

"This might seem like an odd question, but did Jesse ever deer hunt that you knew of?"

"Not that I knew of. Maybe if he'd had a dad around to take him hunting, he might have turned out different," she said.

"Where is his father?" Roy asked.

"He was killed in Vietnam in '69. I'd just given birth to Jesse a few months before. Grew up without a dad. I never got married, so Jesse never had a dad around." She said it flatly.

Roy had seen a lot of fatherless children over the years. Their stories had ended a lot like Pud's. Not necessarily suicide, but dead before your time is still dead.

"Do you know if he ever tried to hurt himself before?" Roy asked.

"Not that I knew of, unless you count thirty years' worth of taking drugs," she answered.

"Where do you think Dina is, or where her body is, if you had to guess?

Normally, Roy would have left a grieving mother alone on this subject, but Lydia was not actively grieving, at least outwardly. If he had to pin an emotion on her it might be relief mixed with regret.

"I don't know. Maybe those bones they found up on the hill by the lake. I read about that in the paper," she said.

"It was a mile and a half by trail to where the bones were found. How big was Dina? I guess I'm asking could Jesse have carried her that far?"

"Well, she got all skinny and frail, probably from those drugs. I don't know. Maybe 115 or so pounds. Jesse was strong. He worked construction."

"Oh, another thing, did Jesse have any siblings?"

"No, just me." She trailed off, looking away again.

Roy stood up and handed a piece of paper to Lydia. "Okay. Listen here are the numbers of the coroner's office in Sonoma County, they've got Jesse's remains there. Here's another number for a police detective who's handling the death investigation for Santa Rosa."

"I don't have any money for a burial or whatever, so they'll have to keep him. I'd just as soon not have him come back."

Lydia had finally washed the last of Jesse "Pud" Wilson off her hands.

Roy left her rocking silently in her easy chair, her hands clasped across her belly, staring straight ahead, and dry-eyed. He wondered if she'd turn the TV back on and search for *A Wonderful Life*. It had to be on some channel, somewhere.

He exhaled a fogbank as he negotiated a slippery walkway back to his SUV. He felt his cell vibrate. After he turned his heater up to rescue level he checked. Kat had texted him with a *Merry Christmas!* Autocorrect helped him stab back with *Thanks! Merry Christmas to you and your family, too!*

His reply, with its exclamation points, made it look as if he were in a great mood, everything going peachy, having a wonderful Christmas Eve.

As long as he had his phone out, he threw in a text to Jake Stern telling him he'd write a supplemental report for the SRPD death investigation, detailing his notification and interview with a relieved mother of the decedent.

Another Kat text popped up.

Thanks for giving me the days off to snowboard! It's been great. Will see you day after Christmas? Any big breaks?

He texted back, taking a minute to get it right.

Been a few developments. Will fill you in on Friday. Btw, did your friend Maddy get hold of you?

Kat shot back.

??? Maddy?

Roy wondered how Kat could answer him so quickly. He typed again, wishing she'd just call. Texting was a giant pain.

Came by sub on Monday looking for you saw you at reunion.

Seconds later Kat was on his screen again.

Yes, she was at reunion then at my house later. I told her and others I was working as intern for police, but I couldn't talk about any cases. Honest!!! Confidentiality first!

Roy thumbed a reply.

No worries. Friday then.

He'd just slipped his phone in his pocket and was trying to back around blindly in Lydia Wilson's whiteout of a front yard when it went off again. Stern had texted him, asking for a callback if he was still on duty.

He managed to get himself pointed back west and downhill. Once back on firm, icy asphalt he turned south and drove about a half mile until he came to the intersection of Old Stage Road and Karuk Lake

Road. He turned west into the empty, pitch-black parking lot of the Mount Shasta Fish Hatchery, a state-run facility used for raising stock to be dumped into hundreds of lakes that lay hidden in the nooks and crannies of northern California ranges. He was happy to let his car idle for a bit while his steering wheel warmed.

He dialed Stern, his cold fingers missing a few numbers causing him to curse and start over.

"Stern."

"What's up?" Roy asked.

"I want to thank you for the OT. My whole Christmas just got paid for. Not sure my wife is going to be happy though."

"Oh man, sorry."

"Nah, it's okay, really. Anyhow, I'm reclassifying this as a Suspicious Death with a pinch of 187 thrown in. Too many unanswered questions. Of course, my sergeant thinks I'm milking it. Not really. I called him at home, and he agrees."

"What changed?" Roy asked, curious.

"Well, besides all your info, I went back to the Rusty Nail, and I drove the route from it to the hanging site. Only one liquor store, unless you go way off course. One bottle of JD purchased last night. Got it on tape."

"Good work."

"Yeah, my screw-up. Should have done it today. But then I didn't have one of the top homicide dicks in California breathin' over my shoulder," Stern chuckled.

"Well, that's a load of b.s.," Roy laughed. "But go on."

"It worked out okay, because the same East Indian clerk is working right now who was on last night. He recalled the dude who came in for the JD, thought he was there to hit a lick."

Roy noted the gangster term for armed robbery, tucked it away. Stern must have worked some gang details to use it so naturally.

"So this dude comes in, wearing a hoodie and dark glasses. Clerk was strapped, starts reaching for the gat under his shirt. He's been taken down before and his cousin was killed during a 211 in one of our 7-11's. The guy says, 'bottle of JD' and pulls out a roll of bills. Clerk watches his hands the whole time and then breathes a sigh of relief when dude turns and walks out the door."

"How do we know this is the bottle from the scene?" Roy asked.

"You're going to love this. Not only did old Singh the owner hook up video for the inside, he's got the outside covered, too.

Guess whose truck was driven by hoodie dude?" Stern asked. Roy could feel the buildup in Stern's voice

"Jesse "Pud" Wilson's truck." Roy said. He could feel the mystery surrounding the death of Wilson creeping forward like tendrils from a black lake.

"Exactly," exclaimed Stern. "Ain't that some shit! But wait, that's not all. If you buy today, I can give you our special."

"Which is?" Roy laughed.

"The outside video is good enough to make out the passenger in Pud's truck. It's Pud, and he's sound asleep against the window. He was already wasted," said Stern.

"I see. I'm buying today's special," murmured Roy.

"Yep. Don't see how a guy that drunk, and that's consistent with how fucked up he looked when he left the bar, could manage to get up on a rickety bucket, tie an expert knot and then hang himself. I'll bet his B.A. comes back at three or four times the legal limit."

"Sounds as if he had help," Roy mused thoughtfully.

"Oh, yeah. But wait, if you call in the next ten minutes," Stern laughed. "I can pay for your Christmas, too!"

Roy didn't tell him he was already working Christmas, once again for Tom Hanlon. It was no big deal and worked out well for him, kept him occupied.

"Go ahead. My credit card and ATM PIN are yours," said Roy.

"Like I said, I went back to the bar to drive the route. After talking to Singh the clerk, I hustled back to the bar to look for any witnesses who are regulars."

"Let me guess. A saloon in Santa Rosa has regulars."

"Yep, got a few girls, well, actually they're older ladies without teeth who don't bite you when you pay for a blowjob. They use the bathroom and the parking lot."

"I see," said Roy.

"So did one of them," said Stern. "She was getting out of her car in the parking lot after a little peace on earth and goodwill toward men. She saw Pud being helped across the lot to his truck. She says she saw Pud drop his keys, and the dude helping him scooped them up, threw them in the air, and said something about Dale Earnhardt. And he drove the truck away. He was not drunk. And she knows drunks the way a Chippie deuce car knows drunks on a freeway."

"Wow," said Roy.

"Wow is right," said Stern, "Deck the halls with bowels of Pud."

CHAPTER 19

Given the overwhelming Judeo-Christian make-up of the American population, Christmas continues to be the most celebrated day in America, with the exception of Super Bowl Sunday. But on Super Bowl Sunday all Americans are pretty much consistent in their activities of overeating and unhinged alcohol consumption. Not so much with the religious celebrations of the birth of Christ, or the more secular celebrations of Santa's early, first day of Spring Break.

Roy Church took an early morning respite from Puma Creek and hit the empty streets and roads of Karuk County. No one moved, save a few lonesome big rigs on the I-5, with Virginia or Arkansas plates telling a story of far from home.

He checked his phone. A thankful Deputy Tom Hanlon had texted him regarding a special, glazed nut bread of some sort left for him on his desk at the sub, along with a surprise gift. Nice.

He wasn't sure what to expect in these parts, but experience and his casebook file had told him that an LA Christmas Day starts all fuzzy smiles and warm hugs. Then the first mimosa or beer in a V-8 goes down. By mid-afternoon, and certainly by dusk, the casebook usually had another entry. Alcohol and family gatherings. Always good for a phone call from LASD Dispatch or a pager vibration. Within minutes Charlie Criss would roll by, and Roy would hop in, prepared to admire Charlie's new cufflinks or tie on the drive to the yellow tape.

♦

Cedar Stock passed *his* Christmas morning at Ma's kitchen table on her HP laptop that he'd bought for her birthday. She lay sacked out in her chair in the other room with the TV on low. He'd checked to make sure she had a blanket before firing up the computer. Earlier she'd opened a gift he'd dropped off. Minutes later, her mouth gaped and drooled as she snored contentedly.

He Googled the Santa Rosa Press Democrat newspaper's local section to read an account of a death investigation by the SRPD. Not a lot of information other than the police were investigating the demise of a construction worker at a job site in the "tony Fountaingrove section" of town. *Pud woulda asked, 'Who the fuck is Tony?'* No identity of the deceased had been released pending notification of next of kin. Unless you knew otherwise, for all the info contained in the short story, the dead worker could have been run over by a forklift. He figured it'd be a day or so after Christmas, before the media would put two and two together and come up with Pud's guilty conscience.

He went back over his movements of the previous several days, looking for any obvious mistakes. It'd been smart loading gas containers in his truck so as not to leave credit card receipts or cash-at-the counter video that could track him south from Sisson. The burner phone had been an obvious must. He chuckled to himself remembering how he'd scared the raghead behind the counter into patting a pistol he had all sneaky up under his shirt. Sure, there might be video, but he'd hoodied up over Raybans. The time spent in the bar was a little dicey, but the place had been packed with construction workers and whores, so he felt okay there.

Switching out plates on his truck had been wise, as well. He laughed out loud when he thought about the Mexican's license plate, he'd lifted in the Costco parking lot in Santa Rosa. He thought the owner was a paisa until he heard him yell, "God damn, mother fucker!" upon rolling up with a cart and finding his Oakland Raiders license plate holder on the asphalt. Fuck the Raiders. Deserters. Had the Mexican looked around, he'd have seen Cedar laughing his ass off two rows back. Of course, it had been dark. Not being seen committing a petty theft was sorta the point.

Even if someone ID'd him as being in Santa Rosa, big fuckin' deal. He knew construction work and would have been just as likely to go there as Ol' Pud on a Stud. So he ran into a friend who was in the same business. Proves nothing. No witnesses to the hanging. No prosecutor anywhere would file charges on that case. All he had to say, if hemmed up, was that of course he'd run into Pud in a bar, and noticed he was real depressed, and that he'd tried to cheer him up as any decent pal would, even drove his truck for him because he'd had too much. Wouldn't want innocent persons or Pud to get injured. Drinking and driving is a crime and a national tragedy. He could conjure up a tear or two over that. He'd been a person of interest so many times in his life that one more wouldn't amount to shit.

Cedar leaned back and settled his sights on a fruitcake that some *fruitcake, ha-ha*, had dropped off for Ma. *Jesus. Who the fuck eats that shit?*

He checked the clock. Half past 9. Gonna be a long day. He should have stayed in the Bay Area a little longer, kicked it with some of the old crew, if he coulda found them. Probably all dope sick these days or taking a break from following Fed Ex trucks all day. Being reduced to a porch pirate was sad, just sad. And what about Sarah? It sorta pissed him off that he'd not been invited to a dinner. But she'd mentioned something about her and Maddy going to the home of that fag Faraday for a dinner. Jesus, didn't she see enough of that worthless cock chugger at work?

He crept into the living room to see that Ma was still breathing. Then he picked up his guitar that he'd set on the Mexican horse blanket. Softly he began to strum and sing in a low, gentle voice.

Silent night, holy night
All is calm, all is bright

Ma stirred, opened her eyes and smiled at him. Then she lowered her lids and went back to a world where maybe, just maybe, she'd raised a son who didn't have to glance over his shoulder regularly.

♦

Jake Stern started his Christmas morning by tearing open presents with his mixed race, Native American wife Rachel and several nearly grown children. Jake had the best of all worlds. Blended Jewish-Christian families basically spend the year around the table feasting and toasting every obscure holiday the two faiths can come up with, and Rachel was one hell of a cook. Stern patted his two cans short of a six-pack stomach as evidence. He swore to get back in the gym and out on the track — after the first of the year. No sense rushing it. He planned to pass a few hours with the family, and then spend a few more paying for presents by pounding out his reports on the Wilson death investigation. After that, he'd lose one more can over Rachel's sumptuous evening meal.

He'd made himself a list of *Things to Do*, as any good detective would. He couldn't wait for businesses to open back up *manana* so he could get started. This was going to be a tough one to prove.

Then his mind turned to Roy Church. Odd that a legend from Southern California should end up in a Podunk county taking reports on vandalized pasture gates and rustled cows. He was naturally curious about people's private lives, a holdover trait from his early days in plainclothes as a sexual assault detective in which the ugliest private of private became public. *Quit being so damn nosy*, he told himself.

He took a huge bite of Rachel's special cream cheese sweetbread that had been pleading at him as it lay on his plate next to its cousin, the Rachel Stern, one of a kind, bacon and egg pastry. *Kosher is for the strong, and I'm not back in the gym yet.*

♦

Kat Hoover slid out of a comfy bed early on Christmas and sat by Paul's fire that he'd stoked an hour before returning to the sheets. In a far corner of the living room, through the verdant branches of a silvertip fir, a twinkling kaleidoscope of colors chased one another, like children at recess. Santa and a bevy of reindeer grinned down at her from a temporary wire strung across the room just under the ceiling. The microwave dinged. She got up, dropped a tea bag in the boiling water, and then returned to her perch next to the flames.

She reflected on the past week and a half. Her morose outlook on life had changed considerably with a heavy, boarder-friendly snowstorm, a surprisingly cheery visit with old classmates, and the strange new world of death investigations as the novice partner of an enigmatic man. Roy Church had come off as such an old gentleman willing to go to lengths to aid her in several times of need. He seemed so reserved at times, humorous and exuberant at others, and always smart. He did not strike her as someone who missed much. She hoped he really believed her when she told him she'd divulged nothing about the Puma Creek case to her former classmates. It was unfortunate that Maddy Stock had come looking for her at the Sheriff's substation. Why hadn't she simply texted?

In spite of Christmas being her favorite day of the year, she eagerly looked forward to throwing open the door to the sub in the morning and hashing out whatever new discoveries Roy had to share with her. He'd sounded a bit cryptic in his texts, which were short but full of meaning. Then it crossed her mind that another characteristic she'd noticed, a distant, underlying sadness, subtle, but there. She realized then that she knew nothing about his personal life other than he'd moved from LA. She had no idea how he lived or where he lived or if he lived alone. Maybe she should have invited him for Christmas dinner. No, that would have been too forward, and Paul would have pestered him about racial profiling or glass ceilings or something from the world that always generated heat in a mixed room.

She crossed her legs and took a sip. A toilet flushed in another room, and she heard her mom cough. She rose and walked into the kitchen where she pulled out a thawed pound of bacon and some special morning pastries that Paul had picked up at the Sisson Bakery. The day was on her.

♦

Wallace Westwood lounged in his easy chair watching his two-year-old destroy a fluorescent green package. His giddy wife leaned over with a digital camera capturing every gyration. His cell buzzed. He tapped in his code and saw the text from Alison Baker along with an attachment.

Did Santa's little helper lose his hat?

He clicked on the attachment.

Oh, fuck!

There was Baker, buck naked wearing his elf hat and holding her iPhone toward the mirror, grinning like a two-year-old tearing open a fluorescent green package.

She looked damned incredible, small athletic tits, but a tight ass, unlike his wife who'd taken the eating for two as a challenge and never looked back.

"Who is it, Wally?" his wife turned to ask from her all fours position on the rug. Two Volkswagens trying to pass one another.

"Work. Just an update on that case I told you about. The one I think I've got solved from the other day."

"They caught those Asians?" she asked, pulling her bleached-blond hair to one side.

"No, this is the one I handled down in Sisson back in October. I've been following up on a few leads in my spare time. Looks like they paid off."

She looked at him with pride but frowned a little. "You're a good detective, Wally. Just wish you didn't have to work so much."

"Goes with the territory," Westwood said. "But you benefit from all those hours. Remember, we'll solve no crime 'til overtime!"

"Well, I'm just thankful I got a shift adjustment in the ER, so we could all be together this morning," she said, blissfully.

Westwood pasted a big smile on his face and replied, "Yeah, this is awesome spending time with you and the baby."

"He's not a baby much longer, Wally. Gonna grow up to be a big strong policeman like your daddy, huh. Of course, you'd make more money if you became an ER doc," she chortled, chucking Wally Jr. under the chin.

"Maybe we should have another," she said thoughtfully.

Jesus, I already gotta roll you in flour just to find the wet spot.

"Maybe that's something we should talk about after the holidays. I think I got a little heartburn right now."

♦

Sheriff Ed Silva, sporting a Santa hat at the old family ranch outside Silverton, turned a sizzling steer on a spit. A big crowd of Silvas and their shirttails were due to converge within the hour. They'd be eager to sample Big Ed's faire and should add to his already plentiful supply of bourbon and Napa Valley wines. A traditional turkey and ham were in the warmer for those skipping the ribeye. They would be the in-laws. True Silvas, all descendants of Karuk County's early pioneers and cattle rustlers, craved beef. It's what's for dinner. Those who didn't stroll in carrying bottles would most likely cradle pies and cakes to round out the assault and battery on his gall bladder.

His cell vibrated. He wiped his hands on his white apron and checked. Tommy Sessions. Sheriff Silva envisioned Tommy wearing his Ram's Jersey under a Dodger cap. *Don't bring that shit up here! Ha ha.*

Got your text re the Puma bone case. Sounds promising. Roy Church thinks it's the real deal?

Sheriff Silva texted back.

Haven't spoken to Roy but Westwood and Savage said SRPD detectives apparently think it fits.

Sessions came back.

Hmm Okay, sounds good. I'm not back in town until Saturday. You all meeting on this tomorrow?

Out of the corner of his eye, Sheriff Silva caught a 4X4, with a red wreath attached to the grill, skid to a stop in his front yard. Jingle Bells blared through nephew Jerry's custom PA system.

Yes. 1500 hours. Will update you. Gotta go. Merry Christmas!

♦

Mid-afternoon with a silent radio, Roy Church checked in at the sub. True to his word, Tom Hanlon had left a loaf of sugary bread waiting for him alongside a gaily wrapped gift the size of a boot box. *Merry Christmas, Roy! And Thanks so Much! Tom and Family.*

He carefully set aside ribbon, bow, and the thoughtful note. After tearing off half the wrapping he was able to see that it was indeed a boot box, from Rocky Boots, Tom Hanlon's size, black, military style. He opened the box. Inside, under thin packing papers of green, pink, and white lay his gift. Roy took it out and admired it. He laughed out loud. A note attached read.

Shot this for you myself, seems fitting. Can't thank you enough for giving me the day off with my family, Tom.

Roy decided right then where he'd put it. The rich, chocolate hued, hollow oak plaque and antler kit, easy to assemble, would look fantastic with Tom Hanlon's four-point antlers attached. He had just the spot over his fireplace in his cabin.

He set the box of plaque and antlers aside and pulled out his iPhone. He stared at it a minute, then glanced away out the window, to study the fleet of white and gray battleships steaming across a cerulean sky. He tapped in the 949 area code followed by seven digits. Apple gave him the choice, call or text. He texted, feeling a tightness in his chest.

Merry Christmas to everyone down there. Hope all are well. Am doing fine up here. Working hard, staying out of trouble, Roy.

He thumbed the send arrow and watched the green line advance across the top of the text. He let out a breath. He refreshed to a new text, again to the 949. This time, no Laguna Beach, instead, the Balboa Island enclave in Newport Beach, just a few miles north on the PCH.

Shalom! A belated Chag Hanukkah! Hope all is well. Am doing fine up north, staying out of trouble. I wish you the very best, and may their memories be a blessing, Roy.

♦

In the late afternoon, as the mottled sky began to lose its dazzle, Maddy and Sarah Stock arrived at the normally closed wrought iron gate across the entrance to an asphalt driveway. No need to buzz. Ronnie expected guests.

It never failed to take Maddy's breath away every time she visited her mother's employer. The five-bedroom log home set high above Karuk Lake, overlooking the whole of the Strawberry Valley and Sisson, approached trophy home status for this part of the state. Vaulted ceilings, exposed limestone fireplaces, a gourmet kitchen, and a huge expanse of windows perfectly framed Mount Shasta across the valley. The spa and fireplace on a covered patio, just outside a walkout basement, were spots on the property she'd frequented over the years. If the CSI thing didn't work out, she'd love to try the real estate business like Ronnie and her mom.

Sarah opened the front door without knocking and yelled, "Merry Christmas, boss man!"

Ronald Faraday, a trim man of medium height, in his mid to late forties, with carefully coiffed salt and pepper hair, wearing a brilliant red and white sweater adorned with green reindeer, turned and grinned widely. He set a champagne glass on a long, decked out dining room table.

"Sarah, Maddy! Merry Christmas!" he cried and hurried forward to hug them both.

Another, much younger, man with short blond hair, dark eyes, and the build of a swimmer, stepped into the room from the pantry. He carried two bottles of red wine.

"Rolf, these are my dear friends, Sarah and her daughter Maddy. Ladies, meet Rolf. I came across him last year during my cruise down the Rhine. He was waiting tables. He did all this," beamed Ronnie with a sweep of his hand.

The aircraft carrier of a table extended over twenty feet from the kitchen into the great room. A colorful red, blue, and gold runner lay down the center of the rich landscape, smothered by elegant greenery next to heavy vanilla, vermillion, and deep green candles. Circling the exterior were twenty-five crimson Mikasa of Portugal plates on their warmers. Each was decorated with a chocolate candy cane with perfectly tied gold bows edging into emerald boughs, all guarded by a precise contingent of noble flutes for champagne, and haughty Fusion Air wine glasses for whatever Rolfie and Ronnie had in store. Water optional.

Rolf poured a delightful glass of Domaine Chandon sparkling Brut, and then the quartet stepped to the fireplace where flames danced the tango.

"To that rascal Santa and Baby Jesus," cried Ronnie, giving the Spanish pronunciation to the newborn's name. "You're the first to arrive, so this is but the beginning!"

Clink.

♦

Lydia Wilson lay slumbering in her lumpy, double bed, alone, next to a tattered photo album partially covered by her flower-patterned bedspread. It was open to a clear plastic covered page of fading Polaroid photos. In one photo, center page, stood a youngster in a Little League uniform proudly mugging bared teeth for the camera. Written shakily in ink under the photo were the words *Jesse the Slugger.*

CHAPTER 20

Early morning after Christmas, when the working stiffs wink at bosses, assuring them they'll actually accomplish something pay worthy between now and New Year's, Jake Stern arrived in the gated, back parking lot of the Santa Rosa Police Department. He strolled quickly through the organized pandemonium still lit by night lights, nodding to a dozen or so Early Days shift guys fanning out toward their black and white patrol cars. Impatient night shift units circled the blocks, eyeing the entry gate, waiting for the signal to stand down.

Once inside the red brick building at 965 Sonoma Avenue, he bounded upstairs to the second floor. The second story housed the Admin and Investigations sections of the SRPD. He walked quickly past the empty sea of cubicles and glassed in supervisors' offices until he came to his own door. On the wall next to the door a small black sign with white lettering read *Violent Crimes Investigations.*

He bent at a copy machine in an alcove and made ten copies of his list of Things to Do. Then he returned to his own cubicle and sat, studying it. Presently a select collection of yawning detectives, along with two sleepy eyed evidence specialists, wandered in. Almost all carried matching Starbucks cups.

"Everybody meet in the conference room in five," said Stern.

He jotted some quick notes for his presentation then walked the thirty feet to the VCI section's exclusive conference room. He took a seat at the head of the table, after laying out the copies of his list at different seats.

Five minutes later, eight Starbucks cups rested next to the lists and stills of a hooded male adult wearing dark glasses inside Singh's Liquors.

Stern heard an evidence specialist snigger, "Sunglasses at night?" to which a detective replied, "When you're cool, the sun always shines."

Stern began.

"As you know, the death on Greenskeeper started out as a suicide. It is now a 187. We're two days behind our killer, so we have some catch up work to do."

There was some murmuring around the table. The evidence specialist raised her hand.

"Are we going back to the scene?" she asked. "With all the construction, it's going to look different."

"That's where we lucked out," Stern replied. "Some of the contractors let their guys go on Christmas Eve since a lot of them have to travel a long way to get home. Then we have Christmas Day. Nothing moved. And a lot of contractors told their boys to not show up until Monday, so we've got very little traffic to deal with today. I've got patrol guys blocking the intersection into Greenskeeper right now, so a house to house search needs to get underway ASAP."

As the mini-task force got up to head out to their various assignments, Stern stopped them.

"One other thing," he added cryptically. "We're all being judged on this one. We can't screw it up."

He smiled ruefully at the puzzled looks.

"This OT, for some of you today, is made possible by the work instincts of an old deputy up in Karuk County who is not really an old deputy out their ridin' the range huntin' for a stagecoach robber named Butch Cassidy. He's a lateral from LA County. Not only that, but some of you sat in his classes at Homicide School. His name's Delroy Church, LASD Homicide, 25 years. He is a freakin' legend down there. He took down their Night Devil and the I-10 Clown Killer, among others. We don't want him clownin' us. May G-d have mercy on our souls. That is all."

♦

Roy Church began his morning after by jotting notes for the Silverton meeting scheduled for 1500 hours in the Sheriff's conference room. He'd just turned the page on his notebook when Kat arrived.

They exchanged pleasantries and small talk for a moment, then Roy handed Kat a manila envelope.

"You're up to bat. What does this mean?" he asked.

She looked at the Chico State University address on the outside and immediately smiled.

"I'll read it and try to dumb it down for you," she laughed. She extracted a thick report from the envelope and laid it in front of her next to her water bottle. She leaned over, elbows on the desk, fingers on her temples and began to read silently.

Roy went back to putting the finishing touches on summarizing what he knew to be fact thus far, leaving Kat to concentrate.

After about ten minutes, she looked up and rubbed her hands together. She turned and took a breath.

"There are some main conclusions to take away from this report. Ready?" she asked.

"I'm all ears. Shoot. Make it so I can understand."

"Well," she said, "first we look at two words, *robust* and *gracile*. If a bone is determined to be *gracile*, it could be a sub-adult or consistent with a medium or smaller boned female adult. The word *robust* is associated with an adult. It could be a very large, big-boned female or more probably, a male adult. It all has to do with the density of the bone fragment as well as the actual length or thickness of the fragment."

"And I take it the lab has designated this bone fragment as one or the other. Keep me in suspense on that one. What other conclusions?" Roy asked.

Kat continued, "The consensus is that the broken pruning saw blade is *not* the same saw used to cut the bone. There were several false start cuts plus the one that went all the way through, so the mismatch was fairly easy to call for someone as experienced as Doctor Godwin."

"Hmm," said Roy. "Anything on the deer bones?"

"Yes, indeed," Kat smiled. "The femur was just indicative of a female *Odocoileus hemionus columbianus*, but the pelvis was positive. The deer remains came from a black tail doe, like the restaurant.

"Hmm," said Roy "Veddy Interesting."

Kat looked at him, question marks where pupils should have been.

"Oh," said Roy, "Just channeling my inner Arte Johnson."

"Who?" Kat asked with a puzzled smile on her face.

"Uh, guess you had to be there. 1968-1973. *Laugh-In*, America's most popular TV show at one time? Nothing but comedy skits the whole way through? No? Not feelin' it?"

"I give up," Kat laughed.

"One of the comedians on the show was Arte Johnson. He played Wolfgang the German soldier who would peer through the branches at some off the wall comedy skit and murmur in a German accent, while holding a cigarette Nazi style, 'Veddy Interesting.' Hey, it got lots of laughs and became part of the national lexicon for decades."

"I see," said Kat. "You do know I was born in 1995?"

"Right," said Roy. "What else do the mad scientists have for us?"

"That's about it from a conclusion standpoint. The rest of the report covers the scene, the dig itself, who was involved in recovering the fragments, et cetera."

"There's nothing in there about the intern short stepping away from the job in a gastrointestinal emergency?" Roy asked with mock seriousness.

"We agreed not to ever bring that up again. It was a condition of my working here!" Kat exclaimed, covering her face with her hands.

"Okay then, moving right along," coughed Roy. "I'm going with robust for the clavicle."

"Robust it is," said Kat, surprised that Roy knew the answer.

"Hey, did you ever get with your pal Maddy?" Roy asked, abruptly changing course.

"Yes, I texted her, and she said she'd stopped by to say hi because she had some ideas she wanted to share about Puma Creek. I swear I only told my friends I was working here as an intern. They had seen in the paper how Chico ID Lab was working on the Puma Creek case and put two and two together. Believe me, they pestered, but I fibbed and told them I had signed a confidentiality agreement. They seemed to respect that, but they all had their theories. None that you hadn't thought of," Kat said, rolling her eyes slightly.

"So Maddy's phone was working okay on Christmas Eve?" Roy asked.

"Of course it was," Kat replied. "People my age? Be serious. Your phone is the first thing you grab in a house fire. Forget dogs and small children. These things are our lives!" she laughed, holding up her latest model from Silicon Valley.

"Hmm," Roy said. "She told me it was on the blink and that's why she had to physically come here."

"Hmm," said Kat. "Veddy interesting."

"So how'd you guys meet anyhow?" Roy asked, smiling at Kat's reference.

Kat answered easily. "Oh, we've known each other since grade school. Let me see, since Kindergarten, maybe even preschool. Forever."

"She spoke highly of you, wanted to follow in your footsteps," Roy said.

She seemed a little embarrassed and replied, "That's so Maddy. Always been a bit of a follower. We had a lot in common as kids. We both lost our dads when we were little." She shrugged and continued, "Mine moved away. He lives in Arizona. I get cards and calls, but rarely see him. Paul has been with my mom for ten years."

"Too bad about your dad," Roy said sympathetically.

Kat waved her hand flippantly. "No, it's okay. Better than Maddy I suppose. Her dad drowned when she was a baby."

"Really?" said Roy, eyebrows raised slightly.

Kat nodded. "Yeah, so we kinda hung out after we found out we were both fatherless. Sort of a kindergarten through fifth grade support group, I guess," Kat said. "Her mom Sarah is super nice. She's a realtor, works for Ronald Faraday Realtors downtown. Been there forever."

"Cool. Didn't mean to pry. I was just wondering," Roy said. "Being new to town, I have no idea who is connected to whom. Small towns are supposed be everybody knows everybody places. I've always lived in the city."

"No, it's okay, really," Kat dismissed his apology. "In fact, Sarah and Mr. Faraday know *everybody*. They might be a good resource for you in your investigation if you're trying to find out who owns what or did own what or what was going on back in '95."

"Okay, great. I'll think about that. Look, I have to go to Silverton this afternoon for a pretty important meeting. As much as I'd love to take you with me, I'm afraid it might get ugly, so you'd have to sit in a waiting room. That'd be no fun." He clapped his hands on his thighs and stood up.

"Is everything okay?" Kat asked, a worried look on her face as she stood up as well.

"Oh, sure, it'll be fine. Just a bump in the road. Comes with the territory," Roy reassured her.

"I hope so. If there's anything I can do to help..." Kat trailed off.

"Remember how I said there had been some developments?"

"Yes, I thought you were talking about the lab report coming in," Kat replied.

Roy was putting some papers together in a neat stack on his desk. He shook his head. "No, that's important all right, but the meeting is about a death investigation down in Santa Rosa. Our main suspect in the Dina Morgan disappearance is dead. Looks to have hanged himself."

"Are you serious?!" Kat exclaimed. "I saw his name in one of the reports. It was weird and short."

"Jesse Dale Wilson, aka Pud," Roy filled in the blank for her.

"What sort of a name is Pud?" Kat asked with mild incredulity that the name actually stood for something. "But he killed himself? Why?"

"Apparently there's a school of thought that he got a guilty conscience over the murder of his girlfriend, saw that bones had been dug up on Puma Creek Trail, and decided to end it all," said Roy doubtfully.

"But that girl Dina Morgan disappeared four or five years after our body parts were dumped. Makes no sense," said Kat with confusion. Her pale face was furrowed in an effort to put the pieces together.

"There you go, using logic again," sighed Roy.

"Surely you don't think this Pud guy had anything to do with our case do you?"

"That I do not know. I know our bone does not belong to Dina Morgan. That is all I know," he said. "Unfortunately, others may have connected dots where there are no dots. Now I have to go disconnect them. It may be painful." He gave her a grimace.

"For you? Oh no," said Kat.

"No, not for me," laughed Roy. "Anyhow, you might as well enjoy the rest of day back up on the slopes. I'll fill you in afterward on how it all went. Get hold of your pal Maddy. A fatherless child needs a lot of love from good people. Too easy for bad people to move in and fill a void."

"Okay, if you're sure," Kat said with hesitation.

"I'm sure, and I've got to make a pleasurable death notification by phone call. Feel free to stick around, but I could be tied up for a while. Otherwise, go shred the gnar!"

Kat was still shaking her head and laughing as she closed the door.

Roy dialed the number.

"Hello, this is Roy Church, Sheriff's Office, again," he said.

"What do you want?" came the sullen reply. He'd gotten a friendlier response from a carload of Grape Street Crips.

"I'm afraid I've got some good news for you."

By the time Roy got off the phone, Lonnie Morgan wanted to buy him the Buck Burger at the Blacktail. Roy had to break it to him that the Sheriff had rules.

CHAPTER 21

At 1440 hours, 20 minutes before go time, Roy pulled into the Main's parking lot. He checked the text he'd gotten from Jake Stern during the drive.

Call me for an update, "Detective" Church. My people are running scared. A few of them had your class.

Roy punched in Stern's cell on his own.

"Stern."

"Yo, Jake, lay it on me," Roy said.

"Got a pen in your hand?" Stern asked.

Twenty minutes later, Roy strolled into the Sheriff's conference room. He checked the clock. 1500 hours. He wasn't late. Everyone else was early. Nerves.

Sheriff Ed Silva sat at the head. At the right hand of God, a satisfied look on his face, sat Lieutenant Cyril Savage. At mid-table, Alison Baker fiddled with her iPhone. Opposite her sat Wally the Wizard studying his notepad, as if it were a sergeant's exam practice test.

"Roy, glad you made it on time. How was the weather in Sisson?" Sheriff Silva called out to him as he walked in.

"Fine, great. No problems getting here by 1500," said Roy.

"Alrighty then," Sheriff Silva said, ~~looking around the table.~~ "How do we wanna do this?" He glanced to his right.

Lieutenant Savage said, "Well, Clint took the call from Santa Rosa, and worked the case initially with Alison. Why don't we let him tell us what his thoughts are? Then maybe Alison can chime in. And

Roy, you made notification. You can fill us in on that."

Sheriff Silva looked around the table again. "That okay?"

Roy nodded, yes.

Of course it's okay. You're the Sheriff.

Westwood cleared his throat, brushed a wrinkle in his shirt flat, and began.

"Well, as you know these deer bones and one human clavicle bone were found on Puma Creek Trail back in October. Alison and I were assigned to run with the case."

Baker nodded at him as if he were doing great so far.

"We immediately responded and put our efforts into identifying any and all missing persons in the Sisson area in the recent past."

Lieutenant Savage nodded his head up and down. Seemed a reasonable course of action to him.

Westwood continued, "We immediately keyed in on the Occam's Razor solution to the situation."

Roy smiled to himself. Wally must have Googled that term last night.

Sheriff Silva said, "Occam's Razor?"

"Yes," said Westwood, puffing himself up a little more. "It's the problem-solving principle that, when presented with competing hypothetical answers to a problem, one should select the one that makes the fewest assumptions."

Great job of clicking on Wikipedia.

Lieutenant Savage smiled the smile of a proud parent at a beginning band concert.

"Meaning?" asked Sheriff Silva.

"Meaning that the shortest route between two points is a straight line," responded Westwood.

"What he's trying to say," Baker broke in, to explain the cryptic words of her North Pole sex slave, "Is that the obvious answer, given the circumstances, is that the found human bone at an obvious body dump site was that of Dina Morgan who disappeared nearby at Karuk Lake in 2004."

Westwood, having freshly gassed up at the pit stop, rejoined the race.

"The suspect in the Dina Morgan case was her boyfriend Jesse Dale Wilson, aka Pud. This department interviewed him and surveilled him over a multi-month period after Morgan's disappearance. He claimed she jumped out of his car after an argument, which we all know is B.S. He's always been the number one and only suspect. We put a lot of pressure on him personally and in the press."

Sheriff Silva, connecting a few dots, said, "So what you're saying is a dead body in Santa Rosa is this Pud character. Jesus, who has a messed-up nickname like that? He killed himself because he thought we were closing in?"

"That's right," said Westwood before throwing Sheriff Silva a bone. "Your press releases did the job. You brought his name back out into the public eye. He's been depressed over what he did all these years. Finally couldn't take it anymore. He cut out at least two articles from our KDN and left them underneath his body when he killed himself, as his way of confessing."

"I think it's pretty self-explanatory, Sheriff," Lieutenant Savage added, a satisfied look on his face.

"Yes, when I spoke to a…," Westwood checked his notes, "Detective Stern in the SRPD's homicide section, he agreed that it was a suicide, and that it appeared a motive for it was the disappearance, aka murder, of his girlfriend Dina Morgan. Sort of a signed and sealed confession, you might say."

Sheriff Silva rubbed his chin with a hand that had roped more than one steer.

"Hmm," he said. "Sounds reasonable, as you said Cyril. What say you Roy?"

"Hmm," said Roy. He opened a black canvas briefcase he'd set at his feet earlier. There was no need to prematurely alarm anyone who might be presenting for the prosecution. He took out several sheets of paper and his notebook. He also removed a flash drive from his shirt pocket and set it on the table.

"We have a computer screen and a whiteboard in here?" he said nodding toward the Dell laptop to one side of the room and the projection screen at the opposite end from Sheriff Silva.

"Sure," said Sheriff Silva. "All warmed up and ready to go. Had a budget meeting in here right before this one. Lieutenant Savage can help you run this system. All Greek to me." Sheriff Silva held his palms up in a gesture of uncertainty. Roy stood up. Class time.

"First, thank you all for coming. It's too bad Lieutenant Lynch from Investigations and Undersheriff Sessions are still out of town. Lieutenant Savage could you please put the flash drive in?" Roy asked as he headed for the light switch by the door. Savage looked rather sour as he plugged in the drive.

He'd purposely mentioned Lynch. It was a cheap and petty shot, yes, but Savage had deserved it.

"I'm going to break this into several parts. First, let's go over the initial crime scene."

Westwood looked at his watch. How long is this going to take?

"Thanks LT," Roy said as the whiteboard screen flickered with the first photo, that of the overall crime scene which included the trail and various bright ribbons and Clif Bar wrappers above and below the bank.

"On October 22nd, three hikers from Sacramento found the skeletal remains of an unknown animal. They poked around initially but basically preserved the scene for me for the following day."

Lieutenant Savage did not look as if he recalled with fondness the phone call from Roy asking to inspect the site earlier. He handed Roy a remote for the Dell.

"I say hikers, because they were on a trail. This is important. The trail was at one time a logging road."

Roy clicked his remote to the next slide, a topographical map of the Puma Creek Trail area.

"In fact, according to Forest Service records it had been a logging road from 1980 through the beginning of 2000 when it was redesigned for recreational purposes at the order of the Forest Ranger Roger Parsons."

He threw in the late Parson's name as a subtle detail pointing to homework done.

"*All* vehicular traffic was cut off, so anyone who dumped anything at the site after 2000 had to carry it about a mile and a half."

Roy let those dates and facts sink in for a second. Westwood was looking at his notebook intently.

"An inspection of the scene revealed a number of bones that have turned out to be *Odocoileus hemionus columbianus*, commonly known, locally, as the black tailed deer. Further, the deer was a doe, cause of death unknown."

Sheriff Silva rubbed his chin some more, but did not blink, training an intent gaze on the screen. He'd never had a deputy who spoke Latin as fluently as he'd just witnessed. Roy clicked to the next slide, a close-up of the partial human collarbone.

"However, as we all know, the sternal end of a clavicular fragment was found among the bones. It had several false start cut marks in addition to the final cut that severed the bone. The fragment was given into the custody of the Chico Human ID Lab under the guidance of Professor Jeffrey Godwin. Godwin is the current president of the National Forensic Anthropology Society and is generally thought of as the ultimate expert in his field."

Alison Baker looked up from her iPhone and set it on the table. She didn't look excited about what might be coming next.

Roy continued, "In anthropology, a human bone, any bone really, can be analyzed on its size, thickness, and density when attempting to determine age or sex. In the *human* cases of a sub-adult, which means birth to late teens, or in the case of a small to moderate adult female, the bones are expected to be what they call gracile. Gracile is just a term for thin or slender when referring to *hominids*, meaning humans.

Professor Roy, in spite of having played the novice with Kat, had been down this road more than once. He noted that Sheriff Silva was nodding his head up and down. Roy wondered if was because he'd suddenly connected the *homi* in hominid and homicide.

"In the case of a very large-boned woman or a normal sized adult male, the fragment is typically what they call robust. And yes, that term means just what it sounds like, strong, brawny, muscular, burly, husky, heavily built. In other words, consistent with a normal adult male or very large-boned female."

Sheriff Silva interrupted, "And this Professor Godwin has determined *what* exactly about this broken piece of bone? That's your collarbone, right?"

"Collarbone, yes. He has designated it as robust and would be prepared to testify as an expert in that regard. It is his opinion that the clavicular fragment in all likelihood belonged to a male, a strong robust male. And as we know from this flier...,"

Roy clicked up a Missing Person flier for Dina Morgan.

"At 34 years old she was 5-4, 110 lbs. — definitely gracile."

In the low light of the room, Westwood looked as if he'd just stepped out of the shower onto fresh cat shit.

"What the heck?" said Sheriff Silva. "I thought this thing was solved. I thought that's why we're all here, that we all agreed this was the missing Morgan woman." He cast a baleful eye on Westwood before turning to Lieutenant Savage.

"Cyril, this has sorta taken me by surprise. Not real happy." He drummed his (robust) fingers on the tabletop.

The Three Musketeers — Savage, Westwood, and Baker —

looked as if Cardinal Richelieu had just ordered up a guillotine prototype, the early pre-Robespierre version, and he required three guinea pigs.

"Sheriff, if you don't mind," Roy said quickly "I'd like to briefly run through the rest of the evidence from Puma Creek and then touch on the related investigation currently taking place in Santa Rosa."

"Please, be my guest," Sheriff Silva said with a backhanded wave of his hand. He slumped back in his chair, but Roy had the feeling that he was continuing to give Savage the stink-eye from his deep peripherals — a rather unique talent.

"Thanks," said Roy, clearing his throat. "I'll just touch on the highlights here. I can spell out chapter and verse for Lieutenant Lynch when he returns on Monday. As you'll see, we have a little work ahead of us."

"Fine. Highlights then," agreed Sheriff Silva.

Roy quickly detailed, using photos on the screen, how the Sony CD player cover pinpointed the start of the time span at about 1995. He then moved on to the dismissal of the broken pruning saw blade as the cutting instrument. He also related that the Chico ID Lab had provided a range of weight for the doe, given the skeletal remains analyzed, as likely between 40 and 70 lbs. max.

"That, plus dead body parts of unknown weight, may be doable for a marine if distributed on the back correctly. Nearly impossible for even the strongest male to carry in arms to the front of his body."

"But you're saying it could be done, if someone wanted to throw us off their tracks," observed Westwood, in a last attempt to rise off the bloody, cage mat, apparently going dick-length memory on the gracile vs robust beat-down he'd just received.

"Of course," said Roy agreeably. "In a homicide case, or any case for that matter, never rule out obscure possibilities. That way you're not surprised down the road if something pops up which ruins your theory of the case."

Both Westwood and Savage brightened a bit at that last part. Could a Coast Guard cutter really happen by them after all, here in shark infested waters?

"But that brings me to the Santa Rosa 187 investigation." The momentary glimmer of hope Westwood and Lieutenant Savage were clinging to was snatched from their desperate fists.

"Thought you said it was a suicide." Sheriff Silva was back to staring directly at Lieutenant Savage.

Savage shrugged his shoulders and turned his head toward Westwood, who wanted to get real small again. There was no place to go.

"Initially, that was the thinking," said Roy. "But we've got a pretty sharp partner in the SRPD detective in charge of their case, fellow by the name of Jake Stern. He's been around a long while, has quite the reputation as a meticulous investigator. He actually teaches some classes on sexual assault investigations and others on gang homicide investigations. Don't see that every day."

"Okay, but this Detective Stein told us suicide to begin with, right?" said Sheriff Silva, directing the conversation back to the issue at hand. A thin layer of sweat was just barely discernible at the height of his receding hairline. An unsolved case would not look good for reelection.

Lieutenant Savage and Detective Westwood were on their knees praying that the next words out of Roy's mouth would resemble that white and red Coast Guard cutter they thought they had sighted moments before.

"Uh Stern, not Stein. Stern means Star and Stein means Stone. Just an aside," said Roy, smiling, not trying to sound condescending but more of an educator. "And yes, he thought suicide could have been a possibility at first."

A dripping wet Savage, stepping on Wally's face, was dragged aboard, just as dorsal fins zipped beneath his toes. Wally wasn't so lucky.

"He was clear, however, that he'd initially classified it as a suspicious death because something felt weird about the scene with the cut out KDN articles. Seemed a little too pat given the fact that one of the articles was from three days earlier, and no mail is delivered to Wilson at the garage he was holed up in while he worked. But let me run down the bullet-points in their case and show you a few photos Stern sent me to illustrate how the thing has blown up in the past 24 hours."

Sheriff Silva was visibly unhappy. "Blown up," is not a politician-friendly term.

Roy began phase two, clicking up a Department of Motor Vehicles license photo of Pud.

"Mid-November, Jesse Dale Wilson, aka Pud, the most likely bad actor in the suspected murder of Dina Morgan back in 2004, leaves Sisson for Santa Rosa to work in the construction biz. They had a huge fire October 2017, thousands of carpenters, et cetera, headed there a year later after re-building permits started issuing.

"Fires in the state been damn terrible last few years," said Sheriff Silva. He caught himself. "Sorry, go on."

"Pud is found by co-workers at 0600 hours on December 24, hanging from a new yellow nylon rope tied to a header beam in a home under construction in one of Santa Rosa's more expensive neighborhoods that burned down."

Roy clicked on a photo of a strangled Pud, neck three inches longer than normal, arms hanging limply at his side, staring down at the sub floor yet seeing nothing. No one around the table was fazed, having seen many gruesome scenes in their lives.

Roy utilized the laser function on the remote clicker. "There is an empty bottle of Jack Daniels whiskey at his feet, along with two cut-out articles from the Karuk Daily News. One from last October, the other from last Saturday, the 20th of December. Both articles are about the skeletal remains found on Puma Creek Trail. Both articles rehash the disappearance of Dina Morgan. Both quote Sheriff Silva extensively."

Roy displayed close-ups of the news clippings and the famous JD black label.

"Based on these facts alone, one *might* conclude that Pud hanged himself over guilt, leaving the news clippings as a map of his conscience. The holidays are a prime time for suicide, death by hanging is pretty popular for men if a gun is not available. Females prefer pills, in my experience."

Roy noted the room was silent and still, except for Wally Westwood, squirming a bit, as if he were sitting on pin worms.

"The fact that Pud was the prime suspect in a suspected 187 up here would seem to put the icing on the suicide cake," Roy said. "*However*, Stern, after talking to *me*, and getting facts I had solid on the Puma Trail case that did not fit with Dina Morgan, did a little more digging."

It was lost on no one in the room that a jump to conclusions had been made by person or persons known, *not* on the inside of an investigation, and that the jump had been accomplished with a faulty parachute.

"Stern and his homeboys have been pounding the pavement for

the past 48 hours. Here is where the cute little suicide set-up has come completely off the tracks," said Roy, building up to the kill shot for Wally's career as sergeant under Ed Silva, and Cyril Savage's chances of ever being the big kahuna of Karuk County.

"One, Pud was drinking in a local saloon with an unknown suspect described by witnesses as a 'hard dude.' Thing is, Pud was getting wasted while hard dude was sandbaggin'.

"Pud left the bar with the suspect. Pud was too drunk to drive. Suspect drove. Suspect was then seen at a liquor store minutes later buying a bottle of JD. And here he is."

Roy punched up the as of yet unnamed Cedar Stock as "hoodie and dark glasses dude," for his attentive audience.

"Looks like a gangster in that get-up, WMA, mid to late forties is my guess." observed Sheriff Silva.

"Yep," Roy replied. "This guy right here, dollars to donuts, has been to the joint. Has a natural look of a con. Clerk thought he was in for a 211."

"Hell, I'd think he was gonna rob me, too," chuckled Sheriff Silva. "I'da slapped leather just on principle."

Roy hit his remote.

"And here is Pud, passed out in the passenger seat of his own truck while the suspect is inside buying more booze. SRPD has the truck in impound right now fine tooth combing it."

"Shit," said Lieutenant Savage under his breath. He glared across the table at Westwood, who was wondering if he would ever get his elf hat back from Baker.

"Wait, there's more, a lot more. Of course, Stern and crew got a search warrant for Pud's living quarters and court orders for his phone records from Verizon. We want to see who called Pud in the last thirty days."

Roy looked around the table.

"Any questions before I continue?"

Silence. Sheriff Silva shook his head and lifted a palm, motioning him to go on.

"Before we leave the scene and check out Pud's neighborhood, Stern got lucky and struck gold in the construction area. Stern enlisted the help of a couple of rookie patrol guys on days off looking for OT. Had them dumpster diving and grid searching the houses under construction. They scored a length of yellow nylon rope in a dumpster about three houses down from our scene. It matches the rope used to hang the victim."

"Nice," murmured Sheriff Silva, looking at the photo of the yellow rope in a dumpster.

"And then we have the biggie of the morning. One of the patrol guys got a wild hair and started walking the whole neighborhood. I suspect he was actually trying to stay awake. A volunteer nightshift holdover. Anyhow, he spotted a brand new come-along, seen here in this photo," Roy said. "We lucked out that the crew at this house had been given the day off for Christmas Eve and Christmas, otherwise that would have been long gone."

"Thank you, Mary and Joseph!" exclaimed Sheriff Silva, slapping his hand on the table and sounding as if he were at a tent revival meeting.

Roy struggled to maintain his composure for a second. "I say biggie, because our suspect didn't take the time to remove the UPC code from the come-a-long. It was brand new. There are a lot of hardware stores in Santa Rosa, but Stern had a sizable work force out for a suspected homicide," Roy said.

"Yeah, those big city departments can afford all that OT," groused Lieutenant Savage, coming off his stony-faced sabbatical.

"Santa Rosa has a Lowes, Home Depot, Ace, Tractor's Supply, you name it. One of the biggies there is a locally grown joint called Friedman Brothers. Stern told me the original brothers are friends of his family, go to temple together, all that. Anyhow, the coppers hit pay dirt at Friedman's. They got our suspect buying a come-along and the yellow nylon rope on video. He's wearing his hoodie and dark glasses get-up as you can see here," said Roy. "He'll be hard to identify from these photos. He's done this before."

Cedar Stock, looking every bit the bank robber from an FBI still, stood in line holding a rope and a come-along.

"These were taken on the afternoon of the 23rd. Pud was hanged later that night or early the next morning," Roy said. "SRPD evidence specialist went back into the crime scene given the come-along discovery and found this."

On the screen appeared a close up of grooves in the wall nailer board.

"These grooves could be consistent with marks left by the cable from the come-along, according to the SRPD evidence specialists. Problem is, there are nicks and grooves all over that construction site. At best, it would be questionable in court, at worst, laughed at out loud by four out of twelve jurors. We'd look as if we were reaching, I'm afraid. The important thing is we know based on our gut these are probably from a cable."

"I'll be damned," said Sheriff Silva, the thin sheen of sweat now gone. "That dirtbag in a hoodie went to a lot of trouble. Why not just put a bullet in that miserable Pud, if it's somebody he pissed off at work? Or even somebody pissed off at him from here who's been nursing a grudge for 13 years?"

"Because," Roy replied. "That guy in the hoodie wanted us to think Pud had committed suicide over the bones found on Puma Creek Trail, to throw us off. His error. He never did his homework with the Forest Service on that road to trail, and he sure as heck has never taken a class in anthropology."

"Anything more?" asked Sheriff Silva.

"Of course," said Roy, lightly. "Cops did a neighborhood door to door around Pud's garage quarters on Clark Street near downtown Santa Rosa. High burg area. They got Neighborhood Watch, all that. People tired of being ripped off while they're at work or on vacation."

"Don't tell me, someone saw the asshole in the hoodie," sighed Sheriff Silva.

"Well, maybe, a strong likelihood. Cops showed photos of our hooded dude in glasses. He matches the description of a suspicious person seen cruising the area of Pud's digs in a black Chevy or GMC pick-up on the afternoon of the 23rd. One neighbor even called it in, and copped a plate," Roy said.

"Yes," Sheriff Silva brought his fist down Napoleon Dynamite style.

"Don't get too excited. But it is critical from a specific intent standpoint. The plate came back to a lost or stolen out of Windsor, California. That's just on the north end of Santa Rosa. SRPD Dispatch sent a unit to check the area but he was UTL," said Roy.

"So he's unable to locate, what about the RO?" asked Sheriff Silva.

Roy noticed that this had now become an intimate conversation between the Sheriff and him. He was waiting for Baker to comment that maybe they oughta get a room.

"Okay, this is hilarious. The registered owner is a Sonoma County Sheriff's lieutenant named Carlos Robledo who was shopping at Costco in Santa Rosa. He'd parked his 1995 Ford one ton in the lot.

Someone lifted his plates. He wouldn't have noticed the theft in the dark if he hadn't stumbled over his Oakland Raiders license plate holder next to his rear bumper. Boy, was he pissed," laughed Roy.

"Wait," said Sheriff Silva, getting all serious. "Let me get this straight. This character in a hood goes to all this trouble to steal a plate, scope out the victim's house, set him up and then murder him in cold blood? And he leaves a Raiders license plate holder behind? Can't believe it 'cause he's gotta be straight outta the Black Hole."

Roy and the Sheriff laughed. No one else did.

Roy said, "A few more things. SRPD has contact with the US Post Office law enforcement arm. They will confirm that no mail has been delivered to Pud. In any event, with the mail, being bogged down for the holidays, it is doubtful that the KDN article from last Saturday could have been delivered by Tuesday. SRPD will give the articles a Ninhydrin work-over to see if they can get a photo of a latent."

Roy looked at his notebook and then up at the shell-shocked audience to see if saturation point had been reached yet. Close.

"Pud couldn't read. According to his mom he had a learning disability that kept him from forming his letters correctly and reading from left to right. Doesn't mean he was stupid, just the sort of guy who wouldn't spend his time reading the KDN. Oh, and also, according to his mom, he'd never gone deer hunting to the best of her knowledge. Not an absolute, but something else to tuck away when looking for our Puma Creek responsible or responsibles."

Roy flicked his remote back to a photo of the missing Dina Morgan.

"One last item. I have a lead on a female cousin or aunt to Dina Morgan. She's somewhere in Washington. If we can find her, we'll get mitochondrial DNA to positively eliminate the Puma Creek Trail bone."

Sheriff Silva stood up. "I gotta get out of here and call that reporter at KDN back and ask her to hold off on her story. I guess I prematurely spoke to the press this morning, telling them we had a substantial lead in the case. Gonna be a little egg on all our faces I'm afraid. Mostly mine."

Roy looked at the Sheriff's drawn features.

What he's really saying is Lieutenant Savage and company might want to consider a lateral transfer to Humboldt County.

CHAPTER 22

America's most famed serial killer, the Zodiac, went to his grave nursing a mad-on after going decades of being stiffed for his outstanding work as a technical advisor on the original Dirty Harry film of 1971. At least he went to his grave a free man. Why did he go to his grave a free man you ask? Well, he didn't get caught. Duh. Why didn't he get caught? It's because the cops in Solano County didn't talk to the cops in Napa County who didn't talk to the cops in Sonoma County who didn't talk to the cops in San Francisco County. Ol' Zodiac hop-scotched his way around Bay Area jurisdictions just a hollerin', lootin', and shootin' without a care in the world because he knew the cops were too busy chasing their own tails to really get serious about the likes of him.

Crooks often get away with their questionable lifestyles because cops don't talk to other cops and sometimes even outright refuse to share valuable case-solving info. But sometimes they *do* talk to one another. Sometimes they do set egos aside for mutual benefit. Occasionally they share intelligence on a "big" case and even smaller ones, smaller ones like the dirty little murder on Greenskeeper Ct. in Santa Rosa. That is why Cedar Stock was now playing the part of Butch Cassidy having his trail sniffed by Charlie Siringo of Karuk County and the entire Bolivian army who'd disguised themselves as Santa Rosa Police detectives.

Reporters are a lot like cops. They try not to share information with other reporters because they want the scoop, aka glory for the arrest. But sometimes they do talk to one another. Sometimes they do set egos aside for mutual benefit. This concept of symbiosis was on full display as Amy Douglas, reporter for the Karuk Daily News, chatted amiably on the phone with Mary Redman, reporter for the Santa Rosa Press Democrat.

Amy had called Mary after seeing her byline on the small article covering a death investigation of an unidentified construction worker. Of course, this was after she'd been on the phone earlier in the day bugging Sheriff Silva who'd hinted that there'd be a big announcement soon regarding the bones on Puma Creek Trail and their relationship to the Dina Morgan case. He said the answer lay in a death investigation currently underway in Santa Rosa. He asked her to hold off on any further articles until it could all be sorted out, but it looked promising.

The newsroom back and forth phone calls hadn't started out all warm hugs and air kisses. Mary had been suspicious of a foreign reporter worming her way into a Sonoma County story she'd spent Christmas Eve on, plus all morning on Return-a-Gift Friday.

Amy hadn't been real excited about giving up what she had put together in Karuk County just so it could be a Sunday exclusive on murder and intrigue by a reporter pulling down twice her salary in the Wine Country. It didn't matter that homes cost four times as much there. Both reporters cagily spoke into their iPhones as they had each other's articles up on their desktop screens.

Initially, Mary wouldn't have given an extra sniff around a run-of-the-mill suicide if she hadn't had a little bug in her ear, otherwise known as her special Deep Throat, ensconced in the SRPD watch commander's office. He'd casually mentioned that the violent crimes detectives were stirred up like a kicked over anthill. Whatever they had going, and they were, as usual, being uncooperative, Mary deduced it had everything to do with the fortuitous call from the reporter up there in redneck country.

After securing a mutual non-aggression pact, the two reporters had eventually agreed to pool their troops and had agreed to insert an "allied reporter so and so contributed to this story," at the end of whatever they'd come up with to thrill their respective subscribers.

Mary let down her guard and revealed that she'd hit up one of the workers who'd found Jesse Dale Wilson at the site of the hanging. He'd also seen two cut-out newspaper articles under the body. He'd scanned them both while waiting for fire, ambulance, and police. He noted they were both about some bones found outside Sisson,

California. The worker did not know the dead man's full name, said everyone just called him Jesse. Mary told Amy she'd tossed in a call to Deep Throat to confirm the name Jesse Dale Wilson as the dead hanger on Greenskeeper Court.

Deep Throat had replied with, "You never got that name from me," essentially confirming the hanger on a stud as Pud.

Amy told Mary this whole thing had the earmarks of a guilty conscience-ridden man who had finally done the right thing by killing himself. The intrepid duo soon pieced together the following scenario. Jesse Dale Wilson of Sisson, California, had committed suicide after police dug up the skeletal remains of his long-lost love. While neither reporter could confirm that this was actually the case, there was more than enough to throw down a teaser article in the next edition, but they agreed to hold off until they could caucus again here at Checkpoint Charlie.

As the info flowed back and forth, Amy heard her phone vibrate. She held it away from her ear and saw Sheriff Silva was trying to call in. She kept this little tidbit to herself. At the same time, Mary heard her phone vibrate. She saw that Deep Throat was trying to get hold of her. She kept this little tidbit to herself.

Amy got off the phone and called Sheriff Silva back, freshly painted red fingernails twiddling with a pen on her desk.

"Oh, really glad you called back. Say, listen, could we hold those thoughts I ran past you earlier? About the Santa Rosa suicide being connected to Puma Creek bones?"

Amy hadn't been a member of the Fourth Estate all that long, but she knew controlled panic in a voice when she heard it.

"Okay," she said slowly, making it more of question.

"I mean, we've done a notification, so it's public record that Jesse Dale Wilson is now dead. It's just that the drawing of conclusions might not be the most helpful right now to our investigators," Sheriff Silva said.

"Just so you know, I got a call from a reporter in Santa Rosa asking for background on Jesse Wilson, so my editor might force us to put out something at least. Jus' sayin'," Amy said. She looked closely at her left pointer finger. Was that a chip already?

"Okay, well make it really generic if you can. Really appreciate it," Sheriff Silva said.

Mary got off the phone with Amy and called Deep Throat back, unaware that Deep Throat had just left an upper management meeting in which the Investigative Lieutenant had brought everyone up to speed and had warned all in the room to keep this whole mess under their hats because it looks as though we might have misinterpreted the scene, initially, and it wouldn't look real great if the press got wind. Feel me?

"Oh, really glad you called back. Say, listen, could we hold those thoughts for a bit on the Greenskeeper Court. suicide ID? I think our detectives need a bit more time to piece some things together," he said with evident desperation.

Mary *had* been a 4th Estate member in good standing for years. In fact, she'd served as treasurer or sergeant at arms at one time. She definitely recognized when she was being told less than all the facts.

"Well, just so you know, I recently got a call from a reporter up in Karuk County who is nosing around on my turf, so my editor is not going to hold off long." Mary tapped her classy French manicured nails on her desk, annoyed.

Deep Throat replied, "It sounds as if kin notification has been made, but I'm not 100% sure. Would really appreciate it if you could give us a bit more space on this one. You owe me for that 187 info on Apple Valley Lane."

Never admonish someone who has authority over you that they owe you jack shit.

"Okay," Mary said sweetly, while wearing arsenic lipstick. "But my editor may need something so that we don't look like buffoons if the reporter up north puts something out."

"Okay, well make it really generic if you can. Really appreciate it," Deep Throat said.

Mary texted Amy just as Amy texted Mary. Their twin messages zipped past each other in cyberspace, both holding friendly twin birds out the window.

My editor is cool with me holding off on too much detail, but I've gotta go with something generic to show we're still in the game.

Mary read Amy's text and then set her phone on her desk.

That redneck bitch is going to backdoor me!

Amy inspected Mary's text and then set her phone on her desk.

That wine sippin' ho is dirty AF! I'd trust her about as much as a wet fart!

Both reporters began typing furiously, respective fingernails in danger of breaking.

♦

Roy Church gathered his flash drive and briefcase. The Three

Musketeers had already left to find salve and apply direct pressure to each other.

"Deputy Church, the Sheriff would like to see you in his office," the Sheriff's secretary said, peeking her head into the conference room.

Not surprised.

"Okay, thanks," said Roy. He followed her down the hallway to the big guy's office.

"Close the door, Roy. Have a seat." Sheriff Silva said, with a note of resigned seriousness in his voice.

Roy sat.

Sheriff Silva let out a huge gust of despair.

"You're the guy with all the experience. Where do we go from here?" he asked.

"We keep on keepin' on, sir," Roy said. "We got this mess right where we want it."

Sheriff Silva stared at Roy. Peaked forefingers tapped the end of his nose.

"From where I'm sitting, my people here in Silverton bent me over a barrel, but maybe you'd like to clue me in on where we exactly are at?"

Lose the 'at' — it's redundant.

"Absolutely, sir. And when Lieutenant Lynch gets back on Monday, I can run it down for him as well," said Roy. He settled back into the leather chair normally occupied by Tommy Sessions or other brass.

"How fucked are we on this thing?" asked Sheriff Silva directly.

"Oh, not at all. I couldn't be happier," smiled Roy with a calmness that Sheriff Silva just couldn't understand.

Sheriff Silva set his large and leathery hands on his desk and leaned forward, wanting Roy to expound.

"What we've done is flushed our prey," Roy said. He figured Sheriff Silva for a hunter.

"How so?"

"By finding the bones on Puma Creek Trail, and by publicizing it as we have, we've made someone very nervous. So nervous in fact that they hurried out and staged a suicide to get us off the trail."

"So you're convinced this Pud fellow was killed by someone from Karuk County?"

"No other conclusion to be drawn. By being smart, our boy has been stupid. He should never have placed the newspaper articles at the scene."

"Why not, it made it look like a suicide to everybody but you," Sheriff Silva said, shrugging. "We'd have been more than happy to close it out as a depressed asshole doing the right thing."

"Our killer didn't count on the lack of a mail delivery system betraying him. He also lacks a working knowledge of the modern techniques for bone fragment analysis," Roy pointed out. "He should have let well enough alone. A hanging Pud Wilson, all by himself, would have driven SRPD toward the conclusion the killer wanted us to make. Even if we'd later determined Pud had help, how could we be sure it wasn't somebody he pissed off in Sonoma County?"

"Okay, so the killer is from Karuk County. How do we know it wasn't revenge, like maybe he was hired by this Dina Morgan's family?" Sheriff Silva asked.

"Only family around here for Dina is her dad Lonnie who doesn't have a pot to piss in. He couldn't pay the kinda killer who did this job. I sprung the death on him. Took him by complete surprise. I've interviewed and interrogated hundreds if not thousands over the years. It came to him as a complete surprise. He started crying. I couldn't get him off my leg," Roy replied.

"I see," said Sheriff Silva, fingers steepled at his nose again.

"Had it been a revenge hit, it would have *looked* like a revenge hit. People who want revenge, have to feel the violence of the act. They crave it. A hanging is about as non-violent as a man can get, even though it's a hell of thing, to strangle. Your brain starts fighting for air. Crappy way to go," Roy continued.

Sheriff Silva subconsciously loosened his collar.

"We're searching for a bad boy. A cunning sort. This makes him very dangerous to anyone who gets in his way, or even on his trail. If he feels threatened, and he has, he won't hesitate to kill again," Roy said. "He's the kinda animal to step off into the brush and wait for the hunter to come trippin' by, head down looking at tracks. Bam!"

He studied Sheriff Silva who was probably thinking about taking in a little target practice later in the day.

"Holy shit," breathed Sheriff Silva.

"From a behavioral perspective, we're dealing with a pretty intelligent, aggressive chess player who's not afraid to shove the board aside, reach across, and stick a piece in your throat."

"Fuck," added Sheriff Silva, ever the poet.

"You saw hoodie dude in the photos. He's older. Been to the joint, I'm positive, and most likely has a number of bodies under his belt, in the penitentiary and on the street."

"Damn," said Sheriff Silva, slowly working his way through the ABC's of curse words. "Do you think you can find him and stop him? I mean, that's what you're known for down south. Am I right?"

And this is exactly why I didn't want back in this business.

"Yes," said Roy, with a bit more certainty than he actually felt. He'd given the same answer to two other Sheriffs named Sherman Block and Lee Baca. He had been uncertain then too, but it had worked out. Third time's the charm. But was this third Sheriff the charm? The bad luck charm?

"Okay, well I'd like you to go full detective then. And who can I give you to help out? Still got a couple of guys on the Asian thing, but Baker and Westwood, as worthless as they are, could lend a hand," Sheriff Silva said.

"I understand what you're saying, but I'd still like to remain in uniform for the time being. This is going to be a long game, so I can still take patrol calls as evidence unfolds. If I have to go plainclothes I will," Roy said.

"Your call," Sheriff Silva replied with another shrug of his shoulders.

"I predict we'll have the Santa Rosa police helping with this one. It's first and foremost their 187," Roy noted.

Sheriff Silva nodded and added helpfully, "I can give their chief a call and extend out cooperation."

"Good move," Roy encouraged.

Sheriff Silva seemed heartened by Roy's agreement. "Yeah, I'm good for *something* around here." He said it as though it were a pep talk for himself rather than an assurance for Roy.

Roy replied, "I'd like to think this suicide mock-up has given us a little breathing room, although I'm not naïve enough to think that it will stay suicide in the press for long."

"I asked the reporter for KDN to keep it all under her hat for a spell," Sheriff Silva volunteered.

"As in keep it a secret?" Roy laughed. "It'll get out. We'll deal with it. Remember, two can keep a secret, but only if one is dead."

CHAPTER 23

Sonoma County residents awoke in shifts on the Saturday morning of the last week of December. They shuffled to the doorstep, soggy lawn, or thorny shrubs to retrieve the normal fire hose of goings on in the Gateway to the Wine Country. Above the fold were the main articles on the myriad of lawsuits in which tort lawyers, paid by the hour, were laying blame on any and all deep pockets for the previous fall's unforeseen act of nature. Billions of dollars in destruction, coupled with scores of deaths, meant the venerable firm of Dewey, Cheethum and Howe could meet payroll for the next decade.

Below the fold was a story under Mary Redman's byline updating residents on what the local cops were doing this fine day to justify their generous salary and benefits package.

The headline **Death Investigation Spurs Out-of-County Probe** beckoned latte sippers to learn more about the lurid motive for a suspected suicide being investigated by the SRPD Violent Crimes Investigations Section.

Cedar Stock grinned to himself as he scanned the Press Democrat's digital edition on Ma's laptop. It was all there. This Redman chick had helped the cause a shitload. He wondered what she looked like. Probably hot. Musta shook her tight cheeks at that carpenter who then laid out the whole kit and caboodle. It was good stuff. Ol' Pud just a swingin' above his obvious confession notes, them getting all damp in the puddle of piss.

He Googled images for Mary Redman. He laughed out loud. Jesus, looks like she got hit in the face with a shovel. Yeah, the one she used to eat with. Must be a slick talker, or else that carpenter is hella hard up. Hey, some dudes like a lotta meat on a bone. Chunky yet funky. Real chubby chasers. More likely some horny wood whose PO had picked him up at the gate and told him, "I got you a job. Don't fuck it up." Hasn't had booty, well, female booty, in years.

Cedar slowly shook his head back and forth in wonder.

All these times together I never knew Pud's middle name was Dale.

He reread Redman's piece. Something about it bothered him though, just a snatch hair. The SRPD spokesperson would not publicly confirm suicide. However, some person in the department "not authorized to speak to the media, but under condition of anonymity…" *You mean a snitch, bitch,* had used the term "suspected suicide."

The article had then gone into chapter and verse on Dina Morgan's disappearance and Pud's firm grasp of first place in the suspect category. Redman had been shut down cold when she called the KCSD. This seemed to piss her off. She called the Sheriff "tight lipped." Yeah, you could read between the lines on that one.

He glanced into the living room to make sure Ma was all comfy and snoring in her favorite spot on Planet Earth. Then he punched up *Bigtits.com* on her laptop to see the day's new babes. Presently, he closed the lid. He stepped outside Ma's front door to see if the local paper had arrived yet.

♦

Roy Church analyzed the above-the-fold story by Amy Douglas in the Karuk Daily News.

Deadly Wine Country Twist in Local Cold Case

Now there was an attention getter, enough to leave your diesel tractor warming an extra minute while you brought yourself up to date on this shit.

Amy Douglas had been rebuffed by the SRPD when she'd called for more information, but it was clear from her knowledge of the facts that Jesse Dale Wilson was dead by suspected suicide. She had a source somewhere. The KDN "suicide notes" which Douglas spoke of with glowing motherly pride, firmly tied Pud to the Puma Creek Trail "skeleton." Skeleton? *Jesus, there was a leap.*

Amy had landed a front yard interview for reaction from Lonnie Morgan. Lonnie succinctly expressed himself using multiple asterisks.

"Doesn't bring Dina back. Glad the sonofab***h is dead."

Roy had told Lonnie Morgan only the bare bones. Pud was dead by hanging, and there was a school of thought that he'd done himself in. No use going into details beyond.

♦

With the upcoming Wednesday being New Year's Eve, the normal mid-week Black Tail coffee klatch crew had an alternate get-together late Saturday morning. Unfortunately, the place was crawling with out-of-towners, either skiers or the freeway crowd headed to and from Portland and Seattle.

An annoyed CPO Mendenhall, first to arrive, had to wait like a run-of-the-mill flatlander for his name to be called so he could grab the table farthest back in the overflow room. *Their* table, the one underneath Johnny Pardeau's photo, was occupied by a group of slack jawed, twenty-somethings who walked to and from the bathroom with their hands buried deep in the front pockets of their gray, saggy-assed jeans. Sad state. CPO had muscle-challenged, eye-rolling grand kids just like them. Never played real ball. Daughter-in-law said it was too violent. Christ.

Seeing the restaurant full meant money in town, so CPO kept his grumbling to a minimum when Ollie Johnson and Georgie Miller showed up. As usual Johnny Pardeau limped in last, but he was smiling like a teenage boy on his first trip to a Nevada cathouse.

CPO noticed first.

"Whoa, did Johnny P. get his big screen TV? Guess we know where we are for the playoffs!" he exclaimed, setting down the menu and his cheaters.

Ollie and Georgie fought each other to high five Johnny first.

"65 inches of well-hung Samsung!" Johnny Pardeau laughed. "Can't afford beer anymore, so I guess we know what you a-holes are bringing!"

They then got down to the biz of studying the lunch menu, as if they hadn't seen it dozens of times each.

"I got yours, Johnny, said Georgie Miller. "Just save me a front row seat. Rams gonna kick some Eagle ass tomorrow!"

"Don't care who wins if my Raiders aren't in it. Just want a good game," added CPO Mendenhall with diplomacy. "This is a rebuilding year for us."

"Ha!" laughed Ollie Johnson. "Your Raiders been rebuilding for over a decade."

"When's the last time your Niners built a winning team?" retorted CPO.

"Hey, speaking of building," interjected Georgie Miller, "Cops musta been building a case against that Wilson fella who hanged himself in Santa Rosa."

"I'll bet he looked better hung than my new Samsung," chuckled Johnny Pardeau.

Ollie Johnson was more interested in the logistics of the original alleged crime., "Why would he carry a dead girl all the way up a trail. Christ. What a load." He shook his head in disbelief.

"No shit," said CPO. "I had a hard enough time packing my ditty bag up a gangplank."

"Maybe it wasn't a trail back then. I don't know," suggested Georgie Miller. "I'm not a hiker, but I thought Ranger Parsons made that a trail in the late 90's or early 2000 before he died."

"My ex-old lady was a hiker," said Ollie Johnson. "Hiked her leg every time she got outta bed."

"Yeah, Ollie, they had to close your block off on a regular basis. Gas leak," laughed Johnny Pardeau.

"Well I haven't hiked since my stiff pecker days," CPO chuckled. "So I don't know if it was trail or road."

"Well if it was a trail, man's gotta be strong like Bigfoot to get a body up that hill," Ollie Johnson declared with finality.

"Not a doubt that boy did it," said CPO, returning to his laser-like analysis of the case evidence. "Been saying that SOB murdered that Morgan girl ever since it happened. Can't believe they never arrested him. Always felt sorry for Lonnie, her dad." He took his glasses off and wiped them on the corner of his plaid flannel shirt.

"Heck. He did us all a favor, saved the taxpayers some money!" exclaimed Ollie Johnson. "Justice has been served."

"Now how about serving us with a little lunch, Jeanie," Johnny Pardeau said to their favorite waitress who'd just arrived. "Georgie's buying for me, so I'm goin' Bull Elk Burger basket and a chocolate Muley milkshake…oh, and just water. Too much sugar in Coke. Gotta watch the ol' bottom line."

♦

Lydia Wilson answered the light rap at her trailer door. She instantly regretted it when she saw the nicely dressed young lady with a notepad in her hand.

"Mrs. Wilson? I'm Amy Douglas with the Karuk Daily News. Can I speak with you for a moment?"

Lydia made sure the door wasn't fully open as she replied, "What about?"

The reporter gripped her notepad with chipped red fingernails. "I know this is a hard time for you and your family, but I was wondering if I could get a sense of your son Jesse."

"What for?" Lydia asked suspiciously.

Amy Douglas pulled her glossy lips into what was meant to be a charming smile. "I'd like to humanize him for our readers."

"*Humanize*? I don't even know what that means. Why can't you people leave me alone?" Lydia cried, upset that she was being forced to relive her memories of Jesse.

Amy put her palms out in front of her in a *I meant no offense* gesture. "You're his mother. You must want people to know the good he might have had in him." She knew what manipulations tended to work on mothers.

It didn't have the effect she wanted. Lydia snapped, "The good in him? He's gone, and I want you gone from my property or I'll call the sheriff." She started to shut her door.

"Okay, I'm leaving, I'm leaving, but do you think he killed himself over his guilt for murdering Dina Morgan?" Amy asked in a bid to get to the heart of her inquiry.

Lydia's face drained of color. "Oh, now I see how you wanted to write about the good in him. Leave! Now!" The stained, white front door slammed so hard the adjacent window panes rattled in their frame.

♦

Sarah Stock sat in her office at Ronald Faraday Real Estate on Sisson's main street, her salt and pepper hair French-braided and twisted into a bun. She'd just finished some last minute paperwork to send off to an escrow company for her latest clients, a stuffy couple from Marin. The couple had insisted on a "full mountain view" for their vacation getaway. In local parlance the word *mountain* meant one thing, *the* mountain, Mount Shasta. Being able to see the mountain out your windows was at the top of every buyer's wish list. Holding a full mountain view card in your hand sat atop every seller's list of reasons for not reducing price, now get out there and earn your outrageous commission.

Sarah sealed a manila envelope and dropped it in her out-basket to be dealt with on Monday. Then she turned her attention to the Karuk Daily News and the account of the dead Jesse Dale Wilson. She hadn't wanted to read the details, such as they were, but a door to her distant past refused to stay latched. Every now and then, she heard the creak of it opening, just wide enough to let unpleasantness in.

She set the paper down and turned to her computer. She Googled the Santa Rosa Press Democrat and intently read the digital version of the tragedy.

She'd left the door to her office open, so she did not hear her boss step in until he spoke.

"Boo!" came a mischievous, male voice. Sarah was startled enough to feel her heart pounding against the faux silk of her navy blue blouse.

"Damn, Ronnie! Everybody tries to startle me. Do I have a sign on my back?" she laughed, hand fluttering lightly to her chest as she tried to settle the adrenaline coursing through her.

Ronnie Faraday smiled apologetically and leaned against her doorframe. His dark hair was gelled perfectly in place. "Why are you still here, sweetie? It's Saturday and the tourists are all lookie loos anyhow. Let them read the window and ooh and aah over what they could afford if they sold their home on the Peninsula," he said.

"I know, I know. But I had to get the Bassett property ready to go to escrow. All done now," Sarah said.

"Whatcha reading?" Ronnie asked, curious as to what had absorbed so much of Sarah's attention that she had been spooked by a single syllable uttered from her door.

"Oh, I was catching up on the suicide of this guy Jesse Wilson and how it has to do with him murdering of his girlfriend," she replied. She shook her head at the tragedy of it all.

"Perfectly awful. I read about it in the KDN," Ronnie said, moving from the doorframe to lean over Sarah's shoulder and read the Santa Rosa paper's take. His eyes scanned quickly over the screen.

"I'm pretty sure I remember those two, this Jesse and Dina, coming by the house when Zack was alive," Sarah said with seriousness.

"You're sure? That was a very long time ago. I can barely remember two weeks ago."

"I'm fairly certain. Funny thing is, when Cedar stopped by the other day he brought it up about how well he knew both of them, and now this guy Jesse is dead. Of course, I guess everyone's been talking about it."

"Cedar is the type of man to know someone as scurrilous as Jesse Wilson, *very* well."

"They were pretty far ahead of us in school. I think they grew up together. They're at least pretty close in age. The way Cedar talked, they most likely got in trouble together way back when," Sarah said. "Anyhow, he was certain Wilson killed his girlfriend."

"Did he say how he knew? Or is he like everyone else and can follow a trail of breadcrumbs?" Ronnie questioned with a little acid in his tone.

Sarah ignored his undertone. "I don't know. It just struck me as odd. Maddy has a good friend, Kat, who is an intern with the Sheriff's Department, and who is working on that Puma Creek Trail case. Maddy is very envious. Cedar told her to tell the detective working on the case that she knew somebody who could provide information if he'd let her work with her friend or something like that."

"That doesn't make any sense. But then when did anything Cedar Stock do or say make sense?" Ronnie said, shaking his head and snorting.

"I know, I know," Sarah said before adding defensively, "Maybe Cedar is just trying to help Maddy get a job. You know how he's been like a surrogate father for Maddy ever since Zack drowned."

"That hurts," exclaimed Ronnie, his hand over his heart in mock pain. He took a step back, and Sarah could tell that he was genuinely a little offended.

"Oh, Ronnie, you know what I mean. No one has been better toward us than you. You're a saint. But Cedar being Zack's cousin, I guess he's always felt some familial responsibility."

"Well he had a funny way of showing it, going back to prison like he did. You'd think he'd have stayed out of trouble for you and Maddy…if he really thought you guys meant anything to him." Ronnie sounded only slightly like a petulant child. Sarah could tell his heart was in the right place, and he truly cared about her welfare and the welfare of Maddy.

"I'm hoping that is all in his past. He's older now, more mature. He's got a true heart, and he takes good care of Jersey. Anyone who watches out for his mother the way he does can't be all bad," she pointed out.

"Sorry, I don't see it. But I guess it's not my place," sighed Ronnie. He patted her shoulder before leaving her in her office.

She heard him call from halfway down the hall, "Go home! It's time to kick your shoes off and relax, girl."

CHAPTER 24

"Your sheriff called my chief," Jake Stern said.

"Normally that's cause for alerting your union rep," laughed Roy.

"No shit. So, anyhow I was wondering, can someone up there do a little research for us?"

"Name it." Roy was intrigued.

"Well," continued Stern. "We agree that whoever killed Pud, and I'm looking at our hooded friend right now, is from your neck of the woods, or your corner of the pasture, or whatever it is you cowpunchers say up there."

"We say our chute at the rodeo or our stall in the horse barn," Roy said, dryly.

"Right, pardner. As we both know in our hearts, Hoodie Dude is an ex-con. If he isn't, then your DA needs to be fired. Meaning–."

"Meaning we have him in Karuk County records, somewhere sometime," Roy finished. "We need someone to comb all records from the time Pud was a twinkle in his daddy's eye and compile a list."

"You should teach a class. Have anyone in mind?" asked Stern.

"I actually have that person sitting at a desk in my office at this very moment. I've just finished bringing her up to speed on the general outline of the mess. She stopped by on a Saturday because she is tired of enjoying life in the great outdoors unlike every other sane child of 22 years," Roy laughed.

"We're already researching all the other counties in California and across the Western US for jurisdictions where Pud might have been contacted by the cops, but Karuk County shows up the most on his rap sheet," Stern said with an audible yawn. Roy figured he must've been putting in long hours.

"Sounds about right. From reading his rap in the Dina Morgan file, looks as if he started his sterling career right here, advanced to the pen once, but it was only YA for a receiving stolen property beef when he was twenty. Since then looks to have been in and out of county jail multiple times, petty theft, coupla burgs, under the influence, lot of fighting in public, misdemeanor battery, and minor drug possession. Low level stuff, never the stomach for anything beyond wobblers."

"Well, alrighty then. I'll leave you to it. I gotta get a search warrant finished for phone records," said Stern. "Verizon is on hold until I fax it to them. So get at me, day or night."

After Roy said goodbye to his new partner from Santa Rosa PD, he turned to Kat who'd been listening intently. She was leaning forward in her seat with her hands clasped around a notebook, and she looked ready for whatever task Roy wanted her to complete. He smiled at her enthusiasm.

"How do you feel about getting into some grunt work?" he asked. "Maybe a little today, but for real on Monday?"

She nodded eagerly. "I'm easy. What did I get volunteered for?"

"You heard me use the term rap."

"Yes."

"It means Pud's California Identification and Information record. We call it CII rap or just rap for short. It's a list of his arrests followed by a court dismissal or conviction and sentencing."

"It shows all the times he's been in trouble?" She raised her eyebrows with interest.

"Unfortunately, no, and in this day and age of technology it's a head scratcher as to how much information is lost or kept in dozens of different record management systems that don't talk to each other."

"What do you mean?" Kat asked.

"Well, the CII rap sheet *only* shows arrests and convictions in the State of California Superior Court system. It doesn't show Pud's juvenile hall record that got sealed. It doesn't show his traffic tickets. We have to go to DMV for that. It doesn't show various police reports around the state where his name may have been entered as a victim, witness, suspect, or simply an involved party. It doesn't show if he was ever contacted by the police in any jurisdiction where an FI card got filled out."

Kat furrowed her brow. "An FI card?"

"FI, field identification. Say officers come upon a group of bad boys drinking after hours in a park. They'll often identify each one and put all their names on a single FI card. That card sits gathering dust for years until some detective *or intern* comes crawling through the dust looking for associates of a particular suspect in a drive-by."

"So you're saying if you know who your drive-by shooter is you might be able to identify the others with him if you find out from the FI card that he was drinking with a group in a park?" asked Kat.

"Exactly. Homeboys in that group are likely to have been the homeboys in the *hooptie* with the shooter while he was spraying a front yard with 9 mm rounds."

"I get it," said Kat. "I never thought about it I guess."

"Don't feel like the lone ranger, apparently the people in this state who set up the myriad of police records systems didn't think about it either," Roy laughed. She smiled at his joke.

"Getting all those records system to talk to one another could be a doctoral thesis for a communications major," Kat joked.

Roy was only half kidding when he replied, "There's a heck of an idea." He paused and then continued, "Now, ever hear sayings about how past performance predicts future behavior?"

"Yes."

"Well maybe it isn't always true in the business world, but it is very true in the criminal investigation world, regardless of what psychology professors, the ACLU, group therapists, and drug diversion counselors might tell you."

"Meaning?" Her lack of knowledge about the criminal sphere was making it difficult for her to follow Roy's implications.

"Meaning time to look for Pud's *crimies*," Roy said.

Kat stared at him, waiting for any reasonable elaboration on what he'd just asked of her.

"Okay, here's a quick lesson on bad guys who run with other bad guys, like our drinker/shooters from the park." Roy said. "They have terms for each other. A homeboy is someone within your criminal organization, often a street gang, who hails from your hood, your clique, your crew, your posse. Then your *dawg* may be a homeboy, but not just any fool, he's very close. You'll rely on him, you're tight, sorta like a BFF."

"Do these people write this down so they know what terms to use?" laughed Kat.

"Actually, they often write it in small notes using mini-writing, that's tiny printing you can barely see, when they hit county lock-up, California Youth Authority, or the penitentiary. We call those notes *kites*. A new arrival at a lock-up wants to get in good with the cons running the place, so he'll send along a note to the shot callers, listing who he ran with on the outside. The shot callers examine the names on the kite and get at those on the outside to see if the NA can be trusted or if he's a POS."

"A kite? Like a Ben Franklin kite?"

"Same spelling. Prison or jail communication is done via these small, obscure, surreptitious notes probably worldwide."

"Like when I was in junior high?" Kat asked, wide-eyed.

"Exactly. Only the con isn't gossiping that Jen doesn't like Josh anymore. He's ordering Josh to stick a shank in Jack's neck. Now, when they get to the pen they are usually in a *house*, meaning cell, with another con. He's called a *cellie*," said Roy.

"Makes sense," said Kat. "I heard you say YA." She trailed off questioningly.

"Right. CYA is California Youth Authority. It's where juveniles charged as adults, or even some young adults up to 25 years of age, can be housed if convicted of felonies. It keeps them separated from the seasoned, predatory cons waiting, just licking their chops, in the Big House."

She wrinkled her nose. "Ooh, yuck. Is there more? You used the term wobbler."

"Wobbler is a crime that can be charged as a misdemeanor or a felony. If convicted, a District Attorney and Judge can get together with the local probation department and go with either county jail or prison. For example, if Pud got caught in a burglary or even beating someone up a judge could have chosen to send him to state prison or leave him to do his time in county jail."

"So Pud went to CYA for stolen property possession but stayed in county jail for all his other convictions?"

"Yes, and that brings me back to *crimey*. This is a term used by a con to refer to his homeboy or dawg he sat with at the defense table while he's smirking at the cops, DA, and witnesses."

Kat had been scribbling notes. She stopped.

"You mean like a defense attorney?" she said.

"Nice," laughed Roy. "In a lot of cases I'd have to agree with you. Defense attorneys are a necessary evil, but some of them are flat out scandalous and might as well be the wheelman in a drive-by."

"So what I am going to do is search back through Jesse Pud Wilson's past and look for his-," She checked her notes. "Homeboys, dawgs, cellies and crimies."

"Yep," said Roy. "The facts of Santa Rosa's case tell us Hoodie Dude here in this photo has to be an HDCC."

"That could be a whole pound's worth of dawgs." Kat chuckled at her own joke.

"Very true," Roy said. "Bad boys know a lot of other bad boys. But in the end, they trust only a very few, if any, since they see their own duplicitous, criminal selves in all the faces around them."

"What a life." Kat shook her head.

Roy continued, "Pud had no siblings, according to his mom, so anyone he'd hug and trust as much as he obviously did, is someone who'd take the time to drive two articles from our local paper to him, and who could get up in his personal space, with what the cons on the yard call false friendship, to murder him. Seems to be someone very close to him at one time or another who is trying to cover up his own sins, maybe even sins Pud knew about or took part in, sins connected to our Puma Creek Trail bones."

"Hence probing Pud's past," said Kat, connecting the dots.

"Nice alliteration! Legwork. Something TV and movie cops never do. Too slow and boring. "

"I guess no one would pay to watch a policeman read and write," Kat agreed.

"Exactly. An audience isn't interested in how we put the puzzle together, and believe me, the names of Pud's past associates play a huge part in this jigsaw case."

"A jigsaw case?" Kat said, dark eyebrows again raised with interest. "I take it you're going to explain that to me."

"Yes," Roy said. "We've got multiple crimes over different time periods connected to one another. It's the sort of big puzzle that made Jigsaw John famous. John St. John was the greatest homicide detective in LA for nearly 50 years. He worked on cases from the 1940's clear through the 1990's, everything from the Black Dahlia to the Hillside Strangler."

"Wow. Long time." She seemed impressed.

"He was 74 years old when he finally retired. But he had a system that many of us in the homicide units of the Southland, heck, around whole the country, copied."

Kat sat in rapt attention.

"Ol' John looked at a time period connected to a corpse and took random events to see if there was any connection. He said he liked to build the case in the form of a pyramid, taking as many seemingly unconnected facts as possible making them the base of his pyramid. As he sorted out the facts and discarded the ones irrelevant, the pyramid slowly formed until at the top, the final bits of firm evidence, pointed to the killer or killers," Roy said.

"You're right. Too complicated for the movies," nodded Kat, rolling her eyes. "Are there any car chases in this system?"

"Rarely," laughed Roy. "When people try to hide crimes, they actually often end up doing things to call attention to themselves instead. Events occur around a murder that look unrelated but are actually indications of panic, over thinking, sloppy cover-up, et cetera."

"And you think Pud and others may have done things in the past, before or after crimes, to call attention to themselves, and there is a record of this and record of them all being associated."

"One hundred percent!" Roy said. "You catch on quickly, for a college kid."

"I pay attention in school," Kat responded proudly.

"We'll be combing police records, the news of the time period we've established for our Puma Creek Trail case, the Dina Morgan case, again, and now the Santa Rosa case. We may get into old social outlets like those school annuals over there," Roy said, pointing to all the White and Golds lined up on the shelf.

"We'll be looking for anybody, anything, and everything that may seem unrelated but may actually be a piece of the jigsaw puzzle. And it starts with who Pud's dawgs have been over the years. I've already requested Sheriff's records people to get me anything and everything with Pud's name on it, and Santa Rosa detectives have gotten court orders together for IRS records to reveal any employer who ever issued a paycheck to him."

Kat picked up Hoodie Dude's liquor and hardware stores' photos. She studied them side by side, bringing them close to her face.

"You said the bartender in Santa Rosa believes this man who

came in to see Pud was someone he knew exceedingly well, well enough to let his guard down. So that person has to be from Karuk County, or someone Pud has closely associated with in the criminal world."

"Like I said, forget grad school. You have the mind of a detective," Roy observed, tapping the side of his nose.

Kat beamed and continued, "This person in these photos might even live here in Sisson?"

"Would be a good bet, but of course Pud bounced around, so he could have rubbed up against this character in another state. But not as likely," Roy said.

Kat looked up at him thoughtfully, "That's you not getting locked into one theory of the case again, isn't it?"

"Never discount those aliens from Planet Zarkon."

"So why don't you put this hooded guy's photo in the paper and see if anyone recognizes him?" Kat asked.

"That would be last resort. Here's why. Hoodie Dude, as I'm calling him, is definitely a person of interest. Right now, he doesn't know we know about him, but he is probably smart enough to know that we can't prove beyond a reasonable doubt that he committed Pud's murder. Sure, we could eventually ID him, bring him in for questioning, and he could tell us straight up that he met Pud in a bar, bought a come-along, even brought the article from the KDN with him," Roy said.

"That's not enough?" Kat asked.

"No. Murder is what they call a specific intent crime. It means we have to show 'beyond a reasonable doubt and to a moral certainty' that Hoodie Dude, through his actions and maybe others we don't yet know about, intended to take Pud's life. There are innocent explanations, farfetched as they may be, for every one of his actions and every piece of physical evidence the SRPD has found."

She scribbled some more notes in her notebook. "Doesn't seem right."

"It may not seem right, but it is the way it is. There is always going to be that one juror who doesn't believe you've proved your case, and you end up with a hung jury. Have to try the case all over again or accept a plea deal or worse yet, dismiss."

"So you think the best way forward is to keep the guy feeling comfortable and try to prove he committed the Pud murder or maybe even others without him knowing you're after him."

"As I keep repeating, smart, for a college kid," Roy laughed.

Kat flushed again, a little embarrassed of all the praise. "My mind is playing tricks on me, I know. I'm probably being silly and suggestible, but I think this person looks familiar, as if I've seen him somewhere before. And before you laugh at me, why couldn't that be? The town is not that big, and I could have bumped into him before. I mean, it's possible, right?'

"Not only possible, but probable if you've lived here your whole life, and so has he. He may have delivered heating fuel to your house, been a clerk behind a counter, worked at the Post Office, changed the oil in your car, or checked your dog for ear mites. There is just no way to positively ID him from these photos," Roy said, sighing.

Kat looked at him seriously. "I know for a fact he has not checked *my* dog for ear mites."

"How can you be sure?"

She smiled wryly. "I haven't got a dog."

CHAPTER 25

Sunday mid-morning, Roy's cell phone lit up. Spokane PD.

A detective in Washington, at Roy's request, had driven to a home near Gonzaga College, knocked on a door and gotten a positive response from an elderly, white female. Yes, she had relatives down in California. Her late sister's husband, Larry or Lenny, still lived there as far as she knew. She didn't really have any contact with him and hadn't been close to her own sister for decades. Yes, there was supposedly a niece who had brought many a tear to her sister's eye.

Dina Morgan's aunt, displaying a wealth of family knowledge, said she had no idea the niece had disappeared *13 years earlier*, but she'd gladly provide a DNA sample if it would help the police in California. She was great believer in supporting the troops and all first responders.

Roy couldn't fault Wally Westwood for failing to find the aunt. Lonnie Morgan had been a hostile contact at best, for years. Victims, friends and family of victims, and spectators in the stands often forget the Constitution and all its pesky Amendments that keep the cops from dragging the obviously guilty party out and hanging him from an oak tree in the town square. When they see the smirking SOB wandering around free, they tend to blame the cops. A bitter citizen is an unhelpful citizen. It had taken the death of Pud to loosen Lonnie up enough to dig through an old address book kept by his late wife.

Cross one more item off the list of *Things to Do.*

Roy had taken the day off, although he kept his cell phone at the ready. When a case was hot, there weren't actual days off. He'd never been successful at breaking from the scent, and there had always been a case. Even in bed in a semi-doze, he'd let his mind wander, as if he were moving down a long, school hallway in the silent afterhours, checking doors to see if one would open onto answers he desperately sought.

Charlie Criss claimed *he* took days off, told Roy he barbecued with his second family or watched a ball game. But Roy knew he was lying. He answered immediately whenever Roy came up with a wild hair that wouldn't wait until Monday.

Patrol had been different. He could put the job on hold and hit the surf, wash the shit off. Not so in the Homicide Bureau. Results were expected. Upper management talked a good game, said personal time, quality time spent with family, was important…*as long as we don't have to answer to the public why your case hasn't been solved.*

Over time Roy had fallen into the trap of measuring up to his own success. He'd scoffed at and fought the label of workaholic, maybe for the same reason a drunk refuses to accept what he has become. The pain and humiliation of having to stand before a group and admit to dereliction and failure as a human were too great to even contemplate…until you reached the bottom of your emotional well and were left with two choices, die or keep living.

In a self-imposed exile of rural deputy sheriff, Roy had hoped to make amends, pay a debt, even if no one was there to collect. Two weeks ago, the Puma Creek Trail had taken the screw cap off another cheap bottle in a long line of bottles. And now Roy the detective drunk had staggered back into that darkened school hallway to shake doors while self-hatred slithered along on the linoleum behind him like a snake in a garden. The pitiable thing was that the extreme dislike for himself and for what he'd become was preferable because it masked a deeper pain that would linger for life, the pain of loss.

Roy scratched some quick notes on Spokane. Then he forced himself to push away from the table and approach a wall of books on one side of his cabin. He selected a heavy, aqua blue, hardbound book with gold lettering. He opened Malka's Torah to Genesis and read again through the agonizing account of Jacob as he wrestled with the torment he felt with the loss of his beloved son Joseph. It had not soothed Malka's grief, but Roy had eventually taken some comfort in reading through to Exodus where God promises that "I will let you count the fullness of your days." Roy had come to know that in death he would find peace.

♦

Sunday morning. Cedar Stock stopped by Ma's place, checked the cat turds and the stove wood. Then he picked up his guitar and sang a few hymns for the ever-snoring Ma. She wasn't yet strong enough to go to services on her own after her latest bout with the flu, and it's not like he could take her himself. He had to draw the line somewhere. He didn't mind strumming a few songs for her if it meant she'd get into Heaven.

He didn't believe all that God and Jesus nonsense, but on the slight chance that it wasn't all bullshit, singing a few hymns for a frail old lady couldn't hurt her or him. Now that's a good joke. He was gonna be one hell of a hard sell when it came to making the cut, that is if there was a cut to be made, and he was pretty certain there wasn't. He reasoned that if there really were this God up there looking out for all the people who spent a shitload of time on their prayer bones, why did some of them lose a child to cancer, or get eaten by a shark, or have their dog run over in the street?

For that matter, why did God let six million of his so-called chosen people get snuffed out by the original peckerwoods in Germany back in the day? He hadn't paid all that much attention in school history classes, but in the pen he'd had time to round out his education in the prison library. One thing was for sure, a Jew parent forced to watch his children executed in front of him said loud and clear that there sure as fuck wasn't any God.

Cedar's theological ruminations were interrupted by Ma who'd come to in her chair. She was watching him, and she cleared some excess phlegm from her throat.

"Cedar, I've been thinking." Her voice was gravelly from sleep and illness.

"What is it, Ma? Whatcha thinking about?"

Her gaze was unwavering though rheumatic. "I'm thinking about Pud, ever since I read the paper yesterday."

"Yeah, it's a shame he had to go out that way," Cedar said, brushing his hand through his greying auburn hair. He shifted in his seat at the kitchen table, so he could see Ma better.

"Yeah. A real shame. But it had to be done," Ma said. "I know you and him were close. It couldn't have been easy."

Cedar paused, cocking his head to the side a little. "Don't get your meaning, Ma."

"I'm not dumb. You're a good boy Cedar. You love your mama. You've always been good to girls. Never worried about you."

"Sure, Ma." Cedar furrowed his brow a little, not sure he liked where this conversation was headed.

"That wasn't Dina up on that mountain," Ma said. "I don't know who it is, but it's not Dina."

"What makes you say that, Ma?" Cedar asked. What the hell was she talking about?

"I don't know what Pud did with her, but he sure didn't pack her body up a long trail. Not the Pud who used to come around here with you." She nodded her head once to herself.

"Maybe it wasn't a trail then, Ma."

"Nope, that's part of what I've been thinking about. That Forest Ranger guy, Parsons, I forget his first name, he turned that into a trail. Really pissed off the loggers. "

"So?" said Cedar, narrowing his dark blue eyes slightly. He wished Ma wouldn't talk so crass sometimes. He'd just sung her some hymns for fuck's sake.

"So he died years before Dina went missing. I told you I read and watch the news. I don't care what Sarah thinks," Ma said. "That was one of our favorite drives, to go up there, take some chairs, chips, and cold beer. You were very young, but you loved it too."

"Couldn't beat the view," Cedar agreed slowly. "Had to watch for log trucks though." Where was this going?

"Remember those times we took Maddy on picnics up there? She was little. You'd bring your guitar. We'd sing. She was so happy. Some of the best days ever. Sarah didn't come much." She added the last sentence sourly and adjusted her air tube.

Cedar watched her and agreed softly, "Good times."

"So my point is, I loved that road, and I remember when the Forest Service screwed us by blocking it off. No way could I hike. I was cut off, like all the other old people."

"Okay, but the other day you were sure it was Dina. What changed your mind?"

"I just thought it was a few feet up that trail. They never said in the paper exactly where it was. Sheriff never gave out that detail. I didn't learn it was over a mile up until yesterday when Maddy came by."

Cedar leaned back in his chair. "Glad Maddy came by, but how does she know where the skeleton was found…? Oh, she talked to her friend who works for the cops. I get it now."

"Right. She has that little friend Kat Hoover who's working with the detective on the case. Maddy met him," Ma said, coughing a little.

"Maddy met the cop? When?"

"Last week. She went to the Sheriff's substation to find Kat. She wasn't there. But she talked to him. He gave her his card. She showed it to me. His name is Delroy Church," said Ma.

"That's a darkie name, Delroy?" said Cedar.

"Or he could just have some southern roots somewhere. Maybe his folks came out from Oklahoma during the Depression," Ma suggested.

Cedar was concerned. "Why would a cop give his card to Maddy? Cops don't just hand out cards to everyone unless they want to be called back," he said. "And why is Maddy even carrying that card around?"

Why hadn't Maddy or Sarah called him about Maddy meeting the cops? Last he'd heard from them, they weren't hot on the idea. He'd actually been sorry he even brought it up. Cedar suddenly felt uneasy, like when he sensed a hit called by the Brand about to go down on the yard, and he didn't know the target, but he could feel it being planned behind the face tattoos close by. Time to be on his 360.

It had been a calculated risk, maybe even foolish, suggesting Maddy get close to her friend in the investigation, sort of a way to get a peek into what the cops were thinking. But if Ma could come to the conclusion that those weren't Dina's bones, how hard was it going to be for the cops to figure it out, and from there how hard would it be for them to ask why the fuck would Pud commit suicide? Still, no witnesses meant no one could testify that he'd done shit. Fuck 'em where they breathe.

Ma was squinting a little at Cedar, trying to make out his facial features in the dimly lit kitchen. "So Maddy told me her friend Kat said this Church fella is a detective from LA."

"So?" said Cedar

"So, you got me that computer, and I read the news on it too. And I can Google. So for fun, I Googled his name."

"And?" The uneasy feeling kicked his insides.

"Uh, he's kinda famous down there. You may want to have a look."

"Why should I care?"

"Trust me. I'm your mother. You should care. Pud had it coming. But you should care."

"You're puttin' something on me–."

"You put it on yourself, Cedar," Ma interrupted sharply. "Not smart bringing me this Wine Country coffee cup for a Christmas gift." She took a sip from a white porcelain cup decorated with vines and bottles and names of various wineries.

Shit.

"And another thing, Cedar," Ma said. "Quit watching those pornos on my laptop. I'm tired of getting ads on it asking if I want to meet some hot little chick from Singapore." With that, she settled more deeply into her chair and closed her eyes.

Ma was back snoring her favorite hymn when Cedar lifted the lid of her laptop and typed in *Detective Delroy Church, Los Angeles*. The first entry to pop up with that name was a series of articles from the LA Times laying out details on some glory seeking asshole nicknamed the I-10 Clown Killer. Thirty minutes later he closed the lid. He sat at the table, slowly tapping his front teeth with the nail edge of a forefinger. He had a bad feeling reading about who was on his ass. A pit bull cop. The worst kind. Calculations had to be made

Presently he reopened the laptop and typed in *Google Earth, Sisson, California*. He pressed the plus sign until he was right above the Karuk County Sheriff's Sisson Substation and the tic tac toe of neighborhood streets that lay to the south of it. He wished this shit had been available to him and Jacky Blue Howard and Koondawg Cutler back in the day. Woulda made the in and out planning a hell of a lot easier.

CHAPTER 26

2003

For the benefit of those reading the digital edition from afar, the reporter for the LA Times threw in a description, a few paragraphs down, of the I-10. Known alternately in SoCal as the Santa Monica Freeway or the San Bernardino Freeway, "the 10" started at the ocean where the wannabe-discovereds congregated for ice cream and amateur photo shoots to send back home. It came to a screeching halt back east where the Jaguars play pro ball in Florida.

However, the main thrust of the stories centered on yet another SoCal serial killer, this one dubbed "The I-10 Clown Killer." Articles on the case appeared as if by magic on Roy Church's desk throughout the trial and the penalty phase. The killer caught death, or as it is known in California, life in the quaint lock-up of San Quentin whilst overlooking the San Francisco Bay where one can smell the sourdough bread from Fisherman's Wharf, and hear the commuters laughing on Friday afternoon aboard the ferry headed back to the Marin landing, right where Dirty Harry wasted Scorpio in '71.

According to the papers, it had taken Sheriff's homicide detectives Charlemagne Criss and Delroy Church, two years of dogged pursuit to run to ground the homophobic, yet surprisingly homosexual, murderer named Randy Sorenson. Displaying the same determination and gutsy instincts they'd shown on the Night Devil case of a few years earlier, the dynamic duo, known in the local cop industry as Ebony and Ivory, had caught Sorenson red handed in the oleander bushes on the freeway shoulder. They'd tapped on *his* shoulder, rudely interrupting him as he dragged a dead boy of 18 whom he'd dressed in a clown outfit.

Roy had testified for eight days at trial. A litter of seven dead and brutalized men who'd frequented the West Hollywood gay bar scene had caused quite the stir in the often prurient minds of the Southern California reader. Roy had dryly described in minute detail the crime scenes, most, but not all, being on the shoulders of the 10 freeway. He'd detailed how the first dead boy had lain there dressed in a colorful clown suit with a hole in the festive seat of his pants so a bloody broom handle could protrude from the rectum, "…as you can see in the photo."

Roy left out the first comments over his shoulder by his partner whose name in the press always got stretched to "Charlemagne Criss, one of the few African American homicide detectives in the LASD."

"Whoa, we got us a fudgesicle!" Charlie Criss had exclaimed.

It was the era when people, especially squeamish supervisors on the fast track, weren't so uptight about gallows humor.

Charlie Criss, on a roll, followed that up with, "Case solved. We gotta go arrest Bozo for knocking off the competition."

During testimony, Roy also left out his own retorts.

"Looks more like the work of Internal Affairs to me. This is gonna be a media circus."

He'd spent a day on the stand outlining the surveillance operations inside and outside gay bars. He'd spent another day running down how he and Charlie Criss had cross-referenced nearly every license plate in West Hollywood parking structures and side streets with the sex offender registration records in the county. That, as they say in the joint, had taken a minute, which is to say it had taken months.

A fortuitous break came when they cross matched the sex registrants with DMV records. A sharp-eyed, quota seeking California Highway Patrol officer at the intersection of Santa Monica Boulevard and Doheny Drive had broken the case wide open, without knowing it. Six blocks west of his favorite hunting grounds, a collection of world famous bars, Randy Sorenson should have taken heed of the Buckle Up for Safety campaign. He fell victim to a violation of 27315 of the California Vehicle Code.

The CHP officer had dutifully filled out the traffic ticket with Randy's "horsepower" followed by a detailed description of his vehicle. What he did not do was conduct a car search, for lack of probable cause. Randy wasn't drunk or high, so after he signed for his copy, he was pretty much free to go, so the officer could get back on the duck pond ASAP. That had been a close one. Randy had a body in his trunk, and he was sitting on a loaded Glock.

Roy had left out the observations of Charlie Criss on the traffic infraction. Charlie said the Chippie probably kicked himself when he eventually found out there'd been a passenger in the trunk, *unsecured in a manner proscribed by law.*

"Coulda hadda twofer stat."

Randy later told Roy and Charlie Criss that he'd considered killing the officer, but that wouldn't have been right. The cop probably had a family, and he was just out there trying to keep everyone safe. Randy had paid the ticket rather than go to traffic school. And now he always buckled up. He'd learned a valuable lesson.

Randy's dark blue BMW had matched the description of a vehicle of interest seen leaving the area of one body dump. The rest was pretty standard. Follow Randy. Stick to him like dog shit in a waffle patterned sole. The big surprise came when they found Randy already had one in the breech. He'd been storing a frozen body in his garage that he'd not yet decided where to dump. It was this young man whom Randy was grunting over in the bushes when the roof caved in.

"Did the defendant make any spontaneous statements to you at the scene of his arrest, detective?"

"Yes. He made a statement the instant I shone my flashlight on him and yelled 'Sheriff's Department.'"

"And what were those statements?"

"He said, 'Lucy, you got some 'splainin' to do.'"

Try as he might, the psychiatrist hired by the defense could not find where Randy had been molested by a circus clown when he was eight years old which could have mitigated his reasons for choosing the path of the wicked. Randy did not take the stand in his own defense even when his confession was played in court.

"Detective Church did you ask the defendant why he dressed his victims in clown suits?"

"Yes, I did."

"And what did he say?"

"As you can see in the transcript here, he said, 'I had to separate myself from the pack, so I thought the clown suits would be a delicious touch.'"

The jury had deliberated for less than a day. During the penalty phase a month after trial, the judge took even less time to sentence Randy Sorenson to death.

Charlie Criss and Roy Church got *attaboys* from Sheriff Baca and a dummied up thank you plaque from the World Clown Association.

CHAPTER 27

Sheriff Silva opened his Monday management meeting by passing out his wife's banana nut bread to compare with the commercially made version, along with some traditional pastries, that his secretary had picked up that morning from the newly opened Starbucks at the bottom of the south Silverton off ramp. Coffee and pastries, a long police tradition. It had begun with the Garden of Eden PD as management there sat to discuss the impending arrest of the son of a prominent citizen on charges of fratricide.

"Tommy, how was the traffic down in Smogville?" he asked thickly while biting off another piece of banana nut bread.

"Jesus, I shoulda moved out of there ten years ago. Can't believe it's worse. A high-speed pursuit is anything over 15 miles per hour," Tommy Sessions said with disgust.

"Ironic. Rich, big city cops got all the fast, new cars and can't go over the speed limit. Here we can afford twenty-year-old rattle traps that get passed by big rigs on a grade, and our pursuits reach a 100 plus on regular basis. Good thing the state's got money for fancy CHP cruisers, or we'd never catch shit," grumbled Cyril Savage.

"A rural sheriff always has to fight for the crumbs," agreed Sheriff Silva. "Speaking of crumbs, you got *cross-ant* in your mustache, Cyril."

"Thanks for the goodies, boss," said Lieutenant Gary Lynch, a compact man of about forty, with a shaved head and quick hazel eyes.

"Shit. It's to celebrate you two gold-brickers getting back from your mini-vacations," laughed Sheriff Silva.

"We're tanned, rested, and ready, boss," said Tommy Sessions amiably.

"Good," said Sheriff Silva. "So, Cyril, are we ready troop-wise for Wednesday night? It'll be its usual shit show come 0200."

"Yep, boss. Got detectives back in uniform, jail at max staff, all leaves cancelled. Buddy Hackett has full strength here in town, and CHP will have all their people out looking for drunks as usual. They'll be available to help when the bars let out."

"Unfortunately," sighed Sheriff Silva, "weather looks to be clear and cold. Booze will flow. I sometimes wonder if we got all the folks out there to switch to *wacky tabbacky* how different it would be."

"We wouldn't have jobs, boss," chuckled Lieutenant Lynch. He quipped, "Dude, did you just put your hand on my wife's ass? Not cool, man, you need to mellow. Take a hit off my bowl and chill, man."

"Speaking of the mean green, leafy substance, where we at on the Hmong murders, Gary?" asked Sheriff Silva.

"Ghosts," Lieutenant Lynch replied. "Arrest warrants in the nationwide system, Fresno PD on watch down there. But they've probably landed in another city in another state by now. FBI has alerted all its offices. Agents are coordinating with locals to hit up any and all informants in Hmong communities around the country, but it's a tight culture."

"Do they know we just want to pass out a reward for them doing us a favor on two super-dirtbags? They did what the justice system couldn't, and it only cost a few dollars in lead," laughed Sheriff Silva.

"We've spent a lotta man hours on this case, but we're drowning in a pool of shit elsewhere. We gotta move on until something breaks," Lieutenant Lynch said. "Let me run down the list of highlights.

He proceeded to describe the buffet of open cases crushing his detectives in the Major Crimes Investigations Division. Burglaries, domestic violence, sex assaults of adults and children, suspected gang activity in a migrant farmworker community, several financial fraud cases, and of course drugs, always drugs. The narcotics officers were up to their ponytails in meth, opioids, and illegal marijuana grows.

"Jesus, when I was kid growing up on the ranch outside Montague we had fights after a few beers. This is ridiculous. What the hell is happening to our country?" Sheriff Silva said, rubbing his forehead with two fingers. When he heard about all the soul sucking crap out there, he wondered if he shouldn't urge Tommy Sessions to give it a go as Sheriff.

"The sixties, boss, the sixties screwed us," Cyril Savage said reproachfully. "No personal responsibility. Everybody do your own thing. No sense of national pride. It was bound to happen."

"Glad my dad is gone and doesn't have to see us now. He lost part of his hand on Omaha Beach for this shit." Sheriff Silva said. "Still, he was a champion roper and made a living raising Herefords, best beef cattle there ever was. Hell, you can't even find them anymore. Angus took over. They over bred the Herefords. Then all the city folks started hollering about fat content in meat. Can't find a decent tasting steak in a store anymore."

The managers all sat silently, waiting for Sheriff Silva to finish his normal Monday lament on the state of the union.

"Sorry, I got off track there," Sheriff Silva smiled, wiping remnants of his pastry from his fingers onto a thin paper napkin. "Gary, are you up to speed on the bone thing Roy Church has going on down in Sisson and Santa Rosa?"

"I need to meet with him on that. I'd understood we thought it had taken a turn toward solution. But now I hear there is more to the story," Lieutenant Lynch said.

"Yeah, we kinda jumped the gun a little bit. Now Cyril, don't start gettin' all hang dog on me. Shit happens," Sheriff Silva said.

"I hate a *told ya so*, but Roy Church is no joke," said Tommy Sessions. "He's a once in a generation detective. Just got a nose for the secret shit assholes have stashed behind their eyes. State pen is full of cons who never saw him coming."

"Don't know much about him," Lieutenant Lynch said. "Like I said, I gotta meet up with him so he can clue me in. Is he in uniform or plain clothes down there?"

"Hell, we've offered him plain clothes a shitload of times, but he seems to prefer uniform," said Sheriff Silva.

"I think it might be more a psychological thing for him. Last time he was in plain clothes it got pretty rough for him," said Tommy Sessions. "Bad family stuff. Too much time away from home on the job."

Tommy Sessions did not elaborate, and no one pried. They'd all sacrificed family at one time or another for an unsympathetic citizenry.

"Hmm. Okay then. Anything else? Otherwise, Tommy and I gotta head over to the jail to meet on some prisoners' rights complaints and the new jail death protocol," said Sheriff Silva. He mindlessly reached in his upper shirt pocket for his chewable.

♦

"Somebody's here's got a big mouth. But I don't know if it hurts us or actually helps us," Jake Stern said in a disgusted tone over the phone.

"If it was in your Monday paper, it'll be in ours tomorrow. Nothing we can do about it. Was bound to happen," Roy said diplomatically. "And you're right. The publicity could force our bad guy to make a move. If we're lucky, we'll see it."

"At least they don't have Hoodie Dude's photo. They just know we're keeping one from them," said Stern. "All they've got solid is that we're refusing to rule the hanging as a suicide and that we've got a person of interest seen leaving the bar with Pud."

"It's one step from that to a citizen placing a call to the paper and telling them he works at Friedman's, and he answered questions from a detective about a suspect in a hood buying rope and a come-along. Or the citizen calls, you know, the one who lives on Pud's street and saw the POI in his neighborhood," Roy said. "We might as well plan on it."

Stern sighed heavily. "Right. Well, I'm expecting word from Verizon today with the calls in and out on Pud's phone, plus subscriber info on who called him, if they were a Verizon customer.

If the calls originated with AT&T or another carrier, it'll take more time. By the way, Post Office cop confirms no mail delivered to Pud in the City of Roses," he said. "The articles were hand delivered."

"Okay, keep me in the loop. I figure we'll land a name or two out of Pud's records before New Year's Eve. Then it'll be up to you on how you want to handle it. Surveillance or frontal attack. It'll be your call," said Roy.

♦

Ira Hand grunted with vague annoyance as he flipped through the copy of the police report that a Karuk County deputy DA had handed him in super court that morning. He scratched a few notes on a yellow legal pad as he digested the words.

The facts seemed simple on their face. Two cowboys, listed as Suspects One and Two, *no doubt wearing hats and shit kickers*, had consumed copious amounts of Coors Light on draft at Kerrigan's Bar on the north outskirts of Silverton. The bartender, listed as Victim-Witness One, had cut them off after his barmaid, listed as Victim-Witness Two, complained that they'd filled an empty beer glass with chewing tobacco spit. Suspect One became angry and threw the contents of the beer glass at the bartender, covering him in some really gross shit. That would be the charge of assault and battery with bodily fluids.

Both suspects fled (*more like staggered, hence the charges of Drunk in Public*) out the front door and crawled inside a 1978 Ford flatbed pickup listed as Suspect Vehicle. Suspect One backed Suspect Vehicle out of the lot, but not before colliding with a silver Mazda Miata belonging to the barmaid. Suspect One then drove away out onto northbound Klamath River Drive. Charges continued to accumulate here with the additions of 20002 CVC, Hit and Run, and 23152 CVC, DUI).

So far, Suspect One's lawyer has his work cut out for him.

Upon heading NB on Klamath River Dr., Suspect One failed to negotiate an immediate left hand turn to WB Poker St. Suspect Vehicle left the roadway, crossed a sidewalk, and collided with a fire hydrant.

Karuk County Sheriff's Sergeant Bo Hansen arrived just as both suspects got out of the Suspect Vehicle. Suspect One attempted to flee on foot WB Poker St. Sergeant Hansen pursued him for about 100 feet, caught up to him, and detained him in handcuffs.

As Sergeant Hansen was walking Suspect One toward his patrol vehicle, Suspect Two approached and tried to drag Suspect One away from Sergeant Hansen, resulting in a charge of 148 PC, Resisting and Obstructing an Officer. Suspect Two, while trying to free Suspect One, grabbed Sergeant Hansen's left wrist which was holding onto Suspect One's upper arm. Charge of Battery on a Peace Officer.

Ira Hand chuckled as he could have predicted the next lines in the police report.

Additional deputies and one CHP officer arrived on the scene. Suspect Two became combative and had to be restrained by several deputies. Suspect Two was placed in handcuffs and leg restraints. He was medically cleared at Silverton Hospital before being transported to the Karuk County Adult Detention Center.

The judge saddled the Karuk County Public Defender's office with Suspect, now Defendant, One. That meant a conflict attorney had to step up. It would be a conflict of interest for the PD's office to represent both defendants. Ira Hand and a few other defense attorneys made their living off the conflict cases, meaning those multiple defendant cases where the client could not pay for a private attorney, so one had to be appointed by the court. Ira Hand hung out in the court rooms during morning calendar, watching arraignments. It didn't necessarily have to be a multiple defendant case. If the Public Defender was already representing Billy Bob's brother on another case, the judge had to appoint a conflict attorney for Billy Bob. That's where Ira Hand came in. The pay was minimal, maybe sixty-five bucks an hour, with a ceiling. But it was a living here in Karuk County where housing was cheap.

Ira Hand set the report down and glanced up at his wall. The beautifully scripted diploma from Sacramento's McGeorge School of Law sometimes mocked him. His silver hair and expensive haircut and suits made him look the part, but he knew classmates who were pulling down six figures and partying in Cabo. Here, he was pulling down five and partying on his garden apartment balcony.

His phone rang. It was Silverton Secretarial Service. SSS handled all the businesses in his back street building, meaning Ira Hand, and Associates (truthfully, he was still in the market for an associate) plus a bookkeeper-tax prep service and one marriage and family counselor.

"Your eleven o'clock is here Mr. Hand," a frumpier version of what he imagined his McGeorge peers' secretaries looked like. It didn't help that his was also male and malcontent.

He waved his hand. "Thanks, Todd. Send him in."

Ira Hand was a bit curious. He occasionally got calls from citizens seeking legal representation. They were usually poor, and he was not legal aid. He would advise them to trot over to the Public Defender's office where they could fill out paperwork that might or might not officially land them back with him, but this time with the State of California footing the bill for a conflict lawyer. Today's prospective new client had simply said over the phone that he wanted to talk about possible pending criminal charges based on a mistaken belief by law enforcement that a crime had been committed.

The caller had said he didn't want to elaborate and would discuss it in person if Ira Hand had the time. Ira's 11 o'clock slot on his desktop daily planner had been clear. Actually, so was pretty much the rest of the day. Ira had informed the caller that an initial thirty-minute consultation would be free, but after that he got a hundred bucks an hour.

His heavy, polished office door opened and a middle-aged man in clean Carhartt pants and a flannel walked in.

"Good morning," he said, rising and coming around the desk to greet his visitor. "I'm Ira Hand."

"Good morning, sir. I'm Cedar Stock."

Thirty minutes later, Ira Hand looked at his watch and said, "I'm very interested in your circumstances. I believe I could be of assistance to you, but I do require a retainer."

"How much?"

"Well, normally I ask for…$2,000, but since this appears to have the makings of a miscarriage of justice…."

"Here's 2 grand," Cedar said, reaching in his coat pocket and extracting a stack of folded bills, the crease neatly dissecting Ben Franklin's left eye. Ira Hand smiled at Cedar politely.

"Let me get you a receipt and have you sign a few spots on my attorney-client agreement."

CHAPTER 28

By noon, Roy and Kat had come to two conclusions. First, many of the records for Jesse Dale Wilson prior to 2000 had been purged from Sheriff's records. Secondly, those that hadn't been destroyed revealed that he had a consistent posse… of one, Dina Marie Morgan. On paper, they were joined at the hip. A deputy on dome light patrol had busted them in a bar parking lot while they snorted coke in the front seat of Pud's truck. Another deputy had arrested both for public drunkenness and assault and battery at a campground on the Klamath River, northwest of Silverton. A deputy in Sisson had arrested Pud after he punched out Dina at Karuk Lake in 2001. The DA had dismissed charges after Dina refused to show up in court to testify against her man. Both had possession of controlled substances under their belts. And they'd shared the same probation officer off and on for years.

"How could she stay with him? Kat said, several times, baffled. "He was a real no-good wasn't he?"

"Very typical relationship. Couples who do drugs together or drink together fight together, sometimes against others, sometimes against each other," Roy explained. "In Police Work 101 you learn about love-hate relationships that seem incredible to everyday citizens. Women stick with men who beat them. And it works the other way as well. All the advocates in the world can't change the defective personalities that attract like opposite ends of a magnet."

Kat didn't seem convinced. "What about women's shelters. Shouldn't she have gone to one?"

Roy gave a slight shrug of his shoulders. "The shelters are a godsend for some. Others have an addiction that can't be broken until they themselves are. They end up dead, like Dina."

"Tragic," said Kat, slumping back in her chair. "My dad never beat my mom that I know of. I heard them argue a lot, and then he just left."

Roy grabbed booking photos, if they existed, for every name that he and Kat came across in the meager number of reports. For those who had not been hooked and booked along with Pud and Dina, he ran through the DMV terminal and checked recent CDL photos. No one even slightly resembled Hoodie Dude.

"Well, we've exhausted what's available to us here. Let's grab lunch, and then we'll stop by the Probation Office, check old reports," Roy suggested.

"I don't understand why all the records get purged," Kat remarked with bewilderment.

"Legislative stupidity and records managers who must get a charge out of mucking up investigations," Roy replied with a sardonic snort of laughter. "None of the politicians who come up with rules on recordkeeping have ever had to solve a case. In many instances state law mandates purging of records after a certain number of years."

"Seems short sighted to me, especially now," Kat said, aghast.

"Precisely. Let me give you an example," Roy said. "We have gang databases around the state. If you want to know if a suspect in a gang murder has ever been involved in gang activity, because you now have him in your sights on a current case, you go to a gang database to see what he's done and who he's run with. Problem is, all his gang activity may have been purged."

"Why?" asked Kat.

"Because they say he hasn't been arrested or Field IDed with gang members in the past five years, therefore he's gone straight and shouldn't be labeled for something he did years ago. Trouble is, he has no street activity because he's *been in prison* for five years."

"Wow," said Kat, thoroughly unimpressed.

"Wow is right. But all I can do is work within the insanity that is the criminal justice system in this state."

"It's as if a bad person's past never existed," said Kat.

"There's only one place they don't play that purge game," said Roy.

"Where?" asked Kat.

"The penitentiary. California Department of Corrections and Rehab keeps a fat file on every con ever bussed through their gates. They do it to protect the staff and the cons. It's a different world there. If you don't know a new arrival's past, he, staff, and or his enemies are at risk of bleeding out on a dirty yard. So his Central File goes with him wherever he's housed. Appropriate staff can access it to see who he is, who his associates are, or have been, so they truly know who they're dealing with."

"That makes sense," said Kat before adding, "Maybe too much sense."

Roy replied, "Do-gooders in this state are so afraid of coming off like Javert in *Les Miserables*, you know, the police inspector obsessed with pursuing a bread stealer, that they've turned us into a virtual confessional for criminals it seems. Forgiveness for all."

Roy's cell phone vibrated. It was the secretary in the Investigations Division. He answered immediately.

"I understand you're here at the Main. Lieutenant Lynch in Investigations would like a word," the secretary said.

I need to stop coming here.

"Certainly. When?"

"He'll be back from lunch in thirty if that works," she said.

"I'll be there."

Roy hung up.

"Quick, out the door for a drive-by before anyone else sees us here."

"Hopefully, you mean a *drive-thru*," Kat giggled, getting quickly to her feet and hot-footing it to the door after Roy.

After McDonald's, Roy dropped Kat off at the Starbucks shop before he headed back to the Main for his meeting. He left her there sitting at a table with her laptop open, next to her caramel macchiato, looking for all the world like the college student he would have had, should have had.

♦

"I'da bitch slapped Westwood if he pulled that shit on me," Lieutenant Lynch fumed. "Trust me, he isn't sitting down for a week."

"Well, don't be too hard on him. His interference actually didn't hurt anything and may have helped shake a tree. He's young," said Roy in a soothing voice.

Lieutenant Lynch didn't seem convinced. "Well, he should have known better. Anyhow, I've been thinking. I want you up here with us. We could use a detective with your background. I can make it happen. The Sheriff would sign off in a flash."

"Lieutenant, I really appreciate the vote of confidence, but this Puma Creek Trail case is a one-time shot for me. After we've put it to bed, I want to go back to the road. I'm done exclusively working a plainclothes unit," Roy said. "I'm not saying I won't have to dress light in this case occasionally, but you know what I mean."

"I get that," Lieutenant Lynch said, slowly. "But if I can ask, why did you volunteer to take it on in the first place if you're done?"

"The Sheriff came to me and asked. Plus, I've got personal reasons why I wanted this last hurrah."

"Have anything to do with your intern? Nothing we should worry about is there? Sheriff would shit if there was a scandal. I mean you're single, she's an attractive young adult from what I've heard, but Christ, and you're damn near old enough to be her grandpa," Lieutenant Lynch said, question in his eyes.

"No worries there, boss, but truthfully, it is partially about her and her outlook on life," Roy said. "She's smart and talented, and I want to show her that being kicked in the teeth the way she has a few times is no obstacle to making a difference."

"Okay," said Lieutenant Lynch. "You vouched for her, and that's good enough for the Sheriff, so it's good enough for me. I won't bug you anymore about it. Just know the investigations offer stands. Could use some help right now on the Hmong mess."

"Never an easy case with the Southeast Asians. They're a whole different set of cultures. But I would say, throw in a call to a Detective Bobby Simons in Rochester, Minnesota. Worked with him on a few 187's. No one knows the Hmongs, Cambodians, Laotians, and Viet Ching like he does. A good resource. Use my name when your guys call."

"Will do, thanks," Lieutenant Lynch said as he wrote on desktop pad. "Let me know if and when you need anything on the Puma Creek Trail thing. I understand Santa Rosa PD has got a hand in it now."

Roy nodded. "Thanks, and yes, got a good crew down there to coordinate with. I suspect they'll be up in the not too distant future."

On the way back to Starbucks for Kat, Roy thought about what Lieutenant Lynch had said about his relationship with her. He realized it might not look wholesome to some outsiders who lived in the gutter themselves. He wondered what her mother and Paul thought. Had they spoken to her about it? Were they concerned? Or did they trust her judgment? Bill Clinton had muddied the waters like a pig rolling down the bank. Roy doubted it would do any good to explain that he saw his own daughter in Kat, and that she'd given him a reason for seeing the future in an optimistic light, something he'd not had in nearly five years.

Kat hustled outside and climbed in.

"All okay?" she asked, a hint of concern in her voice. She had no idea the machinations Roy dealt with, but she'd sensed him sniffing the air when he got the phone call from Investigations.

"It's all good, homes." Roy laughed. "Just a *carnal* watching out for his *soldado*."

"Ha, sometimes you talk like a gangster." Kat grinned and buckled her seatbelt.

"Too many years spent in the mix," Roy chuckled.

♦

The Karuk County Probation Department was not much more enlightening on Pud and his running mates than the Sheriff's records had been. Various pre-sentencing reports, follow-up interviews, searches, and arrest for probation violations served only to validate the Pud and Dina Show. Various probation officers had expressed concern that the two adults were exceedingly childlike in their approaches to taking responsibility and attempts at becoming passable citizens who should be allowed their freedom.

Neither had held a job long. Pud had shown promise in that he had worked enough to make a meager living. He'd demonstrated passable abilities as a rough carpenter, had set chokers on a logging crew, planted seedlings for various private government contractors in treeless areas devastated by forest fire or clear cut by loggers. He'd listed blue collar skills with carpentry tools, some heavy equipment and mechanic knowledge, and, like most men in Karuk County, could wield a chainsaw and maul for firewood production. His problem, it seemed, was understanding that an employee should show up for work more than three days out of five, and that being on time was not just a suggestion.

Where Pud had at least gotten a paycheck, Dina had failed miserably, violating probation a number of times by stealing from her employers, early on in the relationship. She was virtually unemployable, ending up on SSI allotments, like a bum under a bridge. Roy estimated that the multiple thirty-day periods in the clink, coupled with 6 months here or there, seemed to be the most productive periods of her life.

It was late afternoon when Roy and Kat finished the fruitless search in Silverton. They headed back south on the I-5 toward Sisson, with a frosty, pink Mount Shasta resembling a gargantuan hood ornament.

Roy's phone chirped a text notification from Jake Stern.

Call ASAP.

Roy pulled into a rest area, across the freeway from the Weed Airport, where a bright orange windsock flipped violently from the ever-present south wind.

"What's happening?" Roy asked, putting Stern on speaker so he could write.

"Verizon came back. Got some names for you," Stern said.

"Go," Roy said, pen at the ready on his pocket notebook.

"Looks as if he had an out-going call or two to his mother Lydia Wilson. Not surprising. Another to the Karuk County Probation Department. Keeping his PO informed. Model citizen. However, we've got an incoming from a phone belonging to a Verizon subscriber named Germaine Stock. Mean anything?"

Roy repeated the name as he wrote. He sensed Kat stiffen.

"Hold on Jake. I've got my intern here. I think I know the name Stock, but not Germaine. Let me check with her."

Roy glanced at Kat whose face, naturally pale from the season, had absolutely blanched.

"Germaine Stock? Is she related to your friend, Maddy?" Roy asked. He held his breath.

She hesitated. "I think so. I think that could be Maddy's great aunt or grandma. I'm not sure. They call her Jersey. That could be short for Germaine. Oh my God."

Roy turned back to his phone. "Okay, Jake. I think we might have a match. Let me call you back in a few. How many calls?"

"One, a couple of weeks back. Got burner calls, at least two in the days leading up to his death. Okay, call me back."

Roy hung up and turned to Kat who appeared to be struggling internally.

"Take it easy, Kat."

Kat's voice broke.

"How stupid could I have been? Is that why Maddy was so interested, why she came by your office? Is she involved in this? I swear I didn't tell her anything about the investigation." Her eyes were serious, pleading with Roy to believe her.

"Whoa, whoa, whoa. I believe you. Let's not jump to conclusions. Remember, never zero in on one explanation," Roy reminded her patiently.

"Sure, but it can't be a coincidence," Kat blustered. She nervously pulled her ponytail over her shoulder and sat holding the end.

"Small town, so we don't know that yet. What do you know about this Germaine or Jersey?"

Kat thought for a moment before answering. "Not a lot. Maddy used to stay at her house after school when we were kids, when her mother Sarah had to work late. She called her Aunt Jersey. Yeah, she was an aunt, a great aunt I think. There was another lady who was her actual grandma-Grandma Becky. It's a big, confusing family."

"Any idea why Aunt Jersey would call or even know a defective character like Pud?" Roy asked.

"It makes no sense. She's got to be in her late 70's or early 80's."

"Okay then, we've got some homework to do. Let me call SRPD back."

Roy dialed Jake Stern.

"No obvious reason for this Germaine, or Jersey, Stock to be calling our boy, she's an old lady, apparently."

"Yeah, I've got her CDL info here. She's 80 years old. Lives there in Sisson. She doesn't look like Ma Barker judging from her photo. Looks more like Ma Bush down in Texas."

"So you're thinking someone used her phone," said Roy.

"We think alike," laughed Stern. "Hoodie Dude maybe?"

"Good possibility. Too thin for a warrant on Jersey's phone?" Roy questioned.

"I'll run it past our DA, but I give it a 50/50," said Stern. "In the meantime, any way you could take a look at this Jersey lady? If you say the word, I can have a surveillance team up there in time to mess up their New Year's Eve parties."

Roy smiled slightly. "Let me get on it, see what we have in our records on this Stock angle."

"Okay, and Roy, one other thing," Stern said seriously.

"Yeah?"

"Get us that road trip, and the best meal up there is on me. We'll solve no crime ‘til overtime!”

Roy didn’t hesitate. “Venison tacos at the Black Tail off the I-5.”

“You can’t be serious. Do I need to wear camo to eat there?” laughed Stern, aghast.

“No, but you gotta bring your own Buck Knife to skin your meal out back.”

CHAPTER 29

Kat stayed silent for several miles as she and Roy sped south on the I-5 toward Sisson. Then she spoke as they were pulling up to the sub.

"I don't understand. The night of our reunion, Maddy was just like several of my friends. They all had theories on whom the bones on the Puma Trail belonged to. Maddy was no more curious than the others. I told them all that I'd been sworn to confidentiality, just like in the Chico ID Lab. Everyone, including Maddy seemed to respect that. No one tried to pry any information out of me."

Roy parked the SUV and turned to look at her. "When Maddy came to the sub she told me you hadn't told her or the others anything about the case, so as I said earlier, no worries."

"I did tell them the embarrassing story of me getting sick and how you came to my rescue and how that led to me getting an offer from you to work as an intern. I thought that would be okay," Kat said, grimacing a little. She clambered out of the vehicle.

"Absolutely," laughed Roy, following her into the sub. "It's a great story."

"A high point in my life to be sure," said Kat, shaking her head.

"So I'm thinking about that. When you told them how sick you were, did you tell them how far you had to walk? What I'm getting at is we did not release the exact spot of the skeletal remains, but someone could have calculated an approximate location based on how far you hustled with your cheeks clenched," Roy suggested.

"Oh my God," said Kat, cringing and shaking her head. "It's

possible, but I'm not sure."

"I don't know why it would make any difference anyhow, since we eventually released the scene, so anyone could have gone up and seen where all the digging took place," Roy mused more to himself than to Kat.

Kat was quiet for a few moments before asking, "Should I call Maddy and ask her about her aunt and her phone?"

Roy appreciated her willingness to help, but he didn't think that would be a good idea. "Why don't we hold off on that for a sec."

"Okay," said Kat. "But I feel as if I was used." She shrugged and pulled on the end of her hair again.

Roy understood how she must be feeling. "Best not to show a hand until you know what game you're playing," Roy advised. "At this point we don't even know if Jersey Stock's phone call to Pud is related to his death. It took place several weeks ago. Obviously, it's highly suspicious, so I've got to do some digging on the name Stock."

"Stocks have been around forever. I think they're like an old pioneer family. I told you Maddy's mom, Sarah, is a real estate agent working for Ronald Faraday Real Estate," Kat said.

"You mentioned Maddy's dad died, right?"

Kat gave him a nod. "Yeah, Maddy's dad drowned in a river when she was a baby. It's one of the reasons Sarah worked so hard and Grandma Becky and Aunt Jersey looked after Maddy a lot. They were all very close when we were in school. I don't know about now. I think Grandma Becky passed away a few years back."

"What about Sarah's parents?" Roy asked, writing while she talked.

"Oh, Sarah's dad is Dr. Fournette. I don't think he's retired. His wife worked with him in their office and at the hospital. She's a nurse. That's why Maddy's other grandma would watch her after school."

"So Sarah was Sarah Fournette before she became Sarah Stock?" Roy scribbled some more notes down in his notebook.

"Yes, Dr. Fournette is supposed to be a good doctor, but I don't think he and his wife got along too well with the Stock family."

This piqued Roy's interested. He looked up from his notebook. "Why is that?"

Kat gave a noncommittal shrug. "Just comments Maddy has made through the years."

"Such as?" Roy prompted.

"She used to complain to those of us close to her that her mom's parents never had anything good to say about her dad. She'd tried to find out about a man she never knew. It's only natural. Grandma Becky and Aunt Jersey were full of information, I'm sure. He was their blood. But I remember Maddy being upset when we were teenagers together because her other grandparents had no photos of her dad at their house. It really offended her."

Roy scratched a few more bullet points down then looked at her thoughtfully. "How do you feel about being used for a good cause?"

"What?" Kat asked, confused.

"Completely voluntary, of course. But do you think you might get hold of Maddy during the rest of your vacation, to ski, or party, or whatever?"

"You want me to go undercover?" Kat raised her eyebrows, a smile starting to warm the features of her face. "I thought you said you didn't want me to talk to Maddy about the phone call from Aunt Jersey."

"I don't," Roy replied. "If I were to *direct* you to do something like that you'd be acting as an agent of the police, going undercover like you said, and that causes all sorts of legal headaches. What I'm asking is for you to keep your ears open only. I don't want you to ask any questions. I just want you to do what would be natural between friends. The point is to see if anyone in the Stock household asks *you* questions."

"Meaning?"

"Meaning I don't believe in coincidence. At least not where I used to work. Here, with the town being so small, I'm not a hundred percent sure." He leaned back in her chair and could see that she didn't fully understand what he was saying.

Her next words confirmed that. "I don't get it."

Roy smiled. "Let me explain by example. We had a missing child in a community called Lancaster in LA County. It's out in the desert by Edwards Air Force Base where the Space Shuttle is. The whole community was up in arms with everyone coming out of the woodwork to help grid search for her, in lines, like you see sometimes on the news or in movies. Days went by. It was not looking good. She'd wandered away from the daycare where she stayed while her parents worked at the base.

"I noticed one kid, about twenty, hanging around our CC,

command center. I guess you could describe him as one of the nerdy, gamer types who sits in a dark room staring all day at a jumping, blasting screen living out his Call of Duty fantasies. Anyhow, he was super helpful. Volunteering to lead search teams, clean trash, and make sure coffee pots were filled. You'd turn around and bump into him asking if we needed anything else.

"I'd been on a number of arson related homicides. I knew that a firebug will stand in a crowd to watch all the fire excitement, not unlike this kid who seemed to be everywhere watching the excitement of a tragedy unfold. He wanted to be close to the action, wanted to know what we knew."

"What happened?" Kat asked, brown eyes wide.

"Eventually, I got him in the box. That means I sat him down for an interview. He confessed to abducting and raping the little girl. He led us to her burial spot in a gully about a hundred yards from the day care center. It was a bad deal," Roy said heavily. He looked down at the wood laminate on the top of his desk as the memory washed over him.

"Oh my God, how horrible," said Kat in a quiet voice.

Roy nodded. "Point is, it was no coincidence that he was underfoot, asking questions, sticking his nose in, and wanting to know what we knew. Get my drift?"

"Maddy only came by once. It's not as if she's stuck her nose in," Kat countered.

"You're right. But if this were back down south, I'd know it was not coincidental. Too many people there for one person to come up twice without it meaning something. Here? Two thousand people plus in the area, it could be just coincidence," Roy said, shrugging.

"But you don't believe in coincidence," Kat replied slowly.

"No, I don't believe in coincidence. Call me cynical," Roy smiled.

"Then I'll do it. I'll go visit Maddy. I just hope her creepy Uncle Cedar isn't there." Kat shuddered slightly.

"Creepy Uncle Cedar? Like the tree?"

"Like the tree," Kat confirmed. She continued, "But I just said that. He's not *really* creepy. He's nice, and Maddy loves him, almost like a father she never had. He plays the guitar and sings and makes her laugh. I haven't seen him in years. He was in and out of Maddy's life when we were younger."

"Got it," said Roy. "But why call him creepy?" He tapped his fingers on his desktop, then picked up a pen, interested.

Kat thought for a moment. "Scary might be a better word. I think it's his tattoos, from what I remember. And I know he got in trouble a long time ago. I think he went to jail even. It wasn't something Maddy wanted to talk about much."

"What's his last name?" Roy asked, feeling adrenalin rise into his fingers as they wrapped tightly around a pen.

"Um…I think it's Stock. Yeah, Cedar Stock," Kat said. "He's Aunt Jersey's son I think."

♦

"Jake. Roy Church here," Roy said into his cell phone as he sat in his chair at the sub staring at his computer screen. Kat had left a half hour earlier.

"Roy? Talk to me. I hear it in your voice." Roy could picture Stern rubbing his hands together with excitement.

"That obvious, huh? Remind me never to get in the box with you," Roy quipped.

"Yeah, I bet I could cop you out," Stern agreed.

"Not a chance. I'd asked for a lawyer right from the gate," Roy chuckled. "Anyway, are you sitting down?"

"Sitting down. You're killin' me."

"Got coffee?" Roy asked.

"Jesus, would you just spit it out?" Stern replied in mock frustration.

"Hey, I'm from Hollywood. It's all about drama and suspense. Anyhow, I think we got Hoodie Dude."

"You're shittin' me. Damn, you work fast!" Stern exclaimed.

"Cedar Robert Stock, aged 49. Former parolee and son to none other than Germaine Stock. He's the registered owner of a 2015 GMC pick-up, per DMV records. Don't know the color, but I'll bet it's black."

"Wait. You're telling me there is a guy actually called Cedar Bob Stock? And he's a suspect in my 187? Bullshit. Does he play the banjo too? I am not going on any canoe trips in Karuk County," Stern sputtered.

"By chance he does play the guitar and apparently has a nice voice from what I'm told," Roy affirmed. "I'm looking at his DMV photo, and he is one hard looking white boy. I'm guessing he was tipped up in the joint. I'm not saying Aryan Brotherhood but more than your run-of-the-mill peckerwood. Could be Dirty White Boys or Nazi Lowrider."

"Holy shit. I'll get his DMV photo and put together a lineup tonight. See if the bartender or Singh the liquor store wit can ID."

"And if you get an ID? What then?" Roy asked.

"Well, you and I know if we arrest him, the clock starts ticking. We gotta have our shit together, enough to make it through a prelim, and I don't think we've got it. Close, but this is Sonoma County where they spoon feed the public on police brutality and corruption, but mostly in the Sheriff's Department, not us."

"Ha," Roy laughed. "Always the Sheriff, except when it's the LAPD's turn, which it has been over the last thirty years."

"Yeah, everyone needs the police, but they don't trust the police. A crazy system," Stern snorted.

"The media types who fan the flames, and the politicians they favor, should try going without the cops for a month," Roy sighed. "Be fine out here in the woods. Hell, everybody's armed. But in the city you got a lot of spongecakes who think owning a gun is worse than owning child porn."

"When they bust down your door and start raping your wife, child porn is not going to change minds," Stern laughed. "Anyhow, if I get an ID, we'll cross that bridge then. I'm thinking surveillance and maybe even a straight up interview. Let's take a wait."

"Okay. Get at me, and if you come up, you're right, don't bring a canoe," said Roy, seriously.

"Why not?" asked Stern.

"'Cause our rivers don't go to Aintree," Roy said in his best *Deliverance* drawl.

CHAPTER 30

Cedar Stock's deep blue eyes, eyes that targeted nothing on the prison yard yet saw everything, stared up at Roy's green eyes from the DMV photo. A tanned, shaved head accented by a drooping Wyatt Earp mustache on the unsmiling, angular face bound for Valhalla reminded Roy of a predator who didn't give a shit about putting a shank or a slug in anyone who stepped in his way, law officer included, law officer especially.

He couldn't see them, but Roy could guess at which blue green tats decorated the prison pumped chest, back, and arms. They'd been earned behind the walls, not like the amusing stolen valor paid for in a parlor by computer keyboard warriors. He imagined the spider webs and clocks, the faces of smile now, cry later, the name *Stock* in Olde English script between the shoulder blades.

He doubted that there'd be a three-leaf clover. True members of the Aryan Brotherhood or the Brand, as they called themselves, numbered in the low hundreds. For the most part those cons were doing *life without.* This was not the face of a lifer but more that of a white boy peckerwood milling with his race for protection. This was a smart guy, someone who'd used prison politics to his advantage for safety and financial gain. A schemer, a master manipulator, a chess player. This remorseless killer was Exhibit A in making the case for law enforcement workouts and time spent on the range.

Roy set the photo down and then picked up Cedar's rap sheet. It was thin. State pen twice. Once for sales of nose candy in 1989, again 11 years later in 2000 for 211 PC, taking somebody's cash through the use of force or fear. No tail. He'd done all his time inside, so a parole officer wasn't in the picture. There had to be a reason he'd completed a full term behind the walls. The state favored parole, even for hardened cons. It saved money and made naïve politicians and citizens in rose-colored glasses feel oh-so-progressive to see second and fifth chances. The only reason to keep an inmate beyond his expected parole date is if he'd been a fuck-up who'd lost his *good time*, time off a sentence earned by an inmate for being, well, good. It might be something to explore down the road. Roy made a note.

Roy rubbed his chin with two fingers. Why was this con so concerned about Puma Creek Trail? He'd killed to throw Roy off the scent. Or had he?

Maybe he's simply a vigilante who demanded justice for Dina. And maybe I'll see winged pigs above the treetops.

The timing on Cedar Stock's rap was right. He'd have been on the street for at least the five years between '95 and 2000, the time period in which Roy was reasonably certain the Puma Creek Trail murder had taken place.

Roy's phone rang. It was Stern.

"Barkeep can't positively ID but picked Stock out a stack of photos as most likely to succeed."

"What about the liquor store witness?" Roy asked, jotting more notes down.

"Not a chance," Stern lamented. "He was too busy watching hands, prepping to slap leather himself."

"So we're looking at surveillance or a straight up request for an interview?" Roy asked.

Roy heard Stern blow his cheeks out. "Looks that way."

"What would we expect to find in a surveillance, besides the truck he drove?" Roy asked.

"Well, we *think* he acted alone, but if it looks as though he has a posse, maybe we can pick one off and get ourselves a source," Stern said.

"Source? You worked with the feds?" Roy said.

"Oh, yeah, picked up the lingo on a fed gang case a few years back. We say informant, the feds say source. Sorta stuck with me. Of course, those who've never worked UC say rat and snitch, like they hear on TV," Stern snorted. "I say show respect for those who make your case for you by wearing the wire."

Roy found himself liking Stern more and more. A man after his own heart. He'd lost count of the cases *he'd* gotten credit for because some sketchy citizen, a lowlife puke in the eyes of most, had helped him out. He'd grown to value the human tools of his trade. Without informants, cops might as well stay in a station and wait for radio calls, like a firefighter.

"You have a team? I can tell you as of now our entire department is on full alert for New Year's Eve and can't spare anyone but me except in an emergency," Roy said.

"Got a good team. CCAIS we call them. Career Criminal Apprehension and Investigation Section. They specialize in following and making cases on our bad boys here."

"Do they realize it's the dead of winter here? Snow tires a must in most places. Street skins won't cut it," Roy warned.

Stern was hesitant. "Hmm. Could be an issue. Might just be me then until I get the lay of the land and see if a team is warranted. We'll cross the tire bridge if and when. They got a hotel up there, or do I gotta build myself a lean-to in the woods?"

"Bring the canoe after all. Sleep under it," Roy joked. "I gotta be honest, I don't know where this cat lives. I have his mom's, Jersey Stock's, address, but he's only got a PO Box on his CDL, and all his local records list Jersey Stock's crib."

"Sounds as though Jersey Stock's in line for a coupla peeping toms named Jake and Roy. Hey, I'm looking at Sisson's top hotels right now on my desktop. Says here Black Tail Inn. Is that related to your deer burger joint?"

"Sure is, right across the street from the restaurant and the new Black Tail Brewery under construction," said Roy.

"Black Tail's got that town sewed up," laughed Stern.

Roy chuckled at yet another gangster doper term flowing naturally from the lips of his new partner in crime. Stern had an interesting history. That was for sure.

"Yep, Black Tail's got the *llaves*," Roy laughed, coming back with the paroled gangster term for "keys" that designated one as having the prison gang-authorized power in a region.

"Okay then, let me get back to you on my ETA after I run all this past my sergeant. Of course, I'll also have to run it past my wife for complete permission. She holds the real juice card. Then we'll see how difficult Cedar Stock the Hoodie Dude is going to be to snatch up," Stern said.

♦

Roy stepped outside the sub. With slow, deliberate steps, he crossed sparkling asphalt toward his SUV, careful not to put full weight on either foot. Too much irony in a broken collar bone at this point in the game. Breathing in the night air was like sucking on a menthol cough drop, and the tops of his ears immediately felt as though they could snap like a tortilla chip. He wondered how long a human could last out here without keys in his or her hand and fuel in a tank. It made sense that nighttime car burgs should drop off for four months of the year in these parts.

He backed the SUV around, listening to the crunch under tires, and then he drove off the lot onto the street fronting the sub. He turned west then south, angling through the neighborhoods toward downtown. No traffic, foot or otherwise. Dead radio. All smart people were inside around roaring flames enjoying pre-New Year's Eve hot totties or cold Bud Lights, or maybe they'd sneaked the cheap champagne early. He shivered as the heater took its sweet time on defrost.

He checked the dash to make sure he had his settings correct, at the same time noting in his rearview mirror the annoying brightness of LED headlights that had popped up and turned behind him a block back. He chuckled to himself. Another habit. When patrolling in the hood you never lost track of tagalongs just because you happened to be searching for the gangstas coagulated on the sidewalks in front of you. 360 swivel became a way of life, a way of survival. He didn't talk to his fellow deputies here in Karuk County about the tactics he been forced to develop in the smog pit. Here in the sticks, they might think him a bit paranoid. In the old days he'd broken leather several times a night until the *Code 4*, all clear, signal. Up here you had to be more discreet about screwing a barrel in an ear.

Roy turned onto Sisson's Main Street and crawled along, looking for any movement on foot or in a car. Patrol was always about the slightest movement that didn't want detection. He'd give the shift another 30 then head home. It had been a long day. He didn't mind. Nothing else to do. With his LASD retirement already under his belt, he wasn't interested in overtime, so he hadn't really calculated how many hours he'd been in the saddle.

He peered to his left through a frosty driver's side window at the afterhours security lights set on low in the office of Ronald Faraday Real Estate, reminding himself that Maddy's mother Sarah Stock worked there. No such thing as a coincidence happening more than once per case. It was a rule you lived by. Maddy Stock, Sarah Stock, Jersey Stock, and now Cedar Stock. Hands had been shown, he didn't care how small this town was and how often you might run into your neighbor. In this case, every time he turned around he ran into a Stock or was about to, like they were all in a phone booth together. That was just plain old, off the hook, blood-red flag time, even for the dumbest rookie he'd ever schooled during his early years as a street training deputy in East LA.

Then he remembered something Kat had said earlier that day about Sarah Stock being an in-law, and how Maddy was resentful of her grandparents for not celebrating the life of her deceased father. He wondered if a visit with the grandparents on that side of the fence might enlighten him on the story of Cedar Stock. The only trouble with this approach was the *cat out of the bag* syndrome. The moment he spoke to one family member, the cans on strings began to rattle, and the element of surprise was completely gone. Still, bushes had to be shaken at times, like when a wiretap operation had gone silent and stale. Sometimes it was good to "tickle the wire," pay a police visit to someone in the mix to get the tongues wagging. What could come out of an unguarded mouth could end up putting it on freeze for 15 to 25.

He resolved to look into the viability of a Dr. Fournette interview somewhere in the near future. You never knew. Said to be a pretty good doctor, he might have his head on straight and want to cooperate. On the other hand, high achievers could possess some quirky traits and need to be handled like a pissed off porcupine. A clue had popped up from the reported frustration of their granddaughter Maddy. No photos of her late father was a sign not to be ignored. A strained relation in a family, when you're trying to break the code of silence, is a godsend for a cop. Relations rarely suffered more than when a darling daughter had been done wrong by, "…that no good sonofabitch she married who treated her like shit." The SOB's family was usually just one step above the SOB, with the lot of them looking up at dog shit on a pedestal in comparison.

Roy slowed even more to check out movement in the Shastafarian Burger joint. Everything seemed Code 4, okay, there. He moved on and noticed the LED lights still in his rearview mirror, way back, matching his speed. Still not unusual. Everyone had to pass through downtown at one time or another, might as well be behind a cop to do it, better than being in front of.

Roy turned west and left the main drag. He passed the Forest Service building. He thought about Sassy Cassie. Out with friends? More likely sitting in her Snuggie in front of the Hallmark Channel, reveling in the perfect romances of perfect looking couples in their perfectly decorated homes. The LED lights turned too. He chided himself for making anything out of it. Who could possibly be following him? Lieutenant Savage? To what, see if the department was getting its money's worth?

Roy took another right and headed back north on the next street. Up ahead the Sisson Hospital complex lit up the night sky destroying any hope of pulling over to gaze at stars. He turned in the first ingress for the hospital and then cruised the lot looking closely at any and all of the several dozen cars, all parked and dark. He meandered in and out of several of the lots, using his last minutes before letting Silverton know he was through for the night. Then he emerged back out onto the street. No sign of any LED lights in his rearview mirror or anywhere. He shook his head slightly, annoyed with his paranoia.

"Victor 12, Silverton."

"Go ahead Victor 12."

"Victor 12, be en route for OD."

"Victor 12, 10-4."

The night was over. Roy tapped the gas pedal and headed for a nearby freeway overcrossing to take him west to Old Stage Road, from there south to Karuk Lake, and then home.

After he crossed the freeway and began winding through the forested roadway, he looked in the rearview. LED lights had reappeared in the distance, flickering through dense foliage he'd passed seconds earlier. The hairs on the back of his neck rose like stealthy soldiers in tall grass.

He continued at his pace well below the speed limit for the next quarter mile until he halted at the sign-controlled intersection with Old Stage Road. He turned south and moseyed — just an old cop doing his rounds — looking for anything amiss…in front of him. He hit the spotlight and lit up a herd of cows huddled together next to an ancient barn, mutual body warmth protecting them from the freeze. Their eyes reflected like shiny marbles he'd collected nearly a half century earlier. Way back at the stop sign the LEDs paused, longer than the lack of traffic called for, and then turned north.

Roy let out an imperceptible breath. He searched his mind for a rationalization, a reason to lower his guard, change his condition back to white for the evening. He couldn't do it. He imagined himself on a board floating a quarter mile from shore as a dorsal fin passes close by but continues on. Just curious and gone or U-turn on a menu selection, he couldn't be sure, but something was wrong. He'd not survived multiple brushes with death on car stops, building searches, and street pat-downs by ignoring the signs. In uniform or plain clothes, it did not matter, he'd geared his being toward expected deadly confrontation at every turn.

Don't get caught slippin'. Have a plan to kill everyone, while you're smiling politely.

The LED lights reappeared. U-turn and menu selection made by a squirming brain.

Roy came to another intersection. Signs pointed back to downtown Sisson to the east, Karuk Lake and a golf course straight ahead, south, the state fish hatchery complex to the right, west. Roy turned into the fish hatchery parking area and spotted up the low, white buildings with green roofs, as if searching for broken windows and a lurking thief. Still an old cop earning his bread. A public toilet building, closed for the season, lay on the south side of the parking lot. He turned and parked on its west side so that most of his SUV was obscured from Old Stage Road. He left the SUV running, lights on. He quickly got out, slinging with him his MP-5 subgun and its 30 round mag. He hurried around the south side of the toilet building. He crept quietly east along its wall until he got to the corner where he could peer and catch a view of the Old Stage Road intersection with its myriad of signs.

The LED lights on the vehicle had stopped at the stop sign, again pausing way too long. Decisions were being made, like a confused tourist? Which way to go? No confused tourist in the vehicle, a confused killer maybe, unsure of what move to make on the cop who'd probably stopped to take a piss behind cover, his guard down, prime for assassination. Momentarily the LEDs continued forward through the intersection, under a streetlight, where Roy could make out the vehicle but not the wheelman or any passengers. The black, shiny, late model GMC pick-up moved on south, slowly, as if ever so cognizant of the icy pavement and the adage *speed kills.*

No, Roy kills, motherfucker. Just keep movin' and we'll do this another day. Too goddamn cold to leave you lying inside a crime scene for the night.

With unblinking eyes, Roy grimly followed the path of Pud's killer as he disappeared south on Old Stage Road. He had no doubt Cedar Stock was the driver, though he had no way to prove it. No ID, no plate. Sure, he could have hopped in his SUV and chased after the Jimmy. There'd be plenty of PC for a stop. A normal citizen was a rolling mass of violations gleaned from the picky sections of the vehicle code. But that strategy would have forced hands, both for Cedar Stock and for Roy. A car stop on a dark night in the woods would most likely end up in a gun fight, one in which Roy had no doubt he'd prevail. But the point was to solve this bitch.

Why was Cedar Stock hell bent on zeroing in on Roy? It had to be because of Puma Creek. Cedar had no way of knowing Roy's connection to the 187 in Santa Rosa, so that meant Puma Creek. Cedar Stock had stupidly shown himself to be ass deep in Puma Creek. Cedar Stock knew about Roy only because Maddy Stock had told him, there was no other way. Roy's name had been mentioned exactly zero times in the press.

Tonight had given Roy direction and marching orders. It was time to take Cedar Stock and every other member of the family apart, examine them like an Amsterdam jeweler on a shiny stone.

It annoyed him to no end that he'd been on the verge of taking yet another life, in a long career that had seen several end beyond his barrel. Had he felt fear? Absolutely not. Anger? Yes. It took years to recover from watching someone's life, even an asshole's, slip away because of a stupid and spur of the moment decision. Roy's occasional cracked teeth told him you never ever really recovered, just pushed it down to a spot where acids could be controlled.

Roy waited in the cold until he thought his hands might weld to the stock, and then he climbed into his SUV and waited some more. The Jimmy never came back. He then drove away from the direction of his home over Karuk Lake. He hit the Reno highway and zoomed under starlight all the way to McCloud, about 12 miles, making sure he'd not been followed.

Had Cedar Stock thought up a better plan? Roy wondered if he'd be lying in wait somewhere along the way back. Did he already know where Roy lived? Had Roy missed being followed days ago? Was he looking at an ambush outside the front door of his cabin? Well, no sleep tonight. He'd have to low crawl his way back home, not the easiest task in a marked police vehicle.

He analyzed the incident some more. What had Cedar Stock's aim been, if in fact it was Stock behind the wheel? Intimidation? Worse? Maybe he'd simply been keeping tabs to see if Roy stopped at any familiar homes, Lydia Wilson's trailer had been close, signaling that Roy was on the scent. Whatever the reason, Cedar Stock was either a man who made mistakes, or a man so sure of himself, he didn't give a hang how many telegraphs he sent.

Roy couldn't exactly call Silverton and whine that he'd had a close call. What could he say? I was tailed by a truck matching the description of a truck of interest in a Santa Rosa 187? In answer to your question, no, I can't ID a driver, and no, I didn't get a plate, but I'm sure someone is out to get me, so could you post up a deputy so I can get my beauty sleep?

He could hear Lieutenant Savage on that one. Why didn't you go after the suspect vehicle and get a plate for us and make a car stop to positively ID? Oh, because you were afraid of a gun fight? Ever hear of asking for mutual aid and then conducting a felony car stop? No? Didn't do that in LA, huh? Sheriff, we need to talk about your boy, uh, behind closed doors.

Light duty on the rubber gun squad did not appeal to Roy. Conversely, seeing Cedar Stock in handcuffs had a certain allure.

After an hour or more of maneuvering stealthily in the dark and checking his tail after every turn, Roy decided on the only course of action. Find Cedar Stock. Turn the tables. He flipped open his pocket notebook and checked two addresses. Maybe he'd get lucky. He'd keep this little cat and mouse game to himself. *Specific intent* could get tricky. There might come a time when he'd want no questions about what did he know and when did he know it.

CHAPTER 31

Downhill from the Sheriff's sub, Cedar Stock tucked back in the parking lot of a closed tractor repair shop. He'd not known how long he'd have to wait so he came prepared with his outdoor snow gear, including hand warmers, hot coffee, jerky, chips and celery. He'd read in a magazine in the pen how celery contained medicinal properties that counteracted the harmful effects of caffeine abuse, like arthritis. A man could pick up pointers when he had spare time to read occasionally. He sometimes regretted his busy life outside prison where he often neglected to sit, relax, and feed his brain with a good book.

He'd also packed an expensive pair of Vanguard Endeavor binoculars that he'd lifted off a dead *coyote* who went squirrely after a clandestine border-crossing near Calexico. The Mexican should have given up the dope carried by his mules whom he'd probably overcharged anyhow. He would still have made *feria* off the human traffic, and he'd still be alive to scarf *frijoles*. Oh well. He shouldn't have tested Koondawg's itchy trigger finger.

He'd gotten lucky this night. The oxidized Honda Accord he'd seen the previous day in the driveway of Kat Hoover's home had been in the Sheriff's sub lot when he'd first cruised by earlier this afternoon. No Sheriff's SUV. That meant Kat was with Detective Church. Cedar puzzled over why a detective of Church's reputation drove a marked police vehicle. Strange. One of life's little mysteries.

He figured 5 p.m. had to be around the latest an intern would work, so he'd passed by a couple of times waiting for the tractor shop to close for the day so he could set up a proper surveillance.

It wasn't that different from scoping a dope house. Actually, it was easier. Dopers were always peeping out of windows or circling the block looking for narcs. Paranoid little fuckers. If they thought they'd spotted an undercover cop they'd sometimes get all bold and stroll up to the dude sitting in a car and then get uppity, like they'd pulled his covers or some shit.

Cedar recalled that long ago time when a hippie prick in the East Bay town of Fremont tapped on Koondawg's window while snapping photos with a Brownie camera and sneering, "Hey, *officer*, I smell pork. Oink. Oink!"

Wrong move, but it had been go time anyhow.

Koondawg popped out of his ride, put his 9 in Hippie Prick's face, and raised his hand over his head in signal for Cedar and Jacky Blue.

A few minutes later Cedar and crew were inside the dope house with everyone on the floor in zip tie handcuffs. Cedar and Jacky Blue cleared the house for dope, money, and firearms while Koondawg stood guard over the pissed off Hippie Prick and his pals who were all acting like sidewalk lawyers, demanding to see a search warrant and threatening civil rights lawsuits.

"And you fucking pigs better provide your full names. Oh, you are so fucked when my lawyer hears about this," Hippie Prick threatened.

Cedar wished he'd shut up. Koondawg only took so much before he went, well, Koondawg.

"I'm gonna take your house, your car, your miserable pension, and I'm gonna fuck your wife in the ass while I'm doing it." Hippie Prick got his facedown pals to giggle over that one.

Cedar called out, "Shut up, dude. You're asking for trouble you don't want. Let us conduct our search and get out of here. Take it up with your attorney." He was feeling benevolent. The haul wasn't half bad for a few days surveillance work. 10 grand in cash, several pounds of high grade weed, and even a sweet 9mm Beretta 92f, worth about 800 bucks. For security, he'd lifted the Brownie camera, plus wallets with ID's from each floor flounder.

"You can't take that camera. That's my evidence, you fucker! Oh, are you the piggy in charge, lieutenant? Lieutenant Piggly Wiggly. Sooo-eeee!"

Everybody spazzed at that one, even Koondawg and Jacky Blue.

Cedar grinned, knowing he'd be called Lt. Piggly Wiggly until at least the next clever victim changed the crew's thinking.

"Maybe we better tape 'em." Jacky Blue said, worriedly, as he pushed the last of the weed into a contractors' black plastic garbage bag.

One of the facedown pals, wearing a tie dye t-shirt, turned out to be a thinker.

"You guys sheriffs or city cops or task force?" Tie Dye asked, trying to turn his head and look at Koondawg.

"Shut the fuck up, bitch," Koondawg growled.

"Hey, you can't talk that way, oinker," Hippie Prick protested. But he wasn't quite as vociferous as before. Even he, the mouthy one, had picked up on a weird vibe.

Tie Dye quietly asked, "You guys sure you're cops? Seriously, what department are you with?"

"We're with the department of Shut the Fuck Up, you little cunt, bitch," Koondawg hissed.

"Let's get the fuck out of here," Jacky Blue said in low tones to Cedar.

"Right," Cedar answered. "Okay, gentlemen, our work is done here. We've got other towns to tame."

"They ain't cops," Cedar heard Tie Dye whisper to Hippie Prick.

"What the fuck!" Hippie Prick shot back. He tried to flip around, like a beached dolphin, to get a look at his captors.

"Surprise, asshole. Looks like you're the pigskin, punk-ass," laughed Koondawg as he reared back and kicked Hippie Prick in the side of his head.

It sounded like Janikowski's winning field goal at the Coliseum. Hippie Prick's head didn't travel through the uprights but came close. He lay limp and silent.

"Let's go, let's go," called Jacky Blue, as he headed quickly for the door.

Cedar, who'd just finished cutting and removing the zip ties, stepped back to follow, but not before warning Tie Dye and the others.

"We got your wallets with your ID's. Stay on the floor for a count of five hundred. If you breathe a word of this, we will visit each of you, and you'll wish all we did was drop kick you like your unfortunate friend there."

"No problem," Tie Dye mumbled, as he turned and looked at the unconscious Hippie Prick who had a strange mucous-like fluid draining from the side of his skull.

Fuckin' Koondawg. A violent mother fucker.

Cedar recalled the first time he actually spoke to Koondawg, in the early 1990's. The afternoon had been sunny and warm in New Folsom Prison, just outside Sacramento. Bare chested cons in white shorts milled the yard. He watched the blacks slapping, laughing, joking, playing netless hoops, doing what they do on one third of the patch of dusty, hard packed dirt and scuffed concrete.

Serious, black-eyed Southern California Mexicans worked out on their half of the yard, sweating through burpees while throwing *fuck you* looks at the *mayates* playing ball. Surenos and their shot callers from the Black Hand, the big dawgs on the block, plotted in little groups that came together and instantly broke apart as word got passed on whatever little plots they always had in the works.

Cedar was relieved that the officers had allowed no northern beaners out or there'd have been a full-scale riot. He could never understand Mexican politics, but one thing was clear, SoCal Mexicans hated NorCal Mexicans and vice versa. It had been like that for decades he'd been told. Fuck, a beaner was a beaner as far as Cedar was concerned. Why not get along and get stronger? Whatever. As long as The Brand, the Aryan Brotherhood, said it was cool to associate with the southern Mexicans it was all good. There was a fuck load of them in the pen. LA had to be empty.

The last spot of turf was a patch around a concrete picnic-style table next to some pull up bars. Cedar's people occupied this area, all pale-skinned peckerwoods, ironically the minority on the yard. Some hailed from the Inland Empire of Riverside and San *Berdoo*, or so their tats said. Others had gotten snatched up by the cops in Orange County or in the rural inland of California's Central Valley or the meth lab dotted foothills of the Sierras. Of course, there strutted the Nazi Low Riders among them all, led by their shot caller Big Red from Oildale, down in Bakersfield. As far as Cedar could tell, the NLR were nothing more than AB wannabes who dreamed of a three-leaf clover, 666, and a one-two tat. Short sighted fuckers. Institutionalized, contented with their little white boy punk bitches.

He had no love for the NLR or the AB but you had to clique up with the gangsters or else you'd be thrown to the wolves sporting brown and black skin. Those boys loved turning ass into pussy on anything inked with a swastika.

In the joint, it seemed race trumped everything. Blacks avoided brown and white. Brown stayed away from black and white, although they actually hated on some browns. White distrusted everybody. Outsiders, especially the public, assumed it was all about race supremacy, especially when it came to whites. Not so. It meant survival. You had to know who wouldn't thrust a blade in you, and who'd have your back when the yard went off. You stuck with your own kind, just to up your odds for survival.

The only exception seemed to be the NorCal Mexicans. Though mostly Mexican, they didn't have rules on ethnic purity in their ranks. Cedar had seen them welcome in white, black, and Indian, the wagon burner kind, not the 7-11 kind. They had some silly notion that *corazon*, or heart, was what mattered. Their big homies were the shot callers in the *Nuestra Familia*, nasty pieces of work who organized along a military structure. They scared the crap out of the other races and the SoCal Mexicans when they worked out in unison on the yard, like freakin' boot camp marines.

Of course, the suspicions got set aside as long as green was involved. Green made skin color disappear. Whites hooked up mostly with Southern brown when it came to prison biz. Blacks usually hooked up with northern brown to sling dope behind the walls. But take away the green, and alliances fell apart. Color could get you killed. So you hung with the fellas of the same color God made you and hoped they stuck *with* you, and did not stick you. If it meant taking an active role in the confusing prison politics of your race, well you did what you had to do to stay alive. Precarious as hell. If you fucked up or pissed off the wrong shot caller, then you were "ass out," and you better run, in a setting where there's no place to run.

Cedar smelled trouble. It wasn't so much a sixth sense as it was the shit smell, the deep-down diarrhea, empty bowel smell. The pungent odor wafting toward him from across the yard told him someone other than a *wood*, a white boy, had shit a piece. All the cons who were *tipped up*, meaning made prison gang members, could stick a cellophane wrapped shank up their asses. Drop your drawers and squat as your brothers surrounded you, like a makeshift curtain, to shield you from the prying eyes of the tower officers. Grunt and push that mother. *Hard candy* coming, time for a move to be made, and a man's wind to be taken.

The other woods smelled the shit just like Cedar. They began milling nervously, eyes clicking, like animals on the Serengeti who sense a lion or a cheetah in the tall, waving grass, and hope it isn't them about to be dragged down and torn into shreds. Big Red stood up on the table and pretended not to scan the black and brown sea across from them while he scanned the black and brown sea across from them. Cedar made sure his own back was to the wall.

Just then, Cedar noticed a door on the other side of the yard open. Two men in street clothes stepped through led by a uniformed correctional officer. They stood watching the yard. One was a squat Mexican, the other was a tall white boy with glasses. Cops of some kind. What the fuck? They here for a tour? Bad timing. If shit jumped off they better get their cop asses off the yard, or the whole place would turn on them and rip their hearts out under the guns. The squat Mexican cop had the confident look of a seasoned CDC officer. The other cop tried to look confident and nonchalant, like he wasn't concerned with the hundred pairs of eyes judging him.

"That's Montalvo, SSU," Big Red announced to his brood, using the initials for the Special Service Unit, high risk parolee hunters of the California Department of Corrections. "Bad motherfucker. Don't know four eyes. He ain't SSU though, but he's a cop. Sure as I got a big dick."

"So Big Red, you're saying he's a 'lawyer'?" another peckerwood laughed nervously. A ripple of anxious chuckling moved through the white boys. Cedar grinned but kept one eye on the black inmates who were elbowing each other driving the rim. He kept the other eye on the Mexicans who were still pin balling one another.

Cedar caught movement from a group of black inmates who'd been watching their brethren dribble, pass, and leap. One black inmate suddenly broke out of that pack pursued by several others who caught him surrounded him and began punching and stabbing him. Cedar couldn't make out the weapons but guessed them to be *one hitter quitters*, small plastic shanks made of heated and rolled plastic dinner ware. The points had been sharpened by scraping them endlessly across the concrete floor of a cell. They weren't as deadly as a full steel *bonecrusher*, but enough punctures could really fuck a dude up.

It never ceased to amaze Cedar how an inmate got set up for the kill. False friendship extended until the target got comfortable. Often times his bestie on the yard had been tasked with the hit, since he could get in close without raising an alarm. It took experience to survive in prison. Trust no motherfucker out here or on the tiers. A smile in your face, an extended hand clasping yours, then a yank forward and shank in the gut or neck. Lights out.

A siren went off. The loudspeaker blared.

"Yard down!"

Every inmate on the yard dropped to the ground and proned out. Lessons had been learned the hard way by new, recalcitrant, arrogant inmates who thought they'd buck the system. If you didn't comply you could catch a wooden block or a rubber bullet or maybe even a .223 round.

The black victim had limped away from his attackers, leaking profusely from multiple gashes on his head and back. He made it to a wall, turned and sank to a sitting position, shock setting in. His attackers had thrown their weapons aside and now lay on their sweating bellies.

A quartet of correctional staff raced to the aid of the injured inmate. Others surrounded his attackers and zip tied them where they lay.

Hundreds of watching inmates lay motionless. It was a moment for stillness. More than a peek was a threat and an invitation for hella pain from the officers and the guns.

Cedar noted that the Mexican cop in plain clothes, the one Big Red had called Montalvo, was assisting the yard cops hook up the black inmates who'd attacked. The white cop with the glasses had stayed by the wall, next to the door, probably scared shitless that he'd gotten trapped with several hundred killers.

"Fuckin' niggers cleanin' house," snickered a white inmate lying next to Cedar. "Shoulda let 'em get busy. Self-cleaning oven. You're Cedar Bob, right?"

"Yeah," Cedar answered, glancing over at the thickset con lying next to him. Jet black hair, piercing dark eyes and the long full beard of a Confederate cavalry general, atop a body decorated with more blue-green tats than Cedar had seen on most. This guy was proud of his convictions.

"Koondawg Cutler,"

"Yo," said Cedar.

"That white cop or lawyer or whatever the fuck he is standing by the door got an eyeful," Koondawg laughed. "Looks like he'd rather be walkin' through fire in a gasoline suit."

"Naw," sniggered Cedar. "He looks like he'd rather be smeared with honey and tied to an anthill."

Koondawg chortled.

Big Red snapped from somewhere behind them, "What's so fuckin' humorous, woods?"

"We're checkin' out that undercover cop who was with Montalvo," Koondawg replied. "He don't wanna be here."

"Yeah," agreed Big Red. "Looks like he'd rather be butt fuckin' a porcupine!"

Relief had begun to ripple through the peckerwoods who were all more than glad to lie on the ground and watch a stretcher haul off a wounded coon.

"That boy's ass out."

"Got caught slippin."

"He best roll it up, and go to walk alone."

"Musta disrespected somebody's baby mama at visiting."

"Or tapped product in the pipeline."

"Or maybe didn't wanna get tapped no more hisself."

Raucous laughter, like open mic comedy night.

Cedar didn't give a shit for the reason the blacks hit their own. In-house biz. Not his concern. Do the time, get the fuck out. He was short to the house, just a couple of months to go, then he'd be ragin' from the gate.

Better them than us! Just glad the Mexicans stayed out of it. Jesus. Fuck. I need outta here!

For days after that, Cedar kicked it in the yard with Koondawg. Koondawg said he hailed from Nevada, had been hooked up with Aryan Warriors in Nevada State pen down in Carson City. He told Cedar he and his boys had taken down a jewelry dealer in the parking lot of a cathouse just off Highway 50. Sweet haul of cash and jewels. Then a bitch who sucked cock for a living dimed him off to the Nevada cops, and he'd done a stretch after a plea deal. When he got out, he found out who the whore witness was and paid her a visit. It was a year before that cunt smoked another pole or sat down without diapers. Ha, ha.

Koondawg was in New Folsom only because California cops had pulled him over on I-80 for a bad taillight, just across the state line outside of Truckee. Fuck. Stolen guns and out on Nevada parole. Oh, and some blow that someone had *hidden* in his trunk. Drug dog sniffed him out. Actually, he suspected the cops of planting it, just to fuck with him because he had FTP, Fuck the Pigs, tattooed on his forearm, next to his FTW, Fuck the World, tat. Cops got no sense of humor. He hoped to blast one someday.

Cedar asked Koondawg about the jeweler.

"How'd you get the jump on him? Them Jews are careful as fuck."

"Easy. Got myself a fake ass badge. Told him the girls inside had complained about his small pecker and he was under arrest. Dumbass let me put handcuffs on him." Koondawg thought that was really funny, and he clasped his hands over his belly as he laughed.

Later on, Cedar made sure Koondawg had his hook-ups just before he hit the gate. Three months after landing back in Karuk County, Cedar got a call from Koondawg who said he and his former cellie Jacky Blue were out, had fucked themselves silly for three weeks, but were now ready to work.

"You boys ever handle a chainsaw or a pair of pruning shears?" Cedar asked.

"What the fuck? We don't mean real work," Koondawg said.

"No shit, Sherlock," Cedar said, "But you've got a tail, so you gotta keep your PO happy. Parole officer's gotta believe you're employed and not out fucking the dog."

"Fucked a dog once. Only once. Won a hundred buck bet in Winnemucca," Koondawg roared. "Had to slit the throat of a motherfucker who called me Cumdawg after that."

Cedar made arrangements to meet Koondawg and his pal Jackson "Jacky Blue" Howard in a Motel Six in Corning, California. They had to make it on the sly. Big no no for three cons to be in association. Cedar suspected Koondawg was a *high control* parolee who had certain stringent requirements for keeping in touch with his PO. He was sure parole would like to *roll up* Koondawg, if they could find any violation of his terms. Six month minimum back to New Folsom or more likely San Quentin. Get rolled up twice and it meant a full year violation. High control meant piss tests on a regular basis and lots of unannounced visits to his home. Koondawg had given his mom's mobile home in Redding, California, as his spot he called home. She'd moved from Yerington, Nevada, to Redding because the welfare paid twice as much. Actually, it was a couch in the trailer that Koondawg called his own. Mom didn't want Koondawg wandering the house. If a PO showed up, all he could legally search was the couch area where Koondawg supposedly slept. Cedar figured

Koondawg was smart enough to stash his shit elsewhere, maybe not even in the trailer.

Jacky Blue he knew nothing about. Koondawg vouched for him, said Jacky Blue had been in on the cathouse jewelry robbery. Cedar said cool but wanted to see paperwork proving it. He wasn't going down behind some undercover cop who'd wormed his way into Koondawg's confidence. Koondawg said he appreciated how cautious Cedar was, that his shit was tight in that regard.

Koondawg had told him over the phone that Jacky Blue had drifted to California from Texas. He'd done a few jobs with the Aryan Warriors in Nevada but had mostly run with the Dirty White Boys and a Barbarian Brotherhood clique from Sacramento.

Jacky Blue was a big, blond, blue-eyed sonofabitch, looked like he could be the lead dog for the Berserkers pounding ashore in England centuries ago, scaring the fuck out of the locals with his horny helmet. A three officer move in the joint. His eyes were a deep ocean blue. Cedar thought he might be wearing fake ass lenses they looked so striking. But no, that's why he had the moniker. He told Cedar he'd picked it up in high school in Buda, Texas, and it had stuck.

Jacky Blue handed Cedar a stack of court papers from Lyon County, Nevada, the essence being that one Jackson Howard had been charged with and convicted on a Class B felony for a violation of NRS 200.380, armed robbery. It all looked legit on crinkled, smudged copies with worn creases. Like every con Cedar had ever been around, Jacky Blue kept his legal papers in a manila envelope, not for the cops to look at, but for fellas along the way who would ask exactly what Cedar had asked. Show me your paperwork. Can you prove you are who and what you say you are, or are you a fucking cell warrior, or worse, an undercover cop?

Satisfied that he had two bad asses sitting in front of him, Cedar laid out his plans. The Cop Robbers gang, the embryo of which had formed in Cedar's mind while face down in the dirt of New Folsom, was born in a grimy motel room off I-5 in a town known for olives and freeway fast food. To think this would not have occurred if Cedar hadn't stepped in and saved Koondawg's life, and his own.

The opening of the substation door interrupted Cedar's waltz down memory lane. Detective Church was on the move.

CHAPTER 32

Cedar watched the Sheriff's SUV far out in front, sliding through downtown Sisson. It seemed to slow slightly when it drew abreast of the closed Faraday Real Estate, or maybe it was his imagination. Did Detective Church know who worked there? Cedar assumed he probably did. A cop of his caliber would be covering all bases, would have uncovered the connections by now, if what they said about him in his press releases was true.

He'd heard the cop's voice on his scanner as he left the substation, letting his dispatcher know he was out and about. Deep, steady voice, like a radio announcer or the guy who used to do voice-overs on movie trailers. He hadn't been able to get a good look at the cop, but figured if he came from LASD, he most likely had seen a weight room a time or two, keeping pace with the cons on the yard who got their prison pump on daily, even after the free weights had all been snatched up in the mid 90's.

Cedar felt comfortable lying way back. Not like following a target in the city where you had to damn near bumper lock or risk losing a payday at a red light. He followed his prey west then back north until the SUV turned into the Sisson Hospital lot. He expected to hear the detective tell his dispatch he was out at the hospital on a call, but that didn't happen. His scanner stayed silent. Must be patrolling only.

Cedar slid to a halt at the curb and waited, his view north along the west side of the hospital complex unobstructed. There was only one direction to come out, so he felt cool at his spot. Time to wait some more. Just like the old days when he and Koondawg and Jacky

Blue and others would follow a dope dealer, a jeweler, a restaurant owner and his receipts, or an armored car. Armored cars got tricky since the guards always expected to get lit up. You had to handle them like a mongoose taking down a cobra.

Koondawg enjoyed the challenge, but Jacky Blue, despite his intimidating size, had a risk aversion to taking on armed victims, not because he was afraid, he didn't scare, but because he was an analyst. Cedar appreciated that quality. Made it easy to bounce strategy off of.

Cedar kept Koondawg in the crew mainly for muscle, quick reacting muscle, a real, blood-loving fucker in a fight. Fearless like Jacky Blue. Of course, he was also there because in the beginning he'd promised needed capital stashed from the jewelry heist, a promise that had saved both their lives.

In the days and weeks following the black attack on one of their own, Cedar had kicked it regularly on the yard with Koondawg and, occasionally, Big Red. Together, they walked the white boys' patch of dirt, keeping an eye out for unusual activity from the jigs who had their shucking and jiving scouts critically analyzing the southsiders who had their own scouts out probing for intel on the other races, intel that could mean the difference between victory or losing soldados the next time the yard went off.

Koondawg's personality and history intrigued Cedar. Many of the lower level white inmates Cedar had shared tiers with whined about the system fucking them. Koondawg embraced his incarceration, declaring he'd been a bad seed that "shoulda dribbled down Mama's leg after whichever dude rocked off while pullin' her hair back and slappin' her ass." Instead, he'd torn through life fucking the system. He was a robber through and through. He laughed heartily recounting tales of ripping off lunch money with his boys in junior high or heisting wallets and purses outside Circus Circus and the El Dorado in downtown Reno.

He'd grown up in a wind rattled double-wide on a sand peppered dirt street in a trailer park called The Tumbleweeds out in Golden Valley, Nevada. Golden Valley lay a stone's throw west of downtown Reno, on Highway 395, over a few dry, low hills. Much of the menial duty, minimum wage help, the backbone of your hotel casino experience, dressed daily in their smart white shirts and black pants in trailer parks like the one where Koondawg dozed until noon, then greeted the day looking for shit to get into.

While his mom labored at her new job as floor help shuttling drinks to high rollers, Koondawg and his boys prowled the concrete canyons of downtown Reno looking for drunks dropping keys in parking lots. Easy targets, fat wallets, and a chance to work over some piss ant if he resisted in the slightest. Koondawg got off turning nose flesh into pulp.

Reno cops and hotel security had been his undoing on a few occasions, handing him over to Juvenile Services for Washoe County. Wittenburg Hall had been a step up from Mama's aluminum cracker box that creaked and shook in the wind. Food was good, not great, but steady. Beds were clean. TV was color. Had to listen to the chaplain preach against sticking your cock in the mouth or ass of another boy, but other than that the place was cool and good for some street schooling with other likeminded thieves.

Koondawg got a charge watching the fear in his victims' eyes when he graduated to pulling robberies with a gun. Once in a while he'd put a bullet in somebody's ass just because it felt good to pull the trigger and hear the scream. He sometimes fantasized about robbing his faceless old man, making dude shit his pants, right before Koondawg busted a cap.

It didn't bother him in the least that his mom had worked the purple trailers inside the concertina wire outside Carson City. What did bother him was her story on how she'd been fired after some big, fat nigger bitch, the one at the door who greets the horny customers, accused her of stealing. She'd lost her job, had to go out on her own and then fuck and suck for cash in back alleys. Disgraceful. Of course, if Mama hadn't got busted for lifting what wasn't hers, Koondawg wouldn't be alive. So there was that. Still, he hated niggers, and every time he got the chance, he'd fuck one up. That's why his boys started calling him Koondawg. Pretty funny right?

Yes, that is quite the story, one fraught with irony, Cedar told him.

"Fart with irony? I don't get it," Koondawg repeated, unimpressed. "Whatever."

Cedar didn't bother correcting him. "So how'd you land on the idea of fake cop?"

"Shit. Was easy. A fucking security goon lied to me, said he was a cop, so I stopped for him. I shoulda run. All it took was that split second thinking the real pigs were on me. The sonofabitch had me in cuffs. I shoulda filed a complaint on his ass for impersonating." Koondawg was rubbing his tatted hands together and shaking his head in disgust.

"I get it. The old light bulb went on."

"Yep, and fake badges are like assholes. They're everywhere. Real cops gotta show an ID card with a photo. No one ever asks to take a close look." Koondawg's pride was evident, and if he didn't know better, Cedar could swear he saw Koondawg's chest puff up a little.

"Hmm," was all Cedar said as he mulled over the idea.

"Yeah, shit, a whore on the inside bird-dogged me on the jeweler, as long as I broke her off later. Then another whore on the inside ratted me out," said Koondawg, picking at some grime under his left thumbnail — not out of cleanliness but out of boredom.

"There goes that old fraught word again," Cedar muttered.

Koondawg cocked his head slightly to the right, a partially amused smile on his face. "Fuck, you talk funny, like you went to school or some shit."

"Yeah, well I read a lot, and I took some courses at a JC," Cedar explained.

Koondawg confided that he'd not spent any of the money from his fence in Vegas after the jewelry robbery. Had to be over a 100-grand hidden. No need to tap it since the state had provided him with a lawyer. Koondawg planned to put together a tight crew when he next got out. Good robbers had to have dirty cash for expenses since none of them qualified for credit cards, and no family ever would fork over a loan for cars, clothes, and guns from a trunk.

"You down for some heavy shit from the gate?" Koondawg asked.

"Fuckin' A," Cedar responded drily.

It was Big Red who palmed Cedar the kite, a one-inch wide slip of paper rolled tight, its diameter smaller than an ink pen refill.

CM to NG KK-9 Needs Change of Scenery Tell him HELLo from his big brother Abbie.

Cedar laid his head back against the wall behind his bunk and took a deep breath. It didn't take a genius, between-the-line reader to see how fucked he was.

Ask for a Cell Move to that No Good Koondawg. He needs to go to Hell on orders from a brother Abbie, the AB, the Aryan Brotherhood.

He'd just been asked to kill Koondawg Cutler. Asked, hell, he'd just been *ordered* to request a cell move and then to murder a fellow inmate, in his cell. Do it, and he'd never see daylight. Tough to claim no knowledge of the crime if you're the only possible suspect in a 6

X 9 cell.

Two thoughts came to mind immediately. One, Koondawg must have really fucked up somewhere along the line. Two, Cedar must have fucked up as well since he'd be *washed up*, done for life, once he went down on an easily proved 187. Then an alternative occurred to him. The Brand may have noticed him. Maybe Big Red had sent word back up the line to the Commission that Cedar could be recruited. To be recruited into the ABs meant violence, lots of it, ruthless, spine-chilling killing. They were testing him to see how he'd handle himself, to see if he could kill in close combat without shitting himself where the odds could be 50/50.

He knew he'd been chosen because of his current relationship with Koondawg. Someone had noted the chumminess. The manipulators behind the scenes made sure the *fish*, the new arrivals, were schooled up on false friendship, getting the target to drop his guard. The shot callers knew full well that Koondawg would go into high alert if someone approached him all buddy, buddy. In this case, however, Koondawg had done the approaching, so he would not suspect a set-up as easily.

Cedar turned the pile of crap over in his mind, searching for a way to come up with fertilizer. No fucking way would he spend the rest of his days in this hell. Rolling it up and requesting walk alone on a sensitive needs yard, like the black dude who'd fallen out of favor, never crossed his mind. Fuck these dudes. He was no punk. Had to be a way. Of course, he couldn't be sure about wiggle room in the kill order. Maybe Koondawg had fucked up so badly he'd become the poster boy for *ass out*. But Cedar had to think and think and think some more of a way out. He felt trapped, as if in a coffin, six feet under.

Then a shaft of light found its way into his tomb. It burned brighter, like a welder's torch, until its brilliance fucking lit up the landscape. Cool breeze swept into his casket. He sucked the air, and he would have cried, "Thank you, Jesus!" if he were inclined toward such foolishness, which he was not. Hell no, he'd come up with this idea on his own. He grabbed a pen and a miniscule slip of paper.

He slipped the kite to Big Red as they passed at chow. Big Red's shoulder bumped his as they passed, a signal that the original kite hadn't required a response other than a formal request to an officer to be moved in with his new butt buddy Koondawg. The officer would check to make sure Koondawg wasn't on single cell status and then check personally with Koondawg to see if he was cool shacking up with Cedar Stock for God knows what reason. If so, and it seemed a way to keep contentment on the unit, staff had no problem. Roll up your shit and stand by for moving day.

Just read my idea before you discount it, you dumb, red headed bitch.

Cedar crossed his fingers that Big Red had a thimble full of integrity and could be trusted to present Cedar's petition to the shot callers, be they in New Folsom or elsewhere. Cedar knew Big Red had the juice card in New Folsom, but he still had to answer to Corcoran and probably the big boys in Pelican Bay. The time between now and whenever an answer came back would be perilous. Cedar could be disciplined at any step for not blindly following his orders, for getting uppity.

Who the fuck you think you are?

Later, Big Red nodded at him on the yard, rolled his eyes toward the whites-only pull-up bars. Cedar stepped away from Koondawg and followed, keeping his head on a subtle swivel, aware that every white boy peckerwood on the yard had questions, wondering what's up? Cedar glanced up at the guns, the tower officer behind the shades stared directly at him. Small comfort. Big Red was all about biz, and right now the biz concerned Cedar for better or worse. Helped to have the officer and his mini-14 monitoring the little get-together.

Cedar felt his heart pumping faster, even as he fought to maintain calm. The fight or flight adrenaline rush approaching. Never show fear or anxiety, or you're through.

If Big Red asked him to work out, it was over, the point being they'd get Cedar tired first, easier prey, like a moose with a broken leg. He might as well hit Big Red with the piece he had hidden in his sleeve before he himself went down in a dusty, crimson frenzy under all those in the circling pack of jackals who'd been assigned the mission of murdering him under the guns.

"You're a smart guy. I think too smart. But it ain't my call," Big Red whispered. "Here's the deal. The brothers bought your plan. But double cross them and they'll see to it you die slow, while watching your momma take it in the ass by niggers."

Cedar felt the blood rushing in his cheeks. The pack of jackals had not moved closer. Big Red's pupils hadn't dilated like those of a predatory cat, and Cedar hadn't been asked to work out with the boss. It was all good.

Cedar resisted the urge to this tell this furry-faced dickhead that the word was *slowly, as in die slowly. It's an adverb, you ignorant asshole.*

"I'll ask for the cell move then. Don't even wanna know how Koondawg fucked up, just hope I never do whatever it is he did," Cedar smirked, trying to sound hella nonchalant.

"Keep your cock outta the wrong, young asshole and you'll be fine," Big Red growled, scanning the yard.

Two weeks later, Cedar showed Koondawg the kill orders kite as the two of them sat in Koondawg's cell, which was now Cedar's house as well.

"Oh, fuck, bro. You saved my life. I fuckin' owe you, man." Koondawg's dark shark eyes were wide.

"No, you owe *them*, and now I do too, and we ain't fucking this up when we hit the gate."

♦

Cedar sat up straight. Detective Church had cruised out of the hospital lot, turned west and headed over the freeway toward Old Stage Road, driving slowly, looking for what? Dedicated. Hadn't he put in a full shift yet? Cedar wondered what time the detective had come on. He thought this was going to be a simple follow and find.

The Sheriff's SUV turned south on Old Stage Road. Cedar, a veteran shadower, turned north on Old Stage. He wished he had his old crew back. Almost impossible to explain why he'd been behind the cop for as many twists and turns. In his rear-view mirror, he saw the stark shafts of the spotlight illuminating a field on the west side of the road. More patrol. No hurry.

Cedar rounded a curve and then flipped a bitch, headed back south with his headlights off, trying to keep on the road solely by light of the stars, thought better of it and turned his lights back on. The taillights of his quarry disappeared around a treed bend far in front. He sped up to close distance.

Coming up on the intersection at the fish hatchery, Cedar looked to his right and saw Detective Church had turned into the fish hatchery parking lot and had parked near the bathrooms.

Old boy has to piss. If I wanted, I'd creep right up on him, get rid of my problems. Maybe.

Cedar paused at the stop sign on the north side of the intersection. Something didn't feel right. Maybe it was the way the SUV was parked. Maybe it was paranoia honed in the joint, when a set-up smelled like a set-up, especially if you'd been in on a few yourself. The hair tingled on his neck.

He ain't takin' a piss, he's fucking watching me. Shit. LA fuckin' Sheriff. How stupid can I get? Dude's a pro.

Cedar eased on through the intersection and continued south on Old Stage. He'd have to think on this whole shitaroo some more. He turned at his first left and drove back into Sisson. After he slid down Sarah's street and made sure her car was in the driveway, and that no strange cars had parked next to it, he made for Ma's, parking in her yard.

Ma was sound asleep in her chair, TV on low. She stirred slightly, snored, farted like the sound of a butterfly's wings flapping, and then turned into the arm, snug for the night.

Cedar sat at Ma's table for the next hour scrolling on her laptop. Done with scanning world events and re-reading the accounts of Pud's demise, he closed the laptop and looked around. He got up and fed the stove. Then he yawned and thought he might grab a piece of Ma's Mexican blanket couch for the night. It was a nice green leather couch, probably the nicest piece of furniture in her house.

He was just about to settle himself onto the cushions when he paused and glanced toward the front window. The flash of distant headlights had lit up Ma's front curtain. Lights coming down the street formed quickly changing geometric shapes highlighting the curtain's lacy swirls. Normally Cedar wouldn't have concerned himself with lights of a passing vehicle, but these lights moved slowly, searching, like a fucking cat.

Cedar quickly crept to the side of the window and peered out just in time to catch the unmistakable fluorescent, six-pointed star on the side of the black and white SUV. A sudden explosion of alley lights from atop the SUV lit up Ma's yard and the whole of Cedar's truck. Then the lights snapped off, and the SUV sauntered on down the street as if the cop driving had not a care in the world.

Mother. Fucker!

Now more than ever, he'd have to consider implementing Plan B.

The following morning, the Tuesday before New Year's Eve, the Karuk Daily News would cement his decision.

CHAPTER 33

Amy Douglas had high hopes of leaving redneck country someday and hooking up with a major media market. She felt her talent level made it possible. Her KDN stories read well. Thorough research and cultivation of sources helped.

She'd been pissed after reading Mary Redman's latest on Monday morning. The bitch had held back on Amy. *Professional courtesy, my ass.* Having to type *according to another news outlet* left a soapy taste. It called for a one up. She dialed Sheriff Silva, mindlessly twisting a strand of bleach-blond highlighted hair around her finger, exposing a number of split ends. She made a mental note to schedule a hair appointment as the line rang.

As soon as Sheriff Silva answered, she jumped into action. "Sheriff, according to the Santa Rosa Press Democrat, you all have got photos of the person who may know something about the Wilson death. Reading between the lines and filling in the blanks, I'd say you actually have a photo of someone who the Santa Rosa police think *may have killed Wilson*, and it has something to do with the skeleton found on Puma Creek Trail. I'd like a comment on that before I run with it."

She detected an audible sigh, a pay dirt sigh. Sheriff Silva sounded as if he were chewing on something, maybe a lifesaver.

"I can't speak for the Santa Rosa investigation. That is their baby, their call on how it's handled. Is there a connection to Karuk County? I can't say for sure other than the victim is from here."

"So you are calling Jesse Dale Wilson a victim?"

"Well he's not a suspect," Sheriff Silva hurriedly said. "Unless you can be a suspect and victim all at the same time when you do yourself in," he chuckled uneasily.

Amy hedged her cards a little.

"According to the reporter in Santa Rosa, the police there have identified the person of interest, and I believe they've shared that information with you."

"Who told you that? I have a strict policy against my staff divulging details of sensitive investigations. If you go with that, there is a chance someone on my staff loses his or her position. Do you want that? Or can you wait until this mess plays out?" Sheriff Silva said harshly.

"I have to echo what the Santa Rosa paper came up with and then some. I don't necessarily have to say you've identified a suspect. But I have to have something newsworthy to take its place," Amy wheedled.

Sheriff Silva sighed again. Amy could hear him scratching an unshaven cheek. "How about if I tell you we've got our best detective on the case, a real legend, new to the north state?"

A smile turned up the corners of her glossed lips. "Who?" she asked sweetly.

♦

Tuesday morning's edition of the Karuk Daily News made Roy Church smile and grimace simultaneously. It had only been a matter of time. He skimmed the various sections of the story.

Local Person Sought in Wine Country Death Investigation

Sheriff Ed Silva confirmed that his department is cooperating with the Santa Rosa Police Department during its investigation of the recent death of Sisson native Jesse Dale Wilson.

Authorities have a photograph of a male adult they believe was with Victim Wilson at or around the time of his death by hanging. Initially thought to be a suicide, detectives have now been following other leads that throw the cause of death into doubt….

The Major Crimes Unit of the Karuk County Sheriff's Department, led by Detective Delroy Church, is interacting with Santa Rosa Police investigators based on a belief that the unknown person of interest sought is from Karuk County. Sources within the Karuk County Sheriff's Department say investigators are of the belief there is a connection with Wilson's death and the discovery of skeletal remains outside Sisson last October on what is known locally as the Puma Creek Trail….

Detective Church, a recent transfer to the Karuk County Sheriff's Department, is somewhat of a celebrity in Southern California. He is known for his key involvement in several notorious cases, including the Night Devil case, the Desert Dump Murders, and the I-10 Clown Killer, for which he received national recognition and acclaim. A number of television documentaries and at least one book have detailed the exploits of Detective Church….

Roy set the paper down and sipped his coffee, staring out the kitchen window at the snowy firs.

Cat's out of the bag.

♦

Cedar Stock set down the Karuk Daily News, retrieved his cell phone and dialed the number. He got a recording, so he left a message.

"Have you read this morning's KDN? We gotta talk."

♦

Kat Hoover had just come down stairs when she heard Paul call from the kitchen table.

"Jesus, Kat, you never told me who you worked with."

Puzzled, she entered the kitchen and looked over Paul's shoulder to see what had caused his outburst.

"This deputy who came to the house is this guy, right? Delroy Church? He's like Sherlock Holmes or something in LA," Paul laughed. "He's pretty famous, and now you're working with him? Whoa. What a great experience for you."

Kat read quickly, and then stepped back.

"Holy cow," she whispered, brown eyes wide and eyebrows raised.

"What the heck is *he* doing in our little town?" Paul asked.

♦

Detective Wallace Westwood, comfortably situated on his porcelain throne, read the Amy Douglas article and immediately hid the paper from his wife. He could hear it now.

I thought you were the lead investigator, Wally.

Fuck.

♦

Alison Baker reread the article before folding it carefully on her desk.

No wonder that old man sounded halfway competent at the crime scene briefing. Good for him. I'll bet Clint just shit himself. She didn't know why, but the thought of his panic made her smile a little.

♦

Undersheriff Tommy Sessions strolled into Sheriff Silva's office and dropped the paper on his desk. Sheriff Silva looked a little guilty.

"Do we have a leak, boss? This isn't going to go over well with Roy Church, outing him like this."

"It's on me, Tommy. I gave Church's name to the press. Didn't have much choice. This Santa Rosa case and the Puma Creek Trail case are connected, and they're heating up. Tips and inquiries will have to be forwarded to Church, so it makes sense to send all directly to Sisson," Sheriff Silva said, covering his mouth with a fist as his indigestion threatened to emerge.

"Normally, cops love seeing their name in lights," Tommy Sessions replied. "Not Roy. He's had enough for three lifetimes. He's got no desire to prove anything to anyone."

"Yeah, I better give him a call and explain my thinking," Sheriff Silva said, reaching for an ever-present chewable in his breast pocket. "Think he's read the paper yet this morning?"

♦

Roy finished listening politely to the "I had no choice" call with Sheriff Silva then dialed Jake Stern and left a message.

"Google this morning's Karuk Daily News. You'll see we both got more leaks than a balloon in a blender. Of course, my leak can't really be called a leak when the Sheriff does it, I guess. Not necessarily helpful, but not fatal."

Roy hung up just in time to answer the substation hard line phone.

"Sheriff's Office, Deputy Church. How may I help you?"

"Just the person I'm looking for, the famous Detective Church. My name is Ira Hand. I'm an attorney in Silverton. I represent Mr. Cedar Stock, someone I believe you and others are interested in speaking with. We would like to make ourselves available to you for an interview at your earliest convenience."

"Can you give me a hint as to why he thinks we'd want to talk to him?" Roy asked, masking his surprise with a tone of professional curiosity.

Roy could practically hear Ira Hand rolling his eyes. "Very funny, detective. How soon can someone from the Santa Rosa Police Department be up here, or should I call them directly?"

"Let me make a call and get back to you, Mr. Hand," Roy said.

"Thanks so much, detective. And one other thing."

"What's that?"

"I think we both agree there is no need to harass or disturb my client any longer by following him at all hours of the night or day. We're cooperating with you. No need for a heavy hand," the lawyer said in a firm and condescending tone.

"Ironic," said Roy, amused.

"What's that?"

"I think we both agree there's irony in someone named Hand coming on heavily demanding no heavy hand," Roy said evenly. "Maybe your client should think better of his own harassing, disturbing, and following at all hours of the night or day."

"I don't get your meaning on that last."

"Check with your client. Tell him I appreciate how he comes to a full and complete stop and looks both ways at a stop sign, especially in the dead of night. Meritorious driving."

Roy hung up and redialed Jake Stern.

"Addendum to my addendum. How soon could you be in Sisson?"

♦

Jake Stern sat in his LT's office.

"We've got no probable cause worth a shit to arrest. On the other hand, we can hope to pin him to a story. He'll have his lawyer with him, so I'm not really hopeful he's going to confess to murdering

Wilson, not unless this criminal defense attorney has suddenly grown a conscience," Stern pointed out.

"Should you take someone with you, or will this Roy Church be in the interview with you?" asked the lieutenant.

"Church will be there. Three would be a crowd. It'll be recorded."

"Okay then. Safe travels and have a great New Year's Eve!" said the lieutenant. "Secretary has got your reservations all set up there? You staying in a trailer park or a hippie commune?"

"Ha, really. No, it's someplace called the Black Tail Inn. Venison steak or burgers next door at the Black Tail Diner. I'll bring a doggie bag. Church says they got something called Doe Tacos for Under a Buck, sounds obscene."

"You can't make this shit up," the LT laughed.

♦

"Mr. Hand? Hello, yeah, heavy handed Roy Church here. Can you have your client at the Sheriff's Substation in Sisson by 1500 today? Great. Yes, it will be recorded."

♦

"Mr. Stock? Yes, Ira Hand. Okay, interview set for 3 p.m. today at Sheriff's office in Sisson. Listen, you'll not be under oath, but you must be truthful in your answers. Only answer those questions you feel comfortable with. Cops love to trick a person into answering the same question a different way. I will object if I don't like the question. You'll have the opportunity to discuss privately with me before any answer."

"I'll see you there," came the deep, calm voice over the line.

"Oh, and Mr. Stock, another thing. Detective Church is the cryptic sort. Thanked you for stopping properly at a stop sign in the middle of the night. What's that all about?"

♦

"Read about you in the paper this morning," Kat said accusingly as she sat at her desk across from Roy. She crossed her arms.

He glanced up at her from his desk. "Never believe everything you read or hear in the media. Their business is to sell advertising, not the truth," Roy reminded her, smiling. He took a sip of coffee and then swiveled in his chair to face her.

"Yeah, right. You worked on some incredible cases. I saw mention of the Desert Dump murders," she continued in an incredulous and awed tone.

Roy shrugged. "Name had a ring to it."

"A professor actually mentioned them in one of my classes this past semester. I had no idea. That is so awesome."

"We got lucky." Roy remained taciturn about his involvement.

"I mean, that is the sort of case I hope to work on someday, uncovering bones, processing them for trauma, helping to determine the cause of death."

"Be careful what you wish for. It's all fun and games until someone loses an eye."

Or loses a family.

Kat ignored his warning and unfolded her arms. "Was there one thing that broke that case? I mean it wasn't all that different than our Puma Creek Trail case, was it?"

"Let's hope they're nothing alike. We really don't want something like that here. We didn't find all the bodies, probably never will in my lifetime."

"It was two guys together from what I read," said Kat, probing for more information.

Roy could see that she wasn't going to give up easily. "Yes, Mitchell Braddock and Sean Bates, two monsters, attached at the hip for decades. Grew up together in Gorman, a burg on the I-5 Grapevine just north of LA, before you get over the mountains to Bakersfield in the Central Valley."

Kat was fascinated. "Wikipedia says they were into drugs."

Roy nodded. "Speed freaks killing mostly other speed freaks and dumping them in shallow, desert graves all over LA and Kern Counties. One or two in San Bernardino County. Several out of state murders. Might have gone unsolved if one hadn't turned on the other."

"Serial killers?" Kat asked, cupping one hand under the right side of her face and staring at Roy.

"Not the classic serial killer you see in the movies. They killed for thrills, profit, boredom, out of sheer meanness, and to stay out of jail. No witness, no crime. That was their motto."

"They'd pick up a hitchhiker, rob him, kill him, bury him, and move on. Somebody in a bar piss them off, they'd take them for a ride, kill him or her, then pull out a shovel. Somebody fail to pay a drug debt. No second chances. Shovel time. Shoot, stab, strangle, bludgeon. No favorite way." Roy clicked his pen slowly a few times, remembering the case.

"Incredible," Kat breathed in a combination of awe and horror.

"Incredible because they scared the hell out of everyone they dealt with. No one came forward for years, even those who suspected that the disappearance of a friend or fellow drug addict or prostitute lay at the hands of these two."

Kat sat for a moment processing the events that Roy was describing. She could think of nothing else to utter than, "Unbelievable."

Roy smiled a little, but it didn't reach his eyes. "Yeah, to be honest, I didn't really believe Bates when he told on Braddock and how the two of them had killed scores of victims over the years. Wasn't until he led us to several clandestine graves that it started to sink in."

Kat, continuing to be nosy, remarked, "I don't mean to be nosy, but why did Bates turn on Braddock?"

"Simple. My partner and I made a capital case on Bates while he was in the pen for a horrific attack on a different victim outside a bar. The victim, suspecting, but not really knowing for sure, had called him Norman, as if he'd never heard *that* before. Apparently a sensitive area, since lord knows, he resembled the real Norman Bates in no way. Yeah, right." Roy rolled his dark green eyes exaggeratedly.

"No sense of humor I take it." Kat smiled and shook her head.

"Once he was in custody, a barfly felt safe enough to put a bug in our ear over her missing boyfriend who'd last been seen with Bates as they headed off to do a deal. Bates robbed and killed the drug dealer. Whole thing went down in Santa Clarita, where the Magic Mountain amusement park is. Tortured him horribly. I won't go into the details. It was bad enough the jury found him guilty of first degree murder, torture, robbery, et cetera. A judge with a conscience recognized a rabid dog and ordered he be put down. He didn't want to go alone." Roy rocked back, forgetting momentarily that that was a very uncomfortable position to be in while sitting in his desk chair.

"Braddock was with him when he killed the drug dealer?" Kat asked, not noticing the wince Roy gave as he sat up again.

Roy rubbed his lower back. "Yes, according to Bates, but we had no evidence on Braddock, and a co-defendant's word alone is never enough PC to arrest, let alone convict."

"I don't understand," replied Kat as she furrowed her brow.

"Well, we couldn't nail Braddock for the drug dealer murder, but we asked Bates if there were any other crimes we could independently attribute to Braddock. That's when he said, 'Better get a Snickers, you're gonna be here a while.' He wasn't kidding."

Kat let out a bark of surprised laughter. "Oh my God."

"No God where those two prowled. Meth heads exist in a hell on this earth. The most difficult task in that case was finding straight or clean family members who cared that we'd found the remains of a son, daughter, sister, or brother who'd been cut loose years earlier."

"That's terrible," said Kat sadly, all trace of amusement vanished.

"Maybe, but understandable. A meth addict steals first from a store, then his or her friends and family–everything not nailed down."

"I've heard the drug destroys families, I mean all drugs hurt families but meth especially," Kat said.

"Modern tragedy. Parents have to lock up a house to keep these scrawny, toothless thieves away who've now become soulless and resemble nothing of the child they brought into this world. When these zombies disappear, they stop torturing their families who find relief instead of anxiety that they've not heard from their once beloved child."

"Perfect victims, like you said," Kat sighed.

"World's full of perfect victims. And you want to dig up their bones." Roy chuckled, pointing at her.

"Preferably just bones. Sooo pleasant when we deal with skeletal remains that still have flesh attached and smell nasty," Kat replied sardonically.

"Appetizing. Mouthwatering in fact," Roy wrinkled his nose, grinning.

"We put them in a tank with beetles. The skin beetles, or dermestids, clean the flesh off and leave us with just the bone to examine. They're really cool! They won't eat anything living, so they can climb all over you and you're safe. But once you start decomposing...." She left the implications unspoken.

Roy shuddered a little. Not his cup of tea. "Desert is full of little critters that clean bones, scatter them to hell and gone, too."

Roy's cell rang. Jake Stern.

"Northbound as we speak," Stern said. "No snow forecast, right? My wife is scared to death she's seen the last of me."

"You're good, as long as you brought long underwear...and a big stick."

"Big stick?" He sounded confused.

Roy grinned. "Yep, Sasquatch mating season is just around the corner."

Roy hung up after making sure Stern had directions. He turned to Kat.

"Hate to do this to you, but we'll need you to stay away from the sub this afternoon."

"I understand," said Kat, picking her small leather purse up off the floor and repacking her notebook into it.

"Cedar Stock requested the meeting. Not sure yet who we're dealing with or how dangerous. Plus, his attorney would object, I'm sure."

Kat smiled and waved her hands, "Seriously, it's no problem."

"At this point we may be dealing simply with small town coincidence, your having met this guy. On the other hand, the Stock family seems to have hopped up front and center in two, maybe three homicide investigations, if we count Dina Morgan. Too much handwriting on the wall for me."

Kat nodded seriously. "I agree completely. Is it odd for a suspect in a case to want to be interviewed?"

"Yes and no. Most suspects want to stay as far away from the cops as possible. They dread the phone call, the knock on the door, or the card left asking for contact. Some come forward because they can't take the tension and want to get it over with so they can eat again. Others, the ones who consider themselves brilliant, revel in the police interview, love the give and take. They fancy themselves modern day Professor Moriartys."

"That's funny. Paul, my stepdad, called you Sherlock Holmes this morning when he was reading about you," Kat said.

"Far from it, but my old partner Charlie Criss and I together could imitate a pretty fair Dr. Watson, or at least Inspector Clouseau."

Kat rolled her eyes a little at Roy's predictably humble response. "So you'll interview Cedar Stock here?" she asked.

"Yes, let me introduce you to our interview room."

Roy then showed Kat yet another converted bedroom that had been fashioned, using Department of Justice grant money, with a table, chairs, carpeted, nearly soundproof walls, and a camera recording system. An alcove outside the room housed a monitor with earphone jacks so outsiders could listen in on the conversation.

"If this were a common interview, I'd let you listen in and watch on the monitor."

"Well, looks as if I win," laughed Kat. "Notice how cold, bright, and prime for snowboarding it is out there? You know where I'll be this afternoon!"

♦

Roy stood on the steps of the sub and watched Jake Stern carefully step out of his white Ford Explorer with its glassy wax job and flatlander tires. Stern wore a black wind breaker and casual shirt and pants over tan mid-cut hiking boots. Perfect look for the city cop visiting the snow country readying to interview a murder suspect. He had his arms spread a little away from his sides, concentrating hard on not losing his balance on any ice.

He glanced up and saw Roy. "Hey, man, whassup? This is freaking gorgeous up here. You get to look at that mountain all day? There can't be any crime," Stern called out, his left boot sliding a few centimeters on a rogue patch of ice.

"Yeah, it's a crime for me to take a paycheck," Roy agreed as he stepped down to shake Stern's hand. "Long time no see."

"Don't gimme that shit. You don't remember me from your class," Stern grinned good-naturedly. Roy was reminded briefly of a golden retriever.

His deep green eyes twinkled as he answered, "Sure I do. Remediation always sticks in the instructor's mind."

After Roy had given Stern a quick tour of the sub they got down to business.

"How do you want to play this?" Stern asked.

"Well, the attorney is going to do what he's going to do, so that might dictate how long or short this thing goes. Your case is the focal point, so you should take lead. I'll sit back, take notes, and only jump in if you give me the nod," Roy said.

Roy thought about mentioning the previous night's encounter with Cedar Stock, but then once again thought better of it. Keep it all conventional for now.

"I'll hop into plain clothes for the interview. In all seriousness, I'm just a uniformed deputy up here who's been thrust into the spotlight by a sheriff who is desperate for votes," Roy chuckled, running a weathered hand over his short, grey hair.

Stern cocked an eyebrow. "So I've noticed. Where's your intern, the one who knows this Jersey Stock gal?"

"I sent her off. Don't want her anywhere around when Stock shows up. Keep her clean for now."

"Good call. Alrighty then, do I have time to grab a bite and see if I can get an early check-in?" Stern asked.

"Give it a shot, and I'll run home to change," Roy said.

♦

Roy examined himself in his bedroom mirror. He hadn't planned on dressing for detectives ever again. But there he was, not LASD compliant, for he had no sport coat and tie. On the other hand, this was 4X4 country. A coat and tie would look suspicious. He stood there, feeling comfortable, ready to invade personal space, again, if need be.

In uniform the object was to never get within a suspect's kill zone, maintain the bladed stance, gun side back. In detectives, all that caution went in the wind. Move your chair right up, knee to knee and beyond, all cultural barriers of distance cast aside. He'd had suspects break down and slobber on his double knits while they gushed on about smothering a baby. Them bawling, him stroking their hair and rubbing their shoulders, whispering to them it would be all right, and that they'd done the right thing, that their conscience would now be clear. He'd done this knowing they were now super-fucked, destined to share tears with a cellie for years, or cry alone while locked in a protective unit, unable to share the yard with those only too eager to tear them apart. Prison didn't go well for child killers.

He smiled inwardly. Cedar Stock, thus far, hadn't struck him as a get-in-close kinda guy, unless there were blades or ropes involved.

As he started from the room, he glanced fearfully over at the smiling photos on his bedside, the illumination in his life he depended on, like light from distant stars that had burned out long ago. He'd left the suit and tie behind because of them. Was this a betrayal of their memories? Would they really judge him harshly for moving on, trying to do right by those still living? Would they forgive him even though he'd never forgiven himself?

Get your shit together. You're a big boy, and you made your choices.

♦

1445 hours. Ira Hand arrived first in his dark blue all-wheel drive Subaru. He shook the hands of both detectives after entering the sub.

"I trust we'll all abide by the ground rules. Cedar wants to clear up some misconceptions and assumptions. I've cautioned him against getting ahead of himself, but he is strong-willed and sure of himself. I will object if I believe either of you has strayed beyond the scope of this interview."

"Well, we're in the dark as to the scope of the interview, since you contacted us telling us he wants to talk…about something," replied Stern. "My belief is that we should wait to see what he has to say before defining the exact scope."

"Fair enough," said Ira Hand. "Anything to add Detective Church?"

Would it do any good to correct detective to deputy?

"Not really, I'm just here to provide a venue for the meeting, although I'm curious as to what your client has to say and why he has to say it."

Roy glanced out the window and saw the now familiar jet-black GMC pick-up turn in and park next to the blue Subaru. Hot blood pulsated through his face as he fought back the adrenalin. He watched Cedar Stock, all 6-2, 235 tattooed pounds of him, nonchalantly stroll across the icy lot, as if he were contemplating which toppings he'd order once he got inside, pepperoni or Hawaiian.

The door opened. Cedar Stock stepped through, saw Ira Hand and smiled, revealing even, white teeth.

"Mr. Hand, thanks for helping set this up. I take it one of these gentlemen is from Santa Rosa?" he said looking back and forth at Roy and Stern.

♦

Stern and Roy sat watching the HD 1080-p version of what had transpired over the past two hours.

"We'll get this transcribed. I think we'll both be scouring it for a minute. Dangerous dude," said Stern, wearily rubbing his face with his hands.

"Dangerous dude," echoed Roy. "Figures all the angles ahead of time."

"Has he actually re-invented the wheel?" Stern asked.

"Nah. Can't improve on the wheel," Roy replied. But even as he said it, he wasn't as sure as he'd like to be.

CHAPTER 34

Transcription Services of Sonoma County

JS: Jacob Stern, detective
DC: Delroy Church, detective
IH: Ira Hall, attorney
CS: Cedar Stock, witness/client

JS: This is Detective Jacob Stern of the Santa Rosa Police Department. The date is December 31, 2018. The time is 1515 hours. This recorded interview is taking place at the Karuk County Sheriff's Department's Sisson Substation. Also present are Detective Delroy Church of the Karuk County Sheriff's Department, Attorney Ira Hand, and his client Cedar Stock.

IH: Gentlemen, before we start, I'd like to highlight the fact that Mr. Cedar Stock approached me and asked that I facilitate this meeting so that he might provide information that could be of use to the Santa Rosa Police Department in its investigation of the death of a Jesse Dale Wilson. I will have a standing objection to any questions that do not pertain to this subject. Mr. Stock is not under arrest and is not being detained. If I feel he should consult with me before answering any questions, I will interrupt.

JS: This is a completely voluntary interview. Mr. Cedar Stock is not under arrest and is free to get up and leave at any time. He has requested this meeting. Since he is not being detained, and since he has his attorney present, I think all here would agree that Miranda rights do not apply. Detective Church do you have anything to add?"

DC: No. I think we should just start by letting Mr. Stock tell us the reasons for requesting this meeting.

CS: Well, here goes. Me and the law haven't always seen eye to eye. You all know that. I've been to the pen twice. I've made mistakes. But I read the paper and seen how Pud killed himself and how you all were looking for someone who was with him before he done it. That was me. In my world talkin' to the cops ain't a good thing. But here I am, to clear it up. So if you got questions, I'll try to answer them.

IH: Again, I'll object when I see fit.

JS: Thank you Mr. Stock, Do I call you Mr. Stock, Cedar, what do you prefer?

CS: Cedar's fine. I seen you before somewhere.

JS: Well, Cedar, that'd be a good one since I've never been to Karuk County. Guess I got one of those faces.

CS: No not here. Somewhere else. Sorry, go ahead with your questions.

JS: If it's okay with Mr. Hand, can you tell us the nature of your relationship with Jesse Dale Wilson?

IH: I have no objection at this time, although relationship is very broad and vague.

CS: Funny, I never knew Pud's middle name was Dale 'til I seen it in the paper.

JS: Okay, instead of relationship, how about telling us how it is that you know Jesse Dale Wilson. Or should we call him Pud? Would that make it easier for everyone if we use the name Cedar here is comfortable with? Where did he get the name Pud anyhow? If you don't mind me asking.

CS: (laughs) This is recorded, right? Don't know if I should say. Aw hell. When we was kids we used to stay overnight, a bunch us. Ol' Jesse was always beatin' his pud, you know, his wang, so we started calling him that. It sorta stuck.
(Laughter)

JS: Alrighty then, moving along. Maybe we better say Jesse. How is it you know Jesse? I gather you grew up together.

CS: Yep, right here in Sisson. Went to school together up until Pud, uh, Jesse, had to go to the other school, that one you go to when you can't get into high school. He had trouble learning, so he never did good in school. He never graduated from nothin' I don't think. But we ran together when we was kids, fished, swam at the lake, hiked, played a lot of ball, mostly baseball. Pud could handle a bat, and he could field a grounder. Later he couldn't play 'cause his grades sucked. That was hard on him. I gotta be honest. We smoked a little weed together and drank beer, lots of beer. In fact, first time I ever got busted it was with Pud when we stole some beer.
(Laughter)

JS: When is the last time you saw Pud?

CS: Shit, you know when. I left him all drunk and pissed off, probably right where you all found him. Where he was working, framing a house there in Santa Rosa. The one he was helping rebuild that burned in that big fire.

JS: Can you tell us the circumstances that brought you to that time and location with Jesse?

CS: Sure. It gets sorta sticky and a whole lotta my bad. But I was trying to right a wrong, and I guess it backfired.

JS: Okay.

CS: Shit. Well, here goes. Look, you're Detective Church. I know you're in charge of that investigation on that skeleton they found on Puma Creek Trail. I read that in the paper. Well, it's pretty simple. It's gotta be Dina, and it's gotta be Pud dumped her there, and I was trying to get him to admit it. I guess I fucked up.

JS: Okay, Cedar, can you slow down and go over that again, sorta one piece at a time?

CS: Yeah, sorry. I went down to see Pud about that body on Puma Creek Trail. Yeah, I went down there to work, too, but I, I seen my chance to make him do the right thing about killin' Dina, and that's why I took some articles from the paper to read to him and show him to see if he'd have a conscience about what he done to her.

JS: Let me interrupt you Cedar, if I may. When you say Dina, who are you talking about?

CS: Dina Morgan. Pud's girlfriend. He killed her and dumped her body up on Puma Ridge. They got in a fight and she jumped outta his truck over at the lake, and he got pissed and I think he run her over or beat her to death or something, and then he got rid of her up there.

JS: And when did this happen, this murder of this girl Dina by Jesse Wilson?

CS: Well, it had to be when they said, back in 2004.

JS: And you know all this how?

CS: Pud said as much.

JS: Jesse Wilson told you he killed a girl named Dina Morgan and took her body to some place called Puma Ridge?

CS: That's what he said. I mean not in them exact words, but it was pretty close to that.

JS: So Cedar, if you knew all this, is there a reason you never came forward with the information?

CS: Shit, you didn't just ask that did you? Seriously? You just don't tell. Not if you're in my life. You ever seen what happens to a rat in the joint?

JS: Okay, I get that, but you're telling us now and you tried to get Jesse to admit it. So what changed?

CS: I'm older. I've paid for my mistakes. I don't never intend to go back to prison, ever. I just want to live a good life for as many years as I got left. Plus, Dina was my friend, too. She deserved justice, and Pud needed to man up and admit what he done, so we could all have closure, especially her old man Lonnie. He was a good dude back in the day. He don't deserve the heartache Pud caused him.

JS: I hear that. Okay then, getting back to Jesse in Santa Rosa. Can you tell us how your meeting with him went? I take it there were some rough spots. You said he got mad.

CS: Yeah. Let me run it down for you. Pud goes to Santa Rosa to help build houses after the big fire. He calls me and says there's lots of work, and I could get on where he's working. So I agree. In the meantime there's all this stuff in the paper about Dina's bones being found on Puma Creek Trail, so I think why don't I do the right thing for once in my life. I mean my mom was pretty upset over the Dina murder back when it happened, and then she had to see it again in the paper, and it dredged up all them bad memories.

JS: Hmm.

CS: So I figure I'll go down and meet with Pud and show him the paper and tell him I've been nursing a mad-on over it myself, and if he admits that it was all a heat of anger thing then he might just get a voluntary or a second degree at best. He ain't gonna do much time. He's never been to the joint, so he'd do easy time in a level one or two, maybe in Avenal or CMC or even Vacaville. If he got lucky he gets Susanville. Not High Desert, but maybe a fire crew or some shit.

JS: Okay, so how did Jesse take your suggestions to man up and admit what he'd done?

CS: He wasn't happy. Surprised me, actually. I figured he'd be all ate up over his conscience bothering him and shit. I mean, he's a bad dude, but he ain't a hard dude. Drugs and gafflin' shit that ain't his, maybe some fights, but nothin' hard.

JS: So where were you when you had this conversation with Jesse, about coming forward, I mean.

CS: Well, we was in a coupla places. A bar for a while. I just sorta hinted about it then. Didn't wanna scare him off by coming on too strong. Then we went up to where he worked. He wanted to show me where the job was and how he was sure we'd be working there together.

JS: Okay.

CS: So we had a lot to drink. I figured that might get him more used to the idea. Heck, I was even gonna record him admitting to killing Dina, but then I remember that shit's illegal.

JS: Okay, then what happened?

CS: Well, like I said, I got him sorta drunk. I told him that I'd have a real hard time working with him knowing all the time that he'd killed my friend Dina, and that I just thought now, this many years after, was the right time for him to clear his conscience and man up.

JS: What was his reaction?

CS: Well, he got all emotional and started crying like a little bitch about Dina and how he missed her. And I told him I missed her too. And then he started saying how sorry he was. Shit, I shoulda recorded that. But I didn't want to get in trouble.

JS: Hmm. And the newspaper articles?

CS: Right. That's when I took out the newspaper pieces I'd brought, and I turned my flashlight on and read them to him about how everyone knew Dina had been found and that it wasn't going away and that he should get ahead of the bullshit and walk in and admit what he done. It would go better for him if he did, you know, admit his mistake in killing her.

JS: Yes, there's a certain logic there. Then what happened?

CS: Well, then he got all depressed and angry and saying he should just solve the whole mess by ending it all for himself, and that way he'd be square with the Lord and shit.

JS: Those were his words?

CS: Well, he said Lord, but I guess he didn't say shit. That's just me telling the story. Any way to edit that comment off the tape?

JS: No worries. It sounds as though it was a very emotional conversation.

CS: Yeah, emotional. And real. Raw you might say. The two of us breakin' down barriers and barin' our souls and shit.

JS: It happens. Then what?

CS: Well, then he got even more depressed, but also started gettin' kinda angry at me for bringing it up, and I thought he might be violent, so I started thinkin' about getting out of there.

JS: Did you fear for your safety? You're a pretty big guy.

CS: That's just it. I'm a big guy, a big guy with a record. Like anyone is going to believe me if I had to whup his ass. So I decide to take the high road. I decide to leave and let him think about it. But I told him when I left that we could no longer be friends unless he did the right thing and gave Dina justice. I just walked away and left him cryin'. I know that was probably the wrong thing to do. I never dreamed he'd kill himself, but I guess he decided to save us all the trouble and cost of a trial. Man, I know that sounds hella cold, but it's the truth.

JS: So you left him there? Where did you go?

CS: I just walked back down the hill to the bar where I'd left my truck.

JS: How far did you walk?

CS: It's like a coupla miles. Froze my azz. But I wasn't goin' back. So that's pretty much my story. I left and came home and then read that Jesse had hung himself. Wasn't surprised the way he was blubberin' when I left him. I ain't in trouble for leavin' him like that am I?

JS: No, you're not in trouble for leaving him like that.

IH: So gentleman, I think that is about that. Mr. Stock, Cedar, is pretty plain in that he was trying to get justice for his presumed-to-have-been-murdered friend by getting the culprit to confess. A bit unconventional, perhaps, but I believe Cedar committed no crimes and in fact was trying to do the right thing, even if he was not successful. He should be commended.

JS: Hmm. Do you mind if I get some clarification in a few areas, Mr. Hand?

IH: As long as we stay within the ground rules and keep it limited to the subject matter previously discussed.

JS: Right. Cedar, can you tell me whose phone you used to communicate with Jesse Wilson about coming down to Santa Rosa for a job?

IH: I'm going to object. Relevance?

JS: Is Cedar willing to answer that or not?

IH: Give me a second will you. Cedar could you step out in the hall?

IH: Okay, I've consulted with my client and he is prepared to answer that question. Cedar?

CS: I used my mom's phone mostly. Germaine Stock. Or Jersey. Most people call her Jersey. I take care of her. She's old and weak and lives alone, so I stay there and care for her a lot. I bought the phone for her, so I use it all the time. Is there a problem with that?

JS: No, no problem. Was just curious since we did a search of Jesse's phone records to see who he called or received calls from. Saw your mom's phone on there.

CS: Yeah, well, see. Like I told you. No mystery right?

JS: No mystery. Just a little detail to clear up for my report. My boss would ask me, and if I didn't ask, then I'm not doing my job thoroughly. I've got a few more minor details like that I'd like to ask you if Mr. Hand doesn't mind.

CS: Ask away. I got nothing to hide.

IH: One question at a time, Cedar. Take your time answering.

CS: Of course.

JS: So when you went to Santa Rosa, where did you first run into Jesse Wilson?

CS: It was at a little bar. Crowded spot on some street in Santa Rosa.

JS: How long did you spend there?

CS: Couple hours, maybe. Drinkin' beers.

JS: How many beers would you say?

CS: Oh, you know a pitcher or two, or three (laughs).

JS: Would you say Jesse was drunk?

CS: Oh hell, yeah. He was lit. I mean not so's he couldn't walk or nothin'. But there's no way I was gonna let him drive. Wouldn't have been safe. I drove when we went to the construction site.

JS: Whose car did you drive in?

CS: His truck.

JS: Why not take yours if he was too drunk to drive his?

CS: That's a good question. Wish I had taken mine. Wouldn't of had to walk so damn far to get back to it. I don't know. Jesse had his keys out, and I just sorta took them from him. I felt it would keep him safer if he didn't have keys to drive with.

IH: Again, commendable, Cedar.

JS: Yes, commendable. Your truck. The one you have outside? That one?

CS: Yep. That's my beauty.

JS: Let's see. Just a few more questions.

IH: Let's make sure of that, shall we, Detective Stern?

JS: Do my best. So Cedar, when you walked away from Jesse, he was at the construction site. Can you describe where at the construction site?

CS: Sure. We was in a big old room on the first floor of the house. All framed in practically, from what I could tell in the dark.

JS: So if you read that Jesse hanged himself, did you notice any rope around anywhere?

CS: What? You mean like the rope I bought for him? Yeah, there was rope. It was like a nylon rope. I bought it and some other shit he told me to bring for the job. He was gonna pay me back but never did.

JS: Jesse asked you to buy rope?

CS: Yep. He asked me pick up some rope and a come-along. Was going to pay me for them. But I got stiffed on that deal looks like.

JS: Why would Jesse ask you to buy a come-along and rope?

CS: You ever work construction? Lookin' at your hands I'd guess not, or you'd know. Hell, you use a come-along for all kinds of shit on the job. You pull together joints, straighten heavy panels while you adjust them. Even use it like a winch to pull together framing while you raise it and nail it.

JS: So you bought and then left a rope and come-along with Jesse?

CS: Yeah, I left the rope. But I sure as shit didn't leave the come-along. I took that with me. It was expensive.

JS: You took the come-along with you? Do you still have it?

CS: Naw. Look, I started down the street and got to thinking. Here I am, a con carrying a new come-along out of a construction site. What does that look like to you? Shit, cops would figure I stole it. Like they're really gonna believe a guy with a record. Doesn't matter that I did my time. They're gonna hem me up for theft. Fuck that. Oops, sorry for the language. So I tossed the come-along in a side yard. Took a loss all the way around. Wasted trip to Santa Rosa. Whole place left a bad taste in my mouth. Shoulda minded my own damn business.

IH: Hey, your motives were pure, Cedar. Your heart was in the right spot. Sometimes no good deed goes unpunished.

JS: That's for sure. So what were you guys drinking all night?

CS: Beer…oh, and Jack of course. That was our favorite. I stopped and grabbed a bottle to help remind Pud of the old days. Now we didn't do no drugs. Pud got into the crank scene for a while. No good for him or Dina. But he was trying to stay clean for his job. I felt sorta bad plyin' him with liquor knowing he'd be sick as hell the next day for work.

JS: So beer, you said a few pitchers, and some Jack, Jack Daniels?

CS: Yep, was our go to drink back in the day.

JS: You said Jesse was pretty drunk. Too drunk to drive?

CS: Yeah. Like I said.

JS: But not too drunk to stand on a bucket and tie a rope with a noose?

CS: Guess not.

IH: I object to that last question detective. Sounds as if you're implying wrongdoing on my client's part.

JS: Oh, not at all. Just trying to see how a guy too drunk to drive with beer and hard liquor in his system could manage the intricate knot and laid out scene that we found. Very hard to imagine.

IH: What was his toxicity level?

JS: Don't know yet. That hasn't been determined. I'd wager it's going to come back fairly high based on what Cedar is telling me.

IH: Well, detective, surely you know of functioning alcoholics. It sounds as if Mr. Wilson had built up quite the tolerance over the years, and he probably could function in conditions that the rest of us, well, I speak for myself, could not. Please discontinue the innuendo or I'll advise my client to cease cooperating with you.

JS: Understood, and I appreciate the criticism Mr. Hand. So Cedar, did you ever go to Jesse's home?

CS: No.

JS: No, never?

CS: You mean his home in Santa Rosa? Don't think he had a house home. He was living in a garage from what he told me. I drove by but never went into his home if you can call it that.

JS: Do you recall when you might have driven past his garage home?

IH: Why is this relevant?

JS: Can your client answer that question? Just trying to establish if he had any other contact with Jesse Wilson where Wilson expressed a dislike for living.

CS: Maybe that day or the next to see if Pud was home. I don't really recall now.

JS: Can you think of a reason why a truck matching your truck's description would stop in front of Jesse's garage home?

CS: I just told you, I drove by his place. Why, someone call in a suspicious person? Yeah, I get that a lot. Goes with the tats I guess. I'm used to it.

IH: Yes, detective I think he told you he went by his friend's place to see if he was there.

JS: Just checking, just checking. Covering bases. I'm almost through.

IH: I'll believe that to be true when I see it.

JS: But Cedar, the truck you drove up in had different plates on it than the one I see out there in the lot. Can you explain that?

IH: Excuse me, detective. Don't answer that, Cedar. Detective Stern what are you trying to say?

JS: I'm not trying to say anything, just that your client's truck may have had different plates on it when it was in front of Jesse's home. A neighbor copied the plates and called it in. The plates had been stolen the night before from a local Costco lot.

IH: And this neighbor has positively identified my client, and he is sure about the plate number? Will he swear that he got the number right? Because I can tell you, eyewitnesses, especially when it comes to license plates, are notoriously inaccurate. I'm requesting that you withdraw the question, and I prefer that Cedar not even address it.

CS: Right. Don't know what to say. I already told you I drove down the street. Your neighborhood watch dude just got the wrong plate is all. Told you I got nothing to hide.

JS: Except maybe your face? Can you view these two photographs, if it's okay with your attorney? The first photograph is from inside a liquor store on Mendocino Avenue, the night that you and Jesse drove to the construction site.

CS: Hey, yeah, that's me. (Laughs). That raghead, sorry, that Middle Eastern dude, thought I was gonna rob him. I get that a lot, too. Tats you know. I bought some Jack. I paid cash for it. Didn't even steal it like I would have back in my crazy days.

JS: Okay. And this photo, taken the same date, only earlier in the day at Friedman's Hardware Store.

CS: Sure, that's me buying the rope and come-along Pud told me to get. So what? You wondering why I'm wearing my hoodie up? Look at the tats on my neck and head. That's why. Get tired of people staring at me, thinking bad things about me, like I'm a violent Nazi or some shit.

IH: All reasonable explanations, Detective Stern. Are we done fishing here? I'm going to advise my client to discontinue this interview. I believe we've given you enough cooperation, and it seems you're reaching for a way to twist facts to justify some negative connotation to what I see as my client's admirable attempt at securing justice for an unfortunate murder victim.

CS: I mean think about it. Friedman's? That's a Jew name, and I got freakin' thunderbolts-

IH: Cedar, it's okay.

CS: -on my neck. You oughta know better than that Detective Stern, as in Howard. Hmm?

IH: Cedar, it's all right. Perfectly understandable. Let's not get personal-

CS: Go to temple do you? Wear one of them little hats? I don't hate Jews. Hell, I don't even know any, well you, and you seem decent, but in the joint, when you're a wood, you gotta play the game or make sure you got your lube, 'cause you in for a worlda hurt.

JS: I apologize if you think I've been a little rough on your client, but a suspicious death requires that the investigator probe in uncomfortable areas sometimes. No offense intended. I don't know if Detective Church has any questions. I hope mine have not precluded him from asking a few if he has any.

IH: Is Detective Church working for the Santa Rosa Police Department on the Wilson death investigation? If not, then I object to his asking any questions. The reason my client is here is for the Wilson matter, nothing else.

DC: I am involved in the Wilson death investigation, since it ties into the investigation I'm conducting of the Puma Creek Trail case. It seems to be the driving reason behind a suggested suicide, per your client. If your client doesn't mind, I was hoping he could help me on that, since he seems to have information that might solve the case for us. Now being a good citizen and all, I think that would be reasonable.

CS: I don't mind.

IH: I'm on the record advising against it. Mr. Stock you do understand that as your attorney I am advising you to end this interview now.

CS: Can we see what the questions are though first? Don't have to answer them.

IH: Okay, in that case, Mr. Stock is taking his own counsel, and I'll remain quiet with a standing objection to any more questions.

DC: Understood. Cedar, if you can recall, what words, precisely, did

Jesse Wilson use that made you believe he had killed Dina Marie Morgan?

CS: That's easy. He told me he had to get rid of Dina.

DC: Those were his words? I had to get rid of Dina?

CS: Something like that. Didn't leave any question in my mind.

DC: And when did he tell you this?

CS: Right after he done it, like a few days I mean, while they were all out looking for her.

DC: Where were the two of you when he told you this?

CS: We were kickin' it at his house.

DC: His house? Street? Address?

CS: Well, it was actually his mom's house where he stayed. He moved around a lot, but usually stayed with Lydia between paychecks.

DC: You went to visit him at his mom's house?

CS: Yeah, see I just barely got out and heard Dina was missing. I knew immediately it had to be Pud, so I went to see him, and that's when he told me.

DC: You'd just gotten out? State pen? Where'd you do your time?

CS: Where didn't I do my time?

IH: Does it do me any good to continually object to these questions?

CS: I don't see no harm. All in my C-file where I done time. Quentin, New Folsom, DVI, The Bay. Moved around a bit. Yard goes off, fools die, and everybody gets shuffled.

DC: So Jesse Wilson told you he got rid of Dina Marie Morgan. Did he say why?

CS: Not really. Made it sound like it was an accident or something. Said they were arguing in his truck, and she jumped out, and he accidentally run her over or some shit. Panicked I guess and took her up on Puma Ridge and buried her. He might have beat her, too. Maybe he just said it was an accident 'cause he could see I was real pissed over it.

DC: You were angry? Why?

CS: Dina Morgan was my friend, too. We all grew up together. She and Pud were a little younger than me, but still she was a nice gal when she wasn't hittin' the pipe.

DC: Okay. He said he buried her on Puma Ridge?

CS: Well, he didn't give no details, but that's what I'm thinking. Makes sense. It's pretty close, a couple of miles, from where he said he done her in.

DC: You said you're friends with Dina's father, Lonnie. Did you ever tell Lonnie what Jesse told you?

CS: Aw, hell no. Lonnie and me wasn't that close. Still, he didn't deserve losing his daughter like that. Made me really tear up sometimes.

DC: Did anyone else hear Jesse confess to you? For example, his mother? You said you were at her home.

CS: Naw, just me. Look, that's about all I know. You want me to swear to what he said? All I can say is what he sorta said. It's been what? 13 years? I can't remember his exact words, but I will swear to what I just told you. Anyhow, I gotta get, 'cause I don't wanna piss off my lawyer no more. We good?

DC: Your interview. Your call.

CS: I don't know, man, it's like you two were trying to put something on me. Man, I'm just tryin' to help. To be a good witness, 'cause you know what they say?

DC: What's that?

CS: No witness, no case.

DC: I've heard that before. And sometimes it's even true.

CS: Oh, Detective Stern?

JS: Yes?

CS: I didn't mean nothin' with that Jew talk. I got nothin' against you people. I feel real sorry for all y'all in Germany and shit. That was messed up.

JS: Appreciate that. No offense taken and thank you for your sympathies.

CS: Yeah, it's fucked, I mean messed up, when you just let yourself get herded into a gas chamber without goin' off.

JS: Yes, it does make one wonder about group think, does it not?

CS: Herd mentality.

JS: Let's hope nothing like that ever happens again.

CS: Yeah, you people gotta stand up for yourselves, like you was on the yard and the BGF's trying to make a move, and you ain't goin' for that shit.

JS: Exactly.

CS: Say, you ever been to New Folsom? I mean on the yard at New Folsom? With an SSU cat named Montalvo?

JS: Why?

CS: 'Cause when them darkies hit their own, you looked like you didn't wanna be there, like you'da rather been doin' anything else, like home scrubbin' your nuts with a handful a razors or some shit. (Laughs).

CHAPTER 35

"So, does he know that we know? Or does he know that we know that he knows that we know?" Stern asked, scratching his chin.

"You ever play chess?" Roy asked, amused.

Stern looked exaggeratedly affronted. "Why, because I'm Jewish? You think all Jews play chess, like Bobby Fischer? Is that it?"

"Okay, let me put it in terms you can understand. Let's try checkers."

"I don't know how to play checkers."

"Well, if you did know chess or checkers, you'd know that he just laid out a full house, reverse end run, with nothing but net. Halftime score: Cedar Stock-one run, Jake Stern and Roy Church-Love."

"Halftime I understood. That means beer time, right?" Stern perked up.

"The Black Tail Brewery isn't set to open until July 4th. Until then, we got the lounge at the Black Tail Inn. I'm a one round kinda guy, but you're my guest, so it's on me."

"Because cow patty deputies make so much more money than us big city cops, I guess I won't fight you for it. But that means I get to pay for dinner!"

"Deal," Roy said. "Got a few phone calls to make first. Need to let my LT know how it went. I'm sure you gotta do the same."

"That's what LTs are for. Always let them know how something went. Not sure of their duties beyond that. I think my wife could be an LT," Stern chuckled.

Roy got on his cell and ran down the essence of the Cedar Stock statement to Lieutenant Gary Lynch.

"With his attorney present, there was no chance to go back over his story, but he's sharp. It was a bit humorous listening to him speak as if he's a dumb old country boy redneck."

"Where do you go from here?" Lynch asked.

"He claimed he's willing to swear in a statement to the truth of the Dina Morgan murder confession by Jesse Wilson. My money says he'll back out if asked, saying he's already given a statement, no need for any other."

"Doesn't sound as if we have hot leads in that one. Can't really spare anyone competent right now anyhow. Can you put that all in a separate report under the Dina Morgan case number?" Lynch asked.

"Absolutely. And LT, if I could…" Roy trailed off.

"What's that?"

"I'd like to go plainclothes for a bit. I'll keep the marked SUV. It's got snow tires, but it's time to soften down a notch. Cedar Stock's interview has given me some room to wiggle."

"No problem. I'll let the Sheriff know, and I'll tell Savage to get you back-filled down there for the street. How's the Santa Rosa detective? Worth a shit?"

"I won't know until the dinner check comes. Nah, he's all right. Been around a while. Funny thing, he and Cedar Stock have a history. Won't bore you with it now."

"Oh, Roy?" Lynch paused.

"Yeah?"

"Nice article today. That's all anyone up here's been talking about. Everyone wants an autograph." Roy could hear Lynch smirking on the other end of the line.

"You're killin' me, boss," Roy shook his head in exasperation, chuckling.

Roy rang off from Silverton and turned to Stern.

He eyed him for a moment. Stern was fruitlessly trying to clean some greasy fingerprints off his phone screen with the edge of his shirt. "What the heck were you doing in New Folsom when Cedar Stock saw you?"

Stern looked up, giving up on the smudges. "Fed and local task force case years ago. We were working the northern Mexican prison gangs and their counterparts on the street. I went to New Folsom to interview a dude. Black on black hit went down on the yard just as we were getting ready to walk to the unit where our witness was supposedly housed. Never got to talk to him."

"You were with Reuben Montalvo at the time? He's a CDC legend."

"Yeah. He and his Special Services guys were helping us on the street and in the pen to get at and transport our cooperators. Funny as hell that Cedar Stock saw me and remembers this many years later."

"You must have made an impression." Roy waggled his eyebrows suggestively.

"Yeah, I gotta admit I cut quite a figure on a prison yard. Glasses, full moist lips, and a gait that belongs on a models' runway."

Roy chuckled.

"So, seriously, where do you guys go from here?" he asked.

"Our Sonoma County DA won't charge. Can't blame her. Cedar is right about one thing. No witness, no case. I'm surprised he didn't bring up reasonable doubt. With what we have right now, I don't even think we could get a well hung jury."

"Agreed," said Roy. "The interview has given him a sense of victory. His lawyer is telling him how great he did. We won't ever get him in the box again, so any case or cases have to be made strictly on evidence and eyewitness testimony, and right now both categories are in short supply."

The door to the sub opened, and Deputy Tom Hanlon walked in. He grinned widely, caffeine-stained teeth on display, when he saw Roy.

"A freakin' celebrity? I had no idea! Not much for braggin', huh? Pam and I read about you this morning, and I about fell out of my chair. Hell, I work with this guy!"

Tom Hanlon shook hands with Stern while pointing at Roy.

"Lies, all lies," Roy protested.

"What? They didn't know who you were up here?" Stern asked, shaking his head.

"Wasn't my intent to make waves," Roy said.

"Hey, Pam Googled some of your cases. That Night Devil sounded like a stone-cold motherfucker!" Tom Hanlon gushed.

"Bad dude. Lotta bad dudes everywhere," Roy said, trailing off.

The other two sensed a sudden downswing in Roy's jocular mood.

"So, I got lucky tonight and pulled swings," Tom Hanlon said, changing the subject. "Can't wait for the fights between now and 0200 when the bars close. Happy New Year, boys!"

Tom Hanlon ducked out after shaking hands all around. He'd known Roy for the past 9 months, but shook his hand anyhow, a silent "Good job" rather than "Hi, how are you?"

"Good man in a back-alley beef, I'd imagine," said Stern.

"Yep. Big ol' farm boy. Stack you like a bale of hay in the back of patrol car."

"Doesn't make sense how they hire Lilliputians these days. Too much relying on tasers and back-up."

"Out here, your back-up can take half an hour or longer. Better be able to talk that long or just handle your biz," said Roy. "I'm reaching the outside limits of the physical part, so I do a lot of gum flapping. Speaking of which, gotta make one more phone call."

Roy dialed a number he'd pulled out of Sheriff's records.

Stern kicked back in a chair checking his smudgy iPhone as he listened to one side of the conversation.

"Dr. Fournette? This is Roy Church with the Karuk County Sheriff's Department. Yes, Delroy Church. Well, thank you. That was all a long time ago, and you know how the media can blow things out of proportion. Gotta sell papers I guess. Listen, sorry to bother you on New Year's Eve, but I wanted to set up a meeting if I might, for some time later this week. I was hoping you could give me some background on some folks who've come up in an investigation I'm conducting. It's the Puma Creek Trail skeletal remains, yes. Oh? Really? Are you sure? Don't you have ball games to watch like the rest of America? I don't want to impose. Just you and your wife? Well, okay. Good, my partner and I will be…wait let me check."

Roy covered the phone and turned to Stern.

"Can you hang for a while tomorrow to interview Cedar's cousin's father-in-law?"

"Hell, yeah. If it'll get me back in the saddle on this case."

"Dr. Fournette, 11 a.m. would be fine. See you then. Yes, I have your address on Volcano View Drive. Big Brother. That's right. Kinda scary. Yes, and Happy New Year to you, too!"

Roy hung up.

"Now there's a man who may be sitting on a volcano of info, and he lives on Volcano View Drive. Poetic and ironic."

"Think he'll spew forth with something to help?" asked Stern.

"Well, I can't *pumice* anything but we'll *ash* him to see what he has," Roy replied.

"I'll just sit back and watch you do your thing. Go with the flow. *Lava* and learn I always say," Stern laughed.

"We'll see if we can get this case to go from dormant to active. Right now your stomach is probably the only thing rumbling. Ready?"

"*Fissure* burgers. Which one do you recommend?"

♦

Roy followed Stern's unmarked as he drove toward the Black Tail Inn. He couldn't help thinking about Charlie Criss and how together they'd fit like a hand and glove. Though he'd only known Stern a short while, he felt a similarity in their styles. All business when it counted, yet able to switch gears from seriousness to humor. The sign of a good, intelligent cop was the ability to see the humor in the darkness while maintaining a focus on the goals. Charlemagne Criss had been a master at it. He could make Roy smile in the bleakest moments, and nearly split a gut when the coast was clear, but he was always mindful of what the job required.

The lounge at the Black Tail Inn, across the street from the Black Tail Diner, buzzed with laughter, high pitched and gruff, *auld lang syne* anticipation setting in five hours early. Roy and Stern found a table by a back wall and ordered a draft beer each.

"Whew, whole lotta people in this town ready to shitcan 2018," laughed Stern.

"Difference between here and East LA is we don't have to find a parking garage to hide in at 2400 hours. Raining lead can make for a crappy night shift," Roy commented.

A waiter who looked college-aged brought them their beers and took their orders.

"Gotta be a lot different for you up here," Stern remarked after taking a long pull from his glass.

"Not really night and day, more like night and late afternoon. Cop work is cop work. More of it in LA, but a lot more guys to handle it when the shit hits the fan. Here? Well, we still have a sewer passing by, more commonly known as the I-5. We get our share leaking down the off ramps, and we're mostly on our own when it does. Hardly ever see a supervisor. That's a plus." Roy smiled and sipped his cold drink.

Stern knowingly shook his head and sat back in his chair, looking around the restaurant with interest.

"Now, not to change the subject, from what I'm gathering, a lot of the folks you work with up here had no idea who you were until this morning's paper. Don't wanna pry, but that's some straight up Steven Segal in the 90's shit right there. What made you take a deputy job here?"

Roy sighed sadly. "No one would believe my cardboard sign on the off ramp. Had to get a job."

Stern raised a palm toward Roy.

"I get it. None of my business. A change of scenery is good sometimes. I transferred from Oakland PD to Santa Rosa back in the day. Needed fresh air."

Roy urged himself to stop, but from a distance he heard his voice disobey. He was in the box. He trusted this man whom he'd only seen in person today for the first time but had formed a bond with nonetheless over the past ten days.

"Guess I needed more than fresh air. I needed life. After the Night Devil case, the one Tom Hanlon was going on about, I had to make a change. Not when that fucker first started his run, but years later, after he'd been convicted and PC-ed up in the cell next door to Charlie Manson at Corcoran State Prison.

His name was Dylan Speaks, and he was as fucked up as they come. It's pretty much true what they said on the news. His thing was to douse his random victims with gasoline. One was at a bus stop. Unfortunately, another had his driver's window down at a red light, but the mother and her baby in a carriage in the park were the worst. While the victims were busy sputtering and going WTF, Speaks was thrusting out his lighter and, voila, screaming, human torch."

"Sounds like a motherfucker," Stern interjected with disgust.

"Exactly," Roy continued. "The paranoia in the Southland got so bad people were attacking homeless dudes carrying those fake gas cans while asking for money. Most of his attacks were at night or about dusk, so the media dubbed him the Night Devil."

"News loves a nickname," Stern nodded his head.

Roy continued, "He disappeared for a while, maybe a few months. What we didn't know is that he'd traveled back to his home state, Oklahoma. Oklahoma City cops thought they might have a copycat. They had one incident. Only one. Incredibly, they never contacted us, and we didn't hear about it. Not all detectives are created equal."

"That's no shit," Stern sighed.

"We caught up with him when a clerk at one of those off brand stations called about a weird guy filling a gas container. The East Indian RP barely spoke English. Those people normally mind their own business, keep their heads down, and work like ants, but this clerk got involved.

My partner and I were in the area already searching. We spotted Speaks as he was walking toward a bus station in Bell Gardens, just south of East Los. We called for uniformed deputies. We surrounded him. He poured gas on himself and threatened to go up in flames. If only. I stupidly negotiated with him for about 30 minutes. He finally put the lighter down.

My partner Charlie Criss and I both testified. A surviving victim testified. Her burns were something out of a war zone. Jury wasn't real happy with Speaks. Deathrow Dylan they began calling him after the trial. Of course, that meant grounds for appeal. Doesn't take much in a death penalty case for the weak sister assholes in this state to look for a way to spare a monster. Ninth Circuit judges found jury misconduct and ordered a new trial.

"DA lost his mud and made a deal. Speaks got Life Without Parole. So off he goes for his LWOP at the protective custody unit at Corcoran. For reals, he celled next to Manson for a spell." Roy took another gulp of his beer. Their food, venison burger baskets, arrived.

"Well, at least he gets to sit and stare at the walls for the rest of his life. I'm surprised the judge didn't send him to a Smokey the Bear rehab program and make him write a heartfelt apology letter of at least five hundred words," Stern said, chewing on some fries. "So that was that, huh? Sounds like you did a good job stopping him, though."

"Except a year or so later, a different Oklahoma City detective took a look at their old case and drew some basic conclusions. Speaks got extradited, and I flew back to Okie City to testify in a jurisdiction where they actually smoke their bad guys who've earned death."

Roy paused and pushed some of his fries around in the basket but didn't eat them.

"I get the feeling it didn't go well. Hey, man you don't have to lay it out if you don't want to," Stern said, hands up.

"Nah, it's okay. It's while I was back in Oklahoma that I lost my little girl, and then, later, her mother, who couldn't cope with the loss."

"Aw, damn," muttered Stern. His basket sat untouched for a while, too.

CHAPTER 36

An only child, Raisa Church, born in 1995 to Delroy and Malka Church, grew up the granddaughter of Robert and Alice Church on one side and David and Deborah Ezekiel on the other. Her renowned father regularly spurred lurid headlines as a cerebral and hard charging homicide detective for the Los Angeles County Sheriff's Department. Her oft feted mother taught at the Pasadena Art Center College of Design. Her successful grandfather Robert Church worked as a certified public accountant in Laguna Beach, California. Her grandmother Alice helmed Robert's staff in their offices overlooking the surf. Her other grandfather, David Ezekiel, owned an exclusive jewelry shop in upscale Newport Beach. Grandma Deborah labored side by side with David, when she wasn't on buying runs to the jewelry wholesale houses in downtown LA. Raisa died on June 12, 2012, taking the light from her parents' and grandparents' lives with her.

The high fever, nausea, confusion, and stiff neck looked to be a bad flu that a few days in bed would solve. Bacterial meningitis, a killer of young people, had disguised itself well enough so that by the time the ambulance slammed hurriedly to a halt in front of San Gabriel Hospital's emergency room doors, it was too late.

Had a mother not been in class administering finals, had a father not been in another state testifying in the trial of a sadistic killer, would it have made a difference? It might have. It could have. It would have. A tormenting cascade of regret and recriminations washed over two parents who were not there when their little girl needed them the most. They'd failed her and themselves.

Roy Church fell into desolation of spirit, but his emptiness, grief, and insurmountable sense of tragic, gut wrenching loss paled in comparison with the complete and utter hatred for life that came to define Malka's existence. The pain became too much, and in spite of Roy's desperate efforts to get her help from counselors, her rabbi, and even her friends, she took her own life two and a half years later on January 12, 2014. The destruction of Delroy Church looked to be complete in a way not even the worst killer he'd ever run to ground could hope for.

♦

Santa Rosa police detective Jacob Stern called his wife from his hotel room before falling tiredly into bed on New Year's Eve. He had no desire to see the clock tick over to 2019. He'd felt an immense emptiness walking back from the parking lot to his room. Dinner had finished silently, and both policemen had called it a night.

"Do me a favor and go hug the kids when you get off the phone. Tell them I miss them and love them, and I'll be home as soon as I can, hopefully tomorrow night," Stern spoke into his phone.

"Everything okay?" his wife, Rachel, asked with concern.

"Fine, well, no, it's not fine. I mean, I'm physically fine. I just feel a bit sick." Stern drew a heavy hand across his face as he sat on the edge of his cheaply outfitted full-size bed.

When Stern finally got off the phone he pulled back the covers, lay on his bed, and stared at the wall. An involuntary tear escaped a corner of an eye. Presently, he undressed and crawled into bed, hoping to sleep but knowing he wouldn't. Unruly firecrackers, one or two distant booms of a big bore firearm, and the raucous sounds of milling, giddy drunks in the parking lot below his window didn't help to distract him from horror he couldn't imagine, carried by a policeman who outwardly appeared stoic and unaffected. He could think of nothing worse happening to a man in this life. He guessed Roy Church had somehow developed a survivor's philosophy of coping with what had to be a myriad of daily reminders of his losses. It worked for Church, but Stern could not imagine anything working for him. He felt himself siding with Malka Church, believing she'd arrived at the only place to find peace and comfort. Indescribable darkness mixed with nothingness. Relief.

♦

Roy Church slept. Recounting the deaths of his daughter and wife, hearing the words said out loud, for the first time since Malka's funeral, he wondered if he'd ever be able to sleep again. Strangely, when he sat at his bedside and gazed at the two lost faces, smiling radiantly in happier times, he certainly felt the familiar melancholy haze descending, but he felt something else. It had been almost cathartic to unburden himself, not in a break down, crying way, but in a manner that proved to himself and to a man who could have been his partner, that he still lived.

For decades he had delivered starkly bad news to men, women, and children. Aware of karma, he'd tried to maintain an empathetic and sympathetic persona every time. He wondered if his strength in the face of his own demons had derived itself from this necessary ugly facet of his occupation. Had he been scarred a little at a time whenever he'd sat with someone who'd just suffered a devastating loss? Had the scars slowly formed a callous-like barrier between him and his emotions? Had it become the only reason he hadn't joined Malka on her walk off the cliff at Dana Point, the spot where the three of them had last stood and hugged together, excitedly watching the whales lumber north?

♦

New Year's Day. Parades and ball games. A day set aside for the hopeful to welcome a fresh chapter, a chapter of renewal and promise. A day that saw Karuk County Sheriff's *Detective* Delroy Church and his partner Santa Rosa Police Detective Jacob Stern alight from a marked patrol unit parked in a snow covered driveway behind a white Mercedes SUV, both sensing a new door to be opened that would lead them closer to Cedar Stock's secrets.

They carefully made their way up the walkway leading to a massive Tudor-style two story. The large, ornate wreath upon the door and general air of upkeep spoke of tasteful and quiet affluence. After ringing a bell and waiting for about thirty seconds, they were greeted at the double door by an older man. Roy estimated the good doctor to be in his late sixties or early seventies based on his gait, paisley tie on at home, and bleached, white as the moon, hair.

"I'm Dr. Fournette. Come in. My wife Emily is waiting for us in the den." He had the smooth tone of voice that implied wealth and comfort with wealth.

Roy and Stern followed Dr. Fournette down a hallway lined with professional looking photographs of nature scenes, including all manner of animals, fish, plant life, and fowl. Roy saw no people in any.

Dr. Fournette led them eventually into a room bathed in natural light where they were greeted by an elderly woman roughly the same age as her husband.

Emily Fournette rose from a pastel colored couch in the comfortable looking room decorated with huge paintings of flamingos, right out of the Miami Vice opening credits, along with South Seas scenes of sunsets and palm trees. Emily was a thin woman wearing cream-colored pants and an asymmetrical grey-striped sweater which accented her bobbed, silver hair. Even with her advanced age, she had a striking resemblance to someone Roy had seen before, recently. Maddy Stock. Unmistakable. But then, of course, this was her grandma.

"Won't you men have a seat," Dr. Fournette said, indicating a chair and a love seat adjacent to the couch his wife had occupied.

Stern grabbed the love seat. Roy lowered himself into the chair and crossed his legs. Emily sat back down on the couch. Dr. Fournette sank beside her.

"Oh, wait," Emily said. "Would either of you like a cup of coffee or a croissant? The coffee is fresh, and the croissant is from this morning's New Year's breakfast."

Both detectives declined on the roll, but each took a cup of coffee. Roy took his black. Stern helped himself to cream. All comfy, as if they were here to talk updating insurance policies. Roy had learned long ago that if a possible witness offered coffee or a soft drink, it was a subtle sign of a cooperative attitude, one to be fostered by acknowledging the gesture.

Roy spoke. Stern listened.

"Dr. Fournette, Mrs. Fournette, first, let me apologize for intruding on a special day like today."

"Oh, it is no bother at all, detective," Dr. Fournette interrupted. "Our curiosity was so piqued at receiving a call from a world-famous detective, we couldn't have waited another day!"

"Well, thank you," Roy grinned. "Just remember newspapers and the like romanticize people and events way beyond reality."

Dr. Fournette leaned forward expectantly. Emily Fournette smiled and didn't move, her intelligent eyes like that of a doe listening to the snap of a twig.

"Well, as I said over the phone, I'm the detective in charge of the investigation into the skeletal remains found last fall on the Puma Creek Trail. Detective Stern here is from Santa Rosa. He is the lead detective on a suspicious death investigation, the death of a Jesse Dale Wilson who recently moved from Sisson to Santa Rosa."

"We've read about them both. We even theorized long before you ever called that this Wilson fella was knee deep in the disappearance of that girl Dina Morgan years ago. I'd say pretty much the entire town knows he had a hand in it," Dr. Fournette said. "But I'm a scientist, and while theories are good to have, that's all they are, until evidence comes available to prove them. Probably not unlike in your jobs. Neither of us has blabbed on about our beliefs, whether we're at parties or with friends or colleagues." Emily Fournette laid a hand on her husband's knee in a subtle gesture of support and agreement.

Roy dipped his head appreciatively toward the Fournettes. "Good policy. Now Doctor, obviously you cannot talk about anyone's confidential medical history, but you've been in this community for a while. I'm new here, about a year. Detective Stern has been here less than twenty-four hours. You know people. Some better than others, and one name has come up consistently in both our investigations. I'm going to ask, even though you're not legally bound, to keep what I'm about to share confidential," Roy continued.

"Of course," Dr. Fournette smiled.

Here's a man used to sensitive info who's seen STD in a file and knows how to keep that shit to himself.

Dr. Fournette clasped his hands together and added, "Conversely, how will any information I might provide be treated? The same I trust."

"Unless you tell me you witnessed someone pull a trigger, what you say will be kept in strictest confidence. Detective Stern and I are simply looking for background and possibly a way forward on our two investigations."

He seemed satisfied and leaned forward. "Okay then, ask away, Detective."

"Does the name Cedar Stock mean anything to you?"

Roy had expected a reaction, but not one so transparent.

"Dear Lord," Emily Fournette gasped quietly, pulling at a necklace under her sweater.

"Not a lot of good to say about that man or, frankly, that last name. Our daughter took it, so we've had to suppress any negative feelings," Dr. Fournette said heavily.

He leaned back on the couch, placed an arm around his wife's shoulders, and pulled her close to him. Emily Fournette leaned into him, the doe eyes staring at Roy.

"The only positive exception in our opinion, for what it's worth, is our granddaughter Maddy. She had no say in her choice of parents, and we've tried to love her unconditionally."

Roy glanced over at Stern, who'd become a statue. Don't do anything to distract the coming narrative they both felt would tumble with the slightest of pushes.

"Then I take it, the name Cedar Stock and the Stock name in general being connected to a law enforcement investigation does not surprise either of you."

"It is expected. Have you ever met Cedar Stock?" Emily Fournette spoke up and shook her head sadly.

"Ah, I believe so," replied Roy.

"You wouldn't forget if you had," said Dr. Fournette in a dark tone. "Our daughter Sarah, our only daughter, became involved with Cedar Stock's cousin when she was in high school nearly twenty-five years ago. She married the cousin, without our knowledge. His name was Zachary Stock, and we've regretted, other than Maddy of course, not being more forceful in our objections. But we didn't want to be that parent who tries to run a child's life. Of course, after Sarah turned 18 there was little we could do or say. For years we felt we'd lost our only daughter."

"Don't beat yourself up. It's the way of human existence. Parents everywhere regret not always being there for their children, not stepping in to keep the boat afloat," Roy said soothingly. "But I learned ages ago some things are out of your control. Children become adults, and they must make decisions. Sometimes those decisions turn out badly. But the lens of time can also reveal brilliance. You may see the decision to marry this Zachary as bad, but time and your granddaughter Maddy have shown its brilliant side too."

"It's no wonder you gained fame, detective, you sound as if you just stepped out of BBC America. We love Inspectors Morse and Lewis!"

"I think our favorite might have been *Foyle's War*," Emily Fournette interjected.

Husband and wife gazed at each other fondly and nodded

affirmatively. Yes, definitely Foyle's War.

I wonder if they have revolving viewing dates with Sassy Cassie.

"So we're not asking that you betray any confidence your daughter might have shared given her association with the Stock family, but what *can* you tell us about Cedar Stock and even Zachary Stock that might help us to get a clearer picture?"

"No betrayal. We made peace with our daughter long ago when she and little Maddy moved back in with us after the death of her so-called husband."

"I understand Zachary drowned long ago? This is all an open-ended question so please, educate us," Roy stated, politely.

Dr. Fournette turned to Emily.

"Honey, could you get a few of the relevant school annuals from my study? Detective Stern, maybe you could help her. I think late 80's to early 90's should do it."

Emily Fournette rose and headed toward a side door. Stern trailed after.

Dr. Fournette's eyes followed them for a moment. Then he returned to Roy.

"Detective Church are you familiar with the White and Gold's? That's what we call the high school yearbooks here in Sisson."

"I am. We have a huge set at our substation."

"I think it would be easier to tell our story with pictures. I've always been a prop user. I learned how effective physical objects can be when I guest lectured at med school."

"I'm a kinesthetic learner myself. Auditory is okay, but hands-on is the better way in my opinion," Roy agreed. "Juries love to see the evidence, handle it even."

Emily and Stern had just returned with a stack of hardback books.

"I never imagined a real detective knowing words like *kinesthetic*," Dr. Fournette laughed, getting comfortable, preparing to read from his tale of woe that had one brilliant passage in it named Maddy.

CHAPTER 37

Penn Fournette never lost track of the fact that his name caught eyes. The door plate reading *Dr. Penn Fournette, General Surgery* looked a hell of a lot more film worthy than say *Dr. Bud Mutz, Ear, Nose, Throat, and Small Engine Repair.* It didn't hurt that he'd exhibited a savant-like knack for medicine along the way. Of course, a name only got you so many patients, and then word got around. He had the intellectual curiosity, self-assurance — some say arrogance — and the steady hand needed for surgery on the Nob Hill set who all had lawyers on retainer.

Money flowed to San Francisco surgeons like crocs to a herd of wildebeest at a Serengeti watering hole. A home view of Mt. Tamalpais out all west side windows and a sailboat (rarely used except for photos designed to impress the office wall) docked at the Tiburon Yacht Club, validated Dr. Penn Fournette as one of Marin County's finest denizens.

But the freeway traffic day in and day out into the decaying morass of *The City*, just to get to his niche in the Pacific Heights Surgery Center, began to take its toll. If he got rear ended one more time on the Golden Gate Bridge or in the bowels of the Waldo Tunnel, or if he turned away from another homeless bum taking a watery crap on a sidewalk on Van Ness, he thought his head might explode. The City by the Bay displayed unmistakable beauty. World travelers spent millions to view its seductive wares. But for him, a cancerous component lurked behind the beckoning facade, one that cut off a little more of his air each day.

Somewhere along the way, Dr. Fournette sat down with his wife Emily, a jail nurse at the Marin County lock-up in San Rafael, along with their fourteen-year-old daughter Sarah. Their future needed tending to. A gilded cage was still a cage.

Dr. Fournette threw in his two cents. We've got more money than we can spend. In fact, we have no time to spend it, and the last time we were out on the sailboat, Sarah had just turned eleven, and she got all sick and frightened in the chop around Alcatraz.

Emily Fournette, who worked with the incarcerated diseased, sick, and injured, out of a sense of social commitment, agreed that a change might be nice. She pointed out that the AIDS epidemic had taken the joy out of daily entering the unique, blue-domed, mostly underground jail in San Rafael, the one designed by the famous architect Frank Lloyd Wright.

Surprisingly, Sarah, normally sullen, brightened considerably at the prospect of switching schools. Sir Francis Drake Secondary School boasted a high academic performance rating when it came to state testing. How could it not? Its feeder families were by and large formed through the union of high achievers, those college educated parents possessing envy inspiring DNA. How could you be in a better spot as a young person aiming high, such as for medical school like your noted father? But roses have thorns.

Sarah had run afoul of the Jennifer-Zoey Mafia, a group of especially loathsome mean-girls who delighted in mental torture, like cats playing with baby mice. Dr. Fournette, occupied as he was with saving lives through organ removal, failed to notice the sloping turn his daughter had taken. Sarah was in full corkscrew mode before Emily Fournette sat her down and demanded to know what her parents had missed. Was she doing drugs? Her manner and dress sure looked as if she were. What next? Full Goth?

As luck would have it, Dr. Fournette found himself on the dais with a formidable spine surgeon from Stanford by the name of Dr. Peter Grahn. Together they led a lively discussion at a conference featuring a break-out room on *Ethics and End of Life Planning*. A major insurance company had underwritten the entire affair, apparently in the hopes of stemming the cash hemorrhage it took to keep elder care facilities solvent.

Over martinis in the hotel lounge, Dr. Grahn listened to Dr. Fournette's lamentations. The Stanford surgeon revealed that he, too, had experienced a crisis of faith in how much fulfillment dead presidents actually provided. The cure for him had come in the form of a decision to spend a few profitable days a month in Stanford, but the rest of his time in a small, far northern California community called Sisson where he reveled in a laid-back practice servicing the rural unwashed. A nearby airport made the commute more than doable, and his family had grown to love him again.

He got lucky; his children couldn't believe the skiing, swimming, horseback riding, and quiet country life. He'd had his fingers crossed. Kids get addicted to the mall. But horses for all had changed that attitude quickly.

Dr. Grahn described a local hospital that would drool at the prospect of getting someone of Penn Fournette's skill level on board. And he could still spice up his bank account with the odd flight into SFO for some custom cutting in his old digs. Hospital administrations understood the mercurial personalities of some of their best and were willing to accommodate as long as they could still list the sought-after doctor in their waiting rooms' literature.

Dr. Fournette wondered if he should explore Bend, Oregon, as long as *goin' country* seemed like the way to navigate toward mental healing. The local papers were filled with tales of this up and coming jewel in the Eastern Oregon desert. The breathless publicity smelled like money. Then he face-slapped himself for forgetting that the unholy pursuit of money had gotten him into the lifestyle trap to begin with.

On a late spring weekend he packed up Emily and Sarah in their spanking new 1990 Mercedes 560 SEL and drove curiously up Interstate 5 toward Dr. Grahn's fabled town. Then, like hundreds of thousands before him, the siren call of Sisson's great white mountain floated toward him, faintly at first when he stopped in Willows for fast food and fuel, but louder and more insistent as he passed through Red Bluff and then Redding. Soon, it grew positively philharmonic, and he was forced to pull over at a vista view or risk wrecking while trying to snap photographs through the windshield. He stood next to a score of other gawking and pointing tourists securing their own breathtaking photos to develop back in the real world.

His heart skipped a beat as the girls commented excitedly at the large number of houseboats streaming and bobbing gently about on the wide expanse of Shasta Lake. Sarah commented that the water looked so calm and inviting she might be willing to give it another go. Dr. Fournette laughed, exclaiming that he had no problem considering a trade of their fifty-foot, floating E-ticket ride in Tiburon for a forty-foot, sleepover vacation home that towed a Ski Natique behind it.

The only fly doing a backstroke in the soup came when they rolled down the car window and experienced a blast from the oven that was the reality of the northern Sacramento Valley in late spring and summer. Dr. Fournette had heard tales of the mythical people who survived in Redding and Red Bluff, the ones who disrespectfully mocked Satan and what he had to offer in the coolness of his lair. The often misty air of Marin and San Francisco had rendered all their skin moist and soft. There was a general concern that they might turn into saddle leather in this heat. But he told the girls that's why air conditioning and swimming pools had been invented, and surely the heat couldn't last more than a few months.

Incredibly, the heat disappeared like bandits on the run as they rose upward in the Sacramento River Canyon. When they finally arrived in Sisson, it was a full twenty degrees cooler. Dr. Fournette was not a religious man per se, but he said a silent prayer in thanks to the Great Spirit for the insulating mountains they'd just passed through.

Sisson, California. For him, it was love at first sight. Two stoplights and no waiting at the gas pumps. Emily had immediate concerns about groceries and a place to buy underwear. Sarah initially offered no opinion but instead dreamily gazed at the now monstrous mountain that cast a friendly eye directly down at them.

They paused at an intersection between two schools, Sisson Middle School on the west side, Sisson High on the east. A tawny, gigantic grizzly bear roared silently at them from the lightly painted side of the high school gym. School was out, so there were no students to be seen milling about on the high school campus, no Jen and Zoey huddled in their malignant clique pointing and laughing at those not worthy of inclusion.

School may have ceased for summer vacation, but that did not mean no children were seen. Between the two schools lay a collection of neatly kempt baseball fields, back to back, side to side, all packed with an entire community seemingly with one goal. Winning. Three games occurring simultaneously spurred shrieks at fly balls, groans at missed grounders, and exhortations to round for home. Vocal partisans filled adjacent stands, some thrilled, some desperate, and others resigned to the bottom of the ninth and the pitcher coming to bat. Tiny and bulky uniforms alike sported individual numbers plus names of what the Fournettes took to be local businesses; Ace Hardware, Faraday Real Estate, Suburban Propane, Cascade Builders, Black Tail Inn, and Shasta Excavation and Septic.

Gravel parking lots around the ball fields held a myriad of vehicles, from Volkswagen bugs to soccer mom vans, four-wheel drive, off-road jeeps, and new and oxidized pick-ups. Cheering fans, maybe adult brothers and uncles, bounced raucously out of chairs in pick-up beds, Igloo coolers between their feet, most likely hiding adult beverages. Dads and frenzied moms had moved closer to the fields to offer shouted advice through chain link fences, advice often countering coaches who roared louder to drown out the familial expertise.

A good time had by all.

Dr. Fournette drove by the ball parks slowly. A few locals turned to eyeball them, suspiciously, it seemed to Emily. It dawned on the family then that just maybe their extravagant car, normal by Marin standards, made them look like wealthy oil sheiks touring their black gold extraction sites. They all laughed at that. It felt good to see Sarah grin.

They checked into their hotel, the Best Western's Black Tail Inn, just off the interstate. Across the street, heavy construction equipment stood silently for the weekend next to a temporary sign that read *Black Tail Restaurant. Coming Fall 1992.* Until then, the

Fournettes contented themselves with a hotel restaurant and a barbecue at the home of Dr. Peter Grahn who'd been thrilled to hear they were checking out the area.

Dr. Grahn's grown children were not at home on his twenty-acre spread northwest of Sisson, but their horses were. Dr. Fournette watched, intrigued, as Sarah stood on the rails of the paddock's fence and whinnied at the buckskin mare and sorrel gelding that danced and bucked playfully in front of her.

Dr. Fournette and Emily queried Dr. Grahn on the state of the local high school. Did it measure up to Bay Area standards? Could a child from the Fournette family get the education she needed to advance successfully onto university and to medical school beyond if she so chose?

Dr. Grahn forcefully made the points that parental involvement, expectations, and predisposed genes determined a student's success whether they be at Sisson High or the Marin Academy. His own children had graduated from Sisson High. Both went on to college. One currently expected acceptance any day now into Stanford's Medical School, following dad's footsteps. The other had gone into the Peace Corps and was traipsing somewhere around Africa helping collect rainwater for dry villages. The years at a rural high school had hindered them not in the least.

Dr. Fournette and Dr. Grahn privately toured the local Sisson Hospital. Dr. Fournette had expected a Civil War era field station good for sawing bones but not much more. The clean, professional state of buildings and state of the art equipment therein pleasantly surprised him. The facilities had the same mobile care 5th wheel hospital stretchers and surgical tables he used at Pacific Heights. He examined the modern defibrillators, the newest model of EKG/ECG machines, up-to-date anesthesia machines and patient monitors. He stopped to inspect an autoclave sterilizer that used its high-powered saturated steam to kill all microbial life on surgical tools. The place impressed him. Would they be as impressed with him? He wondered.

For much of the rest of the weekend, the Fournettes explored the area further, taking in Karuk Lake, the McCloud River and its spectacular sets of falls that led downward to yet another deep forest lake, this one with breathtaking, turquoise colored water. All the while, the splendid mountain stood over them, seemingly amused at their every move, its gaze inescapable.

They stopped in at the Sisson Museum and scanned the history of what had gone on outside the building. Early Indians, late from the land bridge, followed by fur trappers and gold miners, loggers, ranchers, and Italian immigrants, snow skiers and builders of power dams. It was all there, a stew of cultures blended to experience the joys, failures, successes, dreams, and frailties that life had to offer, everyone inspired by and under the constant guard of the magnificent, snow adorned mountain called Shasta.

On the walls of the museum they read the words of two famous pioneers who'd been overcome with the mountain's beauty.

Nineteenth century historian Joaquin Miller described her thus, *As lone as God and as white as the winter moon.*

John Muir penned in his diary, *When I first caught sight of her over the braided folds of the Sacramento Valley, I was fifty miles away and afoot, alone and weary. Yet all my blood turned to wine, and I have not been weary since.*

The Fournettes's next step followed the path of every family before them who'd become enthralled with the prospects of living in this nature's paradise. They went real estate window shopping. They found themselves staring at the collection of photos in the front window at Ronald Faraday Real Estate on Sisson's main street.

That day in the real estate office, Sarah met a friend for life, Ronnie Faraday Jr., and through him, her life and the lives of the Fournettes, and more than one Stock, would be altered forever.

CHAPTER 38

"Ronald Faraday Real Estate has been there quite a while?" Roy asked, interested.

"Long time. Ron Sr. passed away about ten years ago. CHF. Uh, that's congestive heart failure. Ron Jr. has run the office since, very successfully I might add, especially with the help of our daughter," Dr. Fournette replied, his unhappiness at past events tempered momentarily with a hint of pride.

"You know, Sarah never had a boyfriend in Marin," Emily spoke for the first time in a while, having remained silent, but approving, during Dr. Fournette's meander through history.

"She was only fifteen by the time we moved here, honey," Dr. Fournette said. "I don't think a boyfriend in Marin would have helped matters."

"I'm just saying she had no experience with boys. Then she met Ronnie," Emily said. "In spite of growing up in the Bay Area, she was still a bit naïve, not sheltered, but more dreamy and bookish. We preferred it that way, believe me. We just had no idea how miserable she'd been at school with those nasty girls."

"Pre-teens and young teens can be the worst," said Roy.

"No kidding." Stern added his succinct thoughts to the discussion on the testosterone and estrogen fueled social melee more commonly referred to as junior high.

"Ronnie Faraday was in his dad's office when we walked in. He was wearing a baseball uniform, all grass stained and dirty. He and his dad were laughing over a stolen base that went horribly wrong for his team. I'll never forget it," Dr. Fournette chuckled. "He looked at Sarah and said, 'Short stop. Am I right?' Took her by complete surprise."

"Ronnie and Sarah chatted, I mean Sarah actually chatted with a boy her own age while Penn and I discussed real estate with his dad," Emily said, still marveling at the memory. "We're not sure if she'd ever spoken to a boy before then."

"We think Ronnie Faraday did more to sell Sarah on a Sisson move than anything we could have said or the mountain could have offered," Dr. Fournette said.

"Ronnie seemed so animated and at ease with her," Emily added.

They're tag teaming the conversation on Ronnie Faraday. They must have really liked the youngster. How would I have reacted to Raisa's first boyfriend? Roy shook his head slightly and focused.

"Of course," Dr. Fournette sighed. "We came to find out why Ronnie was so at ease with girls. Not that we're judging. We are very open-minded about sexuality. We lived in the Bay Area for crying out loud. I made a tremendous living off of the gay and straight communities alike. People are people, and you don't choose how you're born. It's what's in your heart and how you treat others that matters. I wish people could see that." Emily patted her husband's leg again and smiled at him.

She leaned forward slightly. "Ronnie was very athletic. Loved baseball most of all. But his mannerisms became a bit more revealing the older he got. We don't know if he suffered for it. We never heard people here make fun of him. He grew up in Sisson. As far as we know the other kids accepted him and moved on. It's funny, rural people are always portrayed as backward and narrow minded in the films we see. The truth is, open, caring people are more readily found here than in some places we experienced in Marin," Emily said.

"You're right about stereotypes," Roy concurred. "I seriously don't know cops who live for donuts, but there we are."

"And Jews are good with money," Stern laughed. "My wife Rachel is one half American Indian, and she handles all our finances. I'm clueless as to how to get into my own bank account."

Emily smiled comfortably, grateful for a comedic break in a solemn tale.

Stern got up and helped himself to another cup of coffee, then paused in front of the tray of croissants, and muttered, "Aw what the heck."

"So you made the move to Sisson okay?" Roy asked after Stern had reseated.

"Yes, Dr. Grahn had been correct. Both hospitals welcomed my new schedule. We bought this property, built this home, and moved here right before the start of Sarah's junior year. For years I made the one-hour flight from Redding to SFO several times a month. I still performed surgeries, not as many, but nearly as lucrative. Emily began work here in Sisson as an RN. I guess we misjudged where the real problems in our daughter's life lay."

"Where was that?" Roy asked.

"Both parents working, one out of town, the other doing odd hour shifts. It is not good for a child's upbringing; I don't care what the so-called experts say. Involved parents don't have to be helicopters, but they are sure needed in a child's life to guide better choices," Emily said, beginning adamantly but ending wistfully.

Agreed.

"You can never get the time back that you missed with your children by working. But then you have to put food on the table. No good choices sometimes," Roy said diplomatically.

Both Fournettes smiled appreciatively.

"Penn, show them Ronnie in the 1991 annual," Emily said.

Dr. Fournette opened the annual marked with *1991*. He flipped to the section labeled *Sisson Bears Athletics* and pointed to a handsome, uniformed boy standing tall at one end of the ball team as it posed for a color photo. The hands firmly held a bat, and the young face smiled mischievously, as opposed to the fifteen others who pushed out their most professional frowns.

"That's Ronnie. Good with a bat and could field a grounder. I guess his problem was he wasn't fast enough to get beyond high school. But he sure loved the game. Go to his office today and he's got baseball memorabilia everywhere, going way back to the teams he starred on and several of the high school teams since. Always sponsors a little league team and underwrites summer ball for older boys," Dr. Fournette said. "Most summer nights he's out there with what they call slo-pitch, for adults."

Roy inspected the team photo and the names in the caption. It was not lost on him that Dr. Fournette had neglected to point out another prominent player, one whom they should naturally have brought to his attention. Zachary Stock.

Roy tapped the photo of Zack Stock.

"And that is…?" he prompted.

"Yes, that is the gentleman who fathered our Maddy."

Dr. Fournette did not say "Sarah's husband" although he'd alluded to marriage earlier. The word *gentleman* in this case most assuredly did not sound like a term of respect, more like Dr. Fournette did not use words like *asshole* and needed an alternative. Roy likened it to the annoying way the NY Times used "Mr." in front of last names, as if it made them sound more objectively journalistic when in reality he knew based on the tenor of the article they held this particular person in contempt. *Mr. Hitler's secret meeting with Mr. Stalin took place at Mr. Nixon's condominium.*

"I guess if we had one bone to pick with Ronnie Faraday, it's that he introduced Sarah to Zack Stock. For some unknown reason, he and Zack were friends. They'd gone to school from kindergarten all the way through high school. Sports in common, I guess," said Dr. Fournette, closing the annual but then reopening it. He flipped back to class photos.

"And here is our lovely Sarah as a junior."

Roy and Stern inspected the image of a stunningly good-looking teen, a cross between Maddy Stock and Emily Fournette, with Dr. Fournette's intelligent eyes and wry smile.

"She was beautiful," Roy said.

"She still is," Emily said proudly.

"Sure didn't take after her dad," Stern observed, which caused Emily to elbow Dr. Fournette.

"That makes it unanimous thus far, Penn." She smiled mischievously.

"I've never contested that opinion!" Dr. Fournette gave his wife an elderly person's peck on the cheek.

"I'd say we've arrived at the reason for the bullying in Marin," Stern said. "Pure, unadulterated envy."

"That's what I said!" exclaimed Emily. "But you couldn't get Sarah to believe it."

"She had so much going for her once she got to school here," Dr. Fournette said. "Her grades improved tremendously. She talked seriously about going on to medical school. Our hearts were warmed considerably by the choice we'd made to move here."

"And then something derailed all that. Something with the last name Stock," Roy said, more of a statement than a question.

"Exactly," Dr. Fournette said with sadness in his voice.

"We don't know where and how Sarah became smitten with Zack," Emily said. "It could have been in class, by a hallway locker, at a ball game. We just don't know. Not that it matters now."

"After we'd been here a few months, students who'd gotten their licenses and were friendly toward Sarah started showing up here at the house," Dr. Fournette said.

"We were pleased Sarah had made friends, and it didn't hurt that they wanted to come here instead of her going someplace where we had no idea the situation." Emily Fournette sighed.

"Parenting 101," said Stern. "Have the party at *your* house where you have control."

Dr. Fournette tilted his head in agreement. "We were more than happy to keep the fridge stocked with soft drinks and ice cream, and we had a home theater upstairs with one of those giant Mitsubishi rear projection TVs. The quality was horrible compared to the 85" Sony UKHD we have up there now. We never watch it. We have a TV in our bedroom, but it's there for when Maddy comes over and brings her friends. Although, most of her friends have gone on to college, so it's during vacations that we see her these days."

Emily broke in.

"Ronnie was a regular here. We had no issue with him spending so much time. We felt Sarah was safe with him. He was so polite and helpful around the house, loved to help in the kitchen, set the table. He vacuumed even. Just a wonderful guy. A great house sitter, too," she said. "There were moments when we prayed we were wrong about him." She and her husband exchanged looks.

"I think we first noticed Zack when he was hanging out after a basketball game with Ronnie and Sarah. One of the things we encouraged Sarah to do was get involved in cheering for her school. She'd never done that in Marin, but here it was different. She and Ronnie went to all the basketball games. He didn't play, but Zack did," Dr. Fournette said. He paused and sipped his coffee.

He continued, "Then Zack started showing up here with Ronnie. He tried to be polite, but he never really made eye contact that much with Emily, never asked her about her day or her life. Seemed he'd only speak to me. We suspected he was a boy who'd not been raised to value women all that much."

"Yes, very reticent when discussing his family. A red flag for us. We had to learn about him and his family mostly from Ronnie who knew a lot," Emily said. "Ronnie gave us what he thought was a fair assessment of the Stock family. But we could read between the lines. Not a lot of good traits in the current generations. The family is old Karuk County pioneer. I think they're even mentioned at the Sisson Museum."

Dr. Fournette said, "Since we knew, or at least strongly suspected, Ronnie's orientation, you can only imagine how our hearts sank when Zack came to our house to see Sarah, without Ronnie. We'd held out hope that maybe, just maybe, it was Ronnie that Zack held a candle for. No such luck. He had used Ronnie to get to our Sarah. It was at that time we knew we had to step in and try to help her see he wasn't right for her. We're not trying to be snobs, but he had no college ambition. He was into off-roading, hunting, fishing, lifting weights, playing ball and drinking beer, lots of beer we found out later. That seemed about it. Grades were tertiary. He was a handsome party boy, not all that concerned with his life ten years hence, not the type of young man with a bright future."

"How'd he drown?" Roy asked.

"Well, he inhaled too much water in his lungs and suffocated," Dr. Fournette said drily, momentarily forgetting his professional station in life.

"Ha! Guess I deserved that," Roy said shooting an amused look at Stern who was wiping choked up coffee from his nose.

"Look, I'm sorry," said Dr. Fournette. "I'm not trying to make light of it. Truth is he died how he lived. He got drunk — there's a surprise — was fishing over on the Klamath, fell in the water and that was that. Took them several days to recover his body."

"We'd be lying if we said seeing our daughter a widow at twenty devastated us," Emily said. "But Zack's death brought her back to us and helped her straighten out her life, even if she never went on to university."

Roy felt sympathy for the Fournettes. He could see they had anguish over the fine line they'd tried to tread, not wanting to overly influence their daughter, but fearing she'd make a fatal mistake by falling for a bad boy. In the end, their good-hearted efforts had driven their daughter into the arms of the very type of person they'd tried so hard to get her to avoid.

"We had some awful fights over Zack," Emily said quietly, regret thick in her voice.

She and Dr. Fournette grew silent, both of them staring out the window for a moment, reflecting on words spoken softly, regretting words shouted angrily those many years before, now seen in wisdom's rearview mirror.

Roy let them have a moment. He caught the look on Stern's face, a pro's expression that clearly said, "Let 'em have a moment."

Dr. Fournette broke the silence.

"Honey, hand me the annual for, uh, I think about '88."

Seeing Roy's puzzled expression, he explained, "Gentlemen, you might think it odd that we have so many of them for those years prior to our daughter being in school, but we collected them for a reason. We felt it was a way to get to know the community a bit better. We wanted to fit in, so seeing who was related to whom, who were the popular people, the movers and shakers in high school…well, I guess, if we're being honest, we fit into the stalker category."

Roy nodded understandingly. He had flipped through a few White and Golds himself when he arrived.

Dr. Fournette chuckled while Emily shook her head approvingly.

Emily searched through the stack of annuals on the coffee table, selected one and handed it to Dr. Fournette.

"Let me find the fellow whose name you used, Cedar Stock. He's Zack's older cousin. A strange, mean one. I think we still see him occasionally. I'm pretty sure he went to prison more than once. Just weird, scary."

Dr. Fournette flipped a few pages and then turned the annual and handed it to Roy while tapping one photo.

Roy had expected to see the nasty sneer of a middle linebacker or elbows thrown during a lay-up in a championship game against Silverton. Instead, there sat a gangly, gregarious looking young man holding a guitar and crooning to what Roy assumed was a classroom of his peers. Whoever they were, they were rapt with attention.

A caption under the photo read: *Cedar Stock, voted most likely to headline the Country Music Awards.*

"He's a musician?" Stern broke in incredulously as he leaned forward to view the page.

"Was quite the artist," Dr. Fournette said. "With potential, we understand. Not your normal convict I'd imagine. Somewhere after high school he went down a long, dangerous path, and music took a back seat."

"We'd have known none of this if he hadn't ensconced himself into Maddy's and Sarah's lives after Zack drowned," Emily added. "It was as if he felt a family obligation to care for them. Of course, we suspected he had more than a protective interest in Sarah once she was single again." She sniffed with obvious distaste.

"We cared for Maddy over the years, and of course she and Sarah stayed with us off and on until Sarah got on her feet in the real estate business with Ronnie. We often heard about the comings and goings of Cedar Stock," Dr. Fournette said. "He scared us to death with his prison tattoos and record. He came here once or twice searching for the girls. He looked so mean, not like this boy you see in the photo at all. We thought he might rob or murder us. Of course, he never did."

"Cedar still visits Sarah and Maddy regularly we understand. We have virtually nothing to do with that side of Maddy's family. The Stocks have a right, Maddy's their blood," Emily sighed.

"So Sarah moved in with you after Zack drowned?" Roy asked as he stared thoughtfully at the photo of Cedar in mid-song.

"Oh, no, she had actually left him, came home with little Maddy. I guess you might say they had a domestic disagreement. It was right after they were separated, the day or day after, that Zack drowned. He took off to fish and drink to console himself. He had no ability to problem solve without alcohol. It was a bad time," Dr. Fournette replied.

"Tragic circumstances, but I guess we have that man there to thank for finally opening Sarah's eyes to the whole Zack Stock mistake," Emily said, pointing at the annual and Cedar's photo.

Roy glanced up.

"Really? How so?"

"Well, don't get me wrong, it's bad for any little girl to lose a father, but Maddy has no memory of her father's death. She was very young. We understand that Zack kept allowing Cedar and his workers to stay with Sarah and Zack at their house. They had a little rental outside of town. That lousy situation led to friction," Emily said.

Roy noticed a glance Emily and her husband shared.

"Cedar and his workers?" Roy probed.

"Yes, he had some sort of traveling landscaping or tree cutting business. I'm not sure which. They went from job to job, but the bunch of them stayed with Zack and Sarah when they had a job locally. We've pieced it together over the years. Cedar was not a nice man, and his workers were really a rough sort. They made Sarah very uncomfortable as you can imagine," Dr. Fournette said. "We never met them or saw them, it's just what Sarah and Ronnie have said over the years."

"When did Zack drown?" Roy asked.

Dr. Fournette thought for a moment.

"94?" He turned to his wife.

"95," she said firmly. "June, 1995, on summer's solstice."

"Cedar's mother, Germaine, Jersey Stock, she'd be an aunt-in-law to Sarah?" Roy asked. "What's her story?"

Dr. Fournette and Emily looked at one another again.

"Jersey Stock, Zack's aunt. Comes off like a harmless, sweet old lady. But she is probably why Cedar is the way Cedar is. She and her sister Becky, Zack's mom, were two peas in a pod," Dr. Fournette said.

"Low women married into a miserable family," Emily declared, a nerve struck.

♦

Black clouds had gathered menacingly throughout the afternoon, obscuring the tops of the Pumas and Mt. Shasta. The mercury had dropped considerably as persistent wind, announcing the first snowstorm of the year, blew up the Sacramento River Canyon.

"Keep me in the loop, boss. I'll meet you there. Coffee on me." Stern glanced up at the darkening sky. "Whoa. Looks as if I'm getting out of here just in time."

Stern shook Roy's hand vigorously, and then he hurriedly slid into his unmarked. He fishtailed on the ice, away from the sub, his headlights revealing the first, sneaky flakes.

Roy turned and re-entered the sub, stepping immediately to the wall heater to rub his hands together. Then he sat at his desk and pulled out his yellow notepad, the one he'd started this case with. He flipped to a page and read one set of notes. He set the pad down and then turned his chair to glance out the window at an increasing volume of flakes teasing the frosty pane. He allowed himself to smile.

Old John St. John didn't believe in coincidence, and neither do I.

♦

Cedar Stock sat on the Mexican blanket in Ma's living room watching the tube and Ma at the same time. He chuckled as she leaned forward, shouting at Coach Nick Saban who'd just whipped off his headset in frustration at the pandemonium around him.

"Ha, ha. No more Roll Tide this year, big boy!" she chortled.

Cedar liked it when Ma showed signs of life. The Orange Bowl featuring Alabama and USC football teams had been what the doctor ordered. The adrenalin surge had brought her back to life. Her illness had definitely receded. Nothing like watching the Darth Vader of the SEC lose on national television to a California team.

Ma muted an ad, one with half naked, well-muscled young people on a beach, laughing and dancing as they made out like beer drinking is better for your physique than time spent on an iron pile.

"So tell me," she said. "How did it go with the cops?"

"Fine, Ma. Couldn't have been better. They've got nothing, and I'm keeping it that way." He drummed his fingers impatiently on his thigh.

"That's good, because I could see them coming around here asking questions. Don't underestimate them though. Delroy Church does not sound like a man to be taken lightly."

"They have to follow the Constitution, Ma. No evidence still means something in this country."

"You better be sure. I'll bet you knew boys inside who thought the same thing."

"They're still there. I'm not. I'll never go back." He said it with force, hoping to quell the conversation.

"Then you do what you have to do. Your ancestors did what they had to do to survive coming across the plains from back East. Only the strong survived," Ma said, turning slightly in her chair to look directly at him. In the darkness, her normally rheumy eyes shown like burnished obsidian in a Sisson rock shop.

Cedar changed topics. "No more ball games on tonight, Ma. Want me to sing something for you?"

She turned back in her chair and shimmied down more comfortably. "Aw, that'd be sweet. Rock of Ages?"

Ma closed her eyes but listened attentively while Cedar picked up his guitar and tuned it. She never missed a single chord.

CHAPTER 39

Currently, in 32 prisons scattered throughout the Golden State, the California Department of Corrections and Rehabilitation (CDCR) houses the worst the state has to offer.

In 1963 there weren't as many prisons. The Mexican Mafia, also known as *La Eme*, was the only established prison gang, but the quality of the inmate was just as low and murderous as it is today. Two of them proved it in March of 1963.

Gregory Powell and Jimmy Smith got the drop on two LAPD officers who'd stopped them because they were acting suspiciously. They brazenly disarmed then kidnapped the officers at gunpoint and drove them to an onion field outside Bakersfield, California, a little over an hour north of LA. There, they executed one of the officers, shooting him five times. The other ran and got away as bullets whizzed. The case changed the way LAPD officers and policemen all around California looked at officer safety tactics, especially when dealing with hard core prison parolees who don't give a fuck because they aren't going back.

It dawned on street cops that along with the duty to serve comes a duty to survive. A warrior's mindset has since permeated the training and thinking of most policemen in California. Never give up your gun, and fight until the bitter end.

Don't let them kill you along some dirty freeway. If you knew you were going to die tomorrow, would it change how you train today?

Too many civilians, and some cop hating reporters, along with their editorial boards, have never faced anything more dangerous than a jalapeno burger at a Red Robin restaurant. They jeer and judge from the stands, even though they have no concept of what it's like to face a cobra in a shower stall. Regardless of analyses banged out by these keyboard warriors, going home at the end of watch to a spouse and family, remains the top priority for every man or woman who dons a uniform.

After the infamous Onion Field Murder, in addition to changes in how the individual police officer approached suspects and dangerous situations, the state of California weighed in with an overdue gift. It created a nightmare for the con on the run. In 1964, the Special Services Unit of the California Department of Corrections hit the street, giving birth to a new era in snatching up rapists, robbers, and lethal psychopaths, all the way from Calexico to the Oregon border.

According to its official, government page, SSU:

"...conducts the major criminal investigations and prosecutions, criminal apprehension efforts of prison escapees and parolees wanted for serious and violent felonies, is the primary departmental gang management unit, conducts complex gang related investigations of inmates and parolees suspected of criminal gang activity; and is the administrative investigative and law enforcement liaison unit."

Over the years parolees have demonstrated the obvious, a man just out of prison can be docile or deadly, but either way, he is likely to reoffend. He's been a screw-up since kindergarten, and leopards don't change spots, no matter what the limousine liberals and professors of criminology have declared. Other truisms. Cons steal, kill, cheat, and give dirty piss tests. Then they go on the run. They abscond and commit their crimes in different cities, across county lines, and even in different states. It takes a special bird dog to bring them back to the gray bar motel where they belong. That bird dog is the special agent of the SSU.

SSU special agents are not your normal policeman. They have all cut their teeth on the toughest beat America has to offer, walking the tiers and yards, *unarmed*, shoulder to shoulder and face to face with men who have made it their lives' missions to shred the fabric of civilized society.

Beginning as young officers in Chino, San Quentin, Folsom, Corcoran, or two dozen other institutions, they start their educations. Picking up the vernacular, learning the habits, and otherwise soaking up the culture of the con makes the SSU special agent akin to an old Texas Ranger or an ancient Indian fighter able to spot trail sign on rock and read a smoke signal above a plateau. The ability to think like a con, talk like a con, and walk like a con has the real menace constantly looking over his shoulder, wondering when a ghost will appear bearing bracelets.

Over the years, the SSU special agent has worked behind the scenes supplementing street cops and detectives, shying away from the publicity of the major bust and the upper management press conferences that follow. They simply want to get the job done, nail the outlaw, then disappear into the mist. They are and have been the Navy SEALs of California law enforcement.

An SSU special agent's, training, experience, and spot on the ladder allows him to open doors for local law enforcement that would otherwise remain locked. Behind one of those doors lies the C-file or central file for every con in or out of the joint. The file chronicles every move that con has ever made, from initial and subsequent crimes of conviction, to the first time at reception centers, to the first parole violations, and to the *115 chronos*, those reports on poor behavior behind the walls. It lists, among other info, the documented reasons behind the validation of a con as a prison gang member or as an associate of a gang.

Inside the central file is something called the confidential file. It is off limits to everyone, except a select few in Admin or SSU special agents. It is accessible to an outside law enforcement agency almost never through court orders, but usually through the cooperation of an SSU special agent working on a particular case with local law enforcement. Even then SSU is selective in who within the law enforcement agency is allowed to view it. The sensitive material contained within the confidential file could get the con or someone else, aka an informant, killed if it became common knowledge. For example, an inmate might have surreptitiously traded some innocuous info for tobacco twenty years earlier while doing time in Tehachapi. That fact is in the file. If it became known, that inmate is as good as dead even though he is now doing time in Pelican Bay and is in good with a gang.

In the confidential file, there can be additional intel on a con. An informant may have identified his running mates when he was in a particular unit, hall, or on a dusty yard. And that is the information Roy Church and Jake Stern had come seeking as they sat in a car outside an obscure, unlabeled building in a boring looking industrial park on a nondescript street in Sacramento.

Jake Stern dialed a number on his cell phone. Momentarily a door on the side of the building opened. Out stepped a grey-haired Latino man, short, built like a brick shithouse, dressed in an oversized, blue jeans shirt buttoned at the top, unbuttoned at the bottom, over baggie blue jeans and black sneakers. Senior Special Agent Reuben Montalvo grinned widely under his thick *broche*. If it hadn't been for the prison get-up, he'd have passed for an army general in a banana republic.

Roy remarked, "The inmates are running a business on Sacramento's east side."

"Can't believe he's still working," Stern said. "He'll die of old age looking like an extra from *American Me*, probably keel over while sitting in a darked out van in some low life hood." Roy could tell Stern greatly respected Montalvo.

"Reuben, you old Harley ridin' sonofabitch! How are you?" Roy called.

"The shit I see when I ain't got a gun!" Montalvo called back. "Wait. I do have a gun here somewhere."

Roy and Stern both pumped Montalvo's hands and bro hugged him, the genuine thing, not like beer swilling, Buffalo Wings wannabes.

"I can't believe you're still on the job," Roy said with incredulity.

"I can't believe either of you are still on the job. Planning for retirement should begin after your rookie year," Stern pointed out, grinning.

"46 years this month. I was a rookie officer on a tier in Chino when the *Familianos* killed *La Eme's* Reuben Cadena. That's when shit broke loose all over the state." Montalvo shook his head and continued, "Man, I gotta get outta here and get me a real job. One that pays the bills."

"Gigolo still on the table?" Roy asked, waggling his eyebrows.

Montalvo scoffed, "You know it."

"Thought you said a job that pays," Stern laughed. "*They're* supposed to pay you, not the other way around."

"Really? I thought being a gigolo was about going in the hole!" Montalvo guffawed, slapping his knee.

"Come inside," he said. "I got what you boys need. Shit, Delroy Church and Jake Stern on the same case? Hell, state needs to open up a whole 'nother facility."

♦

Roy, Stern, and Montalvo sat in a windowless room around a conference table, barren save for a single brown accordion file about eight inches thick.

"Cedar Robert Stock, Brand associate known as Cedar Bob, armed robber, and very smart. Those add up to extremely dangerous for a street cop stumbling across him or any detective who takes him too lightly," Montalvo said grimly as he pulled out several sheaths of paper.

"Recruited by the Aryan Brotherhood? Where? When? Do we know?" Roy asked.

"Mid-90's, New Folsom most likely. Did a minute at The Bay in early 2000's, so he got up close and personal with some of the big boys. Full terms. No tails from the gate either time he discharged," Montalvo said.

"Weird about New Folsom," Stern said, remembering how Cedar Stock had recognized him.

"Yeah, I laughed when you told me that over the phone. I remember that time. BGF hit a 415 Kumi out of Oakland right in front of us. Shows Stock's got a memory like a steel trap."

"Stern's got a face and a sashaying stroll you don't forget," Roy laughed.

"Okay, so prison security squad hit a house in L-Wing, second tier, at DVI in Tracy, found a Nazi Low Rider and his cellie dirty as fuck with dope, kites, and a couple of bone crushers. Dude flipped for 'em on the under, gave up a ton of shit. One of them was intel on your boy Stock," Montalvo said.

"Odd for a white boy to cooperate?" asked Stern.

"Nah, not if they're just a peckerwood. But this inmate was Nazi Lowrider which made it more noteworthy. NLR is always trying to come up on the AB's, so sometimes we get lucky there. Half the NLR wants to fall up under the AB's, half wants to go its own path. Lotta prison politics get in the way. That's when we can pick off a few informants."

"Nothing like the fog of a civil war for grabbing sources," Stern remarked.

"You proved that with Operation Brown Recluse," Montalvo agreed, smiling.

"Couldn't have done it without SSU, no way," replied Stern.

"And FBI money," laughed Montalvo. "Good times." He turned to Roy.

"Jake and his FBI boys recruited me back in the early 90's to take the blame for their clusterfuck of an operation against a prison gang. We went after the *Nuestra Familia* generals and captains. Don't know how many times I almost lost my job," Montalvo grinned. Stern shook his head in mock dismay.

Roy, with an appreciative chuckle, forced himself to break in on the war story reunion of the two cops who'd obviously enjoyed themselves back in the day.

"So your informant said what exactly?"

"Well, says here the NLR informant actually personally passed on a kite to Cedar Stock in the early 90's while the two of them were in New Folsom, telling him to kill his cellie, some peckerwood named Koondawg. Security Squad guys IDed Koondawg as one Kelly Cutler out of Nevada. I got his C-file, too. Had been an Aryan Warrior associate there in Nevada."

"Did he? Kill this Koondawg?" Roy asked.

"No, and that's where Stock showed some balls, big brass balls he could sit on. He stood up to the shot caller for the AB who'd sent down the order," Montalvo replied.

"And lived to tell about it?" Stern said, incredulously. "Do we know who and why in the AB?"

"The informant thought the orders originated with an up-and-comer in the Brand by the name of Dale "Moonshine" Tankersley. He wasn't on the Commission then, the top tier, but may be now. Apparently Koondawg was known for his occasional sexual assaults on white boys who weren't protected. Guess he raped the wrong one somewhere along the line. Word got back to Pelican Bay, that's where the big boys live, and Koondawg had to go."

"And they chose Cedar Stock for the hit?" Stern asked.

"Yep. According to the informant, the AB wanted Stock to kill this Koondawg as a test to see if he was ripe for their ranks. It would have meant Stock committing the *ultimate sacrifice*, murder in the joint, with witnesses, resulting in a life sentence. Stock turned tables."

"How so?" asked Roy, leaning back in his chair. Jesus, even SSU had better chairs than him.

"Apparently Koondawg had robbed a jewelry salesman in Nevada and squirreled away the *feria* from it," Montalvo said. "Koondawg told Stock about it. Stock then promised the AB that he'd get the money for them once he paroled and once Koondawg paroled and began working with him. His plan was to pay his way out a life sentence using another con's stolen bread."

"Smart, but you're right, beyond ballsy. They could just as easily killed him on the spot for refusing an order," Roy said. "So Cedar got out, Koondawg got out, and they retrieved the loot, paid off the debt, and it was all good, right?"

Montalvo scoffed. "Uh, nothing is ever quite as simple as it should be. Best laid plans and all that shit. Ol' Koondawg was a bullshitter. Imagine that, a con being less than truthful. Anyhow, the money he claimed he had socked away didn't exist. There was maybe 10% of it, at best. Now Cedar Stock was on the hook with the Aryan Brotherhood for the whole magilla," Montalvo said.

"Which explains his bad attitude," Stern said slowly.

"Yeah, it wasn't just the money he owed to the AB, it was the fact that they took a little of his hide up front in exchange for the deal. They had him beat the fuck out of Koondawg on the yard, right under the officers. Hell of a fight. Officers had to physically break it up. Of course, Stock gets a 115 violation out of it and ends up doing a full term. No good time, but also no parole, no tail."

"But Cedar still has to pay back the AB," Roy said. "So he gets out and starts earning. Right?"

"Right. His next and last case was a 211 armed. He and Koondawg and some others were robbing drug dealers while pretending to be cops, presumably to live and to pay off the AB debt," Montalvo said, scouring the paperwork in front of him.

"Impersonating a police officer is against the law. Did they at least Mirandize their victims?" Stern asked, throwing his hands up in exaggerated disgust.

"I'll bet most of their arrests were tossed by some weak-chinned DA," Roy observed, shaking his head.

"Any idea who all was in his takedown crew?" Stern asked, after high-fiving Roy.

"That's why you comedians are here talkin' to me. Koondawg Cutler for sure, and a cold motherfucker named Jackson Howard. They called him Jacky Blue, a peckerwood out here from Texas. First went up for robbery back in the 90's. He and Koondawg hooked up in the joint and then joined Cedar Stock when they got out." Montalvo opened a bottle of water and took a long drink.

"Illegally robbing drug dealers for their illegal money to illegally give money to an illegal organization who had asked for an illegal hit on a guy named Koondawg, and that's got to be an illegal name somewhere," Roy joked.

"Somebody ought to arrest these fools," Montalvo said. "Of course, the only ones still out are Koondawg and Stock. Everybody else all locked up tight, going nowhere for life, as short as that life may be."

"Meaning?" Roy asked.

"Well, in 2014, Koondawg and Jacky Blue hit a dope pad in Del Rio, Texas. Tied up four, ended up putting bullets in four. Shouldn't have been so stingy with the rounds. Three died, but one survived. The survivor testified against Jacky Blue. Koondawg escaped. He's been on the run. We've got an absconding warrant in the system for him because he's wanted in California. Texas Rangers want him worse than we do. We sent some guys down there to help find him. No luck. Jacky Blue is sitting in Huntsville, quickly running out of appeals. About to be smoke I'd think."

"Gotta love Texas. They handle their biz," nodded Stern appreciatively.

"The *get a rope* state," laughed Montalvo. "No wonder we got so many incarcerated in California. We need to turn more of them into pope smoke."

"So Cedar Stock gets out of the pen in 2004 and has evaded prosecution for fourteen years? Incredible," said Roy. "We know he's been capering, because he really has no visible means of support, just a front handyman business."

"He got smart, learned the system, keeps himself insulated," Stern said.

"So the rough crew Dr. Fournette spoke of has got to be Koondawg and Jacky Blue and a few others off and on. Pud Wilson, maybe? We'll grab some photos of both of them. I'll get at Sarah Stock for an ID," Roy said as he leaned back and ran a hand front to back over his hair.

"Or her boss, Ronnie," suggested Stern.

"Yep, but from a political standpoint I'd have to approach Sarah first, so Ronnie Faraday doesn't think he's going behind her back," Roy pointed out.

Stern was thoughtful for a moment. "So none of this makes any sense to me. I'm kinda thick I guess. Why kill Pud Wilson, and who the hell are your bones on Puma Ridge?" Stern asked, looking at Montalvo who threw his hands up.

"Why you lookin' at me? You're the dicks," Montalvo laughed. "And hey, Jake, Cedar Stock was right."

"How's that?" Stern asked.

"On that yard at New Folsom you looked like youda rather been any place else, like maybe somewhere crawlin' naked through broken glass."

"I gotta admit," laughed Stern, "At that moment, sitting safely at home passing a slim jim through my sinuses had a certain appeal."

CHAPTER 40

Kat looked up from her desk to a white board that Roy had scrawled a web diagram on. He'd printed Cedar Stock in the center of the web. Spokes extended from Cedar's name and ended variously at *Puma Ridge, Pud Wilson, Dina Morgan, New Folsom, Jacky Blue/Texas, Koondawg Cutler, Sarah Stock/Zack Stock, Cops-Robbers Crew, AB (Moonshine Tankersley), Germaine Stock, and Planet Zarkon*

"Well? Have you figured it out, yet?" Roy asked, with a twinkle in his eye.

"I think so," Kat said, tapping her pen on her notebook. "Aliens from Planet Zarkon were conducting experiments on kidnapped humans and animals from Planet Earth. When they were through, they deposited bones on Puma Ridge. Pud Wilson and Dina Morgan were getting high one night and saw their spaceship leaving the area and had to be eliminated because they'd also seen that three of the aliens had taken on human form because they'd been sent to infiltrate the human race. Those three were Aryan Brotherhood members Cedar Stock, Jacky Blue, and Koondawg."

Roy laughed heartily. "You're smarter than you look. Type that up. I'll sign it, and then I can retire, and you can get on with your life as a science fiction writer."

"If you don't mind me asking, why do you have Sarah and Zack Stock up there?" Kat asked.

"Because Old John St. John would have put them up there. Some of their movements over time have been abnormal. When you see abnormal actions in a case, you examine them until you can eliminate them as relevant."

"I'm not sure I follow," Kat said, cocking her head to one side and furrowing her eyebrows.

"That's okay. Look, we know Cedar Stock is at the center of this mess which contains elements of cold and hot cases. He and his crew of robbers stayed with Sarah and Zack Stock back in the day. Around the same time, Sarah and Zack have a break-up; Zack then drinks himself into a stupor, falls in a river, and drowns. These are not everyday occurrences, but they are somehow connected to our main suspect, Cedar Stock. Therefore, they have to be examined and ruled out."

"It's so cool that you came up with those names of Cedar's partners from so long ago," Kat said.

"Too bad you couldn't have come with me, but there are some places that are simply off limits, even to most cops. That's the beauty of the CDCR, they don't destroy records. They're problem solvers first and foremost. Can't afford not to be. We're lucky as a state to have at least one law enforcement organization that has its act together."

"So what's next?" Kat asked.

"Stocks. All day, every day," Roy replied. "Stock family is key before I try to pull an ace. Unfortunately, that means I'll be going it alone on some interviews. I wouldn't want to put you in an awkward position, plus it could get dicey from a safety standpoint. The Sheriff is cool with you being here or at the Main, just not out in the field."

"So, is there anything more I can do to help?" Kat asked.

"Yes. I'll pay for your gas, but someone needs to go to Silverton and pick up an accidental death report and a coroner's report on Zack Stock. They've been pulled and are waiting. A death investigation report is the one document that doesn't get purged. No worries if you can't do it. I can have it brought down by a deputy leaving court up there."

"I'm on it!" Kat declared, rising from her seat.

Inwardly, Roy grinned at her boundless enthusiasm. She was a gem, no doubt. The parallels with Raisa were heartbreaking.

"Is it off limits, or do you mind if I take a peek at it?"

"Zack Stock won't care. Go ahead, check it out. If I'm not here when you get back, leave a note. Let me know what you think."

"By the way," Kat turned as she got to the door. "Maddy Stock invited me over for dinner tonight? That okay?"

"Absolutely. Just remember what I said, don't ask any questions. Ears only. Deal?"

"Deal, Dad!"

And she was gone.

Again? Don't do that, please.

♦

Roy dialed the number. He'd made sensitive phone calls for decades yet still felt the quiver of anticipation mixed with doubt, like some poor mope trying to make a living cold calling from a boiler room. The next few seconds could mean the difference between success and failure.

"Ronald Faraday Real Estate. How may I help you?"

"Sarah Stock, please."

"One moment,"

So far, so good. No gatekeepers to lie to.

"This is Sarah Stock. May I help you?"

"Sarah, my name is Roy Church. I'm a detective with Karuk County Sheriff's Department. Do you have a moment?"

There was a brief moment of silence.

"Uh, well, I guess so. I can't imagine what this is about. Did I list a property with marijuana growing on it? That's legal now, right?" Sarah laughed a little anxiously.

Good. Just the right amount of nervous chatter. Minimal hostility.

"I'm relatively new in Karuk County, and I was hoping to pick your brain on some folks and a property from way back, but only if you have time, and it's convenient."

"Who are these people? Which property?"

"If it's all the same, I'd like to talk to you in person about them. Would it be okay if I came by your office? Again, that's only if you're not busy."

"It's mid-winter. Not showing a lot of properties right now. Sure, why not. Come on by this afternoon, right after lunch?"

"I'll be there. 1 p.m.?"

"Sounds good. Wait. You're the famous detective from LA who was in the paper a few days ago. Now I'm really good and nervous." Her voice had a low, musical quality to it. It was pleasant.

"Don't be. I'm harmless, and you can't trust anything the news puts out," Roy said for the hundredth time since that article came out.

"Okay, I'll be here. Do I need a lawyer?"

Roy smiled. "I hope not. You have reported your commissions properly, I trust."

Not one mention of her parents' interview. They'd kept up their end.

♦

Roy parked the Sheriff's SUV around the corner on a street that T-ed in just north on Main Street. No use advertising where he was with the marked rig. He walked the fifty yards to Ronald Faraday Real Estate, being mindful of the salted areas merchants had kindly spread out on the frosty sidewalks fronting their doors.

Five minutes later, Roy found himself seated in Sarah Stock's office, the scent of a pleasing fragrance in the air. Roy was again struck by family resemblances. He imagined Maddy on the left, Emily on the right and Sarah smack dab in the middle. Time lapse photography at its most human.

Sarah had lost little of her youthful beauty that he recalled from her school photos. Her hair was shorter, the length of Emily's, but a salt and pepper mixture. She sat back in her business suit with white teeth and glittering, curious green eyes. She wore the practiced smile of a professional used to calmly dealing with emotional and demanding buyers and sellers, one side selling the Taj Mahal, the other purchasing an outhouse. Her job was to get them to meet in the middle at the single story, three bedroom, two and a half bath ranch on .25 acres. Roy suspected that she did her job well.

"Thanks for seeing me on such short notice," Roy began.

Sarah smiled politely, said nothing, and looked at him intently. Hard to read.

He continued.

"You may have heard about some skeletal remains found last fall up on Puma Ridge?"

"Yes." Short answer but not rude.

"I'm the detective currently assigned to the case which is why I wanted to sit down with you and see if you could help me."

"Me? Help? How? I guess I'm at a loss here," Sarah said, her palms up in front of her.

"Trust me, I'm confused a bit myself. You may also have read that the Santa Rosa Police, and I tend to agree with them, believe there is a connection to a death investigation they are conducting down in the Wine Country. A Jesse Dale Wilson died there under questionable circumstances a few weeks back. I believe here, locally, he might have been known as Pud Wilson."

"Yes, I know the name, but I don't really know him. I may even have met him or seen him decades ago. I really only know of him because everyone says he killed his girlfriend Dina Morgan. Pud and Dina were older than me when I was in school back in the early 90's. I don't think they went to high school when I was going there. I may have met them through mutual friends at one time or another, but that is about it."

Roy jotted some notes. "Do you know where you might have met Mr. Wilson?"

"I'm still very confused as to why you think I can help. I mean it is possible he and Dina might have come by our house once when my husband Zack was still alive, but that was over 20 years ago."

"And where exactly was that? Here in Sisson?"

"Yes, we lived in a house we were renting right after we got married. It's off of North Old Stage Road, about two miles from town."

"Your husband? You say he's passed away. I'm sorry."

"Thanks, it was a long time ago. He drowned over on the Klamath River."

Sarah's words came out fast and direct. She met Roy's eyes yet did not blink, her face impassive today. He suspected she'd given in to tears regularly at one time but had finally learned to fight back. She'd reached that mental point where she could power through when this painful subject inevitably came up years later. Simple survival strategy. He knew it well.

"I really am sorry for your loss," Roy said, quietly.

Sarah smiled slightly.

Moving on, Roy asked, "Jesse Wilson and Dina Morgan were acquaintances of your husband?"

"Well, more so friends of my husband's cousin Cedar. Cedar used to stay with us occasionally. That is probably when I met Jesse Wilson and Dina Morgan. But that many years ago, I can't be sure."

"Hmm," said Roy.

"I don't know how that helps you. I guess that is Dina's skeleton up on Puma Ridge? That's what everyone says and what it says in the paper, sort of."

"Actually, we do not have an identity on the skeletal remains, but an awful lot of people seem sure it is Dina Morgan. I was not around when she disappeared, so all I have to go on are old reports until I get actual confirmation from a lab," Roy said, shaving the truth just a hair.

"Okay, but she disappeared about ten years after my husband drowned and I moved out of that house we rented. I didn't know her or Jesse Wilson, so I guess I'm not much help," said Sarah, glancing at the clock.

"Well, I'm trying to cover all leads. In a cold case, you have to go back and recreate the past. It's sort of like building a model, so you can walk around it and look for the answers you seek," Roy said, taking it easy and smiling warmly.

"I guess that certainly makes sense, and from what the paper says you seem to know what you're doing. I'll bet you have a lot of good stories. You should write a book." She was meeting him halfway now, her guard slowly lowering.

"Maybe someday. Yes, the stories are interesting, but not good. Lots of human tragedy. Sometimes it's hard to live with old memories," Roy said, slowly working from his old recipe book.

"Oh, I didn't mean good. Of course, the poor people you must have seen," Sarah said, hurriedly.

"It's the ones left behind that you feel sorry for. The victims of a deadly crime are gone. It's the ones left to question why or to live with survivor's guilt, depression, loneliness, the desperate longing. Those are the ones I work for. I work to give them a measure of relief that the person or persons responsible for the death of their loved one did not get away, are held to account."

Sarah stared directly at Roy as he spoke, letting him talk, suddenly not worried about the clock.

He had found that most people were fascinated by the subject matter of a world they'd only paid to peek into at a movie theater or with a cable bill, and they would let you talk about it for a while, softening in the process without even realizing.

Roy continued. "Take for example the skeletal remains on the mountain or Dina Morgan, if they're not one and the same. Loved ones exist, somewhere. Husbands, wives, kids, parents maybe who wake up every day wondering. They go about their lives with a sadness gnawing a hole in their hearts."

"That's terrible," Sarah shook her head sadly. "But I know what you mean. It's been over twenty years, and I still sometimes wake up thinking about Zack and how things might have been if he'd not gone fishing, if we'd not fought before he died. I'll live with that forever."

Now.

"I guess that brings me back to that time and your cousin-in-law Cedar. Well, not so much Cedar, but maybe some who were around him back then."

Sarah was back to staring at him, but she did glance briefly at her hands where two thumbs were now rolling around each other.

"I don't understand," she said. Her go-to position.

"Would you mind looking at two photos and telling me if you recognize anyone?"

"I guess, yes, okay," Sarah said, thumbs kicking it up a notch, like beaters on dough.

Roy opened a manila folder he'd brought with him. He removed the CDCR ID photos of Kelly Cutler and Jackson Howard, both taken in the early 1990's. He'd covered their names. He leaned forward and placed them on the desk in front of Sarah who glanced quickly at them.

"Oh my God," she whispered.

CHAPTER 41

Rule *Numero Uno* in witness interviewing is to never interview two or more witnesses at a time. Otherwise, the statements of one completely undermine the integrity of the second. Are you getting the truth or a parrot? It amused Roy to see films or TV shows where witnesses were called out of a courtroom audience or where the police took statements from several people sitting on a living room couch (often with crime scene techs dusting and photographing everything in sight in the background).

Sometimes Rule One gets fractured, especially when there is an uncontrolled eruption such as the one Roy was now experiencing in Sarah's office.

In fairness, Roy had not gotten far enough into the chat with Sarah where he felt he needed to ask for exclusivity, and he *had* interviewed the Fournettes together. In addition, he had not come across an actual witness to anything resembling a crime, other than Cedar Stock, so there'd been no need for cautionary admonishments. He was not sure where this pandemonium would lead, but sometimes it was best to strap up and enjoy the ride.

Upon seeing the photos of Koondawg Cutler and Jacky Blue Howard, Sarah leaped from her chair and sprinted to her door. Throwing it open, she called out.

"Ronnie! Come here, quick."

Within seconds Ronnie Faraday, owner and CEO of Ronald Faraday Real Estate, had rushed into the room, concern flashing in his eyes. He looked first at Sarah then at Roy, as if he were a burglar holding an office laptop, and then back again to Sarah. She had retreated to the front of her desk, half sitting as she leaned back on it holding the photos in her left hand, her right hand tucked under her left elbow in a subconscious attempt to shield herself from whatever it was that had pulled her fire alarm.

"What is it? What's wrong?" he asked in a worried voice.

"Here," she said, handing him the photos.

Roy had studied body language for decades. His life in patrol and solving cases in the Homicide Bureau depended on the ability to read the unspoken words of body movement. Quick interpretations had to be made if you saw feet shifting position prepping for fight or flight, or a hand cupped to a mouth stifling a cry, or in the present case, a man's shoulders slumping, along with a full body shudder.

Paydirt.

"What's this about?" Ronnie asked, with a distinct weakness in his voice.

Roy glanced at Sarah who was staring down at the carpet, digging one toe in.

Apparently, Miss Sarah, you did not tell your boss the cops were coming to interview you regarding the disappearance of Jimmy Hoffa.

"May I close the door?" Roy asked.

Without looking, Ronnie threw up an underhanded palm in acquiescence, and Roy reached over and slowly closed the door.

"I had no intention of alarming anyone. I was simply looking for some background information for a cold case I'm working on. By the way, I'm Roy Church, Sheriff's Department."

Roy stepped to Ronnie and shook a moist hand.

"What, what case? Sarah? What case?" Ronnie's drained face and quavering voice said he definitely could not think on his feet well enough to join a covert CIA operation to infiltrate and discern who in the Russian mob had the missing nuclear fission material. Better stick to selling overpriced lake fronts.

"I'm just finding out about it myself, Ronnie," Sarah said. "It has to do with the skeleton they found on Puma Ridge and the death of that man Jesse Wilson. Apparently these two did it."

"Oh my God," Ronnie exclaimed.

"Wait, wait" Roy said. "I think we all need to count to ten and take a seat while I explain why I have an interest in these two. To be clear, I have no information that they are suspects in Jesse Wilson's death."

"What? Okay," Ronnie said, "I'm sorry. I'm just in a little bit of shock, I guess. I thought we'd seen the last of these two."

"I can't believe they've resurfaced. It's been what, twenty-two, almost twenty-three years?" Sarah said. "Horrid men."

Sarah sat back down at her desk and put her fingers up to her temples. Ronnie slumped in a chair and stared at the carpet, his mind miles away.

Roy grabbed a chair and then contemplated the two distraught realtors.

Well this has ruined their day. But why?

"I guess I should ask how it is you two recognize these fellas, and I'd like to make sure I get a complete understanding. Normally, I'd ask to talk to you each separately," Roy looked from one to the other noting that Ronnie's eyes had found a fascinating stain on the carpet between his feet.

"I'd like Ronnie with me if it's okay," Sarah spoke more loudly than necessary. Anxiety.

"Yes, if that's okay," Ronnie looked up, with moisture in his eyes — not tears, but not dry for sure. Pressure. Strain.

"Detective, you must think we're overreacting. I'm sorry," Sarah said, smiling feebly.

"No, no, it's obvious that you both had a negative reaction to the photos. I did not mean to upset you. Of course, I am curious now," said Roy with easy diplomacy.

"It's just that we hold these two responsible for the death of her husband and my best friend," Ronnie said. He crossed then uncrossed his legs, grey knit pants lifting to bare expensive looking, silk dress socks.

"Over twenty years of pain," Sarah added.

"Now, it's my turn to say I don't understand," Roy said, his brow knit slightly.

"Simply put, if these two had not been living in my house against my wishes, Zack and I would not have fought about it, I would not have moved out, and he would not have gone off fishing all upset and drowned," Sarah said dejectedly. She pushed her mid-length hair behind her ears as if to free her eyes for better viewing of her memories.

Ronnie got up and moved to Sarah, leaned over, and hugged her. She pressed her head into his hip.

"I'm sorry sweetie," he whispered down to her, rubbing her back.

"You guys take all the time you want. Fill me in whenever you feel you can," Roy said. He settled back, the way he had a hundred times. People in shock needed time, but it was this shock time where unguarded words came tumbling out.

"Do you want me to tell him, or do you feel strong enough, hon?" Ronnie asked Sarah, concern shadowing his face.

"I'll tell him," Sarah said looking up. She took a deep breath and quickly wiped at a moistened eye.

"When my folks moved me here from Marin County in 1990, that's when I first met Ronnie. His dad ran this office. I met him the first day we came in that door over there. He was wearing his baseball uniform," Sarah said. She smiled at Ronnie and wiped another tear. Ronnie leaned over and patted her hand.

"When I got to high school, Ronnie was there. It was tough being a new girl in a strange school not really knowing anyone. Thank *God* Ronnie was there. I'd say we became inseparable. We've been inseparable ever since, haven't we," Sarah grinned through tears.

"We have, we have," Ronnie said reassuringly.

"Ronnie introduced me to his best friend Zack Stock. Zack and I fell in love in high school. We got married as soon as I turned 18, and we moved in together."

Sorta glossing over the Ronnie and I being inseparable. Maybe they know I can read between lines.

"Wow, young," was all Roy said.

"Yes, my parents, as you can imagine, were not happy. To be honest, they didn't like Zack, especially after we ran off to Reno and got married."

"You were an adult and in love," Roy said agreeably.

I would have been less than thrilled.

"They saw him as from the wrong side of the tracks and a derailment of my college ambitions. He didn't come from a blue blood family like we had in Marin County where we lived before. But he was kind, gentle, funny, and adventuresome. A real outdoorsman. He had no desire to go to college. He wanted to work building houses. He would have, too, if the economy had been better. He drove a gas truck when we first got married. That was the job he had, delivering gas, propane, to people around Sisson."

"Sounds like a fine young man, a hard worker," Roy encouraged.

"Yes, a good provider for his family. He was a very good hunter and fisherman. We always had duck and quail and deer and fish. He loved the outdoors."

Finally, at least one deer hunter!

"He was very athletic. Good ball player. Excellent third baseman, could field like that old time Oriole, Brooks Robinson," Ronnie added.

"I used some of my money. Honestly, I had a huge bank account by 18-year-old standards, and we rented a nice home on a couple of acres on Solari Lane over off of Old Stage. It was on part of a working dairy farm. We had no one around us. A great view of the mountain. It was heaven, and even more so when I found out I was pregnant with my daughter, Maddy."

"I've met your daughter," Roy said.

"That's right, you're the one she stopped by and spoke to about how our family thought the bones on Puma Ridge might belong to Dina Morgan."

"But you didn't really know Dina Morgan," Roy said, glancing at his notebook.

"Right," Sarah said. "But a family member who had speculated on it being Dina wanted to make sure you got that information. The family member isn't the most reputable I'm afraid and didn't want to come forward himself."

Cedar Stock sent Maddy to me way back then. Interesting. Veddy Interesting.

"Hmm," said Roy, noncommittally.

"Ronnie came by a lot, not as much as he used to when I was at my parents' home, but for a year it was good times. I even made up with my parents enough that I could at least visit them."

"Well that's good," Roy said.

Sarah nodded and hesitated before saying, "That's when Zack's cousin Cedar came into our lives. Do you know him? Cedar Stock?"

So Cedar, who Dr. Fournette said is still a part of Sarah's life, has not let her in on his new friends in law enforcement.

"I've heard the name," Roy replied evenly.

"Not surprising," Sarah said, without pausing to look questioningly at Roy and wonder if he'd not been forthcoming.

She continued, "He has a good heart, he really does. He was musically inclined in school, but he got into trouble with drugs right out of high school, began dealing them when he was going to our local community college. He really messed up his future. He was very bright and could have gone on. Sadly, he went to prison instead."

"Drugs have destroyed more than one set of dreams I'm afraid," Roy said in an understanding tone.

"When he got out, he really tried to turn his life around. He opened his own business falling and trimming trees. He worked so hard. He had to travel out of the area for work often." Sarah was settling into the rhythm of recounting a long history, old memories.

"Sounds great. Not often a guy gets out of the pen and finds a steady stream of work."

Steady stream of drug dealers to rob though.

Roy noticed Ronnie had looked away from Sarah as she got into the subject of Cedar. Did he share the same fawning attitude toward a rehabbed felon? He was picking at some lint on his sleeve. Roy suspected not.

"Cedar needed help, and he felt sorry for other former inmates who were down on their luck. He hired several of them to help him in his business. Unfortunately, he hired two of the worst, those two there. I just don't think they wanted to go straight the way Cedar did," Sarah said.

Look up the word naiveté in the dictionary and find your picture.

"None of this would have mattered to me that much if Zack hadn't felt sorry for Cedar. He tried to help him by letting him stay at our house while he was in this area working. We had a nice three bedroom, two and half bath with a very large yard that rolled into the old dairy pasture. We had no neighbors on the lane to complain about the work trucks.

I was okay with just Cedar staying, a few days here and there, but it became more regular, and then he brought those two with him. It really went downhill in a short amount of time." Sarah sighed and shook her head slightly. Ronnie leaned back against the edge of the desk, his eyes searching the carpet once more for the elusive stain.

"And it was during this time that you think Dina Morgan and Jesse Wilson might have stopped by?" Roy asked.

"Yes," Sarah answered. "Had to be. No other time would I have had a reason to run into them. They knew Cedar well."

"Let me show you some more photos," Roy said.

He removed Pud's and Dina's DMV photos from a folder and handed them to Sarah.

"They look very familiar. I'm pretty sure they came by the house when Cedar and his workers were there. Yes, that is definitely them."

"I didn't know them at all," Ronnie broke in. "I stopped going to visit regularly after Zack began allowing Cedar to stay there. From what I've heard, Dina and this Wilson character didn't sound like the types who would need a realtor."

"That was almost the worst part, Ronnie. Not seeing you. I missed you terribly."

Ronnie smiled sadly at her.

"But these two guys definitely took advantage of Cedar's good nature," Sarah said emphatically, pointing at Jacky Blue and Koondawg.

Poor Cedar, a real missionary among cannibals.

"Do you recall names?

"I don't know their real names, but Cedar called this one Coon and this one Jacky."

Roy looked at Ronnie.

"What about you Mr. Faraday? Do you remember their names?"

His eyes slid away. "Oh, no. I saw them once, maybe twice, just enough to remember their faces. I didn't even know that they went by those, what are they nicknames? As I said, I stayed away. They gave off a bad vibe."

"Oh, Ronnie, I'm so sorry," said Sarah.

"It's okay, sweetie. I worried so for you and Maddy, and it turns out, we should have been worried for poor Zack, too."

"Are you able to tell me what happened next?" Roy asked in a low voice.

Sarah looked out the window for a moment. She reached behind her, fumbling for a box of tissues. She pulled one out and used it to wipe her eyes and nose.

She took a deep breath. "One of them, this man Jacky, made a pass at me. I told Zack when he came home. Zack didn't believe me. He thought I said it just to get him to kick them out because I'd been asking for him to do that for weeks. I stupidly told him it was either them or me. He stomped off. I gathered a few things, along with Maddy, and left. I never saw him again."

Tears rolled freely but silently down her face. Ronnie stood up and hugged her, letting her bury her head in his shoulder. He reached around her and grabbed a tissue for himself.

Nice going, Roy. Maybe I should go get a real job with Reuben Montalvo. Move to Reno. Reuben and Roy's South of the Border Deli and Wedding Chapel.

Roy studied the two souls comforting each other. Now was the time to let them have their hugs and mutual support, but at some point, he'd have to speak to them individually. Just not today. He waited, knowing what came next. Charlie Criss had warned him decades earlier that the bearer of bad tidings gets a momentary pass, then it dawns on the mourner that this person in the room with them, this policeman, is the one responsible for how they feel at this moment. As irrational as it might seem, the messenger gets the blame and had been getting the blame as far back as Sophocles.

Ronnie straightened up and took the lead.

"Why was this necessary, to come here and dredge up horrible memories, why?" he asked, throwing a dark look at Roy.

"This is where you apologize profusely, son," Charlie Criss had taught him.

Roy began in his softest voice, "I am beyond sorry, can you please accept my apology? I'm only following a lead in trying to solve the murder of a victim whose family probably still grieves much like you still do. It was not my intention to upset you in any way. I had no idea of the connection to your past tragedy in losing your friend and husband. It's the part of this job I hate. Can you forgive me?"

Yes, we forgive you. It's not your fault.

"Oh, it's not your fault," Sarah said through her sniffles.

"Of course, we forgive you," Ronnie said, his eyes red. "It's just so upsetting to have it all boil back up."

"I know, and I'm truly sorry," Roy said. He leaned forward and extended open hands, palms up. A universal sign of openness, of soliciting forgiveness, or in some cases a sign for *I have questions, tell me more.*

"A fateful set of circumstances unintentionally put into motion by Zack simply trying to help his cousin out. But his cousin bears some responsibility, too," Ronnie said pointedly.

"Ronnie, he's tried to atone over the years," Sarah gently separated herself from Ronnie's arms. "Cedar did bad things, it's true. But he paid his debt and has been good to Maddy and me ever since."

Roy noted that Ronnie shook his head ever so slightly, maybe not even aware that he'd sent up a smoke signal that read, *not buying it.*

Roy wondered which one of these people it would dawn on first. Which one would finally ask the question he'd been waiting for? In their dealing with pain, they'd completely forgotten the obvious. Sarah was still too distraught over distant memories, but Ronnie had a moment of clarity.

"So why are these two connected to the death of Jesse Wilson in Santa Rosa and the body on Puma Ridge if they didn't do it," Ronnie asked, getting to the heart of the matter.

I love how an entire body has been found on Puma Ridge. It's one little bone, people.

"Someone put a tiny bug in our ear," Roy said, leaving out the part about it being Reuben Montalvo.

"They said these two guys, Jacky Blue and Koondawg with a K, as they're known, were acquaintances with Dina Morgan and Jesse Wilson aka Pud. Both Morgan and Wilson ended up dead or missing, and both names came up as we're examining the Puma Ridge skeletal remains, so it is simply good investigative strategy to retrace the steps Jacky Blue and Koondawg took," Roy said, making sure to emphasize the monikers for both cons.

"That's right, now I remember, Jacky Blue and Koondawg, that's what Cedar called them," Sarah said, her face blotched and puffy.

"If you say so," Ronnie said, somewhat glumly it seemed to Roy. He really wasn't buying the Cedar as outreach pastor.

"So this rat or snitch or whatever you guys call them, wouldn't he or she be able to tell you who did what to whom?" Sarah asked.

"We're hoping soon, very soon, but we have to be able to corroborate what this person tells us. If and when they get us the information we need, we have to be able to trust it," Roy said, really getting into the manufacturing of this wonderfully helpful informant.

"That whole life of crime and drugs. What a waste," Sarah sighed.

"Yes, it is." Roy paused, clicking his pen. "By the way, do you recall the name of Cedar's business, the one where these guys worked trimming trees?"

"Oh, yes, *Cedar Trims*. I thought at the time how clever it was, you know cedar trees and all being part of what they cleared or cleaned up," Sarah answered.

"Catchy name for sure. So they worked all over the Sisson area?" Roy asked. He marveled at how his violation of the sacred rule of interviewing one witness at a time had yielded so much, verbal and non-verbal.

"Actually, I'm not sure. It was a long time ago. Seems to me they traveled up into Oregon for work, and down south. They had to go where people like them could get work. It wasn't easy, but Cedar was determined to go straight and do what he had to do, travel where he had to travel, to make it work," Sarah said, highlighting Cedar's walk down the straight and narrow again.

"Except he went back to prison for robbery," Ronnie interjected, "Guess he fell off the wagon."

Sarah looked at Ronnie sharply but said nothing.

Ronnie does not like Cedar. Good to know.

"Would it be okay if I contacted either of you, if and when more information comes in related to Koondawg, Jacky Blue, Pud Wilson or Dina Morgan? Having only been here a year, I really don't know the lay of the land yet, relationships, et cetera. I'd hate to make another mistake like I did upsetting you two today," Roy said with a practiced apologetic tone.

"Sure," Sarah said, smiling. Ronnie remained silent but nodded in the affirmative. Deep thinking going on under that hat rack.

"Do you think Cedar Stock would talk to me?" Roy asked.

"I'd be surprised," Sarah said. "He's is not the cooperative citizen type.

"You can say that again," Ronnie added darkly.

"Ronnie, please," Sarah said reproachfully. "Be nice."

Why? Cedar Stock and nice have nothing in common.

CHAPTER 42

Roy sat at his desk thumbing through the summary of the Karuk County Sheriff's Department investigation into the accidental drowning death of Zachary Hughson Stock, aged 21, on or about June 21st, 1995. He'd set aside a yellow sticky note from Kat on the cover page.

Fascinating reading. I marked a few spots with stickies.

It appeared straight forward enough. Presumably the young man had gone fishing alone on the Klamath River after a domestic altercation with his wife, Sarah Stock, aged 20. Sarah had filed a missing person's report on June 24th. Then on June 25th a Sheriff's deputy had spotted Zachary Stock's parked pick-up alongside a fishing beach called Skeahan Bar on the Klamath River, fifteen miles northwest of Silverton. It was unlocked, had no keys inside, and a bed littered with empty beer cans and debris.

Roy shook his head. From what he could gather by studying an overall scene diagram, Zack Stock's pick-up had been visible from the main river highway. Not until a *Be on the Look-out*, a BOLO, had been issued did the beat deputy muster enough curiosity to check it out. Apparently, Deputy Savage had been too busy studying for an upcoming sergeants' exam.

Kat sticky: *Is this deputy related to the lieutenant I met?*

Yes, Kat, one and the same.

After a several day search, Sheriff's divers recovered the body of Zachary Stock five miles west of where his truck had been found.

The autopsy showed fractures and abrasions consistent with a body having tumbled over the thousands of rocks in the various sets of rapids between Skeahan Bar and the body recovery location. Water in the lungs indicated suffocation. A toxicity report was inconclusive based on the time the body had spent in the water or possibly hung out of the water on a branch. Fermentation can occur in a body if it is not kept cool, so there was no way to tell actual blood alcohol level at the time of death. Drowning was listed as cause of death.

Roy set down the investigating deputy's report. It appeared that Detective Edward Silva had done a thorough job.

Kat Sticky: *Wow! Our Sheriff Silva?*

Detective Silva had interviewed multiple Stock family members. All agreed the victim had probably been upset over a fight with his wife. He'd gone fishing to find solace. He drank too much, fell in the water, and drowned. One floated the idea of suicide because of marital problems, but a search of the victim's residence and truck revealed no suicide note, and none had ever heard him make suicidal comments.

An interview with his young widow did not reveal anything out of the ordinary. The facts, statements, and views of any and all connected to the incident were consistent. No foul play, no suicide. A tragedy brought on by domestic strife and alcohol.

Roy flipped to the actual witness statements. Unable to write out her own, due to emotional trauma, Detective Silva had taken an "in essence" statement from the new widow.

In essence, Sarah Stock told me the following. On June 20, 1995, at about 1600 hours, she and her husband Victim Stock got into an argument. The argument centered on guests at the home that her husband allowed to stay there. She said her husband's cousin Cedar Stock and at least two of his workers, white male adults about 30 yrs., identified only as "Jacky" and "Coondog," stayed off and on at the Stock residence. Cedar Stock runs a landscaping business called Cedar Trims.

Sarah Stock did not want Cedar Stock and his workers staying at her home due to their drinking and foul language. She and Victim Stock had apparently argued over this issue prior.

One of the workers, described by Sarah Stock as Jacky (WMA, 30, 6-2, 230, Bln, Blu, Multiple tattoos) made sexually suggestive remarks to her earlier in the afternoon on June 20, 1995 (No investigation desired by Sarah Stock. Reported for information purposes only).

Sarah reported the incident with Jacky to Victim Stock when he got home from work. Victim Stock apparently did not believe her, stating to her that it was an attempt by her to drive a wedge between him and his cousin. They argued, verbal only. No physical confrontation occurred according to Sarah.

Sarah decided to pack up their infant daughter Madison, aka Maddy, and go stay with her parents, Dr. Penn and R.N. Emily Fournette of Sisson.

Sarah last heard from her husband when he called her on the morning of June 21st, telling her to come home. They argued over the phone again about Cedar Stock and his crew of workers hanging out at their home. Sarah told Victim Stock she was not coming back until he got rid of the Cedar Trims crew. She did not speak to or see Victim Stock again.

At about 1700 hours on June 21st a mutual friend, Ronald Faraday, WMA, 21 yrs., of Sisson, stopped by Dr. Fournette's house to check on her. She told Faraday about the argument, and that her daughter Maddy was very upset over not having her favorite toy that Sarah had forgotten when she packed up to leave Victim Stock. Faraday offered to go get the toy.

Faraday returned about two hours later without the toy, stating that the Cedar Trims crew had been at the home drinking and being rowdy, and that he'd felt unsafe retrieving the toy. Faraday told Sarah that Victim Stock's truck (the one found abandoned on the Klamath) was in the driveway. He did not see or speak to Victim Stock.

The following day, June 22, 1995, Sarah Stock went to her home and saw that everyone was gone. She went in the home and got the child's toy. She noticed nothing amiss.

On June 24, 1995, at about 1500 hours, Sarah Stock saw her cousin-in-law Cedar Stock in the Safeway parking lot in Sisson. She asked him if he had seen Victim Stock because she had not heard from him since June 21st. Cedar Stock told her he last saw Victim Stock heading out to fish on the evening of June 21st. Victim Stock had been upset over the separation and told Cedar Stock he was going to "fish and drink." Cedar Stock and his crew of workers had left early the next morning for a job in Oregon and had returned on June 24th. He had not seen Victim Stock since returning.

Sarah Stock called Victim Stock's employer, Karuk Propane, and was told Victim Stock had not shown up for work for four days.

On June 24th, 1995, Sarah Stock called the Sheriff's Department and made a missing person's report.

End of statement.

Roy set the report down and rubbed his chin in thought. He then scribbled some notes on his ever-present yellow pad.

Next, he read a short statement taken by Detective Silva from Ronald Faraday. It, too, was an in essence statement, not uncommon in an investigation lacking obvious criminal wrong doing.

On June 27, 1995, I interviewed Witness Ronald Faraday at his home in Sisson. Faraday told me he was extremely upset over the death of his friend and that talking about it made him even more upset. However, he was able to give me a short statement. In essence, he told me the following.

On June 21st, 1995, in the late afternoon he left an adult baseball game at the Sisson School ball field. He passed by the home of Dr. Penn Fournette on Volcano View Drive. He saw his friend Sarah Stock's car parked in front. He stopped to say hello. He learned that she had separated from her husband. This was very upsetting to him since her husband, Victim Stock, was also a very good friend. He told me Sarah and Zachary Stock are his two best friends.

Sarah Stock told Faraday that she and Victim Stock had argued over Victim Stock letting his cousin Cedar and his friends stay at her house. Faraday was familiar with the problem in that he'd stopped by the Stock home on Solari Lane several times in the recent past and had witnessed Cedar Stock and his friends at the home. Sarah Stock had told Faraday before that she was unhappy about the arrangement.

Sarah Stock told Faraday she'd forgotten a toy for her daughter when she left her home. Faraday offered to go get it for her and speak to Victim Stock about the situation.

Faraday went to the Stock home on Solari Lane and saw Victim Stock's pick-up in the driveway leading him to believe that Victim Stock was in fact home. However, when he got out of his car, he saw that several of the men in question were at the home drinking, listening to loud music, and being rowdy. He decided against going into the home while they were there.

He did not know the names of the men he saw but described them as members of Cedar Stock's work crew, WMA's about 30, with multiple tattoos on arms, necks and backs. This was consistent with how Sarah Stock had described the unidentified Jacky and Coondog, members of Cedar Stock's work crew.

Faraday left without speaking to Victim Stock but had no reason to believe he was not there since his truck was parked in the driveway.

End of statement.

Roy considered Detective, now Sheriff, Silva's report. He had gone into more detail than normal, when documenting the witnesses' movements and descriptions, almost as if he were investigating a suspicious death.

Roy jotted a note on his pad reminding himself to interview Sheriff Silva ASAP to see what he recalled about the case. It was fair to say Sheriff Silva would be shocked to find that he had a part in this whole train wreck.

It did not surprise him that Detective Silva was able to get a statement from Cedar Stock, short as it was. Even back then, Cedar would have known to act cooperatively if somewhere in there he'd committed a crime he was trying to keep brush over.

He began reading yet another in essence statement.

After the funeral for Victim Stock, I was able to speak with Witness Cedar Stock, cousin to Victim Stock. He told me the following, in essence.

He last saw his cousin Victim Stock at Victim Stock's house on Solari Lane on the evening of

June 20 or 21st. He wasn't sure which. He said it was a day or so after "Zack and his old lady split." He said Victim Stock told him he was going over to the Klamath River to "fish and get fucked up, over his old lady leaving with the kid."

He found out Victim Stock was missing when he returned to Sisson on June 24th from a tree trimming job and ran into Sarah Stock at Safeway in Sisson.

Witness Stock said he didn't know the real reasons why Victim Stock and Sarah Stock had problems, although it might have had to do with his or his workers' loud music at the house. He said he and his workers occasionally stayed with Victim Stock and Sarah Stock.

He owns a tree trimming business called Cedar Trims. He employs two, sometimes three, employees at a time, depending on the size of the job.

He told me he has been to prison, and that it is difficult to get hired, so he works for himself. He is not on parole. He also told me two of his employees had also been to prison and could not find work. He hired them to keep them out of trouble. He knows them only as Jack and Coondog. He met them in prison. He described them as "White guys about my age, with tats."

Witness Stock admitted that he paid Jack and Coondog under the table, so he never bothered to get them set up as legitimate employees who have real paychecks.

He said it was difficult to find enough work locally, so he and his crew travel around the state and into Oregon on tree trimming and landscaping jobs.

When asked where Jack and Coondog are now, he said he did not know. After learning that Victim Stock had drowned, and then hearing that Jack might have "tried to get up on" Sarah Stock, he fired both, since they seemed to be more trouble than they were worth.

He said, "As far as I'm concerned those two caused this whole thing. My cousin Zack is dead, so those two can go back to the pen for all I care."

End of statement.

There was no indication anywhere in the report that Detective Silva had attempted to further identify Jacky and Coondog. Roy had no issue with this. Without a suspicion of foul play, Detective Silva would have been wasting time by chasing them down. Whatever skullduggery they'd been up to with Cedar Stock remained undiscovered.

Roy scanned the pathologist report and found nothing remarkable in it. The autopsy had been performed an hour south down the I-5 in Redding, California, by a contract pathology group. It read like the standard medical examiner's report. Roy pictured the doc dictating into a hanging microphone as he cracked open the chest cavity, removed and weighed organs, zipped the skull open, weighed the brain, examined stomach contents, took fluid samples, remarked on fractured and broken bones, and stated how the damage to the body looked consistent with someone who'd been battered and broken in the giant washing machine known as the Klamath River. All a big yawn. Roy could imagine this doctor had at least one or two other "grand openings" to complete before day's end.

He flipped to the evidence sheet of the report. He laughed when he saw Kat's yellow sticky note along with the familiar initials next to numbers.

Kat Sticky: *Dead Fred!*

Fred Cavanaugh must have had hair and a lot fewer pounds as a young evidence technician.

Several 8" X 10" photos taken by the youthful Dead Fred showed Zachary Stock's pick-up, an oxidized red 1984 Ford F-250. Parked in a wooded area with a wide river in the background, it could have been a photo from a family camping trip where memories are made and all return home safely, tired, and dirty.

He held his breath as he examined the close-up photo taken of the trash in the pick-up's bed.

Kat Sticky: *Is that what I think it is?*

Yes, Kat. Yes, it is.

Roy felt the ghost of Charlie Criss looking over his shoulder working on a mirthful quote. He heard the familiar, anguished clamoring for revenge rising from beyond the yellow tape, coming from those who gyrated uncontrollably under vermillion head rags because they'd lost one of their *boyz in the hood.*

Lying among the stacks of crushed aluminum beer cans, the 40 ounce Olde English 800 Malt Liquor bottle, twin to the one recovered on Puma Ridge, stood out like a glittering nugget in a stream.

Kat Sticky: *Read Mr. Cavanaugh's report on what else he saw in the bed!*

Roy scanned the report

Item FC 12: *Blood sample (sent to lab) found in bed of Victim Stock's vehicle*

Item FC 13: *Hair sample (sent to lab) found in bed of Victim Stock's vehicle*

Attached to the Dead Fred's report was the California Department of Justice, Forensic Lab's report on the two items. A precipitin test, or standard serological test, had determined the blood to be non-human.

Test on the hair samples revealed dense pigmentation toward the medulla accompanied by the lattice commonly found in a four-legged North American animal.

Conclusion: the blood and hair came from a deer.

Roy sat back and whistled.

A dead deer and a forty ounce Olde English 800.

No coincidences. Holy shit.

CHAPTER 43

"My mom has come down ill with a migraine. She gets them. I guess she had a rough day at work."

"Maddy, it's okay. No worries," Kat said into her phone, assuming their plans were cancelled altogether.

But Maddy had other plans. "My Uncle Cedar is here and wants to take us out. Is that okay?"

Kat's heart raced. She paused.

"I feel bad taking his money, but sure, where do you think we ought to go?" She tried to keep her voice light.

"Nothing special. He was going to take us for burgers at the Black Tail. Does that sound good?"

"Yes. I can meet you there. What time?"

"7 p.m. okay?"

"I'll be there. Can't wait." Kat hung up and stared at her phone for a minute, unsure of how to proceed.

♦

Roy's cell phone buzzed. Kat had texted.

Did you read the report?

Yes, great work Detective Hoover!

Thanks! BTW, I told Maddy I'd go to her house for dinner. Didn't know they actually wanted to go out instead. Now her mom's not feeling well. Can't go. Unfortunately, her uncle Cedar Stock was coming over for dinner too. I didn't know, or I'd have made excuses. Now he's going with us. Is this okay?

Roy waited for a minute before replying. Warning bells clanged in his head like a five-alarm fire in Bel Air.

Not a good idea? Terrible idea? It seemed like a good idea at the time?

In *any* universe when does an investigating detective think it is okay for his intern to have dinner with a violent murder suspect in his current and only case? How about never. In LA County you could count on the Times and above the fold when it went to shit. In Karuk County they'd rename the county after the plaintiff, for starters. At the memorial they'd most likely make you run the gauntlet naked just to warm you up for your punishment. Would you be fortunate enough to land a six-week suspension or should you hand in your badge and ID before your union rep and attorney arrived? Oh, and the fact that your texts were completely discoverable and would be viewable for a jury deciding on punitive damages shouldn't matter, right? What could go wrong?

I'm not sure that's a good idea, Cedar Stock is murder suspect.

Roy quickly erased that text. Jesus, not a lot of plausible deniability there. He should drive over to Kat's house, block her Honda in the driveway and show the powers that be he'd learned to use common sense.

Have a good time!

He erased that text.

He could hear the plaintiff's lawyer, "Former Detective Church, is it true you told your intern to have a good time with a suspect in at least one murder and a person of interest in others? Is it dark and hard to breathe up there? You know, there where you have your head, up your ass?"

Call me.

♦

Roy sat tucked back in the dark of a Rite Aid drugstore parking lot on the north side of Lake Street. From his vantage point he had a clear view of the Black Tail and the patrons within through the massive glass windows. He wondered if this is how Cedar Stock had felt the night he followed Roy, waiting, watching, and calculating.

Turnabout is fair play, fucker.

Kat, Maddy, and Cedar had been in the restaurant for twenty minutes. Kat and Maddy sat on one side of the booth, Cedar on the other, facing toward the front door. The conversation looked lively through the scope. Had this been a legitimate surveillance and UC meet, Kat would have been wired, but wiring up your intern on a strictly prohibited operation would only have added an extra layer of cashier's checks to damages should this go awry.

Roy cursed himself for a quickened pulse. Had this been a legitimate surveillance, instead of what was shaping up to be a totally predictable, self-inflicted end of his storied career, he'd have been at least sitting in an unmarked. It would be his luck that a citizen would spot him and ask for the time, something citizens always seemed to do when they spotted a cop and could think of nothing else to say. He prayed that wouldn't happen. He could not afford to take his eye off the meeting.

Roy had been clear with Kat, not that it would ever matter to attorneys. He could not sanction the dinner. She had to make the decision herself with no input from him. It would be up to her to decide if she felt comfortable having dinner with her friend and so-called uncle. Under no circumstances should Kat talk about the case. Under no circumstances should she do anything other than eat dinner, get back in her car, parked out front, and drive straight home. Only then could Roy breathe.

♦

Kat sat next to Maddy, checking out her own menu. She kept it flat on the table for fear of trembling hands betraying nervousness.

"I'm independently wealthy, so you girls order anything you like," Cedar Stock laughed from across the table. "And Kitty Kat, get a Buck Burger Basket to-go order for your boss. He's probably working late tonight on his mysteries and would appreciate it."

Kat looked up, directly into Cedar Stock's leaden blue eyes, a shark considering a seal pup in deep water.

He smiled at her, but it did not touch his inky eyes. "Don't look so surprised. Yeah, I actually met with the notorious Detective Delroy Church to help him out a bit on the body they found on Puma Ridge. He didn't tell you? Sorry, not good dinner conversation," he said in a friendly voice, like a spider chatting up a fly.

"Uncle Cedar, I didn't know you met with Detective Church," Maddy said with surprise, setting her menu down and looking across the table.

"I know, it's against my nature, but I'd like to see justice done. I'm just an ordinary citizen these days trying to make my community safer." He shrugged and picked up his menu again.

"I can't imagine you getting in trouble again. In fact, I can't even remember you ever getting in trouble. I was pretty young. I really just heard stories," Maddy remarked.

"Yep," said Cedar with a sigh, "I got out of the pen in 2004 when you were about 8 or 9. Been a good boy ever since. That was a wasted time." He shook his head at his own apparent stupidity, but Kat had a strange sensation that his regret was more for show than out of true remorse.

"You should give talks at the high school," Maddy said enthusiastically.

Cedar flashed a brilliant smile at her, exposing his straight, white teeth. "Now there's an idea. Give back to the community," said Cedar the Magnanimous.

Kat retained a polite expression but had not said a word during the exchange, still surprised at how open and determined Cedar Stock was in letting her know he'd been to prison, and how aware he was of her current role with the Sheriff's Department. She'd been around him several times over the years at Maddy's home and had never known him to speak of his time in custody. In fact, it had always been a taboo subject as far as she could tell.

"That's so cool of you to help out," Maddy continued with warmth. "And Kat you know how envious I am of you getting to work on a big case."

"Yeah, Kat," Cedar broke in. "Must be fascinating. You going to be a police officer someday?"

"No, no, nothing like that," Kat said. "I want to study ancient bones to learn more about previous cultures and how they differed from our own. That way we can learn more about things like changes in nutrition and the movements of early peoples. It's more like I'll be a history buff sifting through hidden graveyards."

"But you are going to help out with murder cases aren't you?" Maddy asked, sounding a bit disappointed and concerned with how Kat was missing out.

"Well, if there happens to be a question about a particular set of bones found by investigators, and they need an expert opinion on them, I'll help out, naturally, but that's not my main goal," Kat replied, completely lying about her career intentions. She hoped to steer the conversation away from Puma Creek by making her future sound oh-so-boring.

"I'll bet you're learning a lot from Delroy," Cedar smiled, sounding as if he and Roy Church were old pals, surfer bros in fact. "Read about him in the paper. Sounds like a total BAMF,"

Maddy snorted with surprised laughter.

"I'd say he's about brilliant," Kat replied, smiling at Cedar sweetly. "I'm so fortunate to have the opportunity."

"I'll bet," Cedar said. Sincerity and sarcasm, or was it fatalism, blended perfectly, like a Reese's Peanut Butter Cup. "He's solved some of the biggest cases in California, that's for sure. Nothing gets past him, from what I've read, of course."

"Hey, maybe the two of you could speak to high schoolers together," Tone Deaf Maddy said.

"I bet that'd pack the gym. The yin and the yang," Cedar said. "I tell them how I screwed up, and Delroy tells them how he hooks up the screw-ups."

"The yin and the yang. Interesting. We studied that in one of my college philosophy classes," Kat said, hoping to change the subject, but not necessarily hopeful with a con on the other end.

"The study of metaphysical notions I've always found to be enlightening. Karma, chi, nirvana, and yes, yin and yang, Asian philosophy opens your eyes to a completely different set of rules and notions of nature, human or otherwise," Cedar said. "Hmm. Mule Deer feels a bit weighty for me tonight. Two venison tacos and a vinaigrette salad. Just the ticket."

"Jeez. You don't sound like a typical Karuk County redneck," Maddy said jokingly but with obvious admiration.

"Hey, I'm not just a country musician who dealt drugs *that are now legal.* I'm a well-read convict. I lived in the prison libraries." Cedar smiled as the waiter approached to take the order.

Kat had the feeling everything Cedar Stock had said since sitting down was intended directly for Roy Church and no one else. It was almost as if Cedar suspected Kat of wearing a wire. She felt like calling his bluff on the take-out order. The notion that he wanted her to go back and report emboldened her, gave her a sense of security.

"I don't mean to be rude, but what was prison like? In anthropology we do more than examine bones, we look at how older societies dealt with those they felt needed incarceration. Old bones tell us how many were treated in that environment. Hopefully we've evolved somewhat in how we conduct our penal institutions."

Cedar studied her for a moment, as if deciding between slitting her throat and asking if she wanted to order a dessert after her Yearling Burger and Fawn Fries, *for the lite eater.*

"Prison kills your spirit if you let it," he said slowly, looking out the dark window, pausing, as if recalling fatal decisions made without consideration.

"When you go to the pen, your life changes forever. That sounds trite, but you're forced to make choices. Are you prey or are you predator? There is no in between. Hearing grown men cry scratches you down deep. You're never the same. The world turns cheap afterward and you don't come back from it."

"I'm so sorry you went through that," Maddy said softly. The lighthearted, out to dinner evening had taken a decided turn.

"When you're new, they call you a fish. The stink of fear is all around. It makes you sick. When you've been there awhile, you smell something else, the stink of power from those who have the reins. They call them *llaves,* keys. That's when you realize what you've become."

"What's that?" Kat asked, finding herself drawn with intrigue into his dark words despite herself.

"An animal willing to fight to the death for survival," Cedar said with disturbing casualty. "You get to where you fear no man, because to show fear invites that man to take all you got, and it ain't pretty."

"Yeah, sounds no fun to me," Kat added, in the understatement of the evening.

"See these," Cedar said placing a finger on his neck.

Kat stared at the two lightning bolts.

"Think they make me a racist Nazi? A lot of fools do. They're wrong. They kept me alive." His navy eyes glinted dangerously in the half-lighting of the Black Tail.

"Why not get them removed? They can do that you know," Kat said, again pushing the boundary of civility.

Once again Cedar looked directly at her before answering, his eyes cutting like the flame of a blowtorch.

"Because they remind me every day of the fools who forced me to put them on, and they're the reason I'll *never* go back," he said in a husky voice that slipped between clenched teeth. His nostrils flared slightly as he and Kat stared at each other.

The tense atmosphere was shattered as a herd of burgers arrived.

"Ah, just in time to lighten the mood," Cedar remarked convivially. "You should call your boss and tell him to join us. On me. And Maddy, I sure hope your mom is feeling better soon."

"I know, she came home from work sorta upset, said she had a bad headache."

"Well, working for Mr. Tutti Frutti could probably do that," Cedar smirked.

"Oh, be nice," Maddy said with a disapproving tone. "Ronnie has been Mom's best friend since high school."

"Maybe she shoulda been a better friend to your dad. Things mighta turned out different."

Maddy stared at him with a look of slight confusion, her smile slipping a little. Kat cleared her throat and issued a warning on the temperature of the fries.

Way to lighten the mood, Cedar Stock. And why do you change your grammar to fit the subject?

CHAPTER 44

"He actually said the word *metaphysical*?" Roy asked.

"It was weird. It's as if he wanted you to know more about him," Kat shook her head.

"And he actually said *yin and yang*, naturally?"

"Yep. Bizarre."

"Check out this transcript. He speaks as if he's barefoot in greasy overalls, with a corncob pipe in his toothless mouth and jug of Who Hit John over his shoulder."

Roy watched Kat devour the transcript. He sensed her growing astonishment as she compared the Cedar Stock she held in her hand to the one who had locked his eyes on her over the meal at the Black Tail.

"Incredible," Kat said, after setting the transcript down. "But he bounced between what I'd call professorial and hillbilly, not to mention downright menacing when talking about prison."

"Well let's try to avoid any more nights out with a bipolar killer, shall we," Roy said. "Took a few years off my life, and I can't afford to lose many more."

"You got a deal. I was so nervous I could hardly eat. I took most of mine home. He even commented that I must have been so nervous I couldn't eat, so I should take it home."

"He was enjoying himself," Roy said. "Thinks he's got the world by the tail. By the way, where's my take-out?"

Kat laughed. "He's a lying, thieving dishonest man, apparently. Who knew?"

"Wow. Poor Cedar Stock. Convicted on scant or no evidence. Hope I never have you on a jury judging me," Roy chastised lightly. "Still, interesting that Cedar doesn't seem to know about my interview with Sarah and Ronnie Faraday the other day."

"I'm sure he would have mentioned it, just to show you how much he knows about what we're doing," Kat observed.

Roy agreed with her.

"Look, I have go meet the Sheriff today, so you're free to scan old missing persons reports, thumb through the file for more dynamite like the deer drinking a forty, or hit the slopes. Your vacation's running short."

"I'll be gone in three days. School won't wait." She grimaced a little.

"You'll get into your grad school. Just keep banging your head against the wall, a door will open."

"You know, it's funny, but not getting in, then meeting you again and working on this case. It's as if it were meant to be. The pause has given me a chance to rethink my direction in life. "

"What do you mean?"

"I guess this case has got me fantasizing about a slightly different path. I think I'm going to check out the FBI."

"Good for you! You're just the type of new blood that outfit needs. Remember, you have be twenty-five, I believe, and you have to have worked in a real job prior, not some fly by night internship with a broken down old door knocker like me."

"I've got you to thank for it if I do. Think you could write me a letter of recommendation if the time ever comes?"

"Sure. It'd be pretty short. Something like 'the time for another Hoover is now, and this time it's okay to dress like a lady.'"

♦

Sheriff Ed Silva looked up at Roy Church who'd just entered his office.

"The famous detective is here. Lemme buzz Sessions and Lynch."

Within minutes Roy found himself looking across at the Sheriff, the Undersheriff, and the LT in charge of Major Crimes Investigations. They all looked across expectantly as if outing his SoCal past had somehow endowed him with magical powers. Time to sprinkle some pixie dust.

"Sheriff, I'm not trying to suck up to you, but I need to commend you on your fine work a few years back," Roy began.

Sheriff Silva tilted his head a little, a quizzical expression on his face.

"Do you remember a kid who drowned over on the Klamath by the name of Zachary Stock? Was fishing, got drunk, and fell in. They found his body downriver at a spot called Skeahan Bar? Left his truck?"

"Oh yeah, yeah, yeah," Sheriff Silva said, turning to the others. "He was from Sisson. Had separated from his old lady. We thought it might be suicide. I think that was Cyril's beat back then. Hell, he probably stopped to take a piss by the kid's truck a few times and never bothered to check it out."

Sheriff Silva turned back to Roy.

"And…?" he prompted.

"And I read through your report and had my intern sift through it too. She's sharp. She spotted a few things, two that are vital in my estimation, that connect the drowning of Zachary Stock to the Puma Ridge bone. If you and Dead Fred hadn't been thorough, we wouldn't be standing here."

Sheriff Silva sat back in his chair, regarding Roy intently. "You shittin' me?"

Tommy Sessions and Lieutenant Lynch looked at each other and briefly exchanged pleasantly surprised expressions.

"Let me run it down."

Roy walked through the highlights of the past few weeks, of course leaving out being stalked by Cedar Stock and then letting his intern break bread with said stalker. Those details went under the heading of *You Had to be There.*

"So who the hell are those bones on Puma Ridge, then?" Sheriff Silva asked.

"Frankly, I do not know. Cedar Stock's crew, including this kid Zachary Stock, may have whacked someone who got in their way who didn't have local roots. Might even have been someone in their gang we don't yet know about who had to go. Whoever it was, those deer and human remains were dumped there by someone close to or by the Cedar Stock gang back when they were busy impersonating police officers in their robberies.

"I think I remember a teletype or two and some news reports on the so-called Cops Robbers," Sheriff Silva said.

Lieutenant Lynch said, "I didn't move here until I was already a deputy. Still, that name Stock is familiar. I haven't had any personal dealings with Cedar Stock, but I've heard of him, and I've heard the last name."

Sheriff Silva lifted one meaty hand and replied, "Stock is a local pioneer name. I think old Hugh Stock came here with my great granddaddy a few years after the Hudson Bay trappers put this little bit of Heaven on the map. Them old boys were tougher 'n cow hide dryin' in the August sun. Some stayed good. A whole bunch went rabid dog bad. Over at the courthouse they got old photos of more 'n one of 'em hangin' out back."

"What are your next steps, Roy? Sounds as if you could use some help beyond your intern," Lieutenant Lynch said, cutting into the Sheriff's history lesson on the outlaw past of Karuk County. "I could maybe shake Westwood loose. He's about as useful as tits on a tomcat up here."

Roy nodded his head in gratitude but said, "Let me think on that. I'm losing my intern to her school semester, and of course she can't really leave the office anyhow."

Except when I have her going all super-secret agent with our prime murder suspect.

"Well Westwood can probably run a copy machine if you need him to. And he could organize your shoe closet or something down there."

"Possibility I could use him," Roy said, sounding about as enthusiastic as the KKK Grand Dragon at a Nation of Islam picnic.

"Just let me know. He's been all mopey since your article came out. He's telling everyone who'll listen that he thinks he oughta give the job up," Lieutenant Lynch rolled his eyes.

"We all make mistakes. His aren't so bad. If he's determined to, he can recover," Roy said diplomatically. "So I have strategy going forward that will involve some interviews. Don't know if I can get the ones I want in the box, at which time I'd like to have someone, maybe Detective Westwood, help me record. Then again, I may have to do them on the fly."

"Even a deaf squirrel finds a nut every now and then," sighed Sheriff Silva. "If he wasn't old Judge Westwood's nephew…."

Roy figured Wally's chances for promotion down the road were probably as good as a steer's chances in a field of cows.

"We gonna solve this thing soon?" Sheriff Silva abruptly got back to business.

Election is two years away, why the hurry?

"Doing my best. You mentioned some state or fed grant money, if I needed to pay an informant or travel?"

"Yeah, we can get you covered. What'd you have in mind?"

♦

On the drive back to Sisson, south on the I-5, Roy weighed his next moves while dialing up Jake Stern to verify what he suspected to be the state of affairs in Santa Rosa.

"Shit storm's settled in over Sonoma County and is dumping on us. We got a couple of gang shootings and an Officer Involved with the Sheriff's Department. Pud Wilson's case has been pushed beyond the back burner all the way to the fridge in the break room."

"Understandable. I'll buzz if you-know-who walks in and confesses."

"Wow, thanks, I bet Lord Voldemort *is* behind this all," Stern joked, having spent the last few nights reading *Harry Potter and the Chamber of Secrets* to his kids. "But really, that's some crazy shit with him and your intern. Glad she's splitting town."

"Yeah, I'm going to miss her. She shook it up for a minute, and she's very bright. Shoulda had her interview Cedar. She'da copped him out," Roy laughed.

"Listen, I'm bringing Rachel up there this summer. That country is incredible. Need to check out retirement spots," Stern said emphatically.

Roy smiled at the thought. "No crime and you can't beat the Herd o' Burgers at the Black Tail."

Stern's tone grew somber.

"I remember from our dinner chat that tomorrow is a bad day for you. It is *Yahrzeit*, a painful anniversary. Rachel and I will light a candle and say *Kaddish*."

"Thanks, I appreciate it."

"Take care, my friend," Stern said. "Shalom."

"Shalom," Roy said and hung up.

Tears rolled down his face intermittently the rest of the way back to Sisson.

When he got back to the sub, he did what he always did to chase away the hurt. He worked. He checked his iPhone history for Lydia Wilson's number.

"Mrs. Wilson, this is Roy Church with the Sheriff's Department again. Do you have a minute? I was hoping I could stop by."

Her wavery, old voice answered, "Detective Church, wow, I read about you. I not going out anywhere, so when would you like to come?"

"How about now?"

Lydia agreed, and Roy rang off. He collected his notepad and keys that he had barely set down on the laminate surface of his desk.

♦

Roy parked behind Lydia's old Explorer. Scant buildup of snow in the tracks behind it said it hadn't moved in at least a day. It didn't look as though Lydia got out much, especially in the dead of winter.

She greeted him at the door with a smile and a cup of tea in her liver-spotted hand. The nightgown from the first encounter had disappeared, replaced with a velour maroon sweat suit fit for a community college nose guard.

"Would you like some, Detective? Fresh steeped."

"Of course, never turn down tea. It's that time of day. Must be my British roots," Roy said warmly, taking note of the cooperative attitude.

He glanced around the interior of the trailer. The cardboard *Merry Christmas* had disappeared along with the decorations. The Season of Joy and Giving had come and gone.

He suspected that he'd made her day by dropping by. Shut-ins took great pleasure in the smallest amount of company. The way he'd treated her the first time had a lot to do with it as well, he was sure. Charlie Criss had burned it into him to leave on a positive note if you could, because you'd always have questions later.

"Reporter came around here a week or so back. I had to threaten to have her arrested for trespassing just to get her to leave," Lydia said in an annoyed voice.

"People in the news media lose their souls sometimes it seems. They want a story and don't care who it affects," Roy said, shaking his head sadly. "I'm sorry that happened to you. Next time tell them to call me if you don't want to talk."

Lydia handed him his cup of tea. He sat in the same straight back chair as before, sipped from the cup, and then set it on a side table.

Lydia shoved herself back into her easy chair while looking directly at him through her coke bottle glasses. The slow blink of her eyes said she expected news from the famous detective, otherwise why would he have driven here?

"Do you remember when I was last here, I asked you about friends Jesse hung around with?"

"Yeah, Dina was about it, I think," Lydia said slowly, looking as if she were scouring her memory again so as not to disappoint the celebrity sitting across from her.

"Have you ever heard the name Cedar Stock?" Roy had no idea what to expect since everyone had an opinion of Cedar it seemed.

She nodded. "Oh, Cedar yes, but that was when they were kids at elementary school together," Lydia said. "They played a lot of baseball together. And Cedar played the guitar from a young age. I remember that. Jesse didn't go on with Cedar to high school, though."

"So you don't recall Cedar ever coming by here as an adult to visit with Jesse, say in 2004, right around the time Dina disappeared?"

"Heavens, no. Jesse was not allowed here then. I told you, he'd gotten into drugs and was a thief. I wouldn't have him on my property except to come by once in a great while for mail."

So Cedar fibbed. Imagine that.

"Okay, what about a Zachary Stock?" Roy asked.

"No. The name Stock, of course. Becky and Jersey Stock, they were ahead of me in school ten years at least. They married into the Stock family. Becky married Artie Stock and Jersey married his brother Donnie, or the other way around. Stock's an old family name here in the county," Lydia said knowledgeably.

"So I've heard. Something about Hugh Stock and the fur trappers back in the day," said Roy.

"Oh, didn't know that," Lydia smiled. "You're a historian too?" Roy's notoriety had awakened senses long thought dead.

Roy shook his head, smiling. "Just to cover my bases, I'd like to show you two photographs. Tell me if you recognize either one," Roy said.

He reached into a manila envelope he'd brought with him and then set the two photos of Jacky Blue and Koondawg in front of her.

She pushed her glasses back up her broad nose and then picked up the prison photo of Jackson Howard.

"The other one, no. This one, a definite maybe. I wish I could remember where. I know I've seen him," she said with an anxious edge to her voice. She was probably worried about letting Roy down.

She reached out to the lamp table by her chair and retrieved a magnifying glass from under the open Bible. Clicking her lamp up a notch, she carefully examined the photo using the glass.

Her face lit up and she said, "The blue eyes! They stand out.

That's why I remember him."

"Do you think you saw him in town, at the market, at a friend's?"

"No, no. I got it! It was here. At that door!" exclaimed Lydia, pointing at her front door. "He was looking for Jesse, only he used that awful name they always called him. Pud. I remember because he'd parked his car or truck down the driveway and walked up, which I thought was strange. There could have been others in the car. I couldn't see. I told him, no, that Jesse was not allowed here. He seemed satisfied, turned and walked back down the driveway. I thought it was probably a drug debt Jesse owed."

"When do think that was?" Roy asked. He felt his pulse quicken but remained calm.

"Well, I don't know. But if I think long enough, I might come up with a sorta time. I'd have to call you with that. My mind's all kinda jumbled right now."

"That's fine. Relax a little tonight. Lie in bed and let yourself float back to that day. Your memories hide out in the recesses of your brain, but if you relax, they will often appear and give you answers."

"I'll do that, and I know it wasn't daytime, sorta dusk, but his eyes reflected and glittered in my porch light, like he was wearing those cataract implants."

Roy decided against telling Lydia what he'd come to tell her originally, that Cedar Stock had been with her son at the time of his death. Right now, he wanted her concentrating on one thing and one thing only — Jacky Blue.

"Okay. Look. I'll be working late into the evening, so if you remember anything, call me," Roy said as he rose to leave.

"Wait, it's coming to me. Remember I said it coulda been a drug debt or something. Well I thought I'd warn Jesse if he telephoned. He called every now and then. I mean, I didn't want to get mixed up in his filthy business, but I didn't want him to get hurt either. So, I was sorta hoping he'd call. He didn't of course. But a few days later a Sheriff's car drove in, and I thought, oh no, it's Jesse. That guy with the blue eyes caught up with him."

Roy was very interested. "But it wasn't?"

"No, they were looking for Dina. That's right. They wanted to know if I'd seen Dina because she'd gone missing."

"So this man with the blue eyes came looking for Jesse in the evening, a few days before you were aware that Dina Morgan had disappeared. In July 2004?"

"Yes, that's the way I remember it." She pushed her glasses back up her nose as they had slipped a little in her excitement.

"Hmm," Roy said.

Cedar and his crew must have kissed and made up nine years after he told Detective Silva they'd parted ways. He forgot to mention that detail to me. Wonder why Cedar didn't get out of the vehicle and ask about Pud instead of sending Jacky Blue?

Roy thanked Lydia for her time and tea. He told her he'd keep in touch if there were any other developments. She actually struggled out of her chair, despite his protests, and walked him to the door. He wasn't surprised. She'd felt useful for a moment, something she probably hadn't felt in years.

♦

Reuben Montalvo answered on the third ring.

"These new phones are so damn cool," he said in awe. "I could see it was you instead of that Nigerian prince or the East Indian dude from the IRS who keep calling."

Roy smiled broadly and said, "Just pay 'em, and they'll leave you alone."

"What can I do you for?"

"I need to milk your brain."

"That don't sound right," Montalvo laughed. "Milk away."

"Our boy Cedar Stock met Koondawg Cutler and Jacky Blue Howard in New Folsom, according to his C-File. In his interview, Cedar told the cops he cut those fools loose in '95 when they had funk over the death of his cousin here in Sisson. Cedar goes back for 211 armed. He ends up in The Bay, does his full term. When he gets out, I'm positive he hooks back up with at least Jacky Blue. I just IDed him tonight as being here in Sisson in 2004 looking for the dude Cedar Stock ends up whacking in 2018."

Montalvo sounded thoughtful. "Okay, sounds like a long term on again, off again marriage. I got one of them. And shit, I couldn't believe it when Stern told me Cedar Stock sat for an interview. Don't make sense."

"You're not alone in that. Anyhow, do you recall Jacky Blue or Koondawg going to The Bay?"

"Hmm. I'll check tomorrow for sure, but I don't think so. I'm thinking Koondawg and Jacky floated back over the border into Nevada and then Texas eventually, where they did their murders on those dope dealers."

"I'd really appreciate it, you checking. While you're at it, any way to see Cedar's associates at The Bay? Was he in A or B Facility or back there in the SHU with the Brand Commission boys?"

"No problem," Montalvo said easily.

"I'm just trying to figure how he got hooked back up with Jacky Blue and Koondawg. Then shit went sideways again somewhere along the line and the other two split for Texas like you said, to do their little capital crimes," Roy added so Montalvo understood the scope of information he was looking for.

"On again, off again. Like I said, story of me and my old lady. Right now we're on, and you interrupted it."

They chatted a few more minutes, Roy apologizing for rudely interrupting Montalvo's marriage, before hanging up.

Roy's next call was to Lonnie Morgan to set up a meet for the next day. His new BFF said he'd clear his schedule.

After Roy hung up from Lonnie, he settled back in his chair, contemplating the changing landscape. Dina Morgan, Pud Wilson, Jacky Blue, Cedar Stock, Koondawg Cutler, Sarah Stock and a Puma Ridge bone — not a body as everyone else liked to call it. Concealed connections or coincidental paths crossed, meant to tease him with promises of truth? Tendrils of fog had begun to float upward. The milky mist left behind still obscured answers, but Roy had been here before. If you hung with it long enough, Braille turned to sight.

He closed up shop for the evening and drove home, checking his 360 the whole way. The threat from Cedar Stock had diminished, given Cedar's hook up with an attorney and his performance in his interview. Still, Roy had not forgotten what could lurk in the brain of a man hell bent on never feeling handcuffs again.

♦

"And Abraham came to mourn Sarah and to weep for her…."

That night Roy read the passages in Genesis from Malka's Torah. On anniversaries he felt smaller, set adrift, and found himself floating toward a whirlpool that would suck him into its void, that black cavity he felt in his heart.

It was late when he put the sacred book aside and picked up his cell phone. He dialed the number.

The elderly voice of David Ezekiel answered. There was no question in his words as to why the late call.

"We wondered about you tonight. I'm on speaker with Deborah."

Together, the three of them cried.

CHAPTER 45

Lonnie Morgan's attitude had changed considerably, much like that of a teenager who's been told he can go to the school dance after all. Someone murdering your daughter's killer can have that effect.

"I tell you, I been sleepin' like a baby. Yeah, I can read between the lines. Pud didn't hang hisself. Them Santa Rosa cops think he had help. If I had any money, I'd post a reward." His chin tilted upward as he said it, pride and a sense of justice emanating from him.

"I won't say you're wrong, Mr. Morgan. It seems it can't be proven either way, so I think you're absolutely justified in thanking an angel of vengeance."

Roy sat in the wooden chair Lonnie motioned to as he settled himself into an old armchair.

"Damn straight I am," Lonnie announced. "Now what's this about Dina?"

"Well, as you know, we initially thought the skeletal remains on Puma Ridge could be Dina, but they're not. They belong to an unknown male. I'm not saying Pud was involved in it, but he could be. I'd hate for him to get away with something, even in death."

Lonnie scowled. "Fuck that asshole. The more we can dirty him up the better. What do you need?"

"You kept in touch with Dina through the years after she left home and was with Pud. Do you know where they lived, traveled, anything about their movements outside of Sisson?"

Lonnie Morgan set down his coffee cup next to an open bottle of Canadian Mist.

"Lemme think. They was up in Oregon for a while. Dina called and said they was gonna pick blueberries. I remember because I laughed at the time. Shit, bent over picking a berry? They ain't Mexicans, for shit's sake. No offense, your Mexican is a hard-working sonofabitch, not like that piece of shit Pud."

"Yep, we wouldn't have food on our tables if someone wasn't willing to do the back-breaking jobs."

Lonnie nodded absently and then continued.

"Uh, damn they was all over. Humboldt, probably growing marijuana. Down in the Central Valley for a while. Fresno? Who the fuck would go to Fresno? You ever been there? Hotter 'n shit and nothin' but Mexicans and raisins." Lonnie shook his head in true disbelief. "Yeah, mostly over on the coast in Crescent City and down in the Valley when they weren't back here in Sisson."

"Dina kept in regular contact with you, though?"

"Yep. She had some issues. Her probation officer was always on her. But it was that fuckin' Pud that kept her in that world. She coulda made a good life here, if she'd found the right man, not some white trash, scum suckin' dummy who couldn't even read a stop sign."

"So, I'd like to show you two photographs. Tell me if you recall ever seeing either one."

Roy pulled out the photos of Jacky Blue and Koondawg. He figured pretty soon the faces would be worn out from continual showings.

"Hell yeah. I seen 'em. Don't remember names. I think they run with that dirty fucker Cedar Stock years ago. Where'd you get them pictures? Those are bookin' photos. Had one or two of them over the years myself. Cops said I was driving drunk once. I only had two beers, but them state freeway cops got tricks with their little tests to show you had more."

Roy smiled sympathetically. That seemed to satisfy Lonnie as though it were a long sought-after exoneration.

"Do you remember when you saw them last?" Roy pressed.

"Uh, no, wait, yeah. The one with the blue eyes came by looking for Pud and Dina. Said he was gonna kick Pud's ass for something. I said good, kick him once for me. Don't know when that was. Around about when Dina died I guess. But they'd all been by here before, years before that. I think Pud tried to work for Cedar Stock. Now there's a sumbitch you need to look at."

"Really? Why would that be?"

Lonnie looked at Roy as if he were dropped on his head as a baby. He waved his arms almost frantically as he said, "Shit. Cedar Stock is a dirty bastard! Been to prison. Part of the Stock clan. His granddaddy stole my family's property way back when. Useless culls."

Roy jotted some notes for the benefit of Lonnie. "Ah, I see, thanks. You said Pud worked for Cedar? When, doing what?"

"Shit, Cedar had some so-called tree trimming business. All bullshit. Those boys never did a lick of tree work in their lives. I dropped timber for a living, and those boys didn't know the first thing about handling a chainsaw or any kind of physical labor. If you ask me, they was using that business as a cover to sell drugs or steal from honest folks. Christ. They all been to prison, the whole bunch of 'em." Lonnie looked disgruntled as he shifted his position in his armchair.

♦

Reuben Montalvo got back to Roy by mid-morning.

"I went in early for the great Delroy Church. I don't do that shit for just anybody," he grunted.

"I appreciate it, Reuben. You ride your Harley to Sisson this spring or summer and beer's on me."

"You're on. Jake Stern says you got a slice of paradise up there."

"Yep. Great food. No crime," Roy reiterated. *Maybe I should consider going into the real estate business when all this is over.*

Montalvo snorted. "Yeah, no crime. All you got is a possible undercover Aryan Brotherhood shot caller for a neighbor."

"Seriously? What the heck?"

"What the heck is right. Hey, I ever tell you that you got a sailor's mouth? Anyhow, you don't cell with Moonshine Tankersley and not get some on you. Your boy Stock started in B facility in '98 but ended up in the SHU for a minute in Moonshine's house. If Moonshine's not on the AB commission he sure as hell is close."

"How'd we miss this in the C-file?"

"Hey, we were looking for his associates in New Folsom pre '95 and then on the street. Facts change in a case, so our search changed. New shit comes to light. Do I still get that beer?"

"A pitcher if you like. Moonshine was the dude who green-lit Koondawg, right?" Roy asked, scribbling notes on his notepad.

"Right. Then Cedar Stock came up with the idea to take Koondawg's money that he never had. Cedar Stock been paying off that debt ever since, it looks like doing the AB's biz on the outside. I'm betting he's one valuable asset to them, and they ain't gonna let him go. Once the Brand gets its hooks in you, you're coming boat side to the harpoon."

"And Moonshine Tankersley got his hooks into Cedar Stock," said Roy, thoughtfully.

"Yep, got his C-file right here in front of me. Thick one. Reads like a trashy novel. Lotta boys have told on him over the years. Their tidbits, along with every psych report and tier officer write-up, say one thing: scandalous motherfucker," Montalvo said. "Lemme run it all down for you. Get comfortable, amigo. Grab popcorn, 'cause you're gonna need to know this bad boy."

♦

Based on personal intake history, court documents, and witness statements, Dale "Moonshine" Tankersley, Commission member of the Aryan Brotherhood, aka The Brand, has been validated by the California Department of Corrections and Rehabilitation as a member of the most feared, white-boy prison gang in the State of California.

Dale Thomas Tankersley was born in Bakersfield, California, to Virginia Cantrell. Cantrell had divorced her first husband in 1968 while pregnant with Tankersley and married Thomas Cantrell, who Tankersley claims is his biological father. Four years later, Virginia divorced Cantrell and married James "Jack" Tankersley, who legally adopted her son.

Tankersley was timid, awkward, shy, and frequently bullied as a child in the lower middle-class neighborhood on Texas Street, just off the Rosemond Highway in east Bakersfield where the family lived.

Virginia Tankersley demanded that her son fight back, telling the boy that if he ever came home again crying because he had been beaten up by a bully, she would be waiting to give him another beating.

Tankersley states, "That's how my mom was. She stood her mud. If someone came at you with a bat, you got your bat, and you both went at it."

At age fourteen, Tankersley got busted for a string of home burglaries. He was sentenced to a California Youth Authority, a reformatory, where he said his attitudes about violence were reinforced. "Anyone not willing to fight was abused. And by abused I don't just mean beat down. You got your ass took. I guess I've took my share along the way. But that's how we roll inside. Fight or get it up the ass. It's about survival."

In 1978, a 19-year-old Tankersley and his cousin Charles Dorfmann, aged 20 years, were convicted of armed robbery after they were taken down by Bakersfield PD. CYA had already taught him the ropes. He never gave up his ass again, even though at 19 there were lots of seasoned cons pointing and laughing at their own stiff wood as he walked by cells on the noisy tiers. Cousin Dorfmann was right beside him when he decided to show a particularly mouthy black inmate, Latrelle Hill, that his white ass was protected territory. He and Dorfmann stabbed the black inmate with "bonecrushers" (huge home-made prison stabbing instruments designed for killing, not wounding) given to them by some older whites who were sporting tattoos of shamrocks and Vikings on their chests and backs. Hill died a painful death on the tier amid all the shouting and cell bar clanging of the other inmates buoyed by the sights and sounds of fatal carnage.

Tankersley and Dorfmann were each charged with first degree murder but ultimately convicted of second degree. The Marin

County DA grew tired of the defense parading white cons onto the stand to testify that the 40 plus stab wounds on Hill were in self-defense. The lawyers reached a deal. Back on San Quentin East Block the white cons celebrated, and Dorfmann earned a nickname. To this day he is called Charles "Fuck 'em Up Chuck" Dorfmann.

The white inmates who'd urged Tankersley and Dorfmann to go off on Latrelle Hill were none other than shot callers for the Aryan Brotherhood, the white prison gang formed in the early sixties as a protective group against the predations of the newly formed Mexican Mafia and the Black Guerilla Family.

The AB shot callers began schooling Tankersley on what it meant to be a white inmate in the joint. You started out as a "peckerwood," a white boy with no protection from the "niggers and beaners who want you bent over." If you wanted some protection, you had to pay or be there when the shit went down on the yard or on the tiers. If you showed enough heart in a fight, you might get noticed by a few of the AB feeder groups in the joint, namely Dirty White Boys, Nazi Lowriders or the like. Put in enough work, show enough initiative, and you might someday become a full-fledged "Berserker," a member of the AB.

At 19, Tankersley had a goal. He craved the title of Berserker, knew he'd someday have the tightest ink displaying Runic phrases, battle axes, Vikings, shamrocks, and of course the universal prison towers and spider-webbed elbows.

In the late seventies and through the eighties, Tankersley the foot soldier took part in a massive number of hits for the AB, ones he did not get tagged for. He loved the smell of blood and loosened shit of the dying victims, if they could be called victims. Their aim would be to kill him if given half a chance. He built his body, getting the reputation as "pig of the iron pile," grunting and sweating under the rusty weight sets on the San Quentin yard, even as the mist off the San Francisco Bay cooled the other thousand cons milling around him.

Tankersley gained a skill. He was taught how to make pruno, prison wine, an alcoholic beverage variously made from apples, oranges, fruit cocktail, candy, ketchup, sugar, milk, and crumbled bread. Bread provided the yeast for the mixture to ferment. Tankersley's was the best on the tier.

An inmate known only to Tankersley as "Sledgehammer" hailed from Tennessee and had been involved with the AB federally at one point. He declared that Tankersley's pruno could match the moonshine he'd grown up with. Dale "Moonshine" Tankersley now had his full prison name.

Fresh out of stir and on parole in the mid-eighties, Moonshine and Fuck 'em Up Chuck rolled into a peckerwood party in the redneck, Kern County town of Oildale. Just north of Bakersfield, Oildale sure as hell hadn't gotten it name because of its wine and cheese. In the 20's and 30's Standard Oil had pulled a fast one on the locals, buying up land cheap, knowing the dumb farmers had no idea they were sitting on a fortune in black gold. Oildale, populated by Texans and Okies, had brought a slew of Southern attitudes with them. Hence, the light skin color of its denizens, and the decided lack of anything darker.

At the party, Tankersley was introduced to a young sweet thing with a bad attitude name Jade Kapplehoff.

"My momma says we're related to Doris Day, her real last name is same as mine," she told Moonshine over a Bud.

"Who the fuck is Doris Day?"

It was love at first sight. One beer-soaked humping in Jade's pick-up truck, and a snort or two of a white powder from a little zip lock baggie, and it was settled. Vegas here we come. Fuck it. Let's get married. Fuck that Doris Day bitch. Meet Jade Tankersley!

Moonshine and Jade hit three liquor stores on the way back west. Cash for the honeymoon. Jade was a hell of a distraction for the clerks with her blouse unbuttoned. Moonshine had Fuck 'em Up's stolen .45 caliber in their faces before they could say, "Hey sweetheart, need some help?"

Moonshine, Fuck 'em Up, and a few Oildale boys put together a sweet little robbery crew. They struck out for the upper Central Valley to hit restaurants in the Sacramento Delta. Jade would always go in first, get the lay of the land. Moonshine and the boys then came in, put everyone on the floor and took the cash, sometimes from the customers

Armed robbery was one thing, manly in fact. But one of the crew, Danny "Farmboy" Sullivan had a perv streak in him. On one robbery he dragged an Asian waitress into the restaurant office and raped her. This pissed off Jade who demanded something be done.

"I don't care if she was a slant. Bitches got rights too."

Just outside of Stockton, on Highway 12, the crew stopped to take a piss alongside the road. Moonshine walked up behind Farmboy and put a slug in his head. Jade was cool with that. She squatted over the dead Farmboy and tinkled. Everybody thought that was funny as fuck. Moonshine wished he'd had a Polaroid camera for that one.

Unfortunately for Moonshine and the gang, video surveillance cameras were coming into vogue. They all, with exception of Jade, went down on armed 211 P.C plus 245 P.C., Assault with Deadly Weapon, after a Denny's in Vacaville handed over the tape that clearly showed Moonshine's and Fuck 'em Up's faces pistol whipping the manager. Photo line ups got shown to a lot of other victims, and both men were convicted on multiple 211 charges. They escaped the 261.2 P.C., forcible rape charges, when the Asian victim could not ID either as her attacker.

"Well, shit, that's something, I guess," Moonshine said to Fuck 'em Up as they were led away to serve another twenty.

In 1991, Tankersley, while in San Quentin, was accused of the murder of Robert Ladoux, a member of the Black Guerilla Family prison gang. Tankersley and another inmate, Clayton Boyce, were convicted, and Tankersley received a life sentence. Tankersley maintained his innocence.

While Tankersley was on trial for Ladoux's murder, the CDC transferred Raymond "Cadillac" Washington, the national leader of the Black Guerilla Family prison gang, from another prison into the control unit in Folsom where Tankersley had been transferred. From the moment Washington arrived in the control unit, prison logs show that he began trying to kill Tankersley.

"I tried to tell Cadillac that I didn't kill Ladoux, but he didn't believe me, and he bragged that he was going to kill me," Tankersley recalled. "Everyone knew what was going on and no one did anything to keep us apart. The guards wanted one of us to kill the other."

Tankersley and Clayton Boyce killed Washington with shanks, stabbing him 67 times. After Washington was dead, they dragged his body up and down the catwalk in front of the cells, displaying it to other prisoners. Tankersley received another life sentence.

In 1992 Moonshine Tankersley was sent to the end of the earth, way up north to Pelican Bay State Prison in Crescent City, California.

It was here, in the Security Housing Unit that he rose toward the top of the white mob. He and the other cons were locked down 22 hours a day. Communication was difficult but manageable, especially if you had someone on the outside who could visit one con one day, get a message, then visit a second con the next day and pass the message on. It helped that Jade was willing to be that gang runner, snort some dope, drive all day and night to get to the pen. She would never get to lay hands on her man again, but she sure loved talking to him through the glass.

It was in the SHU that Moonshine learned to put aside any racial animus he might have toward brown and black inmates in the name of the only color that mattered. Green. Drugs, tobacco, communication routes on the inside were all currency and came under the color heading green. Drugs, guns, robberies, any dirty money on the outside was fair game for cooperation with the "muds." All the major gangs had an understanding. If we see each other in person, we try to kill one another. If we are locked up and can only threaten each other like bitch-ass cell soldiers then we might as well make money together.

Moonshine learned that the AB, based on its philosophy born on the inside, guided the outside. All the prison gangs controlled their outside turf. How? Fear, simple fear. If a gangster-white, brown, yellow, or purple-on the street knew that he would one day come to the joint (an occupational hazard) then he better follow direction handed down from the pen. Otherwise he was going to have a very sore ass at the end of his bid. Or be dead. Which was probably better. The peckerwoods on the street all knew the stories out there of white boys, who'd fuck up, being sold to the coons to pay a debt. Holy shit, Jesus!

So, Moonshine had the inside track for all those years, with Jade willing to do his dirt on the outside, help set up communications with the Mexicans who were taking over the meth biz, but needed white enforcers occasionally in white neighborhoods to get the shit moved.

Still, not a lot of two-way streets with the niggers. His people basically just sold them shit in bulk when they could. The blacks and whites just couldn't seem to forge any alliances the way the whites and southern Mexicans (Surenos) could. Of course, fuck them Nortenos, Northern Mexicans. For some reason Moonshine could not figure, they ran with the niggers. He guessed it might have something to do with the 415 Kumi in Oakland and the Nuestra Familia (leaders of the Nortenos) in the Bay Area having an undercover drug dealing agreement of some sort. Or maybe it was that rap shit they were both putting out. Who knew?

Moonshine's people were making bank when in the mid 2000's they began a pretty successful relationship with the Mexican Mafia (La Eme) from LA and Syndicato Fronteras Califas, (SCF) the front group in California for the Tijuana cartel known as the Felix-Arellano group.

Even after Felix-Arellano got wasted by the Sinaloa, Gulf, and Los Zetas cartels, the AB continued to make money with La Eme and SCF. The Mexicans were expert meth cooks and had great wacky-tabacky gardens. AB had a whole hell of a lot of white boys who wanted to get fucked up on the stuff.

And Jade kept it all moving smoothly on the outside for him. A true "featherwood" if ever there was one. There were times Moonshine wished Jade could be a full member of the AB. Of course, the others on the commission would shit themselves over that. They'd remind him that MoB stood for Money over Bitches.

It was all going along swimmingly. Jade and a few other featherwoods she'd recruited would run messages back and forth for the boys on certain weekends. Visit Moonshine one day in SHU C-facility, get a message through the glass, come back the next day and pass that message to Hillbilly though the glass at SHU D-Facility.

Then it all came crumbling down. Jade got busted holding a kite up to a window for a brother. That fucking Jew warden, Arlo Myers, banned her from visits. A fucking disaster.

Moonshine banged on his cell door to get a passing correctional officer's attention.

"Hey, need you to get a message to Warden Myers. We have to meet. Don't want anyone hurt."

♦

"So the warden met with Moonshine? Did he give in? Did he let Jade back on the visitor's list?" Roy asked.

"No, not at first, even after Moonshine said it could get rough on staff with shanking and gassing, you know, throwing piss and shit on officers. But they managed to come to an agreement that Jade had to spend some time in the penalty box," Montalvo replied.

"And this leads us where?" Roy questioned.

"And this leads us to Moonshine needing a temporary female runner."

"One to take messages from Pelican Bay in Crescent City to, say, oh, I don't know, how about Corcoran down by Fresno?" Roy asked casually.

Montalvo was surprised. "How'd you know?"

"And the temp runner went by the name Dina Morgan, friend to Moonshine's cellie Cedar Stock."

"Damn, dude! You are the man! No wonder they miss you in LA!"

♦

"Sarah? This is Roy Church again. I'm really sorry to bother you, and I know how tough it was last time, but I really need to pick your brain again if I could."

"I don't know what more I can add," Sarah said in a voice that revealed she'd rather be fighting a migraine than speaking to him.

"Some evidence has emerged that I didn't have last time we spoke. I really need to get your take on it and see if that helps jog your memory. Again, I wouldn't ask if I didn't think there are some things you may know but just don't know you know. Some very small details may be vital."

"Well, okay. But Ronnie…."

"I need to speak to you, alone, here at the Sheriff's substation if that's okay. We have our evidence lockers here with the items I'd like you to view."

She sighed. "Okay. I just want to get it over with. I'm free right now. Can I drive over there? You're up on the hill right?"

♦

Roy watched through the window as Sarah Stock parked her green Subaru Outback in the lot next to his SUV. She didn't immediately get out of the car, probably gathering herself to put on a professional air. This would not be a time for professionalism. He needed her to return to her youth, the youth of indiscretion, mistakes, and promises of the future dying on a whim of fate.

CHAPTER 46

June, 1995

Zack Stock stepped from his pick-up truck and fell to his knees. Maddy Stock waddled toward him, pausing to fall forward, hands to the ground. She pushed herself up and struggled forward.

"Daddy!" the little girl babbled excitedly.

"Come here you little honey bunny," Zack said, gathering the child in his arms and kissing her forehead.

"Ooh, you're all sweaty and gross. Put her down before she has to have another bath!" Sarah shouted with a smile. "Dinner ready in twenty. Get a shower so you can sit at our table."

"Shower and a Bud!" Zack said as he approached Sarah on the porch and gave her a smack on the bottom. "And after dinner, dessert!"

"Stop. You're such a pig," Sarah laughed. "Don't set a bad example for our daughter. She'll think it's okay for men to paw women."

"Oh, I'm gonna do more than paw," Zack grinned lasciviously as he passed her, quickly unbuttoning his shirt and heading for the bathroom and a shower.

At dinner, Zack massaged the mood like an overweight drunk with a pocket protector and a flip phone.

"I thought I better tell you. Cedar and his men will be back here for a bit. They've got work lined up in Redding, but not until the twenty-third."

"No, honey. Oh no. You promised it was going to be a one time thing. Those guys creep me out every time they're here," she pleaded with him.

Zack slapped his hand on the table with annoyance. "Damn it, Sarah. He's my cousin, he's trying to get on his feet. He pays us very well. It's not like he's free loading. I mean last time he rolled in with that television you probably been watching all day." He mumbled the last part of his sentence as though it was more for his own ears than for hers.

Sarah's mouth fell open at his insult. "That's bullshit, Zack. I don't watch TV during the day. I read, yes, but I clean and do laundry and I take care of Maddy and I cook meals for you. And we don't need the money. I've got plenty." She was clearly hurt.

"Oh, great. Now I gotta get on my knees and kiss your daddy's ass for his little girl's Marin County money. 'Oh, please, Dr. Fournette, could I have a pretty penny?' Well, no thanks."

Her face splotched red. "That is money I saved from my allowance. It's mine."

"Who the fuck gets a thousand dollars a month in allowance?"

"It was for my college fund, too, not just for going shopping."

"Well, I'm fucking sorry, but I already told Cedar it was cool. Don't make me choose, Sarah. Fuck! Why you gotta be so difficult? Oh, because he's been in jail. I suppose no one in your high and mighty family ever made a mistake!" Zack tilted his chair back, looking away from her and staring steadfastly into the small living room.

"That's not fair. This is our house, our life, and those men are not nice!" Sarah cried.

He looked back at her sharply and raised a finger accusatorily. He jabbed it with each short sentence. "This is my house. I'm the one working. All you gotta do is cook and spread your legs once in a while. Shit, even that ain't what it used to be. When's the last time you even gave me some head?"

"You're nasty and mean. Look, you made Maddy cry!" Sarah turned away, blinking rapidly. She picked up Maddy and tried to soothe her.

Zach shrugged. "Not my fault. I was having a good day at work, all happy to come home, and then I gotta listen to your shit over trying to help a couple of guys out. Fuck. I'm outta here. I'm gonna get a beer where I don't have to be reminded I'm a fucking loser all the time!"

"Zack, honey. Don't go!" Sarah lunged for his arm, but he shook her off. He slammed the front door as he left, causing Maddy to cry even harder.

Several hours later Zack Stock slid naked into bed, rubbed Sarah's ass and whispered, "Baby, I'm sorry. Let me make it up to you."

She turned away from him and pulled herself into a ball. "No, you stink like stale beer and garlic. I'm going to sleep. You hurt my feelings."

He sighed exasperatedly. "Fine. Just fucking fine. I'm going to the couch."

Zack farted long and loudly, polluting the bedroom on his way out, and then he stumbled and cursed as his toe banged a chair leg.

The following day, a sullen Zack left for work, but not before eating the breakfast Sarah had cooked for him and not before grabbing the lunchbox she'd packed. He passed her by without kissing her, got in his truck and drove off.

Later that afternoon, a mini-pickup with the words *Sisson Nursery* painted on the side slid to a halt. The driver got out with a rosebush and card. He left it on Sarah's porch.

Babe, I'm really sorry. Just sometimes I get all crazy trying to help my family out. I hope this lets you know how sorry I am. Love and kisses, Zack Attack.

When Zack got home that afternoon Sarah didn't mention the fact that the rosebush was what they called appurtenant to the land, meaning if they ever left, the rosebush stayed. It was the thought that counted. She kissed Zack and made love to him that night.

The next day Cedar Stock and the Cedar Trims crew arrived in three trucks before Zack got home from work.

Cedar stepped up to her, hugged her, and kissed her on the cheek. Jack with the blue eyes and Coon with the scowl nodded briefly and smiled at her. Within minutes, a fourth truck arrived. Out stepped Jesse "Pud" Wilson and his girlfriend Dina.

Cedar spoke to Pud behind one truck, out of earshot of Sarah, while Jack and Coon took their overnight bags into the house and into a back bedroom. They knew the way and did not ask Sarah if they could enter.

Pud and Dina left without coming in.

That night, Zack came home on time, just as earnest beer drinking started in the backyard around a fire pit. A giant boom box set the tone. An odd mix of old-time country alternating with head banger music filled the property, pausing only for a knock at the front door when the Sacred Mountain Pizza delivery guy brought three extra-large. Sarah noticed Jack and Coon get up and step into the shadows as Cedar followed Zack to the front door. Cedar peeled off a number of bills. Sarah couldn't see what he paid but heard the pizza guy say, "Whoa, thanks, man!"

Sarah acted as waitress and bar maid to Zack and the partying tree trimmers. She brought the beer out to them to keep them from traipsing into the fridge and making noise that would wake little Maddy, as if the music wasn't enough.

The date had just flipped forward when Sarah closed the fridge with her knee, while holding beers in her hands. She straightened, turned, and ran directly into Cedar Stock. He stepped back, putting his hands out to steady her. He stared at her with dark blue eyes, like cold and empty ocean crevices. She wondered what lay within those crevices. Remorse? She hoped so.

He spoke softly. "We appreciate your hospitality. Zack got himself a good one. That sumbitch married up, for sure."

"It's no trouble, really. Whatever we can do to help," she said, uncomfortable with his proximity.

"We shouldn't be here too long — Jack and Coon been told to stay on good behavior. Got a little one in the house."

Cedar reached down and kissed her on the cheek, and it seemed to linger longer than was necessary.

She did not react, chalking it up to drunkenness. He turned and slid out of the kitchen holding the beers she's just grabbed. She did not remember them slipping from her grasp.

Sarah fell asleep in Maddy's room. The last thing she heard was a play fight between Cedar and the others over choice of music. When she got up in the morning everyone was gone, but one truck had been left behind. The backyard resembled a small Oklahoma town that had run out of luck in twister season. She spent the balance of the morning picking up empties, turning over chairs, and slipping leftover pizza slices into freezer bags.

In the early afternoon one truck returned. Jack parked, and Coon emerged from the passenger side. He strolled into the house without saying a word and closed the door to the bedroom he shared with Jack. Sarah heard the television in that room snap on.

Jack walked in and stood next to Sarah in the kitchen where she was bathing Maddy.

"My, what a cute kid, Miss Sarah," he said. His speech pattern hinted of out of state, maybe some place where the summer's scorch calls for sweet tea, and the slow water flows where cottonmouths twist and tangle. Arkansas? Mississippi? Texas?

"Thank you," Sarah replied. She could smell him up close to her, Walmart's top of-the-line cologne. He moved nearer. His shoulder rubbed hers. He cupped his hand in the soapy water then poured some over little Maddy's bare chest. She looked up all bright eyes, giggling at him.

Jack stepped back, opened the fridge and grabbed a beer. Sarah watched him walk out front and fish around in the bed of the truck. A magnetic sign on the driver's door read *Cedar Trims*, with a phone number running underneath.

Sarah rinsed and dried Maddy, and then dressed her in a sunsuit. She walked Maddy to the front door and sat with her on the steps, gazing across the gravel lane in front of the house at the pasture across the way, beyond the trucks. Black Angus and Hereford mingled, munching and frolicking, to Maddy's delight.

"Moo cows," she pointed excitedly.

"Yes, Maddy, Moo cows."

Maddy squealed with delight, and Sarah smiled fondly at her, running her fingers through her fine baby hair.

The phone in the house rang.

"Go get that phone Miss Sarah, I'll watch the little one out here," Jack called from the rear of the truck. He came around carrying a hard hat and a chainsaw.

"Thanks!"

Sarah jumped up and grabbed the phone on the wall by the fridge. Through the window she could see Jack kneeling by Maddy, pointing back at the cows. Her mother was on the phone. Her mom called every day or so, midday, while Zack was at work. Nothing important, just a check in to see how the only child was faring, and of course, when would Grandma and Grandpa get to see their granddaughter again.

Sarah cut the call short instead of the usual thirty minutes, avoiding that normal negative phase of the calls that somehow always wound its way to the subjects of wasted futures and missed opportunities.

Sarah stepped back outside where Jack was sitting on the grass next to the gravel drive. Maddy was tottering around him swinging something in her hand, a shiny piece of metal that Jacky had given her to whack at weeds with.

"Oh, I think I better take that," said Sarah, scooping Maddy up and turning back to the door. She dropped the metal piece in the kitchen garbage. She then took Maddy to her bedroom and laid her down for her nap.

When she came back out in the kitchen, Jack was standing there. The friendly southern charm had leaked away, and his magnetic blue eyes had taken on the glint of a prairie coyote stalking a whistle pig.

"You are so fine. I thought a lot about you since we was last here."

Sarah felt her stomach flip.

"I'm pretty sure you feel something, Miss Sarah, 'cause I don't think that boy of yours treats you right. I seen the way he ignored you last night when you was waitin' on us scalawags out back. That's a damn shame," he said in an oily voice that slipped over her skin like used grease.

Sarah froze, not knowing what to say or do.

Jack stepped forward and touched her hair. She pushed his hand away.

"Please, Jack, don't." She smiled nervously at him to soften the rejection.

"Call me Jacky Blue, everybody does." He let his hand drop to her shoulder and gave it a soft caress that felt to her like she'd been touched by boulders rolling downhill. His thumb played over toward her breast, and she could hear his breathing quicken. The smell of stale beer fumigated her, like Zack's had two nights earlier.

She stepped back and slapped his hand.

"No!"

Jack stepped back, throwing up his palms as if she were a highwayman.

"All right, all right. Was just gonna show you to a little sweet southern love. No big deal. Your husband'd never find out, 'less you told him. Like they say where I'm from, he ain't gonna miss one piece off a sliced loaf."

Jack turned and walked nonchalantly back outside humming a tune.

Sarah stood in shock for a few moments then went in and sat on the bed next to a snoring Maddy.

She heard a truck start up. She went to the door and saw Jack and Coon driving away.

"No doubt to get more beer," she muttered to herself. "Jack, Jacky Blue, you arrogant wolf, with the polite, Southern manners."

Zack came home about an hour later.

As he walked in through the front door, Sarah said, "If they don't leave tonight, I do!"

Zack pursed his lips and tossed his lunchbox onto the counter. "Hell you talkin' about?"

Sarah told Zack what had happened.

"Bullshit. He didn't mean nothin' by it. If it actually happened like you say that is."

Sarah stared at him, incredulous. "What? What? Are you calling me a liar?"

"I ain't calling you a liar, I just think you took some little comment and blew it up because you hate them being here, and you know how I feel about, and you're just trying to piss me off again."

"You are calling me, your own wife, a liar. You son of a bitch!" Her eyes filled with angry tears.

Zack puffed his cheeks out. "Oh, here we go. I just been waitin' for something like this. I knew you'd figure out a way to come up with some bullshit. Well here it is."

"That's it, I'm taking Maddy and going to my parents' house tonight. You can have fun with your convicts all you want."

"Go ahead then, get out, and see if I give a fuck! And where the hell is my damn cousin?!"

♦

Roy handed a box of tissues to Sarah.

"That was the last time you saw Zack?" He asked gently.

She nodded and blew her nose.

"I'm so sorry for making you relive that, but if it's okay, I've got a few more questions."

She sniffed. "I can't believe all the details I remember from so long ago. How did you do that?"

"I didn't, you did it. It was there. You'd simply pushed it way down. A cognitive interview has a way of working magic. Mind relaxation. Think of those old memories as gold nuggets that the 49ers would swish around in a pan. Gold is heavy, it sinks to the bottom. Wash away the top sand and gravel and it's the gold that remains."

"Amazing. But I kind of wish I didn't remember all that." Sarah gave him a thin smile to indicate she was alright.

Roy looked at his notes.

"So now you remember Jacky Blue instead of simply Jack with the blue eyes. That's good."

"It is?"

"Yes, and you recalled Jesse Wilson and Dina Morgan being at the home at least the one time, talking to Cedar."

"Yes. Yes I do, now." She shook her hair out of her face, clearly trying to collect herself.

"And you recall the excessive drinking and the room that Jacky Blue and the one you call Coon staying in."

"I can still see them." She nodded, more to herself than to Roy.

"How about the beer bottles those two were drinking out of?"

"Zack drank Bud or Coors Light in a can. The others most certainly did not. I remember how disgusting their drinks looked, so excessive."

"Bottle size?"

"Big, very big."

"I want to show you something. See if it jogs your memory any," Roy said.

He slipped on nitrile gloves and then opened an evidence bag. He retrieved the item marked by Dead Fred and set it on the table in front of Sarah.

"Oh my God, that's what they were drinking. Those big bottles!"

"It's called a forty ouncer, in street parlance," Roy said.

He then pulled out a cropped copy of the photo from the back of Zack's pick up and showed it to Sarah. All that was visible was the Olde English 800 Malt Liquor bottle, label intact. Her eyes widened.

"That's it, that's it! That's what Jacky Blue and Coon drank, all the time they were at our house. My garbage overflowed with them. Where did you get that bottle, and where did you get the photo?"

"Not just yet," Roy said. "I do have another question. The shiny piece of metal. Any idea what it could have been, the one Maddy was playing with?"

"No, I think Jack, Jacky Blue, got it out of his truck, though."

"I want to show you one more item," Roy said. "But first, I need you to put these gloves on," He handed her a pair of nitrile gloves.

He pulled out the evidence bag that he'd gotten back from the Chico ID lab and laid it on the table. Opening it, he removed the broken pruning saw blade.

Sarah gasped. She clasped her hands together to quell sudden trembling.

"Oh my God," she whispered, for the umpteenth time since he'd met her. "Where on earth…?"

"Well?" Roy prompted, not unkindly.

"That's it, I think that's the piece of metal Maddy was playing with, only it was shinier back then, but I remember being alarmed that she might cut herself on the teeth. They don't look too sharp now, and they're rusty, but this is it, I'm sure of it."

"Do you remember what you did with this?"

"Like I said, I threw it in the trash in my kitchen. I remember because it was right after that that Jacky Blue came in and assaulted me. Well, right after I came back in the kitchen after putting Maddy down."

"Did you use baby wipes for Maddy?"

"Of course, boxes and boxes."

Roy showed her the plastic container he felt belonged to a baby wipe box.

"I mean, it could be, but I can't say. Looks like a part of a baby wipe box, but they all sorta look alike."

"Okay," Roy replied evenly.

Sarah was still examining the piece of plastic container closely.

"I have one other item to show you. Just tell me if it looks familiar in any aspect."

Roy removed the Item FC-3, the broken partial hard plastic he believed to be the lid of a Sony Discman.

Sarah looked at it, then picked it up, turned it over, and studied it carefully.

"What is it?" she asked.

"What do you think it might be?" Roy asked.

"I just don't know. I'm sorry," Sarah said, setting the piece down.

"Did Zack listen to music?"

"Sure, we both did. We had that boom box I told you about. We kept it in the house. We were going to get a stereo for the living room, but decided it was too extravagant and would keep Maddy awake anyhow. We decided to wait."

"Hmm," said Roy. "No other musical devices you can recall?"

"No, I don't think so. I'm sorry," she said with an apologetic tone.

"No, no. That is perfectly all right."

"Are you going to tell me where you found my trash?" Sarah asked. "That is unbelievable."

"In due time. I can't right now simply to keep the integrity of the investigation intact. It has nothing to do with your honesty or keeping a secret. If I were ever to be asked on the stand if I divulged confidential information in this matter, I'd want to be able to truthfully say, no."

"I understand."

"One other question. You said Zack was a hunter, fisherman, outdoors sorta guy,"

"Yes, absolutely," Sarah's brow furrowed in a way that Roy could tell she was trying to piece these questions together.

"Would he ever bag a buck out of season?"

"Oh. I don't know. I'd like to think not, but I knew he fished without a license sometimes. He bragged about that, said the government had no right to keep him from what nature provided in the river. He and his whole family weren't real keen on following the letter of the law, as you know."

"And Ronnie went back the following night to retrieve a toy?" Roy watched Sarah intently.

"A stuffed animal for Maddy, right."

"But decided against contacting Zack when he saw Cedar, Jacky Blue, and Coon."

"Yes, I tried to get her to forget the toy when I found I'd left it behind, but children that age are hard to reason with. Until I went back a few days later, it was tough dealing with her. I appreciated Ronnie's efforts, and I don't blame him for leaving when he saw those men there. They were scary and mean." Sarah gave a small involuntary shudder.

"Even Cedar?" Roy asked in a casual tone.

"Cedar's changed since then. I have to tell myself that. He's been so kind to Maddy and me. He was broken up over Zack's passing," Sarah stated adamantly.

"They were close?"

"Yes. I know he felt responsible because of his workers and how they came between Zack and me. That guilt has affected him greatly."

"Hey, mistakes get made." Roy put his hands up in a conciliatory manner.

"I get what he looks like with his tattoos, and I know he did bad things long ago, but he's not been in trouble since Maddy was a little girl. That speaks highly of him. He turned himself around. He's got a sensitive side to him that people don't really see. You hear it in his music when he sings. There's deepness there." Sarah's eyes were dark and serious.

"Well, again, I'm sorry for how life batted you about back then, but you seem to have made the best of what you were dealt."

"Thanks. And I didn't mean to make Zack sound so bad. He really was a good father, and he never laid a hand on me, in spite of our arguments. I still miss him." Sarah sighed.

"You'll miss him forever. That's the tough part about being left behind."

□

CHAPTER 47

A partial sun peeked over the crystalline top of Mount Shasta, its morning rays negotiating the streaks of clouds, precursors to yet another approaching storm system. Cedar Stock stopped in to check on Ma, as he did most mornings, when he didn't have shit to wrap up from the previous night's work. She had her remote, her juice, and her oxygen bottle. She looked all set for the day.

He played a few songs on his guitar, including the opening chords for "Stairway to Heaven." He stopped before the rock-out, rough stuff.

Afterward he slipped into her garage and grabbed some cash from the disguised wall safe behind the electrical outlet over the tool bench. A quick count told him he'd have to get busy before long. All this bullshit with Detective Delroy Church had taken his attention for a minute. Jade Tankersley had texted him twice with a go for the *joyeria* dope drop in Modesto.

He pondered his current environment. He'd gotten lucky anticipating an answer for almost every criminal move he'd made with the Pud situation. The neighborhood watch cat grabbing the bad license plate nearly threw him, but he figured if they had anything from that, he'd have been in irons before they sprung the question. Typical cop bluff. He smirked to himself. They only interviewed you if they couldn't make the case without a confession or admissions.

Turn the tables and give a reasonable doubt explanation when cornered. They'd have to read that shit in a transcript to the jury showing you'd been cooperative. Your attorney could yell cop spin. Somebody sitting in the citizen's box would be sure to buy it. Hung at the very least. Plea deals or straight up drop of charges, two other distinct possibilities.

Cedar and the other inmates had spent hours, hell, years, strategizing for the next time they had to mount a defense. He thought it comical that lifers, the ones they called "washed up," really got into to it, as if they'd ever again smell daylight. Exercise for the brain he guessed.

Sarah Stock concerned him, though. She'd grown distant. She thought she hadn't shown it, but he was a man used to smelling mood change. A matter of survival in the joint. An eye wink, a nod, a turn at the last moment on the yard, moving out of the line of fire, a friendly handshake, too friendly, and of course the old invite to work out. What was she up to? Should he corner her? Ask what's up? Nah. Let it go for a minute, like a strange sound under a hubcap. Let it develop.

Cedar tucked his ten grand into a zip up leather wallet attached to the chain on his belt. He let himself out of Ma's garage and climbed into his truck. He sat there for a second before firing it up, letting the cold hug his face. Nothing like mid-winter in the Sisson air to keep the senses keen. Still, he admitted to himself that he'd grown tired of hopping across rivers on the heads of crocs. How long could his good fortune last? He wondered if he ought to sign up for one of those genealogical outfits on Ma's computer and check out his roots. Stock? A lucky Irish name? Cedar O'Stock the Lepre-Con. Now that's some funny shit right there.

He turned the engine over and cursed Moonshine Tankersley and Koondawg Cutler while backing out of Ma's driveway. He scanned the Black Tail right before hitting the southbound onramp to I-5. A jammed parking lot said hungry customers and money for the town. Time for him to do his part. Time to bring some of that Mexican cartel money back up north whether those fuckers liked it or not.

With his gun in the mules' faces they probably weren't too happy about it. Fuck 'em. Stay the hell outta my country or pay.

♦

Roy Church dialed Ronnie Faraday.

"Yes, Detective? What can I do for you? Are you interested in a vacant lot or maybe a single family home with a view?" His voice sounded hopeful.

"Uh, neither."

"I didn't think so," Ronnie replied flatly.

"Do you mind if I drop by with a few more questions? Just you. I don't want to upset Sarah again."

"She's not here today, but we can't do it over the phone?" Ronnie's voice was tinged with uncertainty.

"I'd rather meet in person. I want to show you some photos."

"Sure, it's just me in the office, slow winter business, so I may have to answer phones while you're here," Ronnie cautioned.

Roy hung up and thought about it. True, he'd fibbed a bit on the photos, but at this stage of an investigation it was best to look people in the eye if you could. He'd throw in one photo for credibility's sake. Also, it had not sounded as though Sarah had told Ronnie about her interview of the day before. Interesting. Maybe they didn't share everything.

Roy's cell phone vibrated. Sarah Stock's name popped up on his screen. Learning to enter contact numbers had made life interesting.

Hmm.

"This is Roy Church."

"Detective Church I'm so glad you answered. I couldn't sleep all night. Something you said, and a photo you showed, bothered me so much I had to get up and pull out all my old family photos. It had to do with the music question." She sounded a little out of breath.

"And?"

"Well, I told you we had the boom box, and that's true. But I got to thinking as I was lying in bed and my mind relaxed even more, just like you told me it would."

"The locks open when you're lying down," Roy replied.

"That is so true. So, I suddenly remembered, just lying there, that the loud music from our boom box kept waking Maddy up from her naps. Zack liked to work out with weights in the garage, he fixed stuff in there too. So he bought one of those personal devices only you can listen to music on. I mean today we all have our iPhones and iPods and MP3s with our ear buds, but back then it was all CDs. He had a portable CD player, I'm sure of it. He only used it, I never did, never had the time. That's why I didn't remember it at first when you asked. Anyhow, I found a photo of him wearing it. Is that helpful?" Her tone was hopeful.

Helpful? That's a bit of an understatement. Like calling DNA a mildly helpful scientific discovery.

♦

At 1000 hours, Roy walked into Ronnie Faraday's office. Ronnie took a seat behind his aircraft carrier made of brass and mahogany, Roy settled into a dark leather chair and stared at the room around him. It was a virtual shrine to Cooperstown and the Boys of Summer. Ronnie loved his baseball that was for sure. Display cases on walls sported autographed balls; baseball cards from multiple eras; mitts made of ancient creased leather; sweat stained caps and chipped Louisville sluggers. Team photos in wood framed displays showcased decades of Sisson Little League and youth leagues as well as farm and major leagues. Ronnie's office rivaled the decor of the Black Tail. Roy expected to see a waitress step into the room with coffee any second.

Ronnie noticed him staring in awe.

"Yes, I love the game," Ronnie said, dropping a pencil into a SF Giants helmet pen holder on his desk.

He sighed.

"I was an infielder, a short-stop for most of my career, which ended at the JC. If I'd only been faster…. My dream was to go on and play at Sac State and then a farm league somewhere, anywhere. These days I try to sponsor as many youth teams as I can. Been doing it for years. Good publicity for the business, I won't deny."

"Impressive," Roy said truthfully.

"If I were a rich man, I'd have pursued the biggie in baseball cards, Honus Waggoner, the Pittsburgh Pirate himself. 2.8 million."

Honus who? I should have paid better attention in school.

"Well thanks for seeing me this morning," Roy said.

"Whatever I can do to help. You said you wanted to show me another photo."

"Yes, but before that I'd like to scratch your memory a tad. Can you walk me through that last night, when you went over to Zack and Sarah's to get the toy animal for Maddy? Reason I ask, is there are details about those guys that may be very important."

Roy noted a sudden tackiness in Ronnie's lips.

"As I told you the other day, I went over to the Zack's house to get the stuffed animal, but when I got there, music was blaring, a party going on, so I decided not to chance it." Ronnie shifted in his leather chair.

"Chance it? I guess I don't understand. Zack was there, right? He was like your best friend? You saw his truck in the driveway?"

"Yes, I believe so."

"Maybe Zack could go get the toy for his daughter while you waited outside?"

"If I'd seen him, yes, I suppose," said Ronnie, brushing his left hand through his neatly combed hair.

"But you didn't even want to knock on the door. What was it about these dudes in the house that spooked you? I don't blame you, it's just that I'm trying to get a picture of these guys around that time. It could very important, so whatever you can tell me…." Roy trailed off with an expectant look.

Roy watched Ronnie's hands. The thumbnail on his right scraped under the nail of his left forefinger.

Ronnie didn't speak for a moment. Then he took a deep breath.

"You know, they were just plain scary. You heard Sarah say they'd been to prison. Tattoos, big guys, drank as if they were angry at the world. Just didn't want them looking at me is all. I guess you had to be there."

"Trust me. I've been there. Dudes who've been to the pen take on an air," Roy said. "It's because they've survived living with the danger of death every day. They smell weakness in an instant. They exploit it if they can. When they come out of the joint, it's hard for them to let that all go. They come up against people in the civilian world who have no clue what they've been through. We're easily intimidated by them because they've learned to take on the look of a coiled snake. They can stare right through you. Get too close, and they hurt you badly. They don't care anymore. We're true prey to their predator," Roy affirmed solemnly.

Ronnie said nothing, but his fingers worked overtime.

"You'd seen them before though, you said. You stopped going over after they showed up the first time, second time?"

"All I remember, I visited Sarah and Zack once when they were at the house. They'd been stopping in a few times, I think. Sarah told me she was not happy about it. Zack had told her they were staying only one night. I guess it turned into a regular thing. She and Zack fought about it."

"So you actually spoke to them, Cedar and his workers?"

Ronnie shook his head. "Well, not really. I mean I met them, and then I left."

"Like shake hands and leave?"

"Yes. Shake hands and left."

"Do you remember what they might have said when you shook their hands?'

"No, I just shook their hands, you know, to welcome them to Sarah's. Then I left."

"This sounds weird, but I don't think they really did tree trimming. So if you shook their hands, did the hands feel all calloused the way a tree cutter's hands might feel? Long time ago, I know," Roy smiled apologetically.

"Oh, no that was too long ago."

Roy noted that Ronnie had taken his hands off the desk and wiped them on his slacks.

"Okay, I want to show you a photo. Tell me if you ever saw something like this at Sarah's and Zack's," Roy said. *What the heck, take a chance, maybe Ronnie had seen them littering the front lawn.*

Roy approached Ronnie's desk and slid over the photo of the 40 ouncer from the back of Zack's truck.

Ronnie left it on the desk, leaned over and glanced at it for a moment, then leaned back.

"Not that I'm aware of."

Roy had shown a thousand photographs over the years. Those who wanted to help, grabbed the photo, held it up, turned it around, got close, asked if this is the only one he had and where he'd gotten it. Uncooperative or frightened individuals, including those who feigned doing their civic duty, glanced, showed no desire to touch, as if it were an earthworm or worse, and never asked a follow up question.

They drank as if they were angry at the world, but not that I'm aware of….

CHAPTER 48

"I'd just as soon you didn't go by yourself. When our guys travel out of state they go in pairs. We got the money to cover sending another person."

Lieutenant Gary Lynch looked across his desk at Roy to see how he'd react to a live hand grenade.

"Anyone in mind?" Roy asked, knowing the answer before he asked.

"Westwood. Would that be a deal breaker for you?"

Roy shrugged. "Hey, you're the boss. If you want him to go with me, he goes with me."

"That's it? No wtf? Anybody ever tell you you're a pro?"

Roy laughed.

"What can I say? I'm just a patrol dawg. Need someone to show me the ropes."

"I'll break it to him." Roy noted a hint of enjoyment in Lynch's tone.

"Okay. I'll make some calls to see if I can set up the meet. Probably have to fight the ACLU or Innocence Project along the way, but we'll get it done."

♦

The Val Verde Sheriff's Department had grown used to finding dead bodies in the arid Texas land along the border. Some died of starvation trying to cross a desert of rock with its sparse greenery, placing it a short step above the surface of the Red Planet. Some had died of thirst, hoping to make it to a minimum wage job in a San

Antonio hotel. Others died of slit throats or lead poisoning, the 9mm kind of lead.

Three bloated, fly covered Mexican Nationals detracting from the ambience of the cheap motel room didn't push the wow meter all that much. The bullet wounds were par for the course in the hit and run game the drug cartels played on both sides of the border with their *sicarios*, their hitmen. The twitching fingers and blood choked moans of a fourth body, however, grabbed the attention of the first deputy on scene who waded in trying not to vomit from the noxious fog hovering above maggots on putrefying flesh.

Texas Department of Public Safety assisted the Sheriff's Office in its investigation. Detectives surveying local motels, searching for the typical, profile group of your south-of-the-border hitmen, stumbled across the short story of two *Anglos* sporting green inked tats. It was probably unrelated, but the detectives took notes anyhow. The white boys had checked into a motel across the street from the crime scene a week earlier. They'd checked out right around the time the Justice of the Peace estimated time of death for the three unfortunate mules employed by the Gulf Cartel.

The room had been rented under the name Kelly Cutler. Cutler had paid cash as he loudly and rudely commented that he thought Winnemucca was a shithole until he saw Del Rio. The white male adult with Cutler had laughed and said, "Welcome to my state of Texas, bro." The clerk remembered the Texan as having penetrating blue eyes, one stark detail in addition to the roll off your tongue word *Winnemucca.*

Dutifully, Texas DPS contacted Nevada cops who readily came up with the name Kelly "Koondawg" Cutler, Aryan Warrior associate. The Nevada cops turned the Texas cops onto the California cops at CDCR who offered to come help find Cutler who had absconded while on parole years before and was suspected in several armed robberies across the Golden State. A CDCR record check revealed that an associate of Cutler who called Texas his birthplace went by "Jacky Blue." He hailed from Buda, Texas, up the 35 freeway from San Antonio, almost clear to Austin. Jackson Howard fit the description of the blue-eyed Texan to a T.

Val Verde Sheriff's detectives, on a whim, because they seriously suspected a violent cartel on cartel dope rip, but couldn't make it fit, eventually got around to checking a box in what had become a dead-end investigation. They showed the surviving mule some photos of six white dudes, four of whom had been selected at random from local booking photos. The other two photos were of Cutler and Howard.

Incredibly, the mule pointed to Howard and said, in broken *Ingles*, that this is the *hombre muy mal con los ojos azul* who'd shot the others in the back of the head and stabbed at least two in the throat. The victims' *manos* had each been zip-tied before death. His own *cabeza* ached like hell from a 9mm slug that had peeled around the back of his skull, took out an eardrum and several molars before coming to rest in his sinus cavity.

In early 2015, Texas Rangers caught up with Jacky Blue just as he was getting kicked out of his mom's home in Buda. Jacky Blue said he and his old friend Koondawg had been in Del Rio looking to get positions with the Minutemen, guarding the border from marauding Mexicans. How is that a crime? And that's bullshit picking me out of a line-up. Eyewitness testimony is for shit. And no, I don't know where your so-called suspect Cutler has gone. Probably got the fuck out of Texas, and by the way, I wished I'd never come back. Place sucks. Too many Californians moving here.

Jacky Blue had been entirely correct. Eyewitness testimony can be notoriously inaccurate in traumatic events. On the other hand, it helped the state's case that Jacky Blue's folding Buck knife had traces of blood in the blade trough. DNA comparisons connected the knife to the two dead Mexicans with the throat wounds.

A racially mixed jury of Texans, sick and tired of the drug industry and its attendant violence, unanimously voted to smoke Jacky Blue for the three counts of murder during the commission of a robbery.

The Texas Court of Criminal Appeals yawned when it read the case. In legalese, its opinion basically said, "Seriously dude? This ain't California. You put four human beings face down on a greasy, jizz-stained carpet in a cockroach infested motel room. You zip-tied their hands and probably tortured them into giving up the location of the dope and money in the room. But that wasn't enough for you, was it? Because you feared cartel retaliation, you stabbed and shot three to death. It would have been four if you'd had better aim. How could you mess that up from point blank range? You're a son of Texas, by God. Anyhow, have fun dining with the Devil. Okay everyone, break for lunch.

Texas Board of Pardon and Paroles wrote one line, "What they said," referring to the TCCA's lengthy analysis, so the Governor of Texas never even got the chance to weigh in with his own thumbs down.

Jacky Blue found himself in waist and ankle chains seated as sole guest of honor on a bus. The prison bus headed to the East Texas Piney Woods along the shores of beautiful Livingston Lake, part of the Trinity River Authority's complex system for supplying drinking water to the city of Houston, but only after straining out all stray water moccasins. He couldn't actually see the lake since they'd checked him into the concrete bunker that resembled an Eastern Bloc apartment complex without the classy push out windows. The Allan B. Polunsky Unit, home for Death Row inmates in Texas, didn't want the condemned getting any ideas about knotting sheets and sliding down a wall.

Jacky Blue's own mother had eventually given up on him, as disappointed mothers with Death Row children are wont to do. Being the point person in the Howard family, Mother Howard called the shots when it came time to cutting blood ties, so no one went against her to talk to him through a window on a phone that smelled of Lysol. His only visitors were a weary prison chaplain and bespectacled, bearded lawyers racking up hours, on principle, since it's pretty hard to defend the premeditated sticking of cold steel into a terrified, bound man's throat.

Suffice it to say, Jacky Blue exhibited mild surprise when the officers came to his cell door and told him he had a visitor, three in fact. He had a choice, he could see what they wanted, or he could refuse the visit, so the officers wouldn't have to gear up to move him.

His obvious question: What, you're too busy? I haven't seen or heard any movement out there all day. Oh, by the way, who are they?

"California cops. I doubt if they're here to help with an appeal." The officers chuckled to themselves.

CHAPTER 49

The corrections officers, all wearing flak jackets, had Jacky Blue kneel facing away from the sliding door port. He extended his hands back through the port, palms out. The cuffs went on, double locked. He scooted forward on his knees until he was told to stop then told to cross his ankles. The door opened behind him. Three officers moved in while a fourth stood by with a video camera. No need to give the ACLU any ammo. His ankle bracelets went on, a chain from them looped up to his cuffed hands. Plainly, he would not be taking part in a sack race.

The officers shuffle-stepped him to Death Row visiting, but instead of the normal Plexiglas with a phone where he got to listen to his lawyer's empty promises of a winning strategy for clemency, they turned him to a knob-less door, opened only with a key. Inside the windowless room was a metal table with an iron hoop in the center and a hard plastic chair just for him. They sat him at the chair. They hooked his cuffs with another set of cuffs to the iron loop. He hoped the place didn't catch fire. He could die of smoke inhalation before they got all the chains and shit off him.

He stared across the table at the three dudes facing him. One had the star of a Texas Ranger. Whoopee. The other two were a puzzlement. The younger one had the look of a baby coyote who wanted to grow up dangerous but preferred to stick by momma for the time being. The third, the old dude, looked at him with dead eyes, prison eyes. A con who'd turned his life around and joined the cops? What the fuck? This dude had the juice card, that's for damn sure.

Jacky Blue said nothing. He stared at the three, then glanced at the officers who had moved to the back of the room but in no way were going to leave it. The video camera's red light went out.

The old dude with the prison eyes said, "Mr. Howard, this gentleman seated to my left is Wade Bagley, Texas Ranger. We two," he gestured to himself and the coyote pup, "are California cops, Karuk County Sheriff's Department to be exact, up in far Northern California. This is Detective Westwood, and I'm Roy Church."

Jacky Blue said nothing. He wondered if this old Roy Church was about to read him his rights. He'd done a lot of dirt in California, and they sure as shit weren't here with a weekend pass. His mind spun.

"Let me speak as plainly as I can," Roy Church said, "Nothing you say to us can change your current status. Texas has passed sentence. Barring some unforeseen legal maneuver by any number of legal organizations that are in your corner, you will be executed as the state here sees fit."

Old Roy didn't bullshit. Jacky Blue appreciated that.

He ignored the Texas Ranger and the baby coyote. He looked directly at Roy Church.

"So why you wastin' my time?" His eyes were narrowed.

"Why did you agree to come out and see us? I'm sure the officers here told you you're under no obligation."

"You tell me," Jacky Blue said coolly, leaning back in his chair as far as the chains would let him.

"For starters, how about curiosity and a way to pass the time not having to think about what lies ahead?"

"You sound like a guy I used to know. We all said *lay* and he'd correct us to say *lie*. Smart sumbitch, but just some power shit he'd play," Jacky Blue remarked with a twist of his mouth. "Go on."

"Also, I'd wager you're wondering if you tell us some bad stuff you know about in California will it get you a stay of sorts."

Old fucker read my mind.

"Well the answer is no. It won't," Roy continued.

"Well, what's in it for me?" Jacky Blue flexed his heavily tattooed forearms.

"Nothing." The prison eyes watching Jacky Blue were unwavering and emotionless.

"Nothing? You flew all the way here from California to tell me you got nothin' *for* me, but you want something *from* me." Jacky Blue was incredulous.

Roy shrugged slightly. "That's about it."

"Well, fuck, why didn't you say so? Let me just unburden my soul to you about every bit of dirt I ever done, and while I'm at it, rat out every crimey I ever done it with? Shit, get me some paper. Let me get to writin'. You gotta be kiddin'."

"Nope, not kidding."

"Shit, get me outta here," Jacky Blue said to the officers, who started forward.

"On the other hand," said Roy, "I could make you a deal."

Jacky Blue snorted. The officers paused.

"What deal?"

"I tell you the name of the grammar Nazi who corrected your language, and you agree to chat with us a bit longer."

"Sheee-it. You couldn't know his name," Jacky Blue smirked.

Roy studied him for a moment. "Cedar Stock."

"What the fuck? How'd you know that? You ain't no hick sheriff."

"Yes, I am a hick sheriff. Sorry to burst your bubble."

Out of the corner of his eye, Jacky Blue detected a suppressed smile on the Ranger's face. Then it went back to stone. The coyote pup's right leg was bouncing slightly.

"Naw, c'mon. Where'd you do *all* your time? Yer pretty long in the tooth. Shouldn't you be rockin' somewhere?"

Roy leaned back. "It's true, I spent a few years elsewhere. Los Angeles County Sheriff's Homicide Bureau, but right now I'm just a regular old deputy sheriff from Karuk County doing his job."

"Bullshit. You ain't no regular old deputy," Jacky Blue laughed. He heard himself laugh, and realized he'd not laughed since the night he wasted them motel beaners.

"How long was you LA County?"

"Thirty-five years with the Department, over two decades in the Bureau."

Jacky Blue hated to admit it, but he was a little impressed. "You seen some shit," he finally said.

Jacky Blue wondered why he was talking to this old man, but what the hell. Speaking of seeing shit, now he had probably caused a lot of the shit this old boy seen. He'd blasted a few coons and beaners in SoCal back when he ran with the Inland Empire crews.

"How you know Cedar Bob?" Jacky Blue asked with suspicion.

"We're pals back home," Roy said simply.

Jacky Blue laughed out loud.

"Cedar Bob's a good old boy. Miss 'im. He ain't pals with no cops. Not the Cedar Bob I know."

"You boys had a good thing going back in the day. Pretending to be cops, taking down dope dealers. You do know it's against the law to impersonate a peace officer, right?"

Jacky Blue grinned, "If I admit to that, can I have that sentence instead the one I'm hemmed up on?"

"I'd ask the governor, but he's not taking my calls. He only talks to Texas Rangers." This time the Ranger smiled openly and bobbed his head.

Jacky Blue chuckled then sighed. Old Roy Church struck him as a man who didn't need shit from the likes of Jacky Blue to earn a rep. He turned to the custodial officers.

"How long we got?"

The officer in charge shrugged, "Your time is yours. We get off shift in five hours. There's a crew who'll take our place."

"So I could talk until they drag me out to shove a needle in my arm? Days even?"

"Theoretically," the officer said.

"Theo what?" Jacky Blue asked. "Never mind."

He turned back to the plainclothes cops.

"You had some big cases I bet," he said to Roy.

Roy made a noncommittal gesture.

"A few."

"Tell me about them."

"How about I tell you one, you tell me one?"

"Sure," Jacky Blue said. "But let's hurry this up."

"Why? You gotta be somewhere?"

"Yeah, I gotta attend the opening of my cell door."

"Well, you're dressed for the occasion," Roy replied drily.

Jacky Blue smirked.

"Shit, man. That's brass. Okay, let's chop it up."

"Before we do that, you do realize anything self-incriminating you tell me while in custody, about another crime, is inadmissible in court and cannot be used against you, unless your attorney is present and agrees that you may answer my questions."

"Fuck my attorney. If I had a good attorney, I wouldn't be sitting here with a belly growlin' for my last supper like ol' Jesus hisself. And what do you mean used against me? You can't kill me twice."

"Ah, that's why they don't call you *Gato*, the Cat. You haven't got nine lives," Roy pointed out as if it were a shame.

"Fuck dude, you're cold," smiled Jacky Blue. "So tell me a story."

"Gotta be Reader's Digest version, though. I'm not going word for word on a transcript of the days I spent on the stand."

"Okay. Gimme the high points."

"Okay. Sex registrant kidnapped a little girl working the counter at a stop and rob in the desert. Took her out and raped and killed her. Buried her in a shallow grave. My partner and I picked him up in Vegas brought him back to LA in chains. On the way we got stuck in a sandstorm. Dude had to piss bad. I refused to let him piss until he told us where he'd hidden the body. He finally gave in. He's now sitting on Death Row in San Quentin."

"What? That shit ain't admissible."

"Didn't say that's what convicted him. That's just a story. Your turn." Roy motioned for him to speak.

"Okay. What the hell. I got one for you. It was in all the papers. It cost me my life. Me and Koondawg waitin' on a cartel drop we knew was comin'. We got a motel across from the drop site. When it went down, we went in, said we was cops. I know, that's against the law. Anyhow, we took 'em by surprise, zipped 'em up, put 'em on the floor, and took their shit. Oh, and I done for three of them. Shit, I thought I killed four. Even put four notches in my pistol grip. If I get outta here, I promise to sand that fourth one out. I cain't live a lie." Jacky Blue grinned toothily.

"That's a good story. Does it bother you that Koondawg got away, and you're sitting here?"

"Hell yeah, it bothers me. Sumbitch is off spending my half on pussy and margaritas."

"Oh, he'll run out of money. Don't worry. Especially since he's still paying off Moonshine and the boys on the Commission."

Roy felt Westwood glance at him from his peripheries.

Jacky Blue eyed Roy again. "No, you ain't no regular old deputy. That's fer damn sure. You really FBI or CIA or some shit?"

Roy shook his head. "Not smart enough for those outfits. Need a four-year degree plus a masters."

"Ain't that the truth? But you might be SSU. So what else you got?"

"Okay, let's see. Russian organized crime wanted to move in on a restaurant business in West Hollywood. Owner didn't want to sell. Owner disappeared. Turns out the nephew of the ROC guy running the show has a contract business with several local veterinarians to incinerate animals. You know, burn 'em, bag up the remains as ashes and return them to the family so they can keep Fido on the mantle. Well, we sifted through the BLI 400 incinerator box and found the restaurant owner's pacemaker. They all got serial numbers."

"That's cool," said Jacky Blue. "I like the first one better, though."

"Oh, but that wasn't the good part. You see, the owner was Catholic, and we happened to scoop his pacemaker out of the incinerator on Ash Wednesday."

"Uh…," said Jacky Blue.

"Okay, I get it. You're not Catholic. Guess you had to be there."

"Catholic? Like them priests in robes that touch little boys? Fuck. Good thing them sumbitches never came to the yard."

"Yeah, something like that. Your turn."

"Okay. Hell, I could match you all day. You mentioned Moonshine, like you know him or some shit. Well he gets word to us about a load coming up with the paisas. You'll like this 'cause it's from your neck of the woods. Anyhow, we watch the mule pick up a drop at a truck stop in Lodi. When the mule goes in the restaurant to pay for his gas, ol' Cedar Bob walks by the car and cracks the taillight so we can follow it in the dark on the freeway. You can see the white light coming through the crack from way back. We follow the mule north 'til he stops at a rest area by that big old lake you got up there with all them houseboats."

"Shasta?"

Yeah, Lake Shasta. So the mule stops to take a whiz. Nobody around so, we roll in and yell 'cops' while he's got his dick in his hands. Lift his keys, take his car and his shit he's got in it. Leave his brown ass zip-tied in a stall. He's all cryin'. Says his *familia's* gonna get whacked in Mexico 'cause he lost a load. Ol' Koondawg, a cold motherfucker, says, 'Sucks to be you, but if your daughters are good lookin' enough maybe they'll just get whored out instead.' I mean, I actually felt sorry for him. Shoulda put a bullet in him. Save him some sorrow." Jacky Blue didn't look all that contrite.

"So why didn't you get rid of the mule. He could ID you to the cartel, just like the ones in Del Rio. Right? They send their *sicarios* to get rid of the nuisance. Why take the chance?" Roy was genuinely interested.

"I don't know. Maybe we should have. But that causes too much publicity, and we didn't have time to take a body out somewhere and dump it right. That takes time."

"Right, takes time. You gotta cut it up, stuff it in bags and then go dump it."

"Oh, you are a clever one, ain't you? "

"How so?"

"Like I don't know why you're here. I might be a dumb ol' Texan with barnyard shit on my boots to you, but I know why you're here. You got a case in your little county, and you think I can help you with it."

"Maybe." Roy noticed Westwood shift in his chair, sit up a bit straighter. He'd have to speak to him about that.

"Yet there ain't a damn thing you can do for me." Jacky Blue interlocked his fingers and fell silent, as if in prayer.

"That's right. I already made that clear. I guess we're appealing to your sense of civic duty, patriotism, and citizenship."

Jacky Blue burst out laughing.

"You know, Roy Church, I'm not gonna lie. I done some bad shit in my life. But I always tried to make sure it was dudes in the game that got it, before they got me."

"I guess the law doesn't look at it that way."

"I know, but see, that's the thing. Your asshole who killed the little girl and buried her in the desert, he's the one who's gotta go. Or the Russians who whacked a restaurant owner, what'd he ever do to deserve that?"

"You got a point," Roy conceded amiably.

"Hey, I ain't no punk, and I'm gonna walk the walk dry eyed, not cryin' like a little bitch, but damn, there needs to be some fools goin' with me."

"Like Koondawg?"

"Fuck Koondawg. Look, I'm getting' tired. Just spit it out what you want. Either I'm gonna tell you or I ain't. Most likely ain't, but I gotta give you props for tryin'."

"That's all I can ask for," Roy said. "So here goes. Let me tell you a story first before any questions. I don't know what part's fiction and what part's truth. You maybe know the difference. And that's why we're here."

"I'm all ears. I love a good story. Maybe it'll put me to sleep like in kindergarten. Got any chocolate milk and crackers? Or am I the only cracker here?" Jacky Blue sniggered at his own joke. Roy smiled wryly with him.

"We could start outside Carson City in the late 80's when Koondawg helped himself to a jeweler's goods without paying," Roy said.

"Old news. I did time for it."

"And if you'd not been hemmed up for Del Rio, I suspect you'd still be doing time, just not state time."

"Don't get your meanin'." Jacky Blue looked annoyed.

"Doing time for the Commission and Moonshine, same as how Cedar Stock is still doing time."

"Done your homework. I respect that, so I'll throw you a bone."

"Anything helps."

"Koondawg fucked up when he told Cedar Bob how much we scored at the cathouse. Of course, if he hadn't lied, Cedar Bob woulda took his wind in New Folsom, and he wouldn't a been out causin' shit for the rest of us goin' forward. I'll leave it at that."

"A man I know once said that when the Brand gets its hooks in you, they don't let go."

"Smart man." Jacky Blue nodded. He bent forward and scratched the side of his face with dark, overly long nails. His wrist chains jingled vigorously.

"So Cedar Bob, as you call him, made a deal with the Devil. But when he found out how much Koondawg didn't have, he was on the hook to Moonshine and the boys in The Bay. From then on, he and you were tied to Koondawg's bullshit, and when Jade Tankersley called, you all came running."

"You that smart man who come up with that sayin' 'bout the hook?"

"No, but I'm going to make it my own from now on. Make it sound original."

"You ain't wrong. The AB, and every other prison outfit for that matter, tells you it's just mostly for inside when you first pledge allegiance. You gotta have protection from the coons and Mexicans, and they gotta have protection from each other, so they pack up too. The officers can't keep us apart, so we gotta do it all ourselves," Jacky Blue said.

"Prison is not for the weak of heart," Roy added superfluously.

"No shit. Along the way they give you a choice to pledge for life or not. No hard feelings. At least that's what you think. But in the beginning, they get you to run down every bit about you and your crimes and your family, especially your family. Now I ain't had the best of relations with my mama and hers. They don't got no skin in this, but when the fellas at the top send you photos of your momma bent over in her garden and tell you how good that ass looks, you listen. Just like the mule in the rest stop, you gotta think about more than yourself."

"So you and your crew of Cedar Bob and Koondawg, and I'm going to guess Pud and Dina, get busy ripping off dope dealers and then breakin' off the fellas in The Bay. Money went on their books for canteen or into an account they got set up somewhere."

"Pud and Dina? Don't know them." Jacky Blue leaned back in his chair. He'd have rocked on the back legs if he had a few more links to work with.

"Right. My guess is Pud and Dina were your stalking horses, meaning they didn't look as if they'd been to the joint, so you sent them in to buy dope at a target house. Also, you probably had them sit bird dogging in Mexican restaurants where the cartel mules meet to exchange car keys belonging to cars in the lot that have money or dope or both in them."

"Don't know Pud. Don't know no one named Dina." Jacky Blue stared straight into Roy's eyes. Jacky Blue blinked first.

"Sure," said Roy. "Which is why you went looking for them, knocking on doors in Sisson in the summer of 2004."

"Oh, that Pud and Dina. Why didn't you say so?" He'd have slapped his forehead in mock remembrance if the damn chains hadn't once again cramped his style.

"Yes, that Pud and Dina, Dina being the one who filled in as a runner for the AB after Jade Tankersley got sacked by the warden at Pelican Bay for passing kites in the visiting room."

"Damn, you're like that Jew magician Copperfield, or else somebody's snitchin.' Is that it? Gotta be Pud tellin'." Jacky Blue's eyes glittered darkly from under his heavy lids.

Roy continued, "I'm guessing you guys first started working with them in about 1995, back when you and Koondawg and Cedar Bob bunked in with Cedar Bob's cousin Zack, you know, the one who drowned while you were there?"

"What do you mean while I was there? I wasn't there when he drowned. Don't know nothin' about that. We were out of town when that shit went down."

"Were you?" Roy questioned.

"Can you prove we weren't?"

"No."

"Damn, that Zack had a good lookin' wife. I remember that. He treated her like shit though." Jacky Blue shook his head.

"Sarah?" Roy asked helpfully.

"Yeah, that was her name, Sarah. I think she had a little girl."

"Maddy."

"Yeah, Maddy, that was it. Fuck, dude, that was a long time ago. Lotta water under the bridge since them days."

"Almost 23 years ago."

"Yeah, can't remember much about that far back, so I guess I ain't a lot of help to you. But I appreciated your stories. Guess that's it, huh?" He pulled his chains upward and glanced back at the officers.

"I'm not done. If you want to hear more, I got more. It's not like you really gotta be somewhere, or did the governor call and I didn't hear the phone ring."

Jacky Blue laughed out loud for at least the third time.

"God damn, you are a ballsy sumbitch. Shit, that chaplain and my attorneys, they come in here all horse faced, mopin' around. Jesus, it's like they're the ones gettin' the needle. Fuckin' pussies. But you, yer straight up."

Westwood shifted uncomfortably, and Jacky Blue's eyes scanned him briefly in distaste.

"So since we're all in a jocular mood, how about telling me what happened to Dina, and who the hell dumped a body and deer carcass on a ridge in my county back in '95?"

"Damn, I'd have to get a clemency to open up about that shit," Jacky Blue laughed. "But good try. Why don't you ask your buddy Pud? He's the one tellin'."

"Pud's dead, been dead for a few months."

"No shit? What the fuck happened to his sorry ass?"

"Died by asphyxia."

"Ass what?"

"Strangulation. They found him hanging."

"Pud killed hisself? Wasn't much use. Dumb sumbitch, couldn't read or write."

"He got help with the noose."

"No way. Who the fuck done that?" Jacky Blue leaned forward, his eyes bright with curiosity.

"Cedar Bob is my guess."

"Fuck you talkin' about? You tellin' me Cedar Bob killed Pud? Well, I ain't surprised. He had it comin'."

"And you're going to tell me all about why, right?"

"Soon as you get me cuff keys, a car, and an hour head start."

"Okay, I admit that was like asking for sex on a first blind date, but I had to try," Roy chuckled. "Can I get serious for a minute?"

"Mean you ain't been serious? Pud ain't really killed by Cedar Bob?"

"No, I'm serious about that, but there's something else I'd like to say."

His face grew somber. "Go ahead. I'll just tell my secretary to hold all calls."

"Okay. Look, you're a tough dude. You're going to walk on your own when it comes time, and at this point it looks like it's going to happen. I mean, this is Texas, not California. You don't owe anybody anything, because you're about to have all you got taken from you."

"Damn, you oughta man a suicide hotline. You are one cheery sumbitch." Jacky Blue muttered and rapped the table with the bottom of a closed fist.

"I get that a lot. What I'm saying is, it would be nice to know, if you know for sure that is, if Pud killed Dina Morgan. It's not for Pud. It's for Pud's mama. Everyone back in Sisson believes he killed her. He's dead. It doesn't matter to him. But his mama goes to the store and people look at her and say, 'There goes the mother who raised a retard killer.' She's stopped going to her church. Lost her friends. They don't come right out and say it to her face. You know how the whisperers in the store aisles are. They love sticking you in the back with their little knives, love watching you slowly bleed."

"Sick fucks. Mean bitches. I know what you're talkin' about. My mama told me the same thing. Lost her friends because they were all pissin' their pants over me. They're all coverin' lips and cuppin' ears sayin' 'Ooooh, there goes the Beast of Buda's mama.'"

"The Beast of Buda?"

"Told you I done some shit in my hometown. Fucked a kid up pretty bad. Hey, there's a story."

"Let's hear it."

"They called me Jacky Blue, on account of my eyes. I'd been in and out jail, the pen even. I come back to town, go to a party, and some kid says real loud, 'Jacky Blue. Hey, he needed a ride'."

"Uh, oh."

"Yeah. Some fuckin' comic was going around gettin' laughs by sayin' 'Little Boy Blew. Hey, he needed a ride.' So I tore open a beer can and sliced the shithead kid's face wide open like I was guttin' a fish. Jacky Blue, the Beast of Buda. They don't tell that joke there no more." He was proud.

"That's a great story."

"Look. Did Pud waste Dina? I ain't gonna say. Is there a difference between killin' someone and gettin' someone killed?"

"Any way to focus that for me a bit more?"

"Shit, you got the answers in all this trickery you laid on me. You're one hell of a detective. I bet you can figure it out."

"They say Pud and Dina got in a fight. A domestic fight. Pud says she hopped out of his truck on a lonely dirt road. Pud never saw her after that. But you're telling me it was not a boyfriend girlfriend argument."

"I ain't told you nothin'. You figure shit out all by your lonesome. I ain't gonna meet ol' Satan, and the first thing he says to me is, 'You was tellin', boy. You ain't welcome here'."

"I guess I'm still confused. You, and probably Cedar Bob who just got out of The Bay and is waiting back in the car, are going around knocking on doors looking for Pud a few days after Dina disappears. Yet you don't think Pud killed Dina in a domestic blow up."

"You can go back and check some records. Everything gets recorded. All I'm gonna say on that."

"Okay, I will, after I figure out what you're talking about."

"You're a smart guy. You'll do your thing."

"Okay, I'll try to work with that. Hey, on another note, remember a friend of Zack's name Ronnie? You guys scared the hell out of him back then."

"Oh, yeah, Cousin Zack's little lover boy. Was that his name? Ronnie? Couldn't forget him," Jacky Blue grinned wolfishly. "Damn for a guy asking a lot of questions, you sure do know a lot."

"So if Ronnie told me he only just barely met you and Koondawg back in the day, he's being less than truthful."

Jacky Blue's grin grew wider and more dangerous.

"Yeah, I'll give you that one. Tasty Ronnie's lyin' like a rug. I'd say he got to know Koondawg pretty damn well. You ever seen that movie Deliverance? Koondawg made that boy squeal like a pig. And that's when shit come off the rails."

Roy paused. "Uh, is there a story there?"

"Don't you know it," replied Jacky Blue before turning to regard Westwood. "So, Roy, your young buck here. He's probably wonderin' why I'm flapping my gums with you," Jacky Blue said, adjusting in his seat. "What's your name again, boy?"

"Detective Westwood." Westwood used his most authoritative voice

"What? Your daddy and momma looked down at you in that hospital bed and said, 'Hey let's name this shriveled up, wet little fella Detective.' Is that right? Old family name, Detective, is it?" Jacky Blue's dirty grin held no warmth.

"No, it's Wallace," Westwood conceded uncomfortably.

"Wallace? Wallace Westwood? Shit, I'll bet they call you Wally, Wally Westwood, and all the time you probably wanna be called Clint. Ha. Anyone ever call you Clint?"

Westwood replied a little too quickly, "As a joke."

"As a joke? But you tell them, no, my name is Wally. Ha. Don't that beat all?"

"Yep, don't that beat all," Westwood repeated in a hard tone.

"Whoa, hoss, don't set yer ears back, now. I'm clownin' ya. Don't take the bait. So now that we established that Wally would not last a night in San Quentin Reception, why don't you tell him why I'm talkin', Roy. School this pup."

Roy cleared his throat.

"Okay. Mr. Howard here is talking because sometimes old cops and old cons grow to respect each other for choices made and lived with, both of them in worlds of extreme shit. He's talking because we didn't come in here trying to run game on him. If we had, he'd have pulled our covers and been gone. He's talking because I introduced myself as Roy. He's talking because isolation with nothing but what's in your head is suffocating, and even the ear and voice of the enemy is preferable," Roy said, not unkindly.

Jacky Blue broke in.

"That's right Wally. You want a con to talk to you? Well you ain't got but the chance God give a shot o' jizz makin' it past rubber. But it happens. So you can't come in badge heavy. Me? Shit, Roy said he couldn't offer me nothin'. He's right. I got three weeks to live. There ain't nothing on this earth you can offer a man who's got three weeks of air between him and the black."

"Yet here we are," said Roy. Westwood was silent.

CHAPTER 50

2000 hours, June 21, 1995

"Fuck time is it?" Koondawg growled. "I'm hungry, I'm horny, and Cedar Bob needs to get back here so we can figure out what the fuck."

"Simmer down, good buddy. You know how Jade is. On time but has to get cock first. If Moonshine found out Cedar Bob was pumpin' his old lady, we'd all be in the shit."

"She ain't even that good lookin'"

"What woman *is* good lookin' to you, ya faggot."

"Your mom. That's why I did her. Only woman I ever made cum. Boy could she handle the Koondawg hog."

"Man, that ain't right," Jacky Blue said, punching Koondawg hard in the arm.

"Throw me a forty, turn down that music, and let's watch another fuck film," Koondawg sighed.

"Okay, but I ain't watchin' your homo shit."

"Whatever. Hey, you as tired of Jade's shit as I am? That bitch is all up in our grill givin' orders, and we're the ones takin' chances."

"Straight up featherwood. Don't cross her is all. One word to her old man and we're takin' a lime nap."

"Where's she getting her info anyhow? I always wondered," Koondawg said, his voice lowering.

"Koondawg, you ask too many questions. What are you, a rat? You wearin' a wire, you traitorous fuck? And no, I don't want you to get naked so I can check. Border Brothers are passin' info to the *eses* inside. They pass it on to Moonshine. He gets at Jade who gets at Cedar Bob then makes him pound her ass before she lays it out."

"Ha, ha. You thought you was gonna pound ass on Zack's old lady. Ooh, she shot you down in flames, bro!" Koondawg grinned at Jacky Blue's failure.

"Dammit Koon, I was just gonna give her a little bitta Texas two-step. You seen she was eyein' me. You know that faggot she's married to ain't deliverin' the goods."

"Where is that motherfucker anyhow?"

"He's out in the garage skinnin' up a deer he blasted today. Thought it'd make hisself feel all better over his old lady bouncin'. Fucker went out and killed a doe, and it ain't even the season."

"Season? You can't shoot a fuckin' doe in this state you stupid armadildo humper," Koondawg scoffed.

"Armadildo? It's *armadillo*," Jacky Blue choked out, laughing heartily at Koondawg's ignorance.

"Whatever, but you do got them little bastards down in the great state of Texas. Even got a town named after them."

"That's Amarillo, not Armadillo, you dumb butt pirate."

"Ha. Little fuckers remind me of armored cars." Koondawg continued, "So what the fuck? Mexicans wanting us to rip off other Mexicans. Man, that's some shit right there."

Jacky Blue shrugged. "Same in Texas. Cartels fightin' each other below the border and rippin' each other above it. Wipe out the competition."

Koondawg slapped Jacky Blue to attention.

"Hey, whoa, Jacky, car's pullin' up. That ain't Cedar Bob."

"Who the fuck is it? Cops?"

"Can't quite see. Oh, wait, dude's wearing a baseball uniform? What the fuck? Oh, it's Zack's boyfriend, Ronnie."

"Fuck's he doin' here?" Jacky Blue mumbled.

"I don't know. Maybe heard Zack's old lady split, and he come to offer some between the sheets comfort."

"He's comin' to the door? Zack's in the garage. He needs to go there not here."

"Yeah, but Zack's got the door closed. Guess he don't want nobody seeing his doe hangin'."

"Well, don't answer it. Maybe his faggot ass will leave. Cedar Bob said to lay low until he got back," Jacky Blue warned Koondawg.

"Fuck that. I'm lettin' that sweet ass in. Gonna get me some. You watch."

Jacky Blue shot him a glance. "Koon, c'mon man. We don't need the trouble if it goes sideways."

"Sideways? You just get ready. You fuckin' owe me. Quick, grab one of them zip ties." There was a knock at the door. "Just a minute. Be right there, Ronnie," he called.

♦

Jacky Blue sat back in his chair as far as he could, about the length of one cuff.

"Fuckin' chains," he said with disgust. "Three more weeks and I don't gotta wear them no more."

"So you're tellin' me Koondawg Cutler sexually assaulted Ronnie, Zack's friend?" Roy asked.

"Is that what they call it? I call it Koondawg zip tyin' him and ridin' ass like he's tryna win a buckle."

"And you didn't try to stop it," Westwood added, with faint disgust. Jacky Blue eyed him and snorted.

"Yeah, guess I bear some responsibility. I shoulda controlled him better. But when Koon got an idea in his head, it was hard to stop him. And truth be told, he hadn't got laid in a while," he said as if it were an understandable excuse.

"Hmm," said Roy.

Jacky Blue returned his hard gaze to Westwood.

"What's the matter, Wally, don't like what one man will do to another? Best keep your nose clean then. Stay outta the pen. That way you never have to hear another man's balls slappin' your bare ass."

Westwood turned away and stared at the wall, shaking his head. The Texas Ranger remained impassive.

"So, I can't imagine Ronnie was too happy after Koondawg got through with him," Roy observed, breaking the tension.

"Geez, Roy. You sure you were only a detective? 'Cause you startin' to sound more like Captain Obvious," chuckled Jacky Blue, flipping the switch back to gregarious.

"Weren't you afraid he'd go to the police?"

"Yeah, I was kinda nervous about that at first. But then I figured him being a known colon commando, what was he gonna say to the cops? My boyfriend got a little rough on my butthole? Shit, them redneck country cops woulda probably kicked his pervert ass for wastin' their time."

"You said earlier that's when it went off the rails."

"Uh, yeah, shit, I guess I'm kinda unburdenin' my soul, but damn, Roy, you're like the first cop I ever really felt like talkin' to besides askin' what I was bein' charged with."

"Well, you got a lot pent up."

"Shit, now, Roy, don't go all faggot psychology on me. I had enough of them candy asses proddin' me in here, tryin' to see if I had childhood issues that gimme an excuse to whack dudes."

"My bad," Roy said with easy humility.

"That's better. So we kinda figured ol' Zack and Ronnie had a little thing goin' the minute we first seen the two of them together at Zack's. Hell, that's why I thought it'd be cool to give some lovin' to his old lady. Shit. I mean you can tell. When you been to the joint, you can tell when a dude is doin' other dudes because there ain't no women or whether he's doin' dudes because that's what he prefers."

"So on top of his wife leaving him, Zack's best friend gets forcibly sodomized by a parolee. He couldn't have been too happy either. Did he find out about it? I mean he was in the house somewhere. The garage you said, skinning a deer."

"Yeah, he come unglued later. Guess he saw Ronnie limpin' away, get in his car, and drive off. Don't think they talked. Zack was wearing some fuckin' thing on his head, listenin' to music, and I don't think he heard Rump Ranger Ronnie screamin'."

"He was wearing something on his head listening to music?"

"Yeah, you know, not like they got them tiny things today, fuck, I can't remember exactly, but it was clipped to his belt and he took them other things out of his ears when he come in the kitchen to ask what the fuck was going on, and why was his friend drivin' away lookin' all pissed off."

"Hmm."

"Koondawg always was his own worst enemy. He says, 'Oh, you jealous? Your boyfriend just gave up some special ass to the Koon man'. He grabs at his own crotch like a rappin' nigger. I mean he was like rubbin' it in his face. That's when ol' Zack went off."

"Went off?"

"Yeah, got kinda intense there for a minute. I stayed out of it. Had to be between two men over their bitch. Know what I mean?" He posed it as a serious question that Roy should address.

Roy decided to go with a vague, "I think so."

Jacky Blue nodded. "Yeah, don't get involved. Well, shit, I mean Zack threw the first punch, let's be honest. Now Koondawg may be a lotta things, but you don't punch him and not expect retaliation. He ain't no punk." Roy noticed a faint note of pride in his voice.

"Apparently not."

"So they went at it in the kitchen, breakin' shit and kickin' and scratchin' and bitin'. Hell, was like a cage match for a minute. Wished I'da had bets goin'."

"But it ended at some point," Roy prompted.

"Yeah, fuck. I mean Zack gave it a pretty good go, but damn, let's face it. Koondawg was a full-growed man who done his time on the yard iron and fucked up a lot of dudes along the way. He pretty much took control, and then it got bad, real bad."

"Bad?"

"Yeah. Koon put the boots to ol' Zack on the kitchen floor. Fucked him up good. I told him to stop."

"So you did step in. That's something at least. Coulda killed him."

Jacky Blue hesitated. "Well, yeah, see there's the thing."

"Uh, oh."

"Yeah. Shit. I mean it was supposed to be a fair fight and I shoulda stopped it when it was over, and knowin' Koon the way I do, I, like I said, bear some responsibility, but I ain't the one who was mad over a boy chicken."

Roy encouraged him to continue. "So what happened?"

"Well, I got Koondawg to ease up by saying I thought I saw a car headin' down the lane and Cedar might be comin'. Course there weren't no car. I just said that." Jacky Blue was clearly proud of his quick thinking. Roy could feel Westwood suppressing an exasperated scoff.

"Okay."

"So, I said we needed to clean this shit up and get Zack out of there because it was gonna look bad for us if Cedar seen it."

"Right," Roy agreed.

"So we sorta dragged Zack out to the front yard so we could clean up the kitchen. Throw all the busted shit away. That's when I took a big sigh of relief, 'cause I seen Zack was still breathin' and moanin' a little. I figured he was sorta stunned, you know, and he'd be all right and shit. So we left him sittin' on the front yard lickin' his wounds. I told him to chill while we cleaned up the mess in the kitchen."

Roy raised his eyebrows. "So he was conscious?"

"Oh, yeah. He said he was having trouble breathin', but hell, I seen worse. How's I s'pose to know he'd bleedin' inside. I ain't a doctor. Figured he had busted ribs is all. I figured he'd come out of it okay and learn his lesson. Bitches ain't worth gettin' an ass kickin'," Jacky Blue said with wisdom in his voice.

"So you went back and cleaned up?"

"Yeah, and got some beers and turned on the music all loud to work by. We wanted to seem all unconcerned when Cedar got back, like it had only been a little misunderstanding, and then we could act all surprised at how bad Zack was hurt."

"You know Zack was going to tell Cedar what happened. Did that concern you?"

"A little, to be honest. But me and Koon had time to get our stories straight, like how Zack had come all ragin' into the kitchen and sucker punched Koon for gettin' busy with his boyfriend."

"So what happened when Cedar got back?"

"Well, it was a little while before he got back, we drank some more beers, watched a fuck film or two, probably fell asleep. I mean it was a minute before ol' Cedar Bob come in the house. Guess Jade wanted more than just a quick dick this time. Anyhow, Cedar Bob had some bad news for us."

"Bad news?" Roy's eyebrows raised again.

"Uh, yeah." Jacky Blue's little fingers tapped quietly on the table.

♦

2130 hours, June 21, 1995

Cedar Stock yelled as he threw open the kitchen door.

"Jacky, Koon! What the fuck happened?! Where the fuck are you?"

"Right here. We're back here in the bedroom. What's wrong?" Jacky Blue said, stepping out of the back bedroom, rubbing his eyes to clear them from a snooze.

"Zack's on the lawn and he ain't breathin! Fuck! He's dead. What the fuck?!"

"What? Hey Koon, get out here. Zack's fuckin' dead!"

Koondawg Cutler emerged from the bedroom, a forty-ounce malt liquor welded to his hand.

"What do you mean dead? Can't be. We just seen him a little while ago. What the fuck?"

"Yeah, what the fuck is right. Better start talkin' now, motherfuckers!" Cedar's fists were clenched.

"Hey, whoa, Cedar Bob. Zack come in here and punched me. All I did was punch him back a few times. He was fine. I swear." Koondawg held his hands up, still clutching the bottle, in a gesture of surrender.

"What the fuck? Why did he punch you? Fuck. I can't leave you assholes on your own. What happened? And don't fuckin' lie to me," Cedar warned, a vein in his forehead pulsating visibly.

"Zack caught me gettin' sugar from his boyfriend Ronnie. Got all pissed. Threw a punch. Hell, I was defending myself," Koondawg said, playing the victim.

"That's right, Cedar. Zack come in here all fists and fury. Koon beat his ass, but later outside he was all fine. It was a good brawl, but nobody shoulda died. I'm serious, man," Jacky Blue tried to add.

"Bullshit. You put the boots to him, didn't you Koon. Just like that dumb ass kid in Fremont. You did, didn't you? Don't fuckin' lie to me, goddammit."

"Yeah, I mean, I kicked him a coupla times, not hard though. In the ribs and shit. Not the head." Koondawg took a swig and swallowed a burp.

"Bullshit. You fucking caved his head in, you cocksucker. I oughta put a bullet in you right here and now. That's my fucking cousin for crissake!"

Koondawg shrugged. "Sorry, man. But not my fault. I swear."

"Mother. Fucker!" Cedar yelled throwing his hands in the air and pacing back and forth. "Like we need this shit right now. We gotta be in Vacaville in two days and we cannot fuck that up. It's big. The *paisas* are moving pounds and keys together and we gotta take them off. I gotta send Pud and Dina south to scout. They're gonna be over here later tonight. I didn't have no money on me, so I gotta fatten 'em up with some cash before they leave."

"Sorry, Cedar, I shoulda stopped the fight I guess," Jacky Blue said, all droopy faced.

"Okay, who all was here? You said Ronnie. Did he see the fight?"

"No, man he took off like a raped ape," Koondawg said, grinning.

"Wipe that fuckin' smirk off your face. This is all your doing," Cedar growled.

"Yeah, Cedar, nobody but us," Jacky Blue said, ever the buffer.

"Okay, look. Good thing. Nobody saw shit who can hurt us. Here's what we gotta do. We gotta get this all cleaned up and be outta here by mid-morning. It's just fortunate Sarah isn't here with little Maddy or I swear, Koon, I'd call the cops myself. Jesus! Fuck!"

"What do we do? Jacky Blue asked.

"First thing is, Koondawg, throw your damn beer in the trash. Jacky, get Zack's truck. Back it up to the lawn. Koon go get his fishing gear out of the garage. Rods, nets, tackle box, get it all. I'm gonna grab plastic tarping that Zack's got out in that shop. We gotta roll him up and get him out of here. His head's bleeding and we can't get any of that shit in his truck. Sorry to say, but we gotta drown him by accident. Koon, you fucking asshole," Cedar spat.

Koondawg swallowed the last of his forty ouncer. He tossed the empty in the kitchen trash.

"Like I said, man, I'm sorry. Musta hit him harder than I thought. It's not even like heat of anger man, voluntary manslaughter at best, maybe even involuntary, 'cause I didn't even have no Pacific intent."

"Jesus H. Christ," said Cedar, shaking his head. "Specific intent."

Koondawg frowned. "That's what I said."

"And I need a map. I know Zack has a map here somewhere. I gotta show you where to dump him. Fuck me. I'm like a daycare operator for fucksticks," Cedar stormed.

♦

Roy stared across the table at Jacky Blue for a moment before commenting.

"So you guys made it look as if Zack had drowned? Smart. Smart because everybody bought it."

"Yeah," said Jacky Blue, smiling wryly. "Sheriff didn't have no Roy Church workin' for him then, or we'da been screwed royal fer sure."

"How'd you do it? Just for education's sake. In case I ever run across this sometime."

"What? Man, you need to retire. You don't need to be runnin' across this shit never. Ain't you got a family that's said enough is enough?

"No. Just me."

"What? You never got married and had kids? Wait. You did but you're divorced, and your kids got raised by some asshole. I heard how all cops get divorced." Jacky Blue nodded sagely.

"No. Not in my case." He felt Westwood side-eyeing him.

"Wait a sec, Roy. You ain't gay or nothin'. If you are, I mean that's cool. But I wanna apologize if I said anything offensive," Jacky Blue said in a sober tone.

"I thought you could tell, being in the joint and all," Roy said conversationally.

"Well, damn. You hide it well," Jacky Blue said in awe.

"Just fucking with you. I'm not gay. My wife and daughter passed away a few years back. Just me now."

Westwood had now fully rotated his torso as he stared at Roy.

"Oh, goddamn. I am sorry to hear that. I truly am," Jacky Blue muttered somberly.

"Thanks, Jacky. Means a lot coming from a man in your shoes."

"Hey, yeah, no problem. You got my condolences."

"So you and Koondawg staged a drowning?"

"Naw. Turned out Koon was too fucked up to drive. I mean we'd been drinkin' forties all day. So Cedar Bob being sober had to take over. Left Koon there to pack his shit. Course he just got through packin' shit, and now he had to do it again," Jacky Blue's belly chains rattled heartily.

"So you and Cedar Bob staged a drowning," Roy said, ignoring the attempt at sick humor.

"Yep. We done it up good too. Some fuckin' river up there. I drove Zack's truck. Cedar followed me in a work truck with Zack in the back. Hey that rhymes. Sounds like that Cat in the Hat dude."

"You've got talent that way," Roy affirmed.

"When we got there, Cedar Bob took a length of hose and poured whiskey into Zack's throat to make it look like he'd been drinkin. He had of course, been drinking beer while he was skinnin' his doe. There was beer bottles and cans all around. But we couldn't be sure how much he had in him. We wanted him to look real drunk when they cut him open."

"Just in case you ever run into that situation again, the alcohol would not be absorbed into his system if he's already dead. Just sayin'."

"Thanks for the tip, Roy. I guess that was a waste of time. But gotta give us an A for effort."

"Yes. An A for effort. But that's just for your ability to drive there. The Cops Robbers gang could have all been undone on a DUI beef if CHP had been on the prowl."

"Yeah, fuck. I surprised myself. But then I've always been able to hold my liquor. Hey Wally, I'd show you how I hold my licker, but my hands are occupied at the moment. Why the fuck am I in such a good mood?" Jacky Blue laughed.

"Maybe because you got away with it?" Roy offered.

"Yeah, we was pretty slick doin' our reverse CSI thing. Cedar collected a bottle of river water and funneled it into Zack so his lungs would be full, like he drowned for real."

Roy nodded approvingly.

"I mean, it's possible, but he may have put it into Zack's stomach to mix with the booze he just put in. On the other hand, if he got lucky and hit the windpipe going down, the water would go to the lungs. I think either you boys got lucky or Zack was still alive when you all tossed him in the drink."

"Fuck, no way was he alive. Side of his head all stove in, a Koondawg specialty."

"Well let's just hope he was dead. Unless a body is decomposed, there are really only three ways to tell for sure if it's dead. Decapitation of course; or pupils fixed and dilated; or postmortem lividity."

"Don't understand a thing you just said. Like I said, I ain't no doctor, although I stayed in a Holiday Inn Express once," Jacky Blue quipped.

He would have slapped his knee if he could have moved his hand more than an inch. The others smiled to be polite.

"So you rolled poor old Zack into the water, left his truck, and that was that?" Roy asked.

"The fat lady sang."

"Then you two went back to Zack's house? Or what?"

"Yep. Got back. Pud and Dina waitin' there for us. Koondawg was sawin' logs. We grabbed some shut eye, hit the road the next morning for Vacaville. After that job, and Jesus was that a score, Koondawg and me figured we better split the state."

"But Cedar stayed behind and caught a case, got out in 2004 just in time to help look for Dina," Roy clarified.

"Yep, that's about it. Jade and me picked him up in Crescent City when he hit the gate. We drove to Sisson to hook up with Pud and Dina. 'Course we didn't on account of Dina disappearin' like that."

"Hmm," said Roy.

"You say that a lot," said Jacky Blue.

"Nervous habit."

"Ha. Well, looky boys, I gotta piss, I'm tired, and I wanna go back to my rabbit hole."

"Okay then. I'd say good luck, but that doesn't seem appropriate under the circumstances," Roy said.

"Nothin' you can say. And Wally, you stay close to this old man. Some of him might just rub off on you. As for you Mr. Texas Ranger, well, shit, I'm proud it was y'all that took me down. Means I go into history leavin' a mark. As for me, a short road trip over to the Huntsville needle room. Be my last look at the world. I plan to enjoy it 'til I go to my reward."

The Texas Ranger nodded his head at Jacky Blue.

"I can't shake your hand, but I do appreciate your candor. I do believe you will walk unassisted when the time comes. That's balls, and that's how these gentlemen standing back here will remember you," Roy said.

Roy, Wally Westwood, and Ranger Bagley stepped out of the room, accompanied by an officer. Before the door closed behind them, Roy turned back to see Jacky Blue nod at him and smile.

CHAPTER 51

Huntsville, Texas, home to the Texas State Prison death chamber and home to none other than the late, great Sam Houston himself, had a nice selection of motels and hotels. Karuk County Admin had booked Roy and Wally Westwood into one room at the Hampton Inn, so for Roy there was no escaping the baby coyote. The two of them kicked back in the lobby of the hotel drinking free coffee and munching on freshly baked chocolate chip cookies.

Roy grinned inwardly at what Wally had become. There was nothing like getting your pee pee whacked to change an attitude.

"Don't know how you do it. How did you even know how to start with a guy like that? I about shit when they walked him in." Westwood was shaking his head incredulously.

"Experience is the only teacher. I fumbled my way the first few times talking to the super cons. After a while it becomes natural. There is no faking it. They can spot a fraud or a rookie the second you open your mouth. Then you are all theirs."

"Yeah, like how he started fucking with me," Westwood muttered with clear resentment.

"Just testing you. He's right, though. Never rise up to an insult. Know that it is not personal even as they try to make it sound personal. It isn't. A con is always probing for weakness. They find it. They exploit. It's up to us to do the same," Roy replied wisely.

"The same?"

"Yes, think of us as copycats almost. Sometimes, if we want to catch him, we have to copy the moves of the criminal. We have to think like them, move with them, and anticipate them. We're like a spider doing push-ups on a mirror."

Roy bit into another cookie. He made a mental note to check out the hotel gym while he was downstairs.

"Okay. He spoke to us, which I didn't think he would do, but he didn't really solve anything for us."

Roy shook his head slightly. "That's where we disagree. He did not give us everything, but he gave us enough to do some real damage and stir the pot."

"What do you mean?" Westwood sounded confused.

Was he sleeping during the interview? And should I caution him on never interrupting during an interview unless prompted by his partner?

"Beyond telling us that a drowning victim is actually a murder victim, there were a few other tidbits. Right now, I have a hunch, but I'll have to call SSU tomorrow morning while we're waiting for our flight to see if they can check a few facts to be sure. In the meantime, I'll have to check to see if Zack was buried or cremated."

"Oh, I see. You want to dig him up. Guess I'm pretty stupid sounding, huh?"

"Nah, not stupid, just inexperienced, but see, you're catching on. We'll get an exhumation order, but not before I have a sit down with the family. Going to be ticklish with Jacky Blue claiming Cedar Stock helped cover up a murder of his own flesh and blood and then went along with the accidental drowning story."

"It's that name Stock. I've heard it before somewhere. When you and Jacky Blue were talking, I felt like I knew this guy, or at least the name."

"Not unusual in our small county," Roy shrugged. "Old Hugh Stock the pioneer—"

"No, I mean recently. I guess Alison and I came across it and put it in the notes somewhere."

"Nope. Not in your case notes anywhere. First time Stock name came up is when Maddy Stock, Zack's daughter, walked through the door of the sub last December."

"Hell, I don't know. I've only really worked on two cases in the last month. This one and the Hmong 187s. Lynch doesn't trust me to work on anything alone. And I didn't do shit on either case, if I'm honest about it, which I haven't been. I really think I belong back in patrol."

"Don't be so hard on yourself."

"Shit. My wife thinks I'm this great detective, but the truth is that I suck at it," he said with a glum tone.

"You want some advice?"

"Yeah, sure," Westwood said as he got up, grabbed a second cookie and sat back down.

"First, examine why it is you want to be a detective. If it's for the status, the hours, the long lunches, the boss or dispatch not looking over your shoulder, then you're in the wrong job. You're right. Go back to patrol. We gotta have good road dawgs. Patrol is the backbone and face of any police department."

"I wanted to solve shit," Westwood said as he wiped crumbs off his mustache, that promptly stuck to his lapel.

"That's a start. Solving shit. It's what we do. But it's more than that. You have to feel something for your victims or surviving family. I mean really feel something for them. They got a raw deal, and it's up to you to give them justice. You are *the* guy. Without you, they walk around with a huge weight hanging on their hearts. You make the weight smaller, easier to carry. If you don't feel something for them, get out. Next, and it may sound strange, you have to be petty. You can't stand to let the other guy win. By other guy, I mean the bad guy. It's gotta piss you off that he's all smug, lying back thinking he's so smart and clever. No, you're the smart and clever boy, not him. So you keep your eye on the ball, aka the case. You follow every lead. You don't get distracted by good looking partners or your relatives all bragging about *their* detective. If you can look at the job that way, you've got a chance. You work hard and make your mistakes along the way. Learn from them every time, and never repeat if possible. Down the road, you wake up one day and you're a detective, a real one. You don't have to fake it with anyone. Your reputation takes care of itself. You don't have to worry about getting your covers pulled. You have become the real deal." Roy took a breath.

"Yeah, I'm so sorry for mucking up your case. You're right, I put on the suit and thought I'd arrived, but I didn't know shit from fat beef." He almost looked teary-eyed.

"Talk like that, you grew up in Karuk County. I can tell," Roy laughed.

"And of course, I made a fuckin' fool of myself getting involved with Baker."

"It happens. She looks very tempting," Roy conceded for Westwood's benefit.

"Was it that obvious?"

"Pretty much." Roy grinned to lighten the mood.

"Shit," grimaced Westwood, crumbs now stuck to both his lapel and tie.

"Look, men and women work closely together, and it happens. But you gotta figure out what your wife and child mean to you, take corrective action, and try not to repeat mistakes."

"I don't get it. You let me come on this trip with you when you could have said the word, and I'd have been back in patrol already. The LT and all the brass are in awe of you and what you've done over your career."

"What good would that have done? Every good cop I know has screwed up along the way. If you haven't, you must be the Sheriff's driver who's married to his daughter."

"I'm gonna tell my wife what a shit-heel I've been when I get home."

"Or, you could let sleeping dogs lie. Save her the heartache; move on, determine to be a good husband and father, and a better detective, if that is what you truly want to be."

"My uncle is Judge Westwood, and I think that might have had something to do with my promotion, not that I've made him very proud either. Shit, all I've done is go through a thousand missing persons fliers with Baker and basically make copies of reports for the other real detectives in the Hmong case."

"So take stock of yourself, work hard from here on out, and make your uncle proud."

"Take stock. Real funny. Hey, not to change the subject, but don't they got that brisket BBQ down here somewhere?" Westwood had perked up thinking about the meal to come.

♦

Detective Wally Westwood sat bolt upright in bed in his hotel room on the second floor of the Huntsville, Texas, Hampton Inn, causing his roommate, Detective Delroy Church, to instinctively reach for his .45 caliber pistol to throw lead at however many Dixie Mafia motherfuckers had invaded their room at 0230 hours. But no one yelled, "Y'all got caught slippin'!"

Roy figured it had to be food related. *Texasized* chocolate chip cookies, mixed with the several pounds of ribs and brisket, along with the corn on the cob, baked beans, and potato salad, followed by peach cobbler, normally called for a midnight kneel at the porcelain throne. Nope. Whatever it was, something had plainly excited the boy.

"Roy, you awake?" came Westwood's loud stage whisper.

"No," Roy grunted.

"The Hmong case. It's the Hmong case. I can't believe it."

"Believe it, Ralph. You ate the whole thing."

"What? That doesn't even make sense, Roy," Westwood said, annoyed

"From an old Alka Seltzer TV ad. Forget it." Roy rolled over, facing away from Westwood.

"It's Stock. The name Stock, I got it. You gotta hear this!" He was close to clapping his hands together with glee, Roy was sure.

Roy grunted back, "I told you I'm not awake."

"Oh, you'll wake up for this," Westwood gloated.

"No I won't."

"It's the Hmong 187."

"Don't know anything about it."

"I'm almost positive Tim Stock is the name of the kid who gave the surviving 211 suspect a ride. The kid who didn't get blasted, the one who waited outside, who was a cousin of a dead robber. Cody something or other. He drove the U-Haul that got all shot up by the Hmongs. I'm pretty sure Tim Stock is the friend who gave him a ride after he dumped the U-Haul in Silverton."

Roy sat up and grumbled, "Okay, now I'm awake for an *almost positive* followed by a *pretty sure*."

♦

The following morning, while awaiting their flight in Houston's George Bush International, a giddy Westwood watched the clock tick over to 1000 hours. He then dialed up the west coast number. Roy noted that he didn't coo or use any other syrupy voice when Alison Baker came on. All business. Maybe there was hope for this sad sack after all. Time would tell. Then, the Napoleon Dynamite fist pump told Roy that Wally Westwood had scored.

♦

Cody Barham, U-Haul wheelman, existed in the netherworld of legal peril versus witness protection fit for a king. He wandered through his days stuck between competing California penal code sections, 664PC and 211PC on one side, 187PC on the other. Since the Ricky Bobby Crew had been shot down in flames at the threshold, they'd been unable to complete the *asportation* of stolen goods required to charge Cody with straight up robbery. But a really honest attempt had been made, hence the 664PC, or *attempted* robbery charge. Of course, not to be trifled with, were the two pitiable, leaking bodies (blood and bowels) of the RBC brain trust that cried out for justice. So, Ol' Cody had hisself an ace up the sleeve. The prosecution, if the cops could ever discover the location of three Hmong gunmen, was prepared to remove hat and hold in hand for the only witness in the *threefer* defendant murder case, the type that careers are made of.

Cody's lawyer, Ira Hand the conflict gadfly, had come about his current status due to the Public Defender's Office having represented both the late Ricky Dunn and late Bobby Dudley on numerous occasions through the years. Their records were sure to pop up if and when the Hmong were brought to heel and hauled into court.

In truth, Ira Hand had been hoping for a Hmong client in a drawn-out murder trial, but a witness would have to do for now. Bills gotta get paid. Ira Hand was sure that Todd, his secretary, was polishing his resume between forwarding client calls. Besides, the Hmong would probably fly in some super, Clarence Darrow types from Fresno to argue self-defense. So, a bird in the hand he'd reasoned. Clever, Ira, clever.

Ira Hand felt his bird flutter, or maybe it was his stomach, when he stepped into the DA's interview room ahead of his client whom he'd asked to sit patiently in the hallway until the lawyer got the lay of the land.

It had sounded fairly straight-forward over the phone. The prosecutor had claimed the cops wanted to explore Cody's memory, wanted to get the back story on the robbery set-up. *Attempted* robbery, sorry.

"So it's Let's Make a Deal time," Ira had stated, not asked, feeling his oats over the phone.

"Could be," Loni Barber, the prosecutor, had said. Ira Hand hadn't appreciated the vagueness. Loni Barber had transferred in from San Jose a year or so earlier and had brought hardnosed Bay Area tactics with her. A real, stiff-tits competitor. Hastings Law School, someone had confided.

Female law enforcement crawled the morning's scene when Ira

arrived at the station. Ira had noted Sheriff's detective Alison Baker lounging in the hallway outside the interview room.

Yeah, baby. Love me some redhead.

"Good morning, Ira," Loni Barber said, rising and extending a hand.

He took the hand then looked to the right of her. Seated at the table was a male detective, he assumed, that he did not know. The other, he fucking sure as hell knew, and something was definitely up. The bird flapped its wings.

Loni Barber gestured at the two men. "This is Detective Westwood, and I believe you know Roy Church."

CHAPTER 52

"So, Ira, you have to make a decision. You can't represent a suspect and an intended victim in the same case," Deputy District Attorney Loni Barber said as she leaned back turning a pen in her hand.

"Could you run this all past me one more time? Doesn't seem right that I'm getting conflicted off a conflict assignment."

"Irony," Loni Barber said drily. "Okay, Detective Church could you give him the Reader's Digest one more time."

Roy checked his notes.

"Reader's Digest. In October 2018, your client, Cody Mitchell Barham, conspired with Richard Franklin Dunn and Robert Dwayne Dudley to commit armed robbery of a marijuana grow slash packaging house in Montague, California. On the night of the actual robbery attempt the tables turned when, based on evidence at the scene, at least three Asian males inside the house fired on Dunn and Dudley, killing them. Your client Barham, who, as the effective getaway driver, was waiting outside in a rental truck when the shots rang out. He fled the scene as he was being fired upon by the Asian male suspects. Your client placed a phone call to a friend, Timothy Earl Stock, as he drove toward Silverton. He parked the rental truck on a street in Silverton and was then given a ride away from that spot by involved party Timothy Stock. Recent investigative leads resulting in compelling evidence have moved Tim Stock from simple involved party into the suspect category. These same leads have revealed your other client, Cedar Stock, to be a possible suspect in the case as well.

He is suspected of conspiring with his nephew Tim Stock to set up your client, Barham, along with Dunn and Dudley, to be ambushed by the Asian males at the marijuana house. Obviously, we cannot share the evidence with you at this time, but of course we'll do so as part of discovery down the line." Roy shuffled his notes back together.

Ira Hand slumped back in his seat a little.

"So, Ira," Loni Barber said. "You have a choice. Represent Cedar Stock or Cody Barham. We need to talk to Cody about anybody, anything, and everything having to do with the selection and planning of the robbery of the Hmong grow house. We are willing to deal his case, now, if he will talk to us and not bullshit us. Otherwise, when the Hmong and their attorneys come into court, I bet my next three paychecks they push for self-defense, and Cody goes down for attempted armed robbery."

"So you're saying you intend to charge one of my clients, Cedar Stock, with the attempted murder of my other client, Cody Barham, as well as the murder of the two victims Ricky Dunn and Bobby Dudley in the Hmong house?"

"Not saying we're charging anyone with anything at this point. But read into it what you will," said Loni Barber brusquely.

"Cody Barham versus Cedar Stock," Roy said. "Not to sound heavy handed or anything, but you've got a real Sophie's Choice before you."

"Or, we get into court and the judge says, looking at the fact that you have represented both defendant and victim, you may have to conflict off the whole mess," Loni pointed out.

"Well, I had Barham long before I had Stock, so how would that be fair?" Ira asked, getting a sinking feeling, like a father's bank account on a daughter's wedding day. He reminded himself to check the whiny tone threatening to break through in his voice.

"Then I'd have to say I disagree with Detective Church, Ira. I'd say you now have a Hobson's choice."

Wally Westwood broke in.

"Look, I didn't go to a fancy law school or work for the LA Sheriff. I'm just a dumb country deputy. What is this Sophie's vs Hobson's stuff?"

"Poor taste, I admit," explained Roy. "Sophie was a mother in a concentration camp who was forced to pick which one of her children lived and which one died."

"Jesus," said Westwood, shifting uncomfortably in his seat.

"Hobson's, on the other hand, simply refers to taking what's offered to you, what is closest, or risk getting nothing at all," said Loni Barber.

"And Hobson is sitting in the hallway," said Roy.

"Hobson is in the hallway," sighed Ira. "Bring him in." He wondered what his balance owed back to Cedar Stock would be. Had he spent it all? He'd have to check.

♦

Cody Barham sauntered in all sullen and tough looking, sporting a black T-shirt with the silk screen print of a giant green leaf under the red letters *Keep One Rolled*. He'd just entered the world of cooperator but didn't want to seem happy about it. Ira Hand had just explained something about a Sophie and a Hobson and how he was now faced with something called Cody's Choice. Sounded like a bunch of educated horseshit to him. Why couldn't lawyers just talk plain English? Still, in exchange for charges dropped, he agreed to lay out the story of the Hmong robbery conspiracy, and how he could see now that he'd been back stabbed by who he thought was a friend, but had turned out to be a dishonest sonofabitch. He felt betrayed.

"So you've never met, as you say, 'an Indian chick with the clap, named Virginia.' Have you ever heard of her before Timothy Stock told you about her?" Roy asked.

"Naw. Never. I shoulda figured it out then, but I thought Tim was my boy," said Cody sullenly.

"So the only source of information on the Hmong marijuana grow and packaging house was Timothy Stock?"

"'Bout the size of it." He glanced at one of the interview walls as if he were bored of the conversation and looking for a distraction.

"Did you do any surveillance of the Hmong house before the robbery?"

"I didn't. Ricky and Bobby done all that. I just got the rental." Cody ran a hand over his head, freshly skinned for the occasion.

"So, Robert Dudley, Bobby, is, was, your cousin?"

"Yep. Me and him were tight."

"But he was quite a bit older than you, had been away to prison for a while."

Cody looked sullenly back. "So."

"Do you know much about his prison experiences or contacts?"

"A little, maybe, from what he said, him and Ricky were straight up NLR."

"Hmm, Nazi Lowrider. I see," said Roy. "Before the actual robbery attempt, before it all went to pieces, when, if you recall, did you last speak to Timothy Stock?"

Cody frowned. "Whadya mean? Like when were we talkin about the lick? Hell, I was on the phone with him on the way there. He called me to make sure it was all good and where should he meet us when it was all over."

"So you kept him in the loop as to the exact time you would hit the Hmong house? Why did he need to know the exact time?"

"Hell, I don't know. He was my dawg. He was nervous about it. Shit, maybe he thought we were gonna cut him out. I wouldn't have, but Ricky and Bobby could be scandalous that way."

"Ricky and Bobby had crossed someone before?" Roy probed.

"Yeah, come to think of it. They thought it was all funny. Bragged about it even."

"Bragged?"

"Yeah. Don't remember too much about it. They were on a crew doin' rips of Mexicans with somebody, and they helped themselves to more than their share on a job. Blew the money on hoes." He shook his head exasperatedly as though he would've had a much more sensible plan for blowing the money.

"Did their rip crew they worked with have anything to do with Timothy Stock?"

"No, not Tim, maybe Tim's uncle. Don't know his name."

♦

Lieutenant Gary Lynch looked across his desk at the three detectives. One a red headed hottie, one a calm green-eyed legend, and one a panting pup with nervous leg syndrome.

"Who wants to start?" he asked.

"Well, Detective Westwood here made an important connection. I think he should tell you about that first," said Roy Church. "Then we can fill you in on what else we know."

Lieutenant Lynch turned toward Westwood, "Wallace, you're on."

Roy was pretty sure Westwood had stopped in the bathroom to piss and comb his hair prior. The stage was his for now.

"Well, as you know, Roy and I flew to Texas to speak to Jackson Howard, aka Jacky Blue, who is on death row down there. Unbelievable experience."

Steer back into the lane safely, Wally. You're heading for an over correction.

"Jacky Blue spoke of Cedar Stock as someone who helped cover up the murder of Zack Stock, his own cousin, twenty some odd years ago. Roy here has readied an exhumation order to be taken before a judge."

"Yes, I have that here on my desk for review," Lieutenant Lynch commented. "Go on."

Westwood drew a breath. "So the name Stock stuck with me. Alison and I hadn't seen it when we first went down to work on the Puma Creek bone case. It didn't come up until we were called back to work on the Hmong case. A Tim Stock drove the surviving robber away after he abandoned his rental truck here in Silverton. I didn't know at the time that Roy had a Cedar Stock in Sisson."

"That's where I saw that name before!" Lieutenant Lynch exclaimed. "I knew I'd heard or seen it somewhere. Reading reports you all submitted."

"Right," said Westwood, winding up for his curve ball. "So it came to me in the middle of the night. I scared the crap out of Roy when I came out of bed."

"That's true," Roy laughed, only half-joking. "I thought he had ODed on Texas brisket, or a gator had gotten in our room."

"I called Alison the next morning, and she confirmed the Tim Stock name in our Hmong case," Westwood said, grinning without showing teeth.

"And this is where the phone records all come in?" Lieutenant Lynch asked.

"Yep," said Westwood. "As you know we got search warrants and court orders for all the phones of all the involved parties in this case. We can show that Cody Barham was keeping Tim Stock up to speed on the timing for the robbery. We can show Tim Stock hung up from Cody Barham and called a number in Sisson. We can show that the number in Sisson called a cell phone with a Fresno area code."

"Sisson number, Fresno? What?" Lieutenant Lynch asked, not following.

"Yes," Roy interjected. "The Sisson number came up in the Santa Rosa Police suspicious death investigation of Jesse Dale "Pud" Wilson. That number belongs to a phone for Germaine "Jersey" Stock which is often used by Cedar Stock. He pays the bill on it, per his own words."

"So it looks like Cedar Stock got a call from Tim Stock," said Westwood, returning to the fray. "And then he turned around and called the Fresno number. The Fresno number is for the cell phone belonging to 187 suspect Touboy Lyfong."

"So Cedar Stock calls the Hmong and tells them the rip crew has just pulled up and to be ready for them. A cold-blooded mother fucker. Whoa," Lieutenant Lynch said. "But why?"

"I think I better let Roy explain," Westwood said, settling back and relinquishing the floor.

"Cedar Stock, ever the opportunist, got himself a twofer," Roy said.

"Uhh, okay," said Lieutenant. Lynch.

Roy continued.

"Ricky Dunn and Bobby Dudley had worked off and on recently for Cedar Stock in his Mexican drug dealer rip off crew. That's what he's done for money for years, I'm convinced. Somewhere along the line the Ricky Bobby boys took more than their fair share and got green lit, probably by the Aryan Brotherhood Commission after Cedar Stock reported them. Then along comes the Puma Creek bone case. Lots of publicity. Dina Morgan case gets re-opened. Cedar Stock knows Karuk County law enforcement pretty well. He knows we're stretched thin. Bingo. His light bulb goes on. He needs to whack Ricky and Bobby, and he needs attention drawn away from cold cases to something hot. What better than three bodies lying in the doorway of a marijuana grow run by out of towners who have pissed off the Sheriff anyhow by skirting proper permits, and so forth? And that's exactly what happened. Westwood and Baker get yanked, the Puma Creek and Dina Morgan cases go back on the shelf."

"Except Cedar Stock never counted on Delroy Church transferring to Karuk County," grinned Lieutenant Lynch.

"We got lucky," Roy said. "And some fine detective work got done along the way by Wallace Westwood."

Roy thought Wally might pop his middle shirt button. He suppressed a smile.

"Why is Cedar Stock concerned so much with the Dina Morgan case?"

"Not sure at this point. But he was concerned enough to fake the suicide of the main suspect, Pud Wilson."

"Okay. But how does Cedar Stock, AB member, associate, or

whatever the hell he is, know the Hmong well enough to call and dime off the Ricky Bobby Crew?"

"Pretty easy, actually. This is white boy country. The Aryan Brotherhood has parolees, eyes and ears of sympathizers, family members et cetera in a lot of rural areas. The Hmong want to set up shop. Somewhere up the line the AB puts a bug in the ear of a family elder and says 'You need protection in Karuk County.' 'From what?' 'From us.' I'm sure that's how it goes."

"So Cedar Stock runs the show here for the AB, and he is the protector?"

"In a manner of speaking. That made it easy for him to throw in the call and tell the three Hmong that a crew had gone rogue, and they gotta do what they gotta do."

"Like I said, cold-blooded. So what does this all mean? Where do we go from here?" asked Lieutenant Lynch, the buzz killer.

"Well, there are a number of avenues to explore. None of them fool proof," said Roy. "*We* know, or at least suspect, the story of the Hmong set up. But a jury would have a hard time buying it wholesale if the right defense attorney shows up alongside Cedar Stock. He is way too smart to get himself in a situation that doesn't reek of reasonable doubt. I found that out firsthand with the Pud Wilson case."

"Surveillance an option?" Lieutenant Lynch asked.

"We're talking long term, costly, and out of town. Cedar Stock is running his crews way out of county, down in the Valley, the Bay Area, maybe even up in Oregon or the whole Western US for that matter. Tailing him would be a nightmare. We could get a court order for a GPS on his rig, but I'm sure he switches out his everyday vehicle for an underbucket when he's capering."

"What do you suggest?" Lieutenant Lynch asked. Westwood and Baker looked expectantly at the SoCal magician, breathlessly awaiting the rabbit.

"We've just now got Cody Barham's story. Let's sit on it for a minute, let it sink in. I've got calls into SSU for some other prison records I suspect may help us some. And I'd like to take a run at Cedar's mama, Jersey."

"Sounds reasonable," said Lieutenant Lynch, checking his notes. "I'll clue in the Sheriff."

"Also, I think Detective Westwood here and I need to go back over the tape of our conversation with Jackson Howard. He's got roughly two and half weeks to live, so if there's anything he said that we missed, we don't have a lot of time."

"Damn that death penalty!" Lieutenant Lynch smiled ruefully.

CHAPTER 53

Cedar Stock tapped END on his cell phone call. He looked out the driver's window at passing corn fields and a sign that said *Modesto 12 miles*.

"Could have a problem," he said thoughtfully.

"What problem?" asked Jade Tankersley, from the front passenger's seat.

"My attorney has dropped me, says he's been conflicted away from representing me."

"Why?"

"Wouldn't say. So that means it has to do with what? Gotta think on this."

"Hell, while you're thinking, take the next off ramp. Foster's Freeze. I feel like a malt," Jade said.

"You didn't *feel* like a malt this morning."

"You're a bad man," Jade laughed.

"Ugh. Get a room," grumbled Tim Stock from the back seat.

"Why? You shoulda joined us Timmy. I'm always down for a little *double pen*," Jade crooned.

"Gross," said Tim Stock with disgust as he went back to swiping right indiscriminately.

"I think I got it," Cedar said suddenly. "Gotta be that little shit, Cody. He's gotta be tellin'. I can feel it."

"What? Me and him are homies. He ain't gonna rat me out. He don't know shit anyhow," Tim sat up and put his iPhone down.

"*He and I* are homies. He *isn't* going to rat you out. And he *doesn't* know shit. Just because you're a lowlife California criminal doesn't mean you have to speak like one."

"Makes me wet when you sound all educated," Jade purred. "Now who is this little shit you speak of?"

"From the Ricky Bobby Crew. One of their cousins. The gooks missed him when the shit hit the fan."

"Lemme call that fucker right now," Tim said, thumbs dancing on his iPhone.

"Put him on speaker," Cedar said.

The phone rang and rang. Then the sound of head banger music came on followed by a voice.

"You've reached Cody. Right now, I'm busy with your mom. Leave a message. If I give a shit I'll get back to you."

"Yo, Codiak. Where the fuck you at? We gotta chop it up. Call me, bitch, after you're through playin' with your dick."

"Screening calls?" asked Jade.

"Fucker knew it was me. He never don't answer. Sorry. He never *doesn't* answer."

"Find him. Dirt nap 'im," said Jade. "Foster Freeze, right there. It's on me. And both of you could be on me, too." She hopped out as Cedar pulled to a stop. "Y'all don't want nothin'? Well, fuck all y'all then."

Jade skipped to the order window.

"Jesus, Uncs, She's freakin' weird," Tim muttered.

Cedar sighed, "Yes, very weird. But you do what you gotta do to stay alive in this game. Right now, what she says goes."

"But she's a crazy ass bitch. I never understood how that shit happens."

"She's also married to Moonshine. That means she calls shots out here."

"I don't get it. What if he found out about you and her?" Tim's eyebrows were raised.

"There is no me and her. Like I said, I do what I gotta do. You ever catch a case to the *pinta* you'll understand." Cedar made eye-contact in the rear-view mirror.

"Chances are I go someday."

"When that happens, you'll have my name. You'll be fine, as long as I'm still good with the boys in The Bay."

"What happens if you're not?" Tim seemed apprehensive.

"Then put a bullet in your mouth rather than go down. You got zero protection behind the walls."

Tim fiddled with his iPhone for a minute.

"What we gonna do about Cody?"

"If we could find him, we'd smoke him. We aren't going to find him. I smell witness protection, and I smell Delroy Church all over this," Cedar sneered with disgust.

"Who's that?"

"A bloodhound."

♦

Roy knocked on the door under the sagging eave. Westwood stood off to the side and behind.

"Hello? Who is it?" A soft voice came from the other side.

"Sheriff's Department, ma'am."

"Come in."

Roy slowly opened the door, conscious of his slightly bladed feet that would allow him to sweep backward with his right hand, draw, and assume a Weaver combat stance in a split second. He'd been reasonably sure no one but the old lady was home. No vehicles in the driveway, and two Karuk County narcs had set up on the place for the last eight hours but had seen nothing.

Based on Germaine Stock's phone being deeply involved in two separate homicide investigations, with a third waiting in the wings, he could easily have gotten a "no knock" search warrant and hit the place with a SWAT team, especially given Cedar Stock's history of prison gang involvement. But that would have overplayed all hands. He only wanted to bump up the pressure, not drop an Egyptian pyramid on the situation.

"I'm Roy Church, and this is Detective Westwood," Roy said as he looked across the room at the old lady lying back in her chair, perpendicular to him, but cocking her head toward him to get a better look. The home smelled of pets and old people.

He saw her right hand reach for the stand next to her on the opposite side of her chair. He wondered how many other cops, at that moment, had a plan to draw and move to the left if she didn't come up with a remote to turn down the TV. Why left? Because her natural motion would be to swing a gun to her left toward him. She'd have to awkwardly reverse course to track him. By then she'd be dead or close to.

If she hadn't spawned the likes of Cedar Stock, maybe he'd have been less paranoid. But why take a chance?

"I've heard of you," she said quietly, nodding her silver head slightly.

"Don't believe all that the papers say," Roy said, going to his standard line.

"Trust me. I don't. They probably blew you all up, made you look good when you really shoulda been sharing the glory all those times. I know how it is." Her voice had kicked up a few notches.

How refreshing.

"You are a hundred percent correct. So is there anyone else in the house?"

"Yeah, the city council's meeting in the bedroom. No, of course not. I live alone."

Salty.

"Do you mind if I sit?"

"Help yourself." She shrugged and tossed up a resigned hand.

Roy sat on the Mexican horse blanket covered couch. Westwood stood, just to the right of the front door.

"Thanks for seeing us, Mrs. Stock," Roy began.

"Normally, I'd tell you to call me Jersey. Everybody does. But for now, you keep with the Mrs. Stock. You're not here on friendly business, so get to whatever it is you want, as if I don't know." Dark, rheumy eyes fixed themselves on him. Her voice sounded tired.

"Well, maybe you tell me why it is I'm here?"

"What? A little word game? Is that how the great Detective Delroy Church made all those cases? I don't fall for that Columbo crap." Her voice sounded less weak. Roy wondered if she over-exaggerated her frailty when it suited her.

All right, Mama!

"Then, Mrs. Stock, I'll get to it. I'm one of the investigators on a number of cases. In those cases, your cell phone number has come up several times. For example, calls on it were made to and from Jesse "Pud" Wilson in the days leading up to his death. Calls were made on it to and from others involved in a double murder case in Silverton involving Asian marijuana growers. Do we have an explanation for that?"

"Don't you need to read me my rights to question me?" she spat.

"Oh, not at all. You're not being detained and you're free to leave at any time. We're just having a friendly conversation."

"Friendly, my tired old butt. And free to leave? You're outta your damn tree, cop."

Ah, the infamous Jersey Stock is on scene. Roy chuckled inwardly.

"I guess I'm not understanding the hostility, Mrs. Stock."

"You're lookin' for evidence on Cedar. Come out and say it. Quit beating around the bush. Cops screwed his life way back when, still screwin' it today. Who'd he ever hurt? He sold some grass after high school, to pay for school. He got busted by narcs at the JC. He ends up in prison, and that's when he went bad."

Roy nodded. "Circumstances and fates from a different era. I appreciate your perspective on that."

"You don't appreciate a damn thing. That grass he got busted with in college? It's legal today. Drive downtown. Dirty hippies smokin' it on the sidewalk. Cops drive by and wave or stop for a hit. Asians flooding the county to grow the stuff. Yeah. I read the paper. No, you and your laws destroyed a man's life. My son's life. Didn't do his mama any favors either."

"We can't go back and change the past. Life can be very unfair, I admit."

"No shit, Sherlock." She looked away, one wrinkled hand gripping the edge of a worn book.

"Isn't that a hymn book, Mrs. Stock?"

"Yeah, so, what do you think, just because I'm a Christian I can't get mad? Did you hear me take the Lord's name in vain? No. But I can say shit and even the F word if I wanted to. Neither one is in the Bible, so there's no rules against it. Ever read the Ten Commandments? I'll bet Moses had a few choice words when God said it was a no go on the Promised Land for him. He got screwed over just like Cedar as far as I'm concerned."

"You'll get no argument from me. But then I always thought Job got the raw deal with God and Satan testing him by killing his family members."

"People were tough back then, not like the pussies we got running the country today."

"Then there's Noah,"

"Noah? He made out fine," she said dismissively.

"Well, yes *he* did, along with his sons and all those animals, but what about the people left behind?"

"Hey, they had a chance to get on board."

"Did they? Did they really? The children? The babies? The women ruled by their husbands? Did they have a choice? Nope. They all drowned. Drowning is a horrible way to go."

"Wouldn't know." She stared at her blank TV screen, resolutely looking away.

"And what about all those Egyptian soldiers just following orders to chase the Israelites across the Red Sea bed? Did they have a choice? Trying to feed their families by working for the government, and look what happens. They drowned."

"Working for the government. Served 'em right. Government has done nothing but screw with my family," she sat, fixing her unwavering gaze back on him.

"Your nephew Zack drowned. That had to be a bad deal."

"Oh, is this where you relate to me and get me to lower my guard?"

"Yeah, something like that. Look we're not your enemy. We're just trying to get justice for a few dead people like Pud and Dina, the skeletal remains on Puma Ridge, and the boys gunned downed by the Asians."

"Justice. Ha!" Jersey snorted. "They were in the game. They got what was coming to them."

"The game? You talk as if you know the game."

"When your son has been hounded by the law and had to fight to survive after what's been done to him, you get bitter, and you learn. You also get smart. Like I know how you're talking Bible stories to me, and about poor Zack, trying to get me to open up."

"Well, it's not working, apparently." Roy leaned back, thinking of what Westwood might be thinking. He gave silent thanks that he'd not butted in.

"Yeah, how'd you get to be so famous anyhow?"

"I didn't ask for it." Roy shrugged.

"Yeah, but you sure got it. Bet that boy over there at the door asked for your autograph."

"Actually, he did. I think he worships the ground I walk on. Isn't that right Detective Westwood?" Roy turned around and winked at Westwood.

"Sure is," replied Westwood.

"Westwood?" Jersey said. "Bet they call you Clint."

"Yep, that's me, Clint Westwood all right. Actually, my name is Wally Westwood. But when I'm on the job I like to be called Dirty Wally. Sorta fits, you know."

Jersey snorted and laughed at the same time.

"Ha. Dirty Wally!"

Nice job, Wally. You're learning

Westwood grinned as he stood checking his iPhone.

"So, Mrs. Stock. Do you want to know why we're really here?"

"Well, duh, as the kids say. You want dirt on Cedar."

"Well, actually it's because we're also trying to get justice for Zack. He didn't drown. He was murdered."

"Bullshit. Cop lies." She waved her hand, as if swatting at a pesky fly.

"It's true. Your son Cedar is said to have helped cover it up, knowing it was a murder."

"Who told you that load of crap?" She snorted again, this time without mirth.

"Your son's crimey."

"His what?"

"Thought you were in the game, Mrs. Stock. His crime partner, Jacky Blue."

"Never heard of him."

"Well, he's heard of you. Of course, he's sitting on death row in Texas right now. He and Koondawg, you must remember him, another friend of your son, well they murdered three Mexicans in Del Rio, Texas, year before last. Jacky Blue got caught. Koondawg is still on the run."

"Never heard of them. And that cell phone's sittin' right there on a charger. Don't anyone else but me uses it. Cedar doesn't even live here. He visits regularly, so of course he's got a few things here."

"Where does Cedar live?"

"How should I know?"

"Uh, because he's your son?" Westwood put in.

Easy, Dirty Wally. Roy still had work to do on the partner tag team thing.

"His business is his business. Do I look like I get out much? Enough to be sticking my nose where it doesn't belong? No. I stay right here, watch TV, read my Bible, and read the paper on how the cops can't solve anything. Maybe you better go back to LA where you got all your little snitches."

"We like to call them informants or sources. Snitches has a poor connotation."

"Big word, connotation," Jersey sneered.

"Seemed to be appropriate."

"Use big words on us poor, backwoods, redneck country folk? That the idea?"

"No, not at all. Your son Cedar seems very educated and would probably not blink an eye at a word like that."

"You're damn right he's educated. Self-educated in prison instead of college where he could have been if you and your kind hadn't screwed him over on a little weed."

"A little weed? From what I can tell in his old probation reports, he was running a network of sales outlets of Humboldt homegrown all the way to Southern California."

"Entrepreneur, ahead of his time. All legal now. You made my point."

"Yes," Roy sighed. "You definitely have a point. But from what I can see, he also dealt methamphetamine. And that is not legal, and it has destroyed more families than I can count. So he was not exactly totally innocent."

"He might have dabbled. But saw the error of his ways. So, you never made a mistake, Mr. Super Detective?" she said accusatorily.

"I thought I did once, but I was wrong," Roy said lightly, eyes twinkling.

Jersey snorted and laughed, again.

"If I see Cedar, I'll tell him you stopped by. Anything else?"

"As a matter of fact, yes. Has to do with our religious discussion a few minutes ago, in relation to the legality of marijuana."

"I know my Bible. What is it?"

"I've always suspected marijuana was made illegal as far back as the Garden of Eden."

"What? They didn't have weed in the Garden of Eden."

"You say that, but how else can we explain Eve taking orders from a snake to bite into an apple?"

"LSD?" volunteered Dirty Wally from across the room.

♦

"He was here? In this room? You let him in without a search warrant? Ma, you gotta be smarter than that."

"I'm sorry, Cedar, but he knocked on the door, and I thought it might be Maddy, so I said come in."

"Maddy doesn't knock. Ma, you gotta understand, never talk to the cops."

"You did. You sat down for an interview."

"That's different. I did that to throw them off my trail. And I had a lawyer with me."

"I'm sorry, I said." She sounded irritated.

"It's just that they are so full of tricks. They come on nice and friendly while trying to trip you up on something they can use against you."

"We talked about the Bible mostly. And he only asked about my phone. You told me they already knew about calls to Pud."

"That's true. Did he say anything else?"

"He said something about calls to some Asian guy, I think?"

"What? Shit. I knew it. Damn that Cody piece of shit." Cedar pounded his fist onto his knee.

"Is that bad?" Jersey turned to look more fully at Cedar.

"Well, actually, Ma, that's good to know. You got some good info out of him. Helps me a lot. Anything else? How long was he here anyhow?"

"Just a few minutes. Sat right there on your blanket. Oh, and he tried to get me all confused talking about Zack."

"Zack? What about Zack?"

"He was talking all crazy stuff about how Zack didn't really drown, and how he was murdered."

"Murdered?!"

"Yeah. And then he started lying some more about how you knew about the murder and helped cover it up."

"Jesus, Ma. You're right. He was lyin', that's just a crazy cop lyin'." Cedar pulled a hand roughly through his hair.

"And he said they were digging Zack up to prove it."

"What the fuck?!" Cedar leapt up.

"Gee, Cedar, honey. I wish you wouldn't swear so much. Where you going? Cedar?" Jersey called, worry creeping into her voice.

But Cedar Stock had already disappeared into the garage.

CHAPTER 54

"Dirty Wally! I'm getting that put on a coffee mug. I never really liked Clint."

"You did well," Roy said, as he looked across his desk at Westwood seated in Kat's old desk. He felt a pang of sadness. He missed her terribly, but Wally had begun to grow on him.

Westwood's enthusiasm could channel into something more. Sometimes that's all it took.

"What's our next move? And is there a reason you told Jersey about the Asians?"

"Couple of things. First, Cedar knows right this instant that the Hmong caper is on the table. He also knows his mother let us into her house without a search warrant. He can't be happy about either. And the biggie is Zack Stock, suspected homicide victim. Cedar's gotta be freaking out. Agitated people make mistakes."

"I see," Westwood said thoughtfully, stroking his mustache.

"So now we have to go talk to Zack Stock's wife, Sarah, to let her know about the exhumation. She may have gotten a frantic phone call from Jersey, but I never got the feeling they were that close. Besides, with the accusation of Cedar being involved in a cover-up, she's not going to want that spread around."

"Lotta moving parts."

"Cases coming to a head always begin moving at breakneck. You have to get your juggling suit on. You operate in the shadows for only so long. Then all hell breaks loose."

Westwood nodded, eyebrows raised. "I'm getting dizzy."

"Dizzy is good."

Roy's cell buzzed in a text. It was Reuben Montalvo

Got the records from The Bay. Checking now. Will get at you ASAP.

"About to get dizzier, I suspect."

"Cool. And I took a photo of you sitting there talking about Eve and shit to the old lady. Thought I'd bust a gut. I'll text it to you. What was that all about anyhow?"

"Difficult Witness Interviewing 101. Find something, anything, to keep a conversation going. Sometimes you get lucky, catch 'em slippin'."

Roy dialed Sarah Stock's cell phone. She answered on the second ring. The slight strain in her voice said she possessed only the normal weariness he expected from someone who'd rather have let sleeping dogs lie but had grown resigned to seeing them rise and shake off a slumber. She definitely had not been told he wanted to dig up her dead husband.

He told her he had to speak to her soon, and he did not want it to be over the phone. She told him she was at her parents' house, and if he wanted to come by it was okay. She'd been reliving the past with them, and she thought they should be allowed to hear what had begun weighing so heavily on her as of late. Apparently the Fournettes had continued their code of silence, for she gave off no clue that they even knew who he was.

Westwood and Roy drove toward Volcano View Drive. An animated Westwood checked the weather on his phone. Clear weather two days out for the scheduled big dig. His mood said he'd be telling his grandkids how he rode the range with Marshal Dillon. Exciting times.

Roy's phone buzzed. He expected a text from Montalvo. It was Kat.

Hope all is well. Miss you and the job! Professor Godwin says you're sending us bones. I'm sooo excited to see and hear how it's been going.

K.

Roy put his phone back in his pocket and concentrated on driving, smiling.

Made my day.

♦

Roy and Westwood sat in the same room that Jake Stern and he had occupied on New Year's Day. Dr. and Emily Fournette sat in their same spots. Sarah pulled up a chair from across the room. Except for the sober air, they could have been planning a giant family reunion.

"This is the detective I told you about," Sarah said. The doctor and Emily nodded politely. Real spies.

"I've told them all about your investigation, at least what I know of it, and how you think it relates to Cedar and those awful men he had working for him way back when."

More nodding.

"Good," Roy began. "There have been a number of developments since then, important enough that I had to see you all in person, and it's nice that we can do this together, one time. Let me explain what I have to do as the investigating detective, and then I'll answer any questions that I can."

The nodding stopped. Dread crept into faces that had suddenly grown stony, yet expectant.

"Kelly Cutler, also known as Koondawg by the white prison gang he associated with, worked for Cedar Stock back in the 90's. They had a robbery crew masquerading as a tree removal, landscaping firm called Cedar Trims. Others in the crew included another prison gang member, Jackson Howard, also known as Jacky Blue. To some degree, and I'm still exploring this avenue, Dina Morgan and Jesse Wilson were also involved."

Roy noted Sarah's hands on her lap gripping each other, like railroad car couplers, the right thumb rubbing a raw spot on her left pinky and ring fingers. The Fournettes looked unsurprised but concerned.

"These were very bad people, I'm afraid. They made a living robbing Mexican cartel drug dealers operating here in the US. Currently, Jacky Blue is on death row in Texas. He's scheduled for execution in ten days or so. Koondawg Cutler is on the run, somewhere in the Deep South most likely. The two of them murdered three Mexicans in Del Rio, Texas, in 2016. Dina Morgan is missing and presumed dead as of 2004. Jesse Wilson is dead as of last December. Cedar Stock, of course, as you know, has supposedly reformed his life and lives here in Sisson, working as a handyman."

At the name Cedar Stock, the doctor and his wife rolled their eyes ever so slightly while Sarah pressed the corner of one eye to keep a tear from cresting.

"Detective Westwood and I flew to Texas two weeks ago. We

interviewed Jackson Howard, that's Jacky Blue, on death row."

"Whoa," said Dr. Fournette under his breath.

"On death row, prisoners who have exhausted all appeals will generally do one of two things when the police come to see them. They will say nothing, in which case the visit is short, or they will want to unburden themselves in some fashion. Their game has come to an end, and they know it. They have come to the realization that all their memories are about to be taken."

Emily Fournette began shaking her head, as if she felt a pang of sympathy.

"They've earned their way to this spot, so I'm not telling you this to make you feel sorry for a killer. I'm telling you this because what Jacky Blue told us, I believe to be the truth."

Sarah's cheeks had grown wet with tears as Roy spoke. Emily Fournette rose and grabbed a box of tissue on a side table. She handed it to Sarah and rubbed her shoulders as she did so. Roy noted Emily took none for the doctor or herself.

"There is no good way to ease into this, so here it is. Jacky Blue claims that your husband and son-in-law Zachary Stock did not drown. He was beaten to death by Koondawg Cutler then dumped in the Klamath River to make it look as if he'd drowned."

"What?" Doctor Fournette gasped.

"Oh my God!" exclaimed Emily Fournette.

Sarah blanched and began crying in earnest.

"We don't understand. What happened? How can this be? How could his own cousin, Cedar Stock, have let this happen?" Dr. Fournette asked, ashen faced.

"In essence, Zack got into an argument with Jacky Blue and Koondawg Cutler about how they were conducting themselves in his house. One thing led to another, Koondawg and Zack began fighting. Koondawg beat Zack very badly. Unfortunately, Zack died from the beating while on the front lawn of your home, Sarah. I have no idea what the exact injuries were, although Jacky Blue described the beating with quite a bit of detail."

"And these two monsters dumped Zack in the river?" Dr. Fournette asked, his face growing steadily paler.

Emily had moved to kneel next to Sarah and was rocking her gently while encircling her with an arm.

"Not exactly. I'll get to that in a second. According to Jacky Blue, Cedar Stock was not at the home when the fight happened. He arrived sometime later, and he is the one who actually found Zack deceased on the front lawn."

"Are you kidding me? And he didn't call for an ambulance. How did he know Zack was deceased? Is he a trained EMT?" Dr. Fournette scoffed.

"That I do not know. He's not talking to me about this, although I did question him on another matter. As I said, I only found out about this claim two weeks ago. Cedar had an attorney who forbade us talking to him."

"You've got to talk to him. He would know the truth. Wouldn't he? His own cousin? It's preposterous. How do we know this Jacky Blue person isn't lying?" Dr. Fournette went on.

"There is more."

"More?" asked Emily Fournette, blinking back tears as she held her sobbing daughter.

"Yes, according to Jacky Blue, he and Cedar Stock took Zack's body to the river and dumped it in."

"Oh my God," Sarah's voice choked, thick with emotion.

She knows it's true, but will she acknowledge it?

"I knew something was wrong. I just knew it!" Sarah cried. "How will I ever tell Maddy?"

Roy felt his cell phone vibrate once. He quickly checked and saw it was Reuben Montalvo. On the screen he could only see the first few words of the text.

Holy Shit Batman! You were…

It would have to wait. He returned his attention to the Fournette drama in front of him. Blood being thicker than water, difficulty arose in spades when telling a family member that another family member had been arrested for, or was suspected of, the murder, or even molestation of, another family member. Domestic violence, sexual assault, and family fights being what they are, this scenario of perpetrator versus related victim was all too common an occurrence.

The notifying officer or detective in a family violence case had to tread carefully. The first instinct is disbelief. The second instinct is anger at the messenger for false accusations. *Protect the family at all costs and return our lives to us!* Resentment toward the police abounds, even in cases where the family suspects or fully believes the accusations to be true. Turning lives upside down is never met with palm fronds and hosannas. So Roy braced himself for bared teeth. Bared teeth that never showed up.

Sarah calmed somewhat, blowing her nose and sniffling while leaning against her mother's breast. A little girl again.

She blurted out, "I played it over in my mind so many times, especially at night when I would lie in bed alone and listen to the rain or the wind or even crickets. I couldn't accept what they said had happened. I had no way to prove otherwise. In my deepest bone marrow, though, I knew something was wrong. Zack drank, but he was so experienced in the outdoors, whether he had a gun or a fishing pole. It made no sense. Yet what could I do? I did not suspect Cedar's involvement at first, but over the years I've wondered. He grew so attentive to Maddy and me. That is, when he wasn't in prison."

"It's okay, sweetheart," Emily said, kissing Sarah's hair.

Sarah continued in a thick voice, "I had this feeling that he'd not shed a tear over the death of his cousin. In fact, there were times I thought he actually preferred life without Zack. It gave him unfettered access to Maddy and me. And I had no way to keep him away, so I let him in. And though I've always kept a small barrier between us, Maddy has completely accepted him and loves him so much. Oh God. What will I do?" She sniffed again, more tears leaking.

From now on she'll flinch whenever she sees me coming.

"Did Cedar ever discuss the circumstances of his last time seeing Zack?" Roy asked softly.

"No, and I found that strange. Rather than express remorse over not seeing warning signs or being there to help his cousin, he simply ignored the whole thing, as if Zack had not existed."

"Strange," murmured Dr. Fournette.

"I even asked him once why he never discussed my dead husband."

"What did he say?"

"Past is the past, and that it was too painful for him to discuss it but that he felt responsible and would see that Maddy and I were always taken care of. I did not completely believe his sincerity, but I acted as though I did. Then, of course, over the years memories and feelings fade, and I grew to accept him being in Maddy's and my life."

"May I make a suggestion?" Roy asked.

Sarah and her parents looked at him, waiting.

"Say nothing. For now."

"I don't understand," said Sarah.

"Give us time to finish our investigation."

"What does that mean?" asked Sarah.

"It means that it does not matter that it has been over twenty years since Zack's death. There is no statute of limitations on murder. He deserves justice. Koondawg Cutler will be found and prosecuted if I can prove that he murdered Zack. I will do my best to see it happen."

Sarah straightened up resolutely. "Okay, I think I understand, and I support you in your investigation. I too want justice for my husband."

"I'm glad you feel that way, because there is something I must do to make that happen."

"What's that?" asked Sarah, sensing another shoe about to drop.

"A judge has ordered an exhumation and second autopsy on Zack. We have been ordered to retrieve and send his remains to the Chico Human Identification Lab for analysis to try and confirm how he died."

"You mean dig him up?" exclaimed Emily.

Roy noted Dr. Fournette nodding in the affirmative. No dummy, he could connect dots.

"Yes. We've been ordered to do so day after tomorrow.

"Oh my God," murmured Sarah, invoking the Creator's name for the third or fourth time. Grief and trauma spurring cries for help. Roy had been there. Tears continued to spill down her face.

Roy had expected resistance, and he'd been careful to put it all on the anonymous judge, leaving out the tiny detail of his advocacy for said dig. It just made it all easier to play the good soldier sadly following orders. Like the absent bared teeth, resistance did not rear its ugly snout.

"When?" Dr. Fournette asked.

"Day after tomorrow. Sarah, as his widow, you may attend if you like. The utmost care and respect will be given to the matter. He'll be taken to Chico where two of the leading experts in the field of forensic anthropology will examine him and render findings on the nature of his injuries."

"Why wouldn't they have seen his injuries to begin with?" asked Emily.

"To be fair, the consensus was death by drowning. No one involved in the incident at the time raised the idea of foul play. In fact, his cousin Cedar was interviewed and gave a consistent statement with the evidence. Zack had been extremely upset over the separation with Sarah and had announced his intention to go fish and drink. Falling in the river and sliding over and into rocks in rapids could have produced broken bones. He had broken bones. It all fit. But now that a different theory of cause of death has arisen, it is imperative that the bones be reexamined to see if the injuries are consistent with a beating."

"Cedar again," Dr. Fournette said under his breath.

Roy had deliberately left out the claim by Jacky Blue that Cedar and he had forced water and alcohol down Zack's throat to make the drowning story more believable. Too much detail and images they did not need to sleep with.

"You're right. I'll say nothing for now." Sarah sighed. She blew her nose and excused herself to go to the bathroom.

When Sarah had gone, Dr. Fournette turned to Roy.

"She can't ever know that you spoke to us."

"Fair enough. I appreciate the way you've handled this. Family issues can be tricky."

"I think I told you before. We never wanted to be those helicopter parents, but from up where we are, we could see all this unfolding. It's just too bad the girls will have to suffer going forward."

"Bad business, and you have my sympathies. People don't ask for the pain dropped on them. It happens in this world, and sometimes there is no good explanation."

"Are you a religious man, Detective?" Emily asked. "In your line of work you've seen so many people in such a sad state. I imagine it has made you turn away."

"Yes and no. But I'm human, and I've been on both ends. I've found comfort at times in writings by those who've gone before us and who, over the ages, have put together words that describe the torture our souls experience and the ways to understand and deal with our grief."

"You're a fine man, and we wish you all the luck." Dr. Fournette said.

"Thank you," Roy responded. "Know that in spite of your daughter's life not following a path you would have chosen, she is a very special woman, and you have no reason not to be proud of her."

♦

When Roy and Westwood got back in Roy's SUV, Westwood let out a whistle.

"You need to wear a helmet cam, so we can study your style. I don't know how you sit and relate to people the way you do. I'd have said it simple. Hey, lady, I think your husband got murdered, and I'm diggin' him up to find out if I'm right. Hope you're cool with that."

"Yeah, that was me early on," Roy grinned. "But I learned from one of the best. Take your time. Develop your life's philosophies. Don't be afraid to share them at the appropriate time. Seem human. Be human. Sometimes that's what folks need. Not a robot."

Roy checked his phone for the Montalvo text.

Holy shit, Batman! You were right. The records show it. Call me ASAP!

"Hang on a sec, Robin. I gotta make a call to SSU"

"Robin? Thought I was Dirty Wally. Hey, Robin works." Westwood shrugged.

Roy checked his recent calls, found Montalvo's number, and tapped it. As the phone rang, he felt the familiar spread of adrenalin warmth.

"Well Delroy Church. When we old bulls are gone, who's gonna service all them cows in the pasture?" Montalvo laughed when he answered the phone. "Hey. I'm just trying to relate to your new digs."

"Ha! I'm actually wearing spurs right now. Next year I plan to try getting on a horse for the first time ever. Baby steps. So what have we got?"

"It took a while. Hand search on old records, but all visitors' logs are stored away at The Bay. Just for this very reason. You were right. Jade Tankersley has been on again off again as a permitted visitor. But on July 9, 2004, she visited Dale "Moonshine" Tankersley, AB shot caller extraordinaire."

"Great," said Roy. "More?"

"Gimme a drum roll please." Montalvo paused for dramatic effect. "That was one of Jade's first visits allowing her back in after being on visitor's probation so to speak. Before that, over a half dozen times. I can't fucking believe it. None other than Miss Dina Morgan of Sisson, California."

"No shit?" said Roy. "So she was definitely a runner for Moonshine while Jade was on ice."

"Yep. And we've got her visiting several of the fellas in Corcoran as well. "

"So she'd get messages in Pelican Bay and run them down to the AB in Corcoran. Most likely driven by Pud Wilson."

"Most likely. Of course, Moonshine wasn't the only person she visited."

"I think I know who."

"Of course you do. You're the great Delroy Church. She visited Cedar Bob Stock every time she visited The Bay. See Moonshine on Saturday morning, come back Sunday and see Cedar Bob. Only time she didn't see Cedar Bob is when he and Moonshine celled together which was about for a coupla months in early to mid-2004. Then there was no need."

"That means she was getting messages for Moonshine to pass to Cedar Bob in The Bay, then heading down to Corcoran to run messages to AB shot callers there."

"Prison mail," said Montalvo, marveling. "Of course, today, we got inmates and some staff smugglin' cell phones in. Not like the old days. Jesus. Time for me to think about retirement." Roy could see him shaking his head.

"Anything else?" asked Roy.

"Oh, were you expecting something more? That wasn't enough? Like a damn kid at Christmas. Always wants one more present. Spoiled are you?"

"That's me, spoiled rotten. Now give me something shiny before I throw a tantrum."

"Okay, okay, simmer down. Mommy and Daddy just want you to be happy. It's what we live for. So how about this? You were right about the other dates too. Went back to the C-File. Your boy Cedar Stock has been fibbing just a little."

"No, not Cedar Bob. Say it's not true. He's reformed. Just ask his mother," Roy replied with a chuckle.

"He's lying when he told you and whoever else that he got out *after* Dina Morgan disappeared. He discharged from The Bay on July 9, 2004. He'd done his full term. No tail, no high-risk parole, so he could associate with whoever he wanted."

"And?"

"Oh, little guy still not satisfied with his presents? You're the poster boy for what's wrong with America's youth."

"Millennial Roy. That's me."

"Guess who picked up Cedar Bob in the parking lot at The Bay when he discharged at 0930 hours? Yep. That's right. Jade

Tankersley."

"And Dina Morgan disappeared the following night," said Roy. "Veddy interesting. Reuben you got beer on me when you get here!"

"Okay brother, let me know if you need anything else."

"Is that all good stuff?" Westwood asked when Roy hung up.

"The game is afoot!" exclaimed Roy.

"Dirty Wally? Robin? Now Watson? Yeah. I can do Watson." Westwood buckled his seatbelt and settled back for the ride.

CHAPTER 55

Once back at the sub, Westwood headed for the freeway north for home while Roy moseyed back inside to sort out recent events, get his bearings, and plan his next moves.

In the quiet, he could think, turn it all over in his mind. He hoped the weather held for the excavation crew at the Sisson cemetery two days hence. What would the bones of the long gone Zack Stock reveal? How would he tie them to Puma Creek Trail? Kat would get in on the examination, a real plus. He'd texted her back.

Miss your smiling face and quick mind. You're a born detective. I don't say that lightly. I've known a few. Have fun with the bones I'm sending downhill!

A text that long had given him carpal tunnel.

How much, if anything had he missed in his chat with Jacky Blue? He wished he could get a do over, spend the day with the condemned Texan. He planned to review the transcript of their chat shortly.

But first, how worried was Cedar Stock at that moment? He had probably never counted on a detective laying the Hmong 187s at his doorsteps. His calculations had seemed correct. Stir up activity to pull resources away from Puma Creek, but the fates had conspired against him. The fates had dropped Roy Church in his lap. So how dangerous had he become? Especially now that he had no attorney, Ira Hand having abandoned him. Roy could feel the desperation within Cedar building, desperation that he would try valiantly to control, to push down deep, and to fight as if he felt bloody punctures on a dusty, roiling yard.

He checked his phone once more before pulling out the Jacky Blue transcript. He saw that Westwood had texted him a photo. There he was, his back to Westwood, leaning earnestly toward the old lady in the chair, she with her hand in the air making a salient point in defense of her beloved boy.

Roy tapped the phone to save the amusing scene. As he did so his finger touched the photo and enlarged it. He paused and studied its upper right corner. He tapped it again to enlarge the corner some more. An item on the fake mantel over the free-standing stove in the middle of an interior wall caught his eye. He'd not seen it when he was in the house, his attention being focused on the old woman and the possibility that Cedar Stock might appear with an Uzi. He'd been seated on the Mexican blanket on the couch, facing Jersey Stock, yet he'd still not noticed the item in his peripheral vision, which he could now make out as a post card leaning against the wall. His pulse beat quicker, like hooves at the derby.

Its brilliant yellow stood out against a desert landscape spread haphazardly under an indigo sky. The flower rising out of the areole displayed nature's warm beauty, juxtaposed with the threat of dangers lurking in the unforgiving spines that surrounded it. Next to the cactus flower, in matching, bright yellow script, were three words missing a single comma, an oversight that Roy was sure irritated Cedar Stock to no end.

Del Rio Texas.

Roy dialed Westwood.

"Hey Roy, what's up?"

"Say, about that photo you snapped inside Jersey Stock's home."

A momentary silence had Roy wondering if he should repeat.

"Uh, did I fuck up?"

"No, young man, you just made detective."

♦

Roy ended his call with a jacked-up Westwood and hurriedly searched through the Jacky Blue interview transcript. He suspected subliminal messages had been sent his way. He'd felt it from the minute he'd walked out of the cell, turned and looked into Jacky

Blue's eyes, acknowledging the nod, the subtle smoke signal of a seasoned con telling his dawg to make a move. He'd taken the look and the nod to mean those records found by Reuben Montalvo confirming Cedar Stock's lie regarding his release date from Pelican Bay and how this figured into the Dina Morgan case. He'd congratulated himself on the coup, had begun believing his own press clippings. He now chided himself for missing the other obvious messages Jacky Blue had sent him from only four feet away.

And there he was, a voice on paper, easy to read. His crafted words had gone in one ear and out the other. Jacky Blue had been wrong about him being this "hell of a detective" from LA. He gave himself another mental boot in the ass.

"Hell yeah, it bothers me. Sumbitch is off spending my half on pussy and margaritas."

Pussy? Koondawg Cutler, the connoisseur of young men, had been nowhere near Del Rio, Texas. Koondawg Cutler had not announced to a motel clerk that he'd been in Winnemucca, Nevada. Roy had even marked that statement as odd and sloppy when reading the Val Verde Sheriff's report on the motel room murders. Two professional thugs bent on a big crime sure as hell didn't announce to the world where they hailed from. Even using the name Kelly Cutler on a motel register smelled of amateur, unless it wasn't. No, those were calculated slips of the tongue uttered by a man laying trail away from himself and behind a pigeon.

Roy dialed Reuben Montalvo.

"Reuben, yes, I know it's late. Your third beer? Okay, sorry about this, but if you'll answer me what I think you can answer me, I can triple that amount for you with high quality Black Tail Ale, the preferred IPA of the big game hunter."

Roy took a breath.

"When did Kelly Koondawg Cutler abscond? I know you know. You've been all over his file. It's your business to know when a con goes on the run. I want my tax money's worth."

Roy waited while Montalvo set his beer down and massaged his memory.

Roy smiled broadly. "Bingo, Reuben! He's our boy. We're about to bust his not so bright ass! Cedar's also our boy, and I can't prove the rest, but I think I know the score."

After explanations that totally screwed with the integrity of Montalvo's cocktail hour, Roy hung up. He leaned back in his chair and peered out the window at the frozen parking lot of the sub. The streetlamp shone, reflecting off the sides of his SUV. It cast a flaxen dome that obscured the stars far above that had just now come into alignment.

♦

At 0600 hours the following morning, Roy dialed a Texas number. Ranger Wade Bagley answered.

"Damn," Ranger Bagley said, after Roy laid out his theory. "I think we can run down the clerk, but I don't know if we can lay hands on the mule. Send me the photo anyhow. We're on it as soon as I can print out a copy and get a line-up together. Val Verde Sheriff is going to love this. Election year down there."

Roy hung up and pressed send within the minute. Thanks to the Apple servers in Cupertino, California, Cedar Stock's prison photos landed seconds later in the Lone Star state on a Texas Ranger's desk.

Wade Bagley, twenty-year Ranger man, dialed his contact, Detective Raul Morales, in the Val Verde Sheriff's Department Investigations Section.

Two hours later, Detective Morales and his partner Detective Jenny Ramirez strolled into the musty smelling lobby of the Del Rio Motel Six, directly across the street from the Super 8 where almost two years earlier three bloated bodies had been carefully placed inside black zip-up bags.

Two hours and ten minutes later, Ranger Bagley's phone vibrated. It was Detective Morales.

"Got us a positive, Wade," reported Detective Morales. "Clerk didn't hesitate except to say the dude in the photo looked a little younger but is definitely the same guy who checked in with the defendant he testified against last year."

"Fantastic, Raul!" said Wade Bagley. "Going to be tough showing the photo to our surviving mule, though, since he's worm food in Nogales. Cartel on cartel bullshit."

"We still got enough for a warrant?" Detective Morales asked.

"We got enough for a warrant. Look outside. All the leaves are brown and the sky is fuckin' gray! California dreamin', homie."

"Hell you talkin' about, Wade?"

"Sorry, I'm an old guy. Only been out there once, but the song always stuck in my mind from when I was a little kid. My folks played Mamas and Papas all the time. I think they were undercover hippies."

"Whatever. If it wasn't Vicente Fernandez, it didn't get no airtime in mi casa. Should I pack shorts and sandals?"

"Uh, I think the California where we're going ain't got surfers."

He was wrong, of course. But then he had no way of knowing the sandy haired past of Delroy Church who still missed those epic days *frothing* with his *brahs.*

♦

Roy stood and surveyed the gathered cops in front of him. Sheriff Ed Silva sat on his normal throne at the far end of the table. Tommy Sessions sat to his right, while Lieutenant Gary Lynch looked up from Sheriff Silva's left. Alison Baker had grabbed the spot next to the LT, while two other detectives from the original Hmong investigation had slipped into seats next to her. A newly minted detective, variously referred to as *Wally, Clint, Dirty Wally, Robin* or *Watson,* sat beaming next to Roy's right leg. Roy shifted a hair to his left to keep Westwood from doing a shoulder to thigh purr rub.

"Texas has just walked through a warrant for the arrest of Cedar Stock on three counts of capital murder. Their case will trump all of ours, but in the event a Texas jury stumbles on the evidence or grows tired of snuffing undesirables, we still have to do our jobs," Roy began.

Smiles formed on the lips of all the cops who, unlike a large swath of the *evolved* civilian population, admired the hell out of those states that actually eliminated vermin instead of coddling them.

"Their evidence is thinner without the surviving victim available to testify, but his original testimony may be entered into evidence to bolster the state's case. In any event, that's their problem. We'll help snatch up Cedar when the Rangers arrive with their warrant. We've got narcs watching Jersey Stock's place now. We don't have an address for Cedar other than his mom's," Roy informed the group.

"Hell, maybe he'll show up and resist. Narcs can put 'im down and save us all a lot of trouble," Sheriff Silva remarked hopefully.

"Of course, we don't want to grab him too early. Rangers want to be on scene with their own bracelets to get any spontaneous statements and to attempt questioning before he's in front of a judge and is assigned an attorney to examine extradition requests," Roy said.

"Don't mess with Texas," Sheriff Silva smiled, nodding around the room. Everyone smiled back and nodded affirmatively.

"Rangers and Val Verde County detectives are in the air as we speak, flew out of San Antonio and will be in Medford in about six hours," Roy said.

"That boy's a one man crime wave. Time for him to say *adios* to Karuk County, that's for damn sure," observed Sheriff Silva, keenly aware that credit for the Texas case would drip all over him come election time. And having another county in another state foot the bill for any trial? Hell, that was just gravy.

"The Sheriff's right, Roy," Lynch said. "Sounds as if Cedar Stock has cut a path like Sherman's march to the sea, only kept himself clean the whole time."

"Been a slick one all right," Roy said. "Has covered his tracks pretty well for a few decades. Here's a rundown of what I believe he's been up to, some provable, some probable, some only Cedar knows.

"For years he's been running crews for the Aryan Brotherhood, ripping Mexican cartel mules in California as well as out of state, for example the murders in Del Rio, Texas. He's been using a gal by the name of Jade Tankersley as his runner to the AB Commission in Pelican Bay and to other AB shot callers in other institutions. She's married to an AB shot caller called Moonshine. Cedar's crews have varied over time with boys like Jacky Blue Howard, Koondawg Cutler, Jesse Pud Wilson, and his girl Dina Morgan. There have been others who have come and gone. We may never know their names. Even your Hmong 187 victims had been involved for a minute, but they got greedy on one job and had to go. So he set them up to be whacked by the Hmong. Tim Stock, his nephew, was in on the set up and is most likely part of his crew as we speak.

"He lied about being around when Dina Morgan disappeared. He was never on the radar back then, so he was never formally interviewed. Why would he be? But anyone he's ever spoken to in the civilian world has gotten the impression that he had great concern for Dina once he rolled back into town, and, like OJ, he's been looking for her killers ever since."

"You mean he killed Dina Morgan?" exclaimed Lieutenant Lynch.

"Not necessarily, but I have no doubt he knows who did, and he knows where her remains are," Roy said.

"You don't think it was Pud Wilson?" Lieutenant Lynch asked.

"Might have been. We may never know."

"He killed Pud Wilson, though" Lieutenant Lynch said. "To shut him up? Seems a little late."

"I think Pud had no idea of Cedar's involvement in Dina Morgan's disappearance. Otherwise you're right, he might have disappeared himself years ago. He was simply a loose end whose death conveniently created diversion just like the Hmong 187s."

"Diversion?" asked Lynch.

"Diversion from Puma Creek Trail," said Roy. "All about covering up dirty deeds. Like maybe the murder of his cousin Zack by Koondawg Cutler, maybe something else."

"Koondawg. Now there's a boy who needs to be drug down to Texas!" Sheriff Silva broke in. "That sorry bastard, my apologies to Detective Baker, is on the run somewhere, still piling up victims."

"Actually, he's still in Karuk County. Thanks to Detective Westwood here, we now know he never left," Roy said quietly, clapping a hand on Westwood's shoulder. Roy suspected Westwood might pee himself with any more excitement.

CHAPTER 56

2330 hours, June 21, 1995

Cedar Stock pulled his work truck to a halt in the driveway of Zack and Sarah's home. Lights were on inside. Two Cedar Trims rigs sat parked in the driveway.

"Shit. Pud and Dina are here. Gotta get rid of them quick," Cedar muttered under his breath.

Jacky Blue said, "Let's hope dumbass didn't say anything to them about Zack."

"We'll know the second we walk in," Cedar said, shaking his head.

"What'll we do then?" asked Jacky Blue.

"They gotta go. Simple as that. Can't take a chance," said Cedar, his voice cold, like a floe in the Bering Sea.

"Just gimme the signal, I'll take Pud. Don't feel like dumpin' a female tonight, though I wouldn't mind gettin' busy with her before we gotta do what we gotta do. Feel me?" Jacky Blue said, patting the nine in his waistband.

"No guns unless I give you a sign. If it comes to it, we gotta go blades, gotta be quiet about it. Get 'em zipped up first. Gunshots carry on a summer's night."

"Fuck, let's hope it don't come to it then. But I got the zips."

Cedar and Jacky Blue walked quickly to the front door. Cedar unlatched the screen door and stepped into the kitchen that opened into the small living room. Pud and Dina slouched back on the couch watching TV, munching Doritos, and swigging beers.

"Yo, boss. All cool?" Pud Wilson asked.

He didn't seem nervous. He made no move toward rising. Dina didn't look up from the TV. Not nervous either. Good signs.

"All cool. Where's Koondawg?"

"Dude crashed in the bedroom. Pretty fucked up from what I can see," Pud laughed. "Said you guys was partyin' without us. That's bullshit. But Dina and me brought our own party."

He held up the chips.

Nope, Koondawg Cutler had not said shit.

"Okay, listen, we gotta get you and Dina on the road. *Serpiente's* gonna meet you early in Vacaville, show you the target house. Then Dina goes in and does her thing. We'll be down tomorrow afternoon after we grab Jade to bring with us. We hit the pad day after tomorrow."

"Man, I hope we know what we're doing, gettin' in with them northern beaners. Them cats scare me a bit," Pud shook his head.

"Don't worry, it's all cool, bro," Cedar said.

"C'mon Dina, let's split," Pud said, getting up. He set his beer bottle on the TV stand.

Dina Morgan tossed the chip bag to the end of the couch, took a pull off her beer, and stood up.

"Could we get a taste this time, Cedar?" Her eyes glinted.

"Work time, baby. Party later, can't have you buggin' on the job," Cedar said.

"Fuck, whatever. Jade's rules? Just 'cause you gettin' jiggy with her don't mean you gotta do what she say."

Cedar responded sharply, "No, *my* rules. Rules to not get busted by. Party later, like I said. And watch your mouth about Jade, Dina. She ain't no bitch to fuck with."

"Then why you dickin' her, huh? She's a married woman. Fuck, Pud, let's get outta here." Dina waved her arm dismissively and made for the door.

"Yeah, Pud, get her outta here. See you in Vacaville," Cedar said, wondering how it was you found good help in the criminal world, help without the mouthiness.

Dina Morgan opened the door with Pud in her ear.

"Dammit Dina, why you always gotta push?"

"Eat my shorts, Pud," Dina snapped back as the two of them shouldered each other and bounced out into the dark. Presently the sound of a truck started, followed by spinning gravel as Pud and Dina took their argument on the road to the Bay Area.

"What a pair," Jacky Blue sighed.

"Yeah, but that bitch can buy dope, anywhere," Cedar said. "Worth her weight in gold."

"Pud had a point. Them *Nuestra Familia carnales* are dangerous as fuck, especially that fucking Snake sumbitch," Jacky Blue said.

"Money in it for him, too. Otherwise we don't even talk. He's gotta pay his people behind the walls just like us. Fucking prison rules. We wouldn't normally fuck with the northerners, but Jade says Moonshine and the big *hombres* on *La Mesa* in The Bay got an understanding on the under. Okay, let's wake dumbass up."

Cedar and Jacky Blue opened the bedroom door. Koondawg Cutler lay face down on his bed fully clothed with footwear still on.

Cedar kicked the bottom of Koondawg's boots. Koondawg farted, then grunted.

"C'mon boy, we gotta get our shit and get outta here," Cedar said, giving the soles another sharp tap.

"What the fuck?" Koondawg said as he slowly rolled over and blinked his eyes.

"Koon," Jacky Blue said "Pud and Dina just left. We gotta talk, bro."

"Talk to this, bitch," Koondawg laughed. He lifted a hip and farted noisily.

"Goddamn. You got one rotten ass, you nasty motherfucker," Jacky Blue said disgustedly, fanning the air with a hand.

Koondawg giggled then sat up.

"What's up boys?"

"You heard Jacky, we gotta talk," said Cedar.

"So fucking talk," said Koondawg, his tone less accommodating now that he'd awakened fully. He stuck a finger in his nose and scraped at an annoyance.

"We took care of Zack, but what did you say to Pud and Dina?" Cedar asked.

"Didn't say shit to them. Told 'em you and Jacky went on a beer run."

"They ask about Zack or Sarah?"

"Yeah. I told 'em Zack took off pissed after he caught Jacky here humpin' his ol' lady Armadildo-style, from behind, on the kitchen table." Koondawg made a crude gesture, undulating his hips and shuffling his fists and arms, brightened by the fantasy.

"You tell 'em about your fight with Zack?"

"Fuck, I can't remember. Maybe told 'em I had to tune that boy up some," Koondawg said. He yawned. "Damn. My mouth tastes like ass."

Koondawg pulled a hair off his tongue, held it up and examined it.

"Might have to buy Ronnie a fist fulla flowers," he chortled. He stood up, facing Cedar and Jacky Blue. "Hey, I'm just fuckin' with ya. Me and Ronnie is probably over with. I guess I fucked up a bit. Sorry."

"Okay, cool. Well look, we gotta make sure this place is all cleaned up before Sarah comes back here. Can't look like nothin' went down," Cedar said.

"Looks clean to me. I gotta piss like a stud horse," Koondawg said, turning to head toward the bathroom.

Koondawg passed through the open bedroom doorway and down the hallway into the living room. As he approached the couch just vacated by Pud and Dina, Cedar moved. With the speed of a snake strike, he gripped Koondawg's left shoulder from behind and kicked him behind the right knee, buckling it. He encircled Koondawg's neck with his right arm and drove the inside of his elbow hard against Koondawg's sternum. They both dropped. Koondawg fell to a seated position with Cedar kneeling behind him, squeezing neck between bony forearm and biceps. Koondawg immediately went limp.

"Gimme the zips, quick. This fucking alligator ain't stayin' out long."

Jacky Blue silently produced a black zip tie. Cedar quickly secured Koondawg's wrists behind his back He took a second zip and sucked it up tight around Koondawg's ankles.

Several seconds later the carotid restraint started wearing off. Koondawg Cutler began shaking like a headless chicken, his nerves, heart, and blood supply all jockeying for their rightful balance. His eyes opened. He shook his head in an attempt to orient himself to his new condition.

"What the fuck, motherfuckers?!" His voice sounded a mixture of anger and bewilderment. "Goddammit! What the fuck?!"

Cedar bent behind him, grasped his shoulders, and pulled him to a sitting position with his back against the couch. He then grabbed a kitchen table chair, placed it in front of Koondawg, and sat firmly on it.

"Damn, boy. You got yourself in a fix this time," Cedar said softly.

"Goddammit bro, what's goin' on? This ain't funny," Koondawg said scratchily, his voice box uncertain as to what the hell had just happened.

"Zack's my cousin, boy, my blood. We've got to address this."

"I didn't do nothin' man, just defendin' myself. I never even hit 'im that hard. Jacky tell him, Jesus."

"Jacky and Jesus have got to stay out of this Koon. This is you and me now."

"But Cedar, I don't get it. I maybe kicked him a few times, sure but not like really hard," Koondawg said, his voice approaching touchdown on the whine runway as it dawned on him that his situation had gone from *ain't funny* to *maybe fucked.*

"Must have punctured a lung with a broken rib. Lots of internal injuries, I'm sure. But you see, Koon, we couldn't call 9-1-1. You're a high control parolee, and here you are with two ex-cons and a dead boy that you beat. Questions get asked, even by these cops out here who couldn't get hired on by big city departments," Cedar continued in a soothing voice, like he'd just slipped a halter on a bronco.

"What do want me to do, Cedar? Man, I'll give up my share on the next job. I'll buy his wife a new washer. Fuck. What can I do to make it right?" His voice trembled.

"Well, Koon. I gotta level with you. This really hurts. It does, man. We been down a few roads together, had some good times."

"Cedar, God, you're fuckin' scarin' me now. I get it. I fucked up, but this ain't right, bro."

"Now, Koon, let me finish what I have to say. It's important that you know how I feel."

"How you feel? What about me. Think I'm happy?"

"Listen, it's only natural to fear death—"

"Death? Fuck Cedar, c'mon man. Jacky? You and me, we're bros. This can't be."

"Sorry, Koon, Cedar Bob's right. This ain't about me no more. Boy, you done made your bed," Jacky Blue offered sympathetically from his spot on the couch.

"Koon, listen to me, son, listen to me. Calm down. Nothing you can say can change what's about to happen. But I want you to know a few things first. I'm going to get your money to your mother. Wouldn't be right for us to take it. You earned it fair and square. You put in the hours and the sweat. Money's yours, and your momma won't be getting anymore. We gotta take care of our moms when we have the opportunity. Am I right?"

"Oh, Jesus, Cedar. Dawg," tears slid down Koondawg's cheeks, and snot bubbles played peek-a-boo at his nostrils.

"C'mon, son, don't do that shit. You're embarrassin' yourself," Jacky Blue said.

"I'm sorry," Koondawg blubbered.

Jacky Blue turned away in disappointment.

"Koon, if it makes any difference, I'm not going to fuck up your face. Look what I have here," Cedar said.

He held up a .45 auto.

Koondawg flinched.

"This would destroy too much flesh. So look, I'm putting it down. I'm going to use this instead. Quick, painless, very little mess."

Cedar pulled a .22 caliber pistol out of a back pocket.

".22 magnum. Good round. Quiet, powerful. I'm going to place it behind your ear. You'll not feel a thing. Now please quit crying. Jacky's right. You've got to be a man at times like these. Be philosophical about your life and its end. So you have about one minute. Is there anything you would like to say? It would be wrong of us if we didn't give you your time to speak."

"I wanna go to Heaven, if there is one," Koondawg sniffled and choked. "That's about it."

"I've got to be honest with you, Koon. I'm not sure there is a Heaven. I'm not sure there's a Valhalla. I'm pretty sure they're made up to make folks feel good about seeing their loved ones again. But if it makes you feel better, I hope you get to Heaven, too. 'Bout the best I can do for you is sing a little song in that regard. Jacky, get my guitar from the corner over there will you please."

Momentarily, Cedar tuned his guitar as a terrified Koondawg looked wildly around the room. His face had turned pasty.

"I gotta piss bad, Cedar. Please!"

"Hold it if you can. If you can't, well we'll clean it up. So here you go."

Cedar played and sang the opening lyrics for "Stairway to Heaven" in as beautiful and sensitive a way as he could.

There's a lady who's sure
All that glitters is gold
And she's buying a stairway to heaven
When she gets there she knows
If the stores are all closed
With a word she can get what she came for
Oh oh oh oh and she's buying a stairway to heaven

Cedar set down his guitar.

"Look we're out of time, son. Now I've got some plastic here that I had left over from Zack, so I gotta get you to roll over onto it. We can't leave any mess for Sarah to clean up here in the living room."

"No, Cedar, no! Jacky, please, help me!" Koondawg screamed in desperation.

Cedar lay a shaking, sobbing Koondawg on his side and rolled him over onto the piece of heavy plastic tarp.

"Son, you had to know you've been living on borrowed time. We both been used by Moonshine and the fellas in The Bay. But at least we got to see daylight. We got that goin' for us."

Koondawg squeezed himself into the fetal position and bawled.

Cedar shook his head, like a disappointed parent checking on the state of a teenager's room. He knelt behind Koondawg and placed the pistol barrel against his head just behind and below the right ear.

"So long, Koondawg."

He pulled the trigger.

Pop!

The snap of the explosion filled the room, but quickly died away without echo. Koondawg kicked out, quivered violently then went limp. Like time lapse photography, a stain expanded away from his pants crotch.

"Let's get him to the bathtub. Drain him first then carve him. Too heavy to carry very far like this," Cedar said, sighing at the prospects of having to find a replacement killer. Koondawg had always stepped up when called upon.

Jacky Blue got up to help, the deep blue in his eyes glistening.

"Damn, when my time comes, I'm gonna remember how not to act. Thought he was better'n that."

"Yeah, surprised he took it so hard. After we get him in the tub, fetch me some knives from the kitchen and, oh yeah, Zack's meat saw there in the garage. Oh, Zack's got those trash bags in the garage. Grab them all, will you? We gotta get rid of Sarah's kitchen trash too, so grab all the bags under the sink except one. This place has got to be spic and span when she comes back. I want her to have a fresh garbage though."

Two hours later Cedar stood back with his hands on his hips after policing the kitchen, living room, and bedrooms.

"I think we're loaded, and it's all good in here. Let's get to dumping bags in the back country," he said to Jacky Blue who had just dropped Pud's empty beer bottle into the black kitchen trash bag in his hand.

"Okie dokie. Let me tie this baby up. Only one little piece of Koon in this one. Probably his pecker." Jacky Blue laughed.

Cedar checked the black bags in the rear of the Cedar Trims work truck to make sure they were secure under a tarp. He sure didn't want a ticket for part of his load flying off on the roadway. He went around the driver's door and hopped in. Jacky Blue slid in on the passenger side.

Cedar began to back out of the driveway. Suddenly he slammed on the brakes. Jacky Blue looked over at him in surprise, then whipped his head around, fearful that the cops had just parked behind them.

"Fuck. Can't do that to Sarah. She doesn't deserve this."

"What don't she deserve?!" exclaimed a concerned Jacky Blue.

"That goddamn deer hanging in the garage. Zack shot that doe. Bad enough to kill a buck out of season. And no telling when Sarah will return. Can you imagine the stinkin' mess? Holy Christ. Go open the garage door. We gotta take the doe with us. Can't believe I almost did that to her. She'd have been so fucked if the Fish and Game found out."

"Well at least somebody woulda got to fuck her," Jacky Blue muttered as he scooted out.

♦

0310 hours, June 22, 1995 0310

The gray fox tore at the dead doe, ignoring, for the time being, the human trash bag that also smelled slightly of freshly killed flesh.

The night hunter sat above on its perch, dispassionately eyeing the fox's quick movements. It swiveled its head slightly to follow the far away taillights that disappeared into the trees deep in the ebony canyon.

CHAPTER 57

"Yep, that was Koondawg's clavicle on the Puma Creek Trail," interjected Detective Wallace Westwood who sat next to his mentor, grinning like the cat who got the cream.

"Pretty easy to confirm. We got mitochondrial DNA from the partial clavicle. SSU has kept tabs on Koondawg's mama over the years. I'm sure she'll want to solve the mystery of her poor missing love child," Roy said.

"But it gets better," Westwood burst out excitedly, like that annoying friend who saw the movie the night before and can't contain himself.

He grew somber quickly when the Sheriff shot him a look.

"Yes, it does get better," smiled Roy. "Our contact at SSU, Reuben Montalvo, has been doing a whole lot of digging for us on this case. Once we suspected it to be Koondawg Cutler, Montalvo scoured all the way through his prison records and struck gold."

"Gold," Westwood silently mouthed, nodding his head.

Baby steps, a work in progress, and Rome wasn't built in a day.

Roy continued, "The AB let Koondawg live under Cedar Stock's promise to deliver money from the Nevada jewelry robbery. But they still wanted a piece of him. Cedar had to beat Koondawg down on the yard in front of the other cons and under the guns. Cedar lost all his good time and did a full term for it. That explains no parole tail when he walked out of the gate."

"And Koondawg?" asked Lieutenant. Lynch.

"Koondawg suffered a broken collarbone in the fight. Cedar really wailed on him. The AB got the piece they wanted. UC Davis Hospital in Sacramento had to treat Koondawg initially then he spent several weeks in the prison infirmary. Montalvo faxed us those medical records this morning, broken collarbone confirmed. CDCR still has his X-rays which will most likely match perfectly with our Puma Creek Trail bone."

"So where's the rest of that piece of crap? All we got is a partial collarbone?" Sheriff Silva asked.

"Who knows? Scattered to the winds or fox dens more likely. Or could be on another road somewhere in another county south. Cedar Stock and Jacky Blue, if Jacky Blue is to be believed, had a date with another gang of thieves the following day in the Bay Area for a drug rip in Vacaville."

"So why the hell did Cedar Stock go to all the trouble to throw us off the scent if Puma Creek Trail is just a lowlife parolee?" Lieutenant Lynch asked.

"Two things. He's *been* Kelly "Koondawg" Cutler for the past 23 years. Similar enough in age and looks. Dropping little Koondawg hints here and there like in the Del Rio motel. A really great way to keep Koondawg alive and kicking while he stays in the shadows. If Koondawg gets IDed as dead, cops ask questions, and some might even follow tracks backward.

"Once we didn't give up on the investigation, he had to switch gears and push us toward the Dina Morgan theory, completely unaware of the forensics involved in showing the bone to be most likely from a male.

"Second, I'm betting Dina Morgan really is up on that mountain somewhere, somewhere close to where we found partial Koondawg, and Cedar miscalculated that we'd actually found part of her remains," Roy answered.

"But you said nobody could carry a body that far up a trail, all dead weight. Not even a marine," said Alison Baker.

"I don't think they carried her. When I first went out to the scene, I called for the Forest Service cop to come along. He wasn't available. He was out investigating a cut chain on a Forest Service gate out off the Reno highway. I'm betting Cedar, or whoever, simply cut the chain on Puma Creek Trail and drove up it. Every good drug rip crew carries bolt cutters. It hadn't been a trail very long. It was still a good road. That's probably why the Forest Service eventually placed huge boulders in front of the gate. Nowadays, even if you cut the chain, you need a tractor to move the boulders," Roy replied.

"I'll be damned," Sheriff Silva said, stroking his chin. "Nobody's looking for bones up there now. Gotta be ten feet of snow."

"At least," said Roy. "When does the snow melt around here? Then we can take our time and look."

"Why would Cedar Stock or his associates dump Dina Morgan near the same spot as Koondawg Cutler?" Baker asked.

"Force of habit. Comfort. Familiarity. Cedar Stock is not your typical serial killer. But make no mistake, he is a killer. Killers repeat what has worked for them in the past. Of course, unless Cedar tells us, we may never know why he picked Puma Creek Trail."

"We'll put the Dina Morgan matter on the calendar for late April," Lieutenant Lynch said, making notes. "Gives me time to get a proper search organized. Civilian search and rescue types will come out of the woodwork for this."

"Well, all this can take a slow-down as long as those Texas Rangers get here, and we find this Cedar Stock pain in my ass." Sheriff Silva said. "Detective Westwood, good work, son. That old boy there rubbed off on you it seems."

Roy figured Wally would strut around with a high hard one for about a week.

♦

Six hours later, two Stetsons and two sets of boots, their leather having taken shape in a Mercedes, Texas, boot shop, moved purposefully through the Medford, Oregon, International Airport. Thirty minutes later they were resting on the floor mats of a Karuk County unmarked driven by Detective Wallace Westwood.

"Damn! Those are some tall trees," remarked Ranger Bagley as the car whizzed southbound on Interstate 5 up and over the heavily wooded Siskiyou Mountains Pass. Traveling down the south side, past the *Welcome to California* sign, both Texans whistled in awe when they first spied the ancient volcano before them guarding the Shasta Valley and judging carefully all those who would pass beyond her into the Golden State.

"I got service. I'm sending photos home right now!" Detective Morales said excitedly as he snapped photos through the windshield.

"Seems we need to expand our borders, Raul. Something that big has just gotta call Texas home," laughed Ranger Bagley.

♦

The Karuk County narcs reported no activity over a 16-hour period at Jersey Stock's home. A huddle by two Texans, one former LA County homicide detective, and the powers that be in the Karuk County Sheriff's Department resulted in a decision. Serve the warrant.

At 1900 hours, under the cover of darkness, a Karuk County Sheriff's SWAT team, led by Tommy Sessions, former LAPD SWAT Commander, moved in.

The home was quiet and dark, save for the lonely, dancing light of a television illuminating the peaceful face of an old woman lying back in her chair as still as cold granite. Her eyes were closed. A Bible rested in her hands under the bright, Mexican horse blanket. No obvious signs of violence disturbed her tranquil, forever slumber, save slight discoloration in the pallid skin on each side of her neck.

Within minutes after the home had been cleared of occupants, yellow crime scene tape encircled the property as if it were a late Christmas present. Twenty minutes later, Dead Fred radioed that he was bucking a headwind, headed south from Silverton on I-5.

The postcard from Del Rio, Texas, conspicuous in its absence, put Detective Sherlock Westwood, upgraded from Watson, on yet a higher pedestal given that he would now be a star witness in Val Verde County, if this bad hombre from California could be run to ground and dragged through the cactus into a West Texas courtroom.

Two bushed Texans retired to the Black Tail Inn while a search of the Jersey Stock home continued through the night. Nary a sign of Cedar Stock or damning evidence appeared, tying him to over two decades as a wily soldier of the Aryan Brotherhood.

At 0600 hours, a California Highway Patrol officer arrived on scene. He opened the back door of his SUV. Out jumped a twister on a leash. Twenty minutes later the drug sniffing canine leaped up on a workbench in Jersey Stock's garage. Thirty minutes later, after Dead Fred's photos and quick measurements had been taken, and after a Sheriff's deputy who trained in the Reserves as a bomb tech had given the go ahead, the former LASD stalwart and the rotund evidence specialist peered into the dark recesses of a hidden wall safe. An old-style cell phone and a thin, unsealed manila envelope stared back. Two words had been printed neatly on the outside of the envelope.

To Delroy

Dead Fred finished his photos and collection of the envelope and cell phone before turning to Roy.

"Mind if I open your love letter? Not my mail. I don't want the feds kickin' my fat ass into a cell."

"Be my guest. But any chocolates inside are mine," replied Roy warningly.

Dead Fred had laid out butcher paper on the spotless floor of Jersey Stock's garage. He removed the contents of the envelope, snapping away with his camera as he did. He placed the several sheets of a neatly printed letter side by side and took photos. He turned them over to expose the words on the back side and took more photos. He then photographed the slightly faded 35 mm photograph that he'd also removed.

"Wonder what that's about?" Dead Fred mused, looking at the photo of a slightly younger, but decidedly mobile, version of Germaine Stock watering flowers in her front yard. The photo looked to have been taken from a distance consistent with the middle of the street fronting her house, as if from a passing car.

"I can guess," Roy said quietly as he peered over Dead Fred's shoulder. "A subtle reminder to work hard and stay loyal. Lives depend on it."

"If you say so. I'm just the tubby tech. No need for me to know state secrets."

Dead Fred gently placed the envelope, letter pages, and photograph into individual evidence bags to save for a ninhydrin treatment later, one that would hopefully reveal Cedar Stock's fingerprints.

"Well, you can now read this bitch," Dead Fred said handing his digital camera to Roy with page one of the letter on the screen.

"And that is how I will describe it on the stand. 'At that time, Evidence Specialist Dead Fred Cavanaugh handed me his camera, and I read the bitch'. Okay, that'll work," joked Roy.

Roy read the letter, printed in a style and neatness that would have made an IBM Selectric envious back in the day. Seasoned cons, used to communicating in tiny hand written kites, could get jobs as elementary school handwriting teachers, if they could just pass that pesky background.

Delroy,

If you're reading this, I'm either dead or on the run. I prefer the latter, but in the case of the former I hope I went down fighting.

Also, if you're reading this, it means someone has been tellin', because bright as you are, you could not have caught onto me without a rat. It's got to be one of two people who have betrayed me, Jacky Blue Howard or Jade Tankersley. Everyone else who could dime me off is dead. Well, actually, Jacky Blue could be dead at the time of your reading this, but I suspect you've turned the house upside down and have found this in a timely fashion.

I do not believe there is a God, but if there is one, I hope he accepts my mother. She had a rough exterior, and many found her to be brusque and bitter. But she was still my mother. I loved her dearly. Yes, she is deceased, and it pains me to admit it, but I helped her along the way. I had no choice. With me gone, she would have suffered greatly, either in the halls of a convalescent hospital or at the hands of the outfit as a way to get back at me.

She and I discussed this problem before I left. It does not matter whether you believe me or not, but this is the truth. She chose to have me end her life in a humane way. She simply went to sleep and never woke up. It doesn't make it right in the eyes of the law, but in the eyes of Jersey Stock, it was the last loving act of a son who failed her early on by choosing the path I did.

I take full responsibility for every bad thing I ever did. I started out in the mistaken belief in high school that selling a little grass on the side was smart and cool. That road eventually led to the pen, and then there was no turning back the clock. Fight or die. Predator or prey, in an environment where laws of the jungle rule, and where circumstances beyond your choosing dictate your next move to stay above ground….

CHAPTER 58

July 9, 2004

Cedar Stock shook Moonshine Tankersley's hand and embraced him.

"Make us proud out there, brother," Moonshine said.

"I won't let you down," Cedar Bob replied to his cellie.

"We know you won't," Moonshine said, all supportive, optimistic, and sinister rolled into one. "Jade'll have some numbers for you. She says Pud and Dina are set to roll. Jacky Blue's got some boys lined up for you to take a look at. Get it together ASAP. They say the Mexicans are on fire out there. Lotta money to be made."

Cedar heard the three officers walking up the stairs.

"Stock. Time to roll. Tankersley on your bunk."

"All right, brother. A report every two weeks. No misses. Okay? And keep an eye on Jade. Make sure that bitch is being faithful to old Moonshine. Don't mind her ridin' a kick start dildo. Anything else and we deal with it. Feel me?"

"Do my best, bro."

Cedar turned and placed his hands through the port.

Cedar wondered if he'd be a three officer move clear to daylight. He was. In spite of it being discharge day, they still ankle and belly chained him all the way to the gate.

In the wide asphalt parking lot on the west side of Pelican Bay's Admin building, Cedar watched an excited Jade Tankersley hop out from behind the wheel of her tan GMC quad cab, its bed loaded with work tools like any other construction outfit. A magnetic sign on the side read *Western States Construction.*

"Hey, Cowboy!" she called. "Welcome to the world!"

She hurried forward and hugged him around his arms. Then she reached down behind him and grabbed his butt cheeks.

"Bet we get our freak on before we hit Willow Creek. Jacky Blue's gonna have to either watch or take part. I don't care. I been itchin' to get me some Cedar Bob knob!"

Jade stopped at a motel a few miles south in Crescent City. Jacky Blue Howard emerged from a room after she honked. He waved heartily at Cedar.

Jade looked mischievously at the two of them hugging in front of the door.

"Long way from here to Willow Creek, boys. Cedar Bob get your ass in there and shower. Wash the Moonshine off you! Hey Jacky, boss man's gotta get busy. You're welcome to hop on in! Nasty Jade bout to get laid!"

A sated Jade, but who knew for how long, drove south on Highway 101 to Arcata, California, where she turned east on Highway 299. It would be a hundred plus mile ride through Sasquatch country and along the clear blue-green of the Trinity River to Redding, California, where they'd catch I-5 and drive the hour north to Sisson.

On the journey, Jade brought Cedar up to speed on the lay of the land.

"Mexicans have padded the fuck outta their gold mine strategy since you were last out. Every cartel has got its own string of restaurants on every major highway from Mexico to Canada. The mules run money and dope north and south. They meet in the restaurants, exchange keys to cars in the lots, turn around and head back the way they came. Then they all got their grows up the ying yang out these old loggin' road all over California. Getting so you have to watch your ass if you're a hunter and stumble onto one of them. Been hella gunfights with dudes trying to rip off weed. That ain't our thing. We stick to the dope houses and mules in restaurant lots."

"Yes, ma'am," said Cedar.

Jade reached over and squeezed his crotch.

"You better say 'Yes ma'am' you devil you. Hey, speaking of loggin' roads. You boys wanna have another go? I can pull off."

Cedar politely declined but said to ask again in another twenty miles. He had to recharge his batteries.

"Whenever," said Jacky Blue from the back seat. He settled back to sleep.

"Open that glove box, boy. Got you a present."

Cedar opened the glove box. Inside he found a small cell phone. He took it out and examined it. Nokia.

"Has a built in camera," said Jade, proudly. Just for you. A gettin' out present.

"No fuckin' way! A camera built into a phone?"

"Takes video too. You can film me while I'm riding your buckin' bronco."

"You gotta be shittin' me. What the hell will they think of next?"

She gave him a huge smile. "All charged up. I'll show you how to use it when we stop for gas or ass. Nobody rides for free."

Three hours later Jade pulled into Jersey Stock's driveway in Sisson, California. Cedar touched down on concrete before she'd put it into park. Jersey met him at the door. He grabbed her off her feet and hugged her long and hard.

Jersey had a steak barbecue for them that night. Cedar ate rib eye and drank a beer, the first in four years. Jade sat and watched TV while Jersey cleaned up. Jacky Blue helped with dishes.

"You are one polite young man," Jersey gushed. "Your mama raised you right."

Jacky Blue smiled.

"Why thank you, ma'am," the murdering, dope robber said, damn near blushing.

Cedar fumbled with his new phone and took an amateurish video or two of Ma and Jacky Blue doing dishes.

"Jacky, you don't want this getting around," he laughed.

"Damn, fool. Turn that shit off. Oops, sorry Mrs. Stock."

Jersey Stock play slapped Jacky Blue on the shoulder.

Out in the living room Jade's cell phone rang.

"Pud!" she said into it. "We're still in Crescent City. Where you at, boy?"

"Where *are* you," corrected Cedar from between the kitchen and living room. "The *at* is redundant."

She ignored him. "What the fuck are you talking about, Pud?" Jade stood up from the couch and turned a half circle to point at Cedar and the phone.

Cedar hurried to where Jade stood. He accepted the phone from her as she covered it and whispered to him.

"Dina giving him shit. We ain't in town. Okay? Don't want those fools knowing where we're at."

"Yo, bro," Cedar said when he took the phone.

"Big homie, how goes it? Glad to be out? Miss you man!" Pud said.

"Cool. Missed you, too, bro. Can't wait to see the town and the trees and the mountains. But it's all good. Gonna crash here tonight, get a seafood dinner. Be home tomorrow. Time to work. So everything cool?"

"Naw, man, Dina, you know man. Dina being Dina. I mean she's happy you're comin' home and all, but she don't wanna get busy with us. I don't know man. Been tellin' her to get it together." Pud's voice had a tone of desperation.

"She spun?"

"Maybe a little, man, I don't know."

Cedar sighed. "Can't work if she's tweakin'. Gotta get straight."

"I told her, man. She's talkin' all crazy. Says she's gonna drive to Crescent City and see Moonshine. Says she's gonna rat you out to Moonshine."

"Rat me out? That's crazy. They ain't gonna let her into see him anyhow. Tell her to get her shit together and then you call me back."

"Okay, man, we're down at Karuk Lake right now. I'm tryin' to be reasonable with her. She's throwin' shit at the ducks."

Pud tried to cover the speaker on his phone as he yelled, "Fuck, Dina leave 'em alone!" He uncovered the speaker and said, "I'll get at you, man."

"You call Jade back in five. No fuck ups."

Cedar hung up without telling Pud he now had his own new number. He handed the phone back to Jade.

"Don't worry, Pud'll get her turned around."

"Fucking better," Jade hissed. "That bitch has lived off us long enough. I'm about up to here with her tweaker shit. And what was the rat shit about? That lowlife cunt better watch her ass if she thinks she can threaten you or me. Did she fuckin' say she's going to see Moonshine?"

"Chill. Pud'll come through."

Jersey dried dishes with a towel, minding her own business. Jacky Blue stood at the entry to the kitchen with question in his eyes.

"All good, brother?" he asked.

Cedar nodded. He'd worried about this shit. Dina had rehabbed before, had started *chippin'* again, had gone back into rehab, had gotten straight then started *slammin'* or smokin' the pipe. A cycle of black tar and crank. A killer combo. Still, when she was on, she could waltz into a dope house and talk a pound or a key out of the most suspicious Mexican or stupid ass biker out there.

Three minutes later, Jade's phone rang again. She handed it to Cedar.

"Wants to talk to you."

Pud sounded totally stressed.

"Fuckin' Dina just jumped out of my truck on Northshore Road. Bitch is all outta control. I'm gonna let her walk her ass home. She'll cool off. She mighta done a line today and didn't tell me about it. Coulda smoked a little too."

"Dammit, Pud. You two have had ample time to get your shit together. Not like it's any secret that I'd be getting out. Okay. Just let her mellow, and I'll see you tomorrow when I get to Sisson. We'll talk to her, get her back on board."

"Okay, bro. I'm sorry. I tried. But Dina gonna be Dina. She could be on a run. I don't know how much she smoked. Always had a head of her own."

"Late," Cedar said and hung up.

"Fuck's going on?" Jade asked, staring at him with eyes of a wraith.

"Dina just hopped out of Pud's truck down at the lake. He's letting her walk to cool off. That's about a mile from here. Let's go. Maybe we can catch up to her before some cop happens by and busts her for being high. We could have an issue if she shoots off her mouth."

Two minutes later, with Cedar driving, since he knew the roads, their headlights reflected off a green and white sign reading *Northshore Road.* Darkness had fallen over the woods on both sides of the gravel road leading around the north side of Karuk Lake, the side used by the locals who wanted separation from the city dwellers at the south side campground. Cedar bounced over potholes, leaving his beams on high. Dust boiled up behind. No other vehicles appeared ahead or to the rear.

"Let's hope she didn't get a ride," Jacky Blue said.

"Let's hope. Not likely," murmured Cedar under his breath,

wondering how he would handle the oft volatile female runner.

Rounding a corner, with the placid darkness of Karuk Lake on one side and a bushy, rocky bank uphill on the other, the headlights illuminated a lone female striding toward them. Dina Morgan raised her hands to shield her eyes from the light. Cedar switched to low beams. Dust caught up and settled slowly around Dina.

Dina, wearing black shorts under a white t-shirt that featured the Twin Towers and an American flag, stumbled toward the headlights. She waved her hands, as if trying for attention, probably looking for a ride.

"Fuck. Here we go," said Cedar as he started to get out of the truck. He heard Jade slide out the passenger door.

"Stay in here," Jade said sharply, "I'll handle her."

Cedar relaxed and sat back. He reached into his shirt pocket and pulled out his new phone. He sensed Jacky Blue leaning forward from the back seat, grinning, eager to get the match started.

"Whatcha doin', Cedar Bob?"

"Let's see how good this camera is. Maybe get us a girl fight on it. But get ready to jump and separate."

"Fuck yeah, mud wrestlin' bitches. Love to see them two naked goin' at it," Jacky Blue laughed. "Kickin' and lickin'!"

Jade walked calmly out of the inkiness into the light.

"Hey, baby," Jade called smoothly. "Are you okay?"

Dina stopped at the sound of Jade's voice. She put her hand over her eyes and ducked her head in question at the backlit figure walking toward her.

"Fuck you doin' here. Pud said you was in Crescent City."

"Oh that Pud, he misunderstood. Told him we had just rolled in from Crescent City. What's goin' on, baby? We came down to party with y'all. You been cryin'?"

Dina threw a hand up slapping the air. She turned to her left and squatted. Sobs shook her shoulders.

"Just leave me alone," she cried.

Jade stepped forward and reached down to place a hand on her shoulder.

"C'mon baby. We can talk about it. You been partyin' without us. Too much, too long. It's okay, baby. Jade's here now."

"Fuck you!" Dina pulled away violently. "Leave me alone. I ain't doin' your shit no more. You can all go fuck yourselves. You and your big man in the pen and all of you. Go to hell."

Dina sobbed louder and sat in the dusty gravel.

Jade looked back at the boys in the truck. She gave a hands up shrug.

"Not much of a fight," said a disappointed sounding Jacky Blue.

Jade looked down at the quivering mess on the ground. She reached into a back pocket and pulled out a pistol. She jammed the pistol barrel against the top of Dina's head and pulled the trigger.

Dina's head snapped, then she slumped over in the dust on her side.

"What the fuck, Jade?!" yelled Jacky Blue.

Cedar jammed the phone in his shirt pocket and sprang from the truck.

"It's cool boys," Jade called, motioning to them. "Help me get this piece of shit in the back of the truck, now!"

Twenty minutes later Cedar had driven up Puma Creek and now sat studying a locked gate across what had once been a logging road.

"Jesus, fucking Christ!" Jacky Blue exclaimed. "Now what?"

"It's just a dinky assed chain keeping it locked. Jade, we got a key, right? Grab the cutters, quick," Cedar said. He got out and began determining the best place to make a cut.

"What makes this place so damn special?" Jade called after him.

"It's close, and parts of Koon need company," Cedar yelled back.

Jacky Blue strode quickly to the gate carrying a pair of bolt cutters he'd fetched from a toolbox in the back of Jade's truck.

The old road, now a trail, had a few more rocks and occasional small trees in the middle. Still, from what Cedar could recall it was basically the same. He came to a halt.

"Zack's doe and a little bit of Koon's about right here," he said, looking at his odometer. "Let's drive up a snatch hair more. Dina can be a nuisance, and Koon, as bad as he was, don't deserve to be *that* close to her."

"Speaking of Koondawg, I still got his ID for you to use whenever, wherever." Jade smirked.

"Koondawg lives," Cedar chuckled.

Jade said, "Okay after we dump her, bury her, or whatever, we head back and crash at Jersey's place. Then tomorrow night we go lookin' for Pud, as if we don't know nothin'. Got it?"

"Yes, ma'am!" said Jacky Blue from the back seat.

Cedar was apprehensive, but he remained expressionless.

"Okay, right about here," said Cedar. "Grab a shovel and a

flashlight, Jade. Flat spot down there past the trees, plenty of rocks to cover her with if we can't get deep. Let's hope the smell don't give us away. You got gloves in here Jade? We gonna need 'em." His heart pounded as he turned away.

♦

Give my best to Detective Stern. He's a smart boy. Pegged me right on Pud. Okay, then. That's about it. Until we meet again.

Cedar Stock,
Aryan Brotherhood, but not by choice.

"When the snow melts," Roy said, thoughtfully.

"Damn, and here is the phone," Dead Fred said, holding up a plastic bag. "Phone this old can't have more than a few minutes of playing time. Pixels were a bit sketch back then too. We'll get it back to the lab and take a gander."

"You gotta cover the big dig today, too? You're going to be one tired man later on," Roy said. "It's set for 1300 hours."

"I'll grab a few winks in my van. Coffee and Black Tail pancakes, I'll be good." Dead Fred grinned and slapped his overhanging belly.

CHAPTER 59

Roy had spent the morning with Dead Fred finishing up at the Jersey Stock murder scene —murder because Cedar Stock had, presumably, usurped the state's rightful task of taking a life without due process and with malice aforethought, no matter what deal mother and son had struck.

At the snow-covered Sisson cemetery, Detectives Westwood and Baker had taken scene command that would include monitoring the dig and then getting the coffin of Zack Stock loaded into a van for transport to the Chico ID lab.

Now, with sand in his eyes, a feeling he'd actually missed, Roy watched Westwood and Baker stamping their feet as the backhoe took its first bite of earth, after scraping away a foot of snow. Then he walked slowly back to his SUV. No need for him to stick around. His priorities were to write some initial reports and get Cedar Stock's *BOLO* on the wire. He wanted every cop in America to be on the look-out for this bad boy just as soon as he entered an arrest warrant in the system. Then he'd get some sleep, not a lot, just enough to get rid of the punchy feeling. Later, he'd write some more reports, and then, for a change of pace, some more, the dreary task they never show in the movies.

♦

The two Texans, now that their quarry had galloped away, became your normal Sisson tourists, and sort of a novelty in the

Black Tail Restaurant, what with their hats and polite Lone Star manners. They were cool with that.

CPO Mendenhall overheard Raul Morales speaking into his phone.

"…*montana muy grande y nevada.*"

CPO turned to Ollie Johnson.

"My Spanish is a bit rusty. Learned some in the Navy, but that man is some kinda confused. Gotta be an illegal. Thinks he's in Nevada."

"No," Ollie said, "Spanish class was next door to me at the school. Pretty sure he said he was in Montana."

"Somebody got a number for ICE?" CPO sniggered.

Georgie Miller smacked him on the shoulder then joined in, "Mooey means very and *grande* means big. He could be saying Nevada is bigger than Montana, which I think it might be." He nodded his head sagely.

Jeanie the waitress set down their breakfasts, shaking her head.

"He's telling his wife or family that he's looking at a very big snowy mountain."

"Damn, Jeanie. Didn't know you were bi…what's the word? Bisexual," exclaimed Johnny Pardeau.

Jeanie snorted a little with laughter. "And they happen to both be Texas Rangers," she sang as she whisked empty plates away, leaving the four awestruck retirees to scramble over one another to buy coffee for the boys from Laredo, which CPO Mendenhall loudly declared had been his favorite TV show in the '60s.

♦

Back in the state of Texas, a gray windowless van pulled to a halt inside the prison walls at Huntsville. A chained Jackson "Jacky Blue" Howard stepped out into the gray dawn for the last time. He blinked and glanced around. He'd hoped to see a tree or a bird or maybe even a damn flower, something besides unfriendly concrete, a murmuring chaplain, and his whiny lawyer who kept apologizing for not doing enough to save his life. All was not lost though. He caught one glimpse of an airliner far above, against a hint of pale blue. He sighed and stepped through the door to the smells of silence.

Forty-eight hours later he shuffled into the death room. He sneered at the hospital bed they had laid out for him. Later, when he'd been all hooked up with IVs, a Texas state official asked him if he had any last words.

"Well, I had a speech all prepared, but I guess I'll just speak from the heart. Don't blame none y'all. I got myself in this fix, and I was free, white, and 21 when I done it. I'da chose another way to go, but, hell, goin' to sleep can't be all that bad. Most important, I want someone here to tell Delroy Church I'm a man of my word. I walked in here on my own, clear-eyed. Now let's do this bitch."

♦

The remains of Zachary Stock were checked in at the Chico State University Human Identification Lab by intern Katherine Hoover under the watchful eye of lab manager Maya Sanchez. A formal request had been made to examine the remains to test the two current theories of Zack's demise. One, he had fallen in the river in a drunken stupor and had suffered skeletal injuries after colliding with any number of dark, mossy rocks under the waterline as he floated five miles west. Two, he had been beaten to death by a vicious, prison gangster who'd joyously punched, kicked, and stomped him into eternity. What fractures, if any, tended to show consistency with which theory?

Now, while the possible murder of Zack Stock may have been front and center in the minds of cops in Karuk County, there were some realities to face when it came to priorities. First, the case was over twenty years old. Secondly, the prime suspect in the murder, if it was indeed a murder, was dead. DNA matches, from the clavicle fragment, with Koondawg Cutler's unmoved mama came back as an unsurprising positive. Yes, it looked as though her little Koondawg had taken his last breath in Karuk County, but he couldn't have asked for a nicer, more scenic burial site. Third, current cases had piled up. For example, victims' charred remains from the October fires in Sonoma County, required immediate attention from the experts in the lab. Family members there actually grieved, and their insurance companies were sitting on a boatload of death bennies.

No one in the Stock family objected to the delay. Zack's mother and aunt were dead. His cousin, Cedar Stock, thought to have assisted in covering up the murder, had not stuck around to answer questions in that regard given his other legal difficulties. He'd been implicated in at least six other homicides. It became difficult to keep track of those he'd killed with his own hand, those he'd knowingly sent to their deaths by the hands of others, and those whose deaths he'd help shield from prying eyes. As for Zack's wife, Sarah Stock, she'd taken a winter vacation from her job at Ronald Faraday Real Estate and had not weighed in either way.

So there Zack lay, as a coy winter considered melting into spring.

♦

Dead Fred Cavanaugh uploaded the contents of Cedar Stock's ancient cell phone. The entire staff of the Karuk County Major Crimes Investigations Section gathered in the room to watch. The grainy color images lasted less than two minutes. Amazingly, there stood the late Jacky Blue Howard washing dishes with the late Germaine Stock. What happened next inspired more than one "Jesus" from the group of detectives. Not even a progressive California jury could deny the capital case against Jade, what with her standing over the seated Dina Morgan and popping her with a pistol as if she were a hapless Polish army officer executed in the Katyn Forest.

A warrant for the arrest of Jade, formally identified as Virginia Jade Tankersley, hit the system at about the time that Roy knocked on the door of a doublewide sitting forlornly at the end of an icy, west Sisson driveway. Lydia Wilson welcomed him in.

When he left ten minutes later, she slowly ambled back and sat in her easy chair. Her glasses fogged over a bit, just enough to blur the Bible page. She reached for a Kleenex on the table beside her and wiped one eye.

♦

At 1530 hours, two Kern County deputies on patrol in the unincorporated town of Oildale, three and half miles north of Bakersfield, spotted a lone white female at the corner of Beardlsey and Plymouth Avenues. She'd just bounced out of a single story, pink stucco house surrounded by a chain link fence. The home, with its dirt front yard tastefully decorated with crushed beer cans and one pit bull, was a known Dirty White Boy hang-out. For shits and grins, the deputies ran the plate of the pickup that the female got in and drove off.

Kern County Dispatch worked quickly.

"10-36, 10-30 Frank, RO Virginia Tankersley wanted for 187."

"Holy shit, that's Jade Tankersley," one deputy exclaimed.

The other radioed, "We'll be following the vehicle prepping 11-95 felony stop."

Multiple deputies in the area keyed mics, whipped around, and started that way Code Three.

The pursuit lasted five minutes, though it seemed longer to citizens who heard the far off sirens screaming from all over town, including even some flying north from a few miles south down in Bakersfield.

Jade led the cops north from Beardsley, hitting Oildale Avenue which turned into McCray Street. She reached speeds of over 90 mile per hour, blowing through multiple stop signs.

Deputies spike-stripped her at the intersection of McCray and Merle Haggard Drive. Her truck lop, lopped to a stop at the northwest corner of the intersection. Two Sheriff's cars pulled in behind her. Three Sheriff's cars pulled in behind them. Car doors open, at least one shotgun racked, and one deputy began to call out the felony stop over his loud speaker.

"Driver. Turn off your engine and throw the keys out the driver's window. Then get your hands up! Do not move again until I tell you to move!"

Jade turned off the engine, then she tossed her keys out the driver's window. She put her hands up.

"Driver! Turn and place both hands out the window and slowly open the door from the outside. Do it, now!"

Jade put both her hands out the driver's open window and pulled up on the driver's door handle.

"Driver! Slowly step out of the vehicle and face away from the sound of my voice! Do it now!"

Jade slowly eased out of the driver's seat but did not face away as ordered.

"Driver, turn and face away from the sound of my voice. Do it now!"

Jade stepped slowly toward the deputies. She lowered her hands.

"Driver. Stop! Turn around and place your hands behind your head and interlock your fingers! Do it now!"

A smile formed on Jade's lips. She reached into her waistband and yanked at the butt of a chrome colored pistol.

The six deputies on scene did not check with each other (as required by the media and civil rights groups) to ask how many rounds each would fire.

Out of the 37 slugs sent her way, she was hit by sixteen that the pathologist later said would have been fatal.

The Sheriff of Kern County said a silent prayer when he heard the downed suspect had not only been white but had been a known associate of the Aryan Brotherhood. The media frenzy would amount to no more than a popcorn fart. *Whew.*

Jade Tankersley died on Merle Haggard Drive. She was not an "Okie from Muskogee," but she did fly away on "Silver Wings."

♦

February, the month school kids and their parents can't spell, disappeared. The favorite month of the AB, with its shamrocks and tricky leprechauns, took over. Still, Cedar Stock proved as elusive as the pot of gold hidden by that wily maker of fairy shoes. The underside of every toadstool had been carefully searched. A school of thought took shape as managers up the line read Roy's reports.

"Think the AB found out Cedar was bangin' the wife of a shot caller and did him in?" Lieutenant Gary Lynch asked in an investigators' early morning meeting. "From what I know, those boys don't put up with any shit."

"Possibly," Roy acknowledged. "A very calculating and slippery guy though. When the jig was up, pardon the Paddy's Day humor, he didn't hesitate. He disappeared in a flash."

"If I got caught with my hand in the boss's cookie jar, I'd take off like a scalded dog, too." agreed Sheriff Silva who'd ducked in to monitor the meeting and see what he might get ambushed with at the day's Rotary Club luncheon.

"Maybe he's been planning his escape for years," offered Tommy Sessions, who'd been shanghaied into accompanying the Sheriff on his rounds. Sheriff Silva had his eye on retirement and would need a suitable replacement.

"No telling how much cash and dope he had squirreled away in his little hiding spot. But cash is cash, takes up room and gets heavy. Just ask *El Chapo*. Cartel money has to be kept in storage facilities. Still, they run out. Cedar has no accounts in his name that the FBI can find, so he'll run out sometime and have to make more money. Of course, he may have great false IDs. Some guys go on the run and don't get found for decades,"

"Like D.B. Cooper," said Lieutenant Cyril Savage, nodding at his own wise reference.

"That boy only took $200,000 in 1971. I'd say with inflation he had to get himself a job at Taco Bell in about 1981, if he was frugal," remarked Sheriff Silva, grinning.

"Warrants are all in the system, so if he ever gets stopped and arrested under a different name, a county jail should bust him, provided they run his prints," Roy said, returning to the more serious topic.

Lieutenant Lynch changed the subject, "Okay, I've got COSR on board to get their people out as soon as the snow melts on Puma Ridge. Maybe a couple of weeks, maybe more."

"COSR?" asked Roy, unfamiliar with the acronym.

"California Oregon Search and Rescue. They got hundreds of volunteers who've got everything from horses, to ATV's, airplanes, helicopters, and boats. Lotta retired cops on board. Lots of experience and know how. They'll find Dina Morgan on that mountain if she's there."

♦

After the investigators' meeting, Lieutenant Lynch pulled Roy into his office and had him close the door.

"So, this is my monthly grovel session with you," he said apologetically, hands raised. "Have you reconsidered moving up to Silverton to join us? Hey, we'd be open to giving you South County investigations if you want to stay around home."

"I'm flattered, and I know you've got my best interests and the best interests of the department in mind, but I really want to go back to full time patrol. I'll step up when any related reports come in, or if we make an arrest on Cedar, but with everyone involved dead or on the run, for the most part, it's time for me to get back and give the patrol guys a hand."

Roy could tell that Lieutenant Lynch wasn't particularly pleased with that response.

"Okay, then. Gotta respect that but expect me to lean on you if the shit ever hits the fan again, which it will."

"Hey, if I don't have a drunk in cuffs in my back seat, I'll be happy to help."

"Right on. And another thing, the Sheriff and I want to thank you for taking the time to straighten out Westwood. He's like a new person. We've all noticed it around here. Don't know how you did it, but boy do we appreciate it."

"Thanks, but all it took were a few little eye openers here and there. I gave him a nudge. The rest is up to him." Roy was proud that Westwood had committed to turning over a new leaf.

♦

St. Paddy's Day made way for Passover and Easter. Holidays, as any suffering person knows, are some of the worst. But Roy sucked it up and sent best wishes on both, *Chag Sameach* to the in-laws and then Happy Bunny Day to his parents. Though he kept his distance from SoCal, he acknowledged that the ebb and flow of the Cedar Stock mess had kept him occupied, engaged in life with little time to sit in despair. The hunt had been a salve for his soul. He chuckled to himself that if he ever saw Cedar Stock again, he'd thank him for the therapy.

♦

Two hundred volunteers from COSR showed up to camp at Lake Karuk on April Fool's Day. The Search and Rescue squads of the various counties in Southern Oregon and Northern California coordinated so as to dovetail training with a practical mission.

Roy watched the hundred plus civilians spread out downhill from the Puma Creek trail in the treed rocky terrain. Scores had become invisible in the trees, but one could hear the chatter as the line slowly progressed north and west around the curve of the mountain away from the Koondawg clavicle discovery site.

Cedar Stock's damning letter of confession had narrowed the search considerably, and it was only 45 minutes later when shouts went up and radios crackled. *Might be something here.*

Clandestine graves present differently depending on the terrain, soil composition, and number of bodies. Still, there are a number of consistencies when dealing with the criminal mind in these cases. Depth of grave in hurried circumstances almost always results in the descriptive word, "shallow." Few killers drive a backhoe to bury a body the normal 6 feet.

In addition to poor grave depth, telltale signs begin their betrayal. Initially, the plants all die, then may come back after 2-4 months, depending on conditions. Nutrients from bodies leech into the soil, promoting plant growth. Bloating from gases can give the soil a rainbow shape. Decomposition can eventually mean soil depression as the space taken by disappearing flesh and fluid grows larger, causing the soil above to fall. Stark disruption of rocks that have taken thousands, even millions, of years to settle mutually can beckon searchers.

In a shallow grave, serious carnivore activity may occur. Soil is further disrupted, remains may be dragged away. Given the lack of conventional cemetery competence, a strip of cloth from a pair of black jean shorts, worn by Dina Morgan and buried almost fourteen years earlier, could grab someone's attention as they're poking a stick among stones and ferns. A soiled and threadbare American flag draping the gracile bones of a defleshed rib cage would reveal itself later.

♦

"Would have been a lot less trouble if Ol' Cedar Stock had turned himself in and then just brought us here," Detective Westwood mused. He and Roy stood on the Puma Creek Trail, looking downhill over a hundred feet where yellow crime scene tape surrounded Dina's grave. Inside the tape, worker bees from the Chico ID Lab, led by Professor Godwin, reveled in their natural habitat.

Roy had hidden his disappointment that Kat couldn't make the trip, but she'd been knee deep in midterms and unable. She'd sent her regrets. He'd texted her back.

Next time you're home, I'll walk you up here to show you the site.

Seconds later he got the patented Kat response.

That would be so cool!

On a hunch, Roy checked his phone. Sure enough, where he and Westwood were standing was almost the exact spot Carrie the Accountant had taken photos of Jerry with a J as he'd hiked toward her after discovering the partial bone that had unleashed this catastrophe. He smiled, thinking how he'd give the CPA mafia a ring to bring them all up to date. It being tax time, what with all the sketchy extensions filed, he wondered if they'd spare the minute to take his call.

Jake Stern called Roy. His DA had decided to hop on board the Let's-Arrest-Cedar-Stock-Express. Positive fingerprints on the old cell phone coupled with authenticated handwriting on the written *sort of a confession* had pushed her over the line. And why not? There was no way Sonoma County would get first crack at Cedar Stock. He could only be executed or do life once. But the more the merrier. It solved a case, and because it was a murder case, evidence would be forever preserved.

Stern said he and his wife Rachel would be en route in mid-July to partake of the Black Tail faire. Roy suggested they try to get Reuben Montalvo up at the same time, so the three of them could sit around telling war stories, boring their wives. He'd even hit up the San Francisco attorney to see if they could reserve the big house. The attorney, after reading about his notorious tenant, had called to reduce his rent to practically nothing and had offered the lodge cheap to FOR (Friends of Roy) on a limited basis.

"Doesn't that fall under graft and police corruption?" Stern had laughed.

"Probably riding the line, but it's like an appreciative restaurant and free coffee. Don't make a scene, just leave a huge tip!"

Stern agreed and after a few more minutes of chat said, "Stay safe. See you in July!"

♦

Amy Douglas tossed back her smooth, freshly highlighted hair and smiled to herself as she looked at *the Small Paper Excellence in Journalism* award that she'd landed. Her series had gotten national play. *Aryan Supremacy in Rural America: How One Prison Gang Turned a Redneck County into its Cash Cow.*

The miscreants who'd made Karuk County their bitch over several decades, and the detective who'd shined his blinding light on their misdeeds, had made for fascinating reading. She had been the envy at the annual gathering of hopeful reporters who'd all worked their tails off but had come up short.

"Mary Redmond had to sit there and clap," she thought, with a satisfied smirk. On top of that, Mary's publisher — in front of Mary — had practically offered her a job!

He'd jested, "Yeah, Mary's getting a little long in the tooth. Hey, I'm joking!"

They'd all chortled. Amy's eyes had done a fox trot while Mary's eyes had formed ice picks. The jocular publisher had taken another drink then asked both ladies if they had *anything* that could take the place of the recent, lurid #MeToo stories since he reckoned that firestorm had started to fade. He had set a heavy hand on Mary's shoulder and sighed, noting that, unfortunately, citizens could only sustain outrage for so long on one subject.

Mary had smiled tightly at him and pulled away. "Hashtag My BBB, boorish, boneheaded, boss," she had whispered, tossing back the last of her martini.

CHAPTER 60

She had lost none of her youthful energy. Her smile beamed delightfully as she skipped up and impulsively threw her arms around him. She stepped back, embarrassed by her show of affection.

He laughed.

"Missed you, too."

She smiled, pink in the face. "My semester's over, I've graduated, and I'm heading to San Marcos, Texas, in August. What could be better?"

Roy furrowed his brow. "Wait, I thought you wanted to go to Knoxville. Didn't they have something there you were interested in?"

"Body farm. Remember? The original. Although calling it that seems a little disrespectful to the body donors. Its real name is the Anthropological Research Facility," she cautioned.

Roy paused and then slapped a hand to his forehead as if remembering. "Oh yeah. I forgot, the girl who wants to hang with the old songwriters."

Kat looked at him quizzically. "Songwriters? You mean Nashville, not Knoxville."

"No, songwriters, as in they never fade away, they just decompose."

"Ouch! Got me! No, I'm going to Texas State. They have a decomposition research facility as well. And, after I get my masters, I'll work for a while then apply to the Bureau."

"Ooh, *the Bureau*. Getting the vernacular down already I see."

She grinned and threw her coffee-colored waves back.

"So it's your day off. Are we going to see these sites or what?" she ribbed him.

"Hop in. Took *Kaopectate* before we leave, I hope!"

"Nooo. Stop!" She laughed heartily, but her face was a little pinker than normal.

♦

As they drove toward the Puma Creek trail head, they chatted about the ID lab's findings on both Zack Stock and Dina Morgan.

"I read the report on Dina's skull. She has the round hole consistent with the .22 caliber magnum round," Roy said.

"Yes, of course the slug had been damaged, from what I heard. Don't know if it was any use," Kat replied.

".22 slugs are notoriously stubborn in giving up which barrel they came from. That's why hit men will use them. But the pistol Jade Tankersley pulled on the Kern County cops was a .22 caliber. Can't believe she hung onto a possible murder weapon all those years," Roy said. "Must have had sentimental value."

"Sick," Kat twisted her mouth. "The video of her killing Dina had to be awful."

"Not pretty, that's for sure. What about Zack? Glad you all finally had time for him." Roy remarked lightly, knowing that the lab had been swamped with determining burn victim identifications.

"Interestingly, Zack's examination showed multiple disruptions in the plasticity of the bone around some of the fracture sites on his ribs and skull. It's as if the bone bends but doesn't quite break when it is struck by a blunt object. The bones tend to fracture more clearly when they come up hard against something sharp, like rocks in rapids."

"So we're looking at consistency with a beating versus rolling over rocks in a river?"

"Both, I'd say. I mean we know he spent several days floating down stream, but the story of him being beaten is also borne out by the bone fracture evidence. He could definitely have sustained nasty blows to ribs and head. The fractures in his skull are on the side. A body floating down stream would be expected to sustain damage to the top, from ramming into a hard rock. But that's not a hundred percent."

"Well, all involved are dead, so as our boy on the run, Cedar Stock, would probably say, 'If you can't get the evidence to fit, you must acquit.'"

Kat looked over at him, and he could see that she was trying to catch the reference.

"Look, it was white Broncos on the run in LA, back in the day. What can I say?" Roy laughed.

"Nice rhyme. You're a mystery, Detective Church," Kat shook her head and looked out the window.

Roy parked his SUV at the trailhead, the only vehicle in the flat, graveled parking area. The boulders had been put back, and the gate reclosed, after the frenetic activity of a month and a half earlier.

Late May meant warmth in the Central Valley and the rest of occupied California, but here at near 5,000 feet in elevation a cooling breeze called for Roy to don a long-sleeved flannel shirt. Kat wore a sweater. Both had hiking boots to negotiate the stones on the hike, even though a Forest Service contracted skip loader had cleared the trail back into road status for all the official traffic headed up to the Dina Morgan burial site.

The sugary smells of Douglas fir and cedar wafted through the air, mixing with the kaleidoscopic scents of Manzanita, ankle high, pale dusty maidens, and lavender colored larkspur. Startled squirrels scampered away, dark hawks soared above, and jingoistic lizards paused and puffed themselves boisterously as the two friends strolled upward, conversing happily.

Roy pointed out the site of the Koondawg clavicle discovery. The area had grown over enough to nearly obscure the human presence from the previous October.

"Cedar Stock and Jacky Blue Howard just tossed him out right here. A sad end. Incredible view, though," Kat said.

"That's the attitude. Dark humor will see you through an outstanding career, young lady."

"Is that how you got through it?"

"Gimme a break, not through yet."

"You know what I mean," Kat said, smiling widely and rolling her eyes.

"I know what you mean. Humor has masked a lot of pain over the years. Anyone in a high stress job has to start off with a sense of humor or grow one quickly. Otherwise it will eat you up."

They turned and continued uphill for another hundred yards or so until they arrived at their destination. Having worked up heat on the hike, Roy unbuttoned his flannel shirt, revealing a white T-shirt.

They paused on the trail overlooking the clandestine gravesite. A fluorescent yellow material fluttered on a crimson Indian paintbrush.

"Question: Why does someone always leave a piece of crime scene tape? Answer: It's tradition." Roy laughed, shaking his head in mock exasperation. "You want to climb down?"

They made their way downhill on the gentle slope, the only such terrain Roy had seen on the hike up. To this point, Cedar Stock had been given few options it seemed.

As opposed to when the first Search and Rescue team had moved in, the area looked as worn and used as a *no reservations needed* campground site.

"How deep did they bury her?" Kat asked.

"Only about eighteen inches. A lot of hard digging in this rocky soil. Then they piled rocks and maybe branches on top of the eighteen. Still, some animal got in and grabbed a hunk covered by cloth. That's what caught the attention of the searcher."

"Really heart breaking, you know. How did her dad take it?"

"You know, he's known she's been dead for fourteen years. Still, when the finality of it hit him, he broke down. Tough old bird, too," Roy said, recalling the way Lonnie Morgan had become immobile at the news, before tears started rolling faster and faster into his wild, white beard. He'd finally broken into silent, heaving sobs. Roy had stepped out of the room to give the weathered man a private minute.

"Always those left behind who suffer the longest isn't it?" Kat said.

"Yep."

They stood in silence for a moment, Kat observing the ground and Roy looking out through the forest. A gentle wind ruffled the upper branches of the fir trees. Somewhere in the distance, a bird was keening for a response. The sound was lonely.

"Well, are you ready to head back down?" Kat asked after a while.

Roy was jarred out of his reverie. He smiled at her. "Sure. You have lunch plans? Be happy to treat."

She pulled her face into an expression of regret. "Yes, I do."

"Oh," said Roy, trying to mask his disappointment.

"I have lunch plans with a famous, former LA Sheriff's homicide detective who turned Karuk County upside down according to the papers," Kat laughed.

"Wasn't me," Roy retorted "Detective Westwood is at fault."

A perfect day he hoped wouldn't end.

As they neared the trail head at a fairly quick pace, Roy felt a sensation climbing up his spine that he couldn't quite place. It tempered his exuberance. Perhaps a slight sense of guilt at enjoying time with Kat? Had he let his daughter's memory slip, just a little? Never. No, that wasn't it. Maybe knowing the hourglass would send Kat away at the end of the day had dosed him with reality. No, something else. A sound maybe? Had he heard a motor, another vehicle?

Then he saw it. Behind his Sheriff's SUV, actually blocking it from an easy back around, sat a gray Dodge van. It had been plucked from the ranks of those 80's and 90's conversion packages, occupied by bearded drivers and dreadlocked passengers who owned the slow lanes up the West Coast from LA to Seattle and back again, stopping and squatting wherever they pleased. Dusty and oxidized, with gasoline cans on a roof rack, and dark tinted windows, it had surely inspired scores of high school girls and boys to point and giggle, "Hey, looks like a serial killer who needs help finding his lost puppy."

Suddenly Roy cursed himself. He reached for Kat's arm to stop her from walking since, though she'd seen the van, she had not processed its meaning.

"Hello, Delroy."

The smooth voice came from behind, and had Kat not been in the way, Roy would have moved immediately. Instead, all he could do was turn, as did a startled Kat, to look into the gaunt, grinning face of Cedar Stock.

"Delroy, caught slippin'," Cedar said easily as he pointed the blue steel semi-auto at him. It looked to be a 9 or better, maybe a .40 cal.

"Kat get behind me," Roy said calmly. He did not take his eyes off Cedar and the pistol, so he sensed rather than saw a terrified Kat step behind him.

"Kitty Kat do as your master says. Seriously Delroy, is her being behind you really going to protect her? I mean, c'mon, if I wanted you dead this second, I'd have shot you both in the back as you slipped by my little hiding place back there behind that big old rock. Damn glad there were no rattlers there. Believe me. I checked first."

Keep talking.

Roy's mind returned to his training. If they have the drop on you, talk, then talk some more. Let them talk. Keep calm. As long as tongues are wagging, rounds aren't flying.

"One bone. One damn bone. It all came down to one damn bone," Cedar said.

Roy estimated Cedar to be ten feet way with the pistol in his right hand. Too far to charge and take a chance.

"So you're judging how far away I am right now, aren't you Delroy. They teach you that in L.A.? Get close? Take a chance. Jesus. I've been robbin' Mexican drug dealers for over twenty years. I think I know my tactics."

Get him to talk more.

"What do you mean one bone?" Roy could almost smell the fear emanating from Kat.

"That's a boy. Keep me talking. Koondawg was never supposed to be up here. I only wanted to dump Zack's doe. But we had a piece of old Koon left over, a shoulder roast I think, and Jacky Blue tossed it in the kitchen trash. Which we also took with us to help clean up Sarah's house a little. We dumped the doe and the kitchen trash back up there. How could one little damn bone, outta how many can there be in the one hunk of meat we put in the trash, still be around twenty years later? What are the odds that some dumbass hiker would find it? When I read all about it in the paper, I about shit. I'd come that close to living a longer life. Damn bad luck!"

Longer life? Talk!

"So you're saying this is not where you left all of Koondawg's remains?"

"What the fuck have I been trying to tell you? We buried Dina up here, not Koondawg. Took most of that sumbitch for a last tour of the Coast Range. Hell, we pitched little bags of Koondawg off every back-road cliff we could find between here and Humboldt on our way to 101 then south for a job in the Bay Area."

"Wow, bad luck is right. Bigfoot country, rugged and remote."

Cedar sneered. "Yeah. Jacky Blue threw out one bag near Happy Camp a hundred miles west of here and said, "Hey, I just gave head to Sasquatch' We laughed about that for years."

"So you thought for sure we'd stumbled on Dina?"

"Of course, everybody said you found a skeleton or a body. The paper, everyone. Nobody said one bone, so it had to be, it shoulda been, Dina's bones."

"Yeah, that's why investigators don't divulge details."

"Well, keeping quiet sure fucked me, and you and the Kitty Kat by default it looks like."

Roy remained calm and still. "So. Cedar, let's cut the b.s. What do you want? You want to give yourself up?"

Don't show fear, dammit.

Cedar laughed, a cold, empty sound that iced Roy's spine into his legs. His heart was hammering against his chest.

"No Delroy, I don't want to give myself up. I guess I'll run as fast and as far as they'll let me. But in the end, you know, killing a cop means the world will be on my ass."

"Then why do it? Why not stay on the under. You've done well so far."

"Thought about it. But Cedar don't run forever. He stops and fights. He ain't no punk. Besides, I've got nothing to really live for, and I've got you to thank for it."

"How so? I didn't sell drugs, steal drugs, go to the pen, join a gang, and kill people."

"No, that's all on me. But you took everything I had."

"Care to explain?"

"Three people in this world ever meant anything to me. My mom, Sarah, and Maddy. You forced me to kill my own mother. Then you turned Sarah and Maddy against me. I got nothing.'" He spat the words out.

Desperate, emotional. Talk!

"Any chance you let Kat go? She's got no dog in this fight."

"Seriously? What have I been saying to you all these months, Delroy? No witness, no crime. Sorta bums me out, but what can I do?"

"Give yourself up. Take your chances in Texas or California. Go for LWOP or even fewer years in a plea deal. I mean life without parole has got the word life in it for a reason."

"You can't be serious. Know what it feels like to take a shank? The fellas behind the walls are just itchin' to get a crack at me. Moonshine has put out the word. I'm as greenlit as any motherfucker has ever been. No, I'm dying from a cop bullet not a rusty bonecrusher."

The longer he talks, the heavier the pistol gets. Right hand gun, move left.

Roy gave thanks to the coolness of the day that had forced him to grab the flannel shirt. A little more fortune had smiled. The heat of the climb had prompted him to unbutton the shirt which he still wore and which now hid his pistol on his right side. It wasn't his duty pistol, which he could draw before Cedar could react, but at least he had a chance. Especially if Cedar kept running his mouth, and the muscles in his forearm began to flag.

"I'm sorry about Sarah and Maddy. Not my intention to turn them on you."

"Jesus, Delroy. You're *sorry*? That's weak. C'mon, you know what it's like to lose someone. Oh, that's right. I spent a lot of time researching you, my man. I can read between the lines in the obits. I know your daughter died, and your wife committed suicide. He ever tell you that about himself Kitty Kat? "

"No," came the quiet, trembling voice from behind Roy.

"So, Delroy, here we are, two men, both lost everything. Both kinda old. But I've got the gun, and you're in plainclothes with no vest. Kinda fucked for you isn't it?"

"Pretty much, but like you said, I lost my wife and daughter. If I get to see them today, I'm a happy man. Just let Kat go. Take her cell phone. Let her hot foot it out of here."

"Speaking of that, Kitty Kat, toss your cell phone over in the rocks."

Roy felt Kat fumbling with something behind him. Then he heard the sound of an object land to his left in the gravel.

Get the damn conversation up and running again!

"Cedar, mind if I ask something?"

"Go ahead, keep me talking while you work on a plan…which won't work." Cedar's tone was one of dull resignation, a bad sign when negotiating with a suicidal, ledge-croucher.

"Why the language and grammar changes?"

He stared at Roy, surprised by the question. "I'm not some dumbass redneck, though I've worked with a few. I speak to fit the occasion or to amuse myself, same way you speak ghetto when you had to back in the day. It's a dystopian nightmare out there sometimes, and you gotta adapt."

"Dystopian? Big word. I'm just a simple cop, didn't get the elite, big prison library education like you."

Cedar chuckled, "Damn, Delroy. You ain't as scared as you should be. You probably coulda held your mud on the yard. Your homeboy Stern? I ain't so sure."

Running out of time.

"Why are you even talking? Why not assassinate us when we walked by?" Roy was genuinely curious.

Stay calm. Show no fear! Fear emboldens the predator.

"You tell me. You're the smart detective with all the insight to human behavior." Cedar rotated the pistol barrel in a lazy circle.

"Okay, for starters, you've never killed anyone, that I know of, outside of your own mother, who wasn't in the game. Am I right?"

"Pretty much. Show me one innocent person."

"The one standing behind me."

"You're right, Delroy. Kitty Kat, you're free to go. Start heading downhill."

"Go Kat, and when you get out of sight, run and hide. Stay hidden," Roy whispered.

"Not going anywhere! I'm not leaving you!" a defiant Kat said in a loud voice, a hint of quaver.

Shit.

Cedar tapped his boot on the ground for a moment. His penetrating gaze bore into Kat's face.

"Then it looks like you gotta die here with your boss, Kitty Kat. My conscience is clear. You made your choice." The tone of his voice didn't match the deadly words. A slight hint of hesitation.

No, Kat!

"No, you made choices, and those choices broke Maddy's heart!" Kat spat at Cedar.

"You have no idea," Cedar shot back.

"You robbed her of her dad!" she shouted.

"I shoulda been her dad. I shoulda been Sarah's husband," retorted Cedar, bitterness dripping off the words like hot lava. It seemed he hadn't planned on this emotional debate.

"I dialed 9-1-1 on my phone before I threw it," Kat said softly.

"Well, that was pretty stupid. But no matter. We're in the country. Cops can't get here for fifteen or twenty minutes at least. If you're even telling the truth."

A hint of uncertainty.

"Gun's getting heavy, Delroy. You counting on that?"

"Yep."

"Damn, an honest man. Hell, we coulda been friends, you and me."

"Is it you and me or you and I?"

"Actually, I'm not sure. But damn, Delroy. I think you could be right, speaking of subject pronouns."

"We all make mistakes. Kat, move away from me," Roy said, his voice going lower, steadier.

"Kat, you move away now. Do like Delroy says. I'm lowering my gun to my side, but it's about to get real loud here."

"Oh God," whispered Kat. "Please, Roy."

"Kat, my daughter Raisa would have been your age."

She took several steps to her right.

Thank God she chose right!

"Neither one of us getting down off this hill upright are we, Delroy."

"Nope, don't think so. Why you giving me a chance?"

"Because I'm tired of the shit, and I bet you are too." Cedar looked much older and more haggard as the truth of his words spread through him.

"No way for us ending this peacefully, is there?" Roy said softly.

"Don't see one."

"Damn. That's too bad. Well, any regrets in your life?"

"I should have played a meaner guitar, and I shoulda done a better job of dumping body parts. Woulda, shoulda, coulda. You?"

"Too many to list, so we better get to gettin'."

"Sorry for how it all turned out, Delroy." Cedar seemed genuinely sad, actually sincere.

"Me too."

A snowball's chance in hell is better than no chance at all, and a man who makes the first move knows when he's going to make that move. Reaction time is not like in the movies, though once again, the media and the hostile fans in the stands think it should be. Cops with guns pointed at suspects have died when the bad guy went for his gun when he should have surrendered. Roy would have preferred to have his duty holster. He would have preferred to have whirled and drawn at the first sound of Cedar's voice. But then snowballs should never test Hell.

Mozambique! Now!

Roy stepped to his left, threw his strong leg back then swept his right hand backward clearing his shirttail and grasping the butt of his .40 caliber Glock. All muscle memory. He heard no shots, did not even see Cedar's hand rise and awkwardly track him right, the unnatural motion for his right elbow and shoulder.

Police one-on-one gunfights take place most often at a range of 3-6 feet, face to face. On car stops, during street detention, or in the living room of an apartment, when the shit hits the fan, even a novice shooter can be quite deadly to a police officer. Create separation, throw in movement, and the chances go out the window for the unskilled shooter.

Cedar had earlier conceded the distance. Roy had now provided the movement. If he stood still in a gunfight, he had an 85% chance of being shot and a greater than 50 % chance of taking a hit in the torso. Move, and he had a roughly a 50% chance of being hit, but only a 10% chance of a torso hit. Seeking cover reduces the chances of being hit to around 25%. There was no cover for Roy, and Cedar was no unskilled shooter.

Roy knew he'd been struck. He felt the jackhammer in his chest even as he squeezed his trigger over and over in the direction of center mass then upwards to the head for the last best hope, the Mozambique failure drill. Cedar's brow snapped back from the impact. He slumped to the dirt ending in the crumpled heap of the instant dead, even as the echoes of explosions bounced off canyon walls.

Roy staggered backward and felt the sudden desire to sit.

With Kat's sobbing help, he slowly lowered himself onto the board and dangled his legs in the warm, salty water. Shaking his naturally bleached and tousled curls, he turned to survey the blue green swells behind him. They rolled his way like determined rows of battlefield soldiers marching bravely into history. The sun's reflection flitted and pirouetted across the ever-shifting surface. Above him, snowy seagulls and pelicans dipped and dived with grace and confusion.

From the beach, plaintive lyrics and a sax solo floated upward and outward as Gerry Rafferty's Baker Street capsulated the magical mood of the day.

He felt the rise under his board. Paddling furiously forward, now on his feet, hands balancing at his sides, he glided ecstatically toward the crashing surf with its roiling sand.

Malka and Raisa waved wildly at him from their colorful towels on the beach. As he drew closer, they were up, dancing arm in arm, all smiles and gaiety. Oh how he wanted to hug them and hold them when he finally stepped on shore! Almost there.

Forever together in the breeze and sun.

He high stepped out of the surf, his board tucked under his arm. They rushed forward toward him, arms outstretched. Charlie Criss stood to one side, clapping and shouting encouragement, his ebony skin glistening in the festive SoCal light.

Never seen Charlemagne Criss at the beach! What fun!

He dropped to his knees and spread his arms, closing his eyes tightly waiting for the impact of their embrace, the sound of the surf pounding nosily in his ears, so noisy. He couldn't hear their cries of joy, the ocean in its violent madness clashing with land, two fierce armies coming together in mayhem.

We've got to move up the beach. I can't hear you! I can't see you!

Raisa! Malka! Please! Don't go! Oh God, please!

"Please, Roy, please," Kat pleaded, the pounding of the helicopter blades nearly wiping out her words. She bent over him, a blurred visage and a gentle, cool hand on his forehead. Her desperate breath in his face mixed with salty teardrops that hit his lips. Like broken icicles, they felt sharp yet cool and soothing against his burning skin.

EPILOGUE

He drove his shoulder into the weights that had trapped his eyelids, while at the same time stretching the spackle that held them shut. She came into view, sitting there beside him, reading a book. He could make out the title.

Enemies: A History of the FBI by Tim Weiner.

"I haven't written your recommendation yet. I'm a slacker," he managed to croak.

For a moment, he wanted it to be Raisa who dropped the book, turned and let out a cry. But then he realized the truth. She and Malka would be there when he was ready. For now, though, Kat Hoover needed his letter to the Bureau.

♦

Roy wheeled himself into his living room. Tom Hanlon had collected his mail which he now placed on the table next to Roy's easy chair. Wallace Westwood and his wife had left earlier after dropping off lasagna and rolls. Tom Hanlon had sniffed at this.

"Stand by to stand by if you want real lasagna. Where'd he get this, Costco?"

"Hey, I'll be up and around in a month or so. Then I'll take you and your wife to the Medford Olive Garden. You two have been incredible. So have Westwood and his wife. We'll make it a fivesome."

"You're on, hero, but I'm warning you, I didn't get this big by eating off the lite menu." He rubbed his belly and grinned.

After Hanlon left, Roy scooted into his easy chair, crying out at the pain still coursing through his chest and stomach every time he exerted himself. Sneezing brought out the worst. When he felt one coming on, he held a pillow to his torso then cursed loudly after the explosion, glad that he had no neighbors to file complaints.

Damn. If I were a TV cop I could have made do with just an arm sling.

The return address on the letter read *Runic Landscaping.*

He opened it, holding his breath as he did. He felt a wave of familiarity descend over him as he saw the small, neatly formed letters.

Delroy,

If you're reading this, congratulations on at least one level: you've survived. But it sucks on another, not for you, but for me, because I'm most likely dead.

Even though you followed a course that forced my hand, I suppose in a way I admire you and wish I could have known you under different circumstances. Had I not thrown in with the AB, maybe I could have been a cop like you. I appreciate talent, and you've got it. I know you had your partner Mr. Criss, but I like to think we'd have made a good team, too. But that's neither here nor there. I'm dead. You're not, and your life goes on.

Please give my regards and regrets to Sarah and Maddy. I have no one else to do it for me. Tell them how utterly ashamed and sorry I am that I made such a mess of my life, and by doing so, made a mess of theirs.

Also, please pass on to Mr. Ronald Faraday, that modern day Ty Cobb, that he owes both those beautiful girls for a lifetime, and that he has to be there for them in their times of need. It's the least he can do given his role.

With best regards,

Cedar Stock,
Aryan Brotherhood Soldier (long term survival was never an option).

P.S. I hope you find my grammar beyond suitable for a con with no college degree.

Roy set the letter down and lay back.

WTF?!

♦

Mr. Ronald Faraday unfolded the professional looking letter. It had come in a white envelope inside an official looking manila envelope from an attorney in Post Falls, Idaho. A cover letter from the attorney stated simply:

Dear Sir,

Our client, Mr. Cedar Stock, requested that we send this confidential letter to you in the event of his death by natural causes or otherwise. This communication is solely between the two of you. We have not been made privy to the letter's contents and could not discuss it in any event due to attorney-client confidentiality rules.

Best regards,

Greg Cooper
Cooper and Hines
A Professional Law Firm.

As Ronnie read, his hands shook uncontrollably.

Ronnie.

If you're reading this, I'm dead, so all I will ever say to you about this matter is in this letter…

♦

2130 hours, June 21, 1995

Cedar Stock sat in his blacked-out truck in the darkness of the open pasture adjacent to Sarah and Zack's house. How would he handle the shit he was watching? Total management headache. These dumb fucking assholes couldn't maintain long enough for him to go set up a business deal? Dealing with Jade was tough enough. Now he had to come back to a fight among drunk employees? They better solve this shit before he walked in there, or discipline would come down hard. Fucking Koondawg and Jacky Blue shoving Zack out the front door onto the lawn? Koondawg yelling like the asshole he was, Jacky Blue trying to calm the situation as he normally did. And wasn't that Light-in-the-loafers Ronnie's little silver Honda Accord speeding away just before Cedar had turned his signal on? Jesus fucking Christ.

Cedar watched Zack struggling to sit up on the lawn. He wondered how badly Zack was hurt. Ribs? Bloody nose? Koondawg could really fuck a dude up, and his violence of late had concerned both Cedar and Jacky Blue. He wondered if Zack had a first aid kit in the house. Maybe ice in a towel and few more cold beers would do the trick.

Aw shit, here comes the Honda. Ronnie coming back to help out his boyfriend? The two of them going to storm the house and take on Koondawg in a real prison yard brawl? This is not good.

Cedar weighed whether he should step in, but sometimes men had to settle their differences as men. The Honda slid to a stop. Ronnie the homo jumped out.

He's not walking right. And he's carrying a bat? You gotta be shittin' me. Dude is serious. Oh. My. God.

Cedar stepped out of his truck and began walking quickly toward the house but paused under the shadows of a cottonwood tree at the side of the house.

Ronnie stood over Zack, the two of them talking, arguing over something.

"They hurt me, Zack!" Ronnie forced through clenched teeth.

Zack looked at him with disgust, holding his right arm across his ribs. "Why were you even here? You looking for love? You brought it on yourself!"

"How could you say that?! I'm your friend! I love you and Sarah. I only came back for Maddy's toy, and they hurt me!" Ronnie's bat hung limply at his side, and his shoulders slumped.

"Fuck you, Ronnie. Ronnie *Fairy Day*!" Zack jeered.

"No!" Ronnie cried, shocked. He stumbled back a step. "Not you, too. I loved you!" His voice grew quieter at the end. Uncertainty crossed his face as Zack's mouth began to twist.

"Fuck you, ya fuckin' fairy faggot. This is all because of you. They kicked my ass because of you, you cocksucking, take-it-in-the-ass, queer!" Zack snarled back, wiping blood from his nose.

Ronnie swung for the fence. A real major leaguer. Cedar heard Zack's skull crack like a melon dropped off a truck on the freeway. He jumped back into the shadows.

Holy shit!

Cedar watched Ronnie Faraday run back to his Honda and speed away down the driveway.

He asked himself why he hadn't rushed forward. He knew the answer.

Pretty simple. In a split second, he'd made the calculations, an amazing ability that had saved his ass in the joint more times than he cared to count. He set out his plan as he walked past Zack who was either dead or was gonna die very soon. No hospitals in his future. Hospitals meant cops. This can of worms would never see the light of day.

And maybe, just maybe, Sarah would be his.

Didn't work out that way for me though, did it? Sarah only saw me as her "friend." Maddy, on the other hand, always loved me. I knew that. In the end I let her down. I let Sarah down. But you will NOT! They both love you. So you be there for them, and treat them as your own for the rest of your guilt-ridden life.

Sincerely,

Cedar Stock

♦

Karuk County Sheriff's Deputy Delroy Church, still out on "4850 time," *Injured on Duty*, parked his Dodge pick-up in a downtown Sisson parking lot. He carefully slid out, gripping the handholds to keep the discomfort at a manageable Nazi torture, level JV.

As he limped away, he stopped to gaze up at the mammoth brown mountain stalking the village. At the peak, thin, white wisps of mist floated north, like lovingly stroked locks of an old woman nearing the end. A thunder and lightning storm the previous night had left a powdered sugar dusting. Just a friendly reminder that the north state's magnificent frosty cone would return in full glory in the weeks and months ahead.

He turned and made his way slowly into Faraday Real Estate. Sarah Stock rose from her desk and rushed forward to hug him tightly, holding on a split second more than necessary. She jumped back when he winced. He regretted his wimpy reaction. She felt nice and smelled even better.

"Oops. So sorry. You're just not gaining the weight back fast enough!" she exclaimed. "More rolls."

"Don't know how I could still be so skinny. I've been sitting on my backside doing nothing but eating for three months. Another few weeks and I'll be back in the saddle."

"Oh, I hope so! Maybe what you need is full time care," she suggested, a twinkle in her eye.

"Let me think on that. Might be on to something. Hey, thanks for dropping food by again. Frankly, my freezer and fridge are full, so I'm good." He smiled kindly at her, long enough to return the unnecessary second.

"It's the least we could do. And I think Maddy will come around eventually. It's been hard for her. I mean it was hard for me at first, but it absolutely killed her."

"I know, tough business, and I'm truly sorry for your pain. Maybe someday I can sit with Maddy and try to explain. On the other hand, sometimes you let sleeping dogs lie."

"Thank you."

She reached out and touched him lightly on the elbow.

"Can you sit here by my desk? Take a load off?" she asked, her voice polished and clean, like new glass.

"I'd love to, but, actually, is your boss in? I need to talk to him real quickly, privately if it's okay. Something's come up regarding a friend of his, thought I'd do him a favor with a little heads up. I owe him that much."

"Sure, he's in there checking Major League scores right now on ESPN."

Sarah turned and opened Ronnie's door.

"Ronnie! Look who's here. I'll leave you two alone. Can't believe he wants to use you, Ronnie, and not me, to find a piece of property. I'm so hurt." She gave a small laugh, and Roy thought the sound tinkled lightly like a windchime.

Sarah squeezed his shoulder softly as he hobbled by.

"Feel better soon, Detective."

Once inside Ronnie's office, Roy closed the door then eased into a chair in front of the desk.

Ronald Faraday Jr., real estate magnet in a small town, stared across at him, a bunny facing a coyote, his face uncharacteristically pale for September.

"I'll make this quick," Roy said as he gave up trying to cross his legs. Stomach muscles not quite there yet. "Got a letter in my mail from our old friend Cedar Stock."

Ronnie Faraday's pallor worsened. He hid his hands under the desk, but Roy could still see muscles in the forearms working the finger twist.

"I won't go into too much detail. He referred to you as Ty Cobb. He asked me to tell you to take good care of Sarah and Maddy since you owe them. I don't suppose you care to tell me what that's all about?"

Ronnie's voice reminded Roy of the common, tiny earthquakes he'd grown up with in the SoCal, shallow, no damage, but still enough rattle to prompt a passing comment at breakfast.

"Cedar? Who knows with that monster? I think he'd always been a little jealous of me. I've tried to be there for both girls over the past two decades. Ty Cobb? I don't know. He knows I love baseball. Ty Cobb goes down as the most aggressive, old time ball player of his era. Some say the dirtiest ball player of all time. Doesn't make sense to me," Ronnie smiled and moistened his lips.

"Yeah, if you know any history of the sport at all, you know he's also famous for sudden, uncontrollable fits of rage," Roy mused.

Ronnie took a shallow breath and forced a chuckle.

"Typical Cedar Stock bullshit. Stirs up emotions even from the grave. I couldn't tell you what he's talking about."

Roy said nothing as he gazed intently at Ronnie who dropped his gaze to look down at an imaginary water well capacity report in front of him

"Well, I thought I'd better pass on his message. Okay, you have a good day."

"Thank you, Detective."

"It's deputy. And oh by the way, I wanted to also pass on to you the results on Zack's second autopsy. It hasn't been made public. I haven't told Sarah all the details, but I thought you oughta know since he was your friend. Looks as if we'll leave it as undetermined for the cause of death. Yes, he could have drowned, and yes, he could have been beaten to death. The injuries on his ribs and skull could have been caused by rocks in the river or fists and boots."

"Horrible," said Ronnie, shaking his head, sitting up straighter.

"Yeah, the injury to his skull was quite severe, what we call blunt force trauma. Something hit his head hard enough to take him out. Guess we'll never know. Boots maybe. Strange though."

"How so?" Ronnie asked, breathily.

"Jacky Blue. You may or may not know I interviewed him before he was executed. He said something that has always bothered me."

"What's that?"

"He said he told Zack to chill out that night on the lawn after the fight with Koondawg."

"So?"

"So anyone with Zack's skull fracture is already chillin'. See what I mean?"

Ronnie blinked. "Yeah, I guess."

"Well, I better get going. I've got physical therapy again this morning."

Ronnie stood up as Roy struggled out of the chair.

"Good luck with your recovery."

"Thanks so much. And say, Ronnie, didn't you used to have a bat hanging on the wall behind your desk? Seems to me I recall it from when I was here before."

"Uh, yeah, but I've got a really valuable collector's item coming to put up there instead, one I got off eBay, cheap. A real steal." He cleared his throat and opened the door for Roy, clearly ending the conversation.

A real steal. I'll bet, Ty. No witness, no evidence, no case.

ABOUT THE AUTHOR

George Collord earned his bachelor's degree in Agricultural Business Management at Cal Poly, San Luis Obispo. Later, he dropped out of the University of San Diego School of Law to help make sparkling wine in the Napa Valley, sell funeral plots in Sacramento, and repossess cars in Nevada. Finally, he found his true calling, police work. He spent over thirty years in law enforcement as a patrolman, a violent crimes detective, a sexual assault and child abuse detective, a street gang/prison gang investigator, a Special Deputy United States Marshal working on an undercover FBI task force, and a trainer/lecturer for law enforcement groups nationwide. He now resides in California's picturesque Siskiyou County, the place he grew up, with his family, two dogs, and a cat.